I0660918

THE ORIGINAL ADVENTURES OF FRANK & JOE HARDY MEGAPACK®

THE TOWER TREASURE

THE HOUSE ON THE CLIFF

THE SECRET OF THE OLD MILL

THE MISSING CHUMS

HUNTING FOR HIDDEN GOLD

THE SHORE ROAD MYSTERY

THE SECRET OF THE CAVES

THE MYSTERY OF CABIN ISLAND

THE ORIGINAL ADVENTURES OF FRANK & JOE HARDY MEGAPACK®

FRANKLIN W. DIXON

WILDSIDE PRESS

The Original Adventures of Frank & Joe Hardy MEGAPACK®
is copyright © 2025 by Wildside Press, LLC.
The MEGAPACK® ebook series name is a registered
trademark of Wildside Press, LLC.
All rights reserved.

CONTENTS

CONTENTS

INTRODUCTION

JOHN BETANCOURT

As a boy growing up in the 1960s and 1970s, I read all of the detective series of the day—the adventures of Frank and Joe Hardy (the "Hardy Boys") being among my favorites (along with The Three Investigators, the Boxcar Children, and so many more). Every week, my mother bought me a new one. The Hardy Boys books I read were the small-sized hardcovers with their iconic blue spines, once very common on the used book market, but growing increasingly harder to find these days, as they have been largely replaced by paperbacks (when you can find them at all).

One day, while visiting relatives in Missouri, my father gave me an old book that had been in storage for decades: a 1939 hardcover in dust jacket of *The Twisted Claw*, a first edition. It had been his as a child, and it had somehow survived in storage till the 1970s. Of course, I had already read that book, but since I'd run out of new things to read, I decided to try it again.

Imagine my surprise when it was an entirely *different* story than the version of *The Twisted Claw* I had already read. So different as to be completely unrelated. Someone had completely replaced the original...with one that was *worse*!

The original had to do with a secret organization of smugglers in the Caribbean. It was action-packed, vibrantly written, and very exciting, with moments of real menace. The modern version had to do with lumber piracy in the North. Incredible! What had happened?

I later found out that the early books in the series had been deliberately rewritten starting in the 1950s, making them less exciting, more politically correct, and generally dumbed-down for a new generation growing up with sanitized TV adventures. Moments of real peril were removed or lessened. The characters were scrubbed and sanitized and repackaged for (I suspect) a less sophisticated audience.

And I suddenly had a whole new series of Hardy Boys adventures to track down and read. It took me years to do it, but I now have a complete collection of the early, original adventures of Frank & Joe Hardy.

And with this volume, I invite you to enjoy an excursion to a past you probably never knew existed: a collection of the first 8 books in the original series, featuring rougher, tougher, more adventurous Frank and Joe Hardy stories from the 1920s. If you think you know the Hardy Boys and already recognize the titles as ones you've read, you're going to be pleasantly surprised.

Enjoy!

****

A note on the texts: We have taken the liberty of lightly modernizing punctuation and spelling where language and usage have changed (for example, replacing archaic words like "clew" with "clue"). These changes should be invisible to mdoern readers.

THE TOWER TREASURE

ORIGINALLY PUBLISHED IN 1927.

CHAPTER I

THE SPEED DEMON

"After the help we gave dad on that forgery case I guess he'll begin to think we *could* be detectives when we grow up."

"Why shouldn't we? Isn't he one of the most famous detectives in the country? And aren't we his sons? If the profession was good enough for him to follow it should be good enough for us."

Two bright-eyed boys on motorcycles were speeding along a shore road in the sunshine of a morning in spring. It was Saturday and they were enjoying a holiday from the Bayport high school. The day was ideal for a motorcycle trip and the lads were combining business with pleasure by going on an errand to a near-by village for their father.

The older of the two boys was a tall, dark youth, about sixteen years of age. His name was Frank Hardy. The other boy, his companion on the motorcycle trip, was his brother Joe, a year younger.

While there was a certain resemblance between the two lads, chiefly in the firm yet good-humored expression of their mouths, in some respects they differed greatly in appearance. While Frank was dark, with straight, black hair and brown eyes, his brother was pink-cheeked, with fair, curly hair and blue eyes.

These were the Hardy boys, sons of Fenton Hardy, an internationally famous detective who had made a name for himself in the years he had spent on the New York police force and who was now, at the age of forty, handling his own practice. The Hardy family lived in Bayport, a city of about fifty thousand inhabitants, located on Barmet Bay, three miles in from the Atlantic, and here the Hardy boys attended high school and dreamed of the days when they, too, should be detectives like their father.

As they sped along the narrow shore road, with the waves breaking on the rocks far below, they discussed their chances of winning over their parents to agreement with their ambition to follow in the footsteps of their father. Like most boys, they speculated frequently on the occupation they should follow when they grew up, and it had always seemed to them that nothing offered so many possibilities of adventure and excitement as the career of a detective.

"But whenever we mention it to dad he just laughs at us," said Joe Hardy. "Tells us to wait until we're through school and then we can think about being detectives."

"Well, at least he's more encouraging than mother," remarked Frank. "She comes out plump and plain and says she wants one of us to be a doctor and the other a lawyer."

"What a fine lawyer either of us would make!" sniffed Joe. "Or a doctor, either! We were both cut out to be detectives and dad knows it."

"As I was saying, the help we gave him in that forgery case proves it. He didn't say much, but I'll bet he's been thinking a lot."

"Of course we didn't actually *do* very much in that case," Joe pointed out.

"But we suggested something that led to a clue, didn't we? That's as much a part of detective work as anything else. Dad himself admitted he would never have thought of examining the city tax receipts for that forged signature. It was just a lucky idea on our part, but it proved to him that we can use our heads for something more than to hang our hats on."

"Oh, I guess he's convinced all right. Once we get out of school he'll probably give his permission. Why, this is a good sign right now, isn't it? He asked us to deliver these papers for him in Willowville. He's letting us help him."

"I'd rather get in on a real, good mystery," said Frank. "It's all right to help dad, but if there's no more excitement in it than delivering papers I'd rather start in studying to be a lawyer and be done with it."

"Never mind, Frank," comforted his brother. "We may get a mystery all of our own to solve some day."

"If we do we'll show that Fenton Hardy's sons are worthy of his name. Oh boy, but what wouldn't I give to be as famous as dad! Why, some of the biggest cases in the country are turned over to him. That forgery case, for instance. Fifty thousand dollars had been stolen right from under the noses of the city officials and all the auditors and city detectives and private detectives they called in had to admit that it was too deep for them."

"Then they called in dad and he cleared it up in three days. Once he got suspicious of that slick bookkeeper whom nobody had been suspecting at all, it was all over but the shouting. Got a confession out of him and everything."

"It was smooth work. I'm glad our suggestion helped him. The case certainly got a lot of attention in the papers."

"And here *we* are," said Joe, "plugging along the shore road on a measly little errand to deliver some legal papers at Willowville. I'd rather be on the track of some diamond thieves or smugglers—or something."

"Well, we have to be satisfied, I suppose," replied Frank, leaning farther over the handlebars. "Perhaps dad may give us a chance on a real case some time."

"Some time! I want to be on a real case *now*!"

The motorcycles roared along the narrow road that skirted the bay. An embankment of tumbled rocks and boulders sloped steeply to the water below, and on the other side of the road was a steep cliff. The roadway itself was narrow, although it was wide enough to permit two cars to meet and pass, and it wound about in frequent curves and turnings. It was a road that was not often traveled, for Willowville was only a small village and this shore road was an offshoot of the main highways to the north and the west.

The Hardy boys dropped their discussion of the probability that some day they would become detectives, and for a while they rode on in silence, occupied with the difficulties of keeping to the road. For the road at this point was dangerous, very rough and rutty, and it sloped sharply upward so that the embankment leading to the ocean far below became steeper and steeper.

"I shouldn't want to go over the edge around here," remarked Frank, as he glanced down the rugged slope.

"It's a hundred-foot drop. You'd be smashed to pieces before you ever hit the shore."

"I'll say! It's best to stay in close to the cliff. These curves are bad medicine."

The motorcycles took the next curve neatly, and then the boys confronted a long, steep slope. The rocky cliffs frowned on one side, and the embankment jutted far down to the tumbling waves below, so that the road was a mere ribbon before them.

"Once we get to the top of the hill we'll be all right. It's all smooth sailing from there to Willowville," remarked Frank, as the motorcycles commenced the climb.

Just then, above the sharp put-put of their own motors, they heard the high humming roar of an automobile approaching at great speed. The car was not yet in sight, but there was no mistaking the fact that it was coursing along with the cut-out open and with no regard for the speed laws.

"What idiot is driving like that on this kind of road!" exclaimed Frank. They looked back.

Even as he spoke the automobile flashed into sight.

It came around the curve behind and so swiftly did the driver take the dangerous turn that two wheels were off the ground as the car shot into view. A cloud of dust and stones arose, the car veered violently from left to right, and then it roared at headlong speed down the slope.

The boys glimpsed a tense figure at the wheel. How he kept the car on the road was a miracle, for the racing automobile swung from side to side. At one moment it would be in imminent danger of crashing over the embankment, down on the rocks below; the next instant the car would be over on the other side of the road, grazing the cliff.

"He'll run us down!" shouted Joe, in alarm. "The idiot!"

Indeed, the position of the two lads was perilous.

The roadway was narrow enough at any time, and this speeding car was taking up every inch of space. In a great cloud of dust it bore directly down on the two motorcyclists. It seemed to leap through the air. The front wheels left a rut, the rear of the car skidded violently about. By a twist of the wheel the driver pulled the car back into the roadway again just as it seemed about to plunge over the embankment. It shot over toward the cliff, swerved back again into the middle of the roadway, and then shot ahead at terrific speed.

Frank and Joe edged their motorcycles as far to the right of the road as they dared. To their horror they saw that the car was skidding again.

The driver made no attempt to slacken speed.

The automobile came hurtling toward them!

CHAPTER II

THE STOLEN ROADSTER

The auto brakes squealed.

The driver of the oncoming car swung the wheel viciously about. For a moment it appeared that the wheels would not respond. Then they gripped the gravel and the automobile swerved, then shot past.

Bits of sand and gravel were flung about the two boys as they crouched by their motorcycles at the edge of the embankment. The car had missed them only by inches!

Frank caught a glimpse of the driver, who turned about at that moment and, in spite of the speed at which the automobile was traveling and in spite of the perils of the road, shouted something they could not catch at them and shook his fist.

The car was traveling at too great a speed to enable the lad to distinguish the driver's features, but he saw that the man was hatless and that he had a shock of red hair blowing in the wind.

Then the automobile disappeared from sight around the curve ahead, roaring away in a cloud of dust.

"The road hog!" gasped Joe, as soon as he had recovered from his surprise.

"He must be crazy!" Frank exclaimed angrily. "Why, he might have pushed us both right over the embankment!"

"At the rate he was going I don't think he cared whether he ran any one down or not."

Both boys were justifiably angry. On such a narrow, treacherous road there was danger enough when an automobile passed them traveling at even a reasonable speed, but the reckless and insane driving of the red-headed motorist was nothing short of criminal.

"If we ever catch up to him I'm going to give him a piece of my mind!" declared Frank. "Not content with almost running us down he had to shake his fist at us."

"Road hog!" muttered Joe again. "Jail is too good for the likes of him. If it was only his own life he endangered it wouldn't be so bad. Good thing we only had motorcycles. If we had been in another car there would have been a smash-up, sure."

The boys resumed their journey and by the time they had reached the curve ahead that enabled them to see the village of Willowville lying in a little valley along the bay beneath them, there was no trace of the reckless motorist.

Frank delivered the legal papers his father had given to him, and then the boys had the rest of the day to themselves.

"It's too early to go back to Bayport just now," he said to Joe. "What say we go out and visit Chet Morton?"

"Good idea," agreed Joe. "He has often asked us to come out and see him."

Chet Morton was a school chum of the Hardy boys. His father was a real estate dealer with an office in Bayport, but the family lived in the country, about a mile from the city. Although Willowville was some distance away, the boys knew of a road that would take them across country to the Morton home, and from there they could return to Bayport. It would make their journey longer, but they would have the pleasure of visiting their chum. Chet was a great favorite with all the boys, not the least of the reasons for his popularity being the fact that he had a roadster of his own, in which he drove to school every day and with which he was very generous in giving rides to his friends after school hours.

The Hardy boys drove along the country roads in the spring sunlight, enjoying the freedom of their holiday as only boys can. When they had reached a culvert not far from the Morton place Frank suddenly brought his motorcycle to a stop and peered down into a clump of bushes in the deep ditch.

"Somebody's had a spill," he remarked.

Down in the bushes lay an upturned automobile. The car was a total wreck, and lay bottom upward, a mass of tangled junk.

"Must have been hitting an awful clip to crumple up like that," Joe commented. "Perhaps there's some one underneath. Let's go and see."

The boys left their motorcycles by the road and went down to the wrecked car. But there was no sign of either driver or passengers.

"If any one was hurt they've been taken away by now. Probably this wreck is a day or so old," said Frank. "Let's go. We can't do any good here."

They left the wreckage and returned to the road again, resuming their journey.

"I thought at first it might be our red-headed speed fiend," said Frank. "If it was, he was sure lucky to get out of it alive."

The boys gave little further thought to the incident and before long they were in sight of the Mortons' house, a big, homelike, rambling old farmhouse with an apple orchard at the rear. When the boys drove down the lane they saw a figure awaiting them at the barnyard gate.

"That's Chet," said Frank. "I'm glad we found him at home. I thought he might have gone out in the car."

"It is strange," Joe agreed. "On a holiday like this he doesn't usually stay around the farm."

As they approached, they saw Chet leave the gate and come down the lane to meet them. Chet was one of the most popular boys at the Bayport high school, one reason for his popularity being his unfailing good nature and his ability to see fun in almost everything. He was full of jokes and good humor and was rarely seen without a smile on his plump, freckled face.

But today the Hardy boys saw that there was something wrong. Chet's face had an anxious expression, and as they brought their motorcycles to a stop they saw that their chum's usually cheery face was clouded.

"What's the matter?" asked Frank, as their friend hastened up to them.

"You're just in time," replied Chet hurriedly. "You didn't meet a fellow driving my roadster, did you?"

The brothers looked at each other blankly.

"*Your* roadster? We'd recognize it anywhere. No, we didn't see it," said Joe. "What's happened?"

"It's been stolen."

"Stolen?"

"An auto thief stole it from the garage not half an hour ago. He just went in as cool as you please and made away with the car. The hired man saw the roadster disappearing down the lane, but he supposed I was in it so he didn't think anything of it. Then he saw me out in the yard a little while later, so he got suspicious—and the roadster was gone."

"Wasn't it locked?"

"That's the strange part of it. The car was locked, although the garage door was open. I can't see how he got away with it."

"A professional job," commented Frank. "These auto thieves always carry scores of keys with them. But we're losing time here. The only thing is to set out in pursuit and to notify the police. The hired man didn't see which way the fellow went, did he?"

"No."

"There is only the one road, and we didn't meet him, so he must have taken the turning to the right at the end of the lane."

"We'll chase him," said Joe. "Climb onto my bike, Chet. We'll get the thief yet."

"Wait a minute," cried Frank suddenly. "I have an idea! Joe, do you remember that car we saw wrecked in the bushes?"

"Sure."

"Perhaps the driver stole the first automobile he could lay his hands on after the wreck."

"What wreck was that?" asked Chet.

The Hardy boys told him of the wrecked car they had found by the roadside. It had occurred to Frank that perhaps the smash-up might have occurred just a short while before and that the driver of the wrecked car had resumed his interrupted journey in a stolen automobile.

"It sounds reasonable," said Chet. "Let's go and take a look at this wreck. We can get the license number and that may help us find the name of the owner."

The motorcycles roared as the three chums set out back along the road toward the place where the upturned automobile had been seen among the bushes. The boys lost no time in reaching the place, for they realized that every second was precious and that the longer they delayed the greater was the advantage to the car thief.

The car had not been disturbed and apparently no one had been near it since the boys had discovered the wreck. They parked their motorcycles by the roadside and again went down into the bushes to examine the wrecked car.

To their disappointment the car bore no license plates.

"That looks suspicious," said Frank.

"It's more than suspicious," said Joe, who had withdrawn a little to one side and was examining the automobile from the rear. "Don't you remember seeing this car before, Frank? It didn't occur to me until you mentioned the matter of license plates."

"I have been wondering if this isn't the same car that passed us on the shore road at the curve," replied Frank slowly.

"It is the same car. There's no doubt of it in my mind. It didn't have a license plate, I noticed at the time, for I wanted to get the fellow's number. And it was a touring car of the same make as this."

"You're right, Joe. There's no mistake. The red-headed driver came to grief in the ditch, just as we said he would, and then he went on to the nearest farmhouse, which happened to be Chet's place, and stole the first car he saw."

"The busted car was the one the fellow was running who nearly sent us over the cliff," Joe declared. "And it's ten chances to one that he's the fellow who stole Chet's roadster. And he's red-headed. We have those clues, anyway."

"And he went on past our farmhouse instead of turning back the way he came," cried Chet. "Come on, fellows—let's get after him! There was only a little bit of gas in the roadster anyway. Perhaps he's stalled by this time."

Thrilling with the excitement of a chase, the boys clambered back onto the motorcycles and within a few moments a cloud of dust rose from the road as the Hardy boys and Chet Morton set out in swift pursuit of the red-headed automobile thief.

CHAPTER III

TRACES OF THE THIEF

Chet Morton's roadster was a brilliant yellow, not easily mistaken, and the Hardy boys were confident that it would not be difficult to pick up the trail of the auto thief.

"The car is pretty well known around Bayport," said Chet. "It was certainly a gay-looking speed-wagon. Any one who saw it would remember it."

"Seems strange that a thief would take a car like that," remarked Frank. "Auto thieves usually take cars of a standard make and standard color. They're easier to get rid of. He would know that a car like yours could be easily traced."

"I don't think he stole the car to sell it," Joe pointed out. "Take it from me, that chap was getting away from some place in a hurry and when his own car was smashed he just took the first one that came to hand. If we keep after him before he has a chance to get rid of it we'll run him to earth."

A number of men in a hay-field near by attracted Frank's attention, and he brought his motorcycle to a stop.

"I'm going to ask these chaps if they saw him pass."

Frank scrambled over the fence and went over to talk to the farmhands, who watched his approach with curiosity.

"Didn't see a yellow roadster pass here within the last hour, did you?"

One of them, a lanky old farmer with a sun-burned nose, carefully laid down his scythe, put his hand to his ear and shouted:

"Eh?"

"Did you see a fellow pass along here in a roadster?" Frank repeated, in a louder tone.

The farmer turned to his companions, removed a plug of tobacco from the pocket of his overalls and took a hearty chew.

"Lad here want to know if we saw a roadster come by here!" he said slowly.

There were three other farmhands and all gathered around. They put down their scythes very deliberately, and the plug of tobacco was duly passed around the group.

Frank waited.

"A roadster, eh?" asked one.

"A yellow roadster," Frank told him.

One of the men removed his hat and mopped his brow.

"Seems to me," he observed, "I *did* see a car come by here a while ago."

"A yellow car?"

"No—twan't a yeller car. It was a delivery truck, if I remember rightly."

Frank strove to conceal his impatience.

"It was a roadster I was asking about. A yellow roadster."

"Not one of them there coops, hey?" asked the oldest man in the group doubtfully.

"No, not a coupé. A roadster."

"Roadster, eh?" remarked the old farmer. "That's one of them there autymobiles with just two seats and a little cupboard in the back, eh?"

"My cousin has one," observed another member of the group. "He got it secondhand in Bayport. I never *could* see why he bought the doggone thing, for you can't take the folks out for a ride in it without havin' 'em all crowded somethin' fearful. Give me the old tourin' car every time."

"Cain't say as I agree with you," returned the old farmer. "What good's a tourin' car if you want to haul a load of grain into town. Once of them leetle trucks is the best, I've always thought. Then, if you want to go on a picnic or anythin' the family can all climb in the back. You get the *use* out of a car like that."

"Nope. Nothin' like a tourin' car."

"Rank extravagance, buyin' tourin' cars," put in another. "Horse and wagon is good enough for me."

"That's what I say," agreed the fourth.

"What with taxes the way they are—"

"And last year's crops wasn't any too good—"

"I tell ye a tourin' car is the only thing nowadays—"

Somewhat astonished by the sudden turn the argument had taken, Frank vainly tried to make himself heard above the uproar.

"But about this roadster?" he asked. "Did any of you see it?"

But the four men in the field were not listening. Instead they were deep in a highly complicated argument regarding the faults and merits of various makes of cars and they paid no further attention to the youth.

"Can't afford to waste any more time here," he said to himself, and turned away. At the fence, he looked back. One of the farmhands was shaking his fist beneath the nose of a companion, while the other two were engrossed in a heated discussion. Their voices floated across the hay-field in the drowsy summer morning.

"It looks as if you started something," laughed Joe, as his brother returned to the motorcycle.

"I certainly did. Just asked them if they had seen a yellow roadster and they started to fight about what was the best car for a farmer to buy."

"And didn't they see the roadster?" asked Chet.

"I don't think so. If they had they would have told me. I guess they were glad of an excuse to quit work."

"Well, we'd better be getting on our way then. We've lost enough time already."

So, while the four farmhands wrangled loudly in the field, in an argument that bade fair to last until dinner-time at least, the three boys set out again in pursuit of the red-headed auto thief.

They were approaching Bayport when they saw a girl walking along the road ahead of them. There was something familiar about her appearance, and as they drew nearer Frank's face lighted up, for he recognized the girl as Callie Shaw, who was in his own class at Bayport high school. Of all the girls at the school, Callie was the one most greatly admired by Frank. She was a pretty girl, with brown hair and brown eyes, always neatly dressed, and quick and vivacious in her manner.

As the boys brought their motorcycles to a stop, Frank saw that Callie was not in her usual bright and cheery humor. Under one arm she was carrying a parcel that had evidently become untied and the paper of which was badly torn. Her face was distressed and it appeared that she had been crying.

Callie looked up and, recognizing the boys, ran over toward them.

"That awful man!" she wailed, even before they had time to ask her what the matter was. "He ran right over my parcel and smashed nearly all the cakes and jelly I was bringing to Mrs. Wills!"

And with that she held out the torn parcel. Frank knew that Callie, who was a generous and good-hearted girl, had been in the habit of taking little delicacies to a widow, Mrs. Wills, who lived just on the outskirts of Bayport.

Now he saw that the parcel had been smashed so that only one glass of jelly and a few of the cakes had been left intact.

"What man, Callie?" he asked. "What happened?"

"He ran right over my parcel!" Just then Callie spied Chet Morton, and she pouted at him. "He was a friend of yours, too, Chet Morton, for he was driving your car!"

"My car!" gasped Chet.

"Your yellow roadster. He came driving along this road at such a terrible speed that I was frightened and I dropped my parcel. Then he ran right over it."

"Why, Callie, that's just the fellow we've been looking for!" said Frank quickly. "Chet's car has been stolen!"

"Well, whoever stole it, came by here not ten minutes ago," said the girl. "And he's a madman—by the way he was driving."

"Why, we're right on his trail then!" declared Frank. "He must have gone into Bayport."

"He was heading that way," Callie told them. "But at the rate he was going, you'll have a hard time catching him. Oh, Chet, I'm so sorry your car was stolen."

"Don't worry. We'll get it back," replied Chet grimly.

"Are you going back home, Callie?" asked Frank.

"No, I'm going on up to Mrs. Wills' place. You needn't bother to drive me up. It's only a few yards farther on. I know you're anxious to chase that awful man."

"We'll chase him, all right!" declared Frank, as the motorcycles roared.

They bade good-bye to the girl and sped on their way into Bayport, leaving Callie to continue her journey to the home of Mrs. Wills, with the remains of the cakes and jelly over which she had spent so much time and care.

They sped down the main street of Bayport and headed directly to the police station, where they intended to report the theft of Chet's car and a description of the thief, assuming him to be the red-headed man who had so nearly run down Frank and Joe on the shore road.

But when they reached the police station a further surprise was in wait for them.

CHAPTER IV

THE HOLD-UP

Chief Ezra Collig, of the Bayport police force, was a burly, red-faced individual, much given to telling long-winded stories.

Usually, Collig was to be found reclining in a swivel chair in his office, with his feet on the desk, reading the comic papers or polishing up his numerous badges, but this day something had happened to shake him out of his customary calm.

When the boys went into his office they found the chief painfully writing in a huge notebook and confronted by three excited figures. One of these was Ike Harrity, the old ticket seller at the city steamboat office. The others were Detective Smuff, of the police force, and Policeman Con Riley, both trying their best to look important and composed.

Ike Harrity was frankly frightened. It was plain that something very much out of the ordinary had happened. Harrity was a timid and inoffensive old chap who had perched on a high stool behind the wicket at the steamboat office day in and day out for as many years as any one in Bayport could remember.

"I was just countin' up the mornin's receipts," he was saying, in a frightened and high-pitched voice, "when in comes this fellow and he sticks a revolver in front of my nose—"

"Just a minute," interrupted the chief grandly, as the boys entered. He dipped his pen in the inkwell and poised it in the air, as he peered at the lads over his spectacles.

"What are you boys doing here? Can't you see we're busy?"

"I came to report a theft," said Chet Morton. "My roadster has been stolen."

"Why, it was a roadster this fellow drove up to my office in!" cried Ike Harrity. "A yellow roadster."

"Ha!" said Detective Smuff. "A clue!" He immediately fished a notebook out of his pocket and began rummaging around for a pencil.

"Never mind, Detective Smuff," observed the chief heavily. "I'll take any notes that are needed."

Detective Smuff, duly squelched, put back his notebook in confusion.

"What fellow?" Frank asked. "Who drove up to your office in a yellow roadster?"

"The hold-up man," declared Harrity. "I was held up this morning. A fellow tried to steal the steamboat money on me."

"Now just a minute. Just a minute!" demanded the chief. "Let *me* say a word here. The situation is this. A man drove up to the steamboat office a little while ago and tried to hold up Mr. Harrity. But a passenger happened to come into the office just then and the fellow got frightened and ran away. Is that right?"

"That's right," said Harrity.

"I'll make a note of it," said the chief, suiting the action to the word. When he had scribbled industriously for some time he raised the pen again and pointed it at Chet.

"Now *you*," he observed, "say that somebody stole a yellow roadster on you this morning."

"Yes, sir! From our farm. He was seen driving into Bayport just a little while ago."

The chief made a note of it.

"And *you*," he said, pointing the pen at Ike Harrity, "say the hold-up man drove up to the office in a yellow roadster?"

"That's right, chief. That's right. A yellow roadster, it was. And now that I come to think of it, I've seen Chet Morton's car before and it was the spittin' image of it."

"Then," declared the chief, putting down his pen with the air of one making a momentous discovery, "it looks to me very much as if the hold-up man and the fellow that stole the car is one and the same man."

Detective Smuff wagged his head solemnly in admiration of this feat of deduction. "I believe you're right, chief," he declared.

"Of course he's right," said Frank. "It couldn't be any one else. The point is this—where did the hold-up man go? Did he leave in the car? Did any one follow him?"

"He left in the car all right," said Harrity. "But nobody followed him. I telephoned for the police."

"Did you notice the color of this man's hair?" asked Frank suddenly.

"What's that got to do with it?" asked Detective Smuff.

"Never mind. It may have a great deal to do with it. Did you notice the color of his hair?" repeated Frank, turning to Harrity.

"It was short," said Harrity firmly. "Short and dark."

Frank and Joe looked blankly at one another.

"Are you sure?" asked Joe.

"I'm positive," declared Harrity. "I was face to face with him. He was a dark-haired man, and his hair was cut awful short. I noticed that."

"You're sure he wasn't red-headed?"

"I'm sure of it."

"What's all this about?" asked Chief Collig suspiciously. "What has the color of his hair to do with it?"

"Well," admitted Frank, "we were pretty sure that the man who stole Chet's car had long, red hair."

"Hum!" muttered the chief doubtfully. "Then if *that* was the case, the man who stole the car and the man who tried to hold up the office *isn't* one and the same fellow after all."

"I don't know what to make of it," confessed Frank.

Just then a short, nervous little man was ushered into the office. He introduced himself as the passenger who had gone into the steamboat office at the time of the attempted hold-up, and he presented himself in answer to a call from the chief.

In reply to questions, the newcomer, who gave the prosaic name of Henry J. Brown and said he was from New York, told of entering the office and seeing a man run away from the wicket with a revolver in his hand.

"What color was his hair? Did you notice?" asked Frank eagerly.

"I can't say I did," answered the little man. "It all happened so quickly I didn't realize that it was a hold-up until the man was out the door. Then I saw him jump into the roadster and drive away. But—wait a minute. I did notice the color of his hair. Just as the car was disappearing down the street. You couldn't help notice. He was red-headed. He had long red hair."

Detective Smuff looked blankly at the chief and the chief looked blankly at everybody else, particularly at Henry J. Brown of New York.

"I knew it!" declared Joe exultantly. "It's the same man!"

"It can't be the same man!" said the chief wearily. "You boys don't know what you're talking about. Mr. Harrity says he had short, dark hair. Now how could he have short, dark hair and long, red hair at the same time? I ask you that! How could he?"

Chief Collig propounded this query with the expression of one who has triumphantly settled all difficulties.

"He had short, dark hair!" said Harrity doggedly.

"And I'm sure he had long, red hair!" shouted Henry J. Brown, very indignantly. "Do you think I'm blind? Do you think I'd tell a lie about it?"

"He had dark hair."

"It was red."

"It was dark."

"It wasn't."

"It was!"

"Stop it!" commanded Chief Collig. "I don't think either of you know what kind of hair he had. Probably he was bald-headed. But I'll send word out to keep a watch for the yellow roadster. I'll notify the police in other towns too. I guess that's all that can be done now."

And with that, the Hardy boys and Chet Morton had to be content.

When they left the office it was with little hope that the thief or the car would be found. Their misgivings were justified. When they returned to see Chief Collig that night they learned that no word had been received concerning the yellow roadster from any of the outlying towns or villages and that despite a diligent search conducted by Detective Smuff and other members of the Bayport force, the roadster had not been located in the city.

CHAPTER V

CHET'S AUTO HORN

Fenton Hardy, the internationally famous detective, was reading in the library of his home that evening when his sons tapped on the door.

Although he was a busy man, Mr. Hardy was not the type of father who maintains an air of aloofness from his family, the result being that he was on as good terms with his boys as though he were an elder brother.

"Come in," he shouted cheerfully, putting aside his book, and when Frank and Joe entered the room he motioned to a deep leather sofa near the window. "Sit down. What have you been doing all day? Burning up all the roads in the country, I suppose?" He grinned amiably at them and puffed vigorously at his pipe.

"Well, we didn't travel very far today, dad," Frank replied. "We were— well, we—we were—"

"Investigating," prompted Joe.

"Aha!" exclaimed Mr. Hardy, in mock surprise. "So my sons were investigating, eh? What was it? A murder? A plot to blow up the White House? A train wreck? Something big, I hope."

"No—not quite that bad," admitted Frank. "It was a car theft."

Mr. Hardy shook his head.

"I'm disappointed in you," he said solemnly. "I really am. To think that sons of mine should investigate a car theft. I thought you wouldn't bother about anything less than a murder!" His eyes twinkled, and the Hardy boys, who were accustomed to their father's good-natured banter, smiled back at him.

"We weren't just practicing detective work, dad," explained Frank. "You see, Chet Morton's roadster was stolen this morning."

"Is that so!" exclaimed Mr. Hardy, genuinely concerned. "Why, that's too bad. Chet was mighty proud of that car, wasn't he?"

"Yes, he was. And it hasn't been found yet."

"No trace of the thief?"

"He tried to hold up the steamboat ticket office after he stole the car."

Mr. Hardy whistled.

"Why you *have* been on a case worth while. Tell me all about it."

He settled back in his chair while his sons told him the story of the day's doings. When they told of the difference of opinion as to the color of the man's hair he did not laugh with them, as they had expected, over the argument between Harrity and Mr. Brown. On the contrary, he knitted his brows and his face wore a serious expression.

"It wasn't any ordinary auto thief you were dealing with," he said slowly. "I've no doubt the man who tried to rob the ticket office and the man who almost ran you down on the shore road were one and the same. And the same man stole Chet Morton's car."

"But how about the color of his hair? There must have been two men," said Joe.

"Think so? I have my own theories. But then—the average witness is very unreliable. For instance, I'll give you a test. You have each seen Superintendent Norton of Bayport high school—well, how often?"

"About two or three thousand times, I guess," answered Frank.

"Over a period of three years. Well, what color is his hair?"

Frank looked blankly at Joe.

"Why, it's—it's—"

Joe scratched his head.

"Brown, isn't it?"

"I think it's black."

"You see?" said Mr. Hardy, smiling. "Your powers of observation have not been trained. A good detective has to school himself to remember all sorts of little facts like that, until it gets to be a habit with him. Both of you have been looking at Mr. Norton for about three years and you don't know the color of his hair. And if I asked you whether he was in the habit of wearing laced shoes or buttoned shoes you would be stumped altogether. As a matter of fact, Mr. Norton is bald and he wears a chestnut wig. You never noticed that? He always wears buttoned shoes, he belongs to the Elks, and his favorite author is Dickens."

The boys looked at their father in amazement.

"But, dad, you've never met him."

"I've never been introduced to him, but I've passed him on the street a number of times. When your powers of observation have been trained as mine have been it's no trick at all to take away a mental photograph of a man after seeing him once. If you are specially observant it isn't hard to notice such details as that regarding the wig. A wig never has the same appearance as natural hair."

"But how do you know he belongs to the Elks?" asked Joe.

"He wears the lodge emblem as a watch charm."

"And how do you know his favorite author is Dickens?"

"On three separate occasions that I met Mr. Norton I noticed that he was carrying a book. Once it was *Oliver Twist*. Another time it was *A Tale of Two Cities*. The third time it was *David Copperfield*. So I judge that his favorite author must be Dickens. Am I right?"

"He always talks Dickens to us at school," said Frank.

"It's simple enough, once you get the habit," remarked Mr. Hardy. "You must train yourselves to be observant, so that in time you will automatically remember little details about people you meet and places you've visited. Now, if Harrity and Mr. Brown had been at all observant, in spite of the fact that they were surprised and frightened, they would have been able to give the police a very thorough description of the man who tried to hold up the steamboat office. And if the man happened to be a professional thief the description would have helped the officers ascertain who he was, because once a man has served a prison term his description is kept on file. As it is, all we know about him is that he is probably red-headed. That isn't very much to go on."

"I'm afraid Chet hasn't much chance of recovering his roadster," said Joe.

"You never can tell," remarked his father. "It may turn up some time. Perhaps the thief will get himself into trouble yet. Keep your ears and eyes open. And now, if you don't mind, I have some reports to write—"

Frank and Joe took the hint and left their father to his work. But although they talked long into the night on possible ways and means of recovering Chet's car, they were able to devise no plan for tracing the thief.

And through the week that followed there were no further clues. Chet had given up all hope of seeing the roadster again.

"I sure miss the old bus," he told the Hardy boys after school on Friday afternoon. "I have to take my chances on catching rides in and out of town now. Why, last night I walked half way home before a car came along and gave me a lift."

"Saturday will be a pretty dull day for you now."

"You just bet your sweet life it will be dull! Nothing to do but sit around the farm."

"Better come with us tomorrow," suggested Joe. "A bunch of us are going fishing up near the dam. You can meet us at the crossroads near Willow River."

"Good idea!" said Chet. "What time?"

"Ten o'clock."

"Fine! I'll be there. Gosh, I see where I get a ride home. There goes a hay wagon, and it's heading right for the next farm."

A long wagon rumbled slowly toward the boys. A lean and solemn farm-er perched on the front seat, half asleep. The horses dawdled along.

"That's Lem Billers—the laziest man in nine counties," said Chet. "Watch me have some fun with him."

Chet took from his pocket an automobile horn. He had originally bought it for the roadster but had not had time to install it before the car was stolen. The horn was of a new type, very small, yet it had a particularly raucous shriek.

The Hardy boys grinned as they saw Chet step out into the road and swing himself lightly up on the back of the wagon. Mr. Billers was bringing some supplies back to the farm and Chet was hidden from view by a bag of flour.

As the wagon rumbled past, Chet sounded the automobile horn.

It shrieked sharply and insistently.

Mr. Billers, being a lazy man, did not even look behind. He simply tugged lightly at the reins and the horses edged over to the side of the road.

Having heard the horn, Mr. Billers expected an automobile would pass. But when no car flashed by he turned indolently in his seat and looked be-hind. The roadway was clear. There was not an automobile in sight. He did not see Chet, doubling up with laughter, on the back of the wagon. He gazed doubtfully at the Hardy boys, who were standing at the curb, trying to con-ceal their smiles.

"Could 'a' swore I heard a horn," grunted Mr. Billers. Then he tugged at the lines and brought the horses into the middle of the road again.

Instantly the horn shrieked again. This time it was even louder and more insistent than before. It seemed that an automobile was right behind the wag-on, clamoring to pass.

Almost automatically, Mr. Billers yanked at the reins and the horses again went to the side of the road.

But again no car went by.

Again Mr. Billers looked behind. Again, to his astonishment, he saw that the roadway was clear.

"Hanged if I didn't think I heard a horn!" exclaimed Mr. Billers, greatly puzzled, as he drove on again. "My ears must be goin' back on me."

But in a few minutes the horn shrieked again. Frank and Joe, who were walking along the sidewalk, keeping abreast of the wagon so as not to miss the fun, chuckled as they saw Mr. Billers once more pull on the reins to guide the horses to the roadside. Then the farmer recollected how he had been fooled on the previous occasions and he looked quickly around. But there was no car in sight.

Mr. Billers gazed down the roadway for a long time. Then he sighed, with the air of one whose patience has been long tried.

"Must be somethin' the matter with my ears," he muttered, and drove on.

At this moment a luxurious sedan swept around a corner and drew up close behind the wagon. There was a chauffeur at the wheel and he sounded his horn impatiently, for the road was narrow and he was unable to get past.

Lem Billers smiled darkly to himself and paid no attention.

"There it goes again," he grumbled. "I *must* be hearin' things. Hang me if I'll turn out any more when there ain't no car there to turn out for."

The wagon continued in the center of the road. The chauffeur of the car glared at Lem Billers' back and sounded the horn again. Still the farmer paid no attention.

Chet, limp with laughter, almost rolled off the wagon. Frank and Joe could control their mirth no longer, and leaned against a telephone post with shouts of glee.

The chauffeur, believing that the boys were laughing at him because he could not get past, became purple with anger. He sounded the horn again and again, and finally, when Lem Billers obstinately refused to pay any attention, he looked wildly about for a policeman.

As luck would have it, Constable Con Riley was ambling along Main Street at that moment, wondering if it would soon be supper time and hoping his wife would serve corned beef and cabbage that evening. He was aroused from his trance by the chauffeur, who brought the sedan to a stop and ran over to him.

"Officer—arrest that man!" roared the chauffeur, pointing to Lem Billers.

"What for?" demanded Con, taking off his helmet and scratching his head.

"Obstructing the traffic. He won't let me pass. I've been sounding my horn for the last five minutes, and he won't let me go past."

"Oh, ho!" said Constable Riley. "He can't get away with that. Not while Con Riley's on the beat." And with that he ran out into the road, shouting to Lem Billers to stop.

At the constable's command, the farmer halted his team and gazed in amazement at the chauffeur and the officer as they came running up to him.

"Why won't you let him pass?" demanded the constable.

"Don't say you didn't hear me?" roared the chauffeur. "I sounded my horn fifty times."

"Sure, I heard a horn," admitted Billers. "But," he added triumphantly, "I didn't see no car."

"Are you blind?" asked Riley. "There's the car."

Lem Billers looked behind. At sight of the sedan, his jaw dropped.

"Well, I'll be hanged!" he declared sadly. "It must be my eyes is goin' back on me. Not my ears. I looked behind three times and I couldn't see no car."

"Don't believe him, officer," said the chauffeur. "He didn't even turn around."

"I did so!" contended Mr. Billers.

"Then why didn't you let me pass?"

"You didn't have no car. I heard a horn but I didn't see no car."

Thereupon the argument grew fast and furious. Constable Riley was vastly puzzled. He didn't know what to make of it. Both the chauffeur and Lem Billers appeared to be telling the truth, yet there was something wrong somewhere. He took it all down in a notebook, while Mr. Billers and the chauffeur grew angrier and angrier at each other until finally they were on the point of settling the matter with their fists.

In the meantime there was a steadily lengthening line of cars and wagons blocking the street, unable to get past because of the hay wagon and the sedan. A constant chorus of automobile horns sounded. Angry drivers roared at the officer to clear the road.

Constable Riley threw up his hands in disgust.

"Get on your way, both of you," he commanded. "I can't stand here arguin' all afternoon."

And while Lem Billers, wondering whether his eyes or his ears had deceived him, drew his horses to the side of the road and muttered strong threats of vengeance against the chauffeur, the traffic tangle gradually abated. When he finally resumed his journey, the Hardy boys could see Chet Morton lying limply in the back of the wagon with tears of laughter running down his face. As for Frank and Joe, they laughed all the way home and during supper that evening their spasmodic outbursts of chuckles puzzled their parents extremely.

CHAPTER VI
TIRE TRACKS

Next day was Saturday, and immediately after breakfast the Hardy boys asked their mother to make up a lunch for them, as they intended to spend the day in the woods with a number of their school chums.

Mrs. Hardy quickly made up a generous package of sandwiches, not forgetting to slip in several big slices of the boys' favorite cake, and the lads started out in the bright morning sunshine, with the whole holiday before them.

They met the other boys, half a dozen in all, on the road at the outskirts of the town and so, whistling and chattering and telling jokes, the group trudged along the dusty highway. Once in a while they would explore along the fences for berry bushes, and occasionally a friendly scuffle would start, to end with both laughing contestants covered with dust.

When they reached the crossroads Chet had not yet appeared, so they rested in the shade of the trees until at length the chubby youth came panting along the road, his lunch under his arm.

"If I only had my roadster I wouldn't be late," he said, as he came up to them. "I've been so used to it that I've forgotten how long it takes to walk this far."

"Well, are we all set?" asked Frank.

"Everybody's here. Where are we going?"

"What do you say to Willow Grove?"

"All those in favor say 'Aye'," demanded Chet, and there was a chorus of "Aye" from the crowd.

"It's unanimous," Chet decided. "Willow Grove it shall be. Let's go."

Willow Grove was about a mile farther on. It was some distance in from the road, and was on the banks of Willow River, from which it got its name. It was an ideal place for a picnic, and as it was somewhat early in the season it was hardly likely that other parties from the city would be in the grove that day.

Frank told the other boys about Chet's adventure with the auto horn and the story was greeted with shouts of laughter, which were redoubled when Chet told how he had later jumped down from the wagon and run along behind, shouting to Lem Billers to give him a ride.

"It was a shame!" he confessed. "The poor old chap reined in his horses and made me come up and sit on the seat beside him. He asked me if I had walked very far and then he told me all about his argument with the policeman and the chauffeur. I could hardly keep my face straight."

When the boys reached the lane that led in toward Willow Grove from the main road they broke into a run and raced into the woods, shouting and yelling like wild Indians. Once in the friendly shade of the trees they capered about in the joy of their Saturday freedom. Chet took charge of the lunches and stored them in a convenient clearing, and then began the rush for the river.

The day passed in the usual fashion of such days. They swam, they ate, they loafed about under the trees, they played games at imminent risk of life and limb, they explored the woods, and otherwise enjoyed themselves with all the happy energy of healthy lads. Joe Hardy, who was an amateur naturalist in his way, went roaming off by himself during the afternoon while the other boys were enjoying their third swim of the day, and penetrated deeper into the woods.

He poked about in the undergrowth, examining various flowers and plants that came to his attention, but discovered no specimens that he had not seen before. He was just on the point of going back to the other lads when he saw before him a small clearing. It was a part of the grove in which he had never been, so he ploughed on through the bushes until he found himself in a clearing that appeared to be part of an abandoned roadway.

It was in a low-lying part of the grove and the ground was wet. At one point it was muddy, and in this mud Joe saw something that aroused his curiosity.

"Tire tracks, eh! There's been an automobile in here," he muttered to himself. "I wonder how on earth a car could get this far into the woods!"

Then he remembered his father's remarks on the value of developing his powers of observation, so he went over closer and examined the marks in the mud.

"That's a strange tread," he thought. "I've never seen a tire mark quite like that before."

He gazed at it until he was sure that if he ever saw a similar auto tread again he would recognize it.

"That just goes to prove that dad was right," said Joe. "Probably I've seen auto tires like that often, but I've never noticed the markings, and now that I do notice one in particular it seems strange to me. But I wonder what an automobile was doing in here and how it came to get here in the first place!"

However, he gave the matter little further thought and retraced his steps through the woods until he returned to the other boys, who were getting dressed after their swim.

"I thought automobiles weren't allowed in Willow Grove," he said casually to Chet Morton.

"Neither they are. You have to park just inside the fence."

"Well, somebody brought a car right down into the grove."

"They couldn't. There's no road."

"Well, there's a sort of clearing over there," said Joe, motioning in the direction from which he had just returned. "It looks as if it had been a road at one time."

"That's probably the old creek road. It hasn't been used for years."

"Well, it was used just this week. I saw the marks of an automobile tire over there not ten minutes ago. And it was a mighty peculiar tread, too. Like this—," and Joe commenced to draw a replica of the design in the sand, using a thin stick of wood as a pencil.

Chet Morton stared.

"Why," he exclaimed, "there's only one car in the city has tires like that!"

"Whose car?"

"Mine!" exclaimed Chet, springing to his feet. "Where *is* this road you found?"

Joe Hardy quickly led the way and all the other boys came trooping along behind, the whole band thrown into a state of great excitement by this unexpected discovery. They all knew that Chet's car was of an unusual make and that the tires were distinctive. When they reached the clearing and Chet had examined the imprint in the mud he exclaimed:

"There's no mistake about it! My car has been here! No other car in the city has a tread like that!"

"Perhaps the car is still around here," suggested Frank quickly. "For all we can tell, the thief may have abandoned it and picked this road as a good place to hide it."

"It would be an ideal place," agreed Chet. "This road leads off the main highway, and it isn't often used. Let's take a look around, anyway."

The boys quickly scattered, some taking one side of the road, the rest taking the other.

For a while the search continued without success, but at last Frank and Chet, who were following the abandoned road farther down, gave a simultaneous cry.

"Here's a bypath!"

Before them was a narrow roadway, over-grown with weeds and low bushes that almost hid it from view. It led from the abandoned road into the very depths of the wood. Without hesitation the two boys plunged into it.

The narrow roadway widened out farther on, then wound about a heavy clump of trees, until it came to an end in a wide clearing.

And in the clearing stood Chet Morton's lost roadster!

"My car!" yelled Chet, in delight.

His shout was heard by all the other boys, and the sound of snapping twigs and crackling branches soon told Frank and Chet that the others were losing no time in reaching the scene.

Chet's delight was boundless. He examined the car with minute care, in every particular, while the other boys crowded about. At last he straightened up with a smile of satisfaction.

"She hasn't been damaged a bit. All ready to run. The thief just hid the old bus in here and made a getaway. Come on, fellows, we don't walk back home today. We ride."

He clamored into the car and in a few seconds the engine roared. There was sufficient room in the clearing to permit him to turn the roadster about, and when he swung the car around and headed up the bypath the boys gave a cheer and hastened to clamber on board.

Lurching and swaying, the roadster reached the abandoned road and from there it was an easy run to the main highway. In spite of the fact that it had been left in the bush for probably a week, the roadster was in perfect condition and the engine ran smoothly. Joe was given the seat of honor beside the driver, because he had discovered the tire marks that had led to the recovery of the car, and the other boys distributed themselves as best they could. They clung to the running boards, hung precariously to the back, and one lad even straddled the hood. In this manner the triumphal procession returned to Bayport.

But as the cheering lads came down the main street they noticed that there was an unwonted air of excitement in the town. People were standing on the street corners in little groups, talking earnestly, and when the boys spied Detective Smuff, of the police force, striding along with a portentous frown, they called out to him.

"What's on your mind today, detective? Chet got his car back!"

"I've got something more important than stolen cars to worry about," declared Detective Smuff. "The Tower Mansion has been robbed."

CHAPTER VII

THE MANSION ROBBERY

Tower Mansion was one of the show places of Bayport. Few people in the city had ever been permitted to enter the place and the admiration the palatial building excited was solely by reason of its exterior appearance, but the first thing a newcomer to Bayport usually asked was, "Who owns that magnificent house on the hill?"

It was an immense, rambling stone structure situated on the top of the hill overlooking the bay, and it could be seen for miles, silhouetted against the skyline, like some ancient feudal castle. This resemblance to a castle was heightened by the fact that at each end of the mansion rose a high tower.

One of these towers had been built when the mansion was first erected by Major Applegate, an eccentric old army man who had made millions by lucky real estate deals and had laid the foundation for the Applegate fortune. The mansion had been the admiration of its day, and in its time had seen much gaiety.

But as the years passed the Applegate family became scattered until at last there remained but Hurd Applegate and his sister Adelia, who continued living in the vast and lonely old mansion.

Hurd Applegate was a man of about sixty years of age. He was a tall, stooped man, eccentric in his ways, and his life seemed to be devoted to the collection of rare stamps. He was an authority on the subject, and nothing else in life appeared to hold a great deal of interest for him. The only visitors at Tower Mansion were philatelists from New York or experts desirous of appraising some new stamp that Hurd Applegate had managed to secure from some remote part of the world. It had often been said in Bayport that Hurd Applegate had accomplished only two things in life—he had collected stamps and he had built a new tower on the mansion. The new tower, a duplicate of the original tower at the opposite end of the great building, had been built but a few years—even well within the memory of the two Hardy boys.

Adelia Applegate, who lived in the Tower Mansion with her brother, was a maiden lady of uncertain years. The records in Bayport's city hall gave her age as fifty-five, but Miss Applegate admitted it to no one. She was as eccentric as her brother, and lived very much to herself, being seldom seen in the city. She was at one time a blonde, but she had endeavored to retain her youth by dyeing her hair, with the result that it was now a sort of dusty black. Chet Morton was fond of saying that "Miss Applegate used to be a blonde but she dyed."

She dressed in all colors of the rainbow, and her infrequent excursions into Bayport stores, when she would order the clerks about like so many soldiers, shouting at them in her high, cracked voice, had become historic on account of the wild and colorful garments she would carry off with her.

These eccentric people were reputed to be enormously wealthy, although they lived simply and kept only a few servants. So when Hurd Applegate came into the Bayport police station that afternoon and reported that the safe in his library had been broken open and that it had been robbed of all the securities and jewels it contained, the rumors that soon spread about the city magnified the actual loss until it became common talk that the loss amounted anywhere from one hundred thousand to a million dollars.

When Frank and Joe Hardy arrived home that evening they met Hurd Applegate just leaving the house. The man tapped the steps with his cane as he came out and when he met the boys he gave them an abrupt and piercing glance.

"Good day!" he growled, in a grudging manner, and went on his way.

"He must have been asking dad to take up the case," said Frank to his brother, as soon as Hurd Applegate was out of earshot.

They hurried into the house, eager to find out more about the robbery, and in the hallway they met Fenton Hardy, who had just seen Mr. Applegate to the door.

"I hear the Tower Mansion was robbed," said Joe.

Mr. Hardy nodded.

"Yes—Mr. Applegate was just here. He wants me to handle the case."

"How much was taken?"

"Quite curious, aren't you?" remarked Mr. Hardy, with a smile. "Well, I don't suppose it will do any harm to tell you. The safe in the Applegate library was opened. The loss will be about forty thousand dollars, I believe."

"We heard it was over a hundred thousand!" exclaimed Joe.

"Rumors always exaggerate. Forty thousand dollars is the figure Mr. Applegate puts it at. And it's quite enough, too. All in securities and jewels."

"Whew!" exclaimed Frank. "Quite a haul! When did it happen?"

"Either last night or this morning. He did not get up until after ten o'clock this morning and he did not go into the library until nearly noon. Then he discovered the theft."

"How was the safe opened?"

"It was either opened by some one who knew the combination or else by a very clever crook. It wasn't dynamited at all. I'm going up to the house in a few minutes. Mr. Applegate is to call for me."

"Can't we go along?" asked Joe eagerly.

Mr. Hardy looked at his sons with a smile.

"Well, if you are so anxious to be detectives, I suppose it is about as good a chance as any to watch a crime investigation from the inside. If Mr. Applegate doesn't object, I suppose you may come along."

In a few minutes an automobile drew up before the Hardy home. Mr. Applegate was sitting in the rear seat, resting his chin on his cane. When Mr. Hardy mentioned the boys' request he merely grunted assent, so Joe and Frank clambered into the car with their father. They were tremendously excited at the prospect of being "on the inside" in the mysterious case.

While the car bowled along over the city roads toward the Tower Mansion that was gloomily silhouetted against the sky, Mr. Hardy and Mr. Applegate discussed the robbery.

"I don't really need a detective in this case," snapped Hurd Applegate. "Don't need one at all. It's as clear as the nose on your face. I *know* who took the stuff. But I can't prove it."

"Whom do you suspect?" asked Fenton Hardy.

"Only.one man in the world could have taken it. Robinson!"

"Robinson?"

"Yes. Henry Robinson—the caretaker. He's the man."

The Hardy boys looked at one another in consternation.

Henry Robinson, the caretaker of the Tower Mansion, was the father of one of their closest chums. Perry Robinson, nick-named "Slim", was to have accompanied them on their jaunt to the woods that day but had failed to appear. The reason was now evident.

But that Henry Robinson should be accused of the robbery seemed absurd. The boys had met Slim's father and he had appeared to them as a good-natured, easy-going man, the soul of truth and honesty.

"I don't believe it," whispered Frank.

"Neither do I," returned his brother.

"What makes you suspect Robinson?" asked Mr. Hardy of Hurd Applegate.

"He's the only person besides my sister and me who ever saw that safe opened and closed. He could have learned the combination if he kept his eyes and ears open. I believe he did."

"But is that your only reason for suspecting him?"

"More than that. This morning he paid off a note at the bank. It was a note for nine hundred dollars, and I know for a fact that he didn't have more than one hundred dollars to his name a few days ago. The Robinsons have been hard up, for they had sickness in the family last winter and Henry Robinson has had a hard time meeting his debts since then. Now where did he raise nine hundred dollars so suddenly?"

"Perhaps he has a good explanation," said Mr. Hardy mildly. "It doesn't do to jump at conclusions."

"Oh, he'll have an explanation all right!" sniffed Mr. Applegate. "But it will have to be a mighty good one to satisfy me."

"Luckily, he'll not have to satisfy Mr. Applegate, but will have to convince a jury—if it gets that far," whispered Joe in his brother's ear.

The automobile was speeding up the wide driveway that led to Tower Mansion, and within a few minutes it drew up at the front entrance. Mr. Applegate dismissed the driver, and Mr. Hardy and the two boys accompanied the eccentric man into the house.

Nothing had been disturbed in the library since the discovery of the theft. Mr. Hardy examined the open safe, then drew a magnifying glass from his pocket and with minute care inspected the dial of the combination lock. Then he examined the windows, the door-knobs, all places where there might be finger-prints. At last he shook his head.

"A smooth job," he observed. "The fellow must have worn gloves. Not a finger-print in the room."

"No need of looking for finger-prints," said Applegate. "It was Robinson—that's who it was."

"Better send for him," advised Mr. Hardy. "I'd like to ask him a few questions."

Mr. Applegate rang for one of the servants and instructed him to tell Mr. Robinson he was wanted in the library at once. Mr. Hardy glanced at the boys.

"You had better wait in the hallway," he suggested. "I want to ask some questions, and it might embarrass Mr. Robinson if you were here."

The lads readily withdrew, and in the hallway they met Henry Robinson, the caretaker, and his son Perry. Mr. Robinson was calm but pale, and at the doorway he patted his son on the shoulder.

"Don't worry, son," he said. "It'll be all right." With that he entered the library.

Slim Robinson turned to his two chums.

"My dad is innocent!" he cried.

CHAPTER VIII

THE ARREST

There was something in Perry Robinson's tone that made Frank and Joe extremely sorry for their chum, for it seemed that the boy realized that the case looked black against his father.

Although the Hardy lads realized that it was only natural that Perry should stand up for his father, they shared some of his conviction that Mr. Robinson was not guilty.

"Of course he's innocent," agreed Frank. "He'll be able to clear himself all right, Perry."

"But everything looks pretty black against him," said Perry, who was pale and shaken. "Unless your father can catch the real thief I'm afraid dad will be blamed for it."

"Everybody knows your father is honest," said Joe consolingly. "He has a good record—even Applegate will have to admit that."

"A good record won't help him very much if he is blamed for this and can't clear himself. And dad admits that he did know the combination of the safe."

"He knew it?"

"Accidentally. He was cleaning the library fireplace one day when he found a slip of paper with numbers marked on it. The combination was so simple that any one could remember it if he read it once. Dad didn't realize what it was until he had studied it a while, and then he put it back on Mr. Applegate's desk. The window was open and the breeze had blown the paper to the floor."

"Does Applegate know that?"

"Not yet. But dad is going to tell him now. He says he knows it will look bad for him, but he's going to tell the truth about it. He knew the combination, although of course he would never think of using it."

From the library came the dull hum of voices. The harsh tones of Hurd Applegate occasionally rose above the murmur of conversation and once the boys heard Mr. Robinson's voice rise sharply.

"I *didn't* do it. I tell you I *didn't* take that money."

"Then where did you get the nine hundred you paid on that note?" demanded Mr. Applegate.

There was silence for a while.

"Where did you get it?"

"I'm not at liberty to tell you."

"You won't tell?"

"I can't."

"Why not?"

"I got the money honestly—that's all I can say about it."

"Oh, ho!" exclaimed Applegate. "You got the money honestly, yet you can't tell me where it came from! That's very likely, isn't it? If you got it honestly you shouldn't be ashamed to tell where you got it."

"I'm not ashamed. But I'm not at liberty to tell."

"Mighty funny thing that you should get nine hundred dollars so quickly. You were pretty hard up last week, weren't you? Had to ask for an advance on your month's wages."

"I admit it."

"And then the day of this robbery you suddenly have nine hundred dollars that you can't explain."

Mr. Hardy's calm voice broke in.

"Of course, I don't like to pry into your private affairs, Mr. Robinson," he said; "but it would be best if you could clear up this matter of the money. You must admit yourself that it doesn't look promising."

"I know it looks bad," replied the caretaker doggedly. "But I can't tell you where that money came from."

"And you admit knowing the combination of the safe, too!" broke in Applegate. "I didn't know that before. Why didn't you tell me?"

"I didn't consider it important enough. I had found the combination by accident and I had no intention of using it. As a matter of fact, I don't think I could remember it accurately right now. I just put the paper back and decided to say nothing about it, to save trouble."

"And yet you come and tell me about it now!"

"I have nothing to conceal. If I had taken the money I wouldn't very likely be telling you now that I knew the combination."

"Yes," agreed Mr. Hardy, "that's a point in your favor."

"Is it?" asked Applegate. "You're just clever enough to think up a trick like that, Robinson. You think that if you come to me now and admit you knew the combination I'll believe that you are so honest that you couldn't have committed this robbery. Very clever. But not clever enough. There's enough evidence right here and now to convict you, and I'm not going to delay another minute."

There was the sound of a telephone receiver being lifted, and then Applegate's voice continued—

"Police station." After a short wait, he went on. "Hello—police station?—This is Applegate speaking—Applegate—Hurd Applegate.—Well,

I think we've found our man.—In that robbery.—Yes, Robinson.—You thought so, eh?—So did I, but I wasn't sure.—He has practically convicted himself by his own story.—Yes, I want him arrested.—You'll be up right away?—Fine.—Good-bye."

The telephone tinkled.

"You're not going to have me arrested, Mr. Applegate?"

"Why not? You took the money!"

"But I'm innocent! I swear it! Haven't I always been honest, ever since I came to work for you? Have you ever had any fault to find with me?"

"Not until now," returned Applegate grimly.

"It might have been better to wait a while," suggested Mr. Hardy mildly. "Of course, it is entirely in your hands, Mr. Applegate, and I admit the case looks rather bad against Mr. Robinson. But perhaps some more evidence may turn up."

"What more evidence do we want? The man's guilty. It's as plain as the nose on your face. If he wants to return the rest of the jewels and securities I'll see what can be done toward having the charge reduced—but that's all."

"But I can't return them! I didn't take them!"

"I suppose you have them hidden safely away by now, hoping to get them when you get out of penitentiary, eh? It'll be a long time, Robinson—a long time."

In the hallway, the boys listened in growing excitement. The case had taken an abrupt and tragic turn. Both the Hardy boys were sorry for their chum Slim, who looked as though he might collapse under the strain.

"He's innocent," muttered the boy, over and over again. "I *know* he's innocent. They can't arrest him. My dad never stole a dollar in his life!"

Frank patted him on the shoulder.

"Brace up, old chap," he advised. "It looks pretty bad just now, but your father will be able to clear himself, never fear."

"I—I'll have to tell mother—," stammered Slim. "This will break her heart. And my sisters—"

Frank and Joe led him down through the hallway and along a corridor that led to a wing of the mansion, where the Robinson family had rooms. There, in a neat, but sparsely furnished apartment, they found Mrs. Robinson, a gentle, kindly-faced woman, somewhat lame, who was sitting anxiously in a chair by the window. Her two daughters, Paula and Tessie, twins, were by her side, and all looked up in expectation as the lads came in.

"What news, son?" asked Mrs. Robinson bravely, after she had greeted the Hardy boys.

"Bad, mother."

"They're not—they're not—arresting him?" cried Paula, springing forward.

Perry nodded, dumbly.

"But they can't!" cried Tessie protestingly. "He's innocent! He *couldn't* do anything like that! It's wrong—"

Mrs. Robinson began to cry, quite silently. Perry went over to his mother and awkwardly patted her shoulder, his face white and stern. The twins gazed at one another with desperate eyes.

Frank and Joe, their hearts too full for utterance, withdrew softly from the room.

CHAPTER IX

RED HAIR

The arrest of Henry Robinson caused a sensation in Bayport, for the caretaker of Tower Mansion was one of the last men in the city whom one would have suspected of dishonesty. There was a great deal of public sympathy for the family, but little for the accused, as most people seemed to take it for granted that he would not have been arrested if he had not had something to do with the crime.

But the Hardy boys were not satisfied.

"I'm positive Henry Robinson is innocent," said Frank to his brother the next morning. "There's a great deal about this case that hasn't come to the surface yet. I have a sort of sneaking idea that the man who stole Chet Morton's car had something to do with this."

"He was a criminal—that much is certain," agreed Joe. "He stole an automobile and he tried to hold up the ticket office."

"I'd like to go back to the place where we saw the wrecked car. You never know what evidence we might find. There might be something there that would identify the chap."

"I'm with you. Let's go this morning."

So within the hour the boys were on their motorcycles, speeding along the shore road toward the place where the speed fiend's car had been wrecked in the bushes.

"I'd certainly like to do something to help clear Mr. Robinson," said Frank. "It's pretty tough on Slim and his mother and sisters."

"We probably won't be able to do very much. If dad can't clear him, I don't think we can help a great deal. But it's worth while trying."

"It sure is. And I've had a hunch all along that we didn't investigate the wreck of that car closely enough."

"Well, we'll make a thorough job of it this time."

When the boys reached the scene of the wreck they found the smashed car just where they had seen it last. The tires had been taken and some of the accessories that had escaped destruction had been stripped from the automobile, but the car had been so badly smashed that there were few evidences of disturbance.

Leaving their motorcycles by the side of the road, the lads plunged down into the bushes and busied themselves examining the wreckage. Joe hunted through the side pockets in the hope that there might be papers or some other means of identification, but in this he was disappointed. There were no license plates, but Frank managed to secure the engine number, and this he jotted down in a notebook he carried.

"Perhaps this will give us a clue. Although I have an idea that the fellow got this car in the same way he got Chet's. It's probably a stolen automobile."

For a time they rummaged around among the wreckage without success. Then, at last, Frank gave a low cry.

"Here's something!" he exclaimed. "Look!"

Joe came over to where he was standing, and Frank plucked something from the front seat of the wrecked car.

"Red hair!"

In his hand Frank held a small tuft of vivid red hair. It was very coarse in texture, and the surprising part of it was that the hairs were not separate but were attached to a sort of tough linen.

"Why, it's part of a wig!" said Frank, examining the hair more closely.

"You're right," agreed his brother. "No human hair ever grew like that."

"Part of the fellow's wig was torn when the car was smashed up!"

"And that explains why Harrity and his witness couldn't agree on the color of the fellow's hair!" exclaimed Joe, in excitement.

"I see it now! The man didn't wear the wig when he held up the steamboat office, and the minute he reached the car he put it on again. That explains why Brown saw a red-haired man driving away in Chet's roadster and why Harrity was positive that man wasn't red-headed."

"That's a *real* clue!" exclaimed Joe. "We ought to tell dad about this."

"And we will, too," said Frank, beginning to scramble through the bushes back toward the road.

He put the fragment of the red wig carefully in an inner pocket, and then the Hardy boys started back toward Bayport. The clue was slight, of course, but, still, it served to clear up the disagreement as to the color of the hold-up man's hair. It also served to prove conclusively that the man who had passed Frank and Joe on the shore road at such break-neck speed, and who had later wrecked his car, was the same man who had stolen Chet's roadster and had attempted to hold up the steamboat ticket office.

"I guess dad will think we aren't such poor detectives after all," Joe exulted, as they brought their motorcycles to a stop in the yard of the Hardy home.

Their father was in the library, but in their excitement the lads forgot to rap at the door and rushed into the room without ceremony.

"Dad, we've found a clue!" cried Joe, when he saw his father sitting at the huge oak desk. Then he fell back, embarrassed, when he saw that there was some one else in the room.

"Beg pardon!" said Frank, and the boys would have retreated, but Mr. Hardy's visitor turned around and they saw that it was Perry Robinson.

"It's only me," said Slim. "Don't go."

"Perry has been trying to shed a little more light on the Tower robbery," explained Mr. Hardy. "But what is this clue you are talking of?"

"It isn't about the robbery," replied Frank. "Although it *might* have something to do with it, for all we know. It's about the red-headed man who stole Chet's car and who tried to hold up the steamboat ticket office."

"What about him?"

"This!" said Frank, taking the fragment of red hair from his pocket and showing it to his father. "The fellow wore a wig."

Mr. Hardy examined the little tuft of hair closely.

"Where did you find it?" he asked.

"In the wreckage of that smashed car."

Mr. Hardy nodded.

"That seems to link up a pretty good chain of evidence. The man who passed you on the shore road wrecked his car, then stole Chet's roadster and afterward tried to hold up the ticket office. When he failed in that he abandoned the roadster. He wore a red wig that he took off occasionally to confuse pursuers. If we could only find the wig we might be able to get further information."

"Do you think it might help us solve the Tower robbery?" asked Perry.

"Possibly."

"The man was evidently a professional thief," explained Frank. "If he was smart enough to wear a wig he was evidently an old-timer at the game. And if he failed in the ticket office hold-up, who knows but what he might have been hanging around the city waiting for another chance."

"Gosh, you may be right, at that!" exclaimed Perry. "I was just telling your father that I saw a strange man lurking about the grounds of Tower Mansion two days before the robbery. I didn't think anything of it at the time, and in the shock of dad's arrest I forgot about it."

"Did you get a good look at him? Could you describe him?" asked the detective.

"I'm afraid I couldn't. It was in the evening, and I was sitting by the window, studying. I happened to look up and I saw this fellow moving about under the trees near the wall. Later on I heard one of the dogs barking in another part of the grounds, and shortly afterward I saw some one running across the lawn. But I thought it was probably just a tramp."

"Did he wear a hat or a cap?"

"As near as I can remember, it was a cap. His clothes were dark."

"And you couldn't see his face?"

"No."

"Well, it's not much to go on, but it might be linked up with Frank's idea that the man who stole the roadster might have still been hanging around." Mr. Hardy thought deeply for a few moments. "I am going to bring all these facts to Mr. Applegate's attention and I am also going to have a talk with the police authorities. I don't think they have enough evidence to warrant holding your father, Perry."

"Do you think you can have him released?" asked the boy eagerly.

"I'm sure of it. In fact, I think Mr. Applegate is beginning to realize now that he made a mistake and I don't think the police are any too anxious to go ahead with the case on the meager evidence in their possession."

"It will be wonderful if we can have dad back with us again," said Perry. "Although it won't be quite the same. He'll be under a cloud as long as this mystery isn't cleared up. And of course Mr. Applegate won't employ him any more."

"All the more reason why we should get busy and clear up the affair," returned Mr. Hardy. "You boys can help."

"How?"

"By keeping your eyes and ears open and by using your wits. That's all there is to detective work."

"Well, you can just bet that if it will clear Slim's dad we'll be listening and looking for every clue there is," Joe assured his father.

CHAPTER X

AN IMPORTANT DISCOVERY

When the Hardy boys returned from school next afternoon they saw that a crowd had collected about the bulletin board in the post office.

"Wonder what's up now?" said Joe, pushing his way forward. Boylike, he was able to make his way through the crowd with the agility of an eel, and Frank was not slow in following.

On the board was a large poster, the ink on which was scarcely dry. At the top, in enormous black letters, they read:

$1000 REWARD

Underneath, in slightly smaller type, came the following:

The above reward will be paid for information leading to the arrest of the person or persons who broke into Tower Mansion and stole from a safe in the library jewels and securities, as follows—

Then came a list of the jewels and negotiable bonds that had been taken from Tower Mansion, the jewels being fully described and the numbers of the bonds being given. It was announced that the reward was offered by Hurd Applegate.

"Why, that must mean that the charge against Mr. Robinson has been dropped!" exclaimed Joe.

"It looks like it. Let's go and see if we can't find Slim."

All about them people were commenting on the size of the reward, and there were many expressions of envy for the person who should be fortunate enough to solve the mystery.

"A thousand dollars!" said Frank, as they made their way out of the post office. "That's a lot of money, Joe."

"I'll say it is."

"And there's no reason why we haven't as good a chance of getting it as any one else."

"Golly—if we only could!"

"Why not? Let's get at this case in real earnest. Of course, we would do what we could anyway, but—"

"A thousand dollars!"

"It's worth trying for."

"Dad and the police are barred from the reward, for it's their duty to find the thief if they can. But if we find him we get the money."

"And we'll have the satisfaction of clearing Mr. Robinson too. Joe, let's get at this case in earnest. We have some clues right now, and we can follow them up."

"I'm with you. But there's Slim now."

Perry Robinson was coming down the street toward them. He looked much happier than he had been the previous evening, and when he saw the Hardy boys his face lighted up.

"Dad is free," he told them. "Thanks to your father. The charge has been dropped."

"Gee, but I'm glad to hear that!" exclaimed Joe. "I see they're offering a reward."

"Your father convinced Mr. Applegate that it must have been an outside job. That is, that it was the work of a professional crook. And the police admitted there wasn't much evidence against dad, so they let him go. I tell you, it was a great thing for my mother and sisters. They were almost crazy with worry."

"No wonder," commented Frank. "What is your father going to do now?"

"I don't know," Slim admitted heavily. "Of course, we've had to move out of Tower Mansion. Mr. Applegate said that while the charge had been dropped, he wasn't altogether convinced in his own mind that dad hadn't had something to do with it. So he dismissed him."

"That's tough luck. But he'll be able to get another job somewhere."

"I'm not so sure about that. People aren't likely to employ a man that's been suspected of stealing. Dad tried two or three places this afternoon, but he was turned down."

The Hardy boys were silent. They were sorry for the Robinsons, for they knew only too well that the family were badly off financially and that in view of the robbery it would indeed be difficult for Mr. Robinson to get another position.

"We've rented a small house just outside the city," went on Slim. "It is cheap, and we'll have to get along." There was no false pride about Perry Robinson. He faced the facts as they came, and made the best of them. "But if dad doesn't get a job it will mean that I'll have to go to work."

"But, Slim—you'd have to quit school!"

"I can't help that. I wouldn't want to, for you know I was trying for the class medal this year. But—oh, well—"

The Hardy boys realized how much it would mean to their chum to leave school at this stage. Perry Robinson was an ambitious boy and one of the cleverest in his class. He had always wanted to continue his studies, go to a university, and his teachers had predicted a brilliant career for him. Now it seemed that all his ambitions would have to be thrown overboard because of this misfortune.

"Don't worry, Slim," comforted Frank. "Joe and I are going to plug away at this affair until we get at the bottom of it."

"It's mighty good of you, fellows," said Slim gratefully. "I won't forget it in a hurry. You've been pretty white to me all through this—"

"Aw, shucks!" muttered Frank, embarrassed. "It's the reward we're after. Applegate is offering a thousand dollars."

"Oh, I know it isn't altogether the reward. You would do it to help us anyway, and you know it. Look what you've already done!"

"Well, we're going to get busy," Joe said hastily. "See you later, Slim. Don't worry too much. I think everything will be all right."

Slim tried to smile, but it was evident that he was deeply worried, and when he walked away it was not with the light, springy, carefree step his chums had previously known.

"What's the first move, Frank?"

"We had better get a full description of those jewels. Perhaps the thief tried to pawn them. We can call at all the pawnshops and see what we can find out. Then we may be able to get a line on the thief. You know, he might pawn something here—if he had to have money with which to get out of town."

"Good idea! Do you think Applegate will give us a list?"

"We won't have to ask him. Dad should have all that information."

"Let's go and ask him right now."

But when the lads returned home and asked their father for a description of the jewels, they met with a disappointment.

"I'm quite willing to give you all that information," said Fenton Hardy; "but I don't think it will be much use. Furthermore, I'll bet I can tell just what you are going to do."

"What?"

"You're going to make the rounds of the pawnshops and see if any of the jewels have been turned in."

The Hardy boys looked at one another in consternation.

"How did you ever guess that?" asked Frank.

Their father smiled.

"Because it is just what I have already done. Not an hour after I was called in on the case I had a full description of all those jewels in every pawnshop in the city. More than that, the description has been sent to jewelry firms and pawnshops in other cities near here, and also to the New York police. Here's a duplicate list if you want it, but you'll just be wasting time by going around to the shops. They are all on the lookout for the stuff."

Mechanically, Frank took the list.

"And I thought it was such a bright idea!"

"It *is* a bright idea. But it has been used before. Most jewel robberies are solved in just this manner—by tracing the thief when he tries to get rid of the gems."

"Well," said Joe gloomily, "I guess *that* plan is all shot to pieces. Come on, Frank. We'll think of something else."

"Out after the reward, eh?" said Mr. Hardy shrewdly.

"Yes; and we'll get it, too!"

"I hope you do. But you can't ask me to help you any more than I've done. It's my case too, remember. So from now on, you are part of my opposition."

"It's a go!"

"More power to you, then," and Mr. Hardy returned to his desk. He had a sheaf of reports from shops and agencies in various parts of the State, through which he had been trying to trace the stolen jewels and securities, but in every case the report was the same. There had been no trace of the gems or bonds taken from Tower Mansion.

When the boys left their father's study they went outside and sat on the back steps, silently regarding their motorcycles.

"What shall we do now?" asked Joe.

"I don't know. Dad sure took the wind out of our sails that time, didn't he?"

"I'll say he did. But it was just as well. Saved us a lot of trouble."

"We might have been going around to all the pawnshops in the city and not getting anywhere."

"Looks as if dad has the inside track on the case, anyway. If any of the jewels are turned in he will be the first to hear of it. What chance have we?"

"I'm hanged if I'll give up!" declared Frank, with determination. "We know that there was a strange man hanging around Tower Mansion and we know that there was a red-headed crook in town. Perhaps those two facts aren't connected, but I think they are. And we know he stole Chet's roadster."

"And left it in the woods."

"Yes—and say, Joe! We didn't take much time to look around when that roadster was found, did we?"

"What was the use? The roadster was there and Chet got it back."

"No, but the man who stole the car had been there too. Perhaps he left some clue."

Joe slapped his knee with an open hand.

"I never thought of that, Frank. Let's go right back there now."

"Come on."

Eagerly, the Hardy boys dashed over to their motorcycles. In a few minutes they were speeding through the streets of Bayport, out toward the woods where Chet Morton's roadster had been abandoned.

They were fired with enthusiasm again, in spite of the momentary setback they had received when their father squelched Frank's plan of going around to the pawnshops. They felt now that they were on a new trail.

They came to the abandoned road that led into the woods and they brought their motorcycles as far as possible, finally leaving them by the roadside and going ahead on foot. Frank located the place where the roadster had been driven off into the woods, for the trees were still bent and broken, and the two boys plunged into the depths of the thickets.

At last the Hardy boys emerged into the little cleared space where the roadster had been found. Everything was just as they had left it. They examined the ground carefully.

"He might have dropped letters from his pocket, or something," said Joe hopefully, as they explored the clearing.

But the auto thief had not been so careless. There was not even a footprint, for the boys had trampled the ground thoroughly after the roadster had been discovered.

"If I had only thought to look for footprints at the time!" groaned Joe, in disappointment.

"Or finger-prints. He must have left finger-prints somewhere about the car. If he was a professional crook we could have traced him easily."

"Too late now. Chet has had the car washed since then—we didn't think of it in time."

Their search was without success, and the Hardy boys were about to give up in disappointment when Frank left the clearing and began to hunt about in the bushes.

"I guess we might as well go home," said Joe. "We've come hunting for clues too late. If we had any sense we would have looked for finger-prints and—"

He was interrupted by a shout from his brother.

"Joe! Come here, quick! I've found something!"

There was no mistaking the excitement in Frank's voice. Joe lost no time in scrambling through the bushes until he reached his brother's side.

Frank was standing in the midst of a thicket, holding up something red and bushy.

It was a wig!

"The red wig!" exclaimed Joe, his eyes widening.

"Not only the wig," replied Frank. "But this—" and he bent over to pick up a battered hat from the ground. "And this!" Whereupon he picked up a worn coat.

"They belong to the crook!"

"It couldn't have been any one else. He must have disguised himself here and left the wig and things in the bush when he abandoned the car."

CHAPTER XI

MR. HARDY INVESTIGATES

The Hardy boys looked at one another in growing excitement.

"What ought we do about it?" asked Joe.

"I'm going to tell dad what we've found."

"But didn't he say he would be working the case on his own and that we would be opposition?"

"This is different. We have a real clue here, but we don't know how to use it. You can bet dad will know what to do. He'll act fairly with us. If it leads to anything, he'll see that we get credit for what we've done."

"I guess you're right, Frank. This is a little too big for us to handle ourselves. But imagine finding that wig! What luck!"

"There's nothing else around, is there? Let's look."

Although the Hardy boys scoured the woods in that vicinity thoroughly, they found nothing more. But the wig, the hat and the coat gave promise of interesting developments. Frank hunted through all the pockets of the coat in the faint hope of finding something that would identify the previous wearer, but in this he was disappointed.

So they went back to the abandoned road and remounted their motorcycles, returning to Bayport with the articles they had found in the woods.

Their disappointment had turned to jubilation, for now they felt that they were definitely on the trail of the mysterious man in the red wig, and while ostensibly there was no connection between this fellow and the thief who had robbed Tower Mansion, Frank had, as he said, "a hunch" that the auto thief and the robber of the mansion were one and the same man.

"If we ever lay our hands on the man who stole Chet's roadster I'm sure we'll have gone a long way toward solving the Tower affair," said Frank to his brother. "I may be wrong, but I have an idea that the fellow was a professional crook who first set out to rob the steamboat office. Then, when he was frightened off, he hung around the city and waited his chance to rob Tower Mansion."

Mr. Hardy was still in the library when the boys returned home. The great detective was frankly surprised when his sons again entered the room, and he looked up with the suspicion of a twinkle in his eyes.

"What! More clues!" he exclaimed. "Surely not so soon."

"You bet we have more clues!" exclaimed Frank eagerly. "And real clues this time. We're going to turn them over to you."

"But I thought the two of you were working on this case in your own way. Remember, I'm the opposition."

"Well, to tell the truth, we don't know just what to do with what we've found," admitted Frank. "And, anyway, we know you'll be fair with us, so it doesn't matter. Look!"

And with that he tossed the red wig on the table. He kept the coat and hat behind his back.

Fenton Hardy leaned forward quickly and picked up the wig with an inquiring glance at his sons.

"So!" he murmured. "You found the wig?"

He examined it intently. Then he opened a drawer of his desk and produced the fragment of wig that the boys had found in the smashed car by the road. This he applied to a torn part of the wig itself. It fitted perfectly.

"It's the wig all right," he declared, looking up. "Where did you find it? By the smashed car?"

"No. Hidden in the bushes near the place where Chet's roadster was found."

Mr. Hardy whistled solemnly.

"Good work." He turned the wig over and over in his hands, carefully examined it under a microscope, and then tossed it back on the desk.

"There aren't so many wigs sold that one can't trace them," he observed. "This happens to be made by a small company that doesn't turn out a great many wigs in a year. It's a sort of side line with them."

"How can you tell?"

"There's a little mark on the inside that distinguishes the manufacturer. Just a trademark—hardly noticeable."

"And we found these as well," said Frank, handing over the coat and hat.

Mr. Hardy's eyes opened wide.

"Well, well!" he exclaimed. "You *have* been busy, haven't you?"

"They were all hidden in the same place."

"And well hidden, too, I'll warrant."

"We were sure there must be clues of some kind around that car, so we searched every inch of the woods roundabout."

"Good!" said Mr. Hardy approvingly. "You didn't miss any chances. I'm not saying these clues will lead to the capture of the fellow, but they will go a long way toward finding him."

"What should we do with them?"

Mr. Hardy looked up at his sons and smiled.

"Well, you've shared your clues with me, so I suppose I may as well share some of my experience with you. What do you say if I go to the city and try to trace up some of these labels? This hat, for instance—" and he picked it up from the table, examining the band intently. "There is a label here. Of course, the hat may have been sold a long time ago, and it isn't likely that the man who sold it would remember who bought it. But there is always the chance that the store may not be far from where the fellow lives. You get my idea? And the coat, too. If we can find any trace of who bought the wig we may be able to connect up the other things as well."

"Gosh, I never thought of that!" admitted Frank.

"It's a slim chance, but, as I said before, we can't afford to overlook any chances. I'll take them to the city and see what I can do. It may mean everything and it may mean nothing. Don't be disappointed if I come back empty-handed. And don't be surprised if I come back with some valuable information."

Mr. Hardy tossed the wig, the coat and the hat into a club bag that was standing open near his desk. The great detective was accustomed to being called away suddenly on strange errands, and he was always prepared to leave at a moment's notice.

"Not much use starting now," he said, glancing at his watch. "But I'll go to the city the first thing in the morning. In the meantime, don't rest on your oars, as the saying is. Keep your eyes and your ears open for more clues. The case isn't over yet by any means."

Mr. Hardy picked up some papers on his desk, as a hint that the interview was over, and the boys left the library. They were in a state of high excitement, for they were confident now that they had made valuable progress in the case and they were sure that if the wig and the garments could be of any use at all toward locating the crook, Mr. Hardy would be the man to use them.

When they went to bed that night they could hardly sleep, so elated were they over their discovery near the abandoned roadway.

"He must have been a pretty smart crook," murmured Joe, after they had talked long into the night. "That idea about the wig was clever. I'll bet he was an experienced guy!"

"The smarter they are, the harder they fall," replied Frank. "It's the experienced crook that the police always look for. If this fellow has any kind of a record at all it won't take long for dad to run him down. I've heard dad say that there is no such thing as a clever crook. If he was really clever he wouldn't be a crook at all."

"Yes, I guess there's something in that, too. But it shows that we're not up against any ordinary amateur. This fellow must be a slippery customer."

"He'll have to be mighty slippery from now on. Once dad has a few clues to work on he never lets up till he gets his man."

"Well, let's hope he gets this one. He'll think a lot more of us as detectives if he does." And with that, the boys fell asleep.

When they went down to breakfast the following morning they found that Fenton Hardy had left for New York on an early morning train.

The Hardy boys went to school, but all through that morning they could scarcely keep their minds on their work. Their thoughts were far afield. They were wondering how Fenton Hardy was faring on his quest in New York and it was not until after Frank had drawn a reprimand from one of his teachers because he absent-mindedly answered, "Red wig," when asked to name the capital of Kansas that they settled down to work and tried to put the affair of the wig and the abandoned clothes from their minds.

Slim Robinson was at school that day, but after four o'clock he confided to the Hardy boys that he was leaving.

"It's no use," he said. "Father can't keep me in school any longer and it's up to me to pitch in and help the family. I'm to start work tomorrow for a grocery company."

"And you wanted to go to college!" exclaimed Frank. "It's a shame, that's what it is!"

"Can't be helped," replied Perry, with a grimace. "I can consider myself lucky I got this far. I guess I'll have to give up all those ideas now and settle down to learn the grocery business. There's one good thing about it—I'll have a chance to learn it from the ground up. I'm starting in the delivery department. Perhaps in about fifty years I'll be head of the firm."

"You'll make good at whatever you tackle," Joe assured him. "But I'm sorry you won't be able to go through college as you wished. Don't give up hope yet, Slim. You never know what may happen. Perhaps they'll find the fellow who *did* rob Tower Mansion."

Both boys wanted to tell their chum about the clues they had discovered the previous day, but the same thought was in their minds—that it would be unwise to raise false hopes. It would go much harder with Perry, they knew, if he began to think the capture of the thief was imminent, only to have the hope dashed to earth again. So they said good-bye to him and wished him good luck. Perry tried hard to be cheerful, but his smile was very faint as he turned away from them and walked off down the street.

"Gosh, but I'm sorry for him," said Frank as they went home. "He was such a hard worker in school and he counted so much on going to college."

"We've just *got* to clear up the Tower robbery, that's all there is to it!" declared his brother.

"Perhaps dad is back by now. There's a train from New York at three o'clock. Let's hurry home and see."

But when the Hardy boys arrived home they found that their father had not yet returned from the city.

"We'll just have to be patient, I guess," said Frank. "No news is good news."

And with this philosophic reflection the Hardy boys were obliged to comfort themselves against the impatience that possessed them to learn what progress their father was making in the city toward following up the clues they had given him.

CHAPTER XII

DAYS OF WAITING

Fenton Hardy had high hopes of a quick solution of the mystery when he went to New York. Possession of the wig, the hat and the coat gave him three clues, any one of which might lead to tracing the previous owner quickly, and the detective was confident that it would not be long before he would unravel the tangled threads. He had not stated his optimism to the boys, being careful not to arouse their hopes, but in his heart he thought it would be but a matter of hours before he ran the owner of the red wig to earth.

But obstacles presented themselves before him in bewildering succession.

The wig appeared to be his chief clue, and when he arrived in the city he went directly to the head office of the company that had manufactured it. When he sent his card in to the manager he was readily admitted, for Fenton Hardy's name was known from the Atlantic to the Pacific.

"Some of our customers in trouble, Mr. Hardy?" asked the manager, when the great detective tossed the red wig on his desk.

"Not yet. But one of your customers *will* be in trouble if I can ever trace the purchaser of this wig."

The manager picked it up. He inspected it carefully and frowned.

"We are not, as you know, a wig-making firm," he said. "That is, the wig department is a very small side line with us."

"The very reason I thought it would be easier to trace this," replied Mr. Hardy. "If you turned out thousands of them every year it might be more difficult. You sell to an exclusive theatrical trade, I believe."

"Exactly. If an actor wants a wig of some special nature, we do our best to please him. We only make the wigs to order."

"Then you will probably have a record of this one."

The manager turned the wig over in his hands, glanced carefully at the inside, felt of the weight and texture, then pressed a button at the side of his desk. A boy came and departed with a message.

"It may be difficult. This wig is not new. In fact, I would say it was turned out about two years ago."

"A long time. But still—"

"I'll do the best I can."

A bespectacled old man shuffled into the office at that moment, in response to the manager's summons, and stood waiting in front of the desk.

"Kauffman, here," said the manager, "is our expert. What he doesn't know about wigs isn't worth knowing." Then, turning to the old man, he handed him the red wig. "Remember it, Kauffman?"

The old man looked at it doubtfully. Then he gazed at the ceiling.

"Red wig…red wig…" he muttered.

"About two years old, isn't it?" prompted the manager.

"Not quite. Year'n a half, I'd say. Looks like a comedy character type. Wait'll I think. There ain't been so many of our customers playin' that kind of a part inside a year and a half. Let's see. Let's see." The old man paced up and down the office, muttering names under his breath. Suddenly, he stopped, snapping his fingers.

"I have it," he said. "It must have been Morley who bought that wig. That's who it was! Harold Morley. He is playing in Shakespearian repertoire with Hamlin's company. Very fussy about his wigs. Has to have 'em just so. I remember he bought this one because he came in here about a month ago and ordered another just like it."

"Why would he do that?" asked Mr. Hardy.

Kauffman shrugged his shoulders.

"Ain't none of my business. Lots of actors keep a double set of wigs. Morley's playin' down at the Crescent Theater right now. Call him up."

"I'll go and see him," said Mr. Hardy, rising. "You're sure he is the man who ordered that wig?"

"Positive!" replied Kauffman, looking hurt. "I know every wig that goes out of my shop. I give 'em all my pers'nal attention. Morley got the wig— and he got another like it a month ago. I remember."

"Kauffman is right," put in the manager. "Morley has a very good account with us. If Kauffman says he remembers the wig, it must be so."

"Well, thank you for your trouble," answered Fenton Hardy. "I may be able to see Mr. Morley in his dressing room if I hurry. It lacks about half an hour of theater time."

"You'll just about make it. Glad to have been of service, Mr. Hardy. Any time we can do anything for you, just ask."

"Thank you," and Fenton Hardy shook hands with Kauffman and the manager, then left the office, bound for the Crescent Theater.

But the detective's hopes were not as high as they had been. He knew that Morley, the actor, was certainly not the man who had worn the wig on the day the roadster was stolen, for the Shakespearian company of which Morley was a member had been playing a three months' run in New York. It would be impossible for the actor to get away from the theater long enough for such an escapade, just as it was improbable that he would even try to do so.

He presented his card to a suspicious doorman at the Crescent and was finally admitted backstage and shown down a brilliantly lighted corridor to the dressing room of Harold Morley. It was a snug little place, the dressing room, for Morley had fitted it up to suit his own tastes once it was assured that the company would remain at the Crescent for an extended run. There were pictures on the walls, a potted plant in the window overlooking the alleyway, and a rug on the floor.

Seated before a mirror with electric lights at either side, was a stout little man, almost totally bald. He was diligently rubbing cold cream on his face, and when Fenton Hardy entered he did not turn around but, eyeing his visitor in the mirror, casually told him to sit down.

"Often heard of you, Mr. Hardy," he said, in a surprisingly deep voice that had a comical effect in contrast to his diminutive appearance. "Often heard of you. Glad to meet you. What kind of call is this? Social—or professional?"

"Professional."

Morley continued rubbing cold cream on his jowls.

"Spill it," he said briefly. "What's it all about?"

"Ever see this wig before?" asked Mr. Hardy, tossing the red wig on the table.

Morley turned from the mirror, and an expression of delight crossed his plump countenance.

"Well, I'll say I've seen it before!" he declared. "Old Kauffman—the best wig-maker in the country—made that for me about a year and a half ago. That's the kind of wig I wear for Launcelot Gobbo in *The Merchant of Venice*. Where did you get it? I sure didn't think I'd ever see *that* wig again."

"Why?"

"Stolen from me. Some low-down egg cleaned out my dressing room one night. During the performance. Nerviest thing I ever heard of. Came right in here while I was doing my stuff out front, grabbed my watch and money and a diamond ring I had lying by the mirror, took this wig and a couple of others that were lying around, and beat it. Nobody saw him come or go. Must have got in by that window."

Morley talked in short, rapid sentences, and there was no mistaking his sincerity.

"How many wigs did he take?"

"About half a dozen. Funny thing about that, too. They were all red. Took nothin' but red wigs. I told the cops to be on the lookout for a red-headed thief. I didn't worry so much about the other wigs, for they were for old plays, but this one was being used right along. Kauffman made it specially for me. I had to get him to make another. But say—where did you find it?"

"Oh, just a little case I'm investigating. The crook left this behind him. I was trying to trace it."

"Well, you've traced it all right. But that's all the help I can give you. The cops never *did* find out who cleaned out my dressing room."

Mr. Hardy was disappointed. The clue of the red wig had led only to a blind alley. But he concealed his chagrin and tossed the wig over to Morley.

"Gee, and I'm sure glad to get it back again," declared the actor. "Things haven't gone right with me at all since I lost that wig. Losing it brought me a whole flock of bad luck. Sorry I can't help you find the guy that took it. What's he been up to now?"

Fenton Hardy evaded the question.

"Oh, I'll probably get him some other way. Give me a list and description of the stuff he took from you. Probably I can trace him through that."

"Hop to it," said Morley breezily. "Hop right to it, old man. Here's a list of the stuff right here." He reached in a drawer and drew out a sheet of paper which he handed over to the detective. "That's the same list I gave to the cops when I reported the robbery. Number of the watch, and everything."

Mr. Hardy folded the list and put it in his pocket. Morley glanced at his watch, lying beside the mirror, face up, and gave an exclamation.

"Suffering Sebastopol! Curtain in five minutes and I'm not half made up yet. Excuse me, Mr. Hardy, but I've got to get busy. In this business 'I'll be ready in a minute' doesn't go."

He seized a stick of grease paint and feverishly resumed the task of altering his appearance to that of the character he was portraying at the matinee that day. Mr. Hardy, smiling at the actor's casual informality, withdrew from the dressing room and made his way out to the street.

"A blind alley!" he muttered. "I was sure I could trace the fellow by means of the wig. Oh, well!" He shrugged his shoulders. "I still have the hat and coat. And if the worst comes to the worst I can try to trace the chap through the stuff he stole from Morley—for it was probably the same man. But it looks like a big job."

It was a big job.

Efforts to trace the purchaser of the hat and coat were fruitless. The search ended at a secondhand store where the owner vainly tried to sell Mr. Hardy a complete outfit of clothing at a bargain, but could not or would not remember who had bought the coat from him. He sold so many coats, and at such bargains, that he could not remember the customers who came into his store. Mr. Hardy was forced to retire, defeated.

The predominating quality of the detective's character was patience. When he found that he could not trace the thief through the wig, the hat or the coat, he doggedly set to work trying to trace the man who had broken into the dressing room of the actor, Morley, and this, in spite of the fact that the police had already given up that case as hopeless.

Then, in his spare time, Mr. Hardy spent hours at police headquarters, poring over records, searching for particulars of hundreds of red-headed criminals.

It was over a week before he found what he wanted and it came from a chance note at the bottom of a police description of a thief who was at that time out on parole. But when Fenton Hardy saw the note he knew he had stumbled on the clue he needed. And he smiled grimly.

"It won't be long now," he remarked, in the popular phrase of the day, as he went back to his hotel.

CHAPTER XIII

IN POOR QUARTERS

In the meantime, the Hardy boys were finding the suspense almost unbearable. They had expected that their father would be away but a day at the most, but when two days dragged by, then three, and finally an entire week, without word from Mr. Hardy further than a brief note from New York stating that he was well and that the case was not as easy of solution as he had hoped, they became depressed.

"If dad can't get the thief, no one can," declared Joe, with conviction, "and I'm beginning to think that even dad is falling down in this affair."

"Better wait till he admits it himself," suggested Frank. "Although I don't mind telling you I'm not very hopeful myself."

Frank's preoccupied air had not gone unobserved. Callie Shaw had noticed his abstraction. More than once, when she had smiled pleasantly at him as they met one another in the hallways or in the classroom at the high school, he had merely nodded moodily. Callie was too sensible to be hurt by this, but she wondered what was worrying Frank. So one afternoon, when they happened to leave school together, she taxed him with it.

"What's on your mind, Frank?" she asked gaily. "You've been going around looking like a human thundercloud for the last week."

"Who, me? I didn't notice," returned Frank heavily.

"Yes, you!" she replied, mimicking his lifeless tone. "You used to be full of fun. What's the matter? Can't I help?" She glanced up at him eagerly.

Frank shook his head.

"No, you can't help, Callie. It's about Slim."

"Slim Robinson! Oh, yes! Wasn't that too bad?" said Callie, with quick sympathy. "He had to leave school. They tell me he's working."

"In a grocery."

"And he was so anxious to be a lawyer!"

"I was talking to him this morning. He pretends he likes the work he's at, but I could tell he wishes he could get back to school again. I'm real sorry for him. And all on account of that confounded Tower robbery!"

"But nobody really believes Mr. Robinson did it!"

"Of course not. Nobody but Hurd Applegate. But until they find who *did* take the stuff, Mr. Robinson is out of a job and nobody will hire him."

"Isn't that too bad? I'm going over to see Paula and Tessie and Mrs. Robinson tonight. Where are they living?"

Frank gave Callie the address. Her eyes widened.

"Why that's in one of the poorest sections of the city! Frank, I had no idea it was that bad!"

"It is—and it'll be a lot worse unless Mr. Robinson gets work pretty soon. Slim's earnings aren't nearly enough to keep the family yet."

"Isn't there any chance that Mr. Robinson will be cleared?"

"That's what's worrying me. Dad is working on the case."

"Then why should you worry?" said Callie triumphantly. "Why, that means it'll be all cleared up. Your father can do anything!"

"I used to think so, too. But he seems to be stuck, this time."

"What's the matter?"

"He went to New York almost a week ago with some clues that Joe and I were certain would clear up the affair, and so far we haven't heard from him, only to know that the case was harder than he expected."

"But he hasn't given up, has he?"

"Well—no—"

"Then what are you worrying about, silly? If your father had given up the case there would be something to worry about. If he is still working on it there's always hope."

They walked on in silence for a while.

"Let's go out to see the Robinsons," Callie said suddenly.

"I've been intending to go, but—I sort of—well—you know—"

"You thought it might embarrass them. Well, it won't. I know Paula and Tessie well, and they're not that kind. They'd appreciate a friendly visit."

Frank hesitated. He had the natural shyness of his age and he felt awkward about visiting the Robinsons in their new home, for he knew they were now in reduced circumstances and might not wish their former friends to see them in their present plight. But Callie's words reassured him.

"All right. I'll go. We can't stay long, though."

"We can't. I must be back in time for supper. We'll just drop in on them so they'll know we haven't forgotten all about them."

"I thought you were going over to see them tonight?"

"I was, but I've changed my mind. I want you to come with me now."

Frank hailed a passing street car bound for the section of the city in which the Robinsons lived and they got on board. It was a long ride and the streets became poorer and meaner as they neared the outskirts of Bayport.

"It's an outrage, that's what it is!" declared Callie abruptly. "Mrs. Robinson and the girls were always accustomed to having everything so nice! And now they have to live away out here! Oh, I hope your father catches the man that committed that robbery!"

Her eyes flashed and for a moment she looked so fierce that Frank laughed.

"I suppose you'd like to be the judge and jury at his trial, eh?" he chuckled.

"I'd give him a hundred years in jail!"

When at length they came to the street to which the Robinsons had moved they found that it was an even poorer thoroughfare than they had expected. There were squalid shacks and tumbledown houses on either side of the narrow street, and ragged children were playing in the roadway. At the far end of the street they came to a small, unpainted cottage that somehow contrived to look neat in spite of the surroundings. The picket fence had been repaired and the yard had been cleaned up.

"This is where they live," said Frank. "It's the neatest place on the whole street."

Paula answered their knock. Her face lighted up with pleasure when she saw who the callers were.

"Frank and Callie!" exclaimed the girl. "You've come to see us! Come in. We're dying of loneliness. There hasn't been a soul out this way since we moved."

Callie flashed Frank a look of triumph, and whispered:

"There, now! Didn't I tell you they'd be glad?" as they went into the house.

They were greeted with kindly dignity by Mrs. Robinson and with girlish good humor by Tessie. Mrs. Robinson received them with the same self-possession she would have shown had they been back at Tower Mansion, and Frank wondered at himself for thinking that these good people might be ashamed to meet their old friends in this new and humbler home.

"We can't stay long," explained Callie. "But Frank and I just thought we'd run out to see how you all are."

"We're all well—that's one mercy to be thankful for," answered Mrs. Robinson. "Perry is working. I suppose you knew that."

"And Mr. Robinson?" inquired Frank.

She shook her head.

"Not yet." Mrs. Robinson's lips quivered. "It's so hard for him," she said. "Without a recommendation, you know. It looks as though he might have to go to another city to get work."

"And leave you here?"

"I suppose so. We don't know what to do."

"It's so unjust!" flared Paula. "Papa didn't have a thing to do with that miserable robbery, and yet he has to suffer for it just the same!"

"Has your father—discovered anything—yet, Frank?" asked Mrs. Robinson hesitantly.

"I'm sorry," admitted Frank. "We haven't heard from him. He's been away in New York following up some clues. But so far there's been nothing. Of course, it isn't often he falls down on a case."

"We hardly dare hope that he'll be able to clear Mr. Robinson. The whole case is so mysterious."

"I've given up thinking of it," Tessie declared. "If it is cleared up, all well and good. If it isn't—we won't starve, at any rate, and papa knows we all believe in him."

"Yes, I suppose it doesn't do much good to keep talking about it," agreed Mrs. Robinson. "We've gone over it all so thoroughly that there is nothing more to say."

So, by tacit consent, the subject was changed, and for the rest of their stay Frank and Callie chatted of doings at school. Mrs. Robinson and the girls invited them to remain for supper, but Callie insisted that she must go. When they left they promised faithfully to pay another visit in the near future. Only once again was the subject that was nearest their hearts brought up, and that was when Mrs. Robinson drew Frank to one side as he was leaving.

"Promise me one thing," she said. "Let me know as soon as your father returns—if he has any news."

"I'll do that, Mrs. Robinson," agreed the boy. "I know what this suspense must be like for you."

"It's terrible. But as long as Fenton Hardy is working on the case I'm sure that it will be cleared up if it is humanly possible."

And with that, the matter rested. Callie was unusually silent all the way home. It was evident that she had been profoundly affected by the change that the Tower Mansion mystery had caused in the lives of the Robinsons. Naturally sympathetic and tender-hearted, she felt keenly the injustice of it all, and she realized even more than Frank what it had meant to Mrs. Robinson and the girls to move from their comfortable home in the Mansion to the squalid and distant part of the city in which they now lived.

Callie lived but a few blocks away from the Hardy home, and Frank accompanied her to the gate.

"Mercy!" she exclaimed, glancing at her watch, "it's after six. I'm away late for supper."

"So am I. See you tomorrow."

"Surely. But, Frank—"

"Yes?"

Callie hesitated, then looked directly into his eyes. "Frank," she said, "if your father, somehow, doesn't clear up this affair, you and Joe simply *must* do it! You *must*! For the Robinsons. It means so much to them."

"Dad won't fall down on it. Don't worry. And Joe and I are giving all the help we can."

His confidence was contagious. Callie brightened up immediately.

"In that case," she said, gaily, "the mystery is as good as solved. The three best detectives in the world are working on it. Good-bye, Frank."

With that she ran lightly into the house.

CHAPTER XIV

RED JACKLEY

It was another week before Fenton Hardy returned to Bayport.

Contrary to the expectations of the boys, he did not arrive from New York. Instead, he came home early one morning, having reached the city by a train from the west. He had sent no advance notice of his arrival, and the first his sons knew of it was when a servant told them that their father had reached the house in the early hours of the morning, plainly careworn and travel-stained. He had gone immediately to bed, leaving orders that he was on no account to be disturbed.

This was at breakfast, and although the boys were wild with impatience to learn the outcome of their father's trip, they were obliged to curb their curiosity. Mr. Hardy was still sleeping when they left for school that morning and, to their surprise, he was asleep when they came back home for lunch.

"He must be mighty tired!" remarked Joe. "I wonder where on earth he came from?"

"Probably been up all night. When dad gets hard at work on a case he forgets all about sleep. I'll bet he found something."

"Hope so. But I wish he'd wake up and tell us. I hate to go back to school without knowing."

But Mr. Hardy had not awakened by the time the boys set out for school again, although they lingered until they were in danger of being late.

All afternoon they were tormented by curiosity. Where had their father been? What had he discovered? As soon as school was out they fled down the steps, broke away from a group of boys anxious to get up a baseball game, and shattered all records in their race for home.

Fenton Hardy was in the library, and as they rushed panting into the room he grinned broadly at his sons, for he was quite well aware that they were impatient to hear an account of his trip.

He looked refreshed after his long sleep and it was evident that his trip had not been entirely without success, for his manner was cheerful. The Hardy boys knew their father well, and they knew that when a case was difficult of solution the great detective became moody and worried.

"What luck, dad?" asked Frank, perching on the arm of an easy chair.

Mr. Hardy raised his eyebrows, pretending not to understand.

"About what?" he inquired.

"About the case. The Tower Mansion case. The red wig. Did you find out who owned it? Did you catch the thief?"

"Whoa! Whoa! Not all at once. A question at a time please. Now, do I understand that you want to know if I found out anything about the Tower Mansion affair?"

"Don't keep us waiting, dad," pleaded Joe. "You know that's what we're asking you about."

"Well," answered Mr. Hardy, "yes—and no!"

"That's not much of an answer," objected Frank, in disappointment.

"It's the best answer I can give, unfortunately. I *did* find out something about the red wig. But as for connecting its wearer with the Tower robbery— that is still to come."

"You traced the fellow who wore the wig?"

"I did. And he turned out to be a well-known criminal—well known to the police, that is."

"What's his name?" asked Joe.

"Jackley. John Jackley—commonly known as 'Red'."

"Because he has red hair?"

"No. Because he *hasn't* red hair. That reverses the usual order of nick-names, I imagine. This fellow Jackley has a fondness for wearing red wigs."

"And was he the man who stole Chet's roadster?"

"It seems almost certain. I traced the wig, which had been originally stolen from an actor in New York. I traced it to Jackley because his habit of wearing red wigs is well known to the police, and by locating him and keeping a close watch on him and paying a call at his room one night when he was out, I managed to find some of the loot that he had taken when he robbed the actor. That seemed to connect everything up very well."

"Where did you find him?" asked Frank.

"In New York. He wasn't in hiding, for he hadn't been sought for any particular crime at the time. The police seemed to overlook him in their investigation of the dressing-room theft."

"Did you accuse him?"

"No. I wanted to learn more. When I found the articles that had been stolen from the actor and knew that the wig found by the roadster had been taken at the same time, I knew Red Jackley was the auto thief. But I wanted to get some information on the Tower Mansion affair if possible. So I took a room in the house in which Jackley was living, and kept a close watch on him."

"Did you learn anything?"

Mr. Hardy shook his head.

"Jackley himself spoiled everything. He got mixed up in a jewel robbery and cleared out of the city. Luckily, I heard him packing up, and I trailed him. The police were watching for him and he couldn't get out by railway—that is, not in the ordinary manner. Instead, he tried to make his escape by jumping a freight."

"And you still followed?"

"I lost him two or three times, but luck was with me, and somehow I managed to pick up his trail again. He got out of the city, out into New Jersey, and then his luck failed him. A railway detective recognized him and then the chase was on. Up to that time I had been content with just keeping behind him, I had hoped to pose as a fellow fugitive and win his confidence. But when the chase started in real earnest I had to join with the other officers."

"And they caught Jackley?"

"Not without a chase. Jackley, by the way, was once a railroad man. Strangely enough, he once worked not many miles from here. He managed to steal a railway gasoline speeder and got away from us. But he didn't last long, for the speeder jumped the tracks on a curve and Jackley was badly smashed up."

"Was he killed?"

"I don't think he'll live. He's in a hospital right now and the doctors say he hasn't much of a chance."

"But he's under arrest."

"Oh, yes. He is being held for the jewel robbery and also for the robbery from the actor's dressing room. But I don't think he'll live to answer either charge."

"Didn't you find out anything that would connect him with the Tower robbery?"

"Not a thing."

The Hardy boys were disappointed, and their expressions showed it. If Red Jackley died, the secret of the Tower robbery would die with him, for by now Frank and Joe were convinced that the notorious criminal had indeed been the thief for whose misdeeds Mr. Robinson was now suffering. And if the secret died with him, Mr. Robinson would be doomed to spend the rest of his life under a cloud, suspected of being a thief.

"Have you seen Jackley yet?" asked Frank.

"After the smash-up. But I didn't have a chance to talk to him."

"You might have been able to get a confession from him."

Fenton Hardy nodded.

"I may be able to get one yet. If he is sure he is going to die he may admit everything. I intend to make an effort to see him in the hospital and ask him about the Tower robbery, anyway."

"Is he far away?"

Mr. Hardy named a small city not far distant from Bayport.

"I explained my mission to the doctor in charge and he promised to telephone me as soon as it was possible for Jackley to see any one. I'm convinced that the fellow had something to do with the Tower affair. It's a certainty that he stole the automobile—the wig proves that. By the same token it's certain that he was the man who tried to hold up the ticket office. Having failed in that attempt, it seems more than likely that an old-time criminal like Jackley would look around for something else to do before he left Bayport."

"You say he used to work near here?" asked Joe.

"He was once employed by the railroad, and he knows all the country around here well. Then he got mixed up in some thefts from freight cars and after he got out of jail he became a professional criminal. It was when I was looking over the records that I found out about his fondness for wearing a red wig. That was what eventually proved his undoing. If he had not robbed the actor's dressing room to get the wig that he used when he was in Bayport, I would never have traced him."

At that moment it was announced that Chief Collig of the Bayport police force wished to see Fenton Hardy. The detective winked at the boys, and told the servant to show the chief in.

Chief Collig entered the room, mopping his brow with a handkerchief, for it was a hot day and he was a stout man. Behind him came Detective Smuff, fanning himself with a straw hat.

"Good afternoon, gentlemen," said Mr. Hardy genially, "Won't you sit down?"

Chief Collig eased himself into an arm chair. Detective Smuff leaned against the table. Both glanced inquiringly at the two boys.

"Unless your business is *very* private, I'd just as soon have the boys stay," suggested Mr. Hardy pleasantly. He did not trust Chief Collig and Detective Smuff, who came to him only in emergencies and who usually took all the credit for themselves whenever he helped them out of their difficulties. He preferred to have the boys present as witnesses.

"How about it, chief?" asked Smuff heavily. "Can they stay?"

"I guess so," grunted Chief Collig, undoing the collar of his uniform. "Can't do no good and they can't do no harm."

"Well, gentlemen, to what do I owe the honor of this visit?" asked Mr. Hardy.

"We've been hearin' things about this Tower Mansion case," observed Chief Collig gravely. "You've been workin' on it, eh?"

"Perhaps."

"You've been out of town for quite a few days. You *must* have been workin' on it."

"That's what we dedooce, anyway," put in Detective Smuff.

"Perhaps it's my own business."

"Police business is everybody's business," declared Collig judicially. "What we want to know is—did you find any clues?"

Detective Smuff fished out the inevitable notebook and pencil.

"I'll note 'em down, chief," he remarked.

"You may as well put back the notebook, Smuff," snapped Fenton Hardy, with annoyance. "If I went away, it is my own business, and if I am still working on the Tower robbery, that's my business too. I'll thank you to keep to your own affairs."

Chief Collig opened his mouth, then closed it again. He took out his handkerchief and mopped his brow, all the while staring at Fenton Hardy. Then he turned and gazed at Smuff.

"Detective Smuff," he said, in a solemn voice, "did you hear that?"

"I did."

"What do you think of it, Detective Smuff?"

"I think—I think—" Detective Smuff groped for an expression that would encompass the magnitude of the offence, "I think Mr. Hardy is guilty of obstructin' the cause of justice," he said grandly.

"Obstructing fiddlesticks!" said Mr. Hardy. "I'm minding my own business. Which is more than some police officers seem capable of doing."

Chief Collig sighed.

"The trouble with you, Mr. Hardy," he said, "is that you won't co-operate. If you co-operated a little more, we would all be farther ahead. There ain't any co-operation at all. Here is me and Smuff, doin' our best to drive crime out of Bayport, and you won't co-operate."

"Perhaps the fact that there is a thousand dollars reward in the case isn't making you anxious for some co-operation?" suggested Fenton Hardy dryly.

"It ain't got nothin' to do with it," replied Chief Collig virtuously. "We're just anxious to see this affair cleared up, that's all. Now, Mr. Hardy, we hear you were with the officers that chased this here notorious criminal Red Jackley."

Mr. Hardy gave a perceptible start. He had no idea that news of the capture of Jackley had reached Bayport, much less that news of his own participation in the chase had reached the city.

"What of it?"

"Did Jackley have anything to do with this here Tower case?"

"How should I know?"

"Wasn't that what you were working on?"

"That's my affair."

Detective Smuff and Chief Collig looked at one another.

"You ain't co-operatin'," complained Chief Collig. "You're goin' to put us to a whole lot of worry and expense just because you won't give us a little co-operation."

"Just what do you mean?"

"Detective Smuff and me was thinkin' of goin' over to the hospital where this man Jackley is and givin' him the third degree about the Tower case."

Fenton Hardy's lips narrowed into a straight line.

"You can't do that. The doctor won't let you see him."

"We're going to try, anyway. There's a train at seven o'clock, and we aim to have a talk with this fellow Jackley tonight."

Mr. Hardy shrugged his shoulders.

"Go ahead. It means nothing to me. But if you take my advice you'll stay away. You'll just spoil everything. Jackley will talk when the time comes."

"Oh, ho!" said Detective Smuff triumphantly. "Then there *is* something to it, hey?"

"I knew there was," said Chief Collig. "Come on, Smuff. We'll make this man Jackley talk yet. We're officers of the law, we are, and I'd like to see any doctor keep us from doin' our duty."

He mopped his brow again, put on his hat, nodded to Fenton Hardy, and clumped out of the room. Detective Smuff, putting his notebook into his pocket, followed. The door closed behind them.

Mr. Hardy sat back with a gesture of despair.

"They'll spoil everything," he said. "They're just so clumsy that Red Jackley will close up like a clam if they try to make him talk."

"Perhaps," remarked Frank significantly, "they'll miss their train."

At that moment the telephone rang. Mr. Hardy answered it.

"Hello—yes, this is Fenton Hardy—yes—oh, yes, doctor—he is—well, well—is that so?—won't live until morning—I can see him?—fine—thank you—good-bye."

He put back the receiver.

"There," he said wearily, "just my luck! Red Jackley is dying, and the doctor says I can see him tonight. But Collig and Smuff will have first right to talk to him, for they are officials and I'm only a private detective. If Jackley confesses, they'll have the credit for it."

"They'll just have to miss their train," said Frank. "Come on, Joe. Let's see what we can do."

CHAPTER XV
THE CHIEF GETS A BOMB

"What's up now?" asked Joe, when the Hardy boys had left the house.

"Chief Collig and Detective Smuff must miss that train."

"But how?"

"I don't know just yet, but they've got to miss it. If they reach the hospital tonight they'll interview Jackley first. One of two things will happen. They'll either get a confession and take all the credit for clearing up the case, or they'll go about it so clumsily that Jackley will say nothing and spoil everything for dad."

The Hardy boys walked along the street in silence. They realized that the situation was urgent, but although they racked their brains trying to think of some way in which to prevent Chief Collig and Detective Smuff from catching the train, it seemed hopeless.

"Let's round up the gang," suggested Joe. "Perhaps they can think of something."

"The gang" consisted of the boys who had been with Frank and Joe the day they held the picnic in the woods. There was, of course, Chet Morton. Besides him were Allen Hooper, otherwise known as "Biff", because of his passion for boxing, Jerry Gilroy, Phil Cohen and Tony Prito, all students at the Bayport high school. They were usually to be found on the school campus after hours, playing ball, and there the Hardy boys soon located them. The game was just breaking up.

"Pikers," grinned Chet Morton when he saw the Hardy boys approaching. "You wouldn't play ball when we asked you to, and now you come around when the game's all over."

"We had something more important on our minds," replied Frank. "We need your help."

"What's the mattah?" asked Tony Prito. Tony was the son of a prosperous Italian building contractor, but he had not yet been in America long enough to talk the language without an accent, and his attempts were frequently the cause of much amusement to his companions. He was quick and good-natured, however, and laughed as much at his own errors as any one else did.

"Chief Collig and Detective Smuff are butting into one of dad's cases," said Frank. "We can't tell you much more about it than that. But the whole thing is that they mustn't catch the seven o'clock train."

"What do you want us to do?" asked Biff Hooper. "Blow up the bridge?"

"We might lock Collig and Smuff in one of their own cells," suggested Phil Cohen.

"And get locked in ourselves," added Jerry Gilroy. "Be sensible. Are you serious about this, Frank?"

"Absolutely. If those two catch that train dad's case will be ruined. And I don't mind telling you it has something to do with Perry Robinson."

Chet Morton whistled.

"Ah, ha! I see now. The Tower affair. In that case, we'll see to it that the seven o'clock train leaves here without our worthy chief and his equally worthy—although dumb—detective." He hated Smuff, for the sleuth had once or twice tried to arrest the boys for bathing in a forbidden section of the bay.

"There is only one question left," said Phil solemnly.

"And what is that?"

"How to keep them from getting on the train."

"Get your brains to work, fellows—if you have any," ordered Jerry Gilroy. "Let's figure out a plan."

A dozen plans were suggested, each wilder than the one before. Biff Hooper was in favor of kidnapping the chief and his detective, binding them hand and foot and setting them adrift in the bay in an open boat.

Phil Cohen suggested putting the chief's watch an hour ahead. That plan, as Frank observed, would have been a good one but for the little difficulty of laying hands on the watch.

Chet Morton thought it would be a good idea to start a fight in front of the police station just as Collig and Smuff were about to leave for the train. The possibility that they might all land in jail as a result made this suggestion unpopular.

"If we were in Italy we could get the Black Hand to help," said Tony Prito.

"The Black Hand!" declared Chet. "That's a good idea!"

"We got no Black Hand society in Bayport," objected Tony.

"Let's get one up. Send the chief a Black Hand letter warning him not to take that train."

"And if he ever found who wrote it, we'd all be up to our necks in trouble," pointed out Joe. "I'd like to put a bomb under his old police station."

"Fine idea!" applauded Tony. "Where we get the bomb?"

"Leave it to me," announced Chet Morton mysteriously. "I'll get a bomb. I'll guarantee to keep the chief in town."

"Not a real bomb?" asked Frank.

"Why not?" said Chet. "Listen to me."

Chet proceeded to lay forth his plan in a stealthy whisper. It was received with chuckles and murmurs of admiration. His companions clapped him on the back, and when he had finished the boys hastened down the street toward the Hardy home.

In the rear of the house were a garage and an old barn. In the barn was a gymnasium that the Hardy boys had fitted out for themselves, and here was the usual collection of old toys, footballs, broken baseball bats and such paraphernalia, to be found wherever boys store their cherished possessions. Frank groped about among the rubbish in one corner until at last he rose with an exclamation of triumph, holding aloft a shining object.

"It's here!" he said. "Let's get busy. There's no time to lose."

An old box was quickly produced, and in it the shining object was placed. The box was then carefully wrapped up, and in a few minutes the boys left the barn, Tony carrying the package under one arm.

Not far from the Bayport police station was a fruit stand over which presided an Italian by the name of Rocco. He was a simple, genial soul, who believed almost everything he heard and, like most of his countrymen, he was of an excitable nature. Toward Rocco's fruit stand the boys made their way. Rocco was sorting over his oranges when they approached. Tony, with the box under his arm, hung in the background, while Chet stepped boldly forward.

"How much are your oranges, Rocco?" he asked.

Rocco, with much explanatory waving of arms, recited the prices of the various grades of oranges.

"Too much. There's a fellow at another fruit stand on the next street sells them a nickel a dozen cheaper."

"He no can do!" shrieked Rocco. "My price is da low." Then, angered by this reflection on the prices of his wares, he burst into a lengthy explanation of the struggles confronting a poor Italian trying to get along in a new country. He grabbed Chet by the coat collar, dragged him to a corner of the fruit stall, bade him inspect the fruit, gabbled off prices, and generally worked himself into a state of high indignation. In the meantime, Tony Prito made good use of his time to shove the mysterious package under the front of the stall. Then he joined the other boys who had screened his movements by gathering about Rocco.

"You'll have the Black Hand after you if you keep on charging such high prices—that's all I can say!" declared Chet, as the boys moved away.

"Poof! W'at do I care for da Blacka Hand. No frighten me!" said Rocco bravely, but he gulped when he said it and there was no doubt that the shot had gone home.

It was now after six o'clock, and the boys decided that in the interests of their plan they would have to brook the parental wrath by being late for supper. Frank had assumed that Chief Collig and Detective Smuff would be leaving to catch the train at about ten minutes to seven, so shortly after six-thirty, Phil Cohen, who had remained in the background during the interview with Rocco, walked smartly up to the fruit stand again. The others were viewing the scene from around the corner of a near-by building.

"Banana," said Phil briefly, tossing a nickel on the counter. When he had received the fruit he began to eat it, at the same time chatting with Rocco.

"W'at you t'ink?" snickered the Italian, "some boys come here a while ago and say da Blacka Hand t'ink I charga too much for da fruit."

"Well, you *do* charge too much, Rocco. Everybody says so."

"I sella da good fruit at da good price."

Phil turned aside and at the same time accidentally knocked an apple to the ground. He bent to pick it up, Rocco eyeing him narrowly in case he tried to slip it into his pocket. But Phil did not get up at once. Instead, he said:

"Oi! What's this?"

"W'at you find?"

"What's this, Rocco?" Phil rose from in front of the stand, with the package in his hands. "I found this under the counter."

Rocco stared. His mouth opened in dismay. For, sounding clearly from the inside of the package, came a steady "tick-tock, tick-tock."

"A bomb!" he shrieked. "Put heem down!"

Thereupon he scrambled wildly over the array of fruit at the back of the stand, knocked over a tray of oranges, and went sprawling over the opposite counter, roaring, "Police!" at the top of his lungs.

Phil, with a fine imitation of fright, put the package on top of the counter and fled.

Rocco, in his white apron, was dancing about in the middle of the street, yelling, "Bombs! Police! Da Blacka Hand!" Then, suddenly fearing that the supposed bomb might explode at any moment, he whirled rapidly about and raced down the street away from the stand, in the general direction of the police station.

He reached the doorway just as Chief Collig and Detective Smuff were leaving for the train. Panting with fear and excitement, Rocco implored them to save him from the Black Handers who had put a bomb under his fruit stand.

"Da bomb, she go 'teek-tock'," he wailed. "She blowa da stand into da little piece!"

"A bomb!" exclaimed Chief Collig. "Surely not in Bayport!"

"I always thought there was Black Handers around here," said Smuff.

"She blowa up da fruit stand! Come queeck!"

Chief Collig and Detective Smuff followed Rocco to the corner. Then they peeped around until they could see the deserted fruit stand, with the package on the counter.

"You say it goes 'tick-tock'?"

"Just lika da clock."

"Must be a bomb, all right," said Smuff. "They run by clockwork."

"Might go off any minute," observed the chief. "I hate to go near it. Smuff, you go and pour a pail of water over it."

"Me?"

"Yes, you. You're not afraid, are you?"

"No—I'm not afraid," muttered Smuff, mopping his brow. "But I got to think of my wife and family."

"Coward!" said the chief. "I'd do it myself, only it wouldn't be right, seein' I'm your superior officer. Bad for discipline."

The worthy officers stared at the package on the fruit stand counter, while Rocco danced with impatience. Neither Collig nor Smuff dared approach closer, but they realized something must be done.

"Where's Riley?" asked the chief at last.

"Out on his beat, around the corner."

"Get him."

Smuff departed hastily, glad of the chance to get away from the vicinity of the bomb. He was some time in locating Con Riley, and when at last that minion of the law was escorted back to the chief, seven o'clock had come and gone. So had the train.

CHAPTER XVI

A CONFESSION

"Riley!" ordered the chief, "see that package on the counter of the fruit stand. Go and get it and pour a pail of water over it."

"Huh?" exclaimed Riley, gaping.

"Pour a pail of water over it."

Riley took off his helmet and scratched his head. He began to wonder if his chief's brain had been affected by the heat.

"Don't stand there staring at me!" snapped Collig. "Hurry up and obey orders."

"This is the meanest job I ever got," observed Con Riley. But he ambled across the street, wondering why a crowd of people had collected—for word had quickly spread that a bomb had been found under Rocco's fruit stand— and when he reached the package he inspected it wonderingly.

"Mebbe she blowa him all to da bits!" suggested Rocco fearfully.

"He has insurance," consoled the chief.

"We'll give him a good funeral," observed Smuff.

Con Riley hunted around the fruit stand until he found a pail, and then he went up the street until he located a tap. Finally, with the pail full of water, he went back to the fruit stand, dumped the water over the package, and stood awaiting further orders.

"Soak it again!" roared the chief, who was taking no chances.

Con Riley sighed, but did as he was told. For five minutes he was kept busy dumping innumerable pails of water over the package, and only then did Chief Collig and Detective Smuff venture forth. Then, with fear and trembling, Chief Collig handed the package to Smuff and bade him open it.

Smuff's hands were shaking so that he could scarcely tear apart the coverings from the water-soaked parcel. The chief withdrew to a safe distance. Con Riley, who had just been told by a friend that he had been pouring water over a live bomb, was trying to achieve a sickly smile as the crowd congratulated him on his bravery.

Detective Smuff opened the package. The coverings fell away. The cardboard box, dripping with water, tumbled apart.

A bright object fell to the pavement with a clatter.

Everybody jumped.

But there was no cause for fear. The bright object was nothing more harmful than an old alarm clock.

The Hardy boys and their chums, mingling with the crowd, roared with laughter, and when the crowd saw how Chief Collig and his assistants had been duped they joined in the merriment.

"An alarm clock!" roared some one. "They thought an alarm clock was a bomb. Pouring water over an alarm clock!"

Chief Collig and Smuff returned to the police station with all the dignity they could muster under the circumstances. The crowd howled and whooped with laughter.

The Hardy boys went home smiling. The seven o'clock train had left half an hour before. Their father was making the trip to the city without the interference of the chief and his assistant, Smuff.

Fenton Hardy returned home late that night, and at the breakfast table next morning he was in high spirits.

"Solved another mystery?" asked Mrs. Hardy gaily, as she poured the coffee. She seldom asked questions about her husband's work, being of a gentle nature that instinctively shrank from any discussion of crime. It frequently distressed her that Mr. Hardy's occupation should be one that meant terms of imprisonment for those whom his cunning and cleverness had brought to justice. But her husband's attitude this morning was so unmistakably jubilant that she was glad for his sake if he had scored another success.

"Practically solved, my dear. If you'd care to hear all about it—"

"Not me. You know I don't care to hear about these terrible things."

"Well, the boys shall hear of it then. They are interested. If they'll come into my den after breakfast I'll tell them all about it."

"That means you succeeded," Frank said.

"Eat your bacon and eggs and don't be impatient."

After breakfast the boys went with their father into the den off the library, eagerly awaiting news of his mission of the previous evening. They had not told him how Chief Collig and Detective Smuff had missed the train, but they were shrewdly certain that their efforts in this respect had been of considerable assistance to Mr. Hardy.

"First of all," said the detective, "Jackley is dead."

"Did he confess?"

"You're not very sympathetic for the poor fellow. Yes, he confessed. Fortunately, Chief Collig and Detective Smuff didn't show up—"

Fenton Hardy saw that Joe and Frank glanced at one another, and he smiled quietly.

"I have an idea that you two scamps know more about that than you would care to tell. However, they failed to show up, and I had a clear field ahead of me. I saw Jackley just before he died. And I questioned him about the Tower robbery."

"He admitted it?"

"He admitted everything. He said he came to Bayport with the intention of robbing the ticket office. When he failed in that attempt he decided to hang around for a few days, and then he hit upon Tower Mansion as his next effort. He entered the place and opened the safe. Then he took the jewels and the bonds."

"What did he do with the loot?"

"That's what I'm coming to. I had quite a time making Jackley confess to the Tower affair, and it was not until he was on the point of death that he admitted it. Then he said, 'Yes, I took the stuff—but I couldn't get away with it. You can get it back easily. I hid it in the old tower—' But that was all he said. He became unconscious then and died in a few minutes. Just why he couldn't get away with the loot and why he hid it in the tower, I don't know. He didn't have time to tell me. But he said it was hidden in the old tower."

"Why, we'll find it in no time!" exclaimed Frank. "Tower Mansion has two towers—the old and the new. We'll search the old tower."

"The story seems likely enough," said Mr. Hardy. "Jackley would gain nothing by lying about it when he was on his deathbed. He probably became frightened after he committed the robbery and hid in the old tower until he saw the coast was clear and he was able to get away. Then no doubt he decided to hide the stuff there and take a chance on coming back for it some time after the affair had blown over."

"That was why he couldn't be traced through the jewels and the bonds," Joe said. "They were never disposed of at all. They've been lying in the old tower all this time."

"I tried to get him to tell me in just what part of the tower the loot was hidden," continued Fenton Hardy, "but he died before he could say any more. 'I hid it in the old tower.' He just managed to gasp that out before he became unconscious."

"It shouldn't be hard to find the stuff, now that we have a general idea of where it is," Frank pointed out. "Probably he didn't hide it very carefully. The old tower has been unoccupied for a long time and it is rarely entered. The stuff would be as safe there as if he had hidden it miles away."

Joe got up from his chair.

"I think we ought to get busy and go search the old tower right away. Oh, boy! If we can only hand old Applegate his jewels and bonds this morning and clear Mr. Robinson. Let's start."

"I'll leave it to you boys to make the search," said Mr. Hardy, with a smile. "I've no doubt the stuff will be easily recovered, and you can have the satisfaction of turning it over to Mr. Applegate. I guess you can get along without me in this case from now on."

"We wouldn't have got very far if it hadn't been for you."

"And I wouldn't have got very far if it hadn't been for you, so we're even," smiled Mr. Hardy. "Be on your way, then, and good luck to you."

"We'll find it, never fear," promised Frank, putting on his cap. "I hope the Applegates don't throw us out when we ask to be allowed to look around in the old tower."

"Just tell them you have a pretty good clue to where the bonds and jewels are hidden and they'll let you search to your heart's content," Mr. Hardy advised.

"Come on then, Joe. We'll have that thousand dollar reward before the morning is over."

Their father glanced at them shrewdly.

"Don't count your chickens before they are hatched," he said. And then, as the boys hastened out of the den, he called after them: "Also, you might remember the old proverb that there is many a slip between the cup and the lip."

But the Hardy boys scarcely heard him, so eager were they to begin searching the old tower and so confident were they that the mystery was about to be cleared up.

CHAPTER XVII

THE SEARCH OF THE TOWER

When the Hardy boys reached Tower Mansion that morning the door was answered by Hurd Applegate himself. The tall, stooped gentleman peered at them through his thick-lensed glasses. In one hand he held a sheet of stamps, for it was his custom to devote the mornings to his collection.

"Yes?" he said testily, for he was annoyed at being disturbed. "What do you boys want here at this hour of day?"

"You remember us, don't you?" asked Frank politely. "We're Mr. Hardy's sons."

"Fenton Hardy, the detective? Are you his boys?"

"Yes, sir."

"Well, what do you want?"

"We'd like to take a look through the old tower, if you don't mind. We've got a new clue about the robbery you had here a while ago."

"Want to look through the old tower? Of all the impudence! What do you want to look through the tower for? And what has that got to do with the robbery?"

"We have evidence that leads us to believe the jewels and bonds were hidden in the tower by the thief."

"Oh! You have evidence, have you?" The old man peered at them very closely. "It's that rascal Robinson, I'll warrant. He hid the stuff there, and now he's put you up to going and finding it, just to clear himself."

The Hardy boys had not considered the affair in this light, and they gazed at Mr. Applegate in consternation. At last Joe found his tongue.

"Mr. Robinson isn't mixed up in this at all," he said. "The real thief was found. He said the stuff was hidden in the old tower. If you will just let us take a look around, we'll find it for you."

"Who was the real thief, then?"

"We can't tell you just now, sir. Wait till we find the stolen goods and we'll tell you the whole story."

Mr. Applegate took off his glasses and wiped them with his handkerchief. He glared at the boys suspiciously for a few moments. Then he called out:

"Adelia!"

A high cracked voice from the dim regions of the hallway answered.

"What d'you want?"

"Come here a minute."

There was a rustle of skirts, and then Adelia Applegate, maiden sister of the owner of Tower Mansion, appeared. She was a faded blonde woman, of thin features, and she was dressed in a gown of a fashion fifteen years back, in which every color of the spectrum fought for supremacy.

"What's the matter now?" she demanded. "Can't a body sit down to do a bit of sewin' without you hollerin' at them?"

"These boys want to look through the old tower."

"What for? Up to some mischief, I'll be bound."

"They think they can find the bonds and jewels."

"Oh, they do, do they?" sniffed the woman. "And what would the bonds and jewels be doin' in the old tower?"

"We have evidence that they were hidden there after the robbery," replied Frank.

Miss Applegate sniffed again and viewed the boys with frank suspicion.

"As if any thief would be fool enough to hide them right in the house he robbed!"

"These are Mr. Hardy's boys," explained Hurd Applegate. "He is the big detective, you know."

"All detectives," said Miss Applegate, "are nosey. Always pryin' into other people's affairs."

"We're just trying to help you," put in Joe politely.

"Go ahead, then. Go ahead," said Miss Applegate, with a sigh. "Come around at this hour of morning, disturbing honest folks. Go ahead, and tear the old tower to pieces if you like. But I'll be bound you won't find anything. It's all foolishness. You won't find anything."

Consent having been given, Hurd Applegate led the way through the gloomy halls and corridors of the mansion toward the old tower. He was inclined to share his sister's view that the boys' search would be in vain.

"Might as well save yourselves the trouble," he declared. "You won't find anything in the old tower. If anything was hidden there it's been taken away by this time."

"We'll make a try at it, anyway, Mr. Applegate."

"Don't ask me to help you. I've got better things to do. Just got some new stamps in this morning and you interrupted me when I was sortin' them out. I've got to get back to my work."

The man led the way into a corridor that was heavy with dust. It had not been in use for a long time and it was bare and unfurnished. Leading off this corridor was a heavy door. It was unlocked, and when Mr. Applegate opened it the boys saw that a flight of stairs lay beyond.

"There you are. Those stairs lead up into the tower. Search away. You won't find anything."

"I hope we do, Mr. Applegate," said Frank. "And I'm pretty sure we shall."

"Yes—boys are always goin' to do wonders. Go ahead. Live and learn. Waste your time."

And with this parting shot, Hurd Applegate turned and hobbled back along the corridor, the sheet of stamps still in his gnarled hand. He was muttering to himself as he departed. The Hardy boys looked at one another.

"Not very encouraging, is he, Frank?"

"Not a bit of it. But it will be so much the better for us if we get the stuff back for him. He won't think we were wasting our time then."

"Let's get up into the tower. I'm anxious to start."

The tower was about five stories in height, as compared with the rest of the mansion, which had but three stories. The lower floor was empty. The floors and walls were heavy with dust. Frank and Joe first examined the stairs carefully for footprints, but there were none to be seen.

"That seems odd," remarked Frank. "If Jackley had been in here within the past month you'd think his footprints would still show. By the appearance of this dust, there hasn't been any one in the tower for at least a year."

"Perhaps the dust collects more quickly than we think. It may have covered his footprints over even within a couple of weeks."

An inspection of the ground floor revealed the fact that there was no place where the loot could have been hidden, save under the stairs, and there was nothing in that place of concealment. Accordingly, the Hardy boys ascended to the next floor, finding themselves in a room as drab and bare as the one they had just left. Here again the dust lay heavy and the murky windows were thick with cobwebs. There was an atmosphere of age and decay about the entire place. It seemed to have been abandoned for years.

"Nothing here," said Frank, after a quick glance around. "On we go."

They made their way up to the next floor, after again poking about under the stairs, but again without success.

The next room was a duplicate of the first. It was bare and cheerless, deep in dust. There was not the slightest sign of a hiding place. Much less was there any indication that another human being had been in the tower for years.

"Doesn't look very promising, Joe. Still, he may have gone right to the top of the tower."

So the search continued, until at last the Hardy boys had reached the top of the tower. Here they emerged into the open air, coming through a trapdoor that led through the roof from the upper room. They were now standing on a platform, and far below them lay the city of Bayport. To the east was Barmet Bay, the waters sparkling in the sun.

The platform was quite bare. The stone walls gave no opportunity of a hiding place. Their search had been in vain.

"We were fooled, I guess," Frank admitted. "There hasn't been any one in this tower for years. I knew it as soon as I saw there were no footprints."

The boys gazed moodily down over the city, and then down over the grounds of Tower Mansion. The roofs of the mansion itself were far below, and directly across from them rose the heavy bulk of the new tower.

"Do you think he might have meant the *new* tower?" exclaimed Joe suddenly.

"Dad said he specified the old one."

"But he may have been mistaken. In the darkness and everything, perhaps he didn't know the difference."

"That's possible, too. It's certain that he didn't hide anything in this tower, at any rate. Although why he should say 'the old tower'—"

"Let's ask Mr. Applegate if we can search the new tower, too."

"What a fine chance we have! He'll crow over us now in real earnest when we go back and tell him we didn't find anything. He'll say 'I told you so', and if we try to get into the new tower he'll just laugh at us."

"It's worth trying, anyway. We can tell him the whole story about Jackley. That ought to convince him."

Disappointed, the Hardy boys descended through the trapdoor, and then made their way down through the tower until at last they were in the long gloomy hallway again. Their clothes were covered with dust and their hands and faces were grimy. Slowly, they trudged back into the main part of the mansion again, and there they met Adelia Applegate, who popped out of a doorway as they were passing and cackled with delight.

"So these are the fine boys who were going to find the stolen stuff for us, eh!" she exclaimed, in her cracked voice. "So these are the boys who were so sure it was hidden in the old tower! Well, well! And they didn't find anything after all!"

"I'm afraid we didn't, Miss Applegate," Frank answered, with a smile. "But if you and Mr. Applegate will let us tell our story I think we can convince you that we really thought the stuff was hidden there. Even yet I believe it is hidden somewhere in the mansion—probably in the new tower."

"In the new tower!" she sniffed. "Absurd! I suppose you'll want to go poking through there now."

"If it wouldn't be too much trouble."

"It *would* be too much trouble, indeed!" she shrilled. "I shan't have any boys rummaging all through *my* house on a wild-goose chase like this. You'd better leave right away, and forget all this nonsense."

Her voice had attracted the attention of Hurd Applegate, who came hobbling out of his study at that moment.

"Now what's the matter?" he demanded. Then, seeing the boys, his face became creased in a triumphant smile.

"Ah, ha! So you didn't find anything after all! Heh! Heh!" he began to chuckle, immensely pleased with himself. "I told you so."

CHAPTER XVIII

THE NEW TOWER

"They have the audacity to want to go looking through the new tower now," said Miss Applegate, in high indignation.

Hurd Applegate's smile vanished.

"You can't do anything of the sort!" he snapped. "Are you boys trying to make a fool out of me? I knew mighty well you wouldn't find anything in the old tower."

"And we were pretty sure we would," answered Frank. "Listen, Mr. Applegate—we'll be fair with you. We'll tell you exactly why we wanted to make this search."

"Go ahead and tell me. Why didn't you tell me before?"

"Because we wanted to work this out ourselves, as far as possible. But the information we had came from the man who stole the jewels and the bonds."

"What! Has he been caught?"

"He was captured—but he will never come to trial."

"Did he escape again?"

"He escaped—by death. The thief is dead."

"Dead? What happened?" asked Hurd Applegate excitedly.

"His name was Red Jackley, and he was a notorious criminal. He was tracked down by our father, and when he tried to escape on a railroad hand-car he got into a smash-up, and he was fatally injured. But before he died, he admitted robbing Tower Mansion."

"He admitted it? He confessed?"

"He confessed everything."

"I don't believe it," sniffed Adelia Applegate. "Nothing will ever convince me that it wasn't that rascal Robinson."

"Jackley confessed the whole business," Frank persisted. "And on his deathbed he said that he hadn't been able to get away with the loot. That he had hidden it."

"Where?"

"In the old tower."

"And it isn't there?"

"Joe and I have just searched the place high and low. The stuff isn't there. And from the fact that there are no footprints or marks of any kind in the dust, I don't think any one has been in the place for a long time."

"The old tower has been closed for years."

"So we thought," Joe interjected, "that he might have been mistaken and that he had really hidden the stuff in the new tower instead."

Hurd Applegate rubbed his chin meditatively. His manner toward the boys had undergone a change, and it was evident that he was impressed by their story.

"So this fellow confessed to the robbery, eh?"

"He admitted everything. He was a man who once worked around Bayport and he knew this locality pretty well. He had been hanging around the city for some days before the robbery."

"Well," said Applegate slowly, "if he says he hid the stuff in the old tower and it isn't there, he must have meant the new tower, just as you say."

"Will you let us search it?"

"I'll do more than that. I'll help you. I'm just as anxious to get the jewels and bonds back as anybody."

"All nonsense!" declared Adelia Applegate. "It's all a pack of falsehoods. I don't believe a word of it."

"Now, now, Adelia," said her brother soothingly, "these boys may be right after all. It won't hurt to take a look around, at any rate."

"And much you'll find, I'm sure! I declare, Hurd Applegate, you're just as bad as those boys are."

"Maybe, maybe," he answered. "But I'm going to help them search the new tower, anyway."

"Don't ask *me* to brush the dust off your clothes when you come back, then. For that's all you'll get. Dust. Nothing more. The jewels and bonds are no more in the new tower than they are back in the safe right now."

"All right, Adelia. Perhaps you're right. But it won't hurt to make a search, anyway. Come on, boys."

With that, Hurd Applegate led the way down the hall and opened the door leading to a corridor that extended toward the new tower. Frank and Joe, tingling with excitement, followed.

Although the new tower had been built just a few years back and although its rooms had been furnished, it had been seldom occupied, save on the rare occasions when the Applegates had visitors from the city. The new caretaker, employed to replace Robinson, was a lazy and slovenly fellow, who did not bother to extend his duties to the tower, knowing that the Applegates seldom went near that part of the mansion and realizing that any laxity in his duties in that respect would scarcely be discovered. It came as a surprise to Hurd Applegate, then, to find out that the new tower was dusty, that the windows had not been cleaned, that there were cobwebs on the ceilings.

In the first room they found nothing, although they rummaged about in all the corners, looked beneath the table, behind the chairs—looked everywhere, in fact. Not until they were quite satisfied that the loot had not been hidden there, did they ascend the stairs to the next room, and there again their search was fruitless.

Hurd Applegate, being a quick-tempered man, fell back into his old mood. The boys' story had convinced him, and he had been even more certain than they that the stolen bonds and jewels would indeed be found in the new tower. But when two of the tower rooms had been thoroughly searched without success, his disappointment increased.

"Don't believe there was anything in that yarn, after all," he muttered, as they went up the stairs to the third room.

"I don't see why he should lie about it, after he confessed," remarked Frank thoughtfully. "Dad told us that he admitted not being able to get away with the stuff."

"Then where did he hide it?" demanded Applegate. "If he wasn't lying, the stuff must be around here some place."

"Perhaps he hid it a little more carefully than we imagine," put in Joe.

"Haven't we hunted carefully enough?" Hurd Applegate snapped.

In the third room their search was again in vain. They even inspected the window ledges and tapped the floors and ceiling in the faint hope of finding some secret cupboard that was unknown to them.

But the loot was not found.

When at last they emerged through the trapdoor in the roof, out on top of the rear tower, and found it to be bare and empty, Applegate could not disguise his chagrin.

"Wild-goose chase!" he snorted. "Adelia was right. I've been made a fool of."

"You don't think we would make up a story like that, do you, Mr. Applegate?" Frank asked.

"I don't see any reason why you should. But there's something wrong somewhere. I've wasted half a morning poking around through this confounded tower—all for nothing."

"So have we."

"If that fellow did hide the stuff in one of the towers, some one else must have come along and got it. That's the only way I can figure it out. He had some one working with him. Or else Robinson found the stuff—That's more likely! Probably Robinson found the loot right after the robbery and kept it for himself."

"I don't think he would do that. He isn't that kind of man," Joe objected.

"With all that money in front of him? I wouldn't put it past him for a minute. Where did he get that nine hundred dollars, then? Explain that. He can't. He won't tell."

As they descended the stairs and went back into the main part of the mansion, Hurd Applegate elaborated on this theory. The fact that the loot had not been found in the face of Red Jackley's story, seemed to strengthen his conviction that Robinson had something to do with the affair.

"Either Robinson found the stuff and kept it, or else he was in league with Jackley!" said Applegate. "He's mixed up in it some way. I'm sure of that."

The boys could say nothing. They realized that the theory was probable, although in their hearts they found it hard to believe that their chum's father could have had anything to do with the theft. They were deeply puzzled and tremendously disappointed, for they had been practically certain that the loot would be found. Now they saw that the only consequence of the whole affair was to involve Mr. Robinson more deeply than ever in the mystery.

Back in the hallway they endured the taunts of Adelia Applegate, who cackled jubilantly when she saw that the searching party had returned empty-handed.

"There now!" she crowed. "Who's right now? Didn't I tell you it was all nonsense? Hurd Applegate, you've simply been made a fool of by these two boys."

"Now, Adelia, I think they meant well—"

"Meant well! Of course they meant well! And what did it gain you? They have prowled through the place all morning and all the good that's come of it is that perhaps you won't be so ready to believe the next cock-and-bull story some one tells you. Go back to your stamps, Hurd Applegate, and let it be a lesson to you. As for you boys, you should be ashamed of yourselves, disturbing folks like this!"

Whereupon she escorted the Hardy boys to the door, while Hurd Applegate, muttering sadly, went back to his study with a puzzled air.

CHAPTER XIX

THE MYSTERY DEEPENS

Fenton Hardy was dumbfounded when his sons returned to him with the news that the loot had been found in neither the old tower nor the new. So implicitly had he believed in the dying confession of Red Jackley that he had not even bothered to join in the search, preferring to let his sons have the satisfaction of recovering the stolen goods that he was positive were hidden in the old tower.

"And you're sure you searched the place thoroughly?" he asked, for the third time.

"Every inch of it. There was nothing in the old tower. No one had been there in weeks," answered Frank.

"How could you tell?"

"By the dust. It hadn't been disturbed. There wasn't a footprint of any kind."

"But you searched anyway."

"We went through the tower from top to bottom," Frank replied. "It wasn't any use. No one had been there. So then we thought Jackley might have been mistaken and that he had left the stuff in the other tower."

"And Applegate let you search that as well?" and Fenton Hardy's eyes twinkled.

"Not until we had told him our reasons. We told him about Jackley, and then he became enthusiastic and even helped us in the search. But we didn't find anything."

"Strange," muttered the detective. "I know Jackley wasn't lying. He had nothing to gain by deceiving me. Absolutely nothing. He was in real earnest if ever a man was. 'I hid it in the old tower.' Those were his words. He would have told more if he had been able. And what could he mean but the old tower of Tower Mansion? Why should he be so careful to say the *old* tower. Every one knows the mansion has two towers, the old and the new."

"Of course, it may be that we didn't search thoroughly enough," Joe said. "The stuff may be hidden in the flooring or behind the walls."

"That's the only solution I can think of," replied Fenton Hardy. "I'm not satisfied yet that the loot isn't there. I'm going to get in touch with Applegate and ask permission for a real, thorough search of both towers. It's to his interest as well as mine."

"Applegate thinks possibly Jackley hid the stuff all right but that Robinson found it and sold it," said Frank. "He hinted that he was of the opinion that Robinson was in league with the thief."

"It does look rather bad," Mr. Hardy admitted. "One couldn't blame Applegate very much for thinking Robinson found the stuff after it was hidden and made away with it."

"Robinson wouldn't do that!" cried Joe. "He's too honest!"

"I don't think he would do it, either. But sometimes, if a man is in need of money and temptation is placed in his way, he gives in. I'd hate to believe that of Robinson, but if that stuff isn't found in the tower I'll have to admit that it looks very much as if he were mixed up in it."

The interview with their father left the Hardy boys feeling far from cheerful, for they saw that Mr. Robinson was now more deeply involved in the affair than before. On the face of it, circumstances seemed to be against the caretaker.

"Just the same," said Frank, as the boys left the house and went down the street, "I don't believe Jackley ever hid the stuff in the tower. If he had ever so much as opened the tower door he would have left some marks in the dust and we would have seen them. So I don't believe Robinson came along later and got the loot."

"As we saw it, the dust in the tower hadn't been disturbed in weeks. Why, there was even dust on the door-knob, when Mr. Applegate let us in."

"Then, why should Jackley say he hid the stuff there?" exclaimed Frank, puzzled.

"Don't ask me. I'm just as much in the dark as you are."

When the boys reached the business section of the city they found that already Jackley's confession had become common property. People were discussing the deathbed confession on the street corners and newsboys were busy selling copies of papers in which the story of the criminal's last statement was featured on the front page under black headlines.

Policeman Con Riley was ambling along Main Street in the morning sunshine, swinging his club with the air of a man without a care in the world. When he saw the boys he frowned, for there was no love lost between the Hardys and the Bayport police department.

"Well," he grunted, "I hear you got the stuff back."

"I wish we had," said Frank.

"What?" said the constable, brightening up at once. "You didn't get it? I thought it said in the paper this morning that this fellow Jackley told where he had hidden it."

"He did."

"And you can't find it! Ho! Ho!" Con Riley indulged in a hearty laugh. "What a fine detective your father is! Didn't Jackley say the stuff was hidden in the old tower? What more does he want?"

"Our father didn't search for the stuff," retorted Frank. "We did. And it wasn't there. Jackley must have made a mistake."

"It wasn't there?" exclaimed Riley, in high delight. "That's a good one. That's the best I've heard in years." He chuckled exceedingly, and slapped his knee. "Jackley put a good one over on your father that time. Ho! Ho! Ho! The stuff wasn't there!"

Riley wiped the tears from his eyes and went on his way, trying to laugh and at the same time retain his dignity as an officer of the law. The joke, he decided, was too good to keep, so as he proceeded back toward the police station, there to edify Chief Collig and Detective Smuff with the tale, he buttonholed various passers-by and poured the story into their willing ears. It was not long before the yarn had spread throughout the city with that swiftness peculiar to stories spread by word of mouth, and in the telling the story was exaggerated, the net effect being that Fenton Hardy was made to look ridiculous by believing a false confession.

Highly colored accounts of the boys' search of the old tower quickly spread, and throughout the day they were subjected to many caustic and sarcastic inquiries on the part of friends and acquaintances alike. They took all these remarks in good part, although they did not enjoy their sudden prominence.

"Never mind," said Frank, "we'll show them yet."

"I hope they find that stuff when they search the towers again," added Joe. "Then the people will have to eat crow. It'll be our turn to laugh."

"Yes," agreed Frank; "but just now our laughter seems to be in a far-distant future."

When they returned home they found that Fenton Hardy had been busy in the meantime and had convinced Hurd Applegate that a thorough search of the towers would be advisable. True, he had not accomplished this without a great deal of opposition on the part of Adelia and without misgivings on the part of Hurd Applegate himself, who had by that time come to the conclusion that Robinson had indeed been mixed up in the affair all along.

In this conviction he was sustained by Chief Collig, who had paid a call at the Applegate home as soon as Collig had told him of the vain search of the towers.

"The chief says Robinson is behind it, and I'm beginnin' to think he's right," said Applegate.

"But how about the confession?" Mr. Hardy asked.

"The chief says that's all a blind. Jackley did it to protect Robinson. They were both working together."

"I know it looks bad for Robinson, but I don't think it would hurt to give the towers another thorough search. I was the one who heard Jackley make the confession and I don't believe he was lying. I believe he was trying to tell me all he knew."

"Maybe. Maybe. I think he was too smart for you, Mr. Hardy, and everybody else thinks so too. It was all a hoax."

"I'll believe that after I've searched the towers inside and out."

"Well, go ahead. Go as far as you like. But I don't think you'll find that treasure."

With that, Mr. Hardy was content. He made preparations for a search of the towers, although Adelia Applegate flatly declared that the detective was making a laughing-stock of her and her brother and that if the nonsense continued she would leave Tower Mansion forever and carry out her oft-expressed intention of going to one of the South Sea Islands as a missionary.

In spite of the protestations of the worthy lady, however, the search was carried out. The old tower was visited first, and for the greater part of the following morning the place was searched from top to bottom. Even the floors were torn up in places in the quest for some secret hiding place in which Jackley might have left the loot.

But although Fenton Hardy, accompanied by the boys and Hurd Applegate, who soon became infected with the dogged enthusiasm of the others and lent every assistance in his power, hunted throughout the old tower in every conceivable place, the missing jewels and bonds were not recovered.

"Nothing left but to search the new tower," Mr. Hardy commented briefly, when the search was over, and throughout the whole afternoon the new tower was the scene of a search that was as thorough as it was fruitless.

Walls and partitions were tapped, floors were sounded, furniture was minutely examined—not an inch of space escaped the minute scrutiny of the detective and his helpers. But as the search wore on and the loot still evaded discovery, the chagrin of Fenton Hardy deepened and Hurd Applegate finally lost his temper.

"A hoax!" he declared. "A hoax from start to finish."

"The man was in earnest!" the detective insisted.

"Then where is the stuff?"

"Some one else may have found it. That's the only explanation I can think of."

"Who else could have taken it but Robinson?"

To this, Mr. Hardy was silent. In spite of his knowledge of and liking for the man, he was beginning to suspect that the caretaker may have had a hand in the affair after all.

"Either that or Jackley simply told that yarn to shield Robinson," declared Applegate.

"I'm not going to give up this search yet," said Mr. Hardy patiently. "Perhaps the loot was hidden somewhere about the grounds."

So the grounds of Tower Mansion, particularly in the vicinity of the two towers, were thoroughly searched. The shrubbery was inspected but to no avail.

The search continued until sundown, and by that time Adelia Applegate was pale with wrath, for the place, as she expressed it, had been "turned upside down," Hurd Applegate was outspoken in his rage and disappointment, while Fenton Hardy was deeply chagrined. As for the boys, although they had expected that the additional search would be without success, they shared their father's bewilderment.

"I can't understand it," admitted the detective. "I could have sworn that Jackley was in earnest when he made that confession. He knew he was near death and that he had nothing to gain by concealment. I can't understand it at all."

And there the mystery remained, deeper than it had ever been.

CHAPTER XX

THE FLASH IN THE TOWER

For two days after the unsuccessful search of Tower Mansion, there were no further developments in the affair of the robbery. But on the third day, Chief Collig took a hand.

The first intimation the Hardy boys had of it was when they met Callie Shaw and Iola Morton on their way to school. Iola, a plump, dark girl, was a sister of Chet Morton and had achieved the honor of being about the only girl Joe Hardy had ever conceded to be anything but an unmitigated nuisance.

Joe, who was shy in the presence of girls, professed a lofty scorn for all members of the other sex, particularly those of high school age, but had once grudgingly admitted that Iola Morton was "all right, for a girl." This, from him, was high praise.

"Have you heard what's happened?" asked Callie, as they met the boys near the school entrance.

"School called off for today?" asked Joe eagerly.

"No, no. Nothing like that. It's about the Robinsons."

"What's happened now?"

"Mr. Robinson has been arrested again."

The Hardy boys stared at her as though thunderstruck.

"What for?" demanded Frank, in astonishment.

"Over that robbery at Tower Mansion. He has been working in the city lately and Chief Collig sent Detective Smuff for him last night. Iola and I were over to see the Robinson girls last night and they told us about it. Smuff should be back by now."

"Well, can you beat that!" exclaimed Frank. "I wonder what's the big idea of arresting him again?"

"It seems the chief has an idea that Mr. Robinson was in league with this man Jackley, the man your father got the confession from. He told Mrs. Robinson last night that he was sure Mr. Robinson had the stuff hidden somewhere and that he was going to find out. He was perfectly mean and nasty about it, and Mrs. Robinson doesn't know what to do."

The Hardy boys looked at one another. The affair had suddenly assumed more serious proportions.

"If Mr. Robinson is brought back, he'll lose his job, and he had a hard time getting it, anyway," said Iola.

"The worst of it is," said Frank slowly, "that the case looks pretty bad against Mr. Robinson."

"You don't think they'll send him to the penitentiary?"

"It looks bad. The thief said he hid the stuff in the old tower. When we looked for it, the stuff wasn't there. About the only person that could have found it and taken it away, was Mr. Robinson himself."

"He wouldn't do it!" declared Iola indignantly.

"We're sure he wouldn't. But a jury mightn't be so easy to convince."

It was time to go into school at that moment and they went to their classrooms, Frank and Joe deeply worried by what they had just heard. At recess that morning they met Jerry, Phil, Tony and Chet Morton, and told them the news. All the boys were highly concerned over this sudden turn in events.

"This will be tough on Perry," said Phil.

"It'll be tough on the whole family," Chet declared. "They've had enough trouble over this dirty affair as it is."

The boys discussed the situation from all angles and racked their brains for some way whereby they could help the Robinsons, but they were reluctantly forced to admit that only by actual discovery of the hidden loot could Mr. Robinson be cleared of suspicion in connection with the robbery.

"Even if he were tried and acquitted, it would be a stain on his reputation for the rest of his life, as long as the treasure isn't recovered," Frank summed up.

"We'll just have to wait and see what happens," Joe said. "We've done all we could, and it hasn't been enough."

"And dad has done the same. I'm sorry, on his account. He was so sure he had cleared the whole thing up when he got the confession from Jackley. But there was something lacking."

"Well, we all helped too," remarked Jerry. "We kept Collig and Smuff from catching that train. Jackley wouldn't have talked at all if they had seen him."

So, reluctantly enough, the boys were forced to admit that they were facing a stone wall. This also was the conclusion of Fenton Hardy, when they talked to him at lunch that day.

"There's nothing to be done," said the detective. "Robinson has been arrested, and while he might be cleared by a skilful lawyer, he hasn't any money to spend on his defence. Whether he is cleared or not, his reputation is ruined."

"Unless the loot is found," put in Joe.

"Yes, unless the loot is found. That is his only hope. But I don't think there's much chance of that."

And there the mystery of Tower Mansion rested for the time being. The arrest of Mr. Robinson furnished a sensation for a day or so and then the case receded into the background, the newspapers finding other things to become excited about. But for the Robinsons it was, naturally enough, a matter of supreme moment. Perry Robinson paid a call at the Hardy home, pleading with the great detective to continue his efforts to clear the accused man.

Mr. Hardy was sympathetic, but, as he said, he was facing a stone wall.

"I've done all I can, my boy," he explained to the grief-stricken lad. "If there was anything more I could do, I would do it. But there are no more clues. If Red Jackley's confession couldn't clear up the affair, then nothing else could. I'm afraid—"

He left the sentence unfinished.

"Do you mean my father will go to jail?"

"I wouldn't say that. But you must be prepared to face the worst."

"He didn't do it," said Perry doggedly.

"I know you have confidence in him. But the law looks only at the facts. Many an innocent man has been convicted on less evidence."

"It will kill my mother."

Mr. Hardy was silent.

"I don't know what to do," said Perry. "I'd do anything to save him. But there's nothing—"

"There is nothing any of us can do now unless by some lucky chance the loot is recovered. That would clear everything up, of course. But in the meantime we just have to wait and hope."

"And you can't do anything more, Mr. Hardy?"

"A detective is not a miracle man, my boy," said Fenton Hardy kindly. "He is only a man who is trained in tracing criminals. He has to go by the facts at his disposal. I have exhausted every line of action in this case. Everything that could be done, has been done."

Perry Robinson got up, twisting his cap nervously in his hands.

"We all thank you very much too, Mr. Hardy," he said huskily. "Don't think I've been ungrateful by coming here and asking you to do more. I guess I didn't realize just how hopeless it is."

"It isn't hopeless, exactly. Don't think that. There's always hope, you know. But—be prepared for the worst."

"I'll have to be."

With that, the boy left. Frank and Joe met him in the hallway and awkwardly tried to express their sympathy. Perry was grateful.

"I know both of you have done a lot for us in this mess," he said. "If it hadn't been for you we wouldn't even have Jackley's story to go on."

"We're only sorry it didn't work out as we hoped, Perry," Frank said. "We thought that would clear the whole thing up. Instead, it seems to have involved your father deeper than ever."

"It wasn't your fault."

"Perhaps something will turn up yet. Joe and I aren't going to lie down on the job now. There isn't much we can do, but we'll have our eyes open for more clues—if there are any."

Perry Robinson shrugged his shoulders dispiritedly. "I guess there isn't much use now," he said. "But I appreciate it of you."

When he went away, the Hardy boys watched him going down the front walk. His carefree stride was gone, and instead he walked mechanically, as though in a daze.

"What a fine pair of detectives we are!" exclaimed Frank, in sudden disgust. "If we had been any good at all we could have got those clues soon enough for dad to have caught Jackley in time."

"No use worrying about that now," replied his brother. "It was just the way things happened."

"Well, there's one thing left. We must find that loot!"

"Haven't we tried?"

"Yes, but we can try some more. We've just *got* to clear Mr. Robinson. And there's only the one way. We must find the loot!"

It was a dull, gloomy day, indicative of rain, and this did not add to the boys' spirits.

To ease their feelings the brothers took a walk, and quite unconsciously their steps took them in the vicinity of Tower Mansion.

"Let's have a squint at the old place from the outside," suggested Joe.

"Don't let Adelia see you, or she'll come after you with a broomstick," chuckled Frank. "Gee, but she's a tartar!"

They walked into the grounds. It was growing darker now and they easily made their way among the trees and bushes to the vicinity of the rambling mansion. They gazed up at the old tower questioningly.

"Some puzzle," was Frank's comment. "Will the case of The Tower Treasure ever be solved?"

"Search me!" was his brother's slangy answer. "Perhaps—oh, Frank, look!" he added suddenly.

He was gazing at the upper windows of the old stone tower. He had seen a strange flash of light. Now this flash was followed by another.

"That's strange," muttered Frank. "What can it mean?"

The light disappeared, then of a sudden it flashed out and downward in the direction of the lads.

"Must be looking for us!" gasped Joe, and started to get behind a bush.

"It's Adelia—and she has a big flashlight," came, a moment later, from Frank. "What do you know about that!"

"She's looking for the treasure herself!" cried Joe. "Huh! And after all she said about our looking being nothing but foolishness!"

They saw the woman gaze out of the window for a few seconds. In one hand she held the flashlight. For a moment she turned the light into her own face, and the boys saw there a look of utter disgust.

"Didn't find it, I'll bet a cookie!" chuckled Joe.

"Come on—let's get away before she spots us," returned his brother, and they were soon on their way.

As they walked home, Joe and Frank talked the matter over. They smiled when they thought of the eccentric woman up in that dusty old tower, but their minds soon went back to Slim and the troubles of the Robinson family.

"We've got to find that loot!" declared Frank emphatically. "No matter where that tower treasure is, we've got to find it!"

"Got to—but can we?"

"We simply have to, I tell you!"

CHAPTER XXI

A NEW IDEA

A week passed, and still the loot was not recovered.

Mr. Robinson had been held for trial at an early court session. The general opinion in Bayport was that he would be sentenced to imprisonment. The fact that he still refused to tell where he had got the nine hundred dollars so near the time of the robbery, weighed heavily against him.

Fenton Hardy was downcast. It was the first case of its kind that he had been unsuccessful in solving completely, and although he was satisfied that he had done good work in tracking down Red Jackley and getting the confession, the result had scarcely been worth the effort.

Chief Collig and Detective Smuff were complacent. They made no effort to conceal their critical opinions of the great detective, who had taken so much time trying to solve the mystery, when the real thief was right under his nose all the time.

"I told you so," was the burden of Chief Collig's song of triumph. "I knew all the time that Robinson was the man. I arrested him right after the robbery, but they all said it couldn't be him. So I let him go. But I knew all the time it couldn't be any one else. Ain't that so, Smuff?"

And the loyal Smuff would dutifully chime in with, "Yes, chief. We have to hand it to you. You had the right man all the time."

"I guess these professional detectives won't think they're so smart after all, eh, Smuff?"

"No, you bet they won't. We can still teach 'em a thing or two."

"I'll say we can, Smuff. I'll say we can."

These stories, naturally enough, reached the ears of Fenton Hardy and the Hardy boys and they felt keenly the arrogant superiority displayed by the Bayport police officials. But they said nothing, suffering their defeat in silence.

On the following Saturday, Frank and Joe decided to take an outing.

"I want to get out of this city for a few hours," said Frank. "We've been so busy worrying about the Tower Mansion case that we've forgotten how to play. Let's take the motorbikes and go out for a run."

"Good idea!" his brother replied. "Mother will make us up some lunch."

Mrs. Hardy, who was in the kitchen with the cook, smiled when they made known their request. Fair-haired and gentle, she had been tolerantly amused by her sons' activities in the Tower affair, but she was glad to see them return to their boyish ways.

"You'll be getting too grownup altogether," she had said to them a few days previously. And now, when they said they were going on a day's outing with the motorcycles, she hastened to prepare a substantial lunch for them.

"We'll be back in time for supper, mother," Frank promised. "We're just going to follow the highway along the railroad. After that we may cut across country to Chet's place, and then home."

"Take care of yourself," she warned. "No speeding."

"We'll be careful," they promised, as Joe stowed the lunch basket on the carrier of his machine. Then, with a sputtering roar, the motorcycles sped out along the driveway and soon the boys were on the concrete highway leading out of the city.

In a short time they had reached the outskirts of Bayport, and then they turned west on to the State highway that ran parallel to the railway tracks. It was a bright, sunny spring morning, and the highway was not congested with traffic.

Freight trains shunted back and forth on the railway tracks below the embankment, and now and then a passenger train steamed by, trailing a cloud of black smoke. Like most boys, Frank and Joe could not help but feel the fascination of the railway, although they admitted that they preferred the comparative freedom of their own motorcycles, which were not bound to follow the steel rails and did not have to obey the beck and call of despatchers.

Out in the open country they put on a little more speed. The highway was like a city pavement beneath them and the cool breeze stung the color into their cheeks. For more than two hours they rode, passing through villages and small towns, until at last they came to a point where another railway intersected the line they had been following. Here, a road also ran parallel to the tracks, branching off the main highway. Always on the alert for new country to explore, the Hardy boys decided to follow this side road.

"It's off the main stream of traffic," said Frank, "and the country seems to be wooded farther on. We can have lunch in the shade of some trees."

This appeared to be an advantage, for there were no trees along the State road, and the constant stream of vehicles made a roadside lunch something of a public affair. Accordingly, the boys turned their motorcycles down the side road which, although it was not paved, was well graded, and led through a quieter countryside.

"What railroad is this, anyway?" asked Frank, as they sped along.

"The Bayport and Coast line. It's mostly freight."

"The Bayport and Coast! Why, that's the railway that Red Jackley used to work for. Don't you remember dad telling us that? His first crime was stealing freight from the road."

"So he did! I'd forgotten all about it."

The boys looked down at the tracks below the embankment with renewed interest, by virtue of the railway's association with the notorious criminal. Mention of Jackley's name revived recollections of the Tower Mansion case, and when the boys finally decided to stop in the shade of a little grove of trees beside the road for lunch, they reviewed every incident of the mysterious affair.

"It would have been better for every one if Jackley had stayed with the railway," Frank observed, as he bit into a thick roastbeef sandwich.

"He sure caused a lot of trouble before he died."

"And he has caused even more since, by the looks of things. The Robinsons will remember his name for a long time to come."

"I wonder if Mr. Robinson really was in league with him, Frank?"

"I don't think so. And I don't believe Mr. Robinson ever found that treasure after the robbery, either. There is some explanation to this whole affair that none has been able to fathom."

"If I remember rightly, it was in this part of the country that Jackley worked."

"That's what dad told us. He said it was along the right of way near the State road. Jackley was a section hand or signalman, or something."

Both boys gazed down the two lines of railway tracks that gleamed in the sun. Far into the distance, the glittering bands of steel extended, vanishing into a common perspective.

The land along the right of way was thickly wooded. It was an attractive part of the country and here and there the wooded spaces were broken by green fields and meadows. The boys were at the top of a slope, and they had a view of a wide expanse of country below them.

In the far distance, along the tracks, they could see a little red railway station, and back of that the roofs and spires of a village. Nearer still they could see the spindly legs and squat bulk of a water tank, painted a bright scarlet. This water tank was not far from the railway station, but half a mile down the track, and only a few hundred yards from the place where the Hardy boys were seated, rose the bulk of another water station.

But this tower—one of the old style built before the modern tanks came into use—was not freshly painted. It had been allowed to fall into a state of disrepair. Some of the rungs were missing from the ladder that led up the side, and the tower itself had a forlorn and weather-beaten aspect, as though it had been deserted. This, indeed, was the case. The new tower tank closer to the station had been erected to replace it, and although the old structure had not been torn down, it was not now used.

Frank took a huge bite out of his sandwich and began to munch it thoughtfully. The sight of the two water stations had given him an idea, but at first it seemed to him to be too absurd for consideration. He was wondering whether he should mention it to his brother.

Then he noticed that Joe, too, was gazing thoughtfully down the railway tracks. Joe raised a sandwich to his lips absently, essayed a bite and missed the sandwich altogether. Still he continued gazing at the two water towers.

Finally Joe turned and looked at his brother.

In the eyes of both was the light of a great discovery. They knew that they were both thinking of the same thing.

"Two water towers," said Frank slowly.

"An old one and a new one."

"And Jackley said—"

"He hid the stuff in the old tower."

"He was a railwayman."

"Why not?" shouted Joe, springing to his feet. "Why couldn't it have been the old water tower? He used to work around here."

"He didn't say the old tower of Tower Mansion, after all. He just said 'the old tower!'"

"Frank, I believe we've stumbled on the clue!"

"It would be the natural thing for him to come to his old haunts after the robbery. And if he found he couldn't get away with the stuff he would hide it somewhere he knew. The old water tower! Why didn't we think of it before, Joe? Why, that *must* be the place!"

CHAPTER XXII

THE SEARCH

Lunch, motorcycles—everything else was forgotten!

With a wild yell of delight, Frank began to scurry down the embankment that flanked the right of way. At his heels ran Joe.

They raced down the grassy slope until they came to the wire fence. They scrambled over it, heedless of tearing their clothes. They dashed up on to the cinder path beside the rails.

"What if we're wrong, Frank?" panted Joe.

"We can't be wrong. I just know that's what Jackley meant. The old tower. It was the old *water* tower he meant all along. He didn't have time to explain."

The Hardy boys were tingling with excitement.

It seemed that they could never reach the water tower. They dashed along the cinder path with all the speed at their command, but the tower still seemed a long distance away.

"If only we *have* stumbled on the secret after all, Joe!"

"It'll clear Mr. Robinson—"

"We'll get the reward—"

"Dad'll be proud of us."

These thoughts gave them new strength and their hopes were high as they neared the tower.

The structure reared gloomily from beside the tracks. At close quarters it was even more decrepit, even more in a state of disrepair than they had imagined. The old tower had been abandoned for some time in favor of the new tank nearer the station. It sagged perilously. The ladder that led to the top lacked so many rungs that at first the boys feared they would be unable to ascend.

"If Jackley got up this ladder, we can do the same," said Frank, as he stopped, panting, at the bottom. "Let's go."

He began to scramble up the flimsy ladder.

Hardly had he ascended four rungs than there came an alarming crack!

"Look out!"

Frank clung to the rung above, just as a rung snapped beneath his weight. He hung in midair for a moment, then drew up his feet and placed them on the next rung. This proved firmer, and he was able to go on.

"Don't break 'em all," called Joe. "I want to be in on this."

Frank continued up the ladder. Occasionally, when he came to a place where a rung had broken off, he was obliged to haul himself upward by main force, but finally he neared the top. The ladder ran up along the side of the tank to the very top of the great, vat-like receptacle, and there it led to a trapdoor.

The Hardy boys did not look down. They were high above the ground now, and the old water tower was swaying alarmingly. They began to realize their peril, for the tower was old and liable to topple over with them. But the thought did not serve to restrain them, and at last Frank scrambled over the last rung and found himself on the upper surface of the tower. He turned around and helped Joe over.

Far below them lay the countryside, the green fields laid out in neat patterns, the roads in the distance like white ribbons, and the railway tracks glistening in the sunlight. The wind seemed much stronger on top of the tower, and it whistled about their ears. The flimsy structure swayed to and fro with every movement they made.

The trapdoor was closed. Frank went over to it and tugged at it, but the timber was heavy and Joe was obliged to help him. Between the two, however, they managed to raise it, revealing a dark gap that led into the recesses of the abandoned water tower.

The upper part of the tank was a space about four feet in depth and separated from the lower, or main portion by a thick floor. Frank lowered himself through the opening, and he was quickly followed by his brother. They crouched down below the roof of the tank and peered about them in the obscurity.

"It must be in here. There's no other place he could have hidden the stuff," said Frank.

"Let's hunt for it, then. I wish we had brought our flashlights."

Frank, however, had matches. Cautiously, he lit one. Then, crawling on hands and knees, he advanced into the darkness of the tower.

In the faint glow of the match they saw that the place was half-filled with rubbish. There was a quantity of old lumber, miscellaneous bits of iron, battered tin pails, crowbars, and other things piled up pellmell in all parts of the tower.

But there was no sign of hidden loot.

"It must be here somewhere!" declared Joe doggedly. "He wouldn't leave it out in the open. Probably it's in behind all this junk."

Frank held the match. They had to be careful, for the place was as dry as tinder and any negligence might have made the whole place a mass of flame from which there would have been no escape. In the glow, then, Joe searched frantically, casting the old pails and the old bits of board and lumber aside with reckless abandon.

One entire side of the tower top was searched without result. Then, on the far side, they spied a number of boards piled up in a peculiar manner. They did not look as though they had been flung there carelessly or accidentally, but rather as though they had been placed to hide something.

Like a terrier after a bone, Joe made for it. Frantically, he tore away the boards.

There, in a neat little hiding place formed by the wood, lay a bag. It was an ordinary gunny sack, but when Joe dragged it forth he knew at once that their search had ended.

"We've found it!" he exulted.

"The Tower treasure!"

"This must be it."

Joe dragged the gunny sack out into the light beneath the trapdoor. They did not even wait to go out on top of the water tower.

"Hurry!" exclaimed Frank, as with trembling fingers Joe began to open the sack.

It was tied with a piece of twine, and Joe tugged at the stubborn knots. At last, however, the twine fell away, and the bag sagged open.

Joe plunged his hand into the recesses of the sack and he first withdrew an old-fashioned bracelet of precious stones.

"Jewelry!"

"How about the bonds?"

Again Joe groped into the sack. His fingers encountered a bulky packet. He withdrew it and the packet proved to be comprised of long, imposing-looking documents, held together by a rubber band. On the surface of the outer document, when they held it up to the light, they read the information that it was a negotiable bond for $5000 issued by the City of Bayport.

"That settles it," said Frank. "We've found the treasure."

The boys looked at one another in triumph.

"Jackley wasn't lying after all. He *did* hide the stuff in the old tower. And Mr. Robinson wasn't in league with him and didn't find it after it was hidden," ruminated Joe. "We can clear up the whole affair now."

"Let's start, then!" Frank exclaimed. "No use sitting here all day patting ourselves on the back. It's up to us to get right back to Bayport and turn this treasure over to the Applegates."

Hastily, he scrambled up through the trap, and Joe passed the bag of treasure up to him. Frank put the sack carefully to one side, then helped his brother up to the top of the tower. After that he tied the treasure sack to his belt, in order that he might have the full use of his two hands in descending the precarious ladder.

They were so excited by their momentous discovery, by the knowledge that all the days of fruitless search had now ended, that they descended the ladder at break-neck speed. The last two rungs of the ladder snapped under Frank's feet and the boys were obliged to undertake a drop of six feet in order to reach the ground, but they hardly noticed it. Scarcely had they picked themselves up than they were off on a run for their motorcycles, parked far back on the hillside.

"We've shown 'em. eh?" gasped Joe.

"I'll say we have! Oh boy, won't this surprise everybody?"

"*Now* I'd like to see dad tell us we're not cut out to be detectives!"

"Wait till Adelia Applegate sees all her jewelry back again. She'll change her opinion of us."

"Wait till Hurd Applegate sees his bonds back. And wait till Chief Collig and Detective Smuff hear about it!"

So the Hardy boys gloated over their prospective return, but beneath it all they were thinking of what this discovery meant to the Robinsons.

They reached the embankment, scrambled over the fence, and made their way up the slope until at last they regained their motorcycles. Although they had only partly finished their lunch, they were too excited to eat any more, so they stowed the remainder away in the basket, lashed the bag of treasure securely to Frank's carrier, and turned the motorcycles around.

"What a lucky chance for us that we decided to go down this road!" declared Frank. "If we had done as we intended and circled around by Chet's place we would never have found the stuff!"

"And it's ten chances to one that neither of us would have thought of that water tower until his dying day."

The rest of their speculations were drowned by the roar of the motorcycles as the Hardy boys set out on their return to Bayport with the Tower treasure.

CHAPTER XXIII

ADELIA APPLEGATE'S COMPLIMENT

The curtain rolled down on the mystery of the Tower treasure that afternoon in the library of the Applegate home.

The Hardy boys had gone directly to their father with the story of the recovery of the loot, and Fenton Hardy had lost no time in acquainting Hurd Applegate with the facts. Between them, they arranged a little surprise for Chief Collig and Detective Smuff, as well as for Henry Robinson. On the invitation of Hurd Applegate, the chief brought Mr. Robinson to Tower Mansion, "to be faced with additional evidence," as Fenton Hardy suavely put it.

Chief Collig and Detective Smuff entered the library with their prisoner between them. They had confidently anticipated that Mr. Applegate had discovered some new facts that would further serve to tighten the web about the unfortunate caretaker, and when they came into the room there was nothing at first to eradicate this impression.

Hurd Applegate and Adelia Applegate sat by the huge library table, and with them were Mr. Hardy and his sons. Chief Collig did not at first notice the gunny sack lying on the table.

"Well, Mr. Applegate," said the chief, fanning himself, as usual, with his hat. "I brought along Mr. Robinson, just as you asked."

"Good. As I mentioned to you, there has been some new evidence in this case."

"I knew something would turn up," grunted Smuff.

"Not that any new evidence is needed, of course," declared the chief. "We got this fellow dead to rights, as it is. He ain't got a chance in the world. But still, it's just as good to make a real strong case of it."

"I'm afraid you don't understand me," went on Hurd Applegate. "This new evidence will *clear* Mr. Robinson. And when he is cleared, I want him back in my employ again."

"Huh?" gasped Chief Collig.

"What's that you say?" exclaimed Smuff.

"The stolen stuff has been found."

"No!"

"Here it is," put in Fenton Hardy, getting up and dumping the gunny sack upside down on the table. There was a tinkle and clatter as jewels came rolling out on the table, and then there was a rustle of paper as the packets of bonds followed.

"Where was it found?" asked the chief. "This doesn't clear him. He probably hid it some place."

"The stuff was found just where Jackley said he hid it. In the old tower."

"But the old tower was searched high and low."

"There is more than one 'old tower'," went on Mr. Hardy. "Only we didn't happen to think of that at the time. It was found in the old water tower, down at the Junction, where Jackley used to work."

Chief Collig was speechless with surprise. He gazed at Smuff, whose jaw had dropped in astonishment.

"Who found it?" asked Smuff at last.

"These two lads," said Mr. Applegate, indicating the Hardy boys. "They found it this morning."

"Them kids?" scoffed Chief Collig. "I don't believe it."

"Well, there's the stuff to prove it," snapped Fenton Hardy.

"I've got my jewelry back, thanks to them," declared Adelia Applegate shrilly. "They were smarter than the whole pack of you. If it wasn't for them, the stuff would never have been found. And I was the one who didn't want to let them search the old tower and who spoke crossly to them. Why, they're *real* detectives, both of them."

In all the talk and excitement that followed the clearing up of the Tower mystery, the Hardy boys received no compliment that they treasured so much as that remark of Adelia Applegate's.

"Well," said Chief Collig, scratching his head, "I'll be bumped!"

He looked at Smuff.

"I'll be bumped, too," declared Smuff.

"This beats all," said the chief.

"It does," agreed his faithful satellite.

"Shut up!" snapped the chief. "Who asked you to say anything?"

"Nobody."

"Well, then, keep quiet. A fine detective you are! Why didn't you think of that? The old tower! Of course he meant the old water tower. What else could he have meant? But *you* wouldn't think of it. Not in a hundred years—you wouldn't think of it. What kind of a detective are you, anyway? Here was a case that was as simple as A B C and you couldn't think of it. You let yourself be beat by a couple of boys!"

Smuff looked properly ashamed of himself, although it was plain that he was struggling with the temptation to ask the chief why *he* had not thought of the water tower, too. But he stifled the impulse and thereby doubtless saved the chief the trouble of dismissing him for impudence and insubordination.

"Yes," said Hurd Applegate, "the Hardy boys recovered the treasure. And I think you will admit that Mr. Robinson is cleared. Personally, I am satisfied that he knew nothing whatever of the theft and I want to apologize to him for any unjust suspicions I may have had. Mr. Robinson, will you let me shake your hand?"

Trembling, Henry Robinson stepped forward. His face had been illuminated by a glow of incredulous hope from the moment he learned of the discovery of the loot.

"Am I really cleared?" he asked. "I knew things looked bad against me all along. I hardly dared hope—"

"I guess you'll be let off now all right," said Chief Collig grudgingly.

"There will be formalities, of course," said Fenton Hardy. "But I'm pretty sure the prosecution won't continue. The discovery of this loot proves Red Jackley's story was correct from start to finish."

"But how about that nine hundred dollars?" demanded Smuff suspiciously.

Mr. Robinson straightened up.

"I'm sorry," he said, "but even yet I can't explain that. I can in a few days, perhaps; but I've promised to keep silent about that money. It's a private matter entirely."

"I don't think we need bother about that," objected Hurd Applegate. "I've checked over the treasure and it's all there. All the bonds and all the jewelry. There is nothing missing. As for the nine hundred dollars, why, that is Mr. Robinson's own affair."

Reluctantly, Smuff subsided into silence.

"Will you come back into my employ, Mr. Robinson?" asked Hurd Applegate. "Of course, I feel very keenly, because you were unjustly accused, and I want to make it up to you. If you will consent to come back to Tower Mansion as caretaker again I will increase your salary, and I'll also insist that you accept back pay for the time you were away."

"Why," stammered Mr. Robinson, "this is good of you, Mr. Applegate. Of course I'll come back, I'll be glad to. It'll mean a lot to my wife and daughters—and to Perry. He'll be able to go back to school again."

"Good!" exclaimed Joe Hardy impulsively, slapping his knee. Then, finding that he had attracted attention to himself, he sank back into his chair, embarrassed.

"And as for the Hardy boys," proceeded Hurd Applegate, "seeing they discovered the treasure—"

"Real detectives," shrilled Adelia. "Real detectives, both of them! Smart lads!"

"Yes, they showed some real detective work, and I hope they grow up to follow in their father's footsteps. But, as I was saying, they discovered the treasure, so of course they will get the reward."

"A thousand bucks!" exclaimed Detective Smuff, in awe.

"Dollars, Mr. Smuff—dollars!" corrected Adelia Applegate severely. "No slang please, not in Tower Mansion."

"One thousand iron men!" declared Smuff, unheeding. "One thousand round, fat, juicy smackers for a couple of kids! And a real detective like me—!"

The thought was too much for him. He sank his head in his hands and groaned aloud.

Frank and Joe did not dare look at each other. They were finding it difficult enough to restrain their laughter without that.

"Yes, a thousand dollars," went on Hurd Applegate. "I'll write the checks now. Five hundred for each."

With that he took out his fountain pen, reached in a drawer of the table for a check book, and soon the silence was broken by the scratching of pen on paper. Hurd Applegate wrote out two checks, each for five hundred dollars and these he handed to the boys. Frank and Joe accepted them with thanks, folded them up and put them in their pockets.

"And that, I think," concluded Mr. Applegate, "finishes the mystery of the Tower robbery."

"Thanks to the Hardy boys!" chimed in his sister. "Real detectives, both of them. I must ask them up for supper some night."

CHAPTER XXIV

THE LAST OF THE TOWER CASE

The discovery of the Tower Mansion treasure was a Bayport sensation for almost a week—and a week is a long time for any sensation to last, even in Bayport.

People said that they knew all along that Mr. Robinson was innocent of the theft, and went as far out of their way to be nice to him as they had gone out of their way to be unkind to him and ignore him when he was accused of crime.

People too, were loud in their praises of the Hardy boys, and everybody predicted a bright future for them and said they knew all along that the lads were bound to solve the mystery if they kept at it long enough. All of this the boys took with a grain of salt, as the saying is, for they knew that the public is fickle and as quick to condemn failure as it is to praise success.

Frank and Joe did not let the adulation turn their heads.

"When we couldn't find the treasure everybody said we were just nuisances—little boys trying to play detective," laughed Frank. "Now that we have found it, all that is forgotten. The main thing is that we've proved to dad that we know how to keep our eyes and ears open."

"And we've got a thousand dollars between us."

"A mighty nice start for a bank account."

"I'll say it is! I wish another mystery would come along."

"We can't expect to get a reward for every case we work on—and we can't expect to solve 'em all, either," Frank pointed out.

"We can't expect to get many cases to try our hand at. We're not professionals just yet."

"No, but we will be, some day."

This conversation took place as the Hardy boys were on their way up to Tower Mansion about a week later. Adelia Applegate, who had taken a great fancy to the lads, in violent contrast to her dislike of them on the day they had gone to make a search of the old tower, had invited them up to the Tower Mansion for supper.

She had also asked them to invite a number of their chums. So Slim Robinson, Chet Morton, Biff Hooper, Jerry Gilroy, Phil Cohen and Tony Prito had all been invited by the brothers to attend.

When the Hardy boys reached the Mansion they found that the others had already arrived.

"We're waiting for you," shrilled Miss Applegate, who was decked out in an ancient yellow gown with remarkable trimmings of black and red. "Everybody's hungry."

She soon led the way to the dining room, where a long table had been prepared for the boys. They gasped when they saw that array, and Miss Applegate beamed.

"I know you don't want an old woman like me watching you while you eat," she cried. "So go right ahead—and put your elbows on the table if you wish."

There was a scramble for places, as a servant came in with the soup, but Frank Hardy sprang to his feet.

"Three cheers for Miss Applegate!"

They were given with vociferous enthusiasm. Miss Applegate blushed with pleasure, and as she left the room the Hardy boys and their chums were sitting down to a banquet the like of which they had never seen before. For more than half an hour they indulged in roast chicken, crisp and brown, huge helpings of fluffy mashed potatoes, pickles, vegetables and salads, pies and puddings to suit every taste, and when the last boy sank back in his chair with a happy sigh there was still food to spare.

"I never thought I'd see the day when I'd quit eating while there was still some chicken on the table," murmured Chet Morton, "but this is the day."

"We have the Hardy boys to thank for this spread," said Jerry. "Let's give 'em three cheers."

The boys roared out their "hip, hip, hurrah!" three times, while Joe and Frank looked acutely uncomfortable. They looked still more uncomfortable when Slim Robinson got up, pushing back his chair.

"I'd like to say something, fellows, if you don't mind."

"Three cheers for Slim!" yelled some one.

So the boys gave Slim three cheers, and he gulped and blushed crimson.

"Speech!"

The cry was taken up.

"Speech! Speech!"

"I'm not going to make any speech," he said. "I only want to say something."

"Go ahead!"

"I'm not going to hand out any compliments to the Hardy boys."

Joe and Frank looked greatly relieved. They had been afraid of being embarrassed by Slim's gratitude.

"Everybody knows what they've done and everybody knows what it means to me and to my family."

"You bet!"

"Sure!"

"But I just wanted to clear up one point on behalf of my father."

"Three cheers for Henry Robinson! He's all right."

The three cheers for Mr. Robinson were perhaps a little weaker than the others, but that was only because some of the boys were beginning to show slight signs of hoarseness by that time.

"It's about the nine hundred dollars that he got just about the time of the robbery. He couldn't explain it at the time and it looked bad against him."

"It doesn't matter where he got it," shouted Biff Hooper. "I'll bet he got it honestly anyway, and if any one else says different, just let him come outside."

No one else said differently.

"Yes, he got it honestly, of course," said Slim. "The money was paid him by a man who owed it to him. But dad couldn't say anything about it because he promised not to. This man owed two other men besides my father, and those debts should have been paid first. He was afraid the others would sue him if they heard he had paid dad, so he made my father promise to say nothing. And when my dad makes a promise he keeps it."

The boys looked at one another. To tell the truth, few of them had thought of the affair of the nine hundred dollars, but now that it was recalled to them they realized that here was the final angle of the Tower Mansion mystery cleared up at last. They cheered Slim to the echo, they pounded on the table with their knives, and when Hurd Applegate came in to see what the racket was about they gave him three cheers and made him sit at the head of the table.

And that ended the affair of Tower Mansion, but it did not end the career of the Hardy boys as amateur detectives. They were soon to be called on to help solve another mystery, and the story of their adventures in this case will be told in the next volume of this series, entitled "The Hardy Boys: The House on the Cliff."

"Speech! Speech!" the boys were shouting to Hurd Applegate.

The old stamp collector got up, smiling.

"It's been a long time since there's been a crowd of boys in Tower Mansion," he said. "I've been in danger of forgetting that I was ever young once myself. So I want you to come back—often. I want you to know that Tower Mansion is always open to the Hardy boys and their chums."

The Hardy boys looked at one another, as the crowd about the table broke into a yell of delight.

"He's a pretty good old scout after all, isn't he?" said Frank.

"You bet he is," replied his brother.

THE HOUSE ON THE CLIFF

ORIGINALLY PUBLISHED IN 1927.

CHAPTER I

THE HAUNTED HOUSE

Three powerful motorcycles sped along the shore road that leads from the city of Bayport, skirting Barmet Bay, on the Atlantic coast. It was a bright Saturday morning in June, and although the city sweltered in the heat, cool breezes blew in from the bay.

Two of the motorcycles carried an extra passenger. All the cyclists were boys of about fifteen and sixteen years of age and all five were students at the Bayport high school. They were enjoying their Saturday holiday by this outing, glad of the chance to get away from the torrid warmth of the city for a few hours.

When the foremost motorcycle reached a place where the shore road formed a junction with another highway leading to the north, the rider brought his machine to a stop and waited for the others to draw alongside. He was a tall, dark youth of sixteen, with a clever, good-natured face. His name was Frank Hardy.

"Where do we go from here?" he called out to the others.

The two remaining motorcycles came to a stop and the drivers mopped their brows while the two other boys dismounted, glad of the chance to stretch their legs. One of the cyclists, a boy of fifteen, fair, with light, curly hair, was Joe Hardy, a brother of Frank's, and the other lad was Chet Morton, a chum of the Hardy boys. The other youths were Jerry Gilroy and "Biff" Hooper, typical, healthy American lads of high school age.

"You're the leader," said Joe to his brother. "We'll follow you."

"I'd rather have it settled. We've started out without any particular place to go. There's not much fun just riding around the countryside."

"I don't much care where we go, as long as we keep on going," said Jerry. "We get a breeze as long as we're traveling, but the minute we stop I begin to sweat."

Chet Morton gazed along the shore road.

"I'll tell you what we can do," he said suddenly. "Let's go and visit the haunted house."

"Polucca's place?"

"Sure. We've never been out there."

"I've passed it," Frank said. "But I didn't go very close to the place, I'll tell you."

Jerry Gilroy, who was a newcomer to Bayport, looked puzzled.

"Where is Polucca's place?"

"You can see it from here. Look," said Chet, taking him by the arm and bringing him over to the side of the road. "See where the shore road dips, away out near the end of Barmet Bay. Do you see that cliff?"

"Yes. There's a stone house at the top."

"Well, that's Polucca's place."

"Who is Polucca?"

"Who *was* Polucca, you mean," interjected Frank. "He used to live there. But he was murdered."

"And that's why the place is supposed to be haunted?"

"Reason enough, isn't it?" said Biff Hooper. "I don't believe in ghosts, but I'll tell the world there are some funny stories going around about that house ever since Polucca was killed."

"He must have been a strange fellow, anyway," commented Jerry, "to build a house in such a place as that."

Indeed, the Polucca place had been built on an unusual site. High above the waters of the bay it stood, built close to the edge of a rocky and inhospitable cliff. It was some distance back from the road, and there was no other house within miles. The boys had traveled a little more than three miles since leaving Bayport, and the Polucca place was at least five miles away. It could hardly have been seen, had it not been for its prominent position on top of the cliff, silhouetted clearly against the sky.

"He *was* a strange fellow," Frank observed. "No one knew very much about him. He didn't welcome visitors. In fact, he always kept a couple of vicious dogs around the place, so nobody cared to hang around there if they weren't invited."

"He was a miser," came from Joe Hardy.

"He may have been. At least that was the theory. Everybody said Polucca had a lot of money, but after his death there wasn't a nickel found in the house."

"Felix Polucca always said he wouldn't trust the banks," put in Biff Hooper. "But if he had any money I don't know where he made it, for he didn't work at anything and he mighty seldom came into the city."

"Perhaps he inherited it," Jerry suggested.

"Maybe. He must have had money at some time, to build that house. It's a great, rambling stone place that must have cost thousands."

"Is anybody living there now?"

The others shook their heads. "No one has lived there since the murder and I don't think any one ever will," said Frank Hardy. "The house is too far out of the way, for one thing, and then—the stories that have been going around—"

"Well, I won't say I believe any place is haunted, but the Polucca place is certainly strange. There have been strange lights seen there at night. On stormy nights, particularly. And once a motorist had a breakdown near there, so he went up to the house for help. He didn't know anything about the history of the place. He got the scare of his life!"

"What happened?"

"He decided when he went into the front yard that the place was deserted, and he was just going to turn away when he saw an old man standing at one of the upper windows, looking at him. He called out, and the old man went away, and although the motorist hunted all through the house he didn't find any trace of the old chap. So he left that place as quickly as he could."

"I don't blame him," remarked Jerry. "But the house sounds interesting. I'm game to visit it."

"So am I!" declared the others.

"Lead on!" laughed Chet. "It'll be a brave ghost that will tackle the whole five of us."

Jerry clambered on behind Chet, and Biff mounted Joe's motorcycle. The machines roared, and the little cavalcade started on its way down the shore road toward the house on the cliff.

Instead of being an aimless trip, the outing had now assumed all the aspects of an adventure. With the exception of Jerry, the boys had all passed by the Polucca place at one time or another, but none had ever ventured off the main road to explore the deserted place.

The lane leading into the Polucca grounds, never kept in good repair even during the owner's lifetime, was now almost indiscernible and was overgrown with weeds and bushes. The house itself was hidden from the roadway by trees. Most people gave the place a wide berth, whether they believed in ghosts or not, for the stories that had been told of the rambling stone building since the murder of Felix Polucca two years before were sufficient to indicate that there had been strange happenings in the old house. Whether or not they were of supernatural origin was a matter of debate.

The murder of Felix Polucca had been particularly brutal. He was an old Italian, suspected, as Frank said, of being a miser. He was very eccentric in his ways and most people considered that he was not quite sound mentally.

Be that as it may, Bayport was shocked one morning to learn that the old man had been found dead in the kitchen of his house, his body riddled with bullets. The motive, apparently, was robbery, for although it was popularly believed that the old man possessed a great deal of money that he kept with him in the house, it was never found, in spite of the most diligent search.

This was the gloomy history of the place the Hardy boys and their chums were now about to visit and explore. To add to the atmosphere of excitement that had possessed them from the moment the old house was mentioned, as they drew closer to the cliff, the sun retired behind a cloud and the sky gradually became darker.

Frank glanced up. Although the sky had been bright and clear when the party left Bayport, clouds had gathered in the east and it was plain that a storm was gathering.

"Looks as if we'll have to go into the Polucca place whether we want to or not," he called out to the others. "It's going to rain."

In a little while they came to the lane that led to the haunted house. In spite of the fact that it was overgrown with weeds and bushes, the boys were able to drive down the faintly defined roadway until at last a rusty iron gate barred their progress.

Frank, who was in the lead, got off his machine and kicked the gate open, the rusty chains clanking dismally as they fell from the staples. Then the party went on into the grounds.

Under the lowering sky that heralded the approaching storm, the grounds of the Polucca place were far from inviting. Dank, tall grass grew beneath the unkempt trees, and thistles and weeds sprouted up in the very center of the roadway. A rising wind stirred among the branches of the trees and the waving grasses rustled mournfully.

"Creepy sort of a place," muttered Jerry.

"Wait till you see the house," Chet advised.

Not one of them could restrain a slight shiver of apprehension when at last they came in view of the old stone building. It was framed in a mass of trees, bushes, and weeds that threatened to engulf it from all sides. Weeds obscured the front door. Bushes grew up level with the sills of the vacant downstairs windows. Trees on either side and beyond the house extended trailing branches down over the roof. A shutter hung by one hinge from an upstairs window, and banged with every passing gust of wind.

A deathlike silence hung over the old building. Under the black clouds that now filled the entire sky it was imbued with an atmosphere of gloom and terror.

"Come on!" said Frank. "Now that we're here we may as well go through the place."

"Haven't seen any ghosts yet," laughed Chet, with an effort at being light-hearted. But in spite of himself, his tone seemed forced.

They left the motorcycles beneath a tree and advanced toward the old stone building. The front door was almost off its hinges, and it swung creakingly open at Frank's touch.

Frank stepped boldly into the hallway. The interior of the house was veiled in gloom, for the rear windows were boarded up, but the lads could see that everything was deep in dust. A staircase was before them, leading to the upper stories of the building. To the left, was a closed door.

"This must be the parlor," said Frank, as he flung the door open.

The room was empty. A stone fireplace was at one side, and as the boys came into the room a rat scuttled out of the fireplace and raced across the floor, disappearing through a hole in the wall. The sound made every one jump, for the boys' nerves were at a tension on account of the forbidding atmosphere.

"Just a rat!" said Frank.

His voice had the effect of calming the others.

They stood hesitantly in the middle of the deserted parlor. Joe went over to the window and looked out, but the view from the front window of the Polucca place was so lonely and gruesome, in its aspect of tangled trees and weeds and undergrowth under the lowering darkness of the sky, that he came back.

"Where shall we go next?" said Chet.

"Nothing much to see around here," said Frank, disappointed. "It's just an ordinary, dirty, old, deserted house. Let's explore upstairs, anyway—"

At that moment there was a startling interruption.

A weird shriek, quavering as if with terror, rang out from the upper part of the haunted house!

CHAPTER II

THE STORM

That shriek was the most fearful and uncanny sound the boys had ever heard. There was a diabolical malignancy about it, like the scream of some bloodthirsty animal, yet there was no mistaking the fact that it was uttered by a human being.

As the quavering notes died away, the bare walls of the old house flung back the echoes so that the shriek seemed to be repeated again and again, but on a smaller scale.

The boys stared at one another, aghast. For a moment they were dumbfounded. Then Jerry muttered:

"I'm getting out of here!" and with that, he started for the door.

"Me too!" declared Biff Hooper, and Chet Morton followed him as he rushed for the doorway.

"What's the big idea?" asked Frank, standing his ground. "Let's stay and find what this is all about."

Joe, seeing his brother remain where he was, made no move to follow the others, although it was plain that the weird shriek had unnerved him.

"You can stay," flung back Jerry. "I'm not. This place is haunted, and I don't mean maybe!"

The three boys hastened through the doorway out into the hall and lost no time in regaining the front yard. Frank and Joe Hardy listened to their retreating footsteps. Frank shrugged his shoulders.

"I guess it gave them a pretty bad scare," he said to his brother. "We may as well go with them."

"I guess so," replied Joe, greatly relieved. They were alone in the gloomy and deserted old house, and as they stepped into the hallway Joe cast a cautious glance up the stairway. But there was nothing to be seen. The upper floor was veiled in shadow. The house was in silence that seemed even heavier than before.

When the two Hardy boys got outside they found the others waiting for them in the shelter of some trees about a hundred yards from the house. The three were discussing the strange occurrence in excited tones, and when the Hardy boys came up to them Jerry said:

"I don't have to be convinced any further. The place is haunted, sure. No other way to explain it."

"There's not much sense in running away from a sound," remarked Frank lightly. "If we had seen something, it might be different. I don't believe in ghosts and I'd like to get to the bottom of this. It's foolish to run away. Let's go back."

Chet Morton and Biff Hooper looked a trifle ashamed of themselves because of their precipitous flight from the house while the Hardy boys had remained.

"I got the scare of my life," Chet confessed. "Just the same, I'm game to go back if you want to."

"How about you, Biff?"

Biff Hooper scratched his head reflectively. "I'm none too anxious to go back in there again," he admitted. "Not that I'm scared, of course!" he added hastily. "But I don't see where we'd learn anything, anyway."

"Well, Joe and I are going back. That's settled," declared Frank. "We want to get to the bottom of this mystery."

"Mysteries are your meat!" observed Biff. "Well, when you come to think of it, this is a good chance for a little detective work."

He alluded to the fact that the Hardy boys were amateur detectives of some renown in Bayport. They came by their gift naturally, for their father, Fenton Hardy, had been for years on the detective staff of the New York police. Of late years he had been living in Bayport conducting a private detective service of his own with great success. He was known from one end of the country to the other as an exceptionally brilliant investigator.

Frank and Joe Hardy, his sons, were ambitious to follow in their father's footsteps, although their mother wished them to prepare themselves for medicine and the law respectively. But the lure of Fenton Hardy's calling was persistent, and the two boys were bent on proving to their parents that they were capable of becoming first-class detectives.

They had given proof of this already by helping their father in a small way on a number of cases, but their first big success had been achieved when they solved the mystery of a jewel and bond robbery from Tower Mansion in Bayport. The story of this has been related in the first and preceding volume of this series, "The Hardy Boys: The Tower Treasure," wherein was recounted how the Hardy boys solved the mystery of the robbery when the Bayport police and even Fenton Hardy himself were baffled.

"I'd rather tackle a good mystery than eat," laughed Frank. "And here is one right to hand. Let's go back."

Biff Hooper did not care to seem guilty of cowardice by staying behind while his companions returned to the house, and he was on the point of a reluctant consent when the matter was suddenly solved for them all by a downpour of rain.

Storm clouds had been gathering in the sky for the past hour and there had been dull rumblings of thunder. Now an uneasy wind stirred the branches of the trees and rustled dismally among the undergrowth. There was a spatter of raindrops, and then the storm broke in abrupt violence. Rain poured down in sheets.

"The motorcycles!" cried Frank.

Turning up their coat collars, the boys ran through the thick grass until they reached the place where their machines had been parked.

"I saw an old shed near the house," called out Joe. "We can put the bikes under cover."

There was an abandoned wagon shed near the rear of the house, and toward this refuge the lads trundled the heavy motorcycles. Although the shed was almost falling to pieces, the roof was still in fairly good condition and the machines were safe from the downpour.

"Come on," said Frank, when the motorcycles had been placed under cover. "Let's go back into the house."

He led the way, running across the open space from the shed, through the driving rain, and Joe followed. The others, after a moment of hesitation, came after them.

The back door of the house was open and the lads ran up the steps into the shelter of the building. They were in a room that had evidently been used as a kitchen, and although rain came in slanting streaks through the open windows, the glass of which had long since been shattered, they were at least sheltered from the downpour that had assumed redoubled violence. The rain drummed on the roof of the old house and poured from black skies on the near-by wagon shed. Thunder rolled and rumbled threateningly, and every once in a while a sheet of lightning tore a band of lurid light across the gloom.

Chet took off his cap, which was drenched, and tried to dry it out. The others stood by the window, looking out at the terrific downpour.

Then came the second shriek!

It rang out suddenly, at a time when none of the lads was talking and it was a replica of the first—a quavering, long drawn out yell, that seemed to freeze the blood in their veins.

No sooner had it died away than there came a terrific clap of thunder, and then the rain seemed to beat down on the roof of the old house in a frenzy.

In the gloomy, dusty kitchen, the boys stared at one another.

Frank broke the silence.

"I'm going to find out about this!" he declared firmly, striding over to the door that led to the interior of the house.

"Me too," said Joe.

Taking heart by the Hardy boys' example, the others crowded at their heels.

Frank flung open the door and strode into the room beyond. It was a very gloomy chamber, for the one window was boarded up, but when their eyes became accustomed to the meager light the boys saw that a door on the far side of the room led into a hallway. It was evidently not the hallway that they had already been in at the front of the house, but presumably one that led to a side door.

"Nothing here," said Frank, "I'd like to find those stairs. That yell came from the upper part of the house."

The boys made their way across the room. Outside they could hear the sweep of the rain and the steady rumblings of the thunder, for the storm was now at its height. Through the chinks of the boards over the window they could occasionally see the lurid glare of lightning.

Suddenly there was a blast of wind that seemed to shake the entire house. A sharp, violent noise immediately behind them made every boy jump with surprise.

They wheeled about.

The door behind them had been blown shut. Biff Hooper, who was nearest, grasped the knob and tried to open it. He wrenched and tugged at the door, but it remained obstinate.

"We're locked in!" he muttered.

"We can get out, all right," said Frank. "There must be a door in this side hall."

He walked across the room and entered the hallway.

At the same instant a maniacal howl rang through the old house. The hollow echoes magnified its volume.

A flash of lightning illuminated the startled faces of the five boys. With one accord they rushed into the hallway. It was a narrow place, heavy with dust, and their feet thudded heavily on the mouldy flooring.

Crash!

At the far end of the hall they had a glimpse of falling plaster that fell in a great heap to the floor. A dense cloud of dust arose and filled the narrow chamber.

"Run for your lives!" yelled Frank.

But no sooner were the words out of his mouth than there came a ripping, crackling sound from overhead. Immediately above them, a large part of the ceiling, disturbed no doubt by the vibrations of their feet as they ran into the hall, had given way. A wide crack that showed in the plaster quickly became wider, and then, with a terrific roar, half the hall ceiling came tumbling down upon the lads.

They were buried in dust and lathes and plaster that came upon them in such an avalanche that they were thrown to the floor. The splintering of wood and ominous crackling that followed, indicated that more of the ceiling was about to go, and then came a roar even louder than the first, as another avalanche of débris rolled down upon them.

Was the Polucca house falling in?

CHAPTER III

EMPTY TOOL BOXES

When he was knocked off his feet by the impact of falling débris, Frank Hardy crouched down, protecting his head as well as possible, until the downfall was over. Although a great deal of rubbish descended, it was not heavy material and when at last the rain of plaster and splintered lathes had ceased Frank knew that he was uninjured, although he was almost buried in the heap and half smothered by the thick dust that rose all about him.

He managed to get to his feet, fighting his way clear of the rubbish, and the first sight that met his eyes was an arm, sticking out of the débris near by. He seized the outstretched hand and dragged the owner to safety, discovering that it was his brother Joe.

By this time the others were beginning to extricate themselves, and within a few minutes all five boys, covered with dust from head to foot, had scrambled out to the clear floor in the middle of the hall. No one was injured, although Joe and Jerry complained of bruises about the head and shoulders.

"Let's get out of here!" exclaimed Chet, as soon as he could get his breath. "I'm not going to fool around this house any longer." He looked about him for some means of escape.

"I don't think it's very healthy myself," Frank agreed. He saw a door at the side of the hall and, going over, tried to open it.

But the door was locked fast, and although he kicked at it and shoved against the panels with all his strength he was unable to budge it.

"There's a window," declared Joe. "Let's break our way out."

The window was boarded over, but the glass was already shattered, so Chet and Jerry, picking up rocks that had tumbled down in the débris from the walls and ceiling, pounded at the boards.

"We'd better keep moving," advised Biff Hooper. "Perhaps the rest of the place will start caving in on us."

There was a splintering sound as one of the boards fell loose, revealing the rain-soaked trees and bushes outside. Another onslaught with the rocks and another board fell away, leaving a space sufficient to admit of the passage of a human body.

"Gee, that looks good to me!"

"Let's get out of here quick!"

"That suits me!"

"Don't lose any time—this whole building may be coming down!"

As the last words were uttered the boys heard another crash behind them. It was so close that it made all of them jump.

"Hurry up, everybody!" yelled Biff Hooper.

"Can't get out any too fast for me," returned Jerry.

"You said it!" muttered Chet.

One by one the boys scrambled up on the window sill and squeezed their way out between the boards until at last all were standing outside the old house. The storm was still raging. Rain poured down in a drenching torrent.

"Now let's get as far away from this place as we can travel!" said Jerry. "Somebody is going to get killed if we stick around here much longer."

He was pale with fright and it was plain that the strange experiences of the past hour had completely unnerved him.

"That's the way I feel about it," agreed Biff Hooper. "I'm not a bit comfortable around here. Let's beat it."

"I'd like to find out what is wrong with the place," persisted Frank doggedly.

"You couldn't drag me back in there with a team of horses," objected Chet. "Let's clear out. I've had enough of it."

"Come on," urged Jerry. "There's no use going back. The whole place will cave in on us if we aren't careful. And, anyway, there's something fishy about the house."

Frank saw that the others were determined on leaving, in spite of the pouring rain, so, reluctantly, he gave in, and the five boys hastened around the side of the house over to the shed where they had left the motorcycles.

"We can at least stay in the shed until the rain goes over," he said.

"Not on your life," declared Chet Morton. "I'm going to put as much distance between little me and that haunted house as I can. That place gets on my nerves."

And with that he began tinkering with the machine, preparatory to starting it.

Frank and Joe decided that no good would be served by arguing the matter, so they prepared to leave with the others, although they privately resolved to return to the Polucca place at the earliest opportunity, to investigate the mystery of the house on the cliff more thoroughly.

Jerry and Biff Hooper took their places, and in a few minutes the three motorcycles drove slowly out of the shed and across the yard toward the lane.

It was then that they heard the laugh!

From the haunted house came a harsh, mocking laugh that rang out in peals of derisive merriment. It continued for several seconds, and could be heard quite plainly even above the noise of the engines and the drumming of the rain on the roof.

Then it stopped, abruptly.

The boys looked at one another.

"Did you hear some one laugh?" asked Frank, unable to believe his ears.

"You bet I did!" exclaimed Chet. "And that *does* settle it. I'm leaving here right away."

"That was the most nerve-racking laugh I ever heard in my life," declared Jerry. "Let's get out of here, quick."

"Somebody's playing a joke on us!" Frank said angrily. "I'm going back."

"Joke, nothing! That place is haunted. Come on."

And with a roar, Chet's motorcycle leaped forward as he headed down the lane toward the main road. Joe, after looking behind and motioning to his brother to stay with the party, followed him. Soon the three motorcycles were speeding down the lane.

And from the haunted house came peal after peal of that same demoniacal laughter, as though mocking their flight. Then, as they rode on through the streaming rain and the haunted house was lost to sight among the wet and sodden trees, the laughter died away.

When they reached the main road the boys turned their motorcycles in the direction of Bayport and for more than five minutes the machines rocked and swerved as they sped along through the muddy ruts. The boys were soaked to the skin and water dripped from the peaks of their caps into their eyes. The rain poured down with redoubled violence and the others could scarcely see Chet's machine through the misty downpour. Chet was making such good time back to Bayport that they found it difficult to keep up with him.

Frank Hardy was still dissatisfied. He had really wanted to remain behind and probe the mystery of the house on the cliff further. He held no stock in the ghost theory. The shrieks and the mocking laugh, he was sure, were of human origin. But what could have been the motive? It may have been that some boys had been in the house when they arrived and had simply seized the opportunity to play a joke on them.

"In that case," he muttered to himself, "the story will be all over the Bayport high school by Monday and we'll be kidded within an inch of our lives for running away. We should have stayed behind."

Something told him, however, that this was no ordinary schoolboy prank. The incident of the fallen ceiling had unnerved him slightly. It was only by good luck that none of them had been seriously hurt. Of course, it may have been entirely accidental, but it seemed to have happened at a strangely opportune time. Then the recollection of the shrieks and the mocking laugh came back to him again and he shivered as he recalled the maniacal intensity of the tones.

"If it was any fellow like ourselves he was a mighty good actor," Frank said to himself. "I've heard of a person's blood running cold, but I never knew what it meant until I heard those yells."

Suddenly his motorcycle began, as he termed it, "acting up." It coughed, lurched, back-fired explosively, and then the engine died.

"What a fine time for a breakdown," Frank said, as he dismounted.

Joe drew up alongside. "What's the matter?" he called.

"Engine broke down."

"Gosh, aren't you lucky!" exclaimed Joe, grinning. "There's a shed over at the side of the road. Bring it over under cover."

He pointed to a tumble-down shed near by. Frank realized that it might take some time to discover the trouble, so he trundled the motorcycle over to the refuge his brother had indicated. In the meantime, Chet Morton had looked back, to find that the others were not following him, and had decided to return. The roar of his machine could be heard through the rain as he rode back toward them.

In the shelter of the shed, Frank first of all took off his coat and cap, which were dripping wet, and hung them up on a projecting board. Then, as Joe and Jerry stood by, glad of the chance to get in out of the rain, he rolled up his sleeves and prepared to find the source of the trouble.

They could hear Chet calling for them, as he drove along the road in the rain.

"Thinks we're lost," laughed Joe. He went over to the front of the shed and hailed their companion. "Come on up here!" he shouted. "Had a break-down."

Grumbling audibly, Chet dismounted and came over toward the shed.

In the meantime, Frank had opened the tool box of his motorcycle.

The others were startled by a sudden exclamation. Frank was staring at the tool box, with a bewildered expression on his face.

"My tools!" he exclaimed. "They're gone!"

The other boys crowded around. The tool box was empty.

"Did you have them when you left Bayport?" asked Joe.

"Of course I did. I never go anywhere without them. Who on earth could have taken them?"

"You can have mine," offered Joe, going over to his own motorcycle. He snapped open the tool box on his machine and then gave a shout of astonishment.

"Mine are gone too!"

CHAPTER IV

THE CHASE IN THE BAY

The boys stared at one another in bewilderment.

"I know my tool box was full when I left home," said Frank.

"And so was mine," came from Joe. "I was using the pliers just before we started out."

"Where could they have gone?"

"They must have been stolen while the motorcycles were in the shed at the Polucca place," Chet suggested.

"It's the only time they could have been taken," declared Frank. "It was the only time they were left unguarded."

Joe was frankly puzzled.

"But we didn't see any one around the place," said Jerry.

"No—but there was some one there. We heard those shrieks and the laugh. Some one stole those tools while we were in the house."

"It's some kind of a practical joke, that's what I'm beginning to think," declared Frank. "Let's go back and get those tools."

"Not on your life," objected Jerry decisively. "This is a little too much. First of all we hear those shrieks, and then the house almost comes down around our ears, and now we find that the tools have been stolen by somebody we didn't see. We're safer away from there."

Biff Hooper nodded agreement.

"That's what I think. There's something odd about that house. We'll get into trouble if we go butting in any more."

"But we want our tools!"

"Good night!" Chet exclaimed. "Perhaps mine are gone too." He ran out of the shed over to the road and hastily examined the tool box on his machine. Then he straightened up with an audible sigh of relief.

"Thank goodness, they're here! Guess whoever took the others figured he had enough."

"I'm going back!" declared Frank.

"If you do, you'll have to excuse me," Chet said. "You're welcome to use my tools to fix up your machine, but I won't go back with you."

"Me neither," chimed in Jerry and Biff simultaneously.

Frank and Joe were silent. They wanted to go back to the Polucca place and investigate the matter further, but they did not want to break up the party, so they decided it would be better policy to remain with their companions.

"All right," Frank said. "Lend me a pair of pliers and I'll have this trouble fixed up in no time."

He went over to Chet's motorcycle and got the desired tools. Then he began to tinker with his machine. It was only a minor defect, and a few minutes' work sufficed to repair the damage. In the meantime it was apparent that the rain was letting up, and by the time the Hardy boys took their motorcycles out of the shed and regained the road, it had died away to a mere drizzle.

"This has been some holiday!" Chet muttered, as he mounted his machine again. "I'm going home. Jerry, you and Biff had better come up to our place for dinner. How about you and Joe, Frank?"

"Thanks just the same, but we couldn't. We promised to be back home this afternoon."

"There's a side road that turns off here that makes a nice short-cut to our farm. I guess I'll go that way. There should be room for three on this bike, with a little crowding."

Jerry and Biff Hooper clambered on the motorcycle with Chet Morton and started off. The Hardy boys followed on their own machines until they reached the side road, about a hundred yards away. There the others left them, after shouting good-bye. Frank and Joe watched Chet's motorcycle, heavily loaded, disappear into the mists that hovered over the road, and then they prepared to continue their journey back to Bayport.

The shore road dipped at that point and wound down along the edge of the bay in a deep spiral, which brought them at one point almost back to the cliff at the top of which the Polucca place was located, although by now they were nearer the water's edge. From there the road sloped directly down to the shore, then ran along the edge of the bay and in toward the city.

Frank looked up toward the top of the cliff that loomed high above them. They could not see the Polucca place from where they were, as it was on the high ground and almost masked by trees, but the mystery of the place still preyed on their minds.

"I'd like to go back there yet," said Frank suddenly. "That affair of the tools has me guessing."

"Me too. But I think we'd better go on home. We can come back some other time and look for them."

"One minute I think it was only a practical joke of some kind. And the next minute I think it's something a whole lot deeper than that. There's something strange going on up there."

"There were sure a lot of strange things going on when we struck the place—that's certain. I can hear those shrieks yet."

"Well, I guess you're right, Joe. We may as well go on home. But I'd like to get to the bottom of it."

"Whoever stole those tools made quick work of it. We weren't in the house very long."

"It proves that it wasn't a ghost, anyway."

"I never did believe in the ghost theory. No, some human being took those tools. And he was watching us, too. He saw us put the bikes in the shed and he took the tools while we were in the house."

"Unless they were taken after we left the bikes under the trees in the first place."

"He wouldn't have had time. We only stepped into the front room and then we all came out after that first shriek. No, the tools were taken when the bikes were in the shed."

The boys rode on. The rain had ceased now, but the road was greasy and they had to call on all their skill to keep from skidding as they drove down the steep road toward the bay, so they did not talk again until they reached the more level highway at the shore.

A sound out in the bay attracted Frank's attention and he looked out over the rolling sweep of waters. He could see a powerful motorboat plunging through the waves about a quarter of a mile out. It was just coming into view around the base of the cliff, and as Frank looked he saw the nose of still another boat emerging into sight. Each craft was traveling at high speed.

"Looks like a race!" remarked Joe.

The Hardy boys stopped their motorcycles and watched the two boats. But it was soon apparent that this was no friendly speed contest. The boat in the lead was zigzagging in a peculiar manner, and the pursuing craft was rapidly overhauling it. The staccato roar of the powerful boats was borne to the lads' ears by the wind.

"See! The other boat is chasing it!" Frank exclaimed. He had caught sight of the figures of two men standing in the bow of the pursuing craft. They were waving their arms frantically.

The first boat turned as though it were about to head inshore at the cliff and then, apparently, the helmsman changed his mind, for at once the nose of the boat pointed out into the open bay again. But the moment of hesitation had given the pursuers the chance they wanted, and swiftly the gap between the racing craft grew smaller and smaller.

The Hardy boys saw that there was but one man in the foremost craft. He was bent over the wheel. In the other boat they caught sight of one figure who had snatched up an object that appeared to be a rifle. To their amazement they saw him aim at the man in the leading craft. Then, across the water, they heard the sharp report.

The lone figure in the first boat dropped out of sight. Whether he had been hit or not the boys could not tell. But the craft did not slacken speed. Instead, it still continued to race madly through the waves.

But the pursuers rapidly drew closer until at last the boats were running side by side. They were so close together that it appeared as if a collision were imminent.

"The whole crowd of them will be killed if they aren't careful!" muttered Frank.

Then, just when it seemed that both boats must crash together, the pursuing craft, as though it had given up the chase, veered abruptly away and headed out toward the middle of the bay.

The speed of the other boat decreased. The roar of its exhaust became intermittent.

"Engine trouble!" suggested Joe.

But there was more than engine trouble.

With startling violence, a sheet of flame leaped high into the air from the motorboat. There was a stunning explosion and a dense puff of smoke. Bits of wreckage were thrown high into the air, and in the midst of it all the Hardy boys, horrified, saw the figure of the man they had noticed before, as he was hurled into the water.

The whole boat was swiftly ablaze. Hardly had the wreckage begun to fall back into the water with spasmodic patterings and splashes than the craft was in flames from bow to stern.

"Look!" shouted Frank. "He's still alive!"

The man of the boat had been killed by neither the rifle shot nor the explosion.

They could see him struggling in the water not far from the blazing craft. His head was a dark oval above the water and he was slowly trying to swim ashore.

"He'll never make it!" gasped Joe.

"We'll have to try to save him!" answered his brother.

CHAPTER V

THE RESCUE

The Hardy boys knew that they had no time to lose.

It was evident from the struggles of the man in the water that he was not an expert swimmer. So far, he had not seen the boys, but they could hear him shouting for help, possibly thinking, however, that it was in vain, for it was a lonely part of the bay and the nearest farmhouse, outside of the deserted Polucca place, was more than half a mile down the road.

"Quick!" shouted Frank. "I see a rowboat up on the shore."

His sharp eyes had discerned a small boat almost hidden in a little cove some distance away at the bottom of a steep declivity that was the beginning of the cliff. It could not be reached by going along the shore, and the boys saw that they would have to go along the high ground and then descend to it, for a huge rock that jutted out of the deep water cut the cove off from the more open part of the beach.

They left their motorcycles on the side of the road and hurried back up the slope, then cut down across a narrow strip of weeds and grass until they came to the top of the declivity. They could still see the victim of the explosion struggling in the waves. The man had seized a piece of wreckage and was able to remain afloat, but the boys knew it was only a matter of time before his strength would give out.

"Looks to be almost all in," remarked Frank.

"I wonder if he's anybody we know," came from his brother.

"It isn't likely." Frank reached out suddenly and caught hold of Joe's arm. "Look out there or you may break a leg."

"It certainly is mighty slippery," answered Joe, as he managed to regain his footing. He had come close to going heels over head on the rocks.

Slipping and scrambling, they made their way down the slope toward the little cove. Rocks went rolling and tumbling ahead of them. The distance was only a few yards, but the slope was steep and a false step might result in broken bones.

But they reached the bottom in safety and there they came upon the rowboat. It was battered and old, but evidently still seaworthy.

"Into the water with her!" said Frank.

They seized the boat and the keel grated on the shingle as the little craft was launched. Swiftly, they fixed the oars in the locks and then they scrambled into their places.

They began to row with strong, steady strokes out toward the man in the bay. He had seen them, and was now shouting to them to hurry.

"He'd be better off if he kept quiet," Joe said. "He's only wasting his strength."

Evidently this thought occurred to the victim of the wreck, or else he was becoming weaker, for his cries died away and the boys did not hear him again.

Frank thought he may have gone beneath the waves, and he cast a quick look around. But the fellow was still in view, clinging desperately to his bit of wreckage.

The motorboat in the background was still blazing fiercely. Flames were shooting high in the air and the craft was plainly doomed. A great pillar of smoke was rolling into the sky from the burning boat.

As for the other motorboat, Frank could hear the roar of its exhaust as it continued its flight out into the bay. For a while he could see its dim shape, when he turned around once in a while, but then the fleeing boat disappeared into the mist and the gloom.

The boys exerted all their strength and the little rowboat fairly leaped over the waves. Both were good oarsmen and it was not long before they had drawn close to the man in the water.

But it looked as though they would be too late.

When they were only a few yards away Frank looked around, to shout encouragement to the victim of the wreck. Even as he looked, he saw the man wearily give up his grasp on the piece of wreckage to which he had been clinging. Frank had a glimpse of the white face and the despairing eyes and then the man sank slowly beneath the waves.

"He's drowning, Joe!" shouted Frank, as he bent to his oar again.

With a mighty effort they brought the boat close by the place where the man had gone down.

Frank leaped to the side of the boat and peered down into the depths. He began taking off his coat, preparatory to diving to the rescue.

Then the fellow came to the surface again, gasping for breath, but so weak that he could scarcely make a struggle. He emerged from the water, right beside the boat and Frank leaned over, grasping him by the hair. This sufficed to prevent the man from sinking for the second time, and Frank managed to get a grip on the collar of his coat.

Then, with Joe helping and in imminent danger of upsetting the boat, he managed to drag the stranger to the side of the craft.

The fellow was a dead weight, for he had lapsed into unconsciousness when Frank seized him, but somehow they contrived to get him into the boat, and there he lay, sprawled helplessly, more dead than alive.

"We'd better get him to shelter some place and revive him," said Joe. "We can't do much for him here."

"How about that farmhouse down the bay?"

"The very place. Where is it?"

They finally located the farmhouse, a snug little building back off the main road some distance down the bay. It meant considerable rowing, but there was a life at stake.

The blazing motorboat near by was a roaring mass of flames. Then it began to sink beneath the waves. There was a great hissing sound and a heavy cloud of steam as the craft sank lower and lower into the water, its blazing embers blackening to the touch of the sea. Swiftly, at last, the boat disappeared. Its stern seemed to hesitate for a moment, and then it slid quickly down into the waves and the only trace was a widening pool of oil and scattered wreckage on the surface of the water.

But the Hardy boys were too busy to give more than passing notice to the spectacle. Their immediate problem was to get the stranger under shelter.

Frank decided that there was no necessity for first aid. The man had been conscious when he rose from the water the first time, so there could not be much water in his lungs. He had simply given in to exhaustion and fatigue resulting from his long struggle in the waves.

They headed the boat down the bay, in a direct line with the little farmhouse, which they could see nestling among the trees. They had already spent much energy in rowing out to the rescue of the stranger, but they fell to the new task with a will. Rowing with machine-like precision, they felt the little boat respond to every effort, and it fairly leaped along. This time they had the wind and the waves with them and they made good time.

The man they had rescued lay face downward in the bottom of the boat. He was a slim, black-haired fellow. His clothes, which of course were soaked with water, were cheap and worn, the sleeves being frayed at the cuffs. They could not see his face, but they judged him to be young. He was still unconscious.

Frank let Joe take his oar for a moment, and crouched down beside the stranger. He turned the man over and the limp form lolled about as helplessly as a bag of salt. As they had surmised, he was a young fellow, with sharp, clean-cut features. He wore a cheap shirt, open at the throat.

Frank pressed his ear to the fellow's chest and listened for signs of life. Finally he straightened up, with a mutter of satisfaction.

"His heart's beating all right," he told Joe. "He's alive, at any rate. Just all in. He'll come to after a while."

He returned to his oar and the little boat skimmed over the waves on toward the farmhouse in the distance.

The boys rowed until the muscles of their arms were aching, but at last they drew near the shore and finally the pebbles grated underneath the keel. Frank leaped out and dragged the boat part way up on the beach. Then, between them, they carried the unconscious man up the rocky shore toward the farmhouse.

They found a path that led through a field up to the back door of the house, and although their burden was heavy they managed to carry the still figure, limp and motionless, across the field.

A gaunt, kindly-faced woman came hurrying out of the house at their approach, and from the orchard near by came a man in overalls. The farmer and his wife had seen them.

"Laws! What's happened now?" asked the woman, wide-eyed, as they came up to her.

"This man was mighty nearly drowned out in the bay," explained Frank. "We saw your house—"

"Bring him in," boomed the farmer. "Bring him indoors."

The woman ran ahead of them and held the door open. With the farmer giving aid, the boys carried the unconscious man into the house and placed him on a couch in the comfortably furnished living room. The farmer's wife glanced dubiously at the stream of water that dripped from the victim's clothes, for she was a tidy soul and she had just scrubbed the floor that morning, but her better nature overcame her housewifely instincts and she hastened out to the kitchen to prepare a hot drink.

"Best rub his hands," suggested the farmer. He was a burly man with a black beard. "It'll bring the blood back to his cheeks. One of you take off his boots and we'll wrap his feet up in warm flannels."

For the next five minutes the house was a scene of excitement as the farmer and his wife bustled about and the Hardy boys rubbed industriously at the hands and feet of the unconscious man, trying to restore him to consciousness. At last there was a sign of reviving life.

The man on the couch stirred feebly. His eyelids fluttered. His lips moved, but no words came. Then the eyes opened and the man stared at them, as though in a daze.

"Where am I?" he muttered faintly.

"You're safe," Frank assured him. "You're with friends."

"Pretty—near—cashed in—didn't I?"

"Yes, you pretty nearly drowned. But you're all right now."

"It was Snackley!" said the stranger, as though talking to himself. "Snackley got me—the rat!"

CHAPTER VI

SNACKLEY

At that moment the farmer's wife appeared, bringing a drink of hot ginger and water, which the man on the couch gulped down gratefully.

"We'll put him in the spare room, Mabel," decided the farmer. "He needs a good warm bed more'n anything else just now. I'll look after him, if these boys here will help me."

"I—I think I was shot—" muttered the stranger. He motioned weakly toward his side.

Frank leaned over.

"Why, there's blood on his coat!" he exclaimed.

A hasty examination showed that the stranger was right. There was a bullet wound in his right side. It was evidently not serious, merely a flesh wound, but it had bled freely and the man was weakened.

Gently, the boys helped removed his clothing, and with warm water and a sponge the farmer bathed the wound. The bullet had passed right through the fellow's coat after searing a path across his side. Disinfectant was then applied, the stranger gritting his teeth with pain, and after that the bandages were put in place.

"Now we can put him to bed. Can you walk, stranger?"

The man made an effort to rise, and then fell back weakly upon the couch.

"I'm afraid—I can't!"

"All right, then, we'll carry you. Give me a hand with him, lads."

Between them, they carried the wounded man upstairs into a plain but comfortably furnished room. Here he was put to bed and covered with warm blankets. With a sigh of relief, he closed his eyes.

"He's weak from loss of blood. That's mostly what's the matter with him," the farmer said. "We'll let him have a good sleep."

They left the room, and when they went out into the kitchen again the Hardy boys told the farmer and his wife of the strange adventure they had just been through. The farmer listened thoughtfully.

"Queer!" he observed. "Mighty strange!" Then, glancing significantly at his wife, he said: "What d'you think of it, Mabel?"

"I think the same as you, Bill, and you know it. Most like it's been another of them smuggling mix-ups."

The farmer nodded. "I've an idea it's somethin' like that."

"Smuggling!" exclaimed Frank.

"Sure! There's quite a bit of smuggling goes on around Barmet Bay, you know. Leastways, there has been in the past few months. That's been *my* suspicions, anyway. I've seen too many motorboats out in the bay of late, and I've heard too many of 'em prowlin' around at night. If it's not smugglin' it's some other kind of unlawful business."

"Do you think this fellow may have been shot in some kind of a smugglers' quarrel?"

The farmer shrugged. "Maybe. Maybe. I ain't sayin' nothin'. It ain't safe to say anythin' when you don't know for certain. But I wouldn't be a mite surprised."

Mr. and Mrs. Kane, as they introduced themselves, were just about to have dinner, and they invited the Hardy boys to stay. This the lads were glad to do, as they were very tired by their exertions of the morning, and were already feeling the pangs of hunger.

They sat down to the simple but ample meal, typical farm fare of roast beef and baked pork and beans, with creamy mashed potatoes, topped off with a rich lemon pie, frothy with meringue, and fragrant coffee. During the meal they discussed the strange affair of the bay. The Hardy boys did not mention their experiences at the Polucca place, for they had learned that one of the chief requisites of a good detective is to keep his ears open and his mouth shut and to hear more than he tells. At that, one mystery was enough for one dinner.

"I'd like to find out more about this affair," said Frank, when the meal was concluded and Mr. Kane sat back luxuriously in his chair and puffed at his pipe. "Perhaps that fellow is awake now."

"Wouldn't do any harm to see. You might ask him some questions. I'm just as curious about it as you are yourself."

They went upstairs. The stranger was sleeping when they looked into the room, but the slight noise they made awakened him and he gazed at them dully.

"Feeling better?" Joe asked.

"Oh, yes," replied the stranger weakly. "I must have lost a lot of blood, though."

"That was when they shot at you just before the boat blew up," said Frank.

The man in the bed nodded, but said nothing.

"What's your name, stranger?" asked Mr. Kane bluntly.

The man in the bed hesitated a moment.

"Jones," he said, at last.

It was so evidently a false name that the Hardy boys glanced at one another, and the farmer scratched his chin doubtfully.

"How come you to be in such a mess as this?" he asked, at last. "What were they shootin' at you for?"

"Don't ask me, please," said the mysterious Jones. "I can't tell you. I can't tell you anything."

"I suppose you know these young fellers saved your life?"

"Yes—I know—and I'm very grateful. But don't ask me any questions. I can't tell you anything about it."

"You won't even tell them? Not after they saved your life?"

Jones shook his head stubbornly.

"I can't explain anything about it. Please go away. Let me sleep."

Frank and Joe signaled to the farmer that it would be best if they withdrew, so they left the room and closed the door. When they went back downstairs the farmer was grumbling to himself.

"I'm hanged if he ain't the most close-mouthed lad I've ever seen!" he declared. "You saved his life and he won't tell you why he come to be racin' around the bay in a motorboat with fellows shootin' at him."

"He must have some good reason. It's his own business, after all," reflected Frank. "We can't force him to explain anything."

"He's in with them smugglers, that's what he is!" declared Mr. Kane, with conviction.

"I guess we had better be getting back home. Do you mind keeping him here? We can have him moved to a hospital."

The farmer shook his head.

"Smuggler or not, he stays here until he gets better. Nobody ever said Bill Kane turned a sick man out of doors, and nobody ever will. He stays here until he gets better."

"We'll come back in a day or so and see how he is getting along," Joe promised.

"He'll have the best of care here. Whether it's smugglin' or not that he's been mixed up in, it doesn't matter. My wife and I will look after him."

The Hardy boys arranged to have the rowboat returned to its mooring place, then took their leave of the good-hearted farmer and his wife and made their way out to the road. Then they went back to the place where they had left their motorcycles, and in a short while were speeding again on their return to Bayport.

"That fellow is certainly an odd stick," remarked Joe, as he and his brother motored toward home.

"I'll say he is!" answered Frank. "There's something mighty strange about all this, and don't you forget it!"

It was mid-afternoon when they turned their motorcycles into the driveway beside the Hardy home, and after they had put the machines in the garage they went into the house. They found their father, Fenton Hardy, in his den just off the library. He was never too busy to talk to his sons, and when they came in he put down the papers he was studying and leaned back in his chair.

"Well, what have you two been up to today?" he inquired, smiling.

"We've had a real adventure, this time, dad," Frank told him. "We were out to the old Polucca place with some of the fellows."

"That's the haunted house, isn't it? See any ghosts?"

The boys looked at one another. "No, we didn't see any ghosts, exactly," said Joe. "But—"

"You don't mean to tell me you heard some!" Fenton Hardy threw back his head and laughed with delight.

"You may laugh; but some mighty strange things happened out there," insisted Joe.

Whereupon the brothers told their father of the strange experiences at the deserted farmhouse. But Mr. Hardy refused to take them seriously.

"Some of your school chums playing a joke on you," he said, dismissing the affair. "They'll be laughing their heads off about it right now."

"But how do you account for the tool boxes being robbed?"

"They just did that to make it a little more mysterious. Probably they will hand you back your tools at school on Monday, just to prove their story."

This aspect of the situation had not occurred to the boys. They began to look a bit sheepish. If it had been the work of practical jokers it was only natural that they would seek something definite whereby to prove the fact that they had been at the farmhouse.

"Gosh, we'll never hear the end of it, if that's the case," sighed Joe. "Oh, well, we'll just have to take it in good part. But we didn't tell you about what happened on the way home. Tell him about it, Frank."

"Another adventure?"

"A real one. No practical joke about this."

Frank thereupon told their father about the two motorboats in Barmet Bay, about the chase and the resulting explosion. He modestly underestimated their own part in the rescue of the victim of the wreck, but Fenton Hardy nodded his head in satisfaction as the story went on.

"Good work! Good work!" he muttered. "You saved the fellow's life, anyway. And it looks as though you've stumbled on a mysterious bit of business in that motorboat chase. What did the man say his name was?"

"Jones," answered Frank doubtfully.

Fenton Hardy raised his eyebrows. "Of course—there are lots of Joneses in the world. It *might* be his real name. But more than likely it isn't. Would he tell you anything about the reason for the chase? Did you question him?"

"He wouldn't tell us anything at all. We made a few inquiries, but he said he couldn't explain."

"Still more mysterious," reflected the detective. "Do you think he will talk when he gets better?"

"I'm afraid not. He seemed quite determined not to tell us anything about himself or about the men who were chasing him."

"Don't you remember, Frank?" exclaimed Joe. "When we brought him into the house, just as he became conscious again. What was it he said?"

"Oh, yes! I had forgotten. He said, 'Snackley got me, the rat!' Whatever that meant."

"Snackley!" exclaimed Fenton Hardy, starting up. "Are you sure he said Snackley? Are you sure that was the name?"

"I'm certain. Aren't you, Joe?"

"Yes, that was the name, all right."

"Well that *does* give us something to work on," the detective said. "Probably you have never heard of Snackley, but I have."

"Who is he?" asked Frank.

"Ganny Snackley is a noted criminal. He is a smuggler—one of the leaders of a ring of smugglers who bring in opium and other drugs from the Orient. Is it possible that he is bringing drugs into the country at Barmet Bay?"

CHAPTER VII

BOUND AND GAGGED

The Hardy boys were astonished by this information. Their father, tapping a pencil quickly on the desk, leaned forward in his chair.

"You may have stumbled on some information of great value," he said to them quietly. "I need hardly tell you that it is best to keep it to yourself. If Ganny Snackley is operating in this vicinity it will be a great feather in our cap to catch him."

"It's an unusual name," remarked Frank. "I'll bet that's the Snackley our man meant, all right."

"And the farmer said there was smuggling going on in the Bay," Joe pointed out.

"Of course, there always has been more or less smuggling carried on in Barmet Bay. But it's been on a small scale. Ganny Snackley and his gang are international smugglers. The last I heard of him he was operating up on the New England coast. But probably things grew too hot for him and he moved down here. He seems to have dropped completely out of sight for the past six months or so."

"Perhaps this man Jones, at the farmhouse, will talk later on."

"I'm going out there to interview him," said Fenton Hardy. "I'll wait a few days until he is feeling better. Of course the matter is one for the United States authorities, and as I haven't been assigned to the case I can't do very much. But perhaps I'll get some information I can use at some other time."

"Joe and I will go out tomorrow and see how he is getting along."

"Do so. But don't ask any questions. Don't let him think you are suspicious of him. Otherwise he'll be liable to sneak away as soon as he can, and we'll lose him altogether. He is under an obligation to you now because you saved his life, so it will seem quite natural for you to come back to see him. If you think he is recovering quickly, let me know and I'll go out right away and talk to him. If you think he will be there for several days yet, we'll just let him stay until he feels better."

"Perhaps he is a detective himself," Frank suggested.

"That had occurred to me," admitted Mr. Hardy. "If that's the case, I'll keep out of the affair. It's just probable that he is a Secret Service man who discovered Snackley's hang-out and was shot for his pains. That would explain why he wouldn't tell you anything about himself. But there's always the possibility that he is one of Snackley's enemies; and in that case I may be able to persuade him to talk."

Fenton Hardy asked the boys more questions about their adventure, but beyond a few trivial details they were unable to throw any further light on the mystery. However, it was decided that they should go back to the Kane farmhouse on the following day, which was Sunday, and report on the condition of the mysterious Mr. Jones.

With that they left their father, spending the rest of the afternoon in eager discussion and speculation concerning the strange events of the day. It had been an eventful holiday for them, and although they went over the incidents time and again they were unable to arrive at any solution of the puzzling affair in Barmet Bay. As for the happenings at the house on the cliff, they were inclined to accept their father's theory that some practical joker had been to blame.

Next morning, after church, they took the motorcycles out of the garage and prepared to ride out to the Kane farmhouse, there to make inquiry as to the condition of the man they had rescued on the previous day.

"Remember!" warned their father. "Don't ask him too many questions or he'll get suspicious. Just find out how long he is likely to remain at the farm. If his injuries aren't very serious he'll be leaving in a day or so and we want to check up on him."

The boys promised to follow the detective's instructions. Unlike the day previous, this Sunday was clear and bright, and the rain of the afternoon before had laid the dust so that they enjoyed their journey out along the shore road.

"It would be a bad joke on us if Mr. Jones left before we got there," remarked Joe.

"I don't think he will. That wound in his side was enough to keep him laid up for a few days. And, anyway, he lost so much blood yesterday that it would take him a while to get back his strength."

"I hope he isn't a detective."

"Why?"

"It would be great if we could get a chance to do some work on this case ourselves. If Ganny Snackley is in this neighborhood and the government detectives don't know of it, we would help dad land him."

"It *would* be a great chance," admitted Frank. "But I think we'll find our friend Jones is a detective. That is, if we ever find out anything definite about him. Why else should Snackley and his men try to kill him? For there's no doubt they left him for dead."

"Perhaps he was another smuggler that they wanted to get rid of."

"Maybe. But I think it's most likely he is a Secret Service man."

At length they arrived at the lane leading from the main road to the farm-house. As their motorcycles roared down the drive they watched for some sign of life about the place. But there was no one in the orchard or in the barnyard. No one came out of the house. The place appeared to be deserted and, although it was a warm day, the doors were closed.

"This is strange," remarked Frank, as they brought their motorcycles to a stop and left them in the shade of a large tree near the back of the house. "Mr. and Mrs. Kane couldn't have gone away and left Jones there alone, could they?"

The boys went up to the door and rapped.

There was no answer.

"Try the front door," Joe suggested.

After a number of futile efforts, they went to the front door of the farm-house. But here, although they banged on the panels, there was likewise no response.

"They must have gone out," said Joe.

"But what about Jones? They wouldn't leave him here alone. I can't understand this."

They went to the back door and rapped again and again. Still there was no answer. Frank tried the doorknob and found that the door swung open.

"They didn't lock the place up, anyway," he said. "Let's go in. If Jones is upstairs we'll go up and see him. Mr. Kane won't mind. Probably they didn't expect callers today."

They went into the kitchen and here they were surprised by the scene of disorder that greeted their gaze. The previous day they had been impressed by the neatness of the room, for Mrs. Kane was evidently the soul of tidiness. Now the kitchen looked as though an earthquake had shaken it.

Pots and pans were strewn about the floor. The table had been overturned. A chair lay upside down in a corner. A few cups and saucers lay in shattered bits beside the stove. The wood-box had been upset and the wood was scat-tered about. One window curtain had been partly torn from its fastenings.

"What on earth has happened here!" Frank exclaimed, in profound as-tonishment.

"Looks as if a cyclone came through."

"There's something off about this! There's been a fight or a struggle of some kind here. Let's see what the rest of the house looks like."

The Hardy boys rushed into the next room. There an unexpected sight met their eyes.

Mr. and Mrs. Kane were seated in chairs in the middle of the room. They were unable to move, unable to speak, scarcely able to make a struggle.

The farmer and his wife were bound and gagged, tied to their chairs!

CHAPTER VIII

THE STOLEN WITNESS

Swiftly, the Hardy boys rushed over to Mr. and Mrs. Kane and began to release them. The farmer and his wife had been trussed up by strong ropes and they had been so well gagged that they had been unable to utter a sound. It was only a matter of a few minutes, however, before their bonds were loosened and the gags removed.

"Thank goodness!" exclaimed Mrs. Kane, with a sigh of relief, as the gag was taken away. Her husband, spluttering with rage, rose from his chair and hurled the ropes to one side.

"What happened?" asked the boys, in amazement.

For a moment Mr. and Mrs. Kane were unable to give a coherent account of their experience, owing to the strain they had undergone, but at last the farmer stumbled over to the window and pointed down the shore road.

"They went that way!" he roared. "That way! Follow them!"

"Who?"

"The rascals that tied us up. They took Jones away with them."

"Kidnapped him?"

"Yes—kidnapped him! There were four of them. They broke in here and tied up my wife and me. Then they went upstairs and carried Jones away with them. They dumped him into an automobile and made a getaway."

"Four men!"

"Four of the ugliest looking scoundrels you ever laid eyes on."

"How long ago?" asked Frank quickly.

"They didn't leave ten minutes ago. If you had been here just a few minutes earlier you would have met the whole crowd of them." The farmer was angry and excited. "But there's time yet. You can catch 'em. They went down the shore road."

"Come on, Joe!" shouted Frank. "Let's chase them. They've kidnapped Jones."

Joe needed no urging. The Hardy boys left the farmer and his wife rubbing their chafed wrists and ankles and hastened out of the house over to their motorcycles. Within a few seconds the staccato roar of the powerful machines broke out on the still air, and then they went rocking and swaying down the lane out on to the shore road.

"Some high-handed proceeding, I'll say," yelled Frank, to make himself heard above the roaring of the motorcycles.

"Those rascals ought to be in prison," returned his brother.

The boys followed in the direction the farmer had indicated. Frank then recollected that just before they had turned in toward the Kane farm he had seen a cloud of dust down the main road, evidently caused by a speeding automobile, but he had thought nothing of it at the time, for traffic along the shore highway occasioned no comment, especially on Sunday.

"If we had only been a little earlier!" he groaned.

"We'll catch up to them. They haven't much of a start. Maybe we can follow them to some town and have the whole gang arrested."

The motorcycles roared along at top speed. Both the Hardy boys were skilful drivers, and for a while Frank was able to follow the course of the car they were pursuing by watching the fresh tread mark in the dust. But when the road came to the place where it intersected with the road leading up to the Morton farm the tread mark became lost, as evidently another car had turned out of the side road in the meantime and obliterated the fresh tread here and there.

They passed the lane that led into the Polucca place and continued on down the shore road until they came to a hilltop that commanded a view of a wide stretch of country. Here they could see the road winding and dipping for a distance of more than a mile, until it was lost to sight in a grove of trees. But there was no sign of the automobile they were seeking.

"They've given us the slip, I guess," said Frank, as he brought his motorcycle to a stop.

"They had a good start and they weren't letting the grass grow under their feet, either. Think we should keep on?"

"There's not much use. We'd better go back to the farmhouse and hear what Mr. and Mrs. Kane have to say about this."

They turned their motorcycles about and headed back toward the farm. On the way they discussed the mysterious kidnapping.

"Evidently those men in the other motorboat saw us rescue Jones, or else they heard that he had been taken to the farmhouse," remarked Joe. "They must be desperate characters."

"I wonder what will happen to poor Jones now," said Frank gravely. "They tried to kill him in the first place. This time—"

"Do you think they'll murder him?"

"It looks like that. They didn't show him any mercy out in the bay. They left him for dead that time. Now they'll make sure of it."

Joe shuddered. "If they were going to kill him they'd hardly go to all that bother of kidnapping him," he pointed out. "Perhaps they just want to keep him out of the way. Perhaps they were afraid he would tell about their chasing him and setting fire to his motorboat."

"They were mighty anxious to get their hands on him, when they would come to the house in broad daylight and tie up Mr. and Mrs. Kane. Gee, it's lucky we came along when we did! They might have been left there for hours without being able to get loose."

When they got back to the farmhouse they found that the farmer and his wife had somewhat recovered from their harrowing experience, although they were still unnerved. Mrs. Kane, ever the true housewife, was already beginning to tidy up the kitchen and living room, for the intruders had upset everything in the struggle.

"We lost them," said Frank.

Kane nodded.

"I didn't think you'd catch them," he said. "They left here in too much of a hurry. But I hoped you would. They had a big, high-powered car and they didn't waste any time getting away."

"There were four of them, you said?"

"Four. Ugly villains."

"What did they look like?"

"I didn't get much of a chance to see. It all happened too quick. One of them came to the door—he was a tall chap with a thin face—and asked if I was looking after a man who was almost drowned yesterday. I said that I was, so he told me he had come to take him away, that he was a brother of the fellow. I got kind of suspicious, and asked him his name. But in the meantime I had stepped outside the door, and before I knew it, some one jumped at me from behind. I put up a fight as best as I could, but the others came at me from around the corner of the house where they had been hidin' and before I knew it I was tied up. Then they tied up my wife and left us in the livin' room while they went upstairs."

"Did Jones put up a fight when they took him away?"

"He tried to. He hollered for help, but of course I couldn't do nothin' and he was too weak to fight much himself. They carried him downstairs and put him in the automobile. Then they drove away."

"There must be more to this affair than we imagine," reflected Frank. "It's getting serious when they break into a private home like this."

"You bet it's gettin' serious!" exclaimed the farmer. "It'll be mighty serious for them if they try it again." He motioned to the table where a shotgun was lying. "I've got that gun loaded and waitin' for the next gang that tries anything like that. I only wish I'd had it ready this morning."

"I don't think you'll have any cause to use it," Frank said reassuringly. "It was Jones they were after. They won't bother you again."

"They'd better not."

"I think the best thing we can do, Joe, is to go right back to Bayport and let dad know about this."

"Good idea. We can't do anything by staying here."

"You boys said yesterday that your name was Hardy, eh?" said the farmer. "Ain't any relation to Fenton Hardy, are you?"

"He's our father."

"The detective?"

The Hardy boys nodded assent.

"Good!" exclaimed Kane. "You go right back and tell him about this. If any one can get to the bottom of this affair it's him. I hate to see them rascals getting away scot-free."

Frank and Joe bade good-bye to the farmer and his wife and returned to their motorcycles. They promised to call again at the Kane farm as soon as they had any further information, and Mr. Kane, in turn, gave his promise to notify them if there were any further trace of the kidnappers or of the mysterious Jones.

When they returned to Bayport the boys lost no time in reaching home. Fenton Hardy was enjoying one of his rare afternoons of leisure in reading, but he put his book aside when the boys rushed into the library.

"Did Mr. Jones talk?" he asked quickly, seeing by their expressions that something unusual had happened.

"We didn't have a chance to see him!" exclaimed Joe.

"What's the matter? Did he clear out?"

"He was kidnapped!"

"Kidnapped!"

"Four men broke into the farmhouse and took him away," said Frank hurriedly.

Then he proceeded to tell the story of the strange events of the morning at the Kane farm, prompted occasionally by Joe.

Mr. Hardy was deeply interested.

"There's only one theory I can think of," he said, at last. "This Jones, or whatever his name is, must have belonged to a gang and either squealed on them or threatened to do so. They tried to get rid of him and he escaped in the motorboat, but they thought they had finished him in the explosion. Then they found out that you had rescued him, so they went to the farmhouse and took him away before he had a chance to talk."

"Do you think they are smugglers?"

"Probably. While you were away this morning I called up one of the government authorities in the city, and he told me that they believe smugglers are operating in Barmet Bay on a big scale."

"Did you tell him about Snackley?"

Mr. Hardy smiled. "Not yet. That information, I thought I would keep to myself for the time being. But I wonder if Snackley can be here. It begins to look like it. He is the kind who wouldn't stop at anything from kidnapping to murder."

"Do the authorities suspect him of being around here?"

"I imagine so. The man I was talking to mentioned the fact that the smugglers they are after are in the drug line. And Snackley is king of the dope smugglers on the Atlantic coast."

"Gee! I wish we could land him."

"Of course," said Fenton Hardy, "no one has asked us to work on this case, and I don't believe in working for nothing—"

"You mean you won't help?" asked Joe, in disappointment.

Fenton Hardy's eyes twinkled as he went on.

"I don't believe in working for nothing," he repeated. "But if we ever caught this man Snackley it would be worth our while."

"Why?"

"The reward."

"Is there a reward offered for him?"

"There has been a standing reward of five thousand dollars offered for Snackley's capture for some time. And if he is operating in Barmet Bay, as I suspect, it's just possible that we might be able to collect that reward."

"Good!" exclaimed Frank. "Let's go after it!"

CHAPTER IX
THE STRANGE MESSAGE

The Hardy boys expected that the next day would find them busy on a more detailed investigation of the circumstances surrounding the mysterious kidnapping. But, to their surprise, when they came down to breakfast next morning they found that their father had gone away.

Mrs. Hardy could not enlighten them.

"He went out early this morning and didn't say when he would be back. But he didn't take any baggage with him, so I imagine he hasn't gone very far. He'll probably be back some time today."

Mrs. Hardy was accustomed to the comings and goings of her husband, and nothing surprised her. She realized that his profession demanded that he do many things that were mysterious enough on the surface but reasonable enough when the time came to explain them. But the boy were taken aback, for they had looked forward to seeing their father in the morning and had hoped that he would lay a plan of campaign before them. They went to school in disappointment.

On the way they met Callie Shaw and Iola Morton, two girls who were particular friends of the boys. Callie Shaw, a brown-eyed, brown-haired girl was an object of special enthusiasm with Frank, who was apt to cast an appreciative eye upon the other sex, while Iola, a plump, dark girl, a sister of Chet Morton's, was "all right, as a girl," in Joe's reluctant opinion.

Chet had told his sister about the affair at the Polucca place on the previous Saturday, and she, in turn, had told Callie.

"Well, how are the ghost-hunters this morning?" asked Callie.

"Fine," replied Frank, with a smile.

"What a brave bunch of boys you all are!" exclaimed the girl. "Running away from an empty house!"

"That house wasn't empty!" put in Joe warmly. "I suppose you think our motorcycle tools walked away!"

"Somebody played a pretty good practical joke on you. Just wait till you get to school. Whoever played that trick will be sure to tell everybody."

"Oh, well, we can stand it. If Chet Morton hadn't been with us at the time I would have blamed him. It's like one of his pet ideas."

"He can prove an alibi this time," said Iola. "He was right with you, and by the way he talked when he got home I think he was as badly frightened as any one."

But when the boys reached school they found that although news of their experience at the house on the cliff had preceded them, no one was laying claim to having originated the joke. Chet and the other boys had told of the escapade, but although they momentarily expected that some practical jester would come forward and take credit for the whole affair, nothing of the sort happened, and when noon came it was as much a mystery as ever.

"I'm beginning to think it wasn't a joke at all," admitted Joe, on the way home. "Believe me, if it had been a trick played on us the fellow who did it wouldn't have lost any time coming around to have the horselaugh."

"It was a little too well done to be a joke. I think some one started this ghost rumor just to keep people away from the Polucca place."

"If everybody gets the same reception we got, I don't blame 'em for staying away. What with weird yells and shrieks, with walls falling in and tool boxes being robbed, it's a mighty active ghost they have on the job."

"I wonder—could it have anything to do with the smugglers, Joe?"

The Hardy boys looked at one another.

"There's a thought!" exclaimed Joe. "We had two mighty strange things happen to us on the same day. Perhaps they *have* something to do with each other."

"It might be only a coincidence. But when you come to think of it, that house on the cliff would be a mighty handy hang-out for smugglers if they could keep strangers away. And what better way than by starting a story that the place is haunted?"

"Gosh, I never thought of that! I wonder what dad thinks of it."

"Perhaps he's at home now. We'll mention it to him."

But when they returned home for lunch, they found that Fenton Hardy had not come back. Neither was he at home when school closed for the day; and when the Hardy boys went to bed that night there had not been the slightest word from their father nor any indication of where he had gone. In spite of the fact that they were accustomed to these sudden absences, the lads felt vaguely uneasy.

"I don't know why," said Frank next morning, "but I have a sort of feeling that everything isn't all right."

"I've been feeling that way myself. Of course, dad has often gone away from home like this without telling where he was going, and he has always turned up all right. But this time—"

"Well, we'll just have to wait and see. He knows his own business best, and it's ten chances to one we're worrying over nothing, but I have a sort of a hunch that there's a problem."

Mrs. Hardy, however, was not alarmed.

"Oh, he'll walk into the house when we're least expecting him," she laughed reassuringly. "You boys are just anxious to get to work on the Snackley case. Perhaps that's what he's working on now, he'll probably come back with a lot of information."

"We'd rather he'd let us in on that," returned Joe.

"And keep you out of school! Oh, no. He doesn't mind letting you do detective work as long as it's in your spare time."

So the Hardy boys had to make the best of it. They concealed their impatience during the remainder of the week, doing their school work faithfully. The following week was the start of vacation, and the lads were deep in examinations for several days so that they had not much time to think of detective activities.

But on Friday afternoon the mystery of their father's absence took a strange turn.

They came back from school to find their mother sitting in the living room, carefully examining a note that she had evidently just received.

"Come here, boys," she said, as they came into the room. "I want you to look at this and tell me what you think of it."

She handed the note over to Frank.

"What is it?" he asked, quickly. "Word from dad?"

"It's supposed to be."

The Hardy boys read the note. It was written in pencil on a torn sheet of paper and the handwriting seemed to be that of Fenton Hardy. The note read:

"I won't be home for several days. Don't worry."

It was signed by the detective. That was all. There was nothing to indicate where he was, nothing to show when the note had been written.

"When did you get this?" asked Frank.

"It came in the afternoon mail. It was addressed to me, and the envelope had a Bayport postmark."

"What is there to worry about?" Joe asked. "It's better than not hearing from him at all."

"But I'm not sure that it's from him."

"Why?"

"Your father has an arrangement with me that he would always put a secret sign beneath his signature any time he had occasion to write to me like this. He was always afraid of people forging his name to letters and notes like this and perhaps getting papers or information that they shouldn't. So we arranged this sign that he would always put beneath his name."

Frank snatched up the note again.

"And there's no sign here. Just his signature."

"It *may* be his signature. If it isn't, it is a very good forgery. And it may have been that he forgot to put in the secret sign, although it isn't like him to do that."

Mrs. Hardy was plainly worried.

"If he didn't write it, then who did?" asked Joe.

"Your father has many enemies. There are relatives of criminals whom he has had arrested and there are criminals who have served their terms and have been released. If there has been foul play the note might be meant to keep us from being suspicious and delay any search."

"Foul play!" exclaimed Frank. "You don't think something has happened to dad?" he added, his face showing his alarm.

"The fact that he didn't put the secret sign underneath his name makes me anxious. What other object could any one have in sending us a note like that, if not to keep us from starting a search for him?"

"Well, whether he wrote that note or not, we *will* start a search for him," declared Frank firmly. "He merely said not to worry about him. He didn't order us not to look for him. If he really did write the note he can't say we were disobeying instructions. And then, the absence of the secret sign makes it all different."

"I'll say we'll look for him!" cried Joe. "Vacation starts next week, and we'll have plenty of time to hunt for him."

"Wait until then, at any rate," Mrs. Hardy advised. "Perhaps he will return in the meanwhile."

But as she glanced at the note again and once more regarded the signature, strangely lacking its secret sign, her forebodings that Fenton Hardy had met with foul play increased.

CHAPTER X

THE VAIN SEARCH

Fenton Hardy was still missing when the summer vacation began.

There had been no word from him. Never, in all his years of detective work, had he vanished from home so completely and for such a length of time. He was an intensely considerate man and his first thought was always for his wife and boys. Occasionally it was necessary for him to leave home suddenly on trips that would keep him away for some length of time, sometimes it seemed wiser to keep the knowledge of his whereabouts to himself. But he always managed to communicate with Mrs. Hardy to assure her of his safety.

But this time, with the exception of the dubious note, there had been no such assurance. From the moment he had left the house on the morning after the kidnapping at the Kane farmhouse he had vanished as utterly as though the earth had swallowed him up.

The Hardy boys questioned many people in and around Bayport, but no one recollected having seen their father on the day in question. At the railway station they ascertained the fact that the detective had not bought a train ticket that day or any day since. The agent admitted it was barely possible that Fenton Hardy might have taken a train and paid his fare on board, but said it was not likely. Inquiries at the steamboat office brought a similar response. The detective had not been seen.

None of the local police officers remembered having seen Mr. Hardy that morning. The detective was a well-known figure in Bayport and it seemed strange that no one had seen him about the streets of the city, in spite of the fact that he had left home at an early hour. The boys questioned every one who was likely to have seen him, even to milkmen who might have been on their routes at that time, but the further they pursued their inquiries the deeper the mystery became.

One of the boys greatly interested in the disappearance of Mr. Hardy was Perry Robinson. Perry was the son of Henry Robinson, who had once gotten into difficulties over the disappearance of some valuables, as related in "The Tower Treasure." All of the Hardys had done much for the Robinson family, and the Robinsons were correspondingly grateful.

"I saw your dad on the street one day, boys," said Perry. "He waved his hand to me."

"When was that?" demanded Frank quickly.

"Oh, a day or two before you say he disappeared. Gee, fellows, I wish I could help you!" went on Perry.

"Well, keep your eyes open and if you learn anything let us know," said Joe, and to this Perry readily agreed.

Shortly after the boys had had their talk with Perry Robinson they ran into a number of their girl friends. One of these girls had likewise seen Mr. Hardy, but after considerable questioning the boys came to the conclusion that the meeting had taken place several days before their father's disappearance.

"Oh, I'm so sorry this happened," said one of the girls, and the others nodded in sympathy.

The Hardy boys extended the search beyond the city. It occurred to them that their father might have gone out to the Kane farm, and they made their way to that place. But the farmer and his wife said no one had called at the house since the eventful Sunday of the kidnapping.

"They've left us in peace, praise be!" declared Mrs. Kane. "No one's been near the house since those rascals went away."

The boys gave the kindly couple a description of their father, but Mr. Kane could not recollect having seen any one resembling Mr. Hardy near the farm at any time within the past week. He had been working in the fields, he said, and would probably have noticed any strangers on the road.

So the boys returned to Bayport, puzzled and downhearted over the failure of their search. They could not imagine where Fenton Hardy could have gone if he had not been near the Kane farm.

"Something has happened to him, I'm sure," said Frank. "It isn't like dad to stay away this long without sending some word."

"Perhaps he *did* write that note."

"He would have explained a little more. And he would have put in the secret sign."

The fact that the Hardy boys were searching for their father gradually became known throughout Bayport, and one evening a thick-set, broad-shouldered man presented himself at the front door of the Hardy home and asked for the boys. Mrs. Hardy bade him step inside and he waited in the hall, nervously twisting his cap in his hands.

When Frank and Joe came out the stranger introduced himself as Sam Bates.

"I'm a truck driver," he told them. "The reason I came around to see you was because I heard you were lookin' for your father."

"Have you seen him?" asked Frank eagerly.

Sam Bates shuffled his feet and looked dubiously at the floor.

"Well, I have and I haven't, you might say," he observed. "I *did* see your father quite a few days ago, but where he is now, I couldn't tell you, for I don't know." Sam was evidently not a man of gigantic intellect. He spoke slowly and painstakingly and his most obvious statements were delivered with the gravity suitable to pearls of wisdom.

"Where did you see him?"

"I'm a truck driver, see?"

"Yes, you told us that," said Frank impatiently. "But where did you see our father?"

Sam Bates was not to be hurried. He had a story to tell and he was bound to tell it.

"I'm a truck driver, see?" he repeated. "Mostly I drive just in and around Bayport, but sometimes they give me a run out to some of them villages. That's how I come to be out there that morning."

"Out where?"

"I'm comin' to that. I just forget what day it was, but I think it was about a week from last Monday. I know it was just after Sunday because when I went home to dinner that day the wife was washin' clothes and dinner was late and I had to eat it out on the back steps anyway for the kitchen was all in a mess. You know how it is on wash day."

Sam Bates regarded them wistfully, as though hoping for some expression of sympathy and understanding. But the Hardy boys were eager for information, and impatient with the worthy truck driver's circuitous method of telling his story.

"But what has this got to do with our father?" demanded Joe.

"I'm comin' to that, see? Give me time. Give me time. As I was sayin', I'm pretty sure it was on a Monday, for it was wash day, and the wife never washes except on Monday. I mean she never washes clothes except on Monday. She herself, why, she washes *every* day, of course. Anyway, it was Monday."

"That was the day dad disappeared," prompted Frank.

"You don't say! Well, I saw him that day."

"Where?"

"I'm comin' to that. As I was sayin', it was Monday, and when I went down to the garage the boss, he says to me, says he, 'Sam, I want you to run a truckload of furniture down the shore road.' So I said, 'Well, boss, I guess that's what I'm here for,' so he told me that this here load of furniture had to go to one of them farmhouses away down near the Point. So we loaded the truck and I filled her up with gas and away I went. It must have been about nine o'clock by then I guess."

"And you went down the shore road?"

"Sure. And it was a nice mornin' for drivin' too. Anyway, I went out past the Tower Mansion—you know, Hurd Applegate's place, them people you and your father got back the Tower treasure for—and I was drivin' along without a care in the world and whistlin' away, quite happy-like, when I sees that I was comin' near that haunted house up on the cliff. You know the place—where old Polucca was murdered."

"The Polucca place!"

"Yeah! Well, anyway, I was comin' by there and I didn't drive slow either, for they say there's ghosts in that place and I ain't takin' no chance with nothin' like that, so the truck was going along at quite a clip, when what should I see but a man walkin' along the road."

"Dad!"

"Yeah, it was your father. Well, anyway, nobody ever said Sam Bates wouldn't give a guy a lift, so I slows down a bit and I says, 'Hey! D'you want a ride?' just like that, see? Then this guy turned around so I seen who it was. I didn't know until then, see? So when I seen who it was I said, 'Good day, Mr. Hardy, would you like a lift?' but he thanked me and said he was just takin' a little walk. So I drove on past him and the last I seen of him he was walkin' along beside the road."

"Did he go down the lane to the Polucca place?"

"I dunno whether he did or not. He hadn't quite reached the lane when I seen him last. But I didn't meet him on my way back, so I don't know where he went. Matter of fact, I didn't think nothin' more of it until this mornin' when a bunch of the boys were sittin' around the garage talkin' and one of them said that you two lads had been huntin' all over the city for your old man—I mean your father—and you couldn't find him. So I says to myself, 'Sam, mebbe you can tell 'em somethin' they don't know.' So I just thought I'd come up."

"And we're very grateful to you," Frank assured him. "You've given us some valuable information. We didn't know whether our father had gone out of the city or not. Now I think we'll know where to look for him."

"Ain't any chance of him nosin' around that Polucca place, is there?" asked Bates. "It's a mighty good place to stay away from if everythin' you hear is true. It's haunted, that place is."

"Oh, that wouldn't matter to him. But I'm glad you told us about seeing him. It gives us a better idea of where to look for him."

"Well, I'm glad if I've helped any. Guess I'll be goin' now," said Sam Bates, putting on his cap. "I hope your dad shows up all right."

The Hardy boys thanked him warmly and Bates shambled away, his hands in his pockets.

Mrs. Hardy came into the hallway.

"Any news?" she asked anxiously.

"We have a clue, anyway," Frank told her. "That fellow says he saw dad on the shore road the morning he left here."

"Where was he?"

"Near the old Polucca place."

"The house on the cliff?"

Frank nodded.

Mrs. Hardy looked grave. "Surely he couldn't have gone there and disappeared!" she said.

"I can't imagine why he would go to the house on the cliff, anyway," observed Joe.

"Oh, I know now!" Mrs. Hardy exclaimed. "I had forgotten all about it. I intended to tell you boys, but somehow it slipped my mind. Now that you mention the Polucca place, I remember."

"What was it?"

"Your father discovered something about Snackley, the smuggler. It seems that Snackley was related to Felix Polucca, the miser."

"Related to him!"

"He was a cousin or nephew, or something of the sort. One of the government men told him that. So your father had an idea that Polucca must have been visited by Snackley at some time or another and that Snackley must have got the idea of using Barmet Bay for his smuggling operations at that time."

"Whew!" exclaimed Joe. "Now we're getting on the right track. Dad must have gone up to the house on the cliff to investigate."

"Why didn't we think of searching there before! Dad put two and two together and figured that there might be some connection between the strange things that happened at the Polucca place the day we visited it and the case of that fellow Jones whom we rescued. Then, when he learned that Snackley was related to Polucca, he was sure of it. It's as clear as daylight. But what on earth could have happened to him?"

"Let's go up to the Polucca place and find out."

But Mrs. Hardy interposed. Her lips were firm.

"Promise me you won't go alone."

"Why not, mother? We can look after ourselves."

"If anything has happened to your father, I don't want you to run the same risk."

"But we *must* go up there and look the place over again."

"Get some of the boys to go with you."

"I guess it would be safer," agreed Joe. "We can round up a bunch of the fellows and go up there tomorrow morning. We'll search that place from top to bottom this time."

Mrs. Hardy gave her consent to this plan and the boys thereupon set out to find their chums and tell them of the proposed trip. Although two or three of the boys backed out when they learned that the destination was to be the haunted house, the majority were willing enough, and by nightfall all was in readiness for the journey on the morrow.

CHAPTER XI

THE CAP ON THE PEG

Next morning the searching party set out.

Jerry Gilroy had not got over the scare he had received on the remarkable Saturday of the boys' first visit to the house on the cliff and he did not show up. But Chet Morton and Biff Hooper appeared, with Phil Cohen and Tony Prito, two more of the Hardy boys' chums at the Bayport high school. Chet had his motorcycle and the party left the Hardy home shortly after breakfast, each machine carrying two.

Before they left, Frank explained the situation fully to the others.

"We know that dad was last seen near the Polucca place and we have every reason to believe that he left here with the intention of searching the house. He hasn't shown up since and no person has seen him, so there may have been foul play."

"If there is any trace of him around the Polucca place we'll find it," declared Chet. "It will take a mighty lively ghost to scare us away this time."

The three motorcycles went out of Bayport past the Tower Mansion, sped along the shore road. There was little talk among the boys. Each realized that this was not a pleasure outing but a serious mission and each recognized the importance of it. The Hardy boys had every confidence in their companions. Chet and Biff, they knew, would not be as easily frightened on this occasion, and as for Phil and Tony, they were noted at school for their fearless, at times even reckless, dispositions.

They passed the Kane farmhouse, nestling among the trees, and at last came in sight of the gloomy cliff that rose from Barmet Bay and at the summit of which perched the rambling stone house where the miser, Felix Polucca, had met his death.

"Lonely looking place, isn't it?" remarked Phil, who was sharing Frank's motorcycle.

"It was an ideal place for a murder. When Felix Polucca lived there, I doubt if he had more than two or three visitors in a year."

"How did he get his food and supplies?"

"He used to drive into the city about once a week in a rattly old buggy, with a horse that must have come out of the Ark. The poor animal looked as if it hadn't had a square meal in a lifetime. Polucca must have been a little bit crazy. How he lived alone up there all the time, nobody could understand. He worked hard enough and he made the farm pay. No one could drive a better bargain when it came to selling his hay and grain."

Phil looked with interest at the old gray house that could be seen more clearly now that they were approaching it. When they were still some distance from the lane, however, Frank brought his motorcycle to a stop and signaled to the others to do likewise.

"What's the idea?" Chet asked.

"We'd better sneak up on the place quietly. If we go any farther they'll hear the motorcycles—that is, if there is any one at the place. We'll leave them here under the trees and go ahead on foot."

The motorcycles were accordingly hidden in a clump of bushes beside the road and the six boys went on toward the lane.

"We'll separate here," Frank decided. "Three of us will take one side of the lane and the rest will take the other side. Keep to the bushes as much as possible and when we get near the house lay low for a while and watch the place. When I whistle we can come out from under cover and go on up to the house."

"That's a good plan," approved Tony. "Joe and Biff and I, we'll go on the left side of the road."

"Good. Chet and Phil and I will take the other side. Remember to keep out of sight of the house as much as possible."

The boys entered the lane, then separated according to the agreement they had made. One group plunged into the weeds and undergrowth at the edge of the lane on one side while the others pushed into the bushes at the opposite side. In a few minutes each group was lost to view and only an occasional snapping and crackling of branches indicated their presence in the heavy undergrowth that flanked the lane.

Frank advanced cautiously. The brushwood was much deeper than he had anticipated and they made slow progress, for he was desirous of creeping up on the house with as little noise as possible. The undergrowth was thick and hampered their movements. They made their way forward, step by step, keeping well in from the lane, and after about ten minutes Frank raised his hand as a warning to the others.

Through the dense thickets he had caught a glimpse of the house.

They went on cautiously until they reached the edge of the bushes and there they crouched behind the screen of leaves, peeping out at the gloomy old stone building in the clearing.

But at the first glance, an expression of surprise crossed Frank's face.

The Polucca house was evidently occupied!

The weeds that had overgrown the yard on their last visit had been completely cleared away, the grass had been cut and the tumble-down fence had been repaired. The gate, which had been hanging by one hinge, had been fixed and the grass along the pathway had been trimmed.

A similar change had overtaken the house.

There was glass in all the windows and the boards had been removed. The front door had been repaired and the steps had been mended. Smoke was rising from the kitchen chimney.

"There must be some one living here," whispered Chet.

Frank was puzzled.

He had not heard that any one had taken the Polucca house. On account of the unenviable fame of the place it was hardly likely that a new tenant could move in without arousing considerable comment in Bayport. But this had evidently happened.

For a while the boys remained at the edge of the bushes watching the place. Then they saw a woman come out to the clothesline at the back of the house. She carried a basket of clothes, and these she began hanging up on the line. Shortly afterward a man came out, strode across the yard to the wood-shed and began chopping wood.

The boys looked at one another in consternation.

They had expected to find the same sinister and deserted place they had visited previously. Instead, they had arrived on a scene of domestic peace and comfort. They could not understand it.

"Not much use staying in hiding," whispered Frank. "Let's get together and walk right up and question these people."

He gave a low whistle, then emerged from the bushes into the lane. His companions followed. In a short time they were joined by Joe and the other boys.

All were deeply puzzled by the remarkable change that had come over the Polucca place.

"This beats anything I ever heard of," declared Joe. "It looks as if some farmer has taken the place, but it's strange we hadn't heard of it. Everybody in Bayport would be talking about it if they knew some one had nerve enough to take over the Polucca farm."

"I'm not satisfied yet," Frank said. "We'll go up and question these people."

Accordingly, the six boys walked boldly out of the lane and across the yard. The man in the woodshed saw them first and put down his axe, staring at them with an expression of annoyance on his face. The woman at the clothesline heard their footsteps and turned, facing them, her hands upon her hips. She was hard-faced and tight-lipped, with gaunt features. She was not prepossessing and her untidy garb did not impress the boys favorably.

"What do you want?" demanded the man, emerging from the woodshed.

He was short and thin with close-cropped hair, and he was in need of a shave. His complexion was swarthy and he had narrow eyes under coarse, black brows. His manner was far from polite as he advanced upon the boys.

At the same time another man came out of the kitchen and stood on the steps. He was stout and red-haired and had a thick mustache. As he stood there in his shirt-sleeves he glared pugnaciously at the sextette.

"Yeah, what's the big idea?" he asked.

"We didn't know any one was living here," explained Frank, edging over to the kitchen door. He wanted to get a look inside the house if possible.

"Well, there is," said the red-haired man. "We're livin' here now, and I can't see that it's any of your business. What are you snooping around here for?"

"We aren't snooping," said Frank quietly. "We are looking for a man who has disappeared from Bayport."

"Humph!" grunted the woman.

"What makes you think he might be around here?" asked the red-headed man.

"He was last seen in this neighborhood."

"What's his name?"

"Hardy."

"What does he look like?"

"Tall and dark. He was wearing a grey suit and a grey cap."

"Ain't been nobody around here since we moved in," said the red-headed man gruffly.

"No, we didn't see him," snapped the woman. "You boys had better go and look somewhere else."

There was nothing to be gained by arguing with the unsociable trio, so the boys started to leave. But Frank, who had edged close to the open door during the course of the conversation, had glanced into the kitchen and something had caught his eye.

It was a gray cap, hanging on a peg!

CHAPTER XII
POINTED QUESTIONS

Frank thought quickly. He must ascertain the truth!

The cap, he was almost sure, was the one his father had worn on the morning he had left home. But he wanted to look at it closely, because he knew he might be mistaken and that it would not do to make any accusations unless he were sure of his ground.

"I'm very thirsty," he said quickly. "Do you mind if I have a drink?"

Redhead and the woman looked at one another without enthusiasm. It was plain that they wished to get rid of their visitors as soon as possible. But they could not refuse such an innocent and reasonable request.

"Come into the kitchen," said Redhead grudgingly.

This was just what Frank wanted. He followed the man into the kitchen of the Polucca place. Redhead pointed to a water tap. A dipper was hanging from a nail near by.

"Go ahead," he grunted.

Frank went over to the tap and as he did so he passed the cap on the peg. He took a swift look at the cap.

He had made no mistake. It was his father's.

Then he received a shock that almost stunned him. For a second he almost stopped in his tracks, but then he recollected himself and moved mechanically on toward the tap.

He had seen bloodstains!

On the lower edge of the cap were three large stains, reddish in color. They could have been made by nothing but blood.

In a daze, Frank turned on the water, filled the dipper and drank. At last he turned away, conscious that Redhead had been eyeing him carefully all the time.

"Thanks," he said, and again cast a glance at the peg.

The cap was gone!

Redhead had undoubtedly snatched it away and hidden it. Frank gave no sign that he noticed anything amiss, and walked out of the kitchen into the yard, where he rejoined the others.

"I guess we may as well be going," he said.

"You might as well," snapped the woman. "There's been no strangers around here."

"We're sorry we troubled you," said Joe. "Good-bye."

Redhead grunted a curt farewell. The woman and the other man said nothing as the boys turned away and retraced their steps out to the lane. For a while they walked on in silence and then, when they were out of sight of the house, Frank turned to the others.

"Do you know why I went into the kitchen?" he asked.

"Why?" they demanded eagerly, and Joe put in:

"I thought there was something fishy about the way you asked for that drink. What did you see?"

"I saw dad's cap hanging on a peg!"

This caused an immediate sensation. Phil Cohen whistled in amazement.

"Then he *has* been here! They were lying!"

"Are you sure it was dad's cap?" asked Joe.

"Positive. I'd recognize it anywhere. And more than that, there were bloodstains on it."

"Bloodstains!"

Frank nodded.

The boys looked at one another in silence.

"This is serious," declared Joe finally. "We can't let them get away with this."

"I'll say we can't," agreed Chet. "Let's go back."

"I was going to argue it out right there and then, but I thought I'd better tell the rest of you first so that you'd know what it was all about," Frank explained.

"He may have been—" Joe left the sentence unfinished.

"He may have been murdered," said Frank firmly. "And we're going to find out about it."

"What do you think we'd better do?"

"I think we'd better go back and tell them we saw that cap and ask how it got there. That'll force a showdown. They don't like us any too well as it is, so we won't have to be over polite to them."

The boys held a council, and it was unanimously agreed that the matter should not be dropped. Each was of the opinion that the trio now occupying the house on the cliff were far from savory and that the fact of Fenton Hardy's cap being seen in the kitchen was a clue of first-rate importance.

"He snatched the cap away when my back was turned," went on Frank.

"That shows there is something wrong," Chet affirmed. "We'll go back and tackle him right away."

"No time like the present. Let's go."

The boys accordingly started back down the lane toward the house. When they emerged into the yard again they found the two men and the woman standing together by the shed, talking earnestly. The boys were almost up to them before the woman caught sight of them and spoke warningly to the red-headed man.

"What do you want now?" demanded Redhead, in a surly manner, as he advanced.

"We want to know about that cap in the kitchen," said Frank firmly.

"What cap? There's no cap in there."

"There isn't now—but there was. It's a grey cap and it was hanging in there when I went in for a drink."

"I don't know anythin' about no cap," persisted Redhead.

"Perhaps you want us to ask the police up to help us find out," put in Tony Prito cheerfully.

Redhead glanced meaningly at the woman. The other man stepped forward.

"I know the cap he means," he said. "It's mine. What about it?"

"It isn't yours, and you know it," declared Frank. "That cap belongs to the man we're looking for."

"I tell you it *is* my cap," snapped the swarthy man, showing his yellow teeth in a snarl. "Don't tell me I'm lying."

Redhead stepped forward diplomatically.

"You're mistaken, Klein," he said. "I know the cap they mean. That's the one I found on the road a few days ago."

"You found it?" asked Frank incredulously.

"Sure, I found it. A grey cap—with bloodstains on it."

"That's the one. But why did you hide it when I went into the kitchen?"

"Well, to tell the truth, them bloodstains made me nervous. I didn't know but what there might be some trouble come of it, so I thought I'd better keep that cap out of sight."

"Where did you find it?" Joe demanded.

"About a mile from here."

"On the shore road?"

"Yes. It was lying right in the middle of the road."

"When was this?"

"A couple of days ago—just after we moved in here."

"Let's see the cap," suggested Chet Morton. "We want to make sure of this."

Redhead moved reluctantly toward the kitchen. The woman sniffed.

"I don't see why you're makin' all this fuss about an old cap," she said. "Comin' around at this hour of the day disturbin' honest folk."

"We're sorry to disturb you, ma'am," said Joe. "But this is a serious matter."

Redhead emerged from the house holding the cap in one hand. He tossed it over to the boys. They examined it eagerly.

Frank turned back the inside flap and there he found what he was looking for—the initials F.H. imprinted in indelible ink on the leather band.

"It's dad's cap, all right."

"I don't like the look of those bloodstains," said Joe, in a low voice. "He must have been badly hurt."

To tell the truth, the inside of the cap gave evidence that the wearer had been severely injured, for the bloodstains were of large extent. The boys examined them gravely.

"Are you sure you found this on the road?" Frank asked doubtfully.

"You don't think I'd lie about it, do you?"

"We can't very well contradict you. I don't mind telling you that we're going to turn this over to the police. This man has disappeared, and by the appearance of this cap he has met with foul play. If you know anything about it you'd better speak up now."

"He doesn't know anything about it," shrilled the woman angrily. "Go away and don't bother us. Didn't he tell you he found the cap on the road? Why should he know anythin' more about it than that?"

"We're going to take the cap with us."

"Take it," snapped Redhead. "I don't want it."

The boys turned away. Nothing further was to be gained by questioning the trio in the yard, and at any rate the lads had gained possession of the cap.

"We'd better go," said Frank in a low voice.

They went back toward the lane. As they entered it they cast a last glance back at the yard.

The woman and the two men were standing just where they had left them. The woman was motionless, her hands on her hips. Redhead was standing with his arms folded and the swarthy man was leaning on the axe.

All three were gazing intently and silently after the departing boys.

CHAPTER XIII

A PLAN OF ATTACK

Back in Bayport the boys discussed their visit to the house on the cliff from all angles.

None was satisfied with the explanation the red-headed man had given about the presence of the bloodstained cap in the house.

"I'm sure he knows more about it than he cares to tell," declared Frank.

"The other chap started to claim it at first, and then he stepped in with his story," Chet pointed out.

"That's the most suspicious part of it. And then, when I went into the kitchen in the first place, why should he have hidden the cap?"

"It's a mighty mysterious thing," Joe said. "The fact that dad has disappeared and the fact that there are bloodstains on that cap—"

"We ought to turn it over to Chief Collig," suggested Phil.

The boys looked at one another doubtfully. Chief of Police Collig was a fat, pompous official who had never been blessed by a super-abundance of brains. His chief satellite and aide-de-camp was Oscar Smuff, a detective of the Bayport police force. As Chet was fond of remarking, "If you put both their brains together you'd have enough for a half-wit."

"I don't think it would do much good," said Frank. "But it wouldn't do any harm either. Collig might be able to throw a scare into them, anyway, if he went up to that house and began asking questions."

The boys, therefore, trooped down to the police station and, after stating their business to the desk sergeant, were admitted to the chief's private office. They found Chief Collig and Detective Smuff deep in a game of checkers.

"It's your move, Smuff," said the chief. "What is it, boys?" he demanded, looking up.

Frank, producing the bloodstained cap, explained how and where it had been found. Smuff, in the meantime, scratched his head diligently for a while, then captured one of his opponent's kings.

Chief Collig grunted, whether in disappointment at the loss of the king or in acknowledgment of the information about the cap, the boys could not say.

"So it's Fenton Hardy's cap, eh?" asked the chief.

"It's his, all right."

"And what do you think has happened to him?"

"We don't know. That's what we want you to help find out. But, by the look of this cap, we're afraid there's been foul play."

"Just a minute, Smuff—just a minute." The chief contemplated the checkerboard for a few minutes, then made a move. He settled back in his chair. "Now try and beat *that*!" he said, and looked up at the boys again. "What do you want me to do?" he inquired.

"Help us find him."

The chief regarded them benevolently.

"Mebbe he'll show up in a day or so."

"He's been missing long enough already," protested Joe. "We want you to go up to the Polucca place and question those people. They know more about the affair than they care to tell."

"The Polucca place!" exclaimed the chief, pursing his lips. "We-ll, you see, it ain't in the city limits."

"But Fenton Hardy is a Bayport citizen."

"What d'you think about it, Smuff?"

"Just a minute—it's my move." Smuff meditated over the checkerboard for a while, made his move, then looked up judicially. "To tell you the truth, chief," he said, "I think we'd be just as well stayin' away from that Polucca place. There's been strange stories about it."

"That's what I think," agreed the chief.

"Do you mean to say you won't help us look for him?" exclaimed Frank.

"Oh, we'll keep our eyes open," the chief promised. "But he'll show up all right. He'll show up. Don't worry."

"He'll never show up if we wait for the Bayport Police Department to get into action," declared Chet warmly.

"Is *that* so?" said Chief Collig, nettled.

"Of course, chief," said Frank smoothly, "if you're afraid to go up to the Polucca place just because it's supposed to be haunted, don't bother. We can tell the newspapers that we believe our father has met with foul play and that you won't bother to look into the matter, but don't let us disturb you at all—"

"What's that about the newspapers?" demanded the chief, getting up from his chair so suddenly that he upset the checkerboard over Smuff's lap. "Don't let this get into the papers." The chief was constantly afraid of publicity unless it was of the most favorable nature.

"The taxpayers mightn't like it," suggested Joe. "They pay you to enforce the law and if they know you're afraid to go up to the Polucca place—"

"Now, now," said the chief nervously. "Who said anythin' about being afraid of the Polucca place? Can't you take a joke? Of course I'll go up and investigate this—at least I'll send Smuff up—"

"Who, me?" demanded Smuff, in alarm.

"Smuff and me, we'll go up together."

"I'm doggone sure I won't go up alone," declared Smuff.

"Well, as long as we're sure you'll investigate, we won't say anything to the newspapers," said Frank, and Chief Collig breathed a sigh of relief.

"That's fine. That's fine," he said. "Smuff and me, we'll go up there first thing tomorrow morning and if we find out anything we'll let you know."

But although Chief Collig and Detective Smuff duly departed from Bayport the next morning in an exceptionally noisy and decrepit flivver, with Smuff perched nervously at the wheel, they returned before noon with the news that they had been able to discover nothing further regarding Fenton Hardy. They had, they said, called at the house, but the people there had given a reasonable explanation as to the finding of the cap.

"Real nice people, they were too," added Chief Collig. "The man said he found the cap on the road, and why should he tell a lie about it? So Smuff and me, we came away."

"Yes," agreed Smuff profoundly, "we came away."

"In a hurry," suggested Joe sarcastically.

Collig and Smuff looked uncomfortable. To tell the truth they had been so impressed by the fearful stories they had heard of the house on the cliff that they had stayed no longer than was necessary. They had merely asked a few perfunctory questions of Redhead, had received his explanation of the finding of the cap, and had then hastened from the farm as quickly as was consistent with dignity.

"We've done our duty," declared Chief Collig. "No man can do more."

And with that the boys had to be content.

But they were not satisfied.

"There's some connection between this smuggling outfit and the house on the cliff," declared Frank. "This man Snackley is mixed up in all this, I'm sure."

"Didn't mother say he was related to Felix Polucca?"

"Yes—and isn't it likely that he inherited the Polucca farm after the old miser died? Perhaps that's what encouraged him to move his smuggling operations here."

"Perhaps Snackley was one of the two men we saw at the farm."

"I wouldn't be surprised," said Frank. "But what I'm thinking of is this—where did these two motorboats come from that day Jones was shot? We didn't see them out in the bay. They seemed to come right out from under the cliff."

"Do you mean you think there is a secret harbor in there?"

"There might be. Look at it this way. Snackley was the man who 'got' Jones that day, as he said. Snackley was related to Polucca, and may now own the farm. Snackley has been smuggling in Barmet Bay from some base that the government men have been unable to find. Perhaps that base is the Polucca farm."

"But it's on top of the cliff!"

"There may be a secret passage from the house to some hidden harbor at the foot of the cliff."

"Gosh, Frank, it sounds reasonable!"

"And perhaps that explains why the kidnappers got away with Jones so quickly that day. If they left the Kane farmhouse just a little while before we did, we should have been able to get within sight of them, anyway. But we didn't."

"You mean they turned in at the Polucca place?"

"Why not? Probably Jones is hidden there right now. That is—if they haven't killed him," he added hesitatingly.

"But what could have happened to dad?"

"That's what we're going to find out. What do you say to asking Tony if his father will lend us his motorboat and let us investigate the foot of that cliff?"

"What do you expect to find?"

"We'll find out if there's any place where motorboats could be hidden. And if we get any information we can turn it over to the government officials and have the Polucca place raided. Then we'll get some satisfaction out of it, anyway, and perhaps find out what happened to dad."

CHAPTER XIV

PRIVATE PROPERTY

The Hardy boys explained their plan to Tony Prito, who promised to ask his father about the motorboat provided they allowed him to go with them.

"I wouldn't miss it for anything," he said. "You let me come along on this trip with you and I'll see that we get the boat."

"We wouldn't go without you, Tony," promised Frank.

"I'll have the boat tomorrow afternoon. Be at the boathouse."

Tony was as good as his word. When Frank and Joe appeared at the little boathouse, one of a long row of ramshackle buildings along the shore, next afternoon, they found Tony clad in a greasy suit of overalls, tinkering with the engine. He was of a mechanical turn of mind and could never see an engine of any kind without investigating its most intricate machinery.

"She'll run as smoothly as a sewing machine," he declared, looking up. "We can start any time."

"Your father let you have the boat, all right."

"You bet. I told him it was to help find your father, and he was almost going to quit work and come along with us."

The boys got into the motorboat, which was a rangy, powerful craft with graceful lines, and the engine was soon roaring. The boat, which was called the *Napoli* in honor of Mr. Prito's birthplace in Italy, moved slowly out into the waters of the bay and then gathered speed as it headed toward the gloomy cliffs at the northern extremity of Barmet Bay.

It was already late in the afternoon. The sky was overcast and the bay was rough. The salt spray dashed over the bows of the *Napoli* as it plunged on through the breakers. Bayport soon became a smoky haze on the hillside. The boys could see the white line of the shore road rising and falling on the coast to the north and at last they came within sight of the Kane farm, nestled among the trees.

The cliff upon which the Polucca place stood was stark and sheer against the background of ocean and sky, and at the top they could see the grove of trees and the roof and chimneys of the haunted house.

"Lonely looking place," remarked Joe.

"Pretty steep cliff," Tony observed. "I can't see how any one could make his way up and down that slope to get to the house."

"That's just why nobody has thought of the possibility of the place as a smuggling base," said Frank, "It doesn't look possible. But perhaps when we look around we'll find that things are different."

Tony steered the boat closer in toward the shore so that it would not be visible from the Polucca place. Then he slackened speed so that the roar of the engine would not be so noticeable, and the craft made its way along toward the bottom of the cliff.

There were currents here that demanded skilful navigation, but Tony brought the *Napoli* through them easily and at last the boat was surging along close to the face of the cliff. The boys scanned the formidable wall of rock eagerly.

It was scarred and seamed and at the base had been eaten away by the battering of the waves. Time passed, and there was no indication of a path and the lads were disappointed.

The cliff jutted up out of very deep water and rose to a great height. From the boat they were unable to see the Polucca place, for it was set in a short distance from the edge of the cliff. The face of the steep rock was uncompromising. There seemed to be no foothold for man or beast. It was just an unscalable, craggy wall.

Suddenly Tony bore down on the wheel. The *Napoli* swerved swiftly to one side and at the same time the engine roared as the craft leaped ahead.

Frank and Joe looked quickly around.

"What's the matter?" they asked, in alarm.

But Tony was gazing fixedly ahead. He was tense and alert. Another shift of the wheel and the *Napoli* swerved again.

Then the Hardy boys saw the danger.

There were rocks at the base of the cliff. One of them, black and sharp, like an ugly tooth, jutted out of the water almost immediately at the side of the boat. Only Tony's quick eye had saved them from striking against it. They had blundered into a veritable maze of reefs which extended for several yards ahead.

They held their breath.

It seemed impossible that they could run the gauntlet of those rocks without tearing the bottom out of the craft. But Tony's steersmanship was marvelous. The motorboat threaded its way accurately among the jutting rocks. There was always the chance that a submerged reef might rip through the hull of the craft, but they had to take chances on that.

But luck was with them. The *Napoli* dodged the last ugly rock, and shot forward into open water.

Tony sank back with a sigh of relief.

"Whew, that was close!" he exclaimed. "I didn't see those rocks until we were right on top of them. If we'd ever struck one of them we would have been goners."

The Hardy boys believed him. Angry waves dashed against the base of the cliff. They would not have lived more than a few minutes if they had been wrecked in this place. They would have been battered to pieces against the rocks.

Suddenly, before them, they saw an opening in the side of the cliff. It was a long, narrow cove.

The entrance was like the neck of a bottle, widening as it led into the cliff, and it was over-shadowed by jutting rocks. It had been quite invisible up to this time, and the boat had gone only a few yards further before it became invisible again, so well was the opening hidden by the rocks.

"Here's a find!" exclaimed Frank, in excitement. "Let's turn back and see where this goes to."

Tony swung the boat around and the craft slowly made its way back toward the hidden cove. Soon the opening in the cliff came into view again.

"It's just large enough for the boat to go through," said Tony. "Want me to try it?"

Frank nodded.

"Go ahead."

The nose of the boat turned toward this strange bay and then the *Napoli* began to enter the cove.

"Maybe I won't be able to get out again," said Tony suddenly. He looked ahead. But the passage widened into a bay of considerable extent, quite sufficient in size to enable him to turn the craft around once he had entered. So he continued.

But the cove proved uninteresting. The sides were steep, although dense bushes grew about the base of the slopes, but there was no path, no trail, no indication that any human being had ever been in the place. Being protected from the wind, the water was calm. The echoes of the motorboat's engine were flung back from every side in a roaring volume.

Suddenly Frank gave a gasp of surprise!

Standing among the thickets at the base of the steepest slope, was a man.

He was very tall and he wore a black felt hat, the wide brim of which obscured the upper part of his face. His countenance was tanned and weatherbeaten, his lips were thin and cruel. He wore a short black jacket, and he stood with his hands plunged into the side-pockets and his feet spread wide apart, in the manner of a seaman.

He was standing there quietly, gazing at them without a shadow of expression on his sinister face, as motionless as a statue.

When he saw that he was observed he called out:

"Leave this place!"

Tony throttled down the engine. The three boys stared at the man in the black hat as though he were an apparition.

"Leave this place!" he repeated, in a curiously metallic voice.

"We aren't doing any harm," replied Frank.

"Not now," said the stranger. "But don't land here."

"Why?"

"You don't have to ask why. This is private property. You can't land here. You'd better leave at once."

The boys hesitated. As though to emphasize his commands, the man in the black hat reached suddenly into his pocket and whipped out a wicked-looking revolver. Then he folded his arms, tapping the barrel of the revolver against one shoulder very deliberately.

"Turn that boat around and get out of here!" he snapped. "Don't come back. Don't ever come back. Don't ever try to land here. This is private property. If you ever *do* land here you'll be shot."

The boys were unarmed. They realized that nothing would be gained by argument. Tony slowly brought the boat around.

"Good-bye," shouted Joe cheerfully.

The stranger did not reply. He stood there, gazing fixedly after them, his arms still folded, still tapping the revolver against his shoulder as the motorboat made its way out of the strange bay, out into open water.

"Looks as if he didn't want us around," remarked Tony, as soon as the *Napoli* was out of the cove.

"I'll say he didn't!" exclaimed Frank. "What a wicked-looking customer he was! I expected to see him start popping at us with that gun of his before we got out."

"I don't want to run into *him* again," Joe declared. "He sure gave us our orders. And he meant 'em, too."

"I wonder who he is," said Tony.

"Do you think— Fellows! Do you think it could have been Snackley?" shouted Frank.

CHAPTER XV

SMUGGLERS

The thought struck Frank Hardy like a thunderbolt!

The appearance of the stranger had been so sinister, he was so evidently a lawless and desperate man who was accustomed to being obeyed, and his presence in this place indicated too clearly that he had some connection with the house on the cliff, that Frank's deduction seemed quite logical.

"Snackley!" exclaimed Joe. "It *must* be him."

"The head of the smugglers!"

"I've never seen a picture of Snackley and I've never heard him described," said Joe. "But that fellow looks just as I had pictured Snackley would look."

"He's a leader of some kind—you can tell that by his manner," put in Tony Prito.

"He's the fellow who chased Jones that day in the motorboat."

"And he'll chase us, too," declared Tony, "if we don't get away from here pretty quick."

"Why should we go now?" demanded Frank. "We've stumbled on something important. That may be the smugglers' cove."

"But how do they get to the house if you think they have anything to do with the Polucca place?" asked Tony. "Those cliffs in there are mighty steep."

"There must be some way that we don't know of. What do you say we hang around here for a while and see what we can do?"

Tony became infected with the enthusiasm of the Hardy boys and he readily agreed to keep the motorboat in the vicinity of the cliff, although it was decided that they should not remain too near, but cruise up and down the shore in case the sharp-eyed man should be watching them.

"It was a good thing we didn't put up an argument with that fellow," said Frank, at last.

"I'll say it was!" Tony agreed emphatically. "We didn't have much chance to argue with that revolver he had."

"I don't mean that. He may think we were just out for a cruise and accidentally wandered into that cove. If he knew we were hunting for dad he might have acted very differently."

"That's true, too," said Joe. "Well, we won't go home just yet."

It was late in the afternoon. The sky was overcast and twilight was falling. A cold wind blew in from the sea.

The motorboat went some distance down the shore and then they turned and, keeping well out in the bay, went on up past the cliff once again. They kept a sharp eye on the location of the cove, and in spite of the fact that they knew just where it was they were scarcely able to distinguish the narrow opening in the rocks.

"No wonder the place hasn't been heard of more often!" Frank said. "It looks like an unbroken wall of rock from this far out."

"You've got to be careful around here, Tony," cried Joe. "First thing you know we'll hit the rocks and be smashed."

"That's right," added Frank. "It's pretty dangerous so close to the cliff."

"You leave it to me," came from their schoolmate. "I know how to handle this boat."

It was true, Tony did know how to handle the motorboat; yet several times they came perilously close to the rocks over which the waves were dashing. In fact, once there came a slight bump followed by a grating sound which made the hearts of all the boys leap into their mouths.

"Narrow squeak, that," admitted Tony. "I guess I'd better keep out a little farther, after all."

"I certainly should," answered Frank.

Although they cruised around for more than an hour, they saw not the slightest sign of life either about the base of the cliff or on the Polucca place, which, keeping well out from shore as they did, they could plainly distinguish. As the gloom deepened they felt that it was almost useless to continue, but Frank decided that they should wait a while longer.

"These fellows aren't likely to move around much in daylight. Night is the time for their operations," he pointed out. "We'll hang around for a while longer."

Twilight deepened into darkness and the lights of Bayport could be seen as a yellow haze through the mist at the distant extremity of the bay. The cliff was but a dark smudge in the night and the waves broke against the rocks with a lonely sound.

Suddenly, through the darkness, they heard a muffled sound. Their own boat was running along quietly and they listened.

"Another boat," remarked Tony, in a whisper.

It was, indeed, another motorboat, and it was near the base of the cliff. At last they could distinguish a faint light, and toward this light they began to move slowly.

They were tense with excitement. Everything might depend on the events of the next few minutes.

When they had gone in toward the cliff as far as they dared, creeping up from the west, they could make out the gloomy outline of the other motorboat, which was making its way slowly out of the very face of the cliff itself.

At first they could not imagine how the craft had got in so close nor where it was coming from. They crept up closer, at imminent danger of discovery, and at imminent danger of being washed ashore on the rocks. Then, finally, they heard the other boat slow down, heard the faint clatter of oars, then voices.

After that, with an abrupt roar that startled them, the other motorboat suddenly plunged on out into the bay. They could hear it threshing on its way out toward sea at an ever-increasing rate of speed.

"Where is it going?" said Tony, in amazement.

Frank cautioned for silence.

"There's a rowboat around here," he whispered. "Lay low."

They waited in silence and at last they heard the rattle of oars again. This time the sound was closer.

The rowboat was drawing near.

Fortunately the wind was from the sea and it blew the sounds toward them, at the same time keeping the men in the boat from hearing the muffled murmur of their own craft.

The rattle of oars continued and at last the boys could see the dim shape of the boat through the gloom. Finally they could distinguish the words of the dark figures in the craft. At a sign from Frank Tony cut off the engine for the time being.

But they could not make out complete sentences. The wind would whisk toward them a fragment of speech and then the rest of the words would be drowned.

"—three hundred pounds—" they heard a harsh voice saying, and then the rest of the sentence was lost.

A dull murmur of voices. Finally—

"I don't know. It's risky—"

The wind died for a moment and then through the gloom the boys saw that the rowboat was heading directly in toward the face of the cliff. It was not many yards away and as it passed by they heard the harsh voice again.

"Li Chang's share—" he was saying.

"No, we mustn't forget that," they heard a gruff voice reply.

"I hope they get away all right."

"What are you worrying about? Of course they'll get away."

"We've been watched, you know."

"It's all your imagination. Nobody suspects."

"Those boys at the house—"

"Just kids. If they come nosing around again we'll knock one of 'em on the head."

"I don't like this rough stuff. It's dangerous."

"We've got to do it or we'll end up in the pen. You can't be white-livered in this game. What's the matter with you tonight? You're nervous."

"I'm worried. I've got a hunch that we'd better clear out of here."

"Clear out!" replied the other contemptuously. "Are you crazy? Why, this place is as safe as a church. We can make a big clean-up before they know we're in this part of the country at all."

"Well, maybe you're right," said the first man doubtfully. "But still—"

His voice died away as the boat went on into the cove.

The boys could hear the rattle of oars and then a dull swishing of bushes, a muttered voice, and then silence fell.

The boys looked at one another through the gloom.

"Smugglers!" exclaimed Frank.

"Sounds mighty like it," replied Tony. "What do you think we should do?"

"Follow them."

"Sure," Joe agreed. "Follow them right into the cove."

But Tony demurred, though as he spoke he started up the engine again.

"Count me out," he said. "I don't like that talk about being knocked on the head. I may be foolish, but I'm not *that* foolish."

"There are three of us."

"And we don't know how many more of them. And they're grown men. I don't want to be trapped in that cove. Besides, the motorboat makes too much noise. They'd hear us coming and then we'd be done for."

This phase of the matter had not occurred to the Hardy boys, but they saw that it was reasonable. In the darkness it would be risky entering the narrow passage to the cove and then, as Tony said, it was probable that their approach would be heard.

"I hate to let them get away when we've got such a clue as this," said Frank. "There's no doubt they are smugglers. The men in that motorboat probably are going out to a ship for a cargo of smuggled goods, or else they have delivered a cargo and are on their way back."

"But where on earth did the motorboat come from!" exclaimed Joe. "There wasn't any boat in the cove when we were in there."

"Probably well hidden," said Frank. "There were a lot of bushes growing close down to the water's edge, I noticed. They'd have some sort of a hiding place fixed up."

"But where did all those men come from?"

"That's what we're going to find out. There must be some connection between this cove and the house on the cliff. I'm going ashore."

"Somebody's got to stay with the motorboat," said Tony. "I'm not afraid to go in there, and if it comes to a dare, I will go, although I don't want to be killed. But we can't leave the boat here, that's certain."

"I'll tell you what to do," said Frank. "Let Joe and me go ashore. Then we'll try to follow those men in the boat and see where they go. If we let them slip out of our hands now we may lose them altogether."

"And shall I wait?"

"No. You go back to Bayport and get help—lots of it."

"The police?"

"The federal men. Tell them we're on the track of the smugglers. If Joe and I discover anything we'll wait here at the entrance to the cove and put the police on the right track when they get here."

"Good!" said Tony. "I'll put you ashore right away."

"Don't go too close or you'll wreck the boat. Joe, I guess you and I will have to swim ashore. Then we'll go around into the cove and find out all we can."

Tony edged the boat in as close to the gloomy shore as he could, and then, with a whispered farewell, the Hardy boys slipped over the side into the water. They were only a few yards from the rocks and after a short swim they emerged, dripping, on the mainland. They looked back. They could see the dim shape of the motorboat as it turned away and then they could hear its dull chugging as Tony Prito turned the craft back in the direction of Bayport.

"Now!" whispered Frank. "Now for the smugglers!"

CHAPTER XVI

THE SECRET PASSAGE

It was very dark.

"I wish we had a light," whispered Joe.

"I have a flashlight in my pocket. But we can't use it now. Those men may be still around."

"Wouldn't the water spoil it?"

"No; I have it in a waterproof case. We can feel our way around these rocks until we get into the cove."

Cautiously, the boys made their way along the treacherous rocks. Once Joe lost his footing and slipped into the water with a splash. Instantly both boys remained motionless, fearing the sound had attracted the attention of the men in the cove. But there was not a sound.

Joe was ankle-deep in water, but he clambered up on the rocks again and they continued their journey.

They had landed at a point some twenty-five yards away from the entrance to the cove, but the rocks were so treacherous and the journey was so difficult that the distance seemed much longer.

"It must be Snackley and his gang, all right," whispered Frank, as they went on through the night. "Didn't you hear one of those men use a Chinese name?"

"He said something about Li Chang's share."

"Li Chang is probably the fellow who brings the dope to the coast. They bring the stuff into this cove by motorboat and rowboat and it is distributed from here. Dad said Snackley was smuggling dope."

"It must have been Snackley who ordered us away from here. He seemed like a leader of some kind."

"Five thousand dollars reward if we lay our hands on him!"

They had now reached the place where the seemingly solid coast line was broken by the indentation of the cove. They had feared that the cliff might be too steep at this point, but they found that it sloped gradually to the water and that there was a narrow ledge on which they could walk, one behind the other.

Here, they realized, the dangerous part of the adventure began.

It was very lonely in the shadow of the steep cliffs, and the loneliness was intensified by the distant moaning of the surf and the beat and wash of the waves against the reefs. Far in the distance they could see the reflection of the lights of Bayport through the mist and once or twice they could hear the murmur of Tony's motorboat as it sped away down the bay.

"I hope they bring back lights and guns with them," muttered Frank.

"Who?"

"The police."

"Don't worry. If they get word that Snackley is cornered they'll send out a squad of militia."

The boys rounded the point and began to make their way directly along the shore of the cove. Dense thickets and bushes grew right to the water's edge and the boys were afraid of making too much noise, as they realized that the two men they had heard talking in the boat might be close by—perhaps even waiting to pounce upon them in the darkness.

Their hearts beat quickly with the knowledge of the risk they were running, but neither lad thought of turning back. They were not thinking of the smugglers alone—they were thinking of their father.

When they reached the first of the thickets they paused. They knew that the crackling of the branches would betray their whereabouts if there was any one within hearing distance. For a while they did not know just what to do. Then Frank began to lower himself from the rock on which he was standing into the water.

"If it isn't too deep we can wade around," he whispered.

The water, fortunately, was shallow, and did not come up to his knees. He signaled to Joe to follow, and Joe accordingly slipped quietly down into the water beside him.

Then, without a word and moving as slowly as possible, Frank went on, wading through the water, close to the outstretched branches that overhung the shore.

It seemed as though they were wading at the bottom of a deep pit, for the high walls of rock ranged all about them and after they had penetrated into the cove some little distance the entrance was lost to view, being hidden by an angle of the cliffs. When they looked up they could see the gloomy greyness of the night sky above.

The cove was still in deep silence, so finally Frank concluded that the men who had entered the place in the boat had retired to some secret hiding place. Inasmuch as they could not hope to discover anything without a light, he withdrew the flashlight from its case, and then switched it on.

The yellow beam of light revealed the pallid leaves of the bushes by the shore and the naked walls of rock above. But although Frank turned the flashlight in every direction about the cove there was no sign of the rowboat in which the two men had arrived.

It had vanished utterly.

Although the lads were prepared for the disappearance of the smugglers, they were not prepared for the disappearance of the rowboat. But they searched for it in vain. The light revealed nothing of the craft.

"I wonder where they hid it!" whispered Frank.

They began a systematic search of the bushes around the cove, remaining as quiet as possible, but although they made almost a tour of the place it was soon evident that the boat had not been beached under cover of any of the thickets.

"It must be hidden in a cave of some kind," Frank decided at last. "And that's where the smugglers are."

Once again they began a search of the bushes.

They were still wading in the water and their feet were now very cold, but they searched patiently and carefully, brushing aside the branches, peering into the bushes, but it seemed they were to find nothing but the uncompromising rocks and moss beyond.

At last, however, as they were approaching a part of the cove which they had not visited before, Frank, who was in the lead, stumbled suddenly forward. His groping feet had failed to encounter bottom and he had lost his balance.

With great presence of mind, he kept the flashlight high in the air. He had stepped into a deep hole, and although he was up to his neck in water he kept his arm raised, keeping the flashlight free of the wetness.

"Here! Take the light," he gasped, in a hoarse whisper.

Joe leaned over and grasped the flashlight.

"Deep water here," muttered Frank, as he tried to scramble back into the shallows.

But the hole into which he had fallen was a sudden drop and it was necessary for Joe to grasp his brother's outstretched hand before he could regain the shallow water. At length, soaked to the skin, Frank again stood beside his brother.

"Good thing it wasn't any deeper," he remarked.

"The bottom is pretty level around here. It's funny there should be a deep hole like that."

Frank gave a sudden exclamation.

"I know how that came to be there," he whispered. "That's a channel! See how close it is to the shore. The water shouldn't be so deep right there."

"Why should it be a channel?"

"To let that motorboat get into shore—or the rowboat. They'd run aground otherwise. Give me the light. I'll bet we've found where that boat was hidden."

He played the flashlight on the surface of the water and then they could see clearly that the bottom of the cove was broken by a deep channel at that point, several feet in width, leading directly toward a clump of bushes at the shore.

Keeping well to the side of the channel and in the shallow water, the Hardy boys made their way over to the bushes.

Then, when the beam of the flashlight was cast on the dense covert of branches, the mystery was clear.

Beyond the bushes was a dark opening in the rock.

"A cave!" exclaimed Frank, in a suppressed tone.

It was so cleverly concealed that it could not have been seen in the clear light of the day except at close quarters. The glare of the flashlight, however, cast the dark opening into prominence behind the screen of leaves.

This, then, was the explanation of the boat's disappearance. There was a channel in the cove enabling the smugglers to row the boat directly into this cave in the rock. This also probably explained the presence of the motorboat.

"They went in here," said Joe.

"We'll explore it."

Having gone so far, there was no going back. The boys were fully determined to keep on the track of the smugglers. They did not know what lay behind the darkness of that silent and mysterious opening in the rock. But they meant to find out, no matter what the risks.

Cautiously, they advanced into the bushes, which gave way protestingly before them. The branches whipped their faces. The water was still shallow, for there was a narrow ledge along the side of the channel and, moreover, it was now low tide.

At last the bushes closed behind them. The Hardy boys were standing in the entrance to a secret passage, pressed close against the rocky wall of the cave.

CHAPTER XVII

THE CHAMBER IN THE CLIFF

Frank switched on the flashlight.

The beam illuminated the depths of the dark passage. Far ahead of the brothers they glimpsed a grey shape just above the surface of the glistening water.

For a moment they were startled, then they recognized that the grey shape was nothing more than the rowboat that had passed by them in the darkness outside the cove. It had been drawn up close to a natural wharf hewn out of the solid rock. It swayed to and fro with the motion of the water.

The boys made their way forward along the ledge, which was wide enough for one person to walk on, until at last the ledge widened out and proved to be a path leading to the wharf.

There was not a sound in the passage but the drip-drip of water from the gloomy walls.

The Hardy boys stole quietly forward along the wharf, passed the boat, and then looked about them.

Frank played the beam of the flashlight all about the place until at last the glare revealed a dark opening immediately ahead.

It was a crude arch in the rock and beyond it he could see a steep flight of wooden steps.

His heart was pounding with excitement. There was no doubt now that they had discovered the smugglers' secret.

"We've found it," he whispered to Joe. "We've found the passage. This must be directly underneath the house on the cliff."

"We'll have to go quietly."

The light cast strange shadows through the gloomy passage in the rocks. Water dripped from the walls. Water dripped from their clothing. They tip-toed quietly forward beneath the archway until they reached the flight of steps.

Then, quietly, almost stealthily, they began to ascend.

The place was in a deathlike silence. It was as if they were in a tomb. So quiet was the strange stairway in the cliff that the boys could hardly believe that men had been there but a short while before.

Step by step they ascended the stairs, and at last Frank's flashlight showed that they were approaching a door. It was set directly in a frame in the wall of rock at which the stairs ended. The passageway curved above them in a rocky ceiling.

They stood on the steps outside the door.

Should they enter?

They did not know what lay beyond. They might be entering the very haunt of the smugglers. In fact, this was most probable. And in that event they would not have a chance of escape.

For a while they remained there, not knowing whether to retreat or go on.

Then Frank stepped forward. He pressed his ear against the door and listened intently.

There was not a sound.

He peered around the sides of the door to see if he could catch a glimpse of light. There was only darkness. At length he decided that there was no one immediately beyond the door and he made up his mind to go ahead.

He whispered his decision to Joe, who nodded.

"I'm with you."

The door was opened by a latch, and Frank tried it cautiously. At first it was obstinate.

Then, with an abrupt clatter that echoed from wall to wall and seemed to the ears of the boys to create a hideous and deafening uproar, the latch snapped and the door swung open.

They did not immediately cross the threshold. Perhaps their approach had been heard. Perhaps the smugglers lay in wait for them beyond. So they remained there in silence for several minutes, listening for the slightest sound.

However, it became apparent that the dark chamber was empty, so Frank switched on the flashlight.

The vivid beam cut the darkness and revealed a gloomy cave in the very center of the cliff, hewn out of the rock. It had been a natural cave, just as the tunnel in the cliff had been a natural passageway, but the roof had been bolstered up by great beams and the sides had been chipped away while the floor had been leveled. It was a secret chamber in the heart of the rock.

The light revealed the fact that this chamber was used as a storeroom, for there were huge boxes, bales and packages distributed about the floor and piled against the walls.

"Smuggled goods!" exclaimed Frank.

His suspicions seemed verified by the fact that the majority of the boxes bore labels of foreign countries. Chinese characters were scribbled across them in practically every case.

Seeing that the chamber was unoccupied, the boys stepped through the doorway and looked about them. The flashlight illuminated the murky corners of the cave.

"This must be where they store all the stuff," Joe said, as he inspected one of the boxes.

"There must be another opening that leads to the top of the cliff. They probably bring the stuff up to the house and then dispose of it from there."

"You'd think they would keep it at the Polucca place instead of down here."

"Probably they are afraid the house might be raided at some time or another. That's why they keep the goods hidden in this place. It would be mighty hard for any one to find it here."

"But how do they get the stuff out of here? There's no doorway that I can see."

The light of the flashlight played upon the walls.

No doorway, no opening of any kind, was revealed.

"That's strange," said Frank. "There must be some way out."

They began to move about the chamber. Across some of the bales of goods had been thrown rich bolts of silk, while valuable tapestries were also lying carelessly on the floor. In one corner were three or four boxes piled on top of one another. Frank accidentally knocked the flashlight against one of these and it gave forth a hollow sound.

"It's empty," he said.

An idea struck him that perhaps these boxes had been piled up to conceal some passage leading out of the secret chamber. He mentioned his suspicion to Joe.

"But how could they pile the boxes up there after they went out?" his brother questioned.

"This gang are smart enough for anything. Let's move these boxes away."

He seized the topmost box. It was very light and he removed it from the top of the pile without difficulty.

"I thought so!" exclaimed Frank, with satisfaction.

For the light revealed the top of a door which had hitherto been hidden from view.

The boys lost no time in moving the rest of the boxes, and the entire door was soon in sight. Then the boys discovered how it was possible for the boxes to be piled up in such a position in spite of the fact that the smugglers had left the chamber and closed the door behind them.

Attached to the bottom of the door was a small wooden platform that projected out some distance over the floor of the cave and on this platform the boxes had been piled.

"They are kept there all the time, as a blind," he said. "Whenever any one leaves the cave and closes the door the boxes swing in with the platform and it looks as though they were piled up on the floor."

The ingenuity of the contrivance won their reluctant admiration.

"What shall we do?" asked Joe, looking through the doorway into the darkness beyond. "Go ahead?"

"We've come this far, and there's no sense in turning back. Let's go."

Frank stepped on into the passage beyond. He had hardly switched on the flashlight, revealing a crude flight of stairs that led from the rocky landing, before he stiffened and laid a warning hand on his brother's arm.

"Voices!" he whispered.

They listened.

They heard a man's voice in the distance. They could not distinguish what he was saying, for he was still too far away, but gradually the tones grew louder. Then, to their alarm, they heard footsteps.

Hastily, they retreated into the secret chamber.

"Quick! The door," snapped Frank.

They closed the door quietly.

"Now the boxes. If they come in here they'll notice that the boxes have been moved. Quick."

Swiftly the Hardy boys began to pile the empty boxes back on the platform that projected from the bottom of the door. They worked as quietly as possible and as they worked they heard the footsteps on the stairs drawing closer and closer.

Finally, the topmost box was in place.

"Out the other door."

They sped across the floor of the chamber toward the door that led to the stairs they had just recently ascended, but hardly had they reached it before they heard a rattle at the latch of the door on the opposite side of the cave.

"We haven't time," whispered Frank. "Hide."

The beam of the flashlight revealed a number of boxes close by the door. Over these boxes had been thrown a heavy bolt of silk, the folds of which hung down to the floor. They scrambled swiftly in behind the boxes, pressing themselves close against the wall. They did not have more than time to hide themselves and switch out the light before they heard the other door open.

"There's a package of dope in that shipment that came in last night," they heard a husky voice saying. "We'll bring it upstairs, for Burke says he can get rid of it for us right away. No use leaving it down here."

"Right," they heard some one else reply. "Anything else to go up?"

"No. We won't start moving the rest of this until the end of the week. It's too dangerous. Let Burke take out the shipment he has, along with this dope, and then we'll lay low for a few days. I'm getting a bit nervous."

"What does the big boss think about it?"

"That's his idea too. Here—wait till I switch on that light."

There was a click, and suddenly the chamber was flooded with light. The cave had been wired for electricity.

The Hardy boys crouched in their hiding place. Their hearts were pounding madly.

Would they be discovered?

Footsteps slowly approached the boxes behind which they were concealed!

CHAPTER XVIII

A STARTLING DISCOVERY

The Hardy boys were tense with a realization of their peril.

The strong electric light that hung from the center of the ceiling cast such a vivid illumination that they were sure they would be seen, particularly when they found that the boxes behind which they were hidden were spaced some distance apart. But for the folds of silk that hung down over the opening they would certainly have been seen.

"Here's some of that special silk," they heard the first man say. "Perhaps I'd better bring it up too. Burke was saying he could handle some more silk."

"We're done for!" thought Frank. "If he ever comes close enough to pick up that silk he'll see us, sure."

But the other man objected.

"What's the use? You won't get any more thanks for carrying all that stuff upstairs, even if Burke does take it. And if he doesn't, you'll just have to cart it all the way down again. My motto in this gang is to do just what Snackley tells me and no more."

"I guess you're right. We'll just bring up the dope."

To the relief of the boys the man turned away and went back to the other side of the chamber. They could hear a rustling sound. Then came the words:

"Well, we've got it. Let's go back up."

The switch snapped and the cavern was steeped in darkness immediately. It was a darkness immeasurably welcome to the lads crouched behind the boxes. They began to breathe more easily. They heard the door close and then they could hear the footsteps of the two men as they ascended the stairs in the passageway.

When the footsteps could be heard no more, Frank switched on the flashlight with a sigh of relief.

"That was a close call. Gosh, but I was sure they had us."

"We wouldn't have had any chance with that pair. You can bet your life they carry guns."

"Well, let's follow them."

"I'm with you. We know we're on the right track."

"And we know we're liable to blunder right into the whole den of smugglers if we don't watch our step. It's going to be ticklish from now on."

"It can't be any more ticklish than it has been. I lived about ten years while that pair was in here."

They crossed the chamber and again opened the door. Cautiously, they stepped out on the landing, closed the door behind them, and again confronted the flight of steps.

"I'll go first," said Frank. "Stick close behind me."

He decided to turn out the flashlight, because it was barely possible that the smugglers might have a guard at the top of the stairs, in which event their approach would be discovered. So, in the inky blackness, they ascended, step after step.

They reached the top of the first flight of stairs and then they found themselves upon a crude landing of planks which ran along the side of the rock wall for some distance until it ended in another flight of steps.

Here the boys stopped again to listen. All was as silent as the tomb save for the distant pounding of the sea upon the cliff.

"I don't hear a sound," whispered Joe.

"Come on," came from his brother.

The passage through the rock was of considerable depth, and they went on up countless steps until their limbs were weary. They had never realized that the cliff was so high until now.

But at length they reached the final landing and there they were confronted by another door. This door, they assumed, either led out into the open or into some cave just below the surface of the ground. Perhaps, thought Frank, it even led into the cellar of the Polucca house.

The boys pressed close to the door, taking care to make no noise, and listened.

They heard not a sound.

Still, with the caution arising from their previous narrow escape, they decided to wait a little while longer. As later events proved, it was well that they did.

For a while they could hear nothing from beyond the door and there was no indication that any one was there. But, after listening intently for as long as five minutes, they heard an odd shuffling sound and then a sigh. That was all.

"Some one there!" breathed Frank, in a low whisper.

Joe nodded in the darkness.

They did not know what to do. It seemed apparent that there was some one beyond the door. Possibly a sentry. If there was only one man it might be possible to attack him and disarm him, although it was scarcely possible that they could do this without noise and without attracting the attention of the smugglers.

The problem was solved for them.

A door thudded in the distance. Then there was a muffled murmur of voices, growing in volume, and a trampling of feet.

"I tell you this nonsense has gone far enough. He'll sign, and he'll sign right now, or I'll know the reason why."

The boys started. For the voice was none other than the voice of the man who had ordered them out of the cove that afternoon.

"That's the stuff, chief!" returned some one. "Make him sign and promise to keep his mouth shut."

"If he doesn't he'll never live to tell about it, that's one thing sure!" snapped the first man coldly.

There was the sound of a switch being snapped, and then the boys could see a yellow beam of light beneath the door at their feet. From the sounds they judged that three or four men had entered the room beyond.

"Well, he's still here," said the man who had been addressed as "chief." He strode across the room and the boys could hear a chair scrape on the board floor. "You'll find that this is an easier place to get into than it is to get out of."

A weary voice answered him. The tones were low. The boys could not make out the words.

"You're a prisoner here and you'll be a prisoner here until you die unless you sign that paper."

Again the weary voice spoke, but, as before, the tones were so low that the words were indistinguishable.

"You won't sign, eh? We'll see about that!"

"Wait till he goes hungry for a few days and then he'll think differently," put in one of the other men. There was a hoarse laugh from his companions.

"Yes, you'll be hungry enough before we're through with you. I can promise you that," said the harsh voice. "Are you going to sign?"

"No," they heard the prisoner in the other room answer.

Who was this man who was evidently held captive by the smugglers in the underground room? The same thought was in the mind of each boy as he listened to the conversation.

"You know too much about us. You've found out too much, and we'll never let you get out of here to use your information. You may as well get that straight. You've read that paper. If you don't sign it you will starve."

The prisoner evidently did not reply.

"Give him a taste of the hot iron," suggested one of the smugglers.

"No, nothing like that. It's too crude. I'm giving him his chance. He can sign this paper now or take the consequences."

Still there was no reply.

"Getting obstinate, are you? Won't you even answer me!" The leader of the gang was evidently getting angry. Suddenly he shouted out:

"Sign this paper, Hardy, or you'll starve—as sure as my name is Snack-ley!"

CHAPTER XIX
CAPTURED

The worst fears of the Hardy boys were realized.

They had been unable to distinguish clearly the voice of the prisoner un-til then, for it had been muffled by the intervening door, but all along they had suspected that it was their father. Now they knew, and they knew also that he was a captive of Snackley, the head of the gang of smugglers.

Joe gave a perceptible start, but Frank laid a warning hand upon his brother's arm. Now, of all times, there was need for caution.

They listened.

"I won't sign it," replied Fenton Hardy clearly.

Snackley replied:

"You heard what I said. Sign or starve."

"I'll starve."

"You'll think differently in a day or so. You're pretty hungry now, Hardy, but you'll be a lot hungrier later on. And thirsty, too. You'll be ready to sell your soul for a drop of water or a bite to eat."

"I won't sign."

"After all, we're not asking very much. You've discovered a number of things that we want you to forget about. It won't hurt you to go back to Bayport and say that you couldn't find out anything about us. Nobody knows where you have been."

"I've found out all I wanted to know about you, Snackley. I've got enough evidence to send you to the penitentiary for the rest of your life. And I have more than that."

"What do you mean—more than that?"

"I know enough to have you sent to the electric chair."

There was a sudden commotion in the room and two or three of the smugglers began talking at once.

"You're crazy!" shouted Snackley, but there was a current of uneasiness in his voice. "You're crazy. You don't know anything about me."

"I know enough to have you sent up for murder."

"All the more reason why you're not going to get out of here without signing this paper. You can count yourself lucky you have even this chance of getting out alive. By all rights we should knock you on the head and heave you over the cliff into the sea."

"I won't sign."

"Don't be foolish. All we ask you to do is to agree that you won't make use of the information you have. I admit that you've stumbled on some of our secrets, and we can't afford to turn you loose and have the federal agents about our ears in no time."

"You must trust me very much. What is to prevent me from signing that paper and then going back on my word?" asked Fenton Hardy curiously.

"We know you too well, Hardy. We know that if you signed that promise you would keep it."

"Exactly. And that is why I won't sign it. I wouldn't be doing my duty if I agreed to any scheme that would protect you."

"How about your family? Are you doing your duty to them by being so obstinate?"

There was silence for a while. Then Fenton Hardy answered slowly:

"They would rather know that I died doing my duty than have me come back to them as a protector of smugglers and criminals."

"You have a very high sense of duty," sneered Snackley. "But perhaps you'll think better of it after a while. Are you thirsty?"

There was no reply.

"Are you hungry?"

Still no answer.

"You know you are. And you'll be hungrier and thirstier before we are through with you. We'll put food and water in your sight but you won't be able to reach it. You'll die of thirst and starvation—unless you sign that paper."

"I'll never sign it."

"All right. Come on, men. We'll leave him to himself and give him time to think about it."

Footsteps resounded as Snackley and the others began to leave the room, and finally they died away and a door banged.

Fenton Hardy was left alone.

Joe made a sudden move toward the door, but Frank restrained him.

"Not just yet," he cautioned. "They may have left some one to guard him."

So the boys waited, listening intently at the door.

But there were no further sounds from within the room. At length, satisfied that his father had indeed been left alone, Frank fumbled for the latch of the door.

Noiselessly, he managed to open it. He pressed in on the door until it was open about an inch, then he peeped through the aperture.

He found himself on the threshold of a sort of cellar, a damp and mouldy chamber, of about the same size as the storage room in the heart of the cliff, with the difference that whereas the first room was a cave in the rock, this place had been dug out of the earth. It was floored with planks and a lone electric light cast a yellowish illumination over the scene. There was a crude table and a few chairs, while in one corner stood a small camp-bed.

On this bed he spied his father.

Fenton Hardy was bound hand and foot to the cot, so tightly trussed up that he was unable to move more than a few inches in any direction. He was lying flat on his back, staring up at the muddy ceiling of his prison. On a chair beside the cot was a large sheet of paper, presumably the document the smugglers were asking him to sign.

The detective did not hear the door open. As Frank looked at him he was conscious of a change in the appearance of his father, a change that shocked him extremely. For Fenton Hardy was thin and pale, his cheeks were sunken and he looked like a man who was famished for want of food.

Frank opened the door a little wider and tiptoed into the room. Joe followed quietly.

They knew that there was danger of the smugglers returning at any moment. They knew that they must work swiftly and quietly if they were to effect the release of their father.

A slight sound attracted Fenton Hardy's attention and he slowly turned his head. When his gaze rested on the figures of the two boys who were stealing across the floor toward him he almost uttered an exclamation of amazement but he managed to check the involuntary utterance, although his face lighted up with relief.

Quickly, the Hardy boys reached his bedside. Frank drew out his pocketknife and, without a word, without even a whisper, began to hack at the ropes that bound his father. But the knife was dull and the ropes were heavy.

Joe had lost his knife in the water soon after they had left Bayport, and although he searched about the room, he was unable to find one, so he set himself to the laborious business of trying to untie the knots.

Every moment was precious. At any second, the boys knew, they might hear the footsteps of the approaching smugglers. They worked with frantic caution, working against time.

Frank hacked at the ropes, but the dull blade seemed to make little progress. Joe fumbled at the obstinate knots until his fingernails were broken, but he could scarcely loosen the strands.

Minutes passed—slowly and agonizingly. Fenton Hardy could give no assistance. He had to lie there in silence, not daring even to encourage the lads by a whisper. The silence was broken only by the heavy breathing of the two boys, by the scarcely audible sound of the knife against the ropes.

At last the knife cut through one of the ropes and Fenton Hardy's feet were free. Frank pulled the ropes away, but a loose end fell on the floor with a light sound.

Slight as the noise was, it seemed to them almost deafening, in view of the necessity for silence. Desperately, Frank prepared to set to work to cut through the ropes that bound Fenton Hardy's arms. And, even as he reached over with the knife, they heard a sound that sent a thrill of terror through them.

It was a heavy footstep beyond the door through which the smugglers had recently disappeared!

Some one was approaching the underground room.

Frank strained at the knife, but the ropes were stubborn. The dull blade made little impression at first. But at last the rope began to give, and finally, as Fenton Hardy gave a mighty effort, it snapped, and the detective was free.

But the footsteps on the stairs had drawn nearer and it was followed by others. The smugglers were returning.

"Quick!" whispered Frank, as he flung the ropes aside.

"I—I can't—hurry!" gasped out Fenton Hardy. "I've been here too—too long." He could hardly utter the words. His face showed his exhaustion.

"But we've got to hurry, dad!" came excitedly from Frank. "See if you can't make it."

"I'll—I'll do my—my best," returned his father.

"If those fellows come back let's fight for it," put in Joe desperately.

"You bet we'll fight," answered Frank in a voice that meant a great deal.

Fenton Hardy got to his feet as hastily as he could, but when he stood up on the floor he reeled and would have fallen had not Joe grasped his arm. He had been lying bound to the cot for so long and he was so weak from hunger that a fit of dizziness had attacked him. It soon passed, however, and the three hastened toward the door through which the Hardy boys had entered.

But the smugglers were very close now. The Hardys could hear the coarse voices just outside the other door.

There was no chance of escape.

Just as the Hardy boys and their father crossed the threshold the door on the opposite side of the room was flung open.

Frank had a confused glimpse of the dark man, Snackley, whom they had seen in the cove that afternoon, with half a dozen rough men crowding behind him. Then he saw Snackley whip a revolver from his pocket.

The chief of the smugglers was filled with astonishment, but he did not lose his presence of mind. The weapon was leveled at Frank before he had time to close the door.

Snackley did not speak. He pressed the trigger and the revolver roared, the echoes crowding on one another in that narrow space. The bullet chipped into the wood of the door.

Frank ducked. Joe, who was in the lead, flung himself to one side. Fenton Hardy stumbled out on to the landing at the top of the stairs.

"Come back!" roared Snackley, plunging across the room. "Come back or I'll fire again!"

As the smuggler drew closer Frank crouched for a spring, and then leaped directly at Snackley. He struck out at the man's wrist and the revolver flew out of the rascal's grasp, skidding across the floor into a corner.

Then they grappled, and so sudden had been Frank's attack that the smuggler was taken by surprise and he reeled up against the wall. But his companions rushed to his rescue. Frank was swiftly overpowered and dragged away, while other smugglers, with drawn revolvers, pursued Joe and Fenton Hardy out on to the landing. Being unarmed, they were forced to submit, otherwise they would have been shot without mercy.

The struggle was short. The menacing revolvers gave the smugglers the upper hand.

Within five minutes Fenton Hardy was bound to the cot again while the Hardy boys were seated, trussed up and unable to move, on two chairs near by. They were captives of the smugglers!

CHAPTER XX

DIRE THREATS

Snackley, once he had recovered from his first consternation and surprise, was in high humor.

"Just in time!" he chuckled, rubbing his hands with satisfaction. "Just in time! If we'd been a few minutes later they'd have been away from us altogether."

The Hardy boys were silent. They were sick with disappointment. It had seemed that escape was certain, and then, in a twinkling, the tables had been turned and now they were all worse off than they had been before.

"What will we do with 'em, chief?" asked one of the men.

The voice sounded familiar to the boys and they looked up. Not altogether to their surprise, they saw that the fellow was none other than Redhead, whom they had seen at the Polucca place the day Frank discovered his father's cap.

"Do with them?" exclaimed Snackley. "That's quite a problem. We have three on our hands now, where we had only one. We have to make three people keep their mouths shut instead of only one. We have three people to keep guard over now."

"We ought to do what I wanted to do in the first place," declared Redhead doggedly. "As long as Hardy is alive, he's dangerous."

"You mean we should get rid of him?"

"Sure, we ought to get rid of him—and get rid of those boys of his, too."

"That's easier said than done," returned Snackley, but with a sinister look at the man on the cot.

"I should think you had enough on your conscience already, Snackley!" exclaimed Fenton Hardy. "But I suppose you're hardened enough for anything," he added bitterly. He was thinking more of his sons and their possible fate than of himself.

"Don't you bother about my conscience," sneered Snackley; but a shadow crossed his face. "What do you know about me, anyhow?" he demanded roughly.

"I know all about what happened to Felix Polucca. He had a big treasure hidden in that house on the cliff and you got it, and then you started to use the place for your smuggling operations."

"O, shut up!" Snackley snapped. "I'm going to fix you, and those kids of yours, too! Just wait and see!"

Four of the smugglers had been whispering among themselves at the back of the room during this talk between the chief smuggler and the detective, and now one of these men stepped forward.

"Got a word to say to you, chief," he began, addressing Snackley.

"What is it now?" The chief smuggler's voice was surly.

"It's about what's to be done with these three, now we have 'em prisoners," returned the man hesitatingly. "Of course, your business is your own and we're not asking any questions about what happened to Felix Polucca, but we're in this game of smuggling, see? We don't stand for anything that's too red-handed."

"That's the truth!" put in another of the men.

"Kind of chicken-hearted," sneered Snackley. "You look out or I'll fire the lot of you!"

"No, you won't, chief," replied the first man who had addressed him. "We've helped in this smuggling, and we're going to have our full share of what's coming to us."

"We've got another plan about those three prisoners," put in a fellow who had not yet spoken. "I think it would work out grand."

"What plan?" questioned the chief smuggler briefly.

"We've been talking about Li Chang."

"What about him?"

"Turn 'em over to Li Chang. He's sailing back to China in the morning. Have 'em put on board his ship."

Snackley scratched his head for a moment. Evidently the idea caught his fancy.

"Not bad," he muttered. "I hadn't thought of Li Chang. Yes, he'd be able to look after them. He'd see to it that they never returned," and he grinned grimly.

"He'd probably dump 'em overboard before they got to China at all," declared Redhead smugly. "Li Chang doesn't like to feed passengers if they can be got rid of."

"So much the better. We won't be responsible."

"Leave it to Li Chang. The old villain would just like to have three white men in his power. He'll attend to them."

Snackley reached over and picked up the document from the floor, where it had fallen in the struggle. He glanced at it and then tore it into pieces.

"We won't need this. You've lost your chance, Hardy. If you had signed it you would have been free by now. But you'll never be free—not with three of you knowing our secret. It's too risky. You'll all be turned over to Li Chang. He brought in a little cargo this week and his ship is to sail in the morning. You will go with him."

Fenton Hardy was silent. He had resolved not to plead for his own safety.

"Well," said Snackley, "haven't you anything to say?"

"Nothing. Do as you wish with me. But let the boys go."

"We'll stick with you, dad," said Frank quickly.

"We sure will!" added Joe.

"You certainly will," declared Snackley. "I'm not going to let one of you have the chance of getting back to Bayport with your story."

The chief of the smugglers stood in the center of the room for a while, contemplating his captives with a bitter smile. Then he turned suddenly on his heel.

"Well, they're safe enough," he said to Redhead. "We have that business with Burke to attend to. You two," he said, speaking to two of his men, "had better go down to the cove and take the rowboat out. Signal to Li Chang that we need the motorboat sent in at once. The rest of you come and help load Burke's truck. If any nosey policeman came along and found it in the lane we'd be done for."

"How about them?" asked Redhead, indicating the prisoners.

"They're safe enough. But I guess we'd better leave one guard, anyway. Malloy, you stay here and keep watch."

Malloy, a surly and truculent fellow in overalls and a ragged sweater, nodded and sat down on a box near the door. This arrangement seemed to satisfy Snackley, and after warning Malloy not to fall asleep on the job and to see to it that the prisoners did not escape, he left the room, followed by Redhead and the other smugglers, with the exception of two who left by the other door. Their footsteps could be heard as they went down the flight of stairs leading to the bottom of the cliff.

A heavy silence fell over the room after the departure of the smugglers. Malloy crouched gloomily on the box, gazing blankly at the floor. The butt of a revolver projected from his hip pocket.

Frank strained against the ropes that bound him to the chair. But the smugglers had done their task well. He could scarcely budge.

"We're done for, I guess," he heard Joe say.

Frank seldom gave up heart, but this time he could see no ray of hope.

"I'm afraid so. Looks as if we'd be with Li Chang by morning."

"But we don't want to go to China, Frank!"

"We may never get to China, Joe. Didn't you hear what they said? For all we know, that rascally Chinaman, whoever he is, may heave us overboard when he gets well out in the ocean."

"You fellows shut up," growled Malloy. "Shut up, I tell you, or I'll make it hot for you," and he tapped his revolver suggestively.

After that an ominous silence fell between the prisoners. Frank and Joe were downhearted. It looked as if their fate were sealed.

CHAPTER XXI

QUICK WORK

The Hardy boys glanced over at their father on the cot.

To their surprise they saw that he was smiling. Frank was on the point of asking him what he found in the situation to smile at when he caught a warning glance. He looked over at the guard.

Malloy was not bothering with the prisoners. He was not even looking in their direction. Instead, his head was already beginning to nod, as though he were going to sleep.

Snackley had made a poor selection when he chose Malloy as guard. The man had been up the entire previous night helping bring in the shipment of smuggled goods from Li Chang's vessel, and he had had no sleep that day. He was very tired. Sleep stole upon him without his being aware of it.

Several times he straightened up and rubbed his eyes, but eventually he would bow his head again and give in to the luxury of a little doze.

In the meantime, Mr. Hardy was busy. He had profited by his previous experience.

When the smugglers seized him and attempted to tie him to the bed for the second time he had made use of a trick frequently employed by magicians and professional "escape" artists, who guarantee to escape from ropes and strait-jackets. He had expanded his chest and held his muscles rigid, keeping his arms as far away from his sides as possible, so that later, when he relaxed, he found that the ropes did not bind him as tightly as his captors had intended.

This gave him a small leeway. He found that the ropes were especially slack about his right wrist, so he began to work laboriously to free himself. For a long time he thought it would be impossible, and the rope chafed his wrist, but at last he managed to slide his hand free.

Joe and Frank watched this performance with amazement, and new hope came into their eyes as they saw their father slowly groping for one of the knots. The detective fumbled at it for a while. It was slow work, for he had but one hand free, but in their haste the smugglers had not tied the knot as firmly as they should, and before long Fenton Hardy had loosened it to such an extent that soon the ends of the rope fell away.

His arms were now free, so he braced himself against the sides of the bed and struggled to release his feet. They had not been bound so securely, being simply tied down under one strand of rope about the cot, and after silently struggling for a few minutes he was able to work his way free.

The detective's next move was to take off his boots, which he did swiftly and quietly, placing them noiselessly on the bed. Then he crept out onto the floor and began to steal over toward the guard.

Malloy was half asleep, but the detective had not gone more than two yards before a slight sound, a slight creaking of the floor, warned the guard that something was amiss.

He turned, blinking.

A look of intense amazement crossed Malloy's face and he opened his mouth to yell for help, but Fenton Hardy leaped across the intervening space and hurled himself upon the smuggler before the guard had time to utter more than a muffled gasp.

He clapped one hand over Malloy's mouth and bore the guard to the floor, where they rolled over and over in a desperate and silent struggle. Although Fenton Hardy was weakened by his imprisonment and privation and although the smuggler was strong and wiry, the detective had the advantage of a surprise attack, and Malloy had no time to collect his faculties.

Joe and Frank watched the battle in an agony of suspense. It was, they knew, their last hope.

Fenton Hardy still kept his hand over the other man's mouth, although Malloy was gasping and gurgling and making frantic efforts to call out for help. The detective dug his knee into Malloy's stomach and when the smuggler tried to wriggle out of the way he snatched for the revolver.

Their hands closed about the butt of the weapon at the same instant.

The struggle was short and bitter.

Malloy tugged at the revolver, trying to draw it from his pocket. Fenton Hardy dug his knee sharply against the man and Malloy loosened his grasp, with a groan of pain. The detective snatched the revolver free and then flung himself back, leveling the weapon at Malloy.

"Not a word out of you!" he whispered.

Malloy's hands rose in the air. He did not utter a sound. He was sitting helplessly on the floor, his mouth opening and closing as he painfully drew breath. He was beaten.

The detective spied a knife in a leather sheath at the smuggler's belt so he reached forward and seized the weapon.

Then, still keeping Malloy covered with the revolver, he walked slowly backward until he reached Joe's side. Without removing his eyes from the smuggler, Fenton Hardy bent down and sliced at the ropes that bound his son.

The knife was sharp and the ropes soon fell apart. Joe leaped from the chair, casting aside the rope ends, and took the proffered knife. Then, while his father still covered Malloy, he went over to Frank and set him free.

Still without saying a word, Fenton Hardy motioned toward the bed and indicated by signs that the smuggler was to lie down on the cot. A gesture of refusal on the part of Malloy was met by a vigorous forward thrust of the revolver and the smuggler hastily retreated.

The ropes on the bed had not been cut, so they were still available for trussing up Malloy just as Mr. Hardy had been bound. The boys did the job with neatness and despatch and they even gagged the smuggler with his own handkerchief and one of the ropes from the chairs.

Within five minutes their erstwhile guard was lying helpless on the bed, bound hand and foot and gagged so firmly that only a muffled and subdued muttering escaped him.

"What now?" asked Frank, in a low tone.

"We can't go out by the cove," replied his father. "There are two men down there now signaling to the motorboat. We'd better go upstairs."

"Where does that lead to?"

"Outside. It will bring us into the shed near the house."

Fenton Hardy moved over toward the door.

"We haven't any time to lose," he said. "I have the revolver. If we meet any one—"

He opened the door cautiously and peeped out. There was no one beyond. There was nothing but a flight of steps leading upward into darkness.

The detective went forward, his sons following close at his heels.

Step by step they made their way on up in the darkness, for Joe had closed the door behind them and Frank did not dare make use of the flashlight.

At last Fenton Hardy came to a stop. He was fumbling at something immediately above.

Then the boys saw a faint opening which grew larger above them and resolved itself into a square of grey light against which the head and shoulders of their father were fully silhouetted. Fenton Hardy had raised the trapdoor that concealed the entrance to the underground caves and passages.

Mr. Hardy looked out carefully. There was no sign of the smugglers. He proceeded to the very top of the steps, then moved clear of the stairway.

Frank and Joe followed, rising out of the ground like mysterious spirits of the earth, and the three stood in the shelter of the shed.

It was a dark night and the trees were moaning in the wind from the sea. Immediately before them rose the gloomy mass of the house on the cliff. There were no lights.

In the direction of the lane they could hear dull sounds, no doubt from the truck that the smugglers were loading with goods which were to be disposed of by the man called Burke.

"Safe so far," whispered the detective to his sons.

They moved out of the shed, after closing the trapdoor, and stood in the shadows.

"We can't go by way of the lane," whispered Frank.

"There's a prisoner in the cellar of that house," said Fenton Hardy. "I hate to go without setting him free."

"A prisoner?"

"I heard them talking about him."

"Why can't we go to town for help?"

"Once they find us gone they'll clear out."

"But three of us can't do much against this gang. They'll just capture us all again."

The detective considered this for a moment. At last he sighed.

"Yes, the risk is too great!" he said. "And I've let you take too many risks already. We'd better go back to town."

Having arrived at this decision, they moved slowly across the grass of the yard, heading toward the bushes that flanked the lane. The great bulk of the old stone house loomed heavily and darkly in the night.

Then, suddenly, they heard a harsh sound that struck terror into their hearts—the clatter of the trapdoor being raised!

CHAPTER XXII

INTO THE HAUNTED HOUSE

A hoarse shout came through the darkness.

"Chief! Redhead! They've got away. Watch for 'em!"

Some one was scrambling through the opening in the shed, bellowing in a frantic voice, warning the other smugglers of the escape.

"Into the house!" snapped Fenton Hardy. He began to run swiftly across the yard toward the big gloomy house. Frank and Joe followed.

The man in the shed saw the moving figures.

The darkness was pierced by a flash of crimson and a revolver barked three times.

From the lane came sounds of running feet. A man was shouting:

"What is it? What's the matter?"

"They've got away! Hardy and them boys! They've escaped. Look! There they are now—running across the yard!"

The revolver spoke again. But the shots were wild, for the detective and his sons were soon lost to view in the shadows of the house.

With the uproar growing in volume behind them, they fled for the shelter of the building. It was their only refuge. If they attempted to escape to the road they would be almost certain of meeting some of the smugglers. They could not go back down the passageway. If they retreated they would be driven to the verge of the cliff.

Fenton Hardy sped around to the back door and flung it open. The fugitives raced into the kitchen and closed the door behind them.

Out of the darkness came a frightened voice.

"Who's there?"

It was so sudden and unexpected that their pulses leaped.

They made no answer.

"Who's there, I say? Is it you, Redhead?"

Still they did not reply. Fenton Hardy crept through the darkness in the direction of the voice.

"Speak! Quick! Speak, or I'll fire!"

The boys heard a sudden, scrambling sound. Their father had thrown himself upon the other man. The boys rushed in on the two struggling figures.

There was a deafening roar and a streak of flame. The man of the house had been armed with a shotgun, and in the struggle it had exploded.

Fortunately, the Hardy boys were not standing in the path of the shot. But the noise had attracted the attention of the smugglers outside the house, and in a few seconds the back door was flung open.

"They're in here!" some one yelled. "They're in the house!"

Fenton Hardy flung to one side the man with whom he had been struggling.

"Upstairs!" he called out to the two boys and ran on into the next room.

A feeble light was burning, a candle standing in its own grease near the bottom of the staircase. Up these stairs they fled, Joe pausing long enough to extinguish the candle. The room was plunged into darkness just as the first of the smugglers rushed through the doorway.

Fenton Hardy waited at the top of the stairs until the boys joined him.

Somebody in the room below lit a match.

The detective fired directly at the spluttering light. There was a muttered exclamation. The match was immediately extinguished by the smuggler who had been so incautious as to reveal his whereabouts in this manner. A whispered conversation followed.

"He's at the top of the stairs!" said one of the smugglers. "We can't rush him. He's got a revolver."

"Only one?"

"Yes. The kids aren't armed."

"Wait till he uses up his ammunition. Then we'll get him."

There was another whispered colloquy and then the smugglers apparently withdrew toward the doorway leading into the kitchen. Then, in a moment, a perfect fusillade of shots broke out.

But Fenton Hardy and the boys had withdrawn past the turn in the staircase and were well protected. They could hear the uproar of gunfire as the smugglers riddled the staircase with bullets.

"That should have finished 'em!" they could hear Snackley saying. "If they're on the stairs at all they're as dead as mutton by now."

"Best be careful," muttered one of the men. "Hardy has a gun."

"Where did he get it?"

"From the guard. They tied him up."

"Lucky they didn't get away altogether. Wait till I talk to Malloy!"

"He was tied fast to the bed when we came back up the stairs. They had taken his gun and gagged him. He said they had just gone, so we made after them and came up through the trapdoor. They were just getting out of the shed when we saw 'em."

"What a fine chase we would have had if they had got out into the woods. Well, we have 'em trapped now."

Whispers followed. The boys listened. Once they heard some one say:

"The back stairs—"

Frank turned to his father.

"They're going to rush us by the back stairs!"

"I hadn't thought of that," said Mr. Hardy. "I wonder if there is any way of reaching the attic."

Frank took the flashlight from his pocket and switched it on. Just a few yards away he could distinguish a flight of stairs leading up to a trapdoor in the ceiling. At the same time he could hear a stealthy noise at the bottom of another flight of steps that led to the kitchen.

"Hurry!" he whispered, and the three moved silently down the hall until they reached the steps.

Joe went up first and Frank followed with the light, while Fenton Hardy stood at the bottom of the steps to cover their retreat with the revolver.

When Joe reached the trapdoor he pushed at it. At first it proved stubborn and would not open. There was an anxious moment while he strove to force it open but in spite of all his efforts it would not budge.

"What's the matter?" asked Frank from below.

"It won't open."

Frank went on up the few remaining steps and added his efforts to those of his brother. Together they shoved at the trapdoor, and at last it moved, then opened, falling back with a loud crash.

There was a yell from the stairs.

"Hurry up, men! They're getting into the attic."

A rush of thudding footsteps followed as the smugglers raced up the steps. Joe scrambled through the opening and Frank followed. Fenton Hardy was only half way up the steps, however, when the first smugglers reached the hallway. The detective fired directly at them.

The smugglers who were in the lead fell back in a desperate attempt to reach cover, and in so doing they collided with those behind. For a few moments confusion prevailed, and Fenton Hardy took advantage of it to spring up the few remaining steps, scramble through the opening and fling the trapdoor back into place.

The Hardys found themselves in the inky darkness of the attic. Frank switched on the flashlight, and in its glare they saw that they were in a dusty chamber immediately below the roof. Old boxes and rubbish lay about.

"Where did they go?" they heard one of the smugglers ask.

"Into the attic," replied another. "Now we've got them where we want them."

"That's what you said last time."

"They can't get out of there. We've got them cornered."

Snackley's voice broke in.

"Hardy!" he shouted.

Mr. Hardy did not answer.

"Listen, Hardy!" went on Snackley. "We'll give you one minute to come down out of there."

Still no answer.

"The floors are thin, Hardy! We can fire right through 'em. You can't get out. We have you cornered. Better come down."

Frank flashed the light from side to side. It was evident that the smuggler spoke the truth. They were indeed cornered.

An interval of silence followed. Then came:

"Your last chance, Hardy!"

Frank flashed the light upon his father. Mr. Hardy was inspecting the chamber of the revolver. He held out the weapon with a gesture of despair. There were no more shells.

A shot sounded from below and a bullet ripped its way savagely through the flooring but a foot or so away from where the three sat. Another bullet tore through the wood of the trapdoor.

The Hardys sprang back and, making as little noise as possible, pressed themselves against the sloping walls of the attic, keeping as far away from the trapdoor as they could.

A few more shots resounded. The bullets were unpleasantly close.

Then Snackley spoke again.

"What do you think of it now, Hardy? Are you and your boys ready to come down?"

They did not answer, for they knew that if they did their voices would reveal where they were standing and might bring a bullet. When they did not reply Snackley spoke to his men.

"Let 'em have a few more!"

An angry chorus of revolver shots followed. In the midst of the uproar some of the smugglers secured a long pole and pushed against the trapdoor with it. Before those above could avert the danger the trapdoor was flung wide open. It fell back with a crash.

A hand appeared through the trapdoor, holding a revolver, and then the head and shoulders of one of the smugglers followed. He peered into the darkness, holding the weapon in readiness. Some one had switched on a light in the hall so that the man's figure could be clearly seen.

"Come out of it!" he snapped, pointing the revolver directly at the dim figure of Frank. "Come out of it, or I'll shoot!"

Further resistance was useless.

With sinking heart Frank advanced toward the edge of the opening in the floor, while Joe and Fenton Hardy followed, with arms upraised. The smuggler backed his way down the steps, still keeping them covered, until he reached the bottom of the stairs.

The Hardys descended, conscious of an array of leveled revolvers that covered every movement. They saw Snackley standing in the forefront of the crowd. They were captured again.

CHAPTER XXIII

RESCUE

Snackley stepped forward.

"So!" he sneered. "You pretty nearly got away with it, didn't you?"

The captives did not answer. They were sick with disappointment. Just when escape had been within their grasp the smugglers had outwitted them.

"You bit off a little more than you could chew when you stacked up against me," bragged Snackley.

"What'll we do with 'em, chief?" asked one of the man.

"Take them back to the cave. We'll get them out to Li Chang right away. If they get away again there'll be trouble for you. Keep an eye on them."

"Shouldn't we tie them up?"

"There's no rope. It doesn't matter. Put a bullet through the first one that makes a false move. You hear that?" he said, turning to Fenton Hardy. "The first one that tries to escape gets a bullet through him."

The three were surrounded by the smugglers. The light shone on their evil, bearded faces and glittered on the drawn revolvers. Fenton Hardy's useless weapon had been snatched from him.

"Downstairs!" snapped Snackley. "Get downstairs with you."

He prodded Frank with the barrel of his revolver as he spoke. The Hardy boys moved toward the stairs, their father in the rear. One of the smugglers went ahead in case the prisoners should by chance make some desperate break for freedom.

When they reached the lower room they paused while the man ahead lit a match. The electric light had been broken. Hardly had the match flared than there came the sound of thudding feet through the kitchen and the back door banged noisily.

Some one rushed into the room, gasping for breath. The light revealed him to be another of the smugglers.

"Police!" he exclaimed, in terror. "They're coming down the lane!"

A babel of voices followed. The smugglers came tumbling down the stairs in their haste. With one bound Snackley leaped forward and seized the man by the collar.

"What!" he exclaimed. "What's that you say? Police?"

"Down the lane!" gasped the man. "They came down the road in a car and they're closing in on the house. I saw them."

With a yell, Snackley flung the man to one side.

"Down into the cave!" he roared. "Quick!"

Confusion prevailed. In the resulting uproar the match went out and the room was plunged into darkness.

Frank resolved on a daring move. He was standing directly beside one of the smugglers, and as soon as the light went out he sprang at the fellow, dashing the revolver from his grasp. It clattered on the floor.

"Help!" roared the fellow, as they grappled together.

Fenton Hardy had also been watching for his chance, and he sprang through the darkness at Snackley. He collided heavily with the chief of the smugglers and they rolled on the floor in a desperate struggle.

It was impossible to distinguish friend from enemy in the darkness. Joe plunged into the midst of the surging figures and his fist smashed against the face of one of the smugglers, who gave a howl of pain.

Then, outside the house, another uproar burst forth.

Some one was banging on the front door. Men could be heard shouting to one another.

Snackley made a desperate effort and managed to get to his feet. He struck out with both fists and managed to break free from the detective. He whirled to one side, stumbled out into the kitchen, and then reached the back door. He flung the door open.

Almost instantly a dark figure appeared in the doorway. It was the figure of a man in the uniform of a state trooper with drawn revolver and Snackley shouted the warning to the smugglers in the other room.

"The police!" he roared. "Every man for himself! Make your getaway!"

The trooper shot through the doorway at him, but Snackley dodged to one side. There was a rush of footsteps from the other room as the rest of the smugglers raced out into the kitchen. The officers tried to hold them back, but they were too many for him and he was hurled against the wall.

Utter confusion prevailed. The place was in absolute darkness and out in the yard shots, shouts and hoarse imprecations mingled in an indescribable uproar.

One of the smugglers managed to reach the shed. He flung open the trap-door and descended the steps. Some of his companions followed, and in the darkness and excitement their escape was unnoticed.

Half a dozen police officers were in the yard. They had been attracted to the house by the sound of the shots when the Hardys were pursued by the smugglers, and they had planned to surround the place. They would have succeeded in capturing the entire gang had it not been for the man on guard outside.

Back in the living room of the house Frank was still struggling with his antagonist. The man was strong and heavy, a rough-and-tumble fighter, and the boy soon found that he had his hands full. They struggled desperately in the darkness, the smuggler frantic with the fear of capture, Frank grimly resolved that the man should not get away.

Fenton Hardy headed toward the door leading into the kitchen. Just then a figure brushed by him. He made a grab for the man, but the fellow evaded him and raced toward the other side of the room.

The detective gave chase. The fugitive kicked open a door and ran toward the front of the house. Mr. Hardy could follow him quite easily by the sound of his footsteps.

The fugitive scurried into a front room and banged the door behind him. Mr. Hardy launched himself against the door, which had a lock that snapped when the door shut. For a moment he was balked. Then he stepped back a few paces and rushed at the door, plunging against it with his shoulder. The woodwork splintered. Another rush, and the door fell open. The detective reeled into the room.

His fugitive had disappeared.

But the room was faintly lighted, as there was a wide window, and in the gloom the detective could see a dark patch in the floor. It was a trapdoor leading evidently to the cellar.

He went down through the opening, finding a flight of stairs which he descended. He could hear footsteps receding through the darkness but he made his way across the uneven floor of the cellar.

The detective stopped and listened. He heard the hurrying footsteps as the smuggler went on to the far end of the cellar. Then, to his great surprise, he heard a voice. In the distance he saw a faint glow of light. Then he saw that the cellar was divided into two parts and that the fugitive had entered a small room.

He crept closer.

"What's happening?" he heard some one say in a weak voice.

"Everything," snarled a voice which he recognized as that of Snackley. The detective's heart leaped. "Everything is happening. The police are here."

"The police!"

"Yes—the police—state troopers, federal officers and all. But don't think you're going to have a chance of squealing on us. I'm going to fix you, as I should have done a long while ago."

The other voice rose, replete with terror.

"No! No! You won't do that, Snackley! Let me live!"

Fenton Hardy crept swiftly over to the door. He saw Snackley standing by a small cot in a cell-like room. On the cot crouched a haggard man whose hands were handcuffed behind him. His feet were shackled to one leg of the iron cot.

Snackley, with a grim look of cruelty on his face, was raising a heavy club he had picked up.

There was no time to lose. The detective sprang through the doorway.

He plunged at Snackley just as the smuggler raised the club to strike.

Snackley reeled against the wall, with Fenton Hardy at his throat. Desperately, the smuggler tried to raise the weapon, but the detective had seized his wrist. They swayed to and fro, stumbling about on the muddy floor. Mr. Hardy had the advantage in that he had taken Snackley by surprise. He pinned the smuggler against the wall, twisting his wrist. The club fell to the floor.

Snackley plunged forward and they lost their footing, rolling about in the mud. Suddenly, Fenton Hardy wrenched his arm free, sprawled over and managed to seize Snackley's revolver. He pressed it against Snackley's side.

The smuggler gave in. He flung his arms above his head.

"I'm licked," he muttered sullenly.

They got slowly to their feet, Fenton Hardy keeping a watchful eye on the captive. Upstairs they could hear the uproar continuing as the police still gave battle to the smugglers.

"Upstairs!" snapped the detective curtly. Without taking his eyes off Snackley he said to the man on the cot.

"We'll come back for you later—Mr. Jones."

CHAPTER XXIV

THE ROUND-UP

The Hardy boys, in the meantime, were in the thick of the struggle.

Frank fought desperately with the smuggler he had assailed in the living room of the house, while Joe raced across the yard toward the trapdoor leading to the underground caves. He found that although three of the smugglers had been captured by officers in the yard and that as many more were fighting to escape, none of the police had as yet learned of the trapdoor down which some of the men had disappeared.

With a shout to a near-by officer who had just succeeded in clapping the handcuffs on one of the smugglers, Joe made his way down the stairs. He heard the officer running over to the edge of the trap and saw the gleam of the flashlight.

"Some of them got out this way!" Joe shouted back to the officer.

The man called to one of his companions and then footsteps clattered on the stairs as Joe went on.

He reached the door that opened into the chamber where his father had been a prisoner, but on entering the room he found it empty. There were evidences of hasty flight and the door on the far side of the room was wide open.

"Secret passages, eh!" exclaimed one of the officers, as he came into the room. He was a state trooper in uniform.

Joe led the way out through the opposite door and down the stairs that led toward the bottom of the cliff. The trooper who had spoken illuminated the way with his flashlight and they clattered on down the stairs until they reached the storage room. Here, everything was in confusion. The escaping smugglers had evidently endeavored to take with them what goods they could, probably the smaller packages containing drugs, for boxes and parcels were overturned and strewn about the floor.

"You seem to know this place pretty well," said one of the troopers, as Joe led the way across to the opposite door and stepped out onto the landing.

"I've been here before—got in this way," he answered. "There's a water cave below this passage. They've probably made their getaway in the boat."

They hastened down the passageway and came at last to the cave. As Joe expected, the boat was gone.

"They got away," he said, in disappointment, as the trooper turned the flashlight on to the channel between the rocks.

There was a shout from the darkness of the cove.

"Give us a light!" they heard.

Joe gave a shout of joy. It was Tony Prito's voice!

Then Joe and the troopers with him heard the steady beat of a motorboat.

Joe seized the flashlight and ran out along the path leading to the entrance of the cave.

The motorboat was not many yards away. Tony had been searching for the channel.

"Right this way!" Joe called out. "Head toward the right of the cave and you'll be in deep water. A little further! Good!"

As the motorboat drew nearer he saw that it was filled with men and that a rowboat was being towed behind.

"We got 'em," cried Tony exultantly. "They were just getting out of the cove in the boat when we came up."

"Who is with you?" asked Joe.

"Police. The rest of them went up the shore road in a car."

"We've caught the whole gang then. They raided the house and got the rest of the smugglers. We thought these fellows had made a getaway."

"No chance. Although it was mighty close. They pretty nearly slipped out of the cove right under our noses."

The boat came to a stop beside the natural wharf of rock. One or two of the officers, revolvers in hand, clambered out. Three of the smugglers had been captured while trying to escape from the cove in the rowboat.

"If they'd got out we would never have caught them," said Joe. "They were heading out toward a ship."

"A ship!" exclaimed one of the officers, a burly man in plain clothes. He stepped forward. "Did they say anything about a ship?"

"A man named Li Chang has a ship lying in wait outside the bay," said Joe. "I heard them talking about it."

"Good!" exclaimed the burly man. "Now we'll capture the whole outfit." He turned to Tony. "I suppose your boat is good for another little run."

"I'll say it is, sir!"

"I want as many officers as we can spare," said the burly man. "We'll go out and find that ship. Li Chang, did you say?" he added, turning to Joe.

"That was the name."

"I know his ship. We've been trying to catch that villain for years. Darst, go on up and see how the rest of the men made out at the house on the cliff and take as many officers as they can spare. There's a passage up through the rocks, I take it?"

"Regular staircase all the way, sir," remarked Darst, one of the raiding officers.

"Good! Don't lose any time."

The three smugglers were taken out of the boat and handcuffed, then escorted up the stairs, while the burly man, who was the chief of a squad of federal agents undertaking a drive against the smugglers on that part of the coast, remained with the motorboat.

Within a short time Darst returned with three more officers. He reported that a clean sweep had been made at the house.

"They have 'em all handcuffed and sittin' in the kitchen," he said. "Mr. Hardy got Snackley—"

"Snackley?" exclaimed the federal man. "Is it *his* gang?"

"Yes, sir. He got Snackley in the cellar. One of his sons tackled Red-head Blount, one of Snackley's sidekicks, and held him down until the police came in. When we brought our three in, that finished the round-up."

"It does, so far. We're going out and grab Li Chang from that ship and that'll clean everything up."

The officers got into the motorboat and Joe clambered in beside Tony Prito, who was at the wheel. The craft backed out of the channel into the deeper water of the cove, then sped out into Barmet Bay.

"Once we get out of the bay we should see her lights," said the federal officer. "Li Chang probably has his ship anchored just off the coast."

This proved to be the case. The lights of the vessel were soon descried and the motorboat sped toward it through the night.

When the boat drew alongside, the federal man roared out:

"Ahoy, there!"

A voice answered in Chinese.

"Speak English!" roared the officer. "Throw over a ladder or we'll open fire on you."

"Who there?"

"The police."

Jabbering voices and running footsteps suddenly created a commotion. One of the troopers fired his revolver into the air and very promptly a ladder was lowered over the side of the vessel.

"That's better!" said the federal man, as he clambered up over the rail, revolver in hand. "I'll just talk to your skipper for a minute."

The capture of Li Chang was without incident. When he was told that Snackley and the gang were captured, the Chinaman, who was a small, wizened little fellow with a villainous countenance, blandly submitted to arrest and consented to be taken ashore. There were only two or three members of the crew aboard, the others having shore leave; so two of the federal men were left in charge of the ship until relief could be sent from Bayport, and the motorboat made its way back to the cove.

The round-up was complete. Snackley's smuggling gang had been completely broken up.

CHAPTER XXV
THE MYSTERY EXPLAINED

The Hardy boys were the heroes of Bayport when the news of the capture of Snackley and his men spread throughout the city next day. As for Tony Prito, he was the envy of all the chums of the two lads.

"Tony had all the luck," bemoaned Chet Morton, as the boys were all sitting in the barn back of the Hardy home next afternoon. This barn, which had been fitted up as a gymnasium, was a meeting place for the lads on occasions of importance.

"We had to have a motorboat," said Frank. "Believe me, I was wishing more than once that the whole crowd was along."

"And you'll get the reward for capturing Snackley?" asked Phil Cohen.

"Not all of it. Dad gets half. Joe and I split the rest."

"You haven't any kick coming. What's going to happen to Snackley?"

"He'll probably go to the electric chair," answered Frank soberly.

"Why?"

"He murdered Felix Polucca, the miser."

"Murdered him?"

"Yes. Dad found that out in his investigations. Dad suspected all along that there was some connection between Snackley and the house on the cliff, especially when he found that Snackley and Polucca had been related. He went out to find out what he could, but the smugglers saw him and captured him."

"What about that fellow they had imprisoned in the cellar?" questioned Biff Hooper. "Didn't you say Snackley was just going to kill him when your father saved him?"

"That was the young fellow we saved in the bay that day. The young chap who told us his name was Jones. It wasn't his real name, at all. His name is Yates and he was one of the smugglers."

"Why was Snackley chasing him that day?" asked Perry Robinson.

"It seems that Yates got angry because he didn't get his full share of the money from the last smuggling trip, so he threatened to tell the police on Snackley. The smugglers locked him up, but he got away in one of the motorboats, so they chased him and ran him down. They thought to have killed him in the explosion or else drown him, but Joe and I managed to bring him ashore. We left him at the Kane farmhouse, but the smugglers came along next day and kidnapped him. They kept him prisoner in the cellar of the Polucca place after that."

"I still can't understand about those yells and shrieks we heard the first day we were out at the farmhouse," put in Phil Cohen.

"That was just to frighten us away. One of the men in the gang is a sort of half-wit and they had him posted there to frighten people off by yelling and shrieking whenever any one showed up around the place. He was the chap who stole our tools from the motorcycles," explained Frank.

"But after our visit there," added Joe, "they thought it was too dangerous and that there might be an investigation, so they put Redhead and his wife and one of their men there to pose as renters of the place."

"So there weren't any ghosts after all," exclaimed Jerry Gilroy.

"Nary a ghost," laughed Frank, "Snackley explained everything this morning in a confession. The whole gang is locked up, even to Li Chang. Yates, the young fellow they had kept prisoner so long, told the whole story first. He turned state's evidence and told how long the smuggling had been going on, how Snackley had made use of the house on the cliff after killing Polucca, how he fixed up the tunnels in the cliff—he told everything. It seems that Polucca had the smuggling idea in the first place and he spent years fixing up those caves and tunnels. When everything was ready, he called in Snackley, but Snackley didn't like to share with any one who had a right to a voice in the affair, so he killed the old man, took his money, and brought the smuggling gang in there."

"Yates told all that?"

"He told so much of it that Snackley saw there was no use bluffing any longer, so he admitted the whole story."

"Gosh!" sighed Chet. "Just my luck! I was there in time to get scared to death by that half-wit, and there in time to get bawled out and chased off the farm by Redhead and his wife, but I missed out on all the fun at the last."

"Not much fun about it," declared Joe. "It didn't seem funny to us when the smugglers caught us in the cave just as we were getting dad free."

"And it wasn't any fun hiding in that attic with the bullets coming through the floor, nineteen to the dozen," added Frank. "I thought every minute was going to be my last."

"No, I guess it wasn't any too funny then," admitted Chet. "You deserve every cent you get out of the reward."

"We'll treat the whole gang to a feed as soon as we collect," Joe promised.

"Whee!" shouted Chet, turning a handspring. "Now you're talking!"

The Hardy boys kept their word. Soon after they had received their share of the reward, which was presented to them with many glowing words and congratulations from the federal authorities who had long been trying to put Snackley behind the bars, they gave a dinner in the barn that eclipsed any similar "feed" in the history of Bayport.

"I hope the Hardy boys solve a mystery every week," said Chet, as he confronted his third dish of ice-cream. "And I hope they celebrate every success the same way."

The Hardy boys were not destined to solve a mystery every week, but it was not long before they were plunged into a maze of events which were fully as exciting as those which led to the finding of the tower treasure and those that followed their first visit to the house on the cliff. The story of their adventures will be told in the next volume of this series, called, "The Hardy Boys: The Secret of the Old Mill."

Tony Prito, conscious of the envying glances of the other lads because he had participated in the eventful climax to the mystery of the house on the cliff, scooped up the last of his ice-cream and said:

"Once I wanted my father to buy an automobile and he bought a motor-boat instead. Now he wants to sell the boat and buy an automobile. Just let him try it! That boat gave me more fun in one day than I'd ever had since we came to the States."

THE SECRET OF
THE OLD MILL

ORIGINALLY PUBLISHED IN 1927.

CHAPTER I

A FIVE DOLLAR BILL

The afternoon express from the north steamed into the Bayport station to the usual accompanying uproar of clanging bells from the lunch room, shouting redcaps, and a bellowing train announcer.

Among the jostling, hurrying crowd on the platform were two pleasant-featured youths who scanned the passing coaches expectantly.

"I don't see him," said Frank Hardy, the older of the pair, as he watched the passengers descending from one of the Pullman coaches.

"Perhaps he stopped at some other town and intends coming in on the local. It's only an hour later," suggested his brother Joe.

The boys waited. They had met the train expecting to greet their father, Fenton Hardy, the nationally famous detective, who had been away from home for the past two weeks on a murder case in New York. It appeared that they were to be disappointed. When the last of the Bayport passengers had left the train Fenton Hardy was not among them.

"We'll come back and meet the local," said Frank at last.

The brothers were about to turn away and retrace their steps down the platform when they saw a tall, well-dressed stranger swing himself down from the steps of the nearest coach. He was a man of about thirty, dark and clean-shaven, and he hastened over toward them.

"I want to pay a fellow a dollar out of this five," remarked the stranger, as he came up to the boys. "Can you change the bill?"

At the same time he produced a five dollar bill from his pocket and held it out inquiringly.

He was a pleasant-spoken young man and he was evidently in a hurry.

"I could try the lunch room, I suppose, but there's such a crowd that I'll have trouble being waited on," he explained, the bill fluttering in his hands.

Frank looked at his brother and began feeling in his pockets.

"I've got three dollars, Joe. How about you?"

Joe dug up the loose change in his possession. There was a dollar bill, a fifty-cent piece and three quarters.

"Two dollars and a quarter," he announced. "I guess we can make it."

He handed over two dollars to Frank, who added it to the three dollars of his own and gave the money to the stranger, who gave Frank the five dollar bill in exchange.

"Thanks, ever so much," said the young man. "You've saved me a lot of trouble. My friend is getting off at this station and I wanted to give him the dollar before he left. Thanks."

"Don't mention it," replied Frank carelessly, putting the bill in his pocket. "We'll get it changed between us."

The young man nodded, smiled at them and hastened back up the steps of the coach, with a carefree wave of his hand.

"I'm glad we were able to help him out," observed Joe. "It was just by chance that I had that small change too. Mother gave me some money to buy some pie-plates."

"Pie-plates!" exclaimed Frank, with a grin. "There's nothing I'd rather see coming into the house than more pie-plates. More pie-plates mean more pie."

"We might as well go down and get them now, before I forget. There's a shop down the street and we can get the plates and get this five dollar bill changed. It'll help kill time before the local comes in."

The two lads went down the platform, out through the station to the main street of Bayport, basking in the summer sunlight. They were healthy, normal American boys of high school age. Frank, being a year older than his brother, was slightly taller. He was slim and dark, while his brother was somewhat stouter of build, with fair, curly hair. As they strolled down the street they received and returned many greetings, for both boys were well-known and popular in Bayport.

Before they reached the store they heard the shriek of the whistle and the clanging of the bell that indicated that the express was resuming its southward journey.

"Our friend can travel in peace," remarked Frank. "He got his five changed anyway."

"And the other fellow got his dollar. Everybody's happy."

They reached the store and paused outside the entrance to examine an assortment of baseball bats, discussing the relative merits and weights of each, then poked around in a tray of mitts, trying them on and agreeing that none equaled the worn and battered mitts they had at home. Finally they entered the shop, where they were greeted by the proprietor, a chubby and genial man named Moss. Mr. Moss was sitting on the counter reading a newspaper, for business was dull that afternoon, but he cast the sheet aside when they came in.

"Looking for clues?" he asked humorously, as they came in.

As sons of Fenton Hardy, and as amateur detectives of some ability in their own right, the boys were frequently the butt of jesting remarks concerning their hobby, but they invariably took them in the spirit of good-natured raillery in which they were meant.

"No clues here," continued Mr. Moss. "You won't find a single, solitary clue in the place. I had a crate of awfully nice bank robbery clues in yesterday, but they've all been snapped up. I expect some nice murder clues in tomorrow morning, if you'd care to wait that long. Or perhaps you'd like me to order you a few kidnapping clues. Size eight and a half, guaranteed not to wear, tear or tarnish."

Mr. Moss rattled on, with an air of great gravity, burst into a roar of laughter at his own joke, then swung his feet against the side of the counter.

"Well, boys, what'll it be?" he asked, rubbing his eyes, as the two brothers grinned at him. "What can I do for you?"

"We want some pie-plates," said Joe. "Three."

"Small ones, I suppose," said Mr. Moss, then chuckled hugely as the boys looked at him in indignation.

"I should say not," returned Frank. "The biggest you've got."

Mr. Moss laughed very much at this also, and swung himself down from the counter and went in search of the pie-plates. He returned eventually with three that seemed to be of the required size and quality.

"Wrap 'em up," said Frank, throwing the five dollar bill on the counter.

Mr. Moss wrapped up the plates, then picked up the bill and went over to the cash register. He rang up the amount of the sale and was about to put the money in the till when he suddenly hesitated, then held the bill up to the light. Slowly, he came back to the counter, rubbing the bill between thumb and forefinger, feeling its texture and minutely examining the surface.

"Where did you get this bill, boys?" he asked seriously.

"We just changed it for a stranger on the train," answered Frank. "What's the matter with it?"

"Looks bad to me," replied Mr. Moss dubiously. "I'm afraid I can't take a chance on it."

He handed the bill back to Frank, then indicated the package on the counter.

"What are you going to do about the plates?" he asked. "Have you any other money besides that bill?"

"Not a nickel," said Joe. "At least, not enough to pay for the plates. But do you really think the bill is no good?"

"I've handled a lot of them. It doesn't look good to me. I tell you what you'd better do. Take it over to the bank across the street and ask the cashier what he thinks of it."

The boys looked at one another in dismay. It had never occurred to them that there might be anything wrong with the money. Now it dawned on them that there had been something suspicious about the affable stranger's request. Had they really been victimized?

"We'll do that," agreed Frank. "Come on, Joe. Keep those plates for us, Mr. Moss. If the bill is bad we'll be back with some real money later on."

They crossed the street to the bank and went up to the cashier's cage. They knew the cashier well and he smiled at them as Frank pushed the five dollar bill under the grating.

"Want it changed?" he asked.

"We want to know if it's good, first."

The cashier, a sharp-featured, elderly man with spectacles, then took a sharp glance at the bill. He pursed up his lips as he felt the texture of the paper. Then he flicked the bill across to them again.

"Sorry," he said. "You've been stung, boys. It's counterfeit."

"Counterfeit!" exclaimed Frank.

"You aren't the first one who has been fooled. There's been a lot of counterfeit money going around the past few days. It's very cleverly done and it's apt to fool any one who isn't used to handling a lot of bills. Where did you get it?"

"A fellow got off the train and asked us to change it for him."

The cashier nodded.

"And by now he is miles away, probably getting ready to work the same trick at the next station. I guess you'll have to pocket your loss, boys. It's tough luck."

CHAPTER II

COUNTERFEIT MONEY

The Hardy boys left the bank, feeling at once foolish and wrathful.

"Stung!" declared Frank. "Stung by a counterfeit bill! Oh, if the fellows hear of this we'll never hear the end of it!"

"What a fine pair of greenhorns we must have looked to that slick stranger! I'd like to lay my hands on him for about five seconds. I'll bet he's been laughing to himself ever since about how easily we were fooled."

"I'll say we were easy. We hadn't a suspicion in the world."

"After all," Joe remarked, "that bill might have fooled any one. You can't deny that it looks mighty like a real five."

They halted on the corner and again examined the money. Only an experienced eye could have detected any difference between the counterfeit bill and a genuine one. It was crisp and new and appeared in every respect identical with any bona fide five dollar bill that had ever been legitimately issued by the Federal Government.

"If we were dishonest we could palm this off on almost any one, just as we had it palmed off on us," said Joe. "Oh, well—live and learn. I hate to think of that fellow laughing at us, though. It's a nice price to pay for a lesson not to be too trustful of strangers after this."

"It cost me more than it cost you," Frank pointed out. "It was just my luck that I had three dollars on me and you had only two."

This phase of the matter had not occurred to Joe before, so he felt considerably more cheerful in the thought that he had not, after all, been the chief loser.

They went back to the store and dolefully reported to Mr. Moss that he had been right in his surmise about the bill.

"It was bad, all right," Frank told him. "The cashier took one look at it, and that was enough."

Mr. Moss nodded sympathetically.

"Well, it's too bad you were stung," he said. "But I'd rather it was you than me. In business, we have to be careful. As a matter of fact, I think it would have fooled me, only the bank warned me this morning that there was some counterfeit money going around and that I'd better be on my guard against any new bills. The minute I saw your five was fresh and new I got suspicious. It's certainly a clever imitation. Whoever is putting the stuff out is a real artist at that game."

"We'll be back for the pie-plates later," promised Joe. "But we didn't want you to think we were trying to pass bad money on you."

Mr. Moss laughed at the idea.

"The Hardy boys pass counterfeit money!" he exclaimed. "I know you better than that, I hope. I'll keep the plates for you, or you can take them now and bring back the money later. *Good* money, though," he added, wagging his finger at them.

"We'll be back," they told him.

They went toward the station to wait for the local train on which they expected their father to arrive, and while they waited, sitting on a platform bench, they gloomily discussed the imposition of which they had been the victims.

"It isn't so much losing my three dollars," declared Frank. "It's the thought of being fooled by such a simple trick. We should have known that the fellow had plenty of time to get his money changed at the lunch counter or at the cigar stand, or even the ticket office. Instead of that we dug into our pockets like lambs—"

"Lambs don't have pockets," Joe pointed out.

"All the better for them. They're so innocent they'd be fleeced of everything they put in 'em. anyway. Just like us. We handed over all our money to a total stranger and let him give us a bad bill that we didn't even take the trouble to look at. I wish somebody would kick me all around the block."

While the Hardy boys are sitting on the bench, gloomily awaiting the arrival of their father and preparing to tell him of how they had been fooled by the stranger, it will not be out of place to introduce them still further to the readers of this volume.

As related in the first volume of this series, "The Hardy Boys: The Tower Treasure," Frank and Joe Hardy were the sons of Fenton Hardy, a private detective of international fame. Mr. Hardy, who had been for many years on the New York police force and who had later resigned to carry on a private detective practice, was a criminologist of note. He knew by sight and by reputation most of the notorious criminals of his day, and his mastery over all the branches of his profession was such as to place him at the very forefront of American detectives. So great had been the demand for his services in solving the mysteries of crimes that had baffled the detective forces of other cities that he had found it much more lucrative to carry on a practice of his own than to remain attached to the service in any one city, even such a city as the great American metropolis.

Fenton Hardy, with his wife, Laura Hardy, and their two sons, Frank and Joe, had accordingly moved to Bayport, a city of about fifty thousand inhabitants, situated on Barmet Bay, on the Atlantic Ocean. There Frank and Joe had gone to school until now they were in the Bayport high school. Both boys were fully conscious of the fame of their father and were eager to follow in his footsteps, although their mother had expressed a desire that they fit themselves for some less hazardous and more conventional profession.

However, the Hardy boys had inherited much of their father's ability and deductive talent. Already they had aided in solving two mysteries that had kept Bayport by the ears. As related in "The Hardy Boys: The Tower Treasure," they had solved the mystery of the theft of valuable jewels and bonds from Tower Mansion, after even Fenton Hardy himself had been unable to discover where the thief had hidden the loot. In the second volume of the series, "The Hardy Boys: The House on the Cliff," has been told how the Hardy boys discovered the haunt of a gang of smugglers who were operating in Barmet Bay. In this case they had received a substantial reward, as Federal agents had tried in vain to locate the smugglers' base of activities for many months.

Following the adventures at the house on the cliff an uneventful winter and spring had passed, the brothers devoting themselves to their studies and to an occasional winter holiday. Christmas had come with many presents, and now warm weather was once more at hand.

Because of the pride they took in their achievements as amateur detectives, the Hardy boys felt very keenly the ignominy of being so easily fooled by the stranger who had passed the counterfeit money upon them.

"Dad will have the laugh on us now," muttered Joe, as they heard the distant whistle of the approaching train.

"Well, we'll tell him about it, anyway. Who knows but what a big case might arise out of this?"

The afternoon local pulled into the station, and Fenton Hardy stepped down from the parlor car, bag in hand, light coat over one arm. He was a tall, dark-haired man of about forty years of age. He had a quick, pleasant smile for his sons and he shook hands with them warmly.

"How's mother?" he asked, after the first greetings.

"She's fine," replied Frank. "She said there'd be something special for supper tonight, seeing you're back."

"Good! And what have you two been doing? Kept out of mischief, I hope."

"Well, we've kept out of mischief," said Joe; "but we haven't kept out of trouble."

"What's the matter?"

"We just got fooled by a smart stranger who stepped off the express. It cost us five dollars."

"How did that happen?"

"He asked us to change a five dollar bill for him—"

"Ah, ha!" exclaimed Fenton Hardy, raising his eyebrows. "And what then?"

"It was counterfeit."

Mr. Hardy looked grave.

"Have you got it with you?"

"Yes," answered Frank, producing the bill. "I don't think we can be blamed such an awful lot for being fooled. It certainly looks mighty like a good one."

Fenton Hardy put down his bag and examined the bill closely for a moment. Then he folded it up and put it in his waistcoat pocket.

"I'll take care of this, if you don't mind," he said, picking up his bag and beginning to walk toward the station exit. "As it happens, I know something about this money."

"What do you mean, dad?" asked Frank quickly.

"I don't mean that I know anything about this particular five dollar bill, but I know something about this counterfeit money in general. As a matter of fact, that is why this trip took me longer than I had thought it would. When I finished the case that originally took me away, the Government called me in on this counterfeit money case."

"Is there a lot of it going around?"

"Too much. Within the past few weeks the East has been flooded with it, and the circulation seems to be spreading. There seems to be a central counterfeiting plant somewhere, with experts in charge of it, and they are turning out imitation bills so clever that the average person can hardly detect them. The Federal authorities are worrying a great deal about it."

"And this is one of the bills?"

"It looks just like some of the others that have been turned in, although chiefly they have been dealing in tens and twenties. The man who stepped off the train was probably one of their agents, trying to convert as much of the counterfeit money into good cash as he could. When he saw that you were only boys he thought there would be a better chance of getting change for five dollars than ten. Then, of course, he may only have been some one who had been fooled by the counterfeit and decided to get rid of it by passing it on to some one else."

"I wish he had asked us to change one of his counterfeit tens, instead," mourned Joe. "We would have been five dollars to the good."

CHAPTER III

THE HARDY BOYS AT SCHOOL

If the boys had any lingering hopes that their school chums would not hear of the manner in which they had been fooled, these hopes were quickly removed next morning.

Scarcely had Frank and Joe ascended the concrete steps of Bayport High than Chet Morton, a stout chubby boy of about sixteen, one of their closest friends, a lad with a passion for practical jokes, came solemnly toward them with a green tobacco coupon in his hand.

"Just the fellows I'm looking for," he chirped. "My great-grandmother just died in Abyssinia and I'm trying to raise the railway fare to go to the funeral. How about changing this hundred?"

There was a roar of laughter from about a dozen boys who were standing about, for Chet had evidently acquainted them all with the affair of the previous day. How he had learned of it, Frank and Joe could not imagine. They grinned good-naturedly, although Joe blushed furiously.

"What's the matter?" asked Chet innocently. "Can't you change it? You don't mean to tell me you can't change my hundred dollar bill? Please, kind young gentlemen, please change my hundred dollar bill, for if you don't I'm sure nobody else will and then I won't be able to go to my great-grandmother's funeral in Abyssinia." He wiped away an imaginary tear.

"Sorry," said Frank gravely. "We're not in the money-changing business."

"You mean you're not in it any more," pointed out Chet. "You were in the business yesterday, I know. What's the matter—retire on your profits?"

"Yes, we quit."

"I don't blame you." Suddenly Chet struck an attitude of exaggerated surprise. "Why, bless my soul, I do believe this bill is bad!" He peered at the flimsy tobacco coupon very closely, then whipped a small magnifying glass from his pocket and squinted through it. At last he raised his head, with a sigh. "Yes, sir, it's bad. It's counterfeit. One of the cleverest counterfeits I ever saw. If it hadn't been for the fact that there is no hundred dollar mark on it and if it hadn't been that there is a picture of the president of the El Ropo Tobacco Company instead of George Washington, I'd have been completely fooled. Isn't it lucky that you boys didn't change it for me? Isn't it lucky? Congratulations, young sirs. Congratulations!"

He shook Frank and Joe warmly by the hand, in the meantime keeping a very solemn face, while the other lads surged about in a laughing group and joined in the "kidding."

They jested unmercifully about the incident of the counterfeit five dollars, but the Hardy boys took it all in good part. The news had leaked out through Mr. Moss, who had told Jerry Gilroy, one of the Hardy boys' chums, about the affair just a short while after they had left the store the previous afternoon. Jerry had lost no time acquainting Chet and the others with the details.

"If you keep on changing money for strangers, you won't have much left out of those rewards," declared Phil Cohen, a diminutive, black-haired Jewish boy who was one of their friends. He was referring to the money the Hardy boys had received in rewards for their work in the Tower Mansion case and for helping run down the smugglers.

"Oh, I guess we still have a few dollars," replied Frank smilingly. "We have enough in the bank to buy a motorboat with, anyway."

"What's that?" asked Chet quickly. "Are you getting a motorboat?"

The Hardy boys nodded. Their chums were immediately interested.

"Put me down for one of the first passengers," shouted "Biff" Hooper, a tall, broad-shouldered boy who had just pushed his way through the circle.

"We're thinking of getting one like Tony Prito's," said Joe.

"I wish it was mine!" exclaimed Tony. His father, one of the most respected citizens in the Italian colony of Bayport, owned a speedy motorboat which had proved of great service to the Hardy boys in their conflict with the smugglers of Barmet Bay. "But if you're getting a boat at all you can't do any better than get one just like it."

"Dad told us last night we could get one as long as we stayed in the bay and along the coast with it. He was afraid we might get ambitious and try crossing the Atlantic."

"Well," remarked Jerry Gilroy, "I see where our summer baseball league is shot to pieces now."

"Why?"

"You'll be out in that boat every minute of your spare time. It was bad enough when you had the motorcycles. You were both always roaming around the country on them, but now we'll never be able to find you at all. There goes the best pitcher and shortstop of my team together."

Jerry looked very glum as he said this, for he was an ardent ball fan and he had been much in the forefront in organizing a league for the summer months. Frank Hardy was one of the best pitchers in the school, and Joe could cover short in a manner that was the envy of his companions, but in spite of their natural ability for the game, the Hardy boys had always shown a preference for outings instead of baseball.

"I'd rather go out for a whole day on a motorcycle or in a motorboat than play a dozen ball games," said Frank.

This was rank heresy to Jerry, who could not bear any reflections on his beloved game.

"Gosh, I don't know what's to become of you two! Can't I count on you for any games at all?"

"Sure you can," promised Frank. "We're not going to *live* in the motorboat."

"If you go fooling around Barmet Reefs on a stormy day in the old tub you'll *die* in it, though," snickered Chet.

"That'll be about enough from you," warned Frank, giving him a friendly dig in the ribs. Then, turning to Jerry, he went on: "We'll play on your team, but we won't spend all our time outside of meal-hours in practising."

"Well, I suppose I should be satisfied. We can't have everything. But I'd imagine you'd *like* to practise."

"They don't need to," declared Chet. "That's why you have to spend all your spare time learning how to catch. Even now you're not much good at it." He winked at Tony Prito, who was standing behind Jerry. "Why, I'll bet you can't catch a measly little fly—like this—look—"

He took a baseball out of his pocket and threw it lightly into the air. It did not go very high and it was a ridiculously easy catch for any one. As for Jerry Gilroy, who was really a star outfielder, it was scarcely worth the effort. He had but to step back a pace and the ball was his.

"Can't I?" he said, somewhat nettled by Chet's words. The ball arched through the air and descended directly toward him. He stepped back, prepared to make the easy catch.

But Tony Prito had caught Chet's wink and knew what it meant, for they had carefully rehearsed the trick between them. As soon as Chet had thrown the ball, Tony knelt on his hands and knees on the grass immediately behind Jerry. For all his seeming carelessness, Chet had thrown the ball just far enough so that Jerry would have to step back to make the catch.

Jerry collided with the recumbent figure behind him, he staggered, lost his balance and tumbled over Tony Prito, while the baseball thumped into the grass. The other boys, who had seen the joke from the start, laughed uproariously as Jerry picked himself up and betook himself in pursuit of the already fleeing Tony, while Chet, with an air of vast satisfaction, picked up the baseball.

"I knew he couldn't catch it," he said, with all the airy disdain of a minor prophet.

Just then the gong in the main hall of Bayport High began to clang, summoning the students to their classes, and the boys crowded through the wide doorway.

CHAPTER IV

ANOTHER VICTIM

When he took his place in class that morning, Frank Hardy glanced over at the desk, two aisles away, where Callie Shaw was sitting.

Callie, a brown-haired, brown-eyed miss with a quick, vivacious manner, was one of the prettiest girls attending Bayport high school. She was Frank's favorite of all the girls in the city, and each morning he glanced over at her desk and never failed to receive a bright and fleeting smile that somehow made the dusty classroom seem a trifle less drab and monotonous, and when she was not there it always seemed that the day had gotten away to a bad start.

She was there this morning, but she was gazing soberly at her books and she failed to return Frank's glance with her usual smile. This was something so utterly extraordinary that Frank gazed at her, open-mouthed, for a second or so until, recollecting himself, he turned to his own books and proceeded to spend much of the time until recess in a state of helpless wonderment. Like the average boy under such circumstances, he racked his brains trying to recollect what he could have done that might have offended Callie. But there seemed to be no solution to the mystery.

Perhaps she had heard of how he had been fooled by the stranger yesterday. Perhaps she felt contempt for him because he had been so easily outwitted. This was one of his wild surmises, but he rejected it because it was not like Callie to be angry about anything unless there was good reason for her displeasure. At last he gave it up and tried to dismiss the matter from his mind, but several times during the morning he cast covert glances in her direction.

But Callie was plainly worried and downcast. She seldom raised her eyes from her books, she answered the teacher's questions in a most abstracted manner, and altogether it appeared that there was something on her mind beyond schoolwork.

When recess came she walked slowly out of the room, not mingling with the other girls. Frank saw her go outside toward the campus, where she sat down on the grass by herself, watching an impromptu basketball game and declining all requests to join in the fun.

He went over to her and flung himself down on the grass beside the girl.

"What's the matter, Callie?"

She looked up at him and smiled faintly.

"Hello, Frank, where did you drop from?"

"I've been sitting right across from you in school all morning and this is the first time you've noticed that I'm alive."

"I'm sorry, Frank. I didn't mean to be rude. I've got something on my mind this morning, that's all."

"Trouble?"

She nodded.

"What about?"

"Money."

He was puzzled by this remark. Callie lived with her cousin, Miss Pollie Shaw, the proprietor of a beauty parlor in the city, and although Miss Shaw was not rich, she made a comfortable living. Therefore, when Frank heard Callie say that she was worried about money he was naturally puzzled. Callie's parents lived in the country, but they sent their daughter frequent remittances to pay the expenses of her education in Bayport.

"What's the matter?" he asked. "Didn't your allowance come?"

"No, it isn't that. I'm all right. It's Pollie. She lost some money. More than she could afford."

"Lost some? How was that?"

"She lost fifty dollars last night."

Frank whistled.

"Whew! That's a lot of money."

"It certainly is. The worst of it is that Pollie had just made the final payment on some new electrical fixtures in the shop and it had left her pretty short of cash. I feel bad about it for her sake."

"How did it happen?"

"A woman came into the store last night and bought some beauty preparations, quite a large order. It amounted to about twelve dollars and she had nothing less than a fifty dollar bill in her purse. Pollie had that much money in the till, for it was near the end of the day, and she didn't like to lose the order, so she changed the bill."

Frank nodded soberly. He knew now what had happened.

"And the money was counterfeit," he said.

"Why, how did you know?" exclaimed Callie.

"I was fooled yesterday myself." Frank then went on to tell Callie how he and Joe had been victimized by the stranger on the station platform. "Dad says there is a lot of this counterfeit money being circulated," he said. "They certainly aren't losing much time in getting rid of it around Bayport. Gee, first a five and now a fifty! I'm sure sorry that Pollie is out that much money."

"Yes, it's a big amount," declared Callie. "Of course, she'll get along, but no one likes to lose that much."

"Did she know the woman?"

"Oh, no. She was a total stranger. She was rather handsome and was well dressed. Pollie didn't suspect anything wrong. As a matter of fact, it wasn't until she picked up the paper after work last night and read that the banks had issued a warning about counterfeit money that she began to think about it. So she called up Mr. Wilkins, who works in one of the banks, and he came over and took a look at the bill. He said right away that it was no good, although he admitted it was so cleverly done that any one might be fooled by it."

"Just what they said about my five. Did Pollie tell the police?"

"I suppose she has told them by now. But she gave me the bill and asked me to turn it over to your father."

"Good! Dad happens to be working along those lines just now. Have you got the bill with you now?"

"It's in my purse in the cloakroom. I'll let you have it at lunch hour."

So when school was dismissed at noon Callie gave Frank the counterfeit fifty dollar bill. Frank examined it closely. Like the five dollar bill he and Joe had changed for the plausible stranger the previous day, it was crisp and new. Frank had seen very few fifty dollar bills in his life, either genuine or otherwise, but he realized that this specimen was a very good imitation. The mere fact that such bills are not often seen by the average person no doubt rendered it easier to pass without being readily detected.

"I'll show this to my father," he promised Callie. "I'm afraid it won't do much good. Pollie will have to stand her loss, unless she can trace the woman who passed the bad bill on her, but perhaps this will help dad find the source of all this counterfeit money."

"Goodness knows how many poor people are being victimized just as Pollie was," said the girl. "I hope they catch the people who are at the bottom of it."

When Joe joined Frank on the school steps Frank told him about the incident at the beauty parlor and of how Pollie Shaw had lost fifty dollars in goods and money to the strange woman.

"Of course," said Frank, "she may have been perfectly innocent in passing that fifty dollar bill, and perhaps she didn't realize it was counterfeit, but I'm beginning to think this gang has a number of people traveling around getting rid of the imitation bills."

"Once they get them into circulation they'll go from hand to hand until the banks check them up. Somebody is bound to lose in the end, and usually it's the honest person who finds out that the money is bad and won't pass it any further. The crooked ones will just try to get rid of it as quickly as they can."

When they reached home Frank told his father about Pollie Shaw and handed over the counterfeit bill.

"So they're dealing in fifties now!" exclaimed Fenton Hardy, as he looked at the money.

"Do you think it's made by the people who turned out that bad five that we got stung on?" Joe asked.

Mr. Hardy drew a magnifying glass from his vest pocket and make a close scrutiny of the bill. "It seems to have been printed on the same press but I'm not sure," he announced at last. "These things are so cleverly done that it would take an expert to notice any differences." He proceeded then to examine the five dollar bill, comparing it closely with the fifty, and at last he put the glass back into his pocket.

"I'm practically certain that these bills were issued from the same press. The paper seems to be of the same kind, just a shade lighter than the paper used in genuine money, and there are certain little differences in the engraving that are almost identical on each bill. Miss Shaw won't mind if I keep this, will she?" he asked Frank.

"She asked me to give it to you."

"I'll send both these bills to an expert in the city and we'll get his opinion on it."

Mrs. Hardy, a pretty, fair-haired woman, sighed.

"I'm sure I don't know what the world's coming to," she said, "when men will make bad money and know that poor people are going to lose by it. It's a shame."

"There's nothing some of them won't stop at when it comes to filling their own pockets," declared her husband. "But perhaps when the expert sends me his report on these bills I'll have something more to work on. If it turns out that there is one central gang circulating this money we'll all have to be on the lookout."

CHAPTER V
CURING THE JOKER

Hard work in school occupied the attention of the boys for the rest of the week, for examination time was near, and even Jerry Gilroy was obliged to dismiss baseball from his mind in a frantic attempt to catch up with his geometry and Latin, that somehow appeared to keep perpetually ahead of him. Frank and Joe sweated over the ablative absolute and grumbled over the heroic exploits that could be resurrected from the deathless lines of Cæsar and Virgil if one could but distinguish verbs from nouns, and wondered, as schoolboys have wondered from time immemorial, why they should be obliged to concern themselves with things that happened two thousand years ago and more when they might better be outside playing.

When Friday night came they emerged from the haze of declensions and vocabularies, axioms and theorems, equations and symbols in which they had been engulfed all week and decided that Saturday should see them as far away from school as possible.

"Let's get out of the city altogether," suggested Frank, as the Hardy boys left the classroom on Friday afternoon. "What say we all go for a hike out into the country?"

"Suits me," agreed Chet. "No motorcycles either. Let's walk."

"Good idea," Jerry Gilroy approved. "Unless," he said hopefully, "you fellows would rather come up to the campus and have baseball practice."

"Another smart remark like that out of you and I'll practise my famous left hook on your jaw," warned Biff Hooper, squaring off in a pugilistic attitude. "We don't want to see or hear of this school again until Monday morning, and that'll be too soon."

"All right, all right," said Jerry placatingly. "I just thought I'd mention it."

"And I just think you'll forget about it," said Chet. "You'll come along on this hike with us. Here, have an apple and keep quiet."

He dug into the inexhaustible recesses of his pockets and produced a slightly shopworn apple, which he thrust into Jerry's hands. "There, see if that'll keep you quiet for a while."

Jerry, who could never resist anything in the nature of food, accepted the donation eagerly.

"Where shall we go on this hike?" he asked, raising the fruit to his lips.

"I was thinking we could go up to Carl Stummer's farm," suggested Joe. "Mother was saying she wondered if Stummer would let her have any cherries to can this year. This would be a good time to ask him."

"Suits me," said Jerry, taking a prodigious bite of the apple.

Then an expression of pained surprise crossed his face to be replaced by a look of ghastly realization. Tears spurted to his eyes and his jaws worked convulsively. Then he emitted a gurgle of agony, spluttered, spat out the apple and began to dance around on the pavement, waving his arms in the air.

"Indian war dance!" commented Chet gravely, clapping his hands. "Fine work, Jerry. Do it again."

"Pepper!" spluttered Jerry. "I'm burning up! Water!"

"Call the fire brigade," advised Chet, bursting into a shriek of laughter.

The other lads gazed at their companion in amazement until his wild antics became too much for them and they all roared as Jerry continued his frantic splutterings. Wildly, the victim turned toward the school again. There was a water fountain near the front door and he headed toward it, but his eyes were so full of tears from the mouthful of red pepper that he had gulped when he bit into the hollow apple that he did not see a flower-bed in his path.

Jerry stumbled over the wire border and sprawled full length among the flowers.

The janitor, a cantankerous individual named MacBane, had been standing near by watching the performance with a broad grin on his usually dour features. But when he saw Jerry fall into his precious flower-bed he gave a roar of fury.

"Awa' wi' ye!" he bellowed. "Awa' frae ma flowers, ye young limb! I'll hae ye reported!"

MacBane always lapsed into broad Scotch when his temper was aroused. The rest of the boys scattered, fearing the wrath to come. Jerry managed to scramble out of the flower-bed just as the janitor reached him. He jumped out of reach of the outstretched hand, with the result that MacBane lost his balance and overstepped the border, treading on some choice blossoms and getting tangled up in the wire.

Jerry made for the fountain and was already taking deep gulps of the cool water when MacBane, now spluttering unintelligible phrases that could only have been understood in the remotest reaches of Caledonia, got out of the flower-bed and thundered toward him. With a longing glance at the spouting water, for his raging thirst was not yet appeased, and with a fearful glance at the approaching janitor, Jerry turned and fled.

He joined his laughing companions at the street corner, and with a shame-faced air admitted that the joke had been on him. MacBane gave up the chase, vowing threats of vengeance on the following Monday.

"He'll forget all about it by then," assured Phil.

"I won't forget about it," declared Jerry. "Next time anybody offers me an apple I'll ask for an orange instead. You can't very well fill *that* with pepper. I'll get even with you, Chet."

"You're welcome to try," replied the practical joker cheerfully. "But in the meantime let's plan this trip for tomorrow."

As a result of their arrangements, the Hardy boys and their chums met in the barn back of the Hardy home early the next morning, all outfitted for a hike into the country. Each lad carried a substantial lunch, their mothers realizing that the noonday meal by the roadside is one of the chief features of such an outing. Phil and Tony were late, and the other boys put in the time by exercising in the Hardy boys' well equipped gymnasium, to which purpose the barn had been converted. Biff Hooper practised left hooks and upper-cuts with desperate intensity and battered the punching bag until it hummed; Chet almost broke his neck attempting some complicated maneuvers on the parallel bars that were meant as an imitation of a circus bareback rider; Jerry contemplated his lunch and wondered if it were too soon after breakfast for a piece of pie.

Phil Cohen and Tony Prito arrived together and the boys started off at last, trudging along the broad highway in the early morning sunlight, whistling away in the best of spirits. They were decorous enough while they were in the city limits, but once they struck the dusty country roads their natural activity asserted itself and they wrestled and tripped one another, ran impromptu races, picked berries by the roadside and laughed and shouted without a care in the world.

The road skirted the Willow River, which ran among the farms and hills back of Bayport, through a pleasant, pastoral country. Toward the middle of the morning the boys left the road and struck out beneath the trees toward a secluded spot on the river, where they enjoyed a swim. For over an hour they splashed about in the cool water. Chet was the first to come ashore, and the others would have remained much longer had it not been for the discovery that their thoughtful companion, after getting dressed, was busying himself in the time-honored pastime of tying their clothes into knots.

Whereupon they scrambled out of the water and chased the chubby one into the shelter of some bushes, whence they were unable to pursue him further because the thorns hurt their bare feet and they were forced to retreat, hopping, toward the river bank while Chet jeered at them from the covert.

"Chaw on the beef!" he cried, in the time-honored way.

"Just you wait!" spluttered Joe, chewing on a knot with all his might.

"Am waiting," was the cheerful retort of the joker.

"We'll skin you alive!" muttered Jerry.

"And salt you," added Frank.

But when they had untied the knots they gave chase and the plump jester was soon winded, although he had a good start. He puffed and panted as they chased him down the road in the dust. They caught up to him at the entrance to the lane leading into Carl Stummer's farm, forcibly divested him of his hiking-boots, socks and necktie and proceeded to wreak revenge.

"We'll cure you of practical jokes for a while," promised Frank, with a grin, as he cast one boot into a field wherein a bad-natured bull was grazing, and the other into a field at the other side of the lane, with a heavy growth of thistles around the fence.

"See if you're as good at untying knots as you are at tying them," added Jerry, as he twisted Chet's necktie into a veritable Chinese puzzle.

"And now see how it feels to walk around in your bare feet," suggested Phil, as he hung one of Chet's socks over the limb of a tree some distance down the road and placed the other in the middle of a clump of brambles.

Biff Hooper and Tony then released the protesting Chet. They had been sitting on him in the middle of the lane while the others were performing their kindly offices. "We'll see you down at the farm," said Biff airily, as the lads went chuckling down the lane in the direction of Stummer's place.

Spluttering and vowing threats, Chet was forced to retrieve his clothes. When he sought to regain his boot from the pasture the bull saw him and rushed toward him with a bellow. Chet, in bare feet, just reached the fence in time and tumbled over into the bushes with the rescued boot. Then he had to step gingerly through the thistle patch in the other field before he could get the other boot. After that he had to climb a tree before he could reach one sock, and go plunging through the brambles before he could regain the other. When the laughing boys last saw him he was sitting by the roadside picking thistles from his feet and gazing hopelessly at his necktie.

"He's cured for a while now," chuckled Joe, as the boys came up into the barnyard of Stummer's farm.

"Cure him? Never!" exclaimed Frank. "He'll be making us all step before the day is out."

CHAPTER VI

THE OLD MILL

Carl Stummer, a lanky, shambling old farmer with drooping shoulders, a drooping mustache and a drooping pipe, was just coming in from the fields when the boys came through the barnyard gate.

How he managed to chew a straw and smoke a pipe perpetually at the same time was always a fascinating mystery, but he could do it and always seemed to derive a great deal of satisfaction from the feat, stopping only to change the straw or fill the pipe at intervals. Some people had been known to have seen him without the straw and some had seen him without the pipe, but no one had ever seen him without one or the other.

Chet Morton always stated it as a grave fact that Carl Stummer slept with his pipe in his mouth and a supply of fresh straws constantly by his bedside and that he changed them in his sleep.

"'Lo, boys!" he called, taking a firmer grip of the pipestem. "And what brings you here?"

"How's the cherry crop, Mr. Stummer?" asked Frank.

"Fair to middlin'," replied Mr. Stummer doubtfully.

This was a good sign, as Carl Stummer was rarely known to express an encouraging opinion about anything. If he said crops were poor, one might be reasonably certain that they were really fair. If he said they were "fair to middlin'" it might be inferred that they were excellent.

"Mother wants to know if you can let her have cherries to can this year."

Mr. Stummer chewed with relish at the straw.

"Most probably she kin," he agreed.

"She wanted to speak for them so that you'd keep her in mind at cherry-picking time."

"I'll remember," promised Stummer. "Mrs. Hardy has always been a good customer of mine. You tell her she can have all of them cherries that she wants."

"Thanks, Mr. Stummer. That's all we called about."

The farmer looked at them. His hands were plunged deep in the pockets of his faded overalls. The straw waggled beneath the drooping mustache.

"Out for a hike?" he ventured.

"Yes. We thought it would be a good day for it."

"Yeah, pretty fair day for hikin'," agreed Mr. Stummer, glancing at the sky to make sure. "Where you thinkin' of goin'?"

"Oh, we don't know. Just around the country."

"Yeah? Not goin' down by the old mill, are you?"

"Turner's old mill?" asked Joe. "Down by the deserted road?"

"That's the place. Down by the river."

"Well, we hadn't thought particularly about going down there. Why do you ask?"

The straw waggled more violently than ever. Mr. Stummer took a long drag at the pipe, which was in imminent danger of going out.

"Oh, I dunno," he said, with a reflective sigh. "Just thought I'd say somethin' about it. I wouldn't go down there if I was you."

"Why not?" inquired Frank. "I know the place is deserted and it's almost falling down, but we can keep out of danger, can't we?"

"It ain't deserted now."

"What do you mean?"

"There's three fellows running the mill now. Funny fellows they are. Been there for a couple of weeks."

The boys looked at one another in surprise. Turner's flour mill was located on a wild part of the Willow River. It had once been on a main road, but the construction of a new highway had left it on a deserted loop which was now seldom traversed. The mill had been abandoned for several years and seemed to have outlived its usefulness. No one had ever expected that the mill wheel would turn again.

"Are they running it as a flour mill?" asked Frank.

Stummer nodded.

"They don't do much outside grindin'. I sent 'em some of my wheat, but their prices was too high. They nearly skinned me alive, so they don't need to expect any more trade from me. I'll send my grain into Bayport after this, where I've always been sendin' it."

"How do they expect to make a living then?"

"They ain't lookin' for trade from the farmers. Matter of fact, I don't think they want it. They told me they're gettin' up some new kind of breakfast foods that the doctors are all goin' to take up. There's somethin' secret about it," went on Stummer, warming to the mystery. "They ain't sayin' anything until they get their patents. Why, they won't even let a man go through the mill."

"Three men, you say?"

"Yeah. Three fellers. Sort of onpleasant lookin' chaps. And there's a boy there too. I forgot about him. Looks somethin' like you," he said, pointing to Joe.

"Have you ever seen any of them before?"

Stummer shook his head.

"I guess they come from the city," he hazarded. "They come away down here so they could be quiet and work at this here breakfast food stuff of theirs without bein' bothered. That's why I said you shouldn't go down there. They don't like people hangin' around."

"Makes me curious to see the place," put in Jerry.

The other boys gave murmurs of agreement.

"Go along if you like," said Stummer, shrugging his shoulders. "It ain't none of my affair. Just thought I'd tell you, that's all. They don't like strangers around."

"We won't bother them," promised Frank. "What do you say, fellows? Should we take a trip around that way or should we not?"

As usual, the mere fact that something of a mystery surrounded the old mill made all the boys eager to turn their steps in that direction.

"We'll go down the old road, anyway," said Joe. "I'd like to get a look at the place. It'll give us somewhere to go."

"Sure," agreed Phil. "We can eat our lunch on the way."

"The vote seems to be in favor of it," said Frank, with a smile.

"Well," drawled Stummer, chewing vigorously at the straw, "don't blame me if you get chased away from the mill. I've warned you."

His eyes twinkled. His whole purpose in telling the lads of the mystery that surrounded the mill had been to send them in that direction, for he realized the attraction the place would have for the boys when they knew that the mill was running again. He was rather curious, too, about the three men who were in charge of the place and he thought that perhaps the boys might pick up some information that he had been unable to get.

"Have a good hike," he said, as he turned to go back to the farmhouse. "Don't get into any trouble."

"We won't," they assured him, and forthwith started back down the lane.

They met Chet, who had by this time managed to retrieve his belongings and was trudging along in the dust meditating ways and means of getting even with his companions. He was not vindictive and he had taken the joke in good part, grinning cheerfully as he saw them approach.

"Think you're pretty smart, don't you?" he said, in mock resentment, as they came near. "I've got so many thistles in my feet you'll have to carry me home now."

With that he began to limp in an exaggerated manner, as though he had been completely crippled by his efforts to regain his socks and shoes.

"We wouldn't carry you to the end of the lane," said Frank promptly. "You'd better keep your feet moving if you want to come with us."

"Where are you going?"

"Down to the old mill. Stummer tells us the place is running again."

"Hurray!" shouted Chet. "I'll race you!" and, forgetting all about his tender foot-soles, he led the crowd in a mad race toward the main road.

CHAPTER VII

IN THE MILL RACE

An hour later, the Hardy boys and their chums reached the vicinity of the old mill.

They had lunch in the shade of the trees along the deserted road, and it was early in the afternoon when they arrived at the top of the hill that over-looked the river.

The old mill was a sturdy structure that had once been strong and impos-ing but was now weatherbeaten and showed the ravages of the years. The mill wheel turned slowly, creaking painfully as though it objected to being forced to labor again after its long rest.

Outside the front door, they could see three figures, two men and a boy. At that distance it was impossible to distinguish their features, but as the lads descended the hillside and drew closer they saw that the men were middle-aged fellows, far from reassuring in appearance.

Because of Stummer's remarks, the Hardy boys and their chums took good care to keep to the shelter of the bushes as they went along the aban-doned roadway, now overgrown with weeds and undergrowth. Their ap-proach was not noticed, and at last they were standing not more than a hun-dred yards away from the mill, effectually concealed by the trees and shrubs.

"I don't like the looks of the men," remarked Frank, in a low voice.

"Neither do I," agreed Joe.

One of the men was apparently about fifty years of age. He had a dirty, greying beard and he wore spectacles. He was clad in a torn and stained pair of overalls and his sleeves were rolled to the elbows, revealing his blackened arms.

"For a miller, there's mighty little flour on his hands," commented Frank. "He looks more like an automobile mechanic."

The other man, who looked older, was similarly attired, but he was of a more benevolent appearance. He did not wear glasses and his shaggy brows almost hid a pair of keen, sharp eyes. He fondled his long white beard reflec-tively as the other man talked to him in low tones.

The boys could not overhear what the pair were saying, but they saw the boy, a fair, curly-headed youth of about fifteen, in ragged clothing, look up at the older man and say something to him.

Instantly the old fellow lost his look of benevolent reflection. He gave the boy a cuff on the ear that almost staggered him.

"Be off with you!" he ordered harshly. "Go away and play. Don't be hanging around here while we're talking."

He spoke so loudly that his words could be clearly heard by the lads hidden in the bushes. The curly-headed boy stood his ground, and evidently repeated what he had said before, for the old man at once became furious.

"Go away and play, I tell you!" he shouted in shrill tones. "I'll call you when I need you. And be sure you come in a hurry when you hear me."

He reached behind him for a heavy cane that was leaning beside the doorway and he struck out viciously at the lad with it. But the boy dodged the blow and ran off toward the mill race, while the old man watched him go, muttering imprecations.

"Leave him alone," said the other man in a guttural voice. "We've got other things to attend to than that brat."

"He's a nuisance, I'll whale the hide off him when he comes back."

"Leave him alone. Markel is waiting for us. Let's go inside."

"All right—all right," muttered the old man peevishly. He turned and followed the other through the doorway.

"Nice tempered old chap," remarked Jerry, when the pair had disappeared into the mill.

"I'll say he is," declared Joe. "I don't think either of them is up to much."

"The young fellow looks all right," Chet said. "He looks as if he has a sweet life here with those men."

Phil said:

"I thought Stummer told us there were three men running the mill."

"They said something about Markel," Frank pointed out. "He's the man who is waiting for them inside the mill. That must be the other partner."

"Let's go up and talk to the kid," suggested Joe. "Perhaps we can dig something out of him about those men. They don't seem to treat him very well, anyway."

The boy was walking along the side of the old mill race. The waters were very swift at this point, for the current was strong and the river was deep. The boy was trudging along the weatherbeaten planks, with his hands in his pockets, looking very disconsolate.

"Lonely looking boy," observed Tony. "They told him to run away and play. He looks as if he'd never played in his life."

"We'll go over and talk to him," Frank decided. "If those old chaps say anything to us about being around here we'll ask them to quote some prices on having some milling done."

"I can do that!" exclaimed Chet. "Dad's a farmer, and he's often said he wished the old Turner mill was running again so he wouldn't have to haul his grain so far."

The boys emerged from the bushes and crossed the weed-grown open space near the front of the mill. The other lad had not yet seen them. He was standing by the mill race, some distance below, gazing into the water, now and then raising his head to look at the clacking wheel that turned monotonously in showers of dripping water.

"I'm curious about this patent food story," Frank said. "It's strange there wasn't anything in the papers about it. Nobody except the farmers, like Stummer, seems to have heard about the mill being taken over."

"Oh, probably they want to keep it to themselves until everything is ready," Jerry pointed out. "I'll bet you're beginning to see some kind of mystery in this already, Frank. Chances are we'll just get kicked off the premises for our pains."

"Oh, I don't think there's any mystery about it," said Frank, with a smile. "But I'm just curious to know what it's all about."

"No law against that," Phil agreed. "If this breakfast food invention of theirs turns out to be something wonderful that makes us all live about twenty years longer, we can say we were among the very first to know about it."

By this time they had drawn closer to the mill race, and the boy standing there had raised his head and seen them.

He was a good-looking fellow, not unlike Joe Hardy in appearance, as Carl Stummer had pointed out. But his face was pinched and drawn and there was a melancholy expression in his eyes.

"Looks as if he hadn't had a square meal in a month," Jerry remarked.

The boy turned and began to move toward Frank and Joe.

He had gone only a few paces, however, when they saw him suddenly stumble. He had stepped upon a loose stone that had rolled from beneath his foot.

He wavered uncertainly, striving to regain his balance. Then, with a shrill cry, he toppled over into the mill race and fell with a splash into the swiftly rushing torrent of water.

"Help!" he shouted, in terror. "Help!"

CHAPTER VIII

JOE'S COURAGE

The accident had happened so quickly that it was not for a few moments that the Hardy boys and their chums realized the lad's danger.

Then, as they saw him struggling in the torrent, they began to run toward the spot to which the lad was being rapidly carried.

Joe was in the lead, and as he ran he was taking off his coat. Just below the mill race the river was full of rocks, and the rapids dashed over them in a boiling fury of spray and foam. If the youth were ever swept into the rapids he would be doomed.

The other lads were not far behind Joe. The accident had not been seen from the mill, for no one appeared in the doorway, and the cries of the boy in the river evidently had not been heard by the men in the building.

"Help!" he was shouting. "Help!"

He was struggling in the water, being swept irresistibly on toward the deadly rapids.

"I can't swim!"

Joe reached the bank, paused to kick off his shoes, then stood poised for a moment above the rushing waters. He dived into the mill race, disappeared beneath the surface, then rose just a few yards away from the struggling boy.

The lad had already gone under once and was gasping for breath. He was just about to go under for the second time when Joe swam toward him with strong, steady strokes and grasped him by the collar.

Frantically, the boy tried to seize his rescuer, but Joe was ready for that. He knew that the unreasoning grip of a drowning person is of the utmost danger, so he managed to stay at arm's length and at the back of the boy.

"Hold steady!" he shouted, above the roar of waters. "Hold steady! Keep cool!"

His words had some effect in restoring the lad to his senses and the boy, feeling the supporting grasp on his collar, ceased his struggles.

But the danger was not yet over. The current was so strong that they were both being carried headlong downstream toward the rapids.

Joe could see the jagged rocks silhouetted against a background of flying spray and foaming water. If once they were swept into that maelstrom they would be battered to death.

He was handicapped by the weight of the boy, but he turned toward the shore and exerted all his efforts in swimming toward the bank. But he made little progress. The current was too strong for him.

The other lads, running along the bank, were watching the scene in consternation.

"He'll never make it!" declared Jerry. "The current is too much for him."

They could see Joe's tense face as he pitted his strength against the force of the current and desperately strove to make his way toward the bank. He was still clinging to the boy, who was commencing his struggles anew.

They were being swept closer to the rapids every moment. There were a number of rocks rising above the surface of the river just a few feet ahead, and beyond that was a smooth, deep, swiftly flowing sheet of water that swept past the willows at the bend and ended in a quarter of a mile of rough, turbulent water, rapids and falls.

"I'm going to help him!" exclaimed Frank, suddenly.

He stopped on the bank and flung off his coat, then started to untie his shoelaces in order to kick his light shoes aside.

But in the meantime Joe had managed to catch at a projecting rock with his free hand, so Chet put a restraining hand on Frank's arm.

For a moment it seemed that the current would make Joe lose his grip, but he clung to the rock and drew himself closer until he had wrapped his arm about it. The rest of the rock was wide and flat and lay just a few inches beneath the surface.

Slowly, Joe clambered on to this precarious refuge, dragging the half-conscious boy with him. The rock was big enough to provide foot-hold for them both.

The boy was unable to help himself, as he was limp and weak from his experience. Just as he was almost on the rock Joe lost his grip on the lad's collar for a second, and the current whirled him to one side. The lad toppled backward, striking his head on the rock, but Joe made a frantic grab for him, at imminent risk of precipitating himself into the water again.

His fingers closed about the back of the lad's shirt and he managed to haul the boy to safety once more.

But the blow had rendered the lad unconscious. He lay limply on the flat rock, with the water breaking about his body, while Joe, his clothes drenched, clung to him.

"Get help! Get a rope!" Joe shouted, to his companions on the bank.

Frank and Chet lost no time.

They fled back toward the old mill.

The affair in the river had passed unnoticed by the millers, and when Chet and Frank rushed up to the front door they found no one in sight.

"I'm going inside," declared Frank. "We'll have to get a rope or they'll be swept off that rock in no time."

The door was closed, but he pushed it open and entered the dim interior of the mill. But hardly had he stepped inside, with Chet at his heels, than he ran into the arms of one of the men whom he had seen outside the doorway some time previously.

"Hi, what do you want?" demanded the man angrily. He seized Frank by the shoulders and tried to push him back, out of the building. At the same time the other man came running out of a near-by door.

"What's going on here?" he shouted wrathfully. "What's all this about? Get out of here, you boys!"

The sound of voices evidently attracted the attention of a third man, for he, too, came running out of the shadows, carrying a heavy club, which he brandished threateningly.

"What do you want here?" he shouted excitedly. He was short and broad-shouldered, with a dirty kerchief knotted about his neck.

"We want a rope," Frank explained, taken aback by this hostile demonstration. "Your boy is drowning in the mill race!"

The three men became immediately concerned. They crowded about, asking questions.

"What boy?"

"Where is he?"

"What do you want a rope for?"

"He fell into the river a few minutes ago. If we don't hurry he'll be drowned. My brother rescued him and they're both on a rock down near the rapids," Frank said hurriedly. "Get a rope—quick!"

"Get a rope, Markel!" shouted the bespectacled old man to the fellow with the club. "Hurry up!"

Markel dropped the club and ran back into the room from which he had come. In a few moments he returned, dragging a length of stout rope.

"Where is he now?" asked the old man. "Lead the way."

The men of the mill had forgotten their first animosity when told of the plight of the boy, and now they followed Chet and Frank as the two boys ran outside again and raced along the bank to the place where the other boys were standing in an excited group, shouting advice and encouragement to Joe, who was still clinging to the rock.

Markel stumbled along the bank with the rope, and when he reached the group of boys they moved back to give him space. He coiled the rope loosely in one hand, then whirled the free end of it about his head and flung it out into the stream.

But the rope fell short. Joe made a frantic grab for it, but Markel had misjudged the distance.

"Here—let me try it," demanded the oldest of the three men, pushing Markel impatiently to one side. He seized the loose end of the rope, drew the remainder of it from the rushing water, then cast it out to Joe.

The rope whirled through the air, missed Joe's outstretched fingers by inches, then splashed into the water.

Again the old man drew the rope back, again he swung it about his head and again it arched out above the river.

This time it fell against Joe's shoulders. The youth, still clinging to the unconscious form on the rock, hastily grabbed at it, seized it, and began hastily tying it about his shoulders, underneath his arms.

He was handicapped by the fact that he had but one arm free, but at last he had the rope securely knotted.

The old man was greatly excited. He had noticed that the boy had not moved and that Joe had to cling to him to keep him from being swept off the rock.

"Lester!" he shouted. "Lester! Are you all right?"

"He hit his head on a rock and it knocked him out," explained Jerry. "I don't think he's badly hurt."

At that moment Joe looked up and waved to them, as a signal that they could begin towing him ashore. He tightened his hold on the unconscious boy, then eased himself off the rock.

The old man, Frank and Markel seized the end of the rope, and as Joe released his hold of the rock they began to pull.

The rope was an old one and Frank noticed, with alarm, that it was worn and frayed. Would it hold?

The figures in the water bobbed up and down in the waves, sometimes submerged completely. Bit by bit, they were drawn toward the bank.

But their combined weight and the strength of the current proved too much for the rope.

When they were but a few yards from shore the rope abruptly snapped.

The men and the boys on the bank staggered back as the loose end of the rope spun through the air.

Joe and Lester were swept away in the swift current!

CHAPTER IX
THE RESCUE

Frank Hardy had seen that the rope was insecure. He had already laid a plan of action in case the rope broke.

The rapids were just around the bend in the river. The stream was narrow at that point and willow trees overhung the bank. The moment the rope broke Frank leaped into action.

He stumbled free of the group and raced along the river bank toward the willows. He could see Joe struggling helplessly in the swiftly flowing stream and he knew that if the current once carried him beyond the willows his brother would be doomed. No human being could live in those tossing rapids.

Could he reach the trees in time? Would the current carry Joe and Lester close enough to the bank to enable him to rescue them? Would he be able to hold them until help arrived?

The bank suddenly dipped and he hurried down the grassy slope toward the willows. He was still in advance of the struggling figure in the stream and he knew that he had a chance, although it was but a slim chance at best, of rescuing his brother and the strange boy.

He reached the willows at last. They grew out over the smooth and rushing water. Frank ran to the edge of the soggy bank, grasped one of the trees, and leaned out over the stream.

So far, luck was with him, for Joe was still a few yards away. But he was still too far out in the water to enable Frank to grasp him as he passed.

But Joe had guessed Frank's intention. As well as he could, in spite of the fact that he was handicapped by the weight of the unconscious Lester, he tried to struggle closer toward the shore.

The current was with him, for it swung close to the bend at this point and it swept Joe directly beneath the overhanging willow to which Frank was clinging, steadying himself with his feet on the bank.

As Joe was swept beneath him, Frank reached far down. For one breathless second he thought he had missed his brother's outstretched hand. Then their fingers met and he gripped Joe tightly, hanging on to him with all his strength.

The willow bent and swayed beneath the added weight, but Frank held firm. The muscles of his arm ached with the strain and he knew that he could not hold out long, but already he could hear shouts and the sounds of running feet that told him the others were coming to the rescue.

"Hang on! We're coming!" Chet was shouting, and a moment later Frank heard his chum threshing through the bushes. Phil and the others were close behind.

With his companions clinging to him, Frank managed to drag Joe ashore, still grasping the clothes of the unconscious boy. Dripping wet, Joe scrambled up on the bank, and together they carried Lester out of the willows on to the grass.

First aid was immediately rendered. Lester was not seriously hurt. He had swallowed a great quantity of water and the blow on the head had stunned him, but after a while he stirred and opened his eyes. The old man looked relieved, although the other two men watched the scene with indifference.

When Lester was finally able to sit up his first question was.

"Who saved me?"

Frank indicated his brother.

"Joe did."

Lester struggled to his feet and gratefully shook Joe's hand.

"I don't know how to thank you," he said simply. "But you know I'm grateful. I would have been drowned if it hadn't been for you."

Joe was embarrassed.

"It was him, really," he said, indicating Frank. "If it hadn't been for him we'd have both been in the rapids by now."

Lester grasped Frank by the hand.

"I have both of you to thank, then. You risked your lives for me."

The old man nodded.

"It was brave work," he said reluctantly. "I'm mighty thankful to you boys for saving the lad. And after this," he said harshly to Lester, "stay away from that mill race. I've told you fifty times that you're liable to get drowned fooling around there. Next time you mightn't be so lucky."

"I'm sorry, Uncle Dock," answered the boy.

The party made their way back toward the mill and the boys were conscious of the sullen glances of the two men who were with "Uncle Dock." It was clear that the pair wished the lads would go away.

"Better take the kid inside and let him dry his clothes," advised Markel roughly, gesturing to Lester. "We'd better get back to work."

Joe's clothes were soaked, but the offer evidently did not include him.

"Have you got a fire in the mill?" he hinted hopefully.

Uncle Dock glanced at Markel, who shook his head in a surly manner.

"No," he answered. "Lester can go to bed until his clothes dry."

"My own clothes are pretty wet."

Markel affected not to hear this remark, but hastened on toward the mill.

"When did you take over the mill?" asked Frank of the old man.

"A few weeks ago."

"What are your prices for milling?" asked Chet. "My father was saying the other day that he wished the old Turner mill would open again. If he had known you were running the place he would have been over by now. He can put a lot of trade your way."

Uncle Dock hesitated and glanced at the other man.

"You'd better talk to him, Kurt."

"Our prices are pretty high," said Kurt shortly. "We're makin' breakfast foods, chiefly."

"But don't you need grain?"

"We're pretty well stocked up."

"What are your milling prices, anyway?" persisted Chet.

Kurt thought for a moment, then gave Chet a list of prices which were so greatly in excess of those charged by the Bayport mills that they were prohibitive.

"Why, that's higher than dad would want to pay," Chet said.

Uncle Dock shrugged his shoulders.

"Take it or leave it. We ain't askin' for his trade."

"You won't get it. Not at those prices."

It was quite evident that Uncle Dock and his strange associates were not desirous of encouraging any outside trade for the old mill, However, Frank realized that the men had a right to manufacture patented food in secret if they wished, so he nudged Chet as a signal against any further questions.

They had reached the door of the mill by now, and Markel hustled Lester inside before he had a chance to say anything further to the boys, although the lad cast an appealing glance behind as though he would have liked again to express his thanks to his rescuers.

"Where do you fellows live?" asked Kurt, peering at them from under his shaggy eyebrows.

"Bayport."

"You're a long way from home."

"We're just on a hike," explained Frank. "We just thought we'd come around this way."

"You'll be late for supper if you don't hurry back."

This broad hint was not lost on the boys. It was clear that the men wanted to get rid of them.

"I guess we'll be on our way. We'll go in for a swim farther up the river so Joe can have a chance to dry his clothes."

This seemed to remind Uncle Dock of the fact that Joe had, after all, saved Lester's life. He reached for his pocket.

"I'd like to reward you for saving the lad," he said, becoming suddenly affable. Joe shook his head, and when Uncle Dock took two five dollar bills from his pocket and offered them to the boys, one to Frank and the other to Joe, they disclaimed any intention of accepting money for what had plainly been their duty.

But no sooner had Uncle Dock extended the bills than the other man, Kurt, gave a muffled exclamation and stepped forward. He snatched the money from Uncle Dock's hands and quickly turned around, with his back to the boys.

The interruption was only of about a second's duration, for Kurt at once wheeled about and again extended the money. He gave a short, nervous laugh.

"My mistake!" he said. "I thought he was only offering you a dollar each. You deserve five. It's all right. Here—take it."

He thrust the money upon them but they refused. Kurt did not press the point. He put the bills back in his own pocket.

"All right. If you won't, I suppose there's no use arguing," he said, with evident relief. "But we're very grateful to you just the same. Well, Dock, what say we get back to work?" he continued, turning to his companion.

Uncle Dock turned away and went back into the mill with Kurt.

"It's plain they don't want *us* hanging around," said Joe, with a rueful glance at his clothes. "Let's go on up the river so I can throw these clothes over a hickory limb and get 'em dried out before we start back home."

CHAPTER X

THE NEW BOAT

A week went by, a week in which the Hardy boys and their chums again wrestled with refractory Latin phrases and geometrical problems, as the examinations drew near. There was little time for fun, even outside school hours. The boys were all overcome by that helpless feeling that comes with the approach of examinations, the feeling that everything they had ever known had somehow escaped their memory and that as fast as they learned one fact they forgot another.

But the week was over at last and on Saturday morning Fenton Hardy looked up from his newspaper with a quiet smile.

"What's the program for today?" he asked of his sons.

"Nothing in particular," said Frank. "I was thinking I'd dig into the Latin for an hour or so, although I'm so sick of the sight of that book that I'd like to throw it out the window."

"I'm away behind in my algebra," spoke up Joe. "But it's too nice a day to study. Anyway, I've been working hard all week."

"Perhaps if you went down to the boathouse you might find something there," suggested their father casually.

The boys stared incredulously. Then they gave a simultaneous whoop of delight.

"You don't mean to say the motorboat is here?" exclaimed Frank.

Their father had taken charge of the buying of the motorboat for them. They had not expected that the craft would arrive until the start of the summer holidays.

Fenton Hardy merely smiled and turned to the financial page.

"It mightn't be a bad idea to go down to the boathouse anyway," he said.

The boys needed no further urging. Within a few seconds they were scrambling for their caps, within the minute they were racing down the front steps, and soon they were hastening toward Barmet Bay.

In preparation for the arrival of the motorboat they had rented a boathouse on the southern shore of the bay, at the foot of the street on which they lived. During the week, Mr. Hardy had obtained the key from them on some pretext, but they had thought nothing of it. Now everything was clear.

"The boat must have arrived here during the week and he had it taken to the boathouse without telling us about it," said Frank.

"I guess he was afraid we wouldn't do much studying for the rest of the week if we knew it was there."

"I guess we wouldn't have, either."

When they reached the boathouse they could hardly contain themselves in their eagerness to see if the boat had indeed arrived. Frank inserted the key in the lock and opened the door. They stepped inside.

There, rocking gently in the waves, was a long, graceful craft, white with gilt trimmings, a motorboat that gave an immediate impression of strength and power without the sacrifice of graceful lines. There was a flag at the bow and at the stern; the fittings glistened; the seats were upholstered in leather, and across the bow was the name of the boat in raised letters: *SLEUTH*. The name had been chosen by the Hardy boys previous to the purchase of the craft and after much argument.

"She's a beauty!" breathed Frank in deep admiration.

"I'll say!"

"The smoothest looking boat on the bay!"

"And I'll bet it's the fastest."

"Oh, boy, if we'd only known this was here all week!"

Without further ado, the boys descended from the landing stage and got into the boat to inspect the craft more closely. Everything they saw only served to confirm their first impression that the *Sleuth* was without doubt the neatest, most compact and most beautiful motorboat ever launched. The fittings were bright and shining, the wheel responded to the lightest touch.

"How's the gas and oil?" asked Frank, settling into the steersman's seat.

"Full up. And look, Frank, even the license is here!"

"All right. Cast off."

Joe opened the boathouse doors, unhooked the chains that kept the craft secure, and then leaped into the *Sleuth* as the engine spluttered and roared. Frank threw in the clutch, the roar died away to a purr, and the boat backed swiftly and smoothly out into the bay.

"The engine runs like a watch!" reported Frank, in delight.

Once outside the boathouse he headed the craft out toward the open bay. It was soon apparent that the engine of the *Sleuth* was very powerful, for the boat leaped forward as Frank increased speed, and yet there was very little noise. The nose of the boat cut the water like a knife and the craft skimmed out into the bay like a swallow.

Both boys were almost inarticulate with delight. The sense of speed and freedom held them spellbound. Frank changed places with Joe and gave his brother a turn at the wheel. Joe was astonished at the immediate response that came to his lightest touch.

In anticipation of getting the boat both lads had taken lessons in running such a craft from Tony Prito and others who had motorboats and, as a consequence, Joe and Frank felt thoroughly at home with both the engine and the steering wheel.

They circled about and came down toward shore again. It was a sunny morning and two or three motorboats were spluttering and backfiring in their shelters near the shore. Out of one boathouse came a rakish black craft that the boys recognized instantly as the motorboat belonging to Tony Prito's father.

"There's Tony!" exclaimed Frank. "He always goes boating on Saturday mornings. Let's give him a race."

"His boat's supposed to be the fastest on the bay."

"I don't care whether it is or not. He'll have to go some to beat the *Sleuth*. We'll challenge him."

Although Tony had seen their boat he had not yet recognized the boys in it and when they drew alongside he gave a shout of surprise.

"Well, gee whiz!" he exclaimed. "Look who's here! I was wondering who owned the swell new tub. Is this the new boat?"

"This is she. And she's fast, boy—she's fast. Want to race?"

Tony laughed.

"I hate to show you up so soon. You won't like your new boat near so well if I beat you the first time you get into a race."

"You won't beat us. You've got a pretty speedy old boat there, all right, but you've met your match this time."

"Do you really think you can lick me?" asked Tony. "You know you haven't a chance. This is a *real* speed boat."

"This is a better one. Come on—we'll start from that buoy."

Frank pointed to a buoy that was riding the waves about a hundred yards away and the two boats sped toward it. They kept on even terms until they came abreast of the buoy and then Tony shouted:

"Now!"

At the same instant, the boats leaped forward. The engine of Tony's craft set up a deafening roar, but the *Sleuth* merely changed from a purr to a growl and sprang swiftly through the water.

Tony had the advantage in that he knew his boat well and he knew just how much power it would stand. Within half a minute he had established a substantial lead, while the *Sleuth* was surging along in his wake.

But Frank knew that the boat was more powerful than it seemed.

Gradually, he "let her out," and the *Sleuth* responded until at last he could see that they were gaining on the craft ahead. By this time Tony was tearing along at the highest speed of which his swift craft was capable, and the boat was almost rising out of the water with the force of its momentum.

Rapidly, the *Sleuth* overhauled the flying craft, swiftly it drew abreast, and the boys had a glimpse of Tony's astonished face as he glanced over the side at them.

The *Sleuth* roared on, rocking and swaying, with spray dashing over the bows. There was no doubt as to which was the swifter craft. Tony was being left behind.

When a gap of three or four hundred yards separated the two boats and when it was apparent that he had no hope of overhauling his rival, Tony lessened the speed of his craft as a signal that he had been beaten. Frank immediately throttled down the *Sleuth* and swung her around in a wide circle. Then, at a more reasonable speed, they went back to meet Tony.

Their chum was astonished beyond all measure.

"I thought you were just kidding when you said you'd race with me," he shouted, as they drew closer.

"No kidding about that race, was there?"

"I'll say there wasn't! I let my old boat out as fast as she'd go. I thought the engine was going to jump out, once or twice. I didn't think there was a motorboat in the bay could beat mine, but I guess that tub of yours has it beat. When did you get it?"

"This is the first time we've been out."

"Wish I could stick around and race with you again," said Tony regretfully. "But I have to go back to the boathouse. I promised my father I'd help him at the warehouse this morning."

"Tough luck," sympathized Frank. "We may see you this afternoon. But no more racing until the engine is worked in a bit better. It was foolish to let her out while she is so stiff."

"Where are you going now?"

"Oh, we'll just cruise around," said Frank. "I was thinking we might go up to Barmet village and back."

"That's a nice run. It'll take you about half an hour if you go easy. About five minutes if you let that speed demon out for all she's worth."

"We'll go easy," laughed Joe. "We don't want to ruin the engine on our first trip."

"Runs pretty smooth," approved Tony. "It'll stand quite a lot. Well, I must be going. Good-bye."

He turned the nose of his craft toward the boathouse and drew swiftly away. The Hardy boys set out in the opposite direction, surging through the water toward Barmet village.

CHAPTER XI

A MAN IN A HURRY

Barmet village lay several miles from Bayport on the shore of Barmet Bay, from which it got its name. It was a small place, inhabited by fishermen chiefly, and it was a distributing center for the farmers who lived in the surrounding area. The Hardy boys had no particular object in going to Barmet, beyond the fact that the village served as a destination and gave their boating trip more of a purpose than there would have been had they merely cruised aimlessly around.

Although the sky had been clear and the sun had been shining when they set out, Frank noticed that already clouds were coming in from the sea and the wind was stiffening. Storms sprang up suddenly along the coast but he was not alarmed for he knew that they would have the wind with them on the return trip.

The *Sleuth* sped smoothly along, the engine purring without a miss. The craft neither rocked nor rolled, but cut the waves cleanly. Both Frank and Joe were delighted beyond measure with their boat, and at that moment would not have traded places with a king.

By the time they reached Barmet, the sky was cloudier than ever and there was a hint of rain, so the boys determined that they would not stay long in the village. They made a landing at the wharf and got out to stretch their legs, being greatly pleased in the meantime by the complimentary remarks passed by such villagers as were about at the time, on the appearance of their boat.

These were not empty compliments, for the Barmet people prided themselves on knowing a good boat when they saw one and there was nothing grudging in their approval of the *Sleuth*. Two old fishermen sat on the wharf with their feet dangling over the water and discussed the motorboat in every detail from bow to stern, agreeing that she combined strength and appearance in a remarkable degree. When they had finally affixed their seal of approval to the *Sleuth* they refilled their pipes and settled down to an endless series of reminiscences concerning boats that they had once sailed.

"The sky's beginning to look black," pointed out Frank to his brother after they had listened to a number of these tales. "I guess we'd better be starting."

Joe moved away reluctantly, for he was fascinated by the highly colored yarns of the two old salts. But when he glanced at the lowering horizon he realized that Frank's apprehensions were justified and that it would be better for them to start back to Bayport without delay.

They got into the boat and were just about to cast off when there came a sudden interruption.

A man came running down the road leading to the dock. He was waving his arms and shouting.

"Hi! Hey there! Wait for me!"

Somewhat puzzled, the Hardy boys waited. They did not recognize the man; he was a complete stranger to them. He was stout and thick-set, florid of face and red of hair, and as he ran out on the wharf he panted from his exertions.

"Whew!" he exclaimed, mopping his brow with a bright silk handkerchief. "I nearly missed you."

"What do you want?" Frank asked.

"I wanted to go to Bayport—right away. I want to catch that train, and if you can get me there in twenty minutes I'll give you ten dollars. Will you take me?"

The Hardy boys looked at one another doubtfully. Both were conversant with the Bayport train schedules and neither was aware of any train that left Bayport at that hour in the morning. Still, the stranger seemed very much in earnest and he drew a ten dollar bill from his pocket as proof of his good faith.

"Come!" he said impatiently. "How about it? Will you take me or will you not? I want to be there in twenty minutes. There's ten dollars in it for you."

Ten dollars, as Frank said later, "is not to be sneezed at." When they bought the motorboat their father made the stipulation that they should not draw on their bank accounts to pay for the gasoline, and every cent was precious for that reason.

"Jump in," Frank said. "I guess we can get you there in twenty minutes, all right."

"Thanks," said the florid-faced man, getting into the boat. "Make it as quick as you can."

Frank slipped into his seat and in a few moments the engine was roaring as the *Sleuth* glided away from the shadow of the wharf and headed out into the bay. She rapidly picked up speed and soon the salt spray was flying as the motorboat tore through the waves, her nose pointing toward Bayport.

The stranger settled back with a sigh of relief.

"Mighty good thing I met you," he said. "I was beginning to think I wouldn't be able to get out at all. There was only a rickety looking flivver in the village and I was afraid to take a chance on it, for I don't think it would have lasted a mile without falling to pieces. It was lucky I saw your boat when I did."

The *Sleuth* sped along under a darkening sky. They were running close to the shore in order to cut off as much distance as possible and keep a bee line for Bayport, and it was possible to have a clear view of the road that ran just above the beach.

Joe noticed that the stranger cast frequent anxious glances toward the shore. Suddenly an expression of alarm crossed the man's face, and Joe saw that he was watching two figures who had appeared on the road and who were running along, waving their arms, evidently trying to attract attention.

"Somebody signaling to us," he said to Frank.

Frank looked up. The two men on the road were making frantic efforts to draw attention, as they waved their arms and leaped about like lunatics.

"Friends of yours?" asked Frank of their passenger.

The florid-faced man laughed. The laugh was meant to be carefree and hearty, but there was no disguising the note of uneasiness beneath it.

"Yes—yes, they're friends of mine," he admitted. "I put one over on them that time." He chuckled nervously. "They're just beginning to realize that I've given them the slip."

"What's the big idea?"

"That's the time I fooled them." The stranger laughed loudly—too loudly, in fact. "You see, I'm going to be married. That's why I have to catch that train. I kept it a secret until this morning, but my friends got wind of it and thought they'd play a practical joke on me. I started out in plenty of time for the train, but they had fixed the engine of my car so it broke down and I had to come back to Barmet. They were trying to hold me back, and for a while I was beginning to think that they had got away with it. But I bested 'em. I fooled 'em that time."

He laughed again, but still there was that note of insincerity in his mirth that had aroused the suspicions of the Hardy boys at first. They said nothing, and the stranger evidently thought his story had been believed, for he sat back in the boat with a complacent air.

But Frank glanced again at the two men on the road. For practical jokers, they seemed to be making a tremendous fuss over their friend's escape. They were still waving their arms, evidently trying to signal to the boat to turn back.

"There's something fishy about this," muttered Frank. "I don't know of any train leaving Bayport at this hour of the day."

"Neither do I," his brother replied, in a low voice.

"Those men on the shore seem mighty agitated over something or other. If it was a practical joke they'd just give up and go back to the village."

"It's a pretty unbelievable story. He seemed in an awful hurry to get away from Barmet."

"I have a good mind to turn back. We may be getting ourselves into trouble."

"He'll be as mad as hops if we do. Tell him we don't want his money, and take him back to Barmet."

The more Frank considered the situation the more he felt that the wisest course would be to turn back to Barmet and wash his hands of the whole affair. The stranger's story about an approaching wedding might be true and it might not, but there was the fact of which he was certain, that there was no train leaving Bayport at that hour of the day. He turned to the passenger.

"What time is your train leaving?"

"About ten-thirty."

"There's no train leaving Bayport at that time," said Frank flatly.

"That's the time my train leaves," insisted the stranger, beginning to look somewhat flustered.

"The earliest train is at noon," put in Joe.

"I tell you, this train leaves at ten-thirty. I just have time to catch it."

"I'm afraid you're going to miss it," said Frank. "I'm going to turn back to Barmet."

"Turn back?" shouted the man in consternation. "What are you going to do that for?"

"I don't like the looks of this affair," said Frank. "Considering that this is supposed to be nothing more than a practical joke, those two men on shore seem to be making quite a fuss over your escape."

"They're hoping they can persuade you to turn back. Then they'll have the joke on me after all."

"They're going to have it anyway," said Frank, with determination. "I've changed my mind about taking you to Bayport. We don't want your ten dollars."

"But you've *got* to take me to Bayport!" exclaimed the stranger, in high excitement. "I must catch my train."

His bullying manner nettled Frank.

"This is our boat, and if we want to turn back we can turn back," he told the passenger. "We didn't ask you to come with us."

"But you promised to take me to Bayport," stormed the stranger. "I've got to be there in time to catch that train."

"There isn't any train at ten-thirty, and we know it. We're going to turn back to Barmet and you'll have ample time to catch the noon train after that."

The stranger gritted his teeth and half rose from his seat. Then he sank back, as though realizing that he was going beyond his rights by objecting.

"A nice trick to play on me!" he snapped. "Bringing me this far and then turning back."

"Your friends on the shore seem anxious to have you back, for some reason or other."

Frank bore down on the wheel and the *Sleuth* slowly began to circle about.

Suddenly the voice of the stranger rasped right at their ears:

"Don't turn this boat around! Keep heading for Bayport."

Startled, they turned. The stranger was standing right behind them, and in his hand he clutched a revolver that was aimed directly at them!

CHAPTER XII

SEASICK

The Hardy boys were not prepared for this sudden change of front on the part of the stranger. They gazed incredulously at the revolver, but the coldly determined face of their passenger convinced them that the man meant to use force if necessary.

"Keep right on toward Bayport!" he ordered. "Don't turn back."

"What's the big idea?" demanded Frank indignantly.

"The idea is that I want to go to Bayport, and if you won't take me there of your own free will, I'll just have to persuade you, that's all. This gun is loaded, so don't make any foolish moves."

The boys looked at one another, and the stranger began to chuckle.

"Be reasonable now," said the man with the gun. "I have to catch that train, or I'll miss the wedding. I can't let you bring me back to the village. My friends would never let me hear the end of that joke. It's just by luck I had this revolver in my pocket—but still, if you turn this boat around, I'll use it."

He was trying to pass the affair off as more or less of a joke but there was no mistaking the steely glint in his eyes or the hardness of his voice.

Frank looked at his brother, and shrugged.

"I guess there's nothing else for it but bring him to Bayport," he muttered. "I don't want to get shot."

"That gun looks bad," agreed Joe. "There's not much joking about that part of it."

Frank bore down on the wheel and corrected the course of the boat so that they were soon bound directly for Bayport again.

"We'll take you to the city," he said to the stranger, "but I'm going to warn you that we'll turn you over to the police if we get a chance. That's a dangerous game you're playing, even if you say it is only a joke. It's a hold up."

"You'll think differently after we reach Bayport," promised the man. "I'll have my wife write you a letter of thanks after the wedding. I hate to use this revolver, but I can't miss that train."

The stranger's insistence on his story that he had to catch a train did not convince the Hardy boys by any means. They were still suspicious of their passenger, the more so now that he used force to induce them to take him to Bayport.

"I'd like to get that gun away from him," whispered Frank, as he bent over the wheel.

"Not much chance. He's watching us too closely."

"Trying to fix up some plot to get hold of this revolver?" asked the stranger. "You needn't bother. I hold the whip hand here."

"We know it," retorted Frank. "But wait till we get to Bayport."

The motorboat raced on down the bay. The storm clouds that had been collecting all morning now hung heavily in the sky. The bay was sullen and slate-colored, and a heavy sea was running. White caps broke on the surface of the water.

"Looks like a storm," Frank muttered. "Perhaps it's just as well we didn't turn back."

A streak of lightning split the sky; it was followed by a distant rumble of thunder. The *Sleuth* was riding the waves well, but there was a rocking motion that could not be avoided. The boat swayed from side to side as it plunged on.

After about five minutes Frank glanced behind.

The stranger was no longer standing up; he was sitting back against the cushions again and he still held the revolver levelled at the Hardy boys, but there was a curious expression on his face, an expression of nausea; his eyes were staring and his face was pallid.

For a moment Frank could not understand what the matter was. Then, as the boat gave a lurch more violent than usual, he understood.

He nudged his brother.

"Getting seasick!" he whispered.

Joe glanced back, and when he saw that the stranger's florid face had changed in hue from a deep red to a greenish white he knew that the motion of the boat was indeed taking its effect. He forebore an impulse to chuckle at their passenger's plight.

"Give her a little more gas," ordered the stranger, in a curiously feeble voice. "You're not going fast enough."

He brandished the revolver threateningly.

Frank obligingly increased the speed of the *Sleuth* but the rocking motion only became more pronounced.

The stranger gulped, but he did not lower the weapon.

"That's better," he said, without enthusiasm.

"I'm going to give him something to be seasick about," whispered Frank.

Without warning he suddenly bore down on the wheel and swung the motorboat about so that it was lying broadside to the waves.

"Here—what's the matter?" asked the stranger. "Where are you going now?"

"We're off our course. I'm heading in toward shore a little more so we can get out of the wind."

This explanation satisfied the stranger, although it became speedily apparent that the new course did not.

The *Sleuth* received the full force of the long rollers. The waves were not high enough to be dangerous, but the swells gave an undulating motion to the craft that swiftly increased the stranger's illness.

"He's slipping," whispered Joe.

Frank glanced back again.

The stranger was indeed "slipping." His teeth were tightly clenched. His face was almost green. His expression was that of a man who is deathly sick. But he still clung to the revolver and he still waved it feebly at the boys.

"Head her in toward Bayport," he demanded. "Do you want to make me sick?"

"This'll fix him," said Frank. "Get ready."

He bore down on the wheel again.

The *Sleuth* swung around at right angles to her previous course. The abrupt, swerving motion finished the stranger.

With a groan, he slumped forward in his seat, and bowed his head on his arms.

Joe sprang up. With one bound he reached the man with the gun.

The stranger realized what was happening, and struggled to his feet. He raised the weapon, but Joe struck out and dashed the revolver from his hand. It described a flashing arc, then fell into the water with a splash.

Sick as he was, the man swung out viciously and his fist caught Joe on the side of the face, staggering him. Joe quickly recovered himself and plunged forward, grappling with the man. They swayed to and fro in the middle of the boat, then fell, still struggling.

But although Joe was young and wiry he was not strong enough to cope with his antagonist and Frank soon saw that the stranger was having the better of the battle. He glanced ahead, saw that the *Sleuth* was heading into a long, low bank of fog but that there were no other boats in sight, then abandoned the wheel.

He leaped back to the assistance of his brother, crooked his elbow about the stranger's neck, and dragged him back. The man struck out, wildly, twisted around and staggered Frank with a blow in the ribs. He managed to struggle to his feet, they saw his hand flash to his pocket, and then he produced a small package and flung it far out over the side.

It had only taken a second, but that second was sufficient to serve for his undoing.

Frank scrambled to his feet in the swaying boat, and for a moment they sparred. Then Frank's right fist shot out and the blow landed directly on the point of the stranger's jaw.

The man was not knocked out, but he staggered back and the wild lurching of the boat sent him off his balance. He stumbled and fell. His head struck against the side of the boat and he crumpled up in a heap.

The blow had knocked him unconscious.

Frank bent over him. He saw that the man was not badly hurt, but that he had been stunned by the impact. He pointed out a coil of rope in the stern.

"Tie his ankles, Joe, in case he wakes up. I've got to get back to the wheel."

The *Sleuth* by this time was off her course, and was wallowing in the trough of the waves. Quickly, Frank swung the craft about, but when he peered ahead to locate Bayport he gave an exclamation of alarm.

The city was nowhere to be seen. The heavy cloud of mist that had been gathering over the bay now totally obscured the shores.

How far the boat had departed from her course he did not know, and in the fog bank he had but a vague idea of their location. He began to look around in hopes of finding a compass, but there was none in the boat.

"Have you got a pocket compass, Joe?"

Joe, who was busily engaged in tying the unconscious stranger's ankles together, looked up and shook his head.

"Isn't there one in the boat?"

"No—and here we are in a fog bank. I don't know whether we're in the right direction for Bayport or not."

CHAPTER XIII

PAUL BLUM

Frank Hardy reduced the speed of the motorboat, because he realized the dangers that lurked in the fog.

Almost any moment they might crash into another boat in the bay. Even worse, they might be so far out of their course that they would pile up on one of the rocky shores.

The fog was impenetrable. Frank did his best to judge their direction by the waves but this did not help greatly, as there were cross currents and the wind was shifting.

The *Sleuth* coursed on, feeling its way blindly through the haze that enveloped the bay. Frank peered ahead into the foggy veil.

Joe concluded his ministrations to the stranger, who was now beginning to stir. The man opened his eyes and groaned.

"Have you had enough?" asked Joe.

"Who hit me?"

"You hit your head against the side of the boat. Are you going to make any more trouble?"

The man groaned again, tried to get to his feet, found that his ankles were tied together, and sank back with a sigh.

"He won't give us any more bother," declared Joe, coming forward. It was plain that there was no more fight left in their captive.

"I wish this fog would lift," said Frank.

As though in answer to his words a sudden gust of wind sent the mist in scurrying wreaths, raising the heavy grey veil long enough to enable him to see Bayport lying almost directly ahead. He could make out the position of the row of boathouses and he headed the *Sleuth* toward them.

The curtain of fog descended again, but Frank was now fairly sure of his position.

"We're heading in the right direction now."

"Should we try to make the boathouse? I don't think we'll be able to find it in this mist."

"I guess you're right. We'll land at the big wharf."

In a short while, the boat was nosing its way through the fog, among the shadowy craft anchored near Bayport wharf. The city loomed up in a ghostly dark mass beyond the water.

Finally the *Sleuth* drew alongside the wharf and nosed its way to one of the slips. To the surprise of the boys they saw several figures running along the wharf.

"What boat is that?" shouted some one from the fog.

"The *Sleuth*!"

"Good! That's them. I thought they'd land here," said the voice, evidently addressing some one else on the wharf.

"Looks as if we're expected," observed Joe.

A man came down the slip, and even in the fog they knew the figure was familiar. When he drew closer they saw that the man was none other than their father.

"Dad!" exclaimed Frank.

"Have you got him with you?" asked the detective quickly.

"Who? Joe?"

"No, no. The man you picked up at Barmet village. I had a telephone message about him."

"Yes, we have him here. He tried to hold us up with a revolver, but we got the better of him."

"Fine!" said Mr. Hardy, peering down into the boat, where the stranger was struggling to sit up. "All right, Chief!" he called, to a burly man who was coming down the slip. "They have him."

Chief Collig, of the Bayport police force, and Con Riley, one of his men, then appeared in view.

"Got him, hey?" said Collig.

"They have him here in the boat."

"All right. Hand him over."

Still wondering how their father had known that the stranger was in the boat with them and wondering also why the police were on hand, the Hardy boys untied the ropes that bound their passenger's ankles, and helped him over the side. He was immediately seized by the officers, who proceeded to search his pockets.

"Here!" he protested. "What's all this about?"

"Well, Paul Blum," said Fenton Hardy, "you thought you'd made a get-away, didn't you?"

The man started.

"You have my name wrong," he muttered.

"Oh, no, I haven't," contradicted Mr. Hardy. "They tell me you were 'shoving the phoney' down in Barmet village this morning."

The Hardy boys had been told by their father that 'shoving the phoney' was the underworld expression for passing counterfeit money.

"Those Secret Service men would have caught you if the boat hadn't been handy," went on Fenton Hardy. He turned to his sons: "What sort of story did this fellow tell you?"

"He said he had to catch a train, as he was going to be married, and some of his friends in the village were trying to hold him back, as a practical joke," answered Frank. "We thought the yarn was rather fishy and I was going to turn back but he drew a revolver on us."

"How did you get him tied up?"

"He got seasick and Joe knocked the gun out of his hand. Then we tackled him."

"Good work," approved Mr. Hardy. "I got a phone call from two Secret Service men this morning. It seems they've been trailing Paul Blum for some time and they were just about to arrest him when he made a bolt for liberty. They chased him down the street, but he disappeared, and the next thing they knew he was in your boat, heading for Bayport. They waved at you and tried to signal to you to come back—"

"So that's why the two fellows were running along the shore!" exclaimed Joe.

"But when you didn't turn back they telephoned to me to meet the boat and arrest him." Fenton Hardy turned to Chief Collig. "Did you find anything?" he asked.

The Chief straightened up, scratching his head.

"Not a thing. Nothin' but a dollar bill and some matches."

"No counterfeit money?" exclaimed Mr. Hardy, in surprise.

"Not a bit."

"That's strange. The detectives told me he had a big roll of bad bills."

"Why, that must have been what he threw overboard," said Frank. "He took something out of his pocket and tossed it over the side of the boat while we were fighting with him. At the time I couldn't imagine what it was."

"I guess that's how he got rid of it." Fenton Hardy turned to Paul Blum, who was standing sullenly, with his pockets turned inside out. "And what have you got to say for yourself, Blum?"

"Nothing. You haven't got anythin' against me."

"Perhaps not just now. But wait till those Secret Service men arrive from Barmet. You were passing counterfeit money in the village."

"Any counterfeit money I passed, I got from some one else," blurted the prisoner. "I'm not in that game."

Fenton Hardy turned to his sons.

"This doesn't happen, by any chance, to be the fellow who tricked you on that bad five dollar bill at the railway station, does it?" he asked.

They shook their heads.

"No, it isn't he."

"I'm convinced that he's associated with the gang in some way."

"You haven't got anything on me," Blum persisted doggedly. "Perhaps I did pass some bad money in the village. What of it? If I did, I didn't know it was bad. I got it from some one else. It ain't my fault."

"If you're so innocent, why did you run from the detectives?"

"I had to catch a train."

"Tell that to the judge," advised Chief Collig roughly. "I think I'll lock you up for a while, my friend, and let you just think things over."

"Yeh, put him in the cooler," piped up Con Riley.

"I don't want any advice from you," said the chief, crushing his subordinate officer with a frown. "Here—put the cuffs on this bird and lock him up."

There was a jingle of handcuffs as they were clapped about Paul Blum's wrists. The man protested, but he was quickly silenced by the chief.

"We're going to keep you until the Secret Service men get here," said Fenton Hardy. "Perhaps they'll have more to tell."

Chief Collig and Constable Riley trudged off, with Paul Blum between them. Fenton Hardy turned to his sons with a smile of approval.

"Good work!" he said. "You haven't lost any time making good use of the new boat, I see."

"I only wish we could have got hold of that roll of counterfeit bills he threw overboard," said Frank disconsolately.

"Well, it can't be helped now—although that would have cinched the case against Blum. He has been operating in this neighborhood for over a week. But I expect the Secret Service men will have enough evidence to have him punished."

The fog was beginning to lift and the Hardy boys had no further doubt of their ability to locate the boathouse. They felt they had enough of motorboating for one morning, so they said good-bye to their father and left the wharf, guiding the *Sleuth* safely to the boathouse.

"If every trip we have in the *Sleuth* is as exciting as that one, we'll have no reason to kick," Frank remarked, as he shut off the engine.

CHAPTER XIV

CON RILEY GUARDS A PACKAGE

Officer Con Riley was at peace with the world.

His heart was full of contentment and his stomach was full of pie. The sun was shining and one of the aldermen had just given him a fairly good cigar. His beat had been free of crime for a week. His wife had gone to the country for a visit and she had taken the children with her. Hence, Con Riley's feeling of deep and lasting satisfaction with the world.

Even the boys, his natural and hereditary enemies, had not tormented him for several days. Perhaps, he argued, it was because they were up to their ears in work, preparing for examinations. If that was the reason, Con Riley decided that examinations were good things and should be encouraged.

As he sauntered along the shady side of Main Street, leisurely swinging his club and gravely responding to the greetings of, "Good afternoon, officer," he reflected that there were worse occupations in life than being on the Bayport police force. He was well content with his lot just then. He exchanged salutations with the traffic cop on the main corner and mentally congratulated himself because he was not a traffic cop; the job exposed one to all manner of weather, from cold, drenching rains to sizzling heat. No, he was just as glad he was on the beat.

A troop of boys came down the street from the direction of the Bayport high school, and Riley instinctively stiffened. If it were not for those confounded boys, life would be very different for him. They did not seem to appreciate the dignity of his position. They were always contriving schemes to make him look ridiculous.

He spied the Hardy boys with their companions, and his frown deepened. Too smart, altogether, those Hardy lads. They weren't mischievous, he had to admit that, but they were meddling in the work of the police a little too much. Already they had been credited with solving a couple of mysteries that he, Con Riley, would certainly have solved alone if he had been given a little more time.

Then there was Chet Morton—a boy who was born to be hanged, if ever there was one. He'd come to a bad end some day, that fellow. So would all the rest of them, Tony Prito, Phil Cohen, Jerry Gilroy, Biff Hooper—the whole pack of 'em.

Still, Con Riley was in a good humor that afternoon, so he unbended sufficiently to bestow a nod of greeting upon the boys. To his surprise they gathered around him.

"What has been done with Paul Blum?" asked Frank.

"He's in jail," said Riley, with the portentous frown he always assumed when discussing matters of crime. "He's in jail, and in jail he'll stay."

"Hasn't he been tried yet?"

The constable shook his head.

"Not yet. The rascal has a lawyer and the case has been adjourned."

"Not much doubt that he'll get a heavy sentence," remarked Chet, who was carrying beneath his arm a package wrapped in brown paper.

"No doubt of it at all," agreed Riley.

"Didn't you fellows tell me that Lieutenant Riley helped capture the counterfeiter?" asked Chet innocently, turning to the Hardy boys.

Riley's chest expanded visibly when he heard himself referred to as "Lieutenant," and when it dawned on him that Chet thought he had a part in the actual capture of Blum he tried to look as modest as possible, although he did not succeed very well.

"Oh, I helped. I helped," he said, with a deprecatory wave of the hand.

"If it hadn't been for Officer Riley the fellow might have got away," said Joe smoothly. "He slapped the handcuffs on Blum in the neatest manner you ever saw. He was waiting for us right at the dock."

Riley beamed. This was praise, however undeserved, and he basked in the admiration of the boys. He told himself that he had perhaps been mistaken in his estimation of these lads after all. They were not mischievous young rascals, but bright, intelligent, high-minded boys who recognized human worth when they saw it and who respected achievement.

"Yes," he said heavily, "I got Blum behind the bars and he won't get out again in a hurry."

He said it as though he had personally been responsible for Blum's capture and personally responsible for seeing that the prisoner was kept safely locked up.

"No, he won't get away on you, Lieutenant Riley," said Chet.

Con Riley's opinion of Chet increased. The boy had mistaken him for a lieutenant. The mistake was natural enough, perhaps, but it would have to be corrected.

"Officer," he pointed out sadly. "Not lieutenant—officer."

"Do you mean to tell me that you're not a lieutenant?" exclaimed Chet in well-assumed amazement.

"Not yet," replied the officer, leaving the impression, however, that it was only a matter of hours before such promotion should be his in the natural course of events.

Chet turned to his companions.

"Can you imagine that!" he exclaimed. "There's the police force for you. They keep a solid, brainy man like Riley here on the beat and let fellows like Collig be chief. It's wrong, I tell you. It's wrong."

The boys gravely agreed that it was scandalous.

"A man's just got to be patient," said Riley, with the air of a martyr, and beginning to feel ill-used.

"There's a limit to patience!" exclaimed Chet. "They're imposing on you, Mr. Riley. If I were you, I'd insist on my rights."

"Never mind," said Riley darkly. "My turn will come."

"You're just right it will. And we'll see that it comes very soon. Let's try to stir up public opinion, fellows, and see if we can't influence the public a little bit. If the public demands that Officer Riley be promoted, he'll be promoted."

"Why, that's very good of you," returned Riley pompously. "A few words in the right place mightn't do any harm at all."

"Those words shall be said," Chet assured him earnestly. "You may depend on us, Mr. Riley. We will see that your qualities of leadership are recognized. You're the only man who can wake this city up."

Con Riley, a trifle dazed by this avalanche of flattery, but nevertheless feeling that every bit of it was deserved and that the boys deserved credit for their perception, beamed with appreciation.

"Why, I never had no idea you lads felt like this," he said. "I always thought you had a sort of grudge against me."

The boys immediately disclaimed any such sentiments.

"We may have been a little bit troublesome at times," agreed Chet regretfully; "but that was because we didn't understand you. After this, you may depend on us. Your time will come, Mr. Riley. Your time will come."

With this fine oratorical effort, Chet produced the package from beneath his arm. "By the way," he said, "I wonder if you would mind guarding this package for me, Mr. Riley? You'll be here for the next ten minutes, won't you?"

A doubt flashed across Riley's mind.

"Why don't your friends look after it?"

"We're all going to be together and we didn't care to wait. If a man by the name of Muggins comes along and asks for it, you'll give it to him, will you?"

Riley took the package. "I'll take care of it," he promised.

"I wouldn't trust it with any one but you," declared Chet solemnly.

"You can trust me. I'll look after it. And if your friend Muggins comes along I'll see that he gets it safely all right."

Chet thanked Riley warmly and the boys hastened off and disappeared around the next corner. Riley, with the package under one arm, leaned against a post and thought well of himself and of the world in general. He completely revised his opinions of boys, and particularly of Chet Morton, whom he now regarded as an exceptionally intelligent lad who would make his mark in the world. Riley was glad that he was able to be of service to Chet by minding the package for him.

The package was not very heavy. Riley was curious as to its contents. Chet had left the impression that it contained something quite valuable. He said he would not trust any one but Riley to guard it. That, in itself, was a compliment.

The late afternoon was warm and as Con Riley leaned against the post and indulged in these pleasant meditations, permitting himself to speculate on what the boys had said about his fitness for promotion, allowing himself to remember how pleasant it had sounded to hear Chet refer to him as "Lieutenant," he became a bit drowsy. He was naturally a sleepy man, and he had long since schooled himself in the art of appearing to be wide awake while on duty while indulging in covert naps of a few minute's duration. The hurrying crowds of people behind him, because it was the five o'clock rush hour, gradually became a blurred impression of tramping feet and chattering voices.

Suddenly the shrill jangle of an alarm clock sounded.

Riley started violently, straightened up, blinked, and looked behind him.

The alarm clock trilled steadily. Riley looked suspiciously at the people near by and the people looked at one another. He looked up into the air, looked down at the pavement, but still the mysterious alarm clock rattled on.

Then Riley became aware that the alarm clock was in the package under his arm.

At the same time the crowd became aware of the fact as well. Some one tittered; some one else laughed outright.

"Carry your own alarm clock with you now, do you?" asked a man.

Riley felt very foolish. He was tempted to throw the package away, but instead he held it gingerly by the string and pushed his way through the crowd. The unremitting alarm clock rang loudly.

"Time to wake up!" shouted a wit in the crowd.

Riley flushed and hastened on down the street. But the alarm clock shrilled relentlessly. That tinkling bell seemed as though it would ring forever. And as Riley hurried on his way people turned and stared and laughed, and small boys began to follow him, while all the time the bell trilled on without a sign of weakening.

His journey down the street was a triumphal procession. The crowd of small boys following him swelled to the proportions of a parade. The bell rang on. Con Riley was the center of interest. He did not know what to do. If he threw away the package now it would be an admission that he had been the victim of a practical joke; the longer he kept the package the more the crowd laughed and the louder the bell seemed to ring.

His steps became faster and faster, as though he were trying to run away from the sound. Every one was staring at him in amazement. The giggles and guffaws of the crowd became louder. The shouts of the small boys were more insistent.

Across Con Riley's mind flitted certain phrases of Chet Morton. "Your time will come.... You're the only man who can wake this city up.... We shall see that your qualities of leadership are recognized...."

With a mutter of wrath he flung the tinkling package into the nearest alley. A uniformed street cleaner who was just emerging from the alley received the package full in the chest and sat down very suddenly. He flung the package back at Riley. The crowd whooped with glee. The package fell into the street, the bell still ringing, and one of the small boys picked it up and ran after Riley, asking if he wanted it back.

Thus he was pursued to the police station until the bell of the alarm clock ceased to ring, and only then did the crowd scatter.

Mopping his brow, flushed with anger, Riley took refuge in the station and vowed vengeance in the future on all the boys in Bayport, particularly high school boys, most especially Chet Morton's gang, and most absolutely and positively Chet Morton himself.

As for that worthy, in company with his chums, he had witnessed the alarm clock parade from a convenient corner across the street and was now limply making his way toward the Hardys' barn, pausing every now and then to burst into shrieks of laughter at the remembrance of Riley's undignified flight.

But when the Hardy boys and their chums reached the house they found their father hastening down the front steps.

"I just had a telephone message from the police station," he said.

"What's the matter?" asked Frank, while the other lads looked at one another guiltily. Had Riley reported them?

"Paul Blum has escaped from jail," said Fenton Hardy.

CHAPTER XV

THE CHASE

"When?" asked the Hardy boys quickly, in response to their father's announcement of Paul Blum's escape.

"Just a few minutes ago. At least that was when they discovered it. He managed to get out into the jail yard for some exercise, and in some way the guard's attention was distracted. Blum piled up a couple of old boxes against the wall and was over before any one saw him."

"I wonder where he would go?"

"The police are watching the roads and the trains. I don't think he can get out of the city that way. But I have an idea he has accomplices here, and if he can he'll join them and they'll see that he is smuggled out all right. I was going to suggest that you fellows take the motorboat and keep an eye on the bay."

"Good idea!" exclaimed Frank, who never needed an excuse to take the boat out. "Come on, Joe. Come on, Chet."

"I'll go out in dad's boat," volunteered Tony Prito.

"Fine!" agreed the others, and the boys hastened down the street in the direction of the boathouses.

Jerry Gilroy and Biff Hooper went with Tony, while Phil Cohen went with Chet and the Hardy boys.

Frank unlocked the door of the boathouse and went inside, followed by the others.

But the familiar shape of the *Sleuth* could not be seen.

The front of the boathouse was open. The motorboat had disappeared.

"The boat's gone!" he exclaimed in consternation.

The other boys stared, amazed at this unexpected development.

"It's been stolen!" cried Frank. "No one has a key to the boathouse but Joe and me."

"It was here at noon!" exclaimed Joe. "I was in here for a few minutes before I went to school."

"Who could have taken it?" asked Chet.

"Do you think it could have been Paul Blum?" suggested Joe.

The same thought had been in Frank's mind.

"That's who it was! He wanted to make a quick getaway, so he figured his best chance would be by boat."

"And perhaps he found out where our boathouse was, just so he could get even because we turned him over to the police," Joe put in.

"He can't be very far away," Phil Cohen pointed out. "Your father said he just escaped a little while ago."

Frank ran along the landing out to the front of the boathouse. For a moment he scanned the bay. Then he gave a sudden shout.

"I see the boat! There's the *Sleuth*! I'd know it anywhere!"

The others ran to his side, and Frank pointed out a flashing white shape heading far up the bay. There were very few boats out that afternoon and there was no mistaking the *Sleuth* as it sped eastward.

"Get Tony to chase him!" exclaimed Joe. "Quick!"

They ran hurriedly out of the boathouse and made their way down to the ramshackle building where Tony Prito kept his craft. The other boys looked up in surprise as the Hardys and their companions entered. Tony had been just on the point of starting.

"Paul Blum has stolen our boat!" Frank told him. "He's making his getaway in it now!"

"Paul Blum!" exclaimed Tony.

"Yes. The escaped prisoner. There's the boat now," declared Joe, as he pointed out toward the bay.

In a flash, Tony grasped the situation. He leaped into the motorboat.

"Jump in! We'll chase him."

The Hardy boys scrambled into the boat, but Chet and the others stayed behind.

"Too many cooks spoil the broth," explained Chet. "You'll need all the speed you can get out of that boat to catch him. We'd only delay you."

Chet was eager to join in the chase, but he realized that the fewer passengers Tony's boat carried, the better would be their chance of capturing the fugitive. The other boys quickly took their cue from his attitude and declared that they would remain behind also.

"We'll telephone to Barmet village," suggested Chet. "Perhaps a boat can put out from there and head him off."

His remarks were drowned in the roar of the engine, as Tony's motorboat began to back slowly out into deeper water. It left the boathouse, then Tony turned the wheel and the motorboat headed about for the open bay.

"Now I guess you wish the *Sleuth* wasn't faster than my boat," he said, with a grin. "We'll have trouble catching him."

He opened the throttle, and the motorboat leaped ahead, leaving a widening trail of foaming water behind.

The white shape of the stolen craft could be seen far out in the bay. Paul Blum was losing no time, and it was evident that his method of escape had not yet been discovered by the police, as Tony's craft was the only boat in pursuit. It was doubtful, too, if the fugitive realized as yet that he was being pursued.

"I'll let her out as fast as she'll go," said Tony, suiting the action to the word.

The boat was drumming along at a high rate of speed and it soon became apparent that they were gaining on the *Sleuth*. This was evidently because Paul Blum thought his flight had passed unnoticed and did not feel it necessary to run the craft at its highest speed.

"If we can only sneak up behind him before he knows we're after him, we'll have a chance," said Joe.

"No such luck," Tony remarked. "He'll be looking behind once in a while."

Frank found a pair of binoculars on one of the seats, and he raised them to his eyes, adjusting them so that Paul Blum and the speeding motorboat were brought within his line of vision. The distant *Sleuth* leaped closer as he looked through the glasses, and he could plainly see the face of the man at the wheel.

They had not been mistaken. The fugitive was Paul Blum.

Even as Frank looked, the man turned, and an expression of alarm crossed his face. He had seen the motorboat pursuing him.

Frank saw Blum lean forward, and the *Sleuth* began to increase its speed. The wing of water cleft by its bow became higher and the spray was flying. Swiftly, the motorboat began to draw away.

"He's seen us," said Frank, lowering the binoculars.

"We'll keep after him, anyway."

"We'll chase him clean across the Atlantic if the gas holds out," declared Tony.

Joe gave an exclamation of delight.

"The gas!" he exclaimed. "The gas! That's where we have him. I went down to the boathouse at noon just to see if there was enough gas in the tank, and it's pretty low. He hasn't enough to take him more than a few miles."

"Good!" exclaimed Tony. "That's where we have the edge. My boat may not be as fast as the *Sleuth* but the gas tank's full and there's some more in that can. We'll chase him till he has to quit."

But if the gas in the *Sleuth's* tank was low, there was no sign of it just then. The motorboat sped on up the bay, gradually widening the distance between itself and the pursuing craft. Tony crouched at the wheel, impassively watching the flashing white streak far ahead.

"I wonder where he's heading for," said Frank.

"Along the coast, probably," Tony answered. "He'll likely get out of the bay, then head up the coast as far as he can and abandon the boat."

"That's probably what he intends to do," put in Joe. "But he'll never get out of the bay. There isn't enough gas."

It was evident that Paul Blum had no intention of seeking refuge in Barmet village. On the contrary, he was heading toward the other side of the bay, in the direction of the mouth of Willow River.

"Perhaps he intends to go up the river," ventured Frank.

Tony shook his head.

"Not if he knows what's good for him. He'd run full plump into the falls and rapids near the old mill."

"That's right, too." Frank had forgotten those obstacles.

But while the *Sleuth* was still some distance away from the mouth of the river, her speed began to slacken.

"Good!" exclaimed Joe. "The gas tank's empty."

"Let us hope so," returned his brother. "What a sell for that man!"

But a moment later the other motorboat began to show signs of life again.

"She's started up!" groaned Joe. "Confound the luck, anyway."

A moment later a splutter came from the other boat.

"Gas must be running low," said Frank. "Gee, I wish he would stop entirely!"

"Same here."

Slower and slower went the white motorboat until at last it was just crawling along.

Frank picked up the binoculars again.

He could see Paul Blum laboring at the motor, trying to locate the source of trouble. The fugitive cast a glance backward; Frank could see the anxious expression on the man's face.

"He's trapped, and he knows it."

Rapidly, they gained on the *Sleuth*, which was now almost at a standstill, drifting back and forth in the waves. Paul Blum seized an oar that was carried in the boat in case of emergency, and frantically began to scull toward the shore.

But his effort was in vain. Tony's motorboat bore swiftly down upon him. The engine of the *Sleuth* had died.

As the other craft drew alongside, Paul Blum cast aside the oar in admission of defeat. He sat sullenly in the boat without looking up.

"Too bad, Blum!" shouted Frank. "We're going to take you back with us."

"I'd have been all right if it hadn't been for the confounded gas running out," gritted the man.

"We weren't so particular about getting you as we were about getting back our boat," said Joe. "Will you come back quietly?"

Paul Blum shrugged his shoulders.

"I suppose I might as well," he said. "I haven't any weapons. If I had, you may depend on it, I'd put up a fight."

"Just as glad you haven't, then," remarked Tony cheerfully. Carefully, he brought the boat alongside the *Sleuth* and Frank and Joe jumped over the side into their own craft.

Paul Blum was resigned. He submitted to having his wrists bound with a piece of stout rope that the boys found on the stern of the boat, and then he sat down philosophically.

"I'll get away yet," he told them. "If I can't escape from that jail myself, my friends will see that I get out."

"How will we get back?" asked Frank, turning to Tony.

Paul Blum laughed.

"That's a problem for you," he said. "The gas tank's empty. What are you going to do about it?"

Tony calmly handed over the can of gasoline from his own boat.

"This should help," he remarked. "I always keep some spare gas on hand."

Paul Blum, beaten, had no more to say. The Hardy boys poured the reserve supply of gasoline into the tank, and in a few minutes the engine was pounding away.

Then, side by side, the two motorboats turned about and put back for Bayport.

CHAPTER XVI

A PLAN OF ACTION

The quick work of the Hardy boys and Tony Prito in capturing Paul Blum won them many compliments within the next few days. Even Chief Collig grudgingly admitted that it had been a smart capture. In this he was perhaps largely prompted by a feeling that had Paul Blum made good his escape he, as chief, would have come in for considerable criticism from the townspeople.

As it was, the laxity at the city jail was forgotten in the excitement surrounding the fugitive's return, and Chief Collig was correspondingly relieved. Had Paul Blum not been recaptured, the police force would have had to bear the brunt of public displeasure for having allowed the man to slip through their fingers.

The connection of the Hardy boys with the affair caused many people to recall their previous activities in the Tower Mansion case and the affair of the house on the cliff.

"Those lads will be smart detectives yet," more than one person was heard to remark.

Nothing could have pleased the boys more than recognition of the fact that they showed some ability in the profession of their famous father, and, in the light of their recent successes, even Mrs. Hardy was beginning to abandon her prejudices against their desire to be some day more than amateur detectives.

But although Paul Blum was safe in jail, counterfeit money was still being circulated in Bayport and Barmet village.

Hardly a day passed that some one did not report to the police or to the banks that they had been the unwitting victims of the counterfeiters by cashing or accepting spurious bills. In one instance it was a garage owner who had changed a twenty dollar bill for a passing motorist who bought gasoline and oil. In another instance even the steamship ticket office had accepted a false five dollar bill for a ticket and the mistake had not been discovered until the following day. When the ticket, which was bought at a cost of eighty cents, was traced by its number it was found that it had never been presented on the steamboat.

So many instances came to light that the entire city was on guard against the counterfeiters, but so excellent were the imitation bills and so plausible were the excuses of those who sought to pass them on that many people were victimized in spite of their caution.

In some cases, merchants were handed counterfeit bills by respectable citizens of Bayport, people who were above reproach, and when the fact was pointed out, the would-be customers explained that they had received the money in good faith from equally reputable citizens. Often the original source of the bad money could not be traced, the counterfeit bills had passed through so many different hands without being discovered.

The boys talked the matter over several times with their father, and one day Fenton Hardy took them into his confidence.

"Don't tell anybody," he said, "but the Federal agents have come across some evidence which makes them think the counterfeiting plant is located somewhere near Barmet village."

"Have they got any definite idea, dad?" asked Joe eagerly.

"They think it is up in the woods—maybe at some farmhouse. You know the country over on the other side of the bay is pretty wild. There would be plenty of hiding places there for counterfeiters."

Mr. Hardy spoke of several places that were being watched, but he admitted that so far the Federal agents had unearthed little of practical value.

"They know that most of the bad money is circulated in this vicinity and in and around Boston," he concluded. "It's just possible the plant may be in the Hub." There the talk came to an end and the boys walked away as they knew their father was getting ready for a hurried trip to the city.

"It's a good chance for us to do some real detective work," said Frank to his brother one afternoon after school, as they were in the gymnasium in the barn back of the Hardy home. "The whole city is worked up over this counterfeit money business."

"Smarter detectives than we are are working on the case," Joe pointed out, "but they haven't found much yet."

"Paul Blum won't talk. If we could get something out of him we might have a clue to go on."

"He won't say a word. It's my opinion he doesn't know much about the source of the counterfeit money, anyway. I think he was only an agent sent out to dispose of as much of it as he could. They probably have a dozen men traveling around the country passing off these bad bills. Once the money gets into circulation it's liable to pass through a dozen hands before it is discovered."

"Perhaps that man who stung the garage owner for twenty dollars had no idea the money was bad. And perhaps it's the same way with the fellow who bought the ticket at the steamboat office."

"It's strange that most of the fuss is being raised right around this city. You don't hear much about it from other places."

"It's my idea," said Frank, "that the counterfeiters have their plant right in this vicinity."

"Do you think so?"

"Just as you said—most of the counterfeit money seems to be passed in and around Bayport."

"Where do you think they could be making the stuff?"

Frank shrugged.

"You never can tell. Perhaps in some cellar of one of the downtown buildings, for all we know. Personally, I've got an idea. It may be foolish, but I've been turning it over in my head for a few days, and the more I think of it, the more reasonable it seems."

"Spring it."

"You remember the day we were at the old mill?"

"I'll say I do! Those fellows wouldn't let me dry my clothes in the mill after I'd fished that precious kid out of the water."

"But one of them offered us a reward, didn't he?"

"Oh, well—you can't take a reward for that."

"That isn't what I'm getting at. Do you remember how the other man grabbed the bills out of his hand and turned his back to us?"

"Sure! He said he wanted to see if they were fives or ones. But it *was* rather funny that he turned his back to us. I thought so at the time. Still, he offered the money to us again."

"But was it the same money?"

Joe was silent. The idea had not occurred to him before.

"Do you mean," he said at last, "that perhaps the fellow changed the bills while he had his back turned?"

"Exactly."

"But why should he do that?"

"Don't you see? Perhaps the first bills were counterfeit. Perhaps the man thought that if we took the counterfeit bills and later found out that they weren't good, we would remember where they came from and start an investigation. This is only a theory, remember; but perhaps the reason he took the bills from the man they called Dock was to change them for good bills, so that we would have no cause for suspicion."

Joe nodded reflectively.

"By gosh, Frank, there may be something to your idea, after all. Say! Perhaps that's where the counterfeiting plant is. Right in the old mill!"

"That's just what I've been driving at. There's something fishy about the old mill, for all their story that they're making a patent kind of breakfast food. That may be true, of course, but still—"

"They didn't look very much like scientists to me."

"To me, either."

"But how can we find out anything more about the place than we know already? They won't let any one inside the mill, and it's quite evident that they don't want any one around the place at all."

"What made me suspicious," said Frank, "was the fact that Paul Blum seemed to be heading for the mouth of Willow River that afternoon he got away in the motorboat. I began to wonder later if he might have been intending to make his way up as far as the old mill. Perhaps he is connected with the gang."

"It looks reasonable. But if we show our noses around there they'll just chase us away."

"There's Lester."

"Lester?"

"The boy we saved from drowning. We have him on our side anyway, I think. If we haven't, he must be a very ungrateful beggar. I'd just like to ask him a few questions about this patent breakfast food yarn."

"That's a good idea!" cried Joe. "If he tells us any kind of story at all we can soon tell if he's lying or not. But, somehow, I don't think he would lie to us. He seemed to me to be a pretty decent sort of boy."

"That's what I thought of him too. Chances are, if these men are counterfeiters, they're keeping him there as a prisoner. He might be only too glad to tell what he knows, if given a chance."

"And if it turns out that those men really are scientists and that the mill is really being used for this breakfast food stunt, we won't be making ourselves foolish by poking around and perhaps getting into all sorts of trouble for suspecting they were counterfeiters."

Frank nodded.

"That was my idea in suggesting Lester. We have to work pretty carefully, for it wouldn't do to start a hue-and-cry and find out that those fellows really are scientists after all. But what do you say to taking the motorcycles tomorrow morning and going up to the old mill to see if we can get to talking to the boy?"

"I'm game. Tomorrow's Saturday. Even if the men at the mill do see us they'll think we're just out on a holiday outing. There's no law against going near the old mill, even if they don't want strangers around."

So the arrangement was made, and the Hardy boys laid their plans for a visit to the old mill on the following day. Each felt that there was something suspicious about the place, some mystery that was not entirely nor satisfactorily solved by the breakfast food explanation. If they could only talk to Lester, who was already under obligation to them for having saved his life, they felt that they would go a long way toward verifying or dispelling their suspicions regarding the three men who were the present occupants of the mill.

CHAPTER XVIII
SUSPICIONS

"What do you think, Joe?" asked Frank, as they were speeding back to Bayport on their motorcycles.

"I don't think Uncle Dock is a scientist any more than I am."

"That's my opinion, too. Why should they have so much secrecy about a new kind of breakfast food? Why won't they even let Lester into the workroom with them?"

"Something fishy about it. And it's plain by now that Uncle Dock doesn't like strangers around the place."

"That poor kid must lead a lonely life with that gang. It's a wonder he doesn't run away from them."

"He has no place else to go, I suppose. He seems a nice sort of chap, too," Joe answered.

"Well, we didn't get anything definite from him, but we know enough to make us mighty suspicious of what's going on in that old mill."

"I'd just like to get a look at that machinery in the secret room the boy mentioned."

Frank was silent for a while.

"I wish Uncle Dock hadn't seen us there today. It'll make it awkward now if we ever go back. He has told us to stay away, and now he'll be suspicious if he ever sees us around there again."

"We might tell dad what we know about the place."

But Frank vetoed this suggestion.

"I'd rather work along our own lines until we get something more definite," he said. "If we get some real evidence we can tell dad about it. So far we have nothing to go on but our own suspicions."

All the way back to Bayport, the Hardy boys discussed the various aspects of the case, and although they agreed that the mysterious activities of the three men at the old mill tended to indicate almost anything but scientific endeavors, they realized that if they investigated too thoroughly they might get into serious trouble.

"We'll just wait a while and keep our ears open," Frank decided. "If those fellows are in the counterfeiting game they'll do something to give themselves away. And then we'll be right on the job."

When the boys arrived home they amused themselves in the gymnasium in the barn for some time, had an impromptu boxing match and finally, after a shower bath, went down the street. It was a sleepy Saturday afternoon and the city was very quiet.

"Nothing much doing around here," remarked Frank. "We should have stayed out in the country."

"We could go out in the motorboat for a while."

"Fine. Let's go."

But at that moment they heard the whistle of the afternoon express. Like most boys, they had a weakness for trains. There was a fascination about the great locomotives that held them spellbound and they liked nothing better than to watch the trains that passed through Bayport and to speculate on the towns and cities they had come from or were bound for. At times when school became exceptionally distasteful they had often gone down to the railway station and wished they could board the first train that came by, to travel on to strange countries. Somehow, they had never been so daring as to do this, common sense invariably coming to the rescue, but the lure of locomotives and shining rails still held them in its grasp.

They moved down the street toward the station and came out on the platform just as the express was pulling in. Idly, they watched the few passengers who emerged from the coaches, envied the engineer who was lolling majestically in the cab, watched the conductor in his smart uniform, and looked at the people who were boarding the train.

Suddenly Frank nudged his brother.

"Isn't that Markel?" he asked.

Joe followed his glance. Near the steps of one of the Pullman coaches was a familiar figure, with cap pulled down over his eyes. There was no mistaking the fellow; he was indeed Markel, one of the associates of Uncle Dock at the old mill.

What particularly attracted the boys' attention, however, was the fact that Markel carried a bulky paper package under his arm.

He had not seen them, but there was something so furtive in his manner that the Hardy boys made themselves as inconspicuous as possible in the shadow of one of the pillars near by.

Markel lounged about near the coach, now and then glancing up anxiously, as though expecting some one.

Within a few minutes, just as the conductor shouted, "All aboard!" a tall, thin-faced man with a neat black mustache, emerged from the coach. He glanced hastily down at Markel, nodded swiftly, said something in a low tone, and Markel forthwith handed him the package. The tall man snatched it from his grasp, turned and retreated quickly into the coach again.

Markel, as soon as this transaction had been completed gave a shrug of his shoulders as though he had been relieved of an unpleasant burden, turned swiftly on his heel and walked away. He disappeared into the station just as the train began to pull out.

The whole affair had occupied but a few seconds and had passed almost unnoticed by any one on the platform save the Hardy boys. Any who may have noticed the handing over of the package doubtless attached little importance to it. The Hardy boys themselves would not have given it more than a passing glance had it not been for Markel's connection with the mystery of the old mill.

"What do you make of that, Frank?"

"Markel must have passed on a sample of the new breakfast food."

"He seemed mighty secretive about it."

"I'll say he did. You'd think it was a bomb he was handing over instead of breakfast food. He waited until the train was just pulling out before the other man came for it."

"No breakfast food about that performance."

"I don't think so either. Evidently Markel and the gang are in touch with some one in the city. You remember that Lester said Markel came into Bayport every little while with a package under his arm. That must have been one of them."

"Well, that's a little more evidence to go on."

"Give them enough rope and they'll hang themselves. I'll just bet dollars to doughnuts that there is counterfeit money in that package instead of breakfast food. This man Markel looks to me like a crook, and his tall friend on the train didn't look any too trustworthy either. My idea is that they are using the mill as a plant where they turn out the money, then they give it to one of their men on the train and he takes it to some other city for distribution."

"That looks like it," Joe agreed. "You could tell that Markel had something on his conscience when he handed that package over. He looked mighty shifty about it."

The boys walked back down the street, still discussing the events of the day. They spent the rest of the afternoon out in Barmet Bay, in the *Sleuth*. For the time being, they dismissed the affair of the mill from their minds, being content, as Frank had said, that the counterfeiters, if they were such, would ultimately betray themselves.

When they returned home that evening for supper they did not tell their father what they had learned. But Fenton Hardy himself brought up the question of counterfeit money when he told them that he had that afternoon received a telegram from Federal authorities asking him to further his investigations.

"They have evidence that more than ten thousand dollars in counterfeit money was put into circulation within the past three days," he told the boys. "The affair is going beyond all bounds."

"And Paul Blum is still silent?" asked Frank.

"Can't get a word out of him. I'm inclined to believe he doesn't know anything about the men who are at the head of the organization. I think he was only a tool, employed to get the money in circulation. But I wish you two lads would keep on the lookout for any clues. It will help me a lot if we can run these counterfeiters to earth. Then, besides, there is a big reward."

"We'll do our best," they promised.

And, secretly, they wondered what Fenton Hardy would think if he knew how much work they had already put on the case and how much evidence they had already gathered, tending to indicate that the old mill on the Willow River was in some way connected with the activities of the counterfeiting gang.

"If you can get anything definite in this case," said Fenton Hardy, with a smile, "I'll be ready to admit that you have some abilities as detectives—"

"Fenton, don't encourage them," objected Mrs. Hardy.

"Nonsense, Laura," he replied. "If they want to be detectives and if they have the talent for it, you might as well try to keep water from running downhill as to stop them. They've done good work on two difficult cases already."

"And I have a hunch that we'll do something on this case, too," said Frank, with confidence.

CHAPTER XIX

THE RUG BUYER

Two days later an event occurred that brought the activities of the counterfeiters much closer home.

Frank and Joe returned from school on Monday afternoon to find their mother in a state of great agitation. The moment they entered the house they could tell that something unusual had happened, for Mrs. Hardy was sitting by the living-room table gazing disconsolately at a great heap of bills in her lap.

"Where'd you get all the money, mother?" asked Frank, jokingly at first. But his expression became serious when he saw the anxiety and distress in Mrs. Hardy's face. Her fingers were trembling as she picked up the bills and put them on the table.

"What's the matter?" asked Joe quickly. "What's wrong?"

Mrs. Hardy got up and walked across the room toward the window. She looked out at the street for a while, then turned to her sons.

"You didn't see a foreign rug buyer around the streets this afternoon, did you?" she asked them.

The Hardy boys shook their heads.

"Just came from school," they told her. "We didn't meet anybody on the way." Suddenly Frank glanced at the floor. "Why, you've sold the rug!" he exclaimed, in surprise.

The living-room floor had hitherto been covered by a valuable old Persian rug, as soft as moss. It had been bought by Mr. Hardy when on a trip to the city, but Mrs. Hardy had never cared for it. Fenton Hardy had thought to surprise his wife when he brought the rug home, but in a masculine indifference to color schemes he had neglected to see to it that the rug matched the rest of the room. Its color was not what Mrs. Hardy wanted, and inasmuch as the rug had been purchased at an exclusive sale, they had found it impossible to exchange it at the time.

Mrs. Hardy had always said that if she had an opportunity she would get rid of the rug and purchase something different. However, the opportunity was long in coming. Although she had received several offers for it, none of these had been for more than five hundred dollars.

"And," as she said, "I refuse to sell a nine hundred dollar rug for that price."

Now, as the Hardy boys noticed, the rug was gone.

"How much did you get for it?" asked Joe eagerly.

"I gave it away."

"Gave it away?" they exclaimed.

Mrs. Hardy nodded.

"Not intentionally. I've been cheated."

"How?" demanded Frank quickly.

Mrs. Hardy motioned toward the money.

"I've just been to the bank to deposit that money—"

"You don't mean to say it's counterfeit?"

"So the bank cashier told me."

Frank sat down heavily in the nearest chair.

"Well I'll be gosh-hanged!" he exclaimed. "How did this happen? How much did they sting you for?"

"Eight hundred dollars," answered Mrs. Hardy gravely.

Joe whistled in surprise.

"How did it happen?"

"He came here shortly after you boys left for school," began Mrs. Hardy. "It must have been a little before two o'clock."

"Who came here?"

"The rug buyer. He was an odd little fellow, very short and dark. He was a foreigner, you could tell by his appearance. He didn't speak very good English. He was dark and swarthy, with little, keen black eyes. He came up to the front door and asked me if I wanted to buy rugs. When I told him that I didn't want to buy he asked if I had any to sell. He said he was a traveling rug merchant and that he went from city to city, buying and selling and trading rugs."

"So you told him about the living-room rug?" suggested Frank.

"I just thought of it then, and I thought it might be a good chance to get rid of it and perhaps get a better rug in its stead. I mentioned that I had a rug that I might sell, but I told him I didn't think he could pay the price."

"And he asked to see it anyway?" Frank went on.

"When I told him I didn't think he could buy it he merely laughed in a very shrewd sort of way and said that money was no object to him, that he had bought rugs costing as much as two thousand dollars and turned them over at a profit. So I asked him to come into the house and the moment he saw the rug he admired it very much. He asked me how much I wanted for it, so I told him I wanted nine hundred dollars. Of course, I didn't expect to get that much, because that is all the rug cost, but these fellows always haggle over price, so it's best to name a good stiff figure right at the start."

The Hardy boys smiled at this evidence of their mother's shrewdness.

"He said he wouldn't give me nine hundred dollars but he offered seven hundred dollars. I told him that his price was ridiculous, but asked if he had any rugs he wanted to trade for it. He looked rather dubious when I mentioned a trade, and said that while he carried some medium priced rugs with him he carried nothing that could equal the one I wished to sell."

"Did he say where he kept these other rugs?" Frank asked.

"He said they were at his hotel but that his more valuable rugs were all in the city and that it would take a day or so before he could have them sent here. However, he said that he would buy the rug from me for eight hundred dollars and take a chance on being able to sell me a good rug when he should have them sent down from the city."

"Fair enough," remarked Joe.

"It seemed fair enough to me, for of course the rug was worth only about eight hundred dollars, perhaps less, because it has been used for several months. I was under no obligation to buy a new rug from him unless I wished, so I accepted his offer and he paid me the money."

"Eight hundred dollars!"

"In cash. He seemed to carry a great deal of money in a heavy leather wallet. He gave me the money in fifties and fives, and I thought very well of myself for making such a good bargain."

"Until you came to bank the money," Frank said.

"Until I came to bank the money. The cashier glanced at the bills, then told me he was sorry, but that he couldn't accept them. For a moment I didn't understand him, because I had forgotten all about this scare about counterfeit money and hadn't given the matter a thought. Then he told me that the bills were counterfeit. So there was nothing left for me to do but come back home, realizing that I had been very neatly tricked."

"But perhaps you haven't been tricked after all," suggested Frank. "It may be possible that the rug buyer didn't realize the money was bad. Did he say what hotel he was staying at?"

"Yes, he told me, but I called up the police and asked them to find him for me. They investigated and found that there had been no rug buyer staying at that hotel all week, nor at any other hotel in Bayport, so far as they could find."

"That doesn't look so good."

"What's more, they made inquiries at the station and found that a man answering to his description had taken the early afternoon train out. He took the rug with him—not only my rug, but a rug that he had bought from another woman in Bayport."

"He'll probably sell them in some other town."

"Just what he did. They found that he had bought a ticket to the next city but when they got in touch with the police there they found that he had sold the two rugs to a wholesale firm and disappeared. He sold my rug for five hundred dollars, and the other one for three hundred dollars."

"Did he give the other woman counterfeit money, too?"

"Yes."

"He cleaned up on that afternoon's work," remarked Frank. "He didn't lose any time in getting away, either."

"If I had only gone to the bank early it might have been different," said Mrs. Hardy. "As it was, I got there only a few minutes before three o'clock, and by the time I got in touch with the police and by the time they had tried to trace the man here and later found where he had gone—you know how slow they are—it was too late."

"I guess there's no chance of seeing him back in two days with the rug he wanted to sell you," observed Frank. "Either he is in league with the counterfeiters or else he was stung himself for a lot of counterfeit money and decided to get rid of it as smoothly as possible."

Mrs. Hardy was downcast.

"I should have been on my guard," she said. "There has been so much of this bad money going around that I should have been on watch for it, especially with a big sum like eight hundred dollars. It's my own fault, I suppose, but it's hard to lose that much money." She glanced at the heap of bills on the table. "It's not worth the paper it's printed on."

Frank picked up one of the bills and examined it.

"Looks just like the five that the fellow passed on to Joe and me at the station," he commented, testing the quality of the paper. "It comes from the same source, I'll bet."

"Eight hundred dollars!" Joe exclaimed. "That's the biggest haul yet. I'd like to have that rug merchant by the back of the neck right this minute. I'd shake the eight hundred out of him in a hurry."

"I guess there's not much chance of catching him now. He has sold the rugs and made his getaway."

Mrs. Hardy was silent. She felt the loss of the valuable rug very keenly, and still more keenly did she feel the ignominy of having been imposed upon after all the warnings that had been circulated regarding counterfeit money. But the rug merchant had been so plausible, and as she was an unsuspecting woman by nature, she had never for a moment considered the possibility of trickery.

"We'll go down and have a chat with the police," said Frank, getting up. "Although I'm afraid it won't do any good."

"Chief Collig will tell us that he is busy following up clues," remarked Joe, with a laugh. "And that's as far as he'll ever get."

This proved to be the case. When the boys reached the police station they found Chief Collig and Detective Smuff in the midst of a game of pinochle and averse to being disturbed.

When they inquired if there had been any further information regarding the rug merchant, Chief Collig shook his head.

"We're following up some clues," he said gravely; "but there hasn't been any more trace of him."

"Not a trace," corroborated Detective Smuff, with a portentous frown.

"Do you think he'll be arrested?" asked Frank.

Chief Collig looked up.

"Of course he'll be arrested," he declared. "Didn't I say we're followin' up clues? We'll have the fellow behind the bars all right."

"I'm workin' on the case myself," said Detective Smuff, examining his cards wearily.

"Rely on us," advised the chief. "Your play, Smuff."

The boys retired. Somehow, they got the impression that the Bayport police department was not exerting a great deal of effort to try to capture the fraudulent rug buyer.

CHAPTER XX

A NOTE OF WARNING

Three days later, Fenton Hardy, who had been away from home on business, received a note.

No one saw the man who left it at the door. The Hardy boys were at school and Mrs. Hardy was busy in the kitchen. She heard the front doorbell ring and went to answer it.

But when she opened the door there was no one in sight.

She looked out and saw a man walking briskly down the opposite side of the street. A woman with a baby-carriage was strolling past the house, and farther down the street two men were standing talking on the corner.

Somewhat surprised, and imagining that her ears must have deceived her, she was about to close the door when she became aware of a white object that had fluttered to her feet.

It was a cheap envelope, sealed, and with the name of Fenton Hardy written on it in pencil.

Mrs. Hardy picked it up, examined it curiously, then brought it into the house and placed it on the table in her husband's study. It was not an unusual occurrence to have letters left at the door in this manner, as occasionally anonymous letters were left for the detective, giving him hints or advice concerning cases on which he was engaged. To most of these he paid no attention, although sometimes valuable information was brought to his notice in this manner.

This, Mrs. Hardy judged, was another such communication, which was why the person who delivered it had been careful to hurry away after ringing the bell.

Mr. Hardy did not return home until late that afternoon. He had been over to Barmet village where the Federal authorities were closely watching two men thought to be in league with the counterfeiters. Mr. Hardy had followed one man to a near-by city and seen the fellow pass a small package to a woman in black, who had quickly disappeared in a crowd. But the noted detective knew the woman and knew where she could be located when wanted.

The boys had arrived back from school, had left their books at the house, and had set out with Chet Morton for a cruise in the motorboat. When Mr. Hardy came back he glanced over his mail and was settling down to read the evening paper when his wife remembered the note that had been left at the door that afternoon.

"Some one left a letter for you this afternoon," she said. "I heard the doorbell ring, but when I went to answer it there was no one at the door. I picked up a letter, though, and I put it on your study table."

Fenton Hardy went into the study and picked up the letter, slitting open the envelope. Within, was a thin sheet of cheap paper on which had been written a few lines in pencil.

He read the message with a slow smile, then handed the paper over to his wife.

"Some one trying to scare me," he said.

She picked up the note. In a crude, ill-formed hand, she read the following:

"Better give up this counterfeit case or we'll take the shirt off your back. We know this game too well. Let this be a warning to you. Poor Blum is a rank outsider. Better let him go."

Mrs. Hardy looked up anxiously.

"What are you going to do about this note?" she asked.

The detective shrugged.

"Ignore it, of course."

"But they may harm you."

"They may try. They won't be the first ones who have tried to frighten me away from a case."

"But they must be right in Bayport, to deliver a note like this."

"I've suspected all along that their headquarters were here. Don't worry, Laura. I'm not afraid of them."

"But I *do* worry. They're desperate men. They'll stop at nothing."

Fenton Hardy laughed.

"It isn't the first time I've been threatened. It's only a bluff. I'll stay right on the case—although so far I haven't been able to make much progress on it. But this matter of the note is adding insult to injury, don't you think? First of all they send one of their men around here to fool us to the extent of eight hundred dollars with their counterfeit money, and now they try to frighten me away from handling the case any further."

Fenton Hardy looked at the note again, then replaced it carefully in the envelope.

"You didn't see any one on the street after the doorbell rang?" he asked.

"Oh, there were three or four people walking by, but I didn't notice any of them particularly. They all seemed quite average people. None of them looked at all suspicious."

"The chap that delivered the note was probably hiding around the corner of the house until you went inside again. That's their usual scheme. It wouldn't have done much good if you had seen him. Probably some chap they picked up on the street and bribed to slip the note into the door."

"I don't like it!"

At that moment Frank and Joe came into the house, flushed from their outing on the bay. They were laughing at the recollection of some remarkable acrobatic feats that Chet Morton had attempted on the bow of the motorboat, the result of which had been the sudden immersion of Chet in the chilly waters of the bay. He had just left them, his clothes dripping wet, heading for home on his motorcycle, vowing that he could have stood on his hands on the bow of the boat if only Frank hadn't steered to the left when he should have steered to the right.

"However," he had said cheerfully, "I missed my bath last Saturday night, anyway, so this will make up for it."

The Hardy boys recounted their adventures and after Fenton Hardy had chuckled over the plight of Chet he tossed over the mysterious letter to them.

"What do you think of that?" he asked of the boys.

Frank and Joe read the scrawled warning with interest.

"Trying to frighten you away from the case, are they?" said Frank, as he gave back the note.

"Looks like it."

"You won't pay any attention to it, of course?"

"Not a bit. Although your mother seems to think I'll be carried home on a stretcher any day."

"When did the note come?" Joe inquired with deep interest.

Mrs. Hardy told them how the strange letter had been delivered, and when they learned that it had been left at the door instead of being sent through the post-office both boys became immediately excited. They did not, however, air their suspicions at the time and it was not until they were alone after supper that they discussed the topic between them.

"That settles it!" declared Frank with finality. "The counterfeiters *must* be right here in Bayport."

"Or near by."

"That's what I mean. If they were out of town, the letter would have been sent by mail."

"It's getting to be a little too much. As dad said, it was adding insult to injury—tricking mother to the extent of eight hundred dollars and now sending an impudent note like that. It's up to us to use what we know."

"You mean to see if we can find out anything more about the mill?"

"I mean to find out everything there is to be found out about it."

"I'm with you. When do we start?"

"When should we?"

"Tonight."

"So soon?"

"Why not?"

"It's all right with me."

"If we're going to go back there at all we may as well get it over with as soon as we can," said Frank. "I've been thinking over a way to get away with it and I think we should be able to get inside that place and investigate it without much trouble."

"How?"

"Do you remember how Carl Stummer remarked that you looked something like Lester?"

"Yes."

"And there is a bit of a resemblance, too. You are of about the same build, and you both have fair, curly hair. I think you should be able to impersonate him if we went around there at night. At a distance, and at night time, they might mistake you for him, even if we were discovered."

"I never thought of that," Joe admitted. "It isn't a bad idea. I'm willing to try it."

"It will be risky, of course. But I'm practically convinced that the old mill is where this counterfeit money is coming from. The only way we'll ever find out is to go there ourselves. If we told the town police what we suspected they would only laugh at us and probably they'd be so clumsy about taking any action that the counterfeiters would get wind of it. The only way is to keep it to ourselves and go out there quietly and see what we can find."

"How can we get out tonight? Mother won't let us go. She'll be afraid we'll get hurt."

"I hate to do anything underhand, but it's our only chance. We'll go out for a motorcycle trip this evening, and as soon as it gets dark we'll head for the mill. We should reach there about ten o'clock. We'll park the bikes a good distance away from the mill, so they won't hear us coming, and then we'll walk the rest of the way."

"If we get the goods on the counterfeiters we'll be heroes. If we don't we'll catch a lecture for staying out late."

"We'll just have to take our chance on that. But I think that if everything goes well we won't get any lecture."

"How'll we get into the mill?" asked Joe.

"We'll have to wait until we get there before we lay our plans. I've sort of forgotten the layout of the place. But if we work it right I think we should be able to get inside. I'd like to get into that mysterious stone room that Lester mentioned, and see what sort of machinery they have in there. I'll bet it's an engraving plant and a printing press instead of a patent breakfast food machine."

"What if we're caught—"

"That's a chance we're taking. We've got to risk it. What if we find that the place is really the headquarters of this counterfeit gang? Look at it that way."

So for the rest of the evening the boys were conspicuously studious. They were occupied with their books until twilight fell, after which Frank yawned and murmured that he would like a breath of fresh air.

"Think I'll go out for a little spin on the motorcycle," he said casually.

"I'll go with you," observed Joe promptly.

Fenton Hardy looked up.

"Yes, you've been in the house all evening. Go ahead."

"Don't be long," advised Mrs. Hardy.

"We won't be any longer than we can help," said Frank mysteriously.

With that, the Hardy boys left the house and went out to the garage for their motorcycles.

They drove around the streets of Bayport for some time until at last it grew darker. Then they headed their machines out toward the shore road. The moon was just rising over the bay when they left the city, and they drove at good speed into the country.

"Now to tackle the old mill!" exclaimed Frank.

CHAPTER XXI

AT THE MILL

The two boys made good time out into the country and when at last they reached the abandoned road that led down to Willow River it was not quite ten o'clock. As they rode they discussed their plan of action and it was agreed that they should leave the motorcycles beside the road at the same place they had left them on the occasion of their previous visit to the mill.

"I'd like to have them closer to the river," said Frank, "for we might have to clear out of there in a hurry. But we can't afford to let them hear us coming."

"And it's a calm night. They could hear a motorcycle for half a mile," opined his brother.

They left the machines in the shade of some trees by the roadside and went the rest of the way on foot. They could see quite clearly, for the moon had risen higher and the grey ribbon of road extended before them.

"I wish it had been a bit darker," Joe said. "We'll have to be careful when we get near the place."

"They may have some one posted on guard. Oh, well, we can look the place over when we get there."

At last they emerged on the hilltop that overlooked Willow River.

Below them lay the stream, with water shining in the moonlight. The deep banks of willow trees along the borders cast heavy shadows, and a light mist overhung the fields and hedges in the distance.

Gloomy and mysterious, the heavy bulk of the old mill rose from beside the river, near the shimmering silver streak of the mill race. Not a light shone from the building and it appeared absolutely deserted.

"Perhaps they've all moved away," suggested Joe.

"I noticed that the buildings were all boarded up when we were here last time. They haven't moved away, never fear."

Cautiously, the boys went down the slope.

They left the road and kept to the shadows of the trees, skirting the open space of meadow that lay between the grove and the mill itself. They did not speak, for the night was so calm and clear that sound carried for a considerable distance. They could hear the dull roar of the rapids and the waterfall, sounding hollow and lonely in the moonlit night.

They came to the edge of the grove and moved slowly about in the deep shadows, the grass sinking beneath their feet. When they had reached a point about two hundred feet from the mill they paused to reconnoitre.

"We've got to cross that open space," whispered Frank.

"And what then?"

"See that willow tree beside the mill?"

Joe nodded.

"It reaches right to the roof. It looks to be our best bet. If we can climb that tree and drop to the roof or get in a window we'll be all right."

"As long as we can get up the tree without being heard."

"We have to take our chances on that," Frank said, in a low voice. "I think it's going to be harder to cross that open space."

For two hundred feet the grassy sward was bathed in moonlight. They could not walk across it without being in full view of any one who might be watching from the mill. But it had to be crossed as the mill itself was isolated on the bank of the river and on this side there was no protecting shade to enable them to creep up closer.

"We'll have to crawl across the grass," Frank whispered. "Ready?"

"I'm ready."

"Go easy and quiet. If you hear a sound, don't move."

They dropped to their hands and knees, then left the shadow of the wood. They began to crawl slowly toward the willow tree at the rear of the mill.

Inch by inch they made their way forward.

The moon was high in the sky and seemed like a giant searchlight. It seemed impossible that they could cross that open space without being discovered. Every blade of grass seemed clearly revealed by the moonlight.

When they were about half way toward the mill they heard a sound in the distance.

It was the banging of a heavy door.

There was a warning whisper from Frank. They lay motionless in the thick grass.

For a moment a deep silence prevailed. Then, from the mill, they heard a surly voice:

"I saw some one out on the hillside."

They were startled. But still they did not move. Their only hope of safety lay in silence and in remaining motionless.

"You're crazy, Markel," replied some one. "There's no one out there."

"I tell you I saw some one crawling down through the grass. I'm sure of it. I saw him from that upper window."

"Whereabouts?"

"Out there—see? Can't you see something dark up there?"

There was silence for a moment or so. Then the second man laughed.

"It's only a log."

"I tell you, it isn't a log. A log doesn't move."

"That isn't moving."

"It was."

"Well, if you're so sure of it, why don't you go on up and see? You're getting so nervous lately that you think people are hanging around here all the time."

"I've got a right to be nervous. We're not safe here, I tell you. We should have moved out of here a week ago."

"We'll never find a place as safe as this."

"Is that so? Ever since those two boys came snooping around here and asking Lester questions I've been suspicious. They've got their eye on this place, let me tell you. They were down at the railway station the day I slipped the package to Burgess, and I'm mighty sure they saw me."

"Just a couple of kids. You're too nervous."

"Well, I'm going up on the hill and take a look at that log, as you call it."

As it happened, there was a log lying in the grass close by Frank. But he realized that if Markel came up to investigate he would have no chance to evade discovery. They could not get up and run away—at least not until capture seemed inevitable. Frank's heart sank. They had been discovered before they had a chance even to reach the mill.

At that moment relief came from a most unexpected quarter.

A dark cloud that had been creeping across the sky began to obscure the moon, and gradually the vivid illumination that bathed the hillside gave way to gloom and darkness. The cloud hid the moon completely.

"Now's our chance!" whispered Frank, to his brother. "Head toward the willow tree."

He scrambled to his feet and together the boys raced down the slope toward the willow tree back of the mill. Their feet made no sound in the deep grass. They were taking a desperate chance, they knew, for, in spite of the cloud that had fallen across the moon, Markel might be able to see them.

But Markel had just emerged from the mill and his eyes were not yet accustomed to the gloom. As the boys reached the shelter of the willow tree, the moon emerged from behind the cloud and slowly the hillside was again bathed in radiance.

Panting, the boys halted beneath the tree and looked back.

They could see the dark figure of Markel as he cut across the slope in a diagonal direction and they watched as he drew near the place where they had been lying.

They saw him stop, kick at something in the grass, then they heard him mutter as he turned away.

"Well, what was it?" called the other man from the doorway of the mill.

"It was a log all right," admitted Markel in a disgruntled tone. "But I could have sworn I saw it move a while ago."

"Better get your eyes tested."

To this pleasantry Markel made no reply, but trudged on down the slope until he again reached the mill. The boys pressed close to the willow tree.

"You may think I'm being too careful," they heard Markel saying. "But we've got good reason to be careful. You know what'll happen to the whole crowd of us if we're caught."

"Sure. About twenty years in the pen. But we're not going to be caught I tell you."

"Don't be too sure. We can't afford to take chances, anyway. I'd rather keep my eyes open and get fooled by a few logs on the hillside than feel too safe and spend the rest of my life behind the bars."

"I guess you're right. Anyway, everything is all right tonight."

"I'm going to take a trip around the mill, anyhow."

"Your nerves must be jumpy."

"They are," snapped Markel. "My nerves are always jumpy when I think I see something moving down toward here from the woods—and I don't care whether that was a log or not, I saw something move."

"Oh, probably a sheep or a cow that strayed from one of the farms. Or even a dog."

"Yes, it might have been a dog," Markel admitted.

"We'd better get to work. Dock is waiting for us."

"I'm going to walk around the mill once, anyway."

"Go ahead. Go ahead, then," said the other man. "I'll be inside with Dock."

The boys heard heavy footsteps as Markel left the doorway, and then they saw his dark figure in the moonlight as he came around the side of the mill.

They pressed close against the willow tree and lowered their heads so that their faces would not be seen. Both were wearing dark clothes and dark caps. They did not look up, for they knew that their faces would be grey against the surrounding darkness and that Markel might see them.

In an agony of suspense they heard the footsteps come closer.

Markel poked around among the rubbish at the side of the mill. It was plain that he was not yet convinced that he had been suffering from a delusion when he saw the moving forms on the hillside and he meant to satisfy himself beyond any shadow of doubt that there was no one lurking in the vicinity of the mill.

Nearer and nearer he came.

His body brushed against the overhanging branches of the willow. He was now only a few yards away from the Hardy boys.

Breathlessly, they waited. They stood, rigid and motionless, not daring to look up.

Markel's footsteps came to a stop. He was standing but a short distance away, listening intently.

Had he seen them?

CHAPTER XXII

THROUGH THE ROOF

The Hardy boys always said that the few seconds in which they stood in the shadow of the willow tree with the suspicious Markel almost within arm's length of them, not knowing whether they had been discovered or not, were the longest seconds they had ever known.

It seemed hours before they finally heard Markel give a grunt of satisfaction and trudge away in the opposite direction.

Even then it was minutes before they dared move, before they ventured to raise their heads and look about them. When at last they did so, Markel was no longer in sight.

They heard him go around the other side of the mill and finally they heard his footsteps as he trudged up into the doorway.

The door banged at last.

Markel was back in the mill. They breathed freely.

"That was a close call," whispered Joe, in relief.

"Not a sound," cautioned Frank. "They may be listening."

They waited in the shadows for a long time. But evidently Markel had given up the search, his suspicions allayed. Finally a strange sound came from the interior of the mill, a strange whirring sound, followed by the muffled rumble of machinery.

"What's that?" whispered Joe.

They listened. The rumbling sound rose and fell with monotonous regularity. Finally Frank nudged his brother and pointed to one of the boarded windows half way up the side of the mill.

A faint streak of light was apparent through a crack in the boards.

"That must be where their workroom is," Frank whispered.

The sound of machinery in motion continued.

"We've struck them at the right time," said Joe, in a low voice. "They must do their work at night."

"We've got to make sure."

"How can we get inside the mill?"

"The willow tree. We'll have to climb it and drop down on the roof."

"What if they hear us? We won't have a chance to get away."

"They won't hear us," said Frank confidently. "The walls are of stone. Anyway, the sound of machinery will drown out any noises from outside. It's our only chance to get into the mill."

"Lead the way, then."

Frank began to ascend the willow tree.

It was difficult work, for although the tree was large, it bent and swayed under his weight. It was impossible for both of them to attempt to climb at the same time, and Joe was forced to wait on guard at the bottom, listening as his brother made his way higher and higher among the springy branches.

The topmost branches drooped over the roof of the mill, and when at length Frank had reached them he swung himself over until his feet touched the top of the building. For a second or so he was uncertain of his footing but at length he was able to stand steadily on the sloping surface. He released his grasp and the branches swished back. So far he had been able to move with a minimum of noise and he was confident that his ascent to the roof had been unheard.

He called softly to Joe, and in a few minutes a rustling among the branches indicated that his brother was also climbing the tree.

Frank waited and directed his brother so that Joe was soon swinging out from the branches. He dropped lightly to the roof of the old mill.

"There should be some sort of trapdoor here," said Frank quietly. "If there isn't we'll have to lower ourselves over the edge to one of the upper windows. I noticed a small open window around at the front. But there is probably a trapdoor."

The mill roof was not on an abrupt slant, so that the boys were able to make their way along among the shingles without a great deal of difficulty. The roof was in a bad state of repair, and once Frank came upon a wide hole, where the shingles had fallen off and where the wood beneath had rotted away.

But there was no trapdoor.

"We'll tackle that hole in the roof," he decided.

The gap was only about a foot square, but when Frank turned his flashlight on it he saw that immediately beneath them was a sort of attic, the topmost room in the mill.

Quietly, they began enlarging the hole in the roof. Fortunately, the effect of rain and wind and weather had been such as to render the roof extremely weak. The shingles broke off easily, and bit by bit they made the hole wider until at last it was a large, black gap.

They did not throw the débris to the ground, but piled it carefully up on the roof near by. The work of enlarging the hole in the roof had taken them some time, as they worked cautiously and deliberately with a view to a minimum of noise. Finally they agreed that there was sufficient space to admit the passage of a human body, and Frank began to lower himself through the opening.

The attic was very low, only about five feet from floor to roof, and when Frank's feet touched the boards beneath he tested their strength. Having satisfied himself that the floor was strong enough to support his weight, he crouched down, flashing the light about him in search of some mode of egress to the lower part of the building.

He cautioned Joe to wait on the roof. The condition of the building was such that the floor might not be strong enough to hold them both, in which event disaster would overtake them.

At first he thought the attic was entirely separated from the rest of the mill. The floor seemed to be solid. There was not the sign of a stairway or opening of any kind.

Frank was bitterly disappointed. To have been successful so far and then find themselves in a narrow little room under the eaves of the mill!

Suddenly he caught sight of a crack between the boards, and he held the flashlight closer to investigate. He found a space about two feet square, evidently a trapdoor cut in the floor, and he tugged at the edges of this until at length he managed to raise one side of it. Then, quietly, he worked at the trapdoor until he was able to lift it out of place. He raised it and put it quietly to one side.

It was very dark beneath the opening and he flashed the light down once for a brief second. It was long enough to show him that a ladder led from the opening to the floor of the musty, unoccupied room below.

So far, so good!

He whispered to Joe.

"All right. Come ahead."

In the aperture in the roof he could see Joe's form silhouetted, and then his brother scrambled down beside him in the attic.

"I've found a trapdoor," Frank whispered.

"Where does it lead to?"

"There's another room directly below us. It's empty. The workroom must be just below that. But there's a door at the far side of the room, and I think it leads to the stairs that run to the bottom of the mill."

"Shall we go ahead?"

"May as well. We haven't been seen yet. Nor heard."

Frank handed the flashlight to his brother, then groped his way to the trapdoor. He managed to place one foot on the top rung of the ladder beneath the opening.

It held beneath his weight, although the ladder creaked warningly.

Cautiously, step by step, he descended.

There was the utmost need for silence. From the position of the flash of light that he had seen through the crack in the boarded window, he judged that the workroom of the counterfeiters was about midway in the mill, immediately below the deserted room into which he was now descending. The mill widened out toward the bottom, and Frank judged that the locked stone room on the ground floor and the room above were those used by the men.

He reached the bottom of the ladder at last, touching the floor without a sound. He whispered back to Joe, and in a few seconds a faint noise from above told him that his brother was also descending into the dark room.

The rumble of machinery was louder and came from directly beneath his feet. Also he could hear a muffled murmur of voices. He had not been mistaken. The workroom was immediately beneath.

Joe reached the bottom of the ladder in silence. Frank groped for the flashlight. He switched it on.

The room in which they were standing was a low-ceilinged, bare chamber, on the far side of which was a doorway that led to a flight of stairs. Frank stepped cautiously over to the door and peered down the stairs. They led to a landing a short distance below, and continued from there to the bottom of the mill. The room beneath the one in which they were standing evidently opened onto the landing.

Frank made a mental note of all these features so that he would have a good idea of the layout of the building in case it became necessary for them to make a hurried retreat.

He heard a whisper from behind him.

He turned quickly.

Joe was crouching on the floor, peering through a crack in the boards. He motioned to Frank to come over.

CHAPTER XXIII

THE ALARM

Frank crouched on the floor beside his brother.

He switched off the flashlight. The room was in darkness. Immediately he could see a glow of light through one of the cracks in the flooring.

By crouching close to the floor he could see through the cracks into the room beneath.

At the sight he saw he almost gave an exclamation of triumph. There were three men in the room, the three men of the mill—Uncle Dock, his companion, and Markel. They were standing beside a machine that looked like a small printing press. Their sleeves were rolled up and they were wearing inky aprons.

The printing press was rumbling steadily and Markel was feeding it with small sheets of peculiar greenish paper.

But it was what was heaped on a low table beside the press that particularly attracted the attention of the Hardy boys.

There they saw neat bundles of crisp, new bills. They were heaped high on the low table, each bundle in a thin, paper wrapper, and their denominations ranged from five to fifty dollars.

"They're printing counterfeit money!" whispered Frank.

Joe nodded. A tingling excitement possessed them. In spite of the fact that they knew the bills were counterfeit there was something fascinating in the sight of those hundreds of crisp, green bills.

Their view of the room was limited, but by moving from side to side they were gradually able to take in all the details of the little chamber. Above the constant rumble of the press they could hear the voices of three men.

"Once we get this shipment sent out we'll be on easy street," said Uncle Dock.

"If we can get it all placed," grumbled Markel.

"We'll get it placed all right," said the other man. "We haven't had any trouble so far. Burgess and his crowd have put over their part of the deal pretty well."

"It'd be better if they'd stay away from Bayport," said Markel. "First thing we know, they'll be figuring the money is coming from here."

"Why should they?" said Uncle Dock. "It's being sent around to the other towns as well as Bayport."

"That fool Paul Blum mighty near gave the game away."

"He can't say anything. He doesn't know where the stuff is coming from. I think he has an idea we're round the mill, but he isn't sure. He won't give us away."

"Just the same," said Markel, "I'll be relieved when the whole thing is over and we can get out of here. This patent breakfast food story is all right for a while, but country people are too curious. The farmers are talking because we won't do any milling for them."

"Let 'em talk. We'll be out of here by the end of the week. That last photo-engraving you made for us is a good one. It would take an expert to tell it from the original. We'll make fifty thousand dollars from that shipment of tens alone."

"It's good enough," admitted Markel, evidently pleased with the compliment, "but I've said all along that our paper is too thin. It should have just a little more body to it. But it's too hard to imitate. The genuine banknote paper is a bit heavier."

"What's the matter with you tonight, Markel?" asked Uncle Dock. "You have been nervous and jumpy all evening. First of all, you think you see some one sneaking around the mill. Now you're afraid we're all going to be pinched. By the end of the week we'll be out of here and living on the fat of the land. This is the biggest counterfeiting deal that has ever been put across in the United States. I'd imagine you'd be feeling proud of yourself. By the time it is all over we should be worth a quarter of a million dollars each."

"All the more reason for being careful. You have to watch your step in a game like this."

"And haven't we watched our step? Who would ever suspect this old mill? Why, there's Hardy, the detective, living right in Bayport. He has never suspected a thing. And the Federal dicks think we have a plant somewhere in the woods back of Barmet village!"

"It was a good idea to take over the mill, I'll admit. But the sooner we're out of here, the better."

"Well, the last batch of bills will be run off tonight. We'll clear out tomorrow morning and send down for the machinery as soon as we can."

Frank nudged his brother. So the counterfeiters were planning an early escape!

They peered through the cracks in the floor and watched the three men moving about as the press rumbled and bill after bill was added to the pile on the table.

"Easier way to make money than working," remarked Uncle Dock, with a satisfied smile.

"I'm going to take a trip around the world with my share," said the second man.

"What are you going to do, Markel?"

"I'll follow the horses. I'm going to visit every race track in America this year. I'll double my money."

"You'll lose every cent of it."

"No chance."

Uncle Dock smiled.

"Wait and see. Smarter men than you have lost all their money on the horses."

Frank and Joe had heard enough and had seen enough to know that there was no further doubt as to the nature of the activities of the three men of the mill. They had seen the counterfeiting plant in operation and from the conversation of the three men there was no doubt but that this was the plant that had been responsible for flooding the East with spurious bills in the past few weeks.

The counterfeiters were evidently running off a last shipment of bills before closing up the plant and moving away. It behooved the Hardy boys to act quickly.

"Where will we go when we clear out?" they heard Markel say.

"We'll separate," answered Uncle Dock. "We'll meet in New York."

"Where?"

"We'll meet Burgess at his apartment. You remember the address don't you?" Uncle Dock gave an address in the Forties, and Frank instantly registered it in his memory. It might come in useful in case the counterfeiters slipped through their hands.

He got up slowly from his cramped position, and Joe followed his example. Frank led the way toward the door that opened on the landing.

"We'd better get out of here," he whispered.

"What will we do?"

"We'll go to Bayport for help. We can't tackle these fellows alone."

"How will we get out? There's no use trying to get out by the roof. We might break our necks trying to reach that tree again."

"We can go down the stairs," said Frank quietly.

"And out the front door?"

"It's probably only bolted on the inside. If we can get past the door of that workroom we should be all right."

"Come on, then."

Frank led the way. He stepped out on the landing. Both boys were wearing light "sneakers" that made little noise.

Step by step, they descended the stairs. Step by step, they drew closer to the landing that led to the counterfeiters' room. They could hear the muffled sound of the printing press and the vague voices of the three men.

They reached the landing at last. A streak of yellow light shone from beneath the door of the workroom. The stairs led on toward the bottom of the mill.

Each lad held his breath as he traversed the dangerous distance to the next flight of stairs. Here, if anywhere, they were in danger of being heard.

But the low voices within the room continued; the steady rumble of the press went on without interruption. Frank gained the top of the steps. Joe followed.

They went slowly down the stairs. Frank could see the dim outlines of the mill machinery in the large room below, with the dark shape of the door in the distance. Once they gained the door they would be comparatively safe.

The thought had hardly crossed his mind when his foot struck suddenly against some solid object.

There was a slight noise, the object moved, then it went clattering down the stairs with an uproar that seemed to awaken the echoes from one end of the mill to the other.

He had kicked over a pail that had been left lying on the steps!

The noise would not be unnoticed—he knew that. With a bound, he had reached the bottom of the steps. There was no time to seek escape by the door, for already he could hear some one running across the floor of the workroom above. They must hide, and hide quickly.

Joe was close behind him.

Frank turned and sped through an open doorway close at hand. The boys found themselves in a gloomy stone room in which several large pieces of machinery could be dimly distinguished in the faint light.

From the floor above they could hear voices. A door opened. Frank glanced back and he could see a beam of light against the wall by the stairs.

"I'm certain I heard a noise!" they heard Markel saying. "I'm going to find out what caused it."

CHAPTER XXIV

TRAPPED

The Hardy boys could see little chance of escape.

Markel was coming down the stairs. They could hear his heavy boots as they clattered on the steps.

Frank glanced around the room. There was one window, but it was boarded up. There was but one door, the one through which they had come.

Markel had reached the foot of the stairs by now. They heard him give a grunt of surprise as he picked up the pail.

"This was what did it," he called back to some one on the landing. "It fell down the stairs."

"Well, what of it?" Uncle Dock called down to him.

"Some one must have knocked it over."

"Couldn't have been any one," sniffed Uncle Dock. "There's nobody around. It's just your nerves."

"Pails don't fall downstairs unless somebody knocks them over," said Markel stubbornly.

"Ask Lester. Perhaps it was him."

They heard Markel go into another room. For a few moments there was silence. Then Markel came out again.

"He's asleep—or shamming. I didn't waken him. But I'm going to take a look around, just the same."

His footsteps drew nearer the room in which the brothers were hiding. Frank sprang lightly in behind the open door, pressing himself close against the wall. Joe wedged in beside him.

Markel came into the room.

He was carrying a flashlight and its beam illuminated the corners of the musty chamber. The Hardy boys waited in suspense. Would he think of looking behind the door?

Suddenly there was a mutter of disgust from Markel and a rustle as something flitted out of a corner.

"Me-e-ow!"

"Only the cat!" grunted Markel.

The animal purred ingratiatingly, but Markel aimed a vicious kick at the cat. It missed its mark, however, and Markel turned and trudged out of the room.

"Find anything?" called Uncle Dock from the top of the stairs.

"It was only the cat," answered Markel sullenly. "The brute must have been prowling around on the stairs and knocked the pail over."

"Well, come back and get to work. I hope you're satisfied now. I knew it must have been something like that."

Markel gave no answer, but went back up the stairs. After a while the door of the workroom banged behind him and soon the roar and rattle of the printing press broke out anew.

Frank took a deep breath.

"That's the closest call I ever went through," he whispered, in relief.

"Let's get out of here. Quick! I'd like to give that cat about a quart of cream for breakfast."

They tiptoed quietly out of the room and made their way to the front door of the mill. It was, as Frank had predicted, bolted on the inside, but he drew the bolt and the door swung slowly open.

Frank placed his fingers on his lips as a sign for silence. To this Joe nodded understandingly.

Then from a distance came an unexpected sound—the mewing of a cat!

Both lads had to grin—indeed, it was all Joe could do to keep from laughing outright.

They slipped outside, closing the door behind them.

"Now to get back to Bayport," whispered Frank. "We'll have to hurry."

They sped across the grass toward the borders of the dark wood, and not until they had reached its friendly shade did they look behind. The ghostly old mill stood by the gleaming river, dark and sinister in the clear moonlight.

"We'll be back," Joe said, as he glanced back at the mill.

"There is going to be a big surprise for that gang before the night is over."

"I'll say. Let's get started on it."

They ran up through the trees until they reached the deserted road, where they had left their motorcycles. Within a few minutes they were in the saddles and roaring back in the direction of Bayport.

They made the journey at full speed, but at that it was late before the gleaming lights of the city came into view. The motorcycles sped down the shore road on to the concrete boulevards, then raced through the city streets, now almost deserted save for an occasional late trolley or nighthawk taxi.

At length they drew up before the Hardy home and raced up the front walk. They found their father in the house, sitting up for them.

"What on earth kept you out so late? Your mother—" Fenton Hardy began, but Frank interrupted him.

"We've found the counterfeiters!"

"The what?" demanded Mr. Hardy, in astonishment.

"The counterfeiters. Get some men and we can catch the whole crowd this very minute."

"Is this right?" asked the detective swiftly.

"We've found their plant. We saw them making money. We can bring you there right away. They don't know that we saw them."

"And they're getting ready to leave in the morning," put in Joe.

"Where are they?" demanded Fenton Hardy.

"In the old Turner mill on Willow River. We've just come from there."

Mr. Hardy was a man who wasted little time once he had grasped the essentials of a situation. Without a word he hurried over to his study and picked up the telephone. He asked for a number and, after it was secured, he held a brief, curt conversation. Then he put down the telephone and the receiver clicked.

"We'll have a posse out there in half an hour," he said to his sons. "Three state troopers and two Secret Service men who have been working on this case are in town. Will that be enough?"

"There are three in the counterfeiting gang," Frank told him.

"We'll have enough. And now tell me how you found out about the old mill."

Briefly, Frank and Joe told him how their suspicions had first been aroused by the mysterious activities about the mill, how they had visited the place and found that strangers were not welcome, how they had finally resolved to investigate for themselves, and how they had that night gone to the mill and seen the counterfeiting plant in actual operation.

Their story was interrupted by the arrival of an automobile which drew up in front of the Hardy home with a squeal of brakes. A man in uniform stepped out and ran up the walk.

"Here are the officers," said Mr. Hardy. "Come along."

They left the house and met the officer on the steps. Mr. Hardy spoke to him.

"They are at the old Turner mill on Willow River," he said quietly. "I suppose you know how to get there."

"Can't say that I do," said the officer. "Not by car."

"Follow the shore road and then cut in on that deserted loop. It used to run right past the mill before the shore road was built."

The trooper nodded.

"I remember now. The deserted road, eh? We'll get there all right."

"Better leave the car back on the road some distance and go the rest of the way on foot," suggested Frank. "We can sneak up on 'em better that way."

They clambered into the automobile. The other men were broad-shouldered, keen-eyed fellows with determined faces. The moonlight glinted on rifle barrels and revolvers.

Through the cool night sped the automobile, out the shore road, leaving Bayport behind, until at last the car turned off into the deserted road, rocking and bumping to and fro in the ruts.

When they reached the place where Frank and Joe had abandoned the motorcycles earlier in the evening the boys spoke to the driver, whereupon he brought the car to a stop.

They got out and stood in a little group in the moonlit road. Fenton Hardy was in charge of the raid, and he gave his orders quickly and with precision. The men were to follow the road until they reached the meadow between the wood and the mill. The troopers were to deploy out so as to come up in the rear of the mill; the Secret Service men and the others were to take the front way.

They trudged down the road until at last they stood at the edge of the wood and they could see the mill below them in the moonlight. Then the three troopers moved off to the right, keeping well in the shade, preparatory to cutting down across the meadow toward the back of the mill.

Fenton Hardy, the two Secret Service men and the boys walked boldly across the meadow.

They were not seen. There was not a sound from the mill.

When they reached the front of the building they could see the dark forms of the three troopers who flitted across the grass and waited in readiness back of the mill in case any one should attempt to escape that way.

Mr. Hardy tried the front door. It swung open. He stepped inside. The Secret Service men followed. The boys crowded close at their heels.

"Which room?" whispered the detective.

"At the top of the stairs," Frank told him.

At that moment the door of the workroom opened and they could see a man run out onto the landing.

"Who's there?" called out a startled voice.

It was Markel. He was clearly silhouetted in the light from the workroom.

"The police," answered Mr. Hardy. "Put up your hands! We have you covered."

In reply, Markel flung himself flat on the floor, there was a streak of crimson, and a revolver shot roared out. Mr. Hardy and the Secret Service men had their weapons ready and they replied with a fusillade of shots.

The light in the room at the head of the landing had gone out. With a bound, Mr. Hardy reached the stairs, then raced up the steps. When he reached the landing, however, he found that it was deserted. Markel had escaped the bullets and had crawled back into the room, for the door was closed.

Fenton Hardy launched himself against the door of the workroom, but it did not budge. He could hear sounds of voices, a noise of banging and of running about in the room beyond.

The Secret Service men and the two boys reached the landing.

"Break in the door!" snapped Mr. Hardy.

Together they launched themselves against the door, and there was a splintering sound, but still the barrier held.

"Again!"

With a concerted rush they plunged forward once more. The door fell in with a crash.

Fenton Hardy switched on his flashlight, for the room was in darkness.

There was the printing press, there was the table with the packages of counterfeit money—but the counterfeiters were gone. The window was wide open. They had made their escape that way.

From beneath the window came the sound of rough voices, a shot, a loud yell. Mr. Hardy ran to the window and looked out.

"We got 'em. sir!" called out a voice.

Underneath the willow tree were six figures, and three of them were troopers. Each man held a prisoner. The counterfeiters had been captured.

CHAPTER XXV

THE RECKONING

When the full story of the activities of the counterfeiters became known next day, Bayport found that the Hardy boys had succeeded in breaking up one of the most dangerous bands that had ever baffled the Federal authorities.

After the capture of Uncle Dock and his associates, Fenton Hardy and the Secret Service men had wasted no time. Frank had remembered the New York address of the mysterious Burgess, that he had heard Uncle Dock mention, and a telegram to the New York police resulted in the arrest of this man, who turned out to be the brains of the gang, the man who had arranged for the distribution of the spurious bills. The crooks in Barmet village, and the rascally woman in black were also apprehended.

"The machinery in the mill," Mr. Hardy told his sons, "was the most complete and efficient they could obtain. Markel, it seems, was at one time an expert photo-engraver. He furnished the engravings that enabled them to make such an excellent imitation of United States currency, while Uncle Dock and the other man helped him turn out the bills. Burgess saw to it that they got the proper paper and also planned the distribution. There were enough bad bills lying on the table when we raided the place to have netted them almost half a million dollars between them."

Thanks to the quick work of the officers, not one member of the gang had escaped. In Burgess' rooms had been found a notebook containing the names and addresses of the agents he had working for him, distributing the counterfeit money throughout the country, and by the next day every man had been apprehended.

The two Secret Service men who had aided in the final round-up of the counterfeiters at the old mill called personally at the Hardy home next day to congratulate the boys.

"We've been working around here for almost a week trying to get the goods on these men," said one, "but never once did we think of the old mill. What made you suspicious of that place?"

Frank told him how they had first learned that strangers had taken over the mill and told of their first visit to the place.

"To tell the truth," he said, "my first suspicions were when Uncle Dock offered to give us a reward for helping save Lester from the river. He took two five dollar bills from his pocket and offered them to us. Then the other man snatched them from him, turned around, and later offered them to us again."

The Secret Service man smiled.

"Uncle Dock offered you two counterfeit bills and the other man was afraid they would be detected and that you would know where they came from."

"I suppose that was his idea. But it made me suspicious. After that, Joe and I kept watching the place and as everything seemed to indicate that something suspicious was going on at the mill we made up our mind to pay them a visit."

"And a very lucky thing it was that you did. It was a smart piece of work and I want to assure you that the Government won't forget it."

The Government did not forget it. Before the month was out, the Hardy boys had received a check for one thousand dollars as a reward for the part they had played in the capture of the counterfeiters.

"Enough money," Chet Morton said when he heard of it, "to buy gas for the motorboat for a couple of years, anyway."

As for Uncle Dock and his gang, they were all sentenced to long terms of imprisonment. Frank and Joe made particular inquiries about Lester and they asked their father to see to it that the boy was well taken care of. The result of Mr. Hardy's efforts in Lester's behalf was the discovery that "Uncle Dock" was not the boy's uncle at all, but a rascally impostor who had made claim for the lad at an orphan asylum and who had planned to bring him up in a life of crime.

A well-to-do citizen of Bayport, who heard of the case, offered to give Lester a home and see that he was sent to school. The boy was accordingly assured of a brighter future than had confronted him while he was with Uncle Dock, and no one was more pleased than the Hardy boys.

"We'll take you out with us in the motorboat, Lester," they told him.

"Will you?" he asked, his face lighting up with pleasure.

"Sure—you're one of the gang now."

"And will you take me with you when you go detectiving?"

"When we go what?" exclaimed Joe.

"When you go detectiving."

The Hardy boys laughed.

"Oh, you mean when we're trying to be detectives. We'll see, Lester. But the chances are we won't have a chance to be detectives for a long while now. Counterfeiters don't start operating around Bayport every day, you know."

"And it's a good thing they don't," Joe added.

But the Hardy boys were destined to have other adventures in which they were to have opportunities of displaying their ability as detectives quite as timely as those which had fallen to their lot in the affair of the old mill. What some of these happenings were will be related in the next volume, called, "The Hardy Boys: The Missing Chums."

When they received their check which was the reward from the Government for their clever work in running the counterfeiters to earth, they were accompanied to the bank by Chet Morton and Lester, Jerry Gilroy and Phil Cohen, Tony Prito and Biff Hooper, for the Hardy boys had promised to celebrate by treating their friends to ice-cream, to be followed by a motorboat race, wherein Tony, in the *Napoli*, was going to make a second attempt to beat the *Sleuth*.

"I guess ten dollars will cover it," said Frank, as he handed the check over to the cashier. "We can buy gas with the money that's left over."

"And you want to deposit nine hundred and ninety dollars?"

"Yes."

The cashier handed over two five dollar bills. Chet Morton seized one, bit it, gazed reflectively at the ceiling for a moment, then gave it back to Frank.

"I guess it's good," he said. "There's so much counterfeit money going around, these days, that one can't be too careful."

THE MISSING CHUMS

ORIGINALLY PUBLISHED IN 1928.

CHAPTER I

THE THREE STRANGERS

"You certainly ought to have a dandy trip."

"I'll say we will, Frank! We sure wish you could come along."

Frank Hardy grinned ruefully and shook his head.

"I'm afraid we're out of luck. Joe and I may take a little trip later on, but we can't make it this time."

"Just think of it!" said Chet Morton, the other speaker. "A whole week motorboating along the coast! We're the lucky boys, eh, Biff?"

Biff Hooper, at the wheel of his father's new motorboat, nodded emphatically.

"You bet we're lucky. I'm glad dad got this boat in time for the summer holidays. I've been dreaming of a trip like that for years."

"It won't be the same without the Hardy Boys," returned Chet. "I had it all planned out that Frank and Joe would be coming along with us in their own boat and we'd make a real party of it."

"Can't be done," observed Joe Hardy, settling himself more comfortably in the back of the boat. "There's nothing Frank and I would like better—but duty calls!" he exclaimed dramatically, slapping himself on the chest.

"Duty, my neck!" grunted Frank. "We just have to stay at home while dad is in Chicago, that's all. It'll be pretty dull without Chet and Biff around to help us kill time."

"You can put in the hours thinking of Biff and me," consoled Chet. "At night you can just picture us sitting around our campfire away up the coast, and in the daytime you can imagine us speeding away out over the bounding main." He postured with one foot on the gunwale. "A sailor's life for me, my hearties! Yo, ho, and a bottle of ink!"

The boat gave a sudden lurch at that moment, for Biff Hooper had not yet mastered the art of navigation and Chet wavered precariously for a few seconds, finally losing his balance and sitting down heavily in a smear of grease at the bottom of the craft.

> *"Yo ho, and a bottle of ink*
> *And he nearly fell into the drink,"*

chanted Frank Hardy, as the boys roared with laughter at their chum's discomfiture.

"Poet!" sniffed Chet, as he got up. Then, as he gingerly felt the seat of his trousers: "Another pair of pants ready for the cleaners. I ought to wear overalls when I go boating." He grinned as he said it, for Chet Morton was the soul of good nature and it took a great deal more than a smear of grease to erase his ready smile.

The four boys, Frank and Joe Hardy, Chet Morton and Biff Hooper, all chums in the same set at the Bayport high school, were out on Barmet Bay in the *Envoy*, the Hooper motorboat, helping Biff learn to run the craft. Their assistance consisted chiefly of mocking criticisms of the luckless Biff's posture at the helm and sundry false alarms to the effect that the boat was springing a leak or that the engine was about to blow up. Each announcement had the effect of precipitating the steersman into a panic of apprehension and sending his tormentors into convulsions of laughter.

Biff had made good progress, however, as he had been with the Hardy boys on previous occasions in their own motorboat, the *Sleuth*, and he had picked up the rudiments of handling the craft. He was anxious to be a first-rate pilot before starting up the coast on his projected trip with Chet Morton the following week. He had an aptitude for mechanics and he was satisfied that he would have a thorough understanding of his boat by the time they were ready to start.

"If the coast guards find two little boys like you roaming around in a great big motorboat they're likely to give you a spanking and send you back home," laughed Frank. "I'll bet you'll be back in Bayport inside of two days."

"Rats!" replied Chet, inelegantly, if forcefully. "If our grub holds out we'll be away more than the week."

"There's no danger of that. Not with you along," Joe remarked, and deftly dodged a wad of waste that Chet flung at him. Chet Morton's enormous appetite was proverbial among the chums.

"Just sore because you can't come along with us," Chet scoffed. "You know mighty well that the two of you would give your eye-teeth to be on this trip. Oh, well, we'll tell you all about it when we get back."

"A lot of comfort that will be!"

"A leak!" roared Chet suddenly, pounding Biff on the back. "The boat has sprung a leak. Get a pail!"

"What!" shouted Biff, in alarm, starting up from the wheel. Then, for the fifth time that afternoon, he realized that he had been fooled and he sank back with a look of disgust on his face.

"Some time that boat *will* spring a leak and I won't believe you," he warned, settling down to his steering again.

"I'll be good," promised Chet, sitting down and looking out over the bay. "Say, there's a big brute of a motorboat coming along behind us, isn't it?"

"I'll say she's big," Frank agreed, looking back. "I don't remember ever having seen that boat around here before."

"Me neither," declared Joe. "I wonder where it came from."

The strange craft was painted a dingy gray. It was large and unwieldy and did not ride easily in the water. Although that boat was some distance in the wake of their own craft the boys could distinguish the figures of three men, all seated well up toward the front. Biff glanced back.

"It's a new one on me," he said. "I've never seen it before."

"Sure has lots of power, anyway," Chet commented. The roar of the engine could be plainly heard across the water. In spite of its clumsy appearance, the big boat ploughed ahead at good speed, and, as Bill had the *Envoy*, his craft, throttled down, the second boat was slowly overtaking them.

"Let's wait till they get abreast of us and give them a race," Chet suggested.

"Not on your life," objected Biff. "I'm only learning to run this tub and I'm not in the racing class yet. Besides, there are too many other boats out in the bay this afternoon. I'd be sure to run into one of them."

The boys watched as the other craft overtook them. The big motorboat ploughed noisily ahead, keeping directly in their wake.

"I wonder if the man at the helm is asleep," said Frank. "He doesn't seem to be making any attempt to pull over."

"He's awake, all right," declared Chet. "I can see him talking to the man beside him. He won't run us down. Don't worry—not with Captain Hooper at the helm, my hearties!"

The roaring of the pursuing craft suddenly took on a new note and the big boat seemed to leap out of the water as it increased its speed and bore rapidly down on the *Envoy*. Spray flew about the heads of the helmsman and his two passengers and a high crest of foam rose from either side of the bow. Biff Hooper shifted the wheel slightly and the *Envoy* veered in toward the shore. To the surprise of the boys, the other boat also changed its course and continued directly in their wake.

"The idiots!" exclaimed Biff.

"I don't get the idea of this at all," muttered Frank Hardy to his brother. "What are they following us so closely for?"

Joe shrugged. "Probably just trying to give us a scare."

The other boat was now almost upon their craft. It nosed out to the right and drew alongside, coming dangerously close. The boys could see the three men clearly and they noticed that all three scrutinized them, seeming to pay particular attention to Chet and Biff.

The men were unsavory looking fellows, unshaven, surly of expression. The man at the helm was sharp-featured and keen-eyed, while the other two were of heavier build. One of the pair wore a cap, while the other man was bare-headed, revealing a scant thatch of carroty hair so close-cropped that it seemed to stick out at all angles to his cranium. This man, the boys saw, nudged his companion and pointed to Biff, who was too busy at the helm of his own craft to notice.

"Not so close!" yelled Chet, seeing that the other boat was running broadside in dangerous proximity to the *Envoy*.

In reply, the man at the helm of the other craft merely sneered and brought his boat in until the two speeding launches were almost touching sides.

"What's the idea?" Joe shouted. "Trying to run us down?"

Biff Hooper shifted the wheel so that the *Envoy* would edge away from the other boat, and in this effort he was successful, for a gap of water was soon apparent between the speeding craft. But in escaping one danger he had risked another.

Two sailboats that had been flitting about Barmet Bay that afternoon were racing with the wind, and they now came threshing along with billowing canvas, immediately into the course of the motorboat. Biff had seen the sailboats previously and had judged his own course accordingly, but in his efforts to get away from the mysterious launch he had unwittingly maneuvered the *Envoy* into such a position that a collision now seemed inevitable.

The sailboats seemed to loom right up before him, not more than a hundred yards away. They were racing close together, one boat but a nose in the lead. They were scudding along with the wind at high speed and the motorboat roared down upon them.

Biff Hooper bent desperately over the helm. He was so close that no matter which way he turned it seemed impossible that he could miss one or the other of the sailboats. If he turned to the right he would crash into them head-on; if he turned to the left he would run before them and a general smash-up might be the result.

The men in the sailboats were also aware of their danger.

The boys had a glimpse of one man waving his arms. One of the boats veered out abruptly and the yardarm swung around. The sailboat was lying directly in the path of the *Envoy*.

The roaring of the engine, the threshing of the sails, the warning shouts of the boys, all created a confusion of sound. The white sails seemed to loom high above the speeding boat. A hideous collision appeared to be inevitable.

CHAPTER II

QUICK THINKING

Every second was precious.

Frank Hardy realized the full extent of their peril and in the same moment he realized the only way of averting it.

Without a word he sprang toward the helm, brushing Biff Hooper aside. In this emergency, Biff was helpless. Swiftly, Frank bore down on the wheel, bringing the boat around into the wind. At the same time, he opened up the throttle so that the *Envoy* leaped forward at her highest speed.

The motorboat passed just a few inches in front of the bow of the first sailboat; so close, Chet Morton said afterward, that he "could count every stitch on the patch in the sailcloth." But the danger was not yet over. There was still the other sailboat to be considered. It was pounding along immediately ahead of them; the man at the tiller was making frantic efforts to get out of the way, but the danger lay in the fact that in trying to guess the possible course of the *Envoy* he might make a false move that would have him shoot directly across its path.

Frank swung the helm around again. Once more, the *Envoy* veered to the left so sharply that a cloud of spray drenched the boys. Another shift of the wheel and the motorboat zig-zagged safely past the sailboat and on out into open water.

Not one of the boys had uttered a word during this. They had been tense and anxious, but now that the peril of a smash-up had been averted, they sank back with sighs of relief.

"I sure thought we were headed for Davy Jones' locker that time!" breathed Chet.

Biff Hooper looked up at Frank.

"Thanks," he said. "I'd have never got out of that mess if you hadn't taken the wheel. I was so rattled that I didn't know what to do."

"After you've run the boat a few more weeks you'll get so used to it that it'll be second nature to you. But that sure was a tight squeeze," Frank admitted. "It mighty near meant that you wouldn't have had any motorboat left to go on that trip with."

"It mighty near meant that we wouldn't have been left to make the trip at all," Chet declared solemnly. "What say we go home? I've had enough excitement for one day."

"It's beginning to rain, anyway," Biff remarked, glancing up at the sky. "I guess we may as well go back."

The sky had clouded over in the past hour and the eastern sky was black, while scurrying masses of ragged clouds flew overhead before the stiffening wind. A few drops of water splashed into the boat, then came a gust of rain, followed by a light shower that passed over in a few minutes. The big motorboat that had crowded them had disappeared.

"A real storm coming up," Frank said. "Let's make for the boathouse."

The *Envoy* headed for Bayport.

"I'd like to tell those three fellows in that other boat what I think of them," declared Biff. "They got us into that jam. They were crowding me so close that I didn't have a chance to keep an eye on the sailboats."

"I still can't see why they drew up alongside," Joe observed. "They seemed mighty inquisitive. Gave us all the once-over."

Chet offered a solution.

"Perhaps they thought we were some one else and when they found out their mistake they went away."

"But they *didn't* go away," Frank pointed out. "They kept crowding us over. And one of them pointed at Biff."

"At me?"

"Yes."

"I didn't notice that."

"He seemed to recognize you and was pointing you out to the other men."

"Well, if he recognized me I can't return the compliment. I never saw any of them before in my life."

"He was probably pointing you out as a unique specimen," ventured Joe, with a grin. "Probably those fellows are from a museum, Biff. They'll likely make an offer for your carcass after you're dead and they'll have it stuffed and put it on display in a glass case. That's why they were so interested."

Joe's suggestion elicited warm words from Biff and a friendly struggle ensued. Inasmuch as Biff Hooper was the champion boxer and wrestler of Bayport High, Joe was at a disadvantage, and paid for his derogatory remarks by being held over the side by the scruff of the neck and given a ducking until he pleaded for mercy.

By the time the boys reached Bayport it was raining heavily, and after leaving the *Envoy* in the boathouse they raced up the street to the Hardy boys' home. The barn in the back yard was a favorite retreat of the chums and there they spent many of their Saturday afternoons. The barn was fitted up as a gymnasium, with parallel bars, a trapeze, boxing gloves and a punching bag, and was an ideal refuge on a rainy day. The thrilling experience with the sailboats and the mystery of the strange motorboat were soon forgotten.

Phil Cohen and Tony Prito, school chums of the Hardy boys, drifted in during the afternoon, as well as Jerry Gilroy and "Slim" Robinson. This comprised the "gang," of which the two Hardy boys were the leading spirits.

Frank and Joe Hardy were the sons of Fenton Hardy, an internationally famous detective. Mr. Hardy had been for many years a detective on the New York police force, where he was so successful that he went into practice for himself. His two sons already showed signs of inheriting his ability and in a number of instances had solved difficult criminal cases.

The first of these was the mystery of the theft of valuable jewels and bonds from Tower Mansion, an old-fashioned building on the outskirts of Bayport. How the Hardy boys solved the mystery has already been related in the first volume of this series, entitled, "The Tower Treasure."

In the second volume, "The House on the Cliff," the Hardy boys and their chums had a thrilling experience in a reputedly haunted house on the cliffs overlooking Barmet Bay. This was the starting point of an exciting chase for smugglers, in which the Hardy boys came to the rescue of their father after undergoing many dangers in the cliff caves.

The third volume of the series, "The Mystery of the Old Mill," which precedes the present book, relates the efforts of the Hardy boys to run to earth a gang of counterfeiters operating in and about Bayport and their efforts to solve the mystery surrounding an abandoned mill in the farming country back of Barmet Bay.

Frank Hardy, a tall, dark-haired boy of sixteen, was a year older than his brother Joe, and usually took the lead in their exploits, although Joe was not a whit behind his brother in shrewdness and in deductive ability.

Mrs. Hardy viewed their passion for detective work with considerable apprehension, preferring that they plan to go to a university and direct their energies toward entering one of the professions; but the success of the lads had been so marked in the cases on which they had been engaged that she had by now almost resigned herself to seeing them destined for careers as private detectives when they should grow older.

Just now, however, detective work was farthest from their thoughts. Frank and Tony Prito were engaged in some complicated maneuvers on the parallel bars, Joe was taking a boxing lesson from Biff Hooper, and Phil Cohen was trying to learn how to walk on his hands, under the guidance of Jerry Gilroy and Slim Robinson.

As for Chet Morton, the mischief-maker, he was sitting on the window-sill, meditating. And when Chet Morton meditated, it usually meant that a practical joke was in the offing.

"I'll bet you can't 'skin the cat' on that trapeze, Jerry," he called out suddenly.

Jerry Gilroy looked up.

"Skin the cat?" he said. "Of course I can."

"Bet you can't."

"Bet I can."

"Can't."

"Can."

"Do it, then."

"Watch me."

As every boy knows, "skinning the cat" is an acrobatic feat that does not necessarily embrace cruelty to animals. Jerry Gilroy was not unjustly proud of his prowess on the trapeze and Chet Morton's doubt of his ability to perform one of the simplest stunts in his repertoire made him resolve to "skin the cat" as slowly and elaborately as lay within his power.

He grasped the trapeze bar with both hands, then swung forward, raising his feet from the floor, bending his knees. Chet edged forward, presumably to get a better view of proceedings, but at the same time he tightened his grip on a long, flat stick that he had found by the window ledge.

Jerry slowly doubled up until his feet were above his head, immediately below the bar, and then commenced the second stage of the elaborate back somersault, coming down slowly toward the floor. At this juncture the rear of his trousers was presented as a tempting mark to the waiting Chet. This was the stage of the feat for which the joker had been waiting and he raised the flat stick, bringing it down with a resounding smack on his human target.

There was a yelp of pain from Jerry and a roar of laughter from Chet. Doubled up on the bar as he was, Jerry could not immediately regain the floor, and Chet managed to belabor him twice more before the unfortunate acrobat finally found his footing. There he stood, bewildered, rubbing the seat of his trousers, with a rueful expression on his face, while Chet leaned against the wall, helpless with laughter.

The other boys joined in the merriment, for they had stopped to witness the incident, and after a while Jerry achieved a wry smile, although he looked reflectively at his tormentor as though wondering just what form his revenge should take.

No one enjoyed Chet Morton's practical jokes more than he did himself. He whooped with laughter, wiped the tears from his eyes, and leaned out of the window, spluttering with mirth.

"Oh, boy!" he giggled. "The expression—on your—face—!" Then he was away again, leaning across the window-sill weakly, shaking with laughter.

Jerry Gilroy tiptoed quietly up behind him. A quick movement and he lowered the window until it was against Chet's back.

The practical joker suddenly stopped laughing, and turned his head.

"Hey! What's the matter?" he inquired.

He was pinned down by the window and he could not see Jerry picking up the flat piece of board that had been the instrument of torture a few minutes previously. But a suspicion of the truth came to him, and a roar of laughter from the other boys warned him that vengeance was due.

It came.

Smack!

Chet Morton wriggled and squirmed, but he was pinned helplessly by the weight of the window against his shoulders, and he presented a more tempting target for Jerry's ministrations with the flat stick, and a more stationary target as well, than Jerry had presented for him.

Smack! Smack! Smack!

He roared with pain and, helpless as he was, danced vainly on the floor in his efforts to escape. Jerry Gilroy belabored him across the rear with that stinging stick until his desire for revenge had been fully satisfied, while the other boys howled with glee at the manner in which the tables had been turned.

Finally, when Jerry tossed the flat stick away and joined the others in their laughter, Chet managed to raise the window and escape.

"Can't see what you're all laughing at," he grumbled, as he sat down carefully on a near-by box. Then he rose hurriedly and rubbed the tender spot.

"He laughs best who laughs last," quoted Jerry Gilroy.

"Guess I've got to get home," announced Biff, a moment later, and soon he and the others were on their way, dodging through the rain.

Then Frank and Joe put the barn in order and went into the house. They felt particularly carefree and never dreamed of the news they were to hear or of how it was to affect them and their chums.

CHAPTER III

A SHADY TRIO

"I am sure my man is in Chicago. I know for a fact that he went West, and the Windy City would naturally be his hiding place."

Fenton Hardy tapped the library table reflectively with a pencil. Mrs. Hardy put aside the magazine she had been reading.

"Are you going to follow him?"

"I'll trail him right to the Pacific Coast if necessary."

Frank and Joe Hardy, who had been standing by the window, disconsolately watching the rain streaking down the pane, looked around.

"Who is he, dad?" asked Frank.

"One of the cleverest and most daring bank robbers in the country. I've been after him for almost a year now and it's only been within the last few weeks that I've ever come anywhere near catching him."

"What's his name?"

Fenton Hardy laughed. "I've made you curious, eh? Well, this chap has about a dozen names. He has a new alias every week, but so far as the police are concerned he's known as Baldy Turk, because he's as bald as an egg. He and his gang held up a bank in a small New Jersey town about a month ago and got away with over ten thousand dollars in broad daylight. That's how I managed to get trace of him again. Even the police didn't know Baldy Turk was mixed up in the affair because he was wearing a wig that day, but he double-crossed one of the members of his gang out of his share in the loot."

"And that fellow told the police," ventured Joe.

Mr. Hardy shook his head.

"Not the police. He didn't dare go near them because he was wanted for two or three robberies himself. But he came to me and tipped me off as to where Baldy Turk could be found. He wanted revenge. I went to New York, where Baldy was in hiding; but evidently some of his friends knew I was on his trail and he disappeared before I could lay my hands on him."

"Where did he go then?" asked Frank, with interest.

"He hid out on Long Island for a while, but I managed to pick up the trail again and went after him, but he was too smart for me. He got away in a fast automobile and took a couple of shots at me in the bargain. I managed to get the number of the car and traced it to Manhattan and later found that Baldy Turk had left the East altogether. He bought a ticket to Cleveland, doubled back to Buffalo and managed to shake me off."

"What makes you think he is in Chicago?"

"Because another member of his gang went to Chicago just a week ago. So I imagine Baldy Turk was to meet him there. In any case, Chicago is a thieves' paradise, so it seems logical that Baldy Turk would make for there."

"And you're going after him! Gee, I wish I could go," declared Joe.

Fenton Hardy smiled.

"It's no job for a boy," he said. "Baldy Turk is a bad man with a gun. If I ever do find him it will take some maneuvering to get the handcuffs on him, I'll tell you."

"You'll be careful, won't you, Fenton," said Mrs. Hardy anxiously. "I'm always frightened whenever I know you're after one of these desperate criminals."

"I'll be as careful as I can, Laura," promised her husband; "but in my business I have to take chances. Baldy Turk knows I'm after him and he doesn't mean to be caught if he can help it. He or any of the men in his gang would shoot me on sight. There's a standing reward of five thousand dollars out for Baldy and, besides, the Bankers' Association have promised me a handsome fee if I can get him behind the bars and break up the gang."

"I won't rest easy in my mind until you're back home safe," Mrs. Hardy declared.

"Don't worry about me," replied her husband, going over to her and patting her shoulder reassuringly. "I'll get back safely all right, and Baldy Turk will be in jail if I have to chase him all over the States. The boys will look after you while I'm away."

"You bet we will!" Frank promised.

"I'm sorry it keeps you from going on that motorboat trip with Chet and Biff," Mr. Hardy remarked. "Perhaps you can arrange another jaunt after I come back."

"We're not worrying about that, dad. We don't mind staying at home."

"That's the spirit," approved their father.

"When do you leave?" Frank asked.

"I'm waiting for a letter from a friend of mine in Chicago. If he writes as I expect he will write, I should be away by the day after tomorrow."

"Then let Baldy Turk watch his step!" observed Joe.

"We'll both have to watch our step," answered Mr. Hardy, smiling. "If I don't get him, he'll probably get me."

"Well, I'm betting on you."

Mrs. Hardy shook her head doubtfully, but said nothing. She knew that her detective husband had escaped death at the hands of desperate criminals many times in the course of his career and there seemed to be no reason why he should not bring Baldy Turk to book just as he had captured many other notorious criminals in the past; but this time she had a vague premonition of danger. She knew that her husband would laugh at her fears if she expressed them, so she remained silent.

The rain had stopped, as Frank noticed when he glanced out the window again.

"It's clearing up. What say we go out for a spin, Joe?"

"Suits me."

"Let's go."

"Don't be late for supper," warned Mrs. Hardy, as the boys started out the door.

"We'll be in time," they promised, and the door closed behind them.

The Hardy boys went out to the shed where they kept their motorcycles. Both Joe and Frank had machines, given to them by their father, and in their spare time they spent many hours speeding about the roads in and around Bayport.

Their native city had a population of about fifty thousand people and was on the Atlantic coast, on Barmet Bay. There were good roads along both northern and southern arms of the bay, besides the State highway and the numerous country roads that led through the farming country back of Bayport.

Chet Morton, whose father was a real estate dealer with an office in the city, lived on a farm some distance off the road along the north arm of the bay, Chet making the daily journey to school and back in a roadster that had been given to him by his father. Chet was as proud of his roadster as the Hardy boys were proud of the motorboat that they had bought from the money they had received as reward for solving the Tower Mystery.

"Where shall we go?" asked Joe, as the Hardy boys rode out of the lane.

"Let's go to the Morton farm and see Chet."

"Good idea. I wonder if he's able to sit down yet," replied Joe, alluding to Chet's practical joke earlier in the day.

The motorcycles roared and spluttered as the boys sped along the gleaming pavements of the city. They rode through the main streets, threading their way easily through the traffic until at last they were at the outskirts of Bayport. Finally they left the city behind and reached the road leading toward the Morton farm. The leaves of the trees were still wet with rain and the luxuriant grass by the road-side glistened with the heavy drops. The air was cool and sweet after the storm. The roads had dried quickly, however, and the boys experienced no inconvenience.

They reached the Morton farmhouse in good time and Chet's sister, Iola, answered their knock. Iola was a pretty girl of about fifteen, one of the few girls at whom Joe Hardy had ever cast more than a passing glance. He lowered his eyes bashfully when she appeared in the doorway.

"Chet just left in the car about ten minutes ago," she said smilingly, in answer to their inquiry. "It's strange you didn't meet him."

"He probably went by the other road. We'll catch up to him."

"Won't you come in?"

"N-no thanks," stammered Joe, blushing. "Guess we'll be going."

"Oh, *do* come in," said Iola coaxingly. "Callie Shaw is here."

"Is she?" Frank brightened up at this intelligence, and at that moment a brown-eyed, dark-haired girl about his own age appeared in the hall.

"Hello!" she called, smiling pleasantly, and displaying small, even teeth of a dazzling whiteness.

"Let's go," muttered Joe, tugging at Frank's sleeve. He was incurably shy in the presence of girls, especially Iola.

But Frank did not go just then. He chatted with Callie Shaw for a while, and Iola tried to make conversation with Joe, whose answers were mumbled and muttered, while he inwardly wished he could talk as freely and without embarrassment as his brother. At length Frank decided to go and Joe sighed with relief. The girls bade them good-bye after again urging them to come inside the house, and the boys departed.

"Whew!" breathed Joe, mopping his brow. "I'm glad that's over."

Frank looked at him in surprise.

"Why, what's the matter? I thought you liked Iola Morton."

"That's just the trouble—I do," answered Joe mysteriously, and Frank wisely forbore further inquiry.

They mounted their motorcycles again and rode down the lane, out to the road. Hardly had they gone more than a few hundred yards, however, than Frank suddenly gestured to his brother and they slowed down.

Pulled up beside the road was an automobile, and as the boys drew near they saw that three men were in the car. The men were talking together and they looked up as the boys approached.

Something in the attitude of the trio aroused Frank's suspicions, and this prompted him to ride slower. There seemed no apparent reason why the men should have pulled their car up beside the road, for they were not repairing a breakdown and they were still a little distance from the lane leading to the Morton farmhouse. Then, as the motorcycles slowly passed the car and the three men sullenly regarded the two boys, Frank suppressed an exclamation of surprise.

The three men in the car were the three men who had pursued the boys in the motorboat earlier in the day!

Frank and Joe drove past, conscious of the scrutiny of the unsavory trio in the automobile. The men did not speak, although Frank noticed that one of them drew his cap down over his eyes and muttered something to one of his companions.

When they had gone by, Joe glanced back. The man were paying no further attention to them, but were leaning close together, evidently having resumed their interrupted conversation. There was something stealthy and secretive in their demeanor that was far from reassuring.

"Did you recognize them?" asked Frank, when they were out of earshot.

"I'll say I did! The same gang that followed us in the motorboat."

"I wonder what they're up to."

"Up to no good, by the looks of them."

"That's a strange place to park their car—so close to the Morton farm, too."

"They look like a bad outfit to me," remarked Joe.

"I'd like to know more about them. There was something funny about the way they chased us in the boat. And don't you remember how closely they looked at Chet and Biff? It seems funny to see them hanging around the farm."

"Well, they haven't done us any harm. I suppose it's none of our business—but I'd sure like to know what their game is. Let's find Chet and tell him."

They increased their speed and before long overtook Chet Morton on the shore road. But Chet laughed at their fears.

"You're too suspicious," he said. "They had probably just stopped to fix a tire when you came along. However, we'll go back to the farm and see if they're still on hand."

But when the boys drove back to the Morton farm they found that the mysterious trio in the automobile were no longer in sight.

CHAPTER IV

THE SEND-OFF

On Monday, Chet Morton and Biff Hooper set out on their motorboat trip up the coast. They were well equipped with provisions and supplies and had been up since six o'clock that morning getting the boat in readiness.

The Hardy boys went down to the dock to bid them good-bye, and although they chaffed the adventurers and laughed with them, neither Frank nor Joe could repress the disappointment they naturally felt at being unable to go with their chums.

Chet was busy stowing away the last of the provisions and Biff was tuning up the engine when the Hardy boys arrived. In a few minutes Tony Prito, at the helm of his own motorboat, arrived on the scene with Jerry Gilroy and Phil Cohen. Then, down the dock, came tripping Iola Morton and Callie Shaw.

"Hail, hail, the gang's all here!" roared Chet, when he saw them.

"Oy, what a fine day you pick for your trip!" exclaimed Phil Cohen, looking up at the clouds. For the sky was overcast and there was no sun.

"That's all right," answered Chet. "We made up our minds to start today and we'd start if there was a thunderstorm on."

"Brave sailors!" mocked Callie Shaw, with a smile.

"How long will you be away?" shouted Frank.

"Until the grub runs out."

"That should be about next December," ventured Iola. "It looks to me as if you have enough provisions there to last you a year."

"Not with Chet Morton on the trip, we haven't," grunted Biff Hooper, looking up from the engine. "We'll be lucky if it lasts us a week. I've seen him eat before."

"I'll do my share," Chet promised modestly.

"We should have had the City Band down to give you a proper send-off," Joe Hardy remarked.

"It doesn't matter. We'll forgive you this time. But be sure and have the band here to welcome us when we come back."

"You'll be back by tomorrow night," declared Iola. "I know you! Why, I'll bet you'll both be scared green when darkness comes on. One night will cure you of sleeping in the open."

"Rats!" replied Chet good-naturedly. "I'm not afraid of the dark."

"Cut out the jawing and let's get started," said Biff Hooper. "No use hanging around here. Are you ready?"

"All set!"

"Let's go then. Good-bye, everybody."

"Good-bye!" every one shouted. Frank and Joe cheered, the girls clapped their hands, and the *Envoy* slowly moved away from the dock, with Chet Morton and Biff Hooper waving to their chums.

Tony Prito swung his motorboat around.

"I'll go along with you to the end of the bay," he shouted.

Frank glanced at Joe.

"Why didn't we think of that?"

"It isn't too late yet. Let's get the boat."

"Would you and Iola care to come?" said Frank to Callie. "We're going to get our boat and follow them down the bay a bit."

"Oh, that'll be great!" exclaimed Callie. "I'd love to go. Wouldn't you, Iola?"

"I'll say!" Iola replied, slangily.

They hurried down from the dock and went along the roadway back of the boathouses until they came to the boathouse where Frank and Joe kept their craft.

In a few minutes, the *Sleuth* was nosing its way out into Barmet Bay, but already Chet and Biff were a considerable distance in the lead.

"We'll have to step on it," said Joe.

"We'll catch them, all right. There isn't a boat on the bay can beat the *Sleuth*."

The engine roared and the boat seemed fairly to leap out of the water as it plunged forward. Spray dashed over the bows as the fleet launch headed out in pursuit of the others.

Frank glanced at the sky.

Biff and Chet had certainly chosen a bad day for their departure. The sky had been none too promising at dawn, but now it was clouding over with every promise of a downpour, and there was a heavy cloud on the horizon. Then, too, there was a suspicious absence of wind, and the bay was in a flat calm.

"I wish they'd picked some other day," he remarked quietly to Joe. "It looks like squally weather out at sea."

"I don't like the looks of the sky myself. However, they're away, so there's no use saying anything. It might alarm Iola."

The *Sleuth* was rapidly overhauling the other boats, although Tony and Biff were engaging in a spirited race down the bay. The girls enjoyed the swift progress and were laughing with excitement as they saw the distance narrowing between Frank and the others.

Suddenly a low rumble of thunder caused Frank to glance up at the sky again. With remarkable rapidity, the huge cloud he had previously noticed had spread over the entire sky, causing gloom to spread over the bay. A few white caps were apparent on the surface of the water and there was a splatter of rain.

"Guess we'd better turn back," he said, turning to the others.

"Why, what's the matter?" asked Callie.

"Storm coming up."

The girls had been so intent on the chase that they had not noticed the lowering clouds, but now Callie gave a murmur of astonishment.

"Why, it's going to *pour*! And I haven't brought my slicker with me. We'll be drenched."

"But what about Biff and Chet?" exclaimed Iola.

"I think they'll turn back too when they see what they're heading into," replied Frank. "It looks like a bad storm."

As though in corroboration of his words, a sheet of lightning and a violent clap of thunder heralded the beginning of the downpour. The wind came in from the sea with a violence that surprised them, came whistling down across the bay over a wide line of tossing whitecaps, driving before it a leaden wall of rain.

The two motorboats in the lead were blotted from view, although Frank had seen that Tony Prito was already turning back before the gloomy wall of rain hid him from sight. Slowly, he brought the motorboat around.

The moaning of the wind rose in volume. Waves slapped at the sides of the boat. White spray rose above the bows. The sky was black. The speeding craft fled before the oncoming storm.

But the wall of rain swept down upon them with a whistle and a howl. The streaming sheets of water poured from the dark sky, whirled onward by the raging wind. The boat rocked in the tossing waves.

Frank crouched at the helm, his jaw set, his face stern. The girls huddled in the stern, seeking protection from the sudden downpour.

Joe found a sheet of tarpaulin in a locker, and gave it to the two girls, who draped it over their heads, and it afforded them some shelter. The boat was swaying madly as it ran on through the huge waves that surged on every side.

Frank could scarcely see Bayport ahead through the blinding rain and gloom.

"Where is the other boat?" shouted Joe, above the clamor of the storm.

Frank looked back.

Tony Prito's boat had disappeared. Frank wondered how the other boys were faring. He had every confidence that Tony would make land in safety, for the Italian lad was skilful at the helm and he had iron nerves, but he was not so sure that Biff Hooper and Chet Morton would weather the gale so easily. Biff had only mastered the rudiments of motorboating and a storm such as this was enough to test the mettle of the most skilful sailors.

He wondered if he should not turn back and go in search of Biff and Chet. When he had last seen them they had been heading directly into the teeth of the gale, out to the open sea. Surely they would not be foolhardy enough to go on!

He glanced back and when he saw Iola's frightened face he knew that it was impossible to turn back now, for he was responsible for the safety of the girls and there was grave peril in braving the storm just then. He opened the throttle further and felt the *Sleuth* respond as it leaped ahead into the tossing whitecaps through the shifting screen of rain.

Thunder rolled and crashed. Lightning flickered across the gray void and rent the dark sky in livid streaks. The waves were tossing like white-crested monsters seeking to devour them. Frank peered through the raging gale and he could vaguely discern the city lying ahead. A few lights were twinkling feebly, for the storm brought the darkness of twilight with it.

The gale had sprung up so suddenly that they had been entirely unprepared. Frank devoutly wished that he had taken heed of the warning given by that ominous sky before he started out in the motorboat. He was greatly alarmed for the safety of the girls, because he knew that the storm was one of the worst that had ever swept over Barmet Bay.

"We'll be lucky if we make it!" he muttered to himself. Then, to reassure the others, he turned and grinned.

"We'll make it, all right!" he shouted, the wind whisking the words away so that the others scarcely heard him.

A great wave broke over the side. The boat reeled as though it had been struck by a giant hand.

CHAPTER V

NO WORD FROM THE CHUMS

Frank Hardy bore down on the helm as the boat heeled over. For a breathless second he thought the craft would be swamped. Water poured over the gunwales. The girls screamed. Joe was thrown off his balance and went sprawling into the stern.

But the *Sleuth* was staunch. In a moment it recovered, righted itself, and surged on through the storm. Frank breathed a sigh of relief. The engine throbbed steadily and, although the boat was rocking and swaying in the turbulent sea, it was drawing nearer shore and already he could distinguish the line of boathouses through the downpour.

For all its violence, the storm was brief. The wind began to die down, although the rain continued as though the heavens had been opened up. In a few minutes Frank was able to pick out his own boathouse and he headed the *Sleuth* directly for it. The sturdy craft sped swiftly toward the open doorway, then Frank shut off the engine and the boat came to rest.

"Some trip!" remarked Joe, shaking himself like a dog emerging from the water, so that spray flew from his clothing in every direction.

"My hair is all wet, and I won't be able to do a thing with it," mourned Callie Shaw, with feminine concern for her appearance first of all. In spite of the shelter afforded by the tarpaulin, both girls were thoroughly drenched. As for the boys, their clothing clung limply to their bodies. Frank clambered out of the boat and moored it fast, while Joe helped the girls up onto the landing.

"We're mighty lucky to be back at all," Iola Morton said. "I was sure the boat would be swamped."

"It takes a pretty big storm to swamp our boat," boasted Joe. "Although, to tell the truth, I was pretty nervous for a while."

"I was so frightened I couldn't speak," confessed the girl. "I do hope Chet and Biff turned back. They would never get through that storm alive."

Frank went to the door.

"No sight of them yet," he reported. Then he peered through the driving screen of rain again. "Just a minute—I hear a boat coming this way."

"Perhaps it's Tony."

"I hope it's one or the other. I couldn't see the *Napoli* at all after the rain started."

In a few minutes they discerned a motorboat heading inshore. It was Tony Prito's craft, the *Napoli*.

"Good!" exclaimed Joe. "Chet and Biff should be along, too. They won't start on that trip today."

"I should hope not!" exclaimed Iola.

But when Tony's boat drew near the entrance of the boathouse on the way to its own shelter a short distance away, Tony shouted to Frank:

"All safe?"

"Everybody's okay! How about you?"

"We're all right. Had a tough time getting back, though."

"So did we," Frank shouted. "Did Biff turn back?"

Tony shook his head. "Not a chance. We signaled to him that he'd better come back but he just shook his head, and Chet pointed to the end of the bay. They kept right on going. The last we saw of them they were heading right into the storm."

"Good night!" Frank exclaimed. "They'll be swamped."

"They're taking an awful chance. Oh, well, perhaps they gave in after all. They may have headed in toward one of the villages along the shore. They'll probably be back."

"Let's hope so!" exclaimed Iola. "I won't have a minute's rest until I'm sure they're safe."

Tony went on toward his own boathouse, with Jerry Gilroy and Phil Cohen, drenched to the skin, sitting ruefully in the stern. The Hardy boys and the two girls left the boathouse and were fortunate enough to meet a school chum who happened to be driving past in his car, so they drove home in shelter from the rain. Frank and Joe got off at their home after the chum had volunteered to drive the girls home.

"And I'll make it snappy, too," he promised. "I guess you're in a hurry to get into dry clothes."

"I feel like a drowned rat," declared Callie. "And I suppose I look like one too."

After the others drove away, the Hardy boys went into the house and made a complete change of clothes so that, fifteen minutes later, in dry garments, they were feeling at peace with the world. When they went downstairs again to tell their parents of the adventure they had just experienced, they found Mr. Hardy just snapping the catch of his club-bag, while a packed suitcase stood near by.

"Going away now?" they asked, in surprise.

"Off to Chicago. I just got a fresh clue as to Baldy's whereabouts."

"He's there all right, is he?"

The detective nodded. "I'll just have time to catch this train."

Mrs. Hardy entered the room at that moment.

"I telephoned for a taxi." Her face was troubled. "I do wish you didn't have to make this journey, Fenton."

Mr. Hardy laughed.

"You've never worried about me so much before, Laura. I've gone away on cases as bad as this dozens of times without causing you as much anxiety."

"I know—but somehow I have a feeling that this case is a good deal more dangerous than any of the others."

"I'll be back in a few days, never fear." Mr. Hardy turned to his sons. "Look after your mother while I'm away, boys. Don't let her get worried."

"There's nothing to be worried about, dad. You'll get your man all right."

Mrs. Hardy shook her head. "You *will* be careful, won't you, Fenton? From what you've told me of this Baldy Turk I imagine he wouldn't stop at anything if he thought you were going to catch him."

"He's a pretty tough character, but I guess I can handle him," said the detective lightly. "Well, here's my taxi. I'll have to be going. Good-bye." He kissed his wife, shook hands with the boys, then picked up his suitcase and club-bag and departed. From the front doorway they watched him clamber into the waiting taxi. He waved at them as the car got under way, then it went speeding out of sight along the shimmering pavement.

Mrs. Hardy turned away. "I expect he'll think I'm foolish for worrying so much about him this time, but I have an odd sort of feeling that this Baldy Turk is the most dangerous criminal he has ever had to deal with."

"He'll deal with him, mother," declared Frank, with conviction. "Trust dad to know what he's doing. He'll clap the handcuffs on Baldy Turk in no time. There's nothing to worry about."

"Well, I hope you're right," she replied. "Still, I can't help but be anxious—"

With that she let the matter drop, and her fears for Fenton Hardy's safety were not expressed again, although the boys knew that anxiety still weighed heavily upon her mind. By evening, however, she appeared to be in better spirits and the boys did their best to amuse her and make her forget their father's absence and his perilous errand.

Next day the boys went down to the boathouse where Biff Hooper kept the *Envoy*, but there was no sign of the craft. The storm of the previous day had lasted well into the afternoon and there had been no doubt in their minds but that Chet and Biff had set back for Bayport, but the absence of the motorboat indicated otherwise.

"Let's go up to Morton's farm and see if they did come back," Frank suggested.

"Iola was saying that Chet promised to send a post card from the first village they stopped at. They were to have spent the night at Hawk Cove and he said he'd drop a line from there so that his folks would know everything was all right."

Hawk Cove was a small fishing village on the coast and, under normal conditions, Chet and Biff should have reached the place early the previous evening. A postal card would have caught the morning mail to Bayport.

"Let's go, then," Frank said. "If they went on to Hawk Cove and wrote from there we'll know that everything is all right."

"I'm with you."

The Hardy boys brought their motorcycles out of the shed and drove out toward the Morton farm. They made speed on the run because both were anxious to learn if anything had been heard of their chums. But when they reached the farmhouse and saw Iola's worried face as she greeted them at the door they knew without being told that no word had been received from Chet.

"They didn't turn back," said Iola, almost tearfully. "We waited all afternoon and evening expecting Chet back, but he didn't come. They must have gone straight ahead into the storm."

"Did the post card come?" asked Joe.

She shook her head.

"We haven't heard from him at all. And Chet promised faithfully he'd write to us from Hawk Cove. The card should have been in the morning mail. Chet always keeps his promises. I'm so afraid something dreadful has happened."

"Oh, there's no need to be alarmed," consoled Frank. "Perhaps the storm delayed them so that they didn't reach Hawk Cove until it was too late to catch the mail. Or perhaps they stopped off at one of the other fishing villages down at the entrance to the bay. A dozen things might have happened. You'll probably hear from him tomorrow—or tonight, perhaps."

"That storm was too terrible!" declared the girl. "They should never have gone on. They should have turned back when the rest of us did."

"I guess they didn't want to turn back once they had started," ventured Joe. "Biff doesn't like to admit he's licked."

"Neither does Chet," the girl replied. "They're both headstrong and I guess they thought we'd make fun of them if they had to come back to Bayport and start over again."

"Well, we'll be back tomorrow. I'm sure you'll hear from him by then," said Frank reassuringly. "And if we hear anything we'll let you know."

"Please do."

The Hardy boys walked back to their motorcycles. When they were out of hearing Frank remarked in a low voice:

"I don't like the looks of this, at all! I'm beginning to think something *has* happened."

CHAPTER VI

MISSING

No word came from Chet Morton or Biff Hooper the following day. Although the parents of the chums tried to allay their fears by assuming that the lads had not stopped off at Hawk Cove after all or had neglected to write, as is the way of boys the world over, when three days passed without further news, the situation became serious.

"They were wrecked in that storm, I know it!" declared Iola Morton, with conviction, when the Hardy boys called at the farmhouse on the third day. "Mother is almost frantic and daddy doesn't know what to do. It isn't like Chet to make us wait this long for some word of where he is, particularly when he knew we'd be anxious."

"The Hoopers are terribly worried about Biff," Joe put in. "We went over there last night to see if they had heard anything. Mr. Hooper had telephoned to nearly all the fishing villages up the coast, but none of them had seen anything of the boat."

Iola turned pale.

"They hadn't seen the boat at all?"

Frank shook his head.

"Either the boys were wrecked or they were swept out to sea," said the girl. She turned away and dabbed at her eyes with a handkerchief. She was on the verge of breaking down. "Oh, can't *something* be done to find trace of them?"

"It's time we were getting busy," Frank agreed. "I think we'd better organize a searching party."

"With the motorboats?" asked Joe.

"Yes. We can take our boat. Perhaps Tony Prito will be able to come along with the *Napoli* and we'll get the rest of the fellows. We can cruise along the bay and up the coast and perhaps we'll find some trace."

"Will you do that?" asked Iola, brightening up. "Oh, if you only will! At least we'll know that some one is searching for them."

"I've been thinking that possibly their boat got wrecked and they were washed up on an island or on some part of the coast a long way from any village," Frank observed. "I don't think they've been drowned. They are both good swimmers and it would take a lot to kill either of them."

"Well, if we're going to go we may as well get started."

"All right, Joe. We'll take some grub with us and count on staying until we find some trace of them. Perhaps two or three days."

A sudden thought struck Joe.

"How about mother?"

Frank whistled.

"Gosh—I'd forgotten! But perhaps she can get some one to stay with her. Seeing it isn't a pleasure trip we're going on, she might let us go."

"Oh, I hope she does!" exclaimed Iola. "As long as we know you boys are out searching for Chet and Biff we'll be a lot easier in our minds."

"Well, let's go back home and see what arrangements we can make," Frank said briskly. "The sooner we get away, the better."

The lads mounted their motorcycles and turned toward the city. The idea of organizing a searching party for the missing chums had occurred to Frank previously, but he had been waiting, hoping against hope that some word might be received regarding the two boys. The fact that Mrs. Hardy would be left alone at home had been the one circumstance that had prevented him from starting out in search of the chums before this, but now the situation seemed to warrant action at all costs.

"If mother is afraid to stay at home alone, I guess the trip is off," he said to Joe. "But when she knows how serious it is, I don't think she'll mind."

"I don't like to leave her alone, myself," replied Joe. "But some one has to organize a searching party. I've been more worried about Chet and Biff than I'd like to admit."

"Me too."

When the lads returned to the house they found Mrs. Hardy opening the morning mail. She had a letter in her hand as they entered the living room and she glanced up with a smile of pleasure.

"We're going to have a visitor."

"Who?"

"Your Aunt Gertrude!"

Frank glanced at his brother.

Well did they know their Aunt Gertrude. She was a maiden lady of middle-age who spent the greater part of her life in a sort of grand circuit series of visits to all her relatives, far and near. Aunt Gertrude had no fixed place of abode. Accompanied by numerous trunks, satchels and a lazy yellow cat by the name of Lavinia, she was apt to drop in at any time in the course of a year, brusquely announcing her intention of remaining for an indefinite stay. Then she would install herself in the guest room and proceed to manage the household until the hour of her departure.

Aunt Gertrude was formidable. Her word was law. And, because she was possessed of a small fortune and a sharp tongue, none dared offend her. Relatives had discovered that the best plan was to suffer her visits in silence and pray for her speedy departure.

Now she was coming to visit the Hardys.

"Aunt Gertrude is coming? Isn't that great?" exclaimed Joe.

Mrs. Hardy looked at her son suspiciously. The Hardy boys had never been known to evince much enthusiasm over Aunt Gertrude's visits before. The worthy lady had a habit of regarding them as though they were still in swaddling clothes and she invariably showed a tendency to dictate as to their food, their hours of rising and going to bed, their companions, and their choice of literature. Many a Sunday afternoon she had thrust on them a weighty volume of Pilgrim's Progress and sat guard over them as they miserably strove to pretend an interest in the allegorical adventures of Bunyan's hero.

"I didn't think you cared for Aunt Gertrude," ventured Mrs. Hardy when she saw that both Frank and Joe were beaming with satisfaction.

"When will she be here?"

"This afternoon, according to her letter. She never gives one a great deal of notice."

"She couldn't have come at a better time. For once in her life, Aunt Gertrude will be useful," Frank declared, and with that, he told his mother of their desire to organize a searching party for the missing chums.

Mrs. Hardy had been deeply concerned over Chet and Biff since their departure from Bayport and now she agreed that a search should indeed be conducted.

"And now that Aunt Gertrude is coming, you won't be afraid to stay here alone," Joe pointed out.

Mrs. Hardy smiled. "And you'll leave me here all alone to the mercies of that managing woman?"

"There's not much use having us *all* here. Aunt Gertrude will run things anyway, whether there's three of us or a hundred."

"Yes, I suppose so. Well, I shan't be afraid to stay here as long as Aunt Gertrude is in the house. I imagine any burglar would rather deal with a vicious bulldog. Go ahead on your trip. When do you intend to start?"

"As soon as we can see Tony Prito and the rest of the boys. We want to make a real searching party of it. By the way, when will Aunt Gertrude arrive?"

"On the four o'clock train, I expect."

"Then we'll leave at about three o'clock," declared Frank, with a grin, for the boys' dislike of their tyrannical aunt was no secret in the Hardy household.

Mrs. Hardy smiled reprovingly, and the lads hustled away in search of Tony and the other boys.

Tony Prito was afire with enthusiasm when they broached the subject to him. A few words with Mr. Prito, and he obtained permission to have the use of the *Napoli* for as long as would be necessary.

"We'll start out as soon as we can get ready," Frank told him. "See if you can get Jerry and Phil to go with you, and we'll go and look up Perry Robinson. Perhaps he'll come along with us. We don't want to lose any time."

Perry Robinson, more familiarly known as "Slim," readily agreed to accompany the boys on the search.

"You bet I'll go," he declared. "When do we start?"

"Three o'clock, if we can be ready by then. Meet us at the boathouse and bring along some grub."

"I'll be there," promised Slim.

The Hardy boys carried blankets and a small tent down to the boat and stowed them away. Then came cooking utensils and a supply of food sufficient to last them for several days. They would, of course, be able to get supplies at the fishing villages along the coast, but as they had no idea where their search would lead them they were determined to take no chances.

"Thank goodness we'll be away from here before Aunt Gertrude arrives," chuckled Frank, as the boys were putting on their outing clothes at two o'clock that afternoon.

"She'll be madder than a wet hen when she finds we've escaped her. If there's anything she likes better than bossing us around and showing us our faults, I don't know what it is."

Alas for the best laid plans! Aunt Gertrude must have had some premonition of the truth. She advanced the time of her arrival by a good two hours. The two o'clock train brought her to Bayport, bags, baggage, and Lavinia, the cat. The boys were first apprised of her advent when they heard a taxicab pull up in front of the house. Joe peeped out the window of their room.

"Sweet spirits of nitre! Aunt Gertrude herself!"

"No!"

"Yes!"

"Let me see!"

Frank rushed to the window in time to see Aunt Gertrude, attired in voluminous garments of a fashion dating back at least a decade, laboriously emerging from the taxicab. She was a large woman with a strident voice, and the Hardy boys could hear her vigorously disputing the amount of the fare. This was a matter of principle with Aunt Gertrude, who always argued with taxi drivers as a matter of course, it being her firm conviction that they were unanimously in a conspiracy to overcharge her and defraud her at all times.

With Lavinia under one arm and a huge umbrella under the other, Aunt Gertrude withered the taxicab driver with a fiery denunciation and, when he helplessly pointed to the meter and declared that figures did not lie, she dropped both cat and umbrella, rummaged about in the manifold recesses of her clothing for a very small purse, produced the exact amount of the fare in silver, counted it out and handed it to the man with the air of one giving alms.

"And, just for your impudence, you shan't have a tip!" she announced. "Carry my bags up to the house."

The driver gazed sadly at the silver in his hand, pocketed it and clambered back into the car.

"Carry 'em up yourself!" he advised, slamming the door. The taxi roared away down the street.

Frank chuckled.

"That's one on Aunt Gertrude!"

But Aunt Gertrude had no intention of carrying the bags up to the house. Suddenly she glared up at the window from which the two boys had been watching the scene.

"You two boys up there!" she shouted. "I see you. Don't think I can't see you! Come down here and carry up my bags. Hustle now!"

They hustled.

CHAPTER VII
WRECKAGE

"Good night! We'll be lucky if we get away on the trip at all!" exclaimed Frank, as he and Joe hastened down the stairs.

Mrs. Hardy was already at the front door welcoming Aunt Gertrude, who was expatiating on the wickedness of taxi drivers in general.

"So!" she cried, as the boys appeared. "Standing up at a front window laughing at your great-aunt instead of coming down and helping carry up her bags like little gentlemen! I'm surprised at you!"

"We were just getting dressed, Aunt Gertrude," explained Frank meekly.

"Getting dressed, eh!" snorted Aunt Gertrude, taking in their attire. "Getting dressed! What kind of an outfit do you call that?" She poked Joe in the ribs with her umbrella, indicating the faded khaki shirt he was wearing. "Speak up, boy! What kind of an outfit is that? No necktie. Holes in your trousers. Shoes not shined."

"We were just getting ready to go on a boat trip, Aunt Gertrude," Joe explained.

"Boat trip! Boat trip! No! That settles it!" declared Aunt Gertrude, coming into the house and banging the umbrella decisively on the floor by way of emphasis. "I shan't allow it. The very idea! Laura," she said, turning to Mrs.

Hardy, "I'm surprised at you. Ab-so-lute-ly astonished! The very idea of letting these children go out in a boat! Don't you remember what happened to my Cousin Peter? He went out in a boat, didn't he? And what happened? The boat upset. He might have been drowned if the water had been deep enough. Thank goodness he was only a few feet from shore. But it only goes to show what *can* happen. If these boys go out in a boat they'll be drowned. I can't permit them to be drowned. They shan't go on any boat trip. That settles it!" She strode into the living room. "Boys—bring in my bags!" she commanded.

Mrs. Hardy smiled, for she was quite accustomed to the eccentricities of Aunt Gertrude, and the Hardy boys scuttled down the front steps for the baggage.

"Do you think she means it?" whispered Joe.

"Sure, she means it. But we'll get out somehow. She'll rave for a while, but she'll forget all about it when she starts to show mother how to run the house."

The boys deposited Aunt Gertrude's luggage in the guest room, then went downstairs for inspection. By this time the old lady had taken off her coat and hat and was seated in the most comfortable chair, fanning herself with a newspaper.

"Boat trip!" she was snorting, as they entered the room. "Never heard of such a thing. Letting little boys like that go out in a boat alone. If they were *my* boys I wouldn't let them out of my sight. Up to some mischief, I'll be bound."

"They are going out to look for two chums of theirs who have been lost for three days," Mrs. Hardy explained.

"And serve them right! I suppose they were out on a boat trip, too. I knew it! And now they're lost. That's what happens when you let children go out in boats. They get lost. Or drowned. And now you would let these two youngsters go out in a boat, too. And I suppose in a few days some of their chums would have to go out in a boat to look for *them*. They'd get lost, too. And then some more little boys would go out to look for *them*. And they'd get lost. By the end of the summer there wouldn't be a boy left in Bayport. Not that it would be much of a loss," sniffed Aunt Gertrude; "but I hate to see people making fools of themselves."

"Did you have a pleasant journey?" asked Mrs. Hardy, anxious to change the subject.

"Did I *ever* have a pleasant journey?" countered Aunt Gertrude. "What with the rudeness of conductors and ticket-sellers and baggage-men and taxi drivers there's no enjoyment in traveling nowadays. But *I* put 'em in their place. I know my rights and I insist on them!"

She glared ferociously about the room as though confronting a multitude of conductors, baggage-men and taxi drivers awaiting judgment.

"Now, boys! What are you staring at? Don't you know it's rude to be staring at people? Run away and play. I want to talk to your mother. Run away and play! Shoo!" She brandished the umbrella at them and the Hardy boys left the room precipitately. Their mother excused herself for a moment and followed them into the hall.

"Run!" she said, smiling. "I'll take care of Aunt Gertrude. Run along while you have the chance."

They kissed their mother good-bye and hastily departed, wondering how she was to explain their flight to the terrible Aunt Gertrude, in view of that lady's melancholy predictions concerning their fate should they venture out in the boat.

They found Slim Robinson waiting for them at the boathouse, and with many chuckles the boys told him of their escape from the tyrant who would have prevented their departure.

"We'd better hurry or she'll be down here after us if she finds we've got away from her," declared Joe.

"Tony and the other fellows are over in the other boathouse," Slim told them. "I think they're ready now."

"All right. Let's be going."

Frank started the engine of the *Sleuth* and the motorboat moved slowly out into the open bay. He steered a course for the entrance to Prito's boathouse, where Tony and the others were waiting. As soon as Tony saw him he started his own craft, and the *Napoli* nosed its way out abreast of them.

"All set?" shouted Frank.

"All set."

"Away we go."

The two boats drummed their way out into Barmet Bay and headed out toward the sea, side by side, picking up speed when they had threaded their way through the shipping near the docks.

It was evening before they reached the first village on the coast, after leaving the bay, and although they made numerous inquiries they failed to find any trace of their chums. No one in the village had seen or heard a motorboat during the storm, although they readily admitted that the craft might have passed without being noticed, owing to the gloom and the violence of the gale. The chums spent the night at this village and resumed their journey the next morning, going farther up the coast.

Their progress was necessarily slow because there were numerous small villages and they stopped at them all to make inquiries.

But in every case the answer was the same.

No motorboat answering to the description of the *Envoy* had been seen. None of the fishermen had heard of the craft.

"It's ten chances to one that they was wrecked in that storm," an old fisherman at one of the villages declared when they told him their story. "Unless they were mighty lucky they wouldn't get past Ragged Reef. They might get this far up the coast, but they'd never get past the Reef."

"Where is that?"

"Not far from here. Up past the next point. Seems to me I heard one of the boys sayin' this mornin' that there was some wreckage on the reef yesterday. There's none of our boats missin' from hereabouts, so mebby it's them young fellers."

The two motorboats thereupon started for Ragged Reef. The lads were downhearted. They had little hope that they would ever find their two companions alive. The words of the old fisherman struck terror into their hearts.

When they rounded the point they saw the black and ominous line of Ragged Reef before them. A jagged and irregular series of rocks jutting above the surface of the water in the form of a huge semicircle—this was the reef on which the *Envoy* might have come to grief.

Fortunately, the day was calm so that the searchers were able to venture more closely to the reef than they might have otherwise dared. Frank edged the *Sleuth* in toward the rocks as closely as possible. Suddenly he gave an exclamation:

"The fisherman was right! There *is* wreckage there!"

He pointed to a few broken fragments of wood that could be discerned against the rocks. Joe picked up the marine glasses and peered at the fragments for some time.

"It's wreckage of a boat of some kind," he declared gravely, lowering the glasses at last. "But whether it's from the *Envoy* or not, I couldn't say."

Slim also looked through the glasses. He was able to see more fragments of wreckage farther along the reef.

"Some boat has been battered to pieces along here. There isn't enough wreckage left to tell whether it was a motorboat or a sailing vessel." He scrutinized the mainland. "Nothing there," he announced finally. "Not a sign of life—nor wreckage either. It's all on the reef."

So interested had the boys been in the fragments of broken wood on the jagged rocks that they had not noticed that the motorboat was edging in closer to the reef. There was a strong current at this point and, unnoticed by the boys, the boat was being carried irresistibly forward.

A warning shout from the lads in the *Napoli* told them of their danger.

Frank had throttled down the engine so that the *Sleuth* had been almost drifting. Now he sprang for the helm, conscious of the peril that had crept so insidiously upon them.

The great black rocks of the reef loomed closer. The motorboat seemed to be dragged mercilessly toward its doom. The powerful current had the craft firmly in its grasp!

CHAPTER VIII

THE STRANGE LETTER

The engine roared as Frank Hardy opened the throttle and bore down on the helm of the *Sleuth*.

The grip of the current about the reef was so strong that, for a moment, it seemed that the motorboat could not fight against it. Then, slowly, the craft swung about, seemed to remain motionless for a moment, and then began to forge ahead, away from the reef.

Fighting against the force of the current, the motorboat made slow progress. Still, it was gaining ground. The boys waited tensely, as the craft struggled out of danger. Gradually, the *Sleuth* drew away from the reef, gradually the grip of the current relaxed. Frank cautiously nosed the boat over to the left and managed to get out of the current altogether.

The whole affair had occurred in a few seconds, but it had seemed an eternity to the boys in the boat and their chums in the other craft. It would only have been a matter of moments before they might have been swept swiftly down onto the treacherous reef.

"That'll teach me to watch where I'm going," said Frank, as he sat back and mopped his brow.

"There was mighty near a lot more wreckage on that reef," remarked Slim soberly. "The boat wouldn't have lasted long if we'd piled up on those rocks."

"I'll say it wouldn't! I think we'd better get away from here. We'll never be able to get close enough to identify that wreckage. Might as well go on up the coast."

They drew up alongside the *Napoli* and, after discussing the narrow escape they had just had from being cast up on the reef, acquainted the other boys with their decision to continue the search.

"There's no use trying to get closer to that wreckage," declared Frank. "It's all in small pieces and we probably wouldn't be able to say whether it was from the *Envoy* or not, if we did reach it. We may as well go on up the coast and keep making inquiries at the other villages."

This plan they followed, but to no avail.

Their inquiries were fruitless. The *Envoy*, with Chet and Biff, seemed to have vanished into thin air. At none of the fishing villages were they able to find any one who had seen or heard of the missing motorboat. As for the wreckage on the reef, no one was found who could enlighten them. Two or three fishing boats had been wrecked during the storm, but they had met their fate farther up the coast and in each case the scene of the wreck was known to the fishermen.

"It might have been your friend's boat, and it might have been only some old wreckage washed down the coast by the storm," said one keen-eyed salt. "You'd best give up the search. If they're drowned, they're drowned, and that's all there is to it. If they were wrecked and managed to save themselves they'll make their way to the nearest village and they'll get home from there without any trouble. If you haven't found any trace of them by now there isn't much use going any further, for they would never have got this far up the coast having been seen by some of the fishermen."

The boys reluctantly agreed that his advice was sound. They turned back for Bayport.

When they returned to the city and reported that their quest had been unsuccessful they were scarcely prepared for the sensation that the news aroused. The Hoopers were frantic with anxiety, as their last hopes were dashed. The Mortons were almost stunned. They had hoped against hope that the search would bring them at least some news of the missing boys.

The local papers featured the story and the city was aroused. In every village and town along the coast, to north and south, people were discussing the mysterious disappearance of the motorboat and its human freight. Fishermen were on the lookout for any trace of the craft. The coast guards promised to do all in their power to clear up the mystery.

But, when three days more went by and there was still not the slightest solution in sight, the opinion became general that the boat had been wrecked in the storm and had gone to the bottom. The two boys were given up for lost. The Hardy boys and their chums were gradually forced to the belief that Chet and Biff had perished.

Then came an incident that temporarily drove the tragic affair from the minds of Frank and Joe, because it concerned their own home more intimately.

Aunt Gertrude had greeted them on their return with a barrage of scathing comment on their disobedience in leaving on the trip in spite of her avowed disapproval, and she expressed the greatest amazement because they had returned alive after all.

"You may thank Providence that you got back," she declared in her characteristically brusque fashion. "It was through no skill of your own, I'll be bound. Your poor mother and me were worried to death all the time you were away—gallivanting over the ocean."

Aunt Gertrude did not add that Mrs. Hardy's worries had been chiefly occasioned by her aunt's dire predictions of the certain death that awaited the boys on the search. However, her tone was modified somewhat when she realized that they had indeed been hunting for the missing chums and she made it her business to call on the Hoopers and the Mortons to condole with them, for she was a good-hearted soul in her own way—although it is to be feared that her condolences did more to add to the certainty that the boys were drowned than they served to cheer up the sorrowing parents.

The third day after the Hardy boys returned she was sorting over the morning mail, having duly taken charge of every department of the household.

"Ha!" she exclaimed, holding a letter up to the light. "Here's a letter addressed to Fenton Hardy. Bad news in it, I'll be bound."

Aunt Gertrude could smell bad news a mile away, Frank often said.

"Bad news in it. I can tell. I dreamed about haystacks last night. Haystacks! Whenever I dream about haystacks it means bad news. I never knew it to fail. Open the letter, Laura."

"But it isn't addressed to me," objected Mrs. Hardy.

"Fiddlesticks! It's addressed to your husband, isn't it? You have as much right to open it as he has. More. It's a wife's duty to help her husband as much as she can and look after his affairs for him. Man and wife are one, aren't they? Open the letter."

Mrs. Hardy, with some misgivings, slit open the envelope and Aunt Gertrude, who was possessed of an insatiable curiosity, immediately seized the letter.

"I'll read it for you!" she offered.

"'Fenton Hardy—Bayport,'" she began. "'Dear Sir: We wish to inform you that we have—' My goodness! What's this? What's this? Gracious me!" She lapsed into unintelligible mutterings as she read the rest of the letter to herself, frequently giving vent to exclamations of surprise while her eyes widened with astonishment.

Mrs. Hardy and the boys could hardly contain their impatience until at last Aunt Gertrude laid down the letter and peered triumphantly at them over her spectacles.

"Didn't I say so?" she demanded stridently. "Didn't I say there was bad news in this letter? Didn't I tell you I dreamed of haystacks last night? Haystacks always mean bad news." She looked at the letter again. "Although for the life of me I can't imagine what the man means. Hum! Kidnapped!" She looked up suddenly at the Hardy boys and glared at them.

"You boys haven't been kidnapped lately? No. Of course not. What nonsense! Has any one tried to kidnap you?"

"No, Aunt Gertrude," said Frank, utterly mystified.

"Then," demanded Aunt Gertrude, pushing the letter across to Mrs. Hardy and folding her arms as though prepared to wait until doomsday for a satisfactory answer, "what does this letter mean?"

Mrs. Hardy picked up the letter and read it aloud, while an expression of amazement crossed her face.

"Fenton Hardy—Bayport," ran the letter. "Dear Sir: We wish to inform you that we are holding your two sons in a safe place and that we will not return them to you unless you agree to the following conditions: You must pay us the sum of $5000 as ransom, you must agree to refuse to give evidence in the Asbury Park bank robbery case, and you must further agree to give up your pursuit of our leader, Baldy Turk. These are our conditions. It will do you no good to attempt to find your sons, for we will not hesitate to put them out of the way if you attempt to discover our hiding place. Furthermore, unless you agree to what we ask, it will go hard with them. You may signify your agreement to the terms of this letter by dropping a package containing the money and a signed statement to the effect that you will drop your pursuit of Baldy Turk and that you will not give evidence against our associates in the robbery case from the 5:15 express from Bayport next Thursday afternoon as it passes the grade crossing at the North Road."

The letter was unsigned.

"What on earth does it mean?" asked Mrs. Hardy.

Frank and Joe looked at one another in astonishment. Frank reached over for the letter and examined it. The strange document was typewritten on an ordinary quality of white paper. The envelope bore the Bayport post-mark, indicating that it had been mailed from the city post-office early that morning.

"It must be a practical joke of some kind," said Mrs. Hardy, in perplexity.

"Practical joke, nothing!" scoffed Aunt Gertrude shrewdly. "Did Fenton Hardy go to Chicago after some criminal?"

"He went to arrest Baldy Turk," replied Frank.

"There!" Aunt Gertrude pounded the table. "That explains the whole thing. The companions of this Baldy person sent that letter in the hope that it would bring Fenton Hardy back from Chicago by the next train."

"But the letter is addressed to Bayport."

"Certainly! Why not? They wouldn't know where to reach him in Chicago, so they sent the letter here and trusted that it would be forwarded to him. And if *I* hadn't been here," said Aunt Gertrude, "it very probably *would* have been forwarded to him. Am I right?"

"I usually forward his personal mail," admitted Mrs. Hardy.

"There! Didn't I know it? And look what would have happened. Fenton Hardy would have fallen right into the trap. He would have come back home, thinking his precious sons were kidnapped, and that would have given this Turk person time to get away. It's a blessing I was here, I tell you. I hope this will be a lesson to you, Laura Hardy. *Always open your husband's mail!* Always!"

CHAPTER IX

BLACKSNAKE ISLAND

In spite of Aunt Gertrude's ingenious explanation of the letter, the Hardy boys were not quite satisfied. When they left the house they walked downtown, discussing the matter.

"Aunt Gertrude may be right, but somehow I think those fellows sent the letter to the house, believing dad was still there," declared Joe.

"But if they knew he was at the house, or thought he was at the house, he would know we weren't kidnapped."

"Yes, that's right," Joe admitted, puzzled. "I'm hanged if I can figure it out, but I still think there is more to that letter than Aunt Gertrude imagines."

"I have that idea myself. You noticed that they were very particular to tell how the ransom money was to be delivered. That was quite an elaborate stunt, to have the money thrown off the train at a grade crossing. That would mean that the crooks could come along in a car, snatch up the package and be away without much risk of capture. They'd hardly go to the trouble of outlining all that if they didn't mean something by it."

"Yes, if the letter was only sent as a blind to bring dad back to Bayport you'd hardly think they'd go into all that detail."

"Still," Frank pointed out, "here we are, safe and sound. Haven't been kidnapped yet, and nobody has tried to kidnap us. If that letter had been sent to Chet's people, for instance, or to the Hoopers, they would have something to worry about." Suddenly he stopped and looked at Joe. "Say!" he exclaimed. "*There's* an idea!"

"What?"

"Chet and Biff!" declared Frank excitedly. "Don't you see? This may have something to do with them. Chet and Biff are missing. Perhaps *they* have been kidnapped."

"But why should any one kidnap them?" Joe looked wonderingly at his brother.

"In mistake for us. Don't you see it? Perhaps this gang mistook Chet and Biff for you and me and kidnapped them! Then they wrote the letter to dad."

"Gee, I never thought of that!" Joe exclaimed. "I'll bet dollars to doughnuts that you're right."

"Don't you remember the day we were all out in the boat and the three men came so close to us? Remember how closely they looked at Chet and Biff? Perhaps those fellows had been tipped off that you and I were in the boat and wanted to get a look at us so they could identify us when they got a chance to kidnap us. And instead of looking at us, they picked on Chet and Biff. They knew we owned a boat, but they wouldn't know that Biff had one. Therefore they'd think that the chap at the wheel would be either you or me."

"It hangs together, all right. And then, remember when we saw those same three men hanging around the Morton farm? They must have trailed Chet home to see where he lived. And all the time they thought he was either you or me!"

"I think we're getting at the truth of it, Joe. When Chet and Biff started on their trip, those fellows followed them or lay in wait for them some place and captured them."

Just then the Hardy boys met Phil Cohen and Tony Prito in front of the fruit stand of their friend, Nick the Greek, each with a bottle of pop.

"Hello," was Tony's greeting. "Have one?" he invited, indicating the pop.

"Don't mind if we do, even if it is just after breakfast."

Nick the Greek dexterously opened two bottles of pop and slapped them down on the counter. "Hot day, eh?" he said, as the boys reached for straws.

"You bet it's hot." After a satisfying gurgle of the ice-cold pop, the Hardy boys turned to their chums. "We have a clue," declared Frank.

"About what?"

"About Chet and Biff."

"Yes?" Tony and Phil were immediately interested. "What's up?"

Frank then told them of the incident of the letter and, often prompted by his brother, explained how they had connected it with the disappearance of their chums.

"And so," he concluded, "we've figured that Chet and Biff may have been kidnapped in mistake for us."

"There's something in that, too," agreed Phil. "And here's something else that may help. I forgot about it when we were searching for the fellows the other day. Just a little while before they went on their trip I was talking to Chet and Biff and I remember that Biff said he had always wanted to visit Blacksnake Island."

"Blacksnake Island!" exclaimed Frank. "That's the place that is overrun with big blacksnakes, isn't it? Nobody ever goes there."

"That's the place, and that's why it's called Blacksnake Island. And you can't blame people for staying away from it—with a name like that. But Biff had read about it and said he wanted to see what the place was like."

"That's Biff all over," agreed Tony. "But did they decide to go?"

"Chet didn't want to go. Blacksnake Island is down the coast, and Chet wanted to go up the coast."

"Sure! That's why we searched up the coast—because Chet said that was where they were going!" Frank declared.

"Well, Biff kept on saying that he wanted to see Blacksnake Island anyway, and while Chet wasn't very much struck with the idea he *might* have gone there."

"Perhaps they went that way after all. I wish we'd known that when we made our first search. They might have started for Blacksnake Island and got captured on the way." Frank drained the last of his bottle of pop. "Say, I'd like to start another search for them, and go down the coast in that direction. What do you say?"

"I guess I can get away all right," said Tony. "How about you, Phil?"

"It's okay with me."

"We'll probably find it hard to get away," said Frank doubtfully. "We'll go home and ask mother, anyway. You see, we're supposed to stay around the house now that dad's away. But Aunt Gertrude is there and if we can make a get-away without her seeing us I guess it'll be all right."

"Look us up if you can make it."

"You bet we will! Let's go home now, Joe, and see if we can go."

The boys separated and Frank and Joe returned home. They found their mother and Aunt Gertrude still discussing the letter.

"It's absolute foolishness, Laura Hardy, that's all it is!" Aunt Gertrude declared. "You'll just scare the man out of his wits and he'll be back here on the first train."

"Well, I've sent the message, and at least I'll know where he is. I haven't had any word from Fenton since he left and it's been making me nervous."

"Fiddlesticks! The man is too busy to write."

"It isn't like him not to drop a line every two or three days. He is usually very particular about it. He always sends me a note at least twice a week while he's away."

"Well," sighed Aunt Gertrude, as though giving it up as a bad job, "I suppose you know your own affairs best; but I'm telling you I would *not* have sent that telegram. There!" and she picked up her knitting, the needles flashing furiously.

"What's the matter?" asked Frank.

"Little boys should be seen and not heard," grunted Aunt Gertrude, glaring at him over the tops of her spectacles.

"I sent a telegram to your father, telling him about the letter," their mother explained. "I think he should know about it. And, besides, I've been worrying because he hasn't written."

"Where did you address the telegram?"

"He gave me two addresses where I would be sure to find him in Chicago," said Mrs. Hardy. "He gave me the name of the hotel he would be staying at and he also said that Police Headquarters would reach him. I sent the same telegram to each place so I'd be sure to get him."

"Waste of money," sniffed Aunt Gertrude.

At that moment the telephone rang. Mrs. Hardy answered it. The phone was in the hallway and the boys could not hear their mother's words, but when she returned to the room a few minutes later they saw that she was pale with apprehension.

"The telegraph company tells me that there is no Fenton Hardy registered at the hotel and that Police Headquarters say he hasn't shown up there either," she announced gravely.

The boys looked at each other in surprise.

"That's strange," said Frank. "And he hasn't written. There's something wrong about this!"

Aunt Gertrude, for once, was at a loss for words. The knitting needles remained suspended in mid-air. Behind the spectacles, her eyes were wide and her mouth remained open in astonishment.

"This affair gets more puzzling every minute," remarked Frank, at last. "Of course dad might have been delayed, or he might have picked up a clue that took him away from Chicago after all. But I think he would have written."

"Perhaps he didn't report at Police Headquarters in Chicago because he was afraid Baldy Turk's gang might find out he was in the city," Joe suggested.

"There's something in that."

"But why wouldn't he be at the hotel?" asked Mrs. Hardy.

"He might be there under an assumed name. If Baldy Turk's gang are on the lookout for him he wouldn't register under his real name. They would be checking up on all the hotels to find him if they thought he was in Chicago," said Frank eagerly. "Perhaps that's why your message didn't reach him."

"Of course, that's why!" sniffed Aunt Gertrude, returning to her knitting, much relieved. "Any one might have known that. It was a waste of time to try to reach him with a telegram, and I said that from the start." The needles clashed.

"Oh, I guess we needn't worry about dad very much. He can look after himself," said Frank, with a warning glance at his brother. Nevertheless, he was deeply worried over the fact that the telegraph company had failed to locate his father. However, he was trying to make light of the matter so as to relieve his mother of worry.

Joe saw his motive.

"Sure, dad can look after himself. There's nothing to be alarmed about. He's probably keeping out of sight in Chicago for fear Baldy Turk's gang will find out he is there. If they ever knew he was on their trail they wouldn't stop at trying to kill him. He said so himself. If he tried to communicate with us it might give them just the clue they are waiting for."

"I suppose you're right," Mrs. Hardy agreed, brightening up. "Well, we won't worry about it."

"Of course we won't worry about it!" declared Aunt Gertrude. "Worry is unhealthy. Worry has sent more people to their graves than anything else. Look at me. I never worry. That's why I'm so healthy. I'll live to be a hundred."

"Yes, it would take quite a lot to kill you, Aunt Gertrude," agreed Frank innocently.

Aunt Gertrude looked up at him suspiciously.

"I don't know just what you mean by that, young man, but I'll warrant there's something behind it! What are you two rascals waiting around here for, anyway? What do you want?"

"We were just wanting to talk to mother."

"Well, go ahead. Who's stopping you? *I* won't listen, I'm sure. If it's none of my business you needn't be afraid that *I'll* listen. Not at all. Not at all. Go right ahead. Talk to your mother if you wish. Of course, if you want to leave your poor old aunt out of everything I'm sure *I* don't mind. I'm not interested, anyway."

Whereupon Aunt Gertrude indignantly hitched her chair around toward the window and knitted vigorously.

"Go ahead! I'm not listening. Talk away. I won't listen to a word of it," she shrilled.

Mrs. Hardy smiled.

"What is it, boys?"

"I'm not listening," declared Aunt Gertrude.

"We think we've found a new clue about Chet and Biff," said Frank. "We wanted to go on another search for them!"

"What!" shrieked Aunt Gertrude, quite forgetting that she had not been listening. She wheeled about in her chair. "Go on another search for those two boys! Of all the idiotic ideas! Laura Hardy, if you let these two children go gallivanting out into the ocean again it will be against my advice."

"Where are you planning to look for them?" asked Mrs. Hardy.

"Blacksnake Island!"

Aunt Gertrude gasped. In her astonishment she dropped her knitting needles. "Blacksnake Island! Frank Hardy, have you gone completely off your head?"

CHAPTER X

THE BOY ON THE DECK

Perhaps it was because Mrs. Hardy was determined to show that she was mistress in her own home. At any rate, she gave her consent to the proposed expedition. This was in spite of all Aunt Gertrude's protests and predictions of disaster. The terrible woman raved for an hour when it was definitely decided that the Hardy boys should go on the trip, but Mrs. Hardy was firm. If there was any chance that they might be able to rescue Chet and Biff she meant that they should avail themselves of it.

They explained their theory regarding the letter, and although Aunt Gertrude derided it as nonsense, Mrs. Hardy was disposed to believe that their deductions might be correct.

"You may go," she said. "But take care of yourselves and don't take any foolish chances. I'm worrying enough about your father, as it is."

So the boys left the house before Aunt Gertrude would have an opportunity to change their mother's mind and joyfully acquainted Phil and Tony with the news.

"We're going to start right away," they told their chums. "Better get ready."

"I was speaking to Slim Robinson and Jerry Gilroy," Tony told them. "They want to come along too."

"There isn't room for all of us in the one boat."

"I was thinking of that. What's the matter with the rest of us making the trip in the *Napoli*? I'll get up another expedition and we'll follow you."

"Good idea. One of the boys can come with us and the rest of you can go in the *Napoli*. Joe and I are starting right away."

But when it came time to check up on the various members of the searching party they discovered that Tony was the only one who could leave that day. Slim Robinson had to work that afternoon, as also had Jerry Gilroy, while Phil Cohen had an engagement for the evening that he was unable to break.

"We'll all leave in the *Napoli* first thing tomorrow morning, then," decided Tony. "You and Joe go ahead in your boat now and head toward Blacksnake Island. We'll be along in the morning."

This was the plan agreed upon, and the Hardy boys lost no time in making ready for the trip. They had the forethought to stock up with provisions for several days, although the run to Blacksnake Island would not take them many hours, because they realized that the search might keep them away from home longer than they expected.

It was afternoon before they were able to get away, and all through the lunch hour they were in a constant state of apprehension lest Aunt Gertrude prevail upon their mother to withdraw her permission for the journey.

"They'll never come back alive, mark my words!" declared their aunt. "They'll be bitten by those snakes on Blacksnake Island, as sure as fate. Why, even grownup men won't go on that island. It's a terrible place. I've read all about it."

"We're not planning to explore the island, Aunt Gertrude," Frank explained. "We're going to cruise around it and see if we can find any sign of the fellows."

"Cruise around it!" their aunt sniffed. "As if I don't know boys! You'll not be satisfied until you've tramped from one end of the island to the other. But go ahead. Go ahead. I wash my hands of the affair. If you want to commit suicide, it's your own lookout," and she swept from the room in great indignation.

Mrs. Hardy did not share her fears. She knew her sons well enough to realize that they would not run into needless dangers, and when she kissed them good-bye her only request was that they would not stay away any longer than was necessary.

The bay was calm when they started out, and the *Sleuth* was running, as Joe expressed it, "like a watch."

It was a beautiful summer afternoon and the cool breeze out on the water was in welcome relief to the sweltering heat of the city streets. Spray flicked into their faces as the motorboat raced along toward the eastern gap. When they passed out of Barmet Bay and reached the open sea Frank headed the boat down the coast in the direction of Blacksnake Island.

"It isn't far from the coast. There's a channel of a little over a mile," he said to his brother. "We won't be able to make it tonight, but we'll stop over at Rock Harbor and go on again in the morning. By that time, Tony and the others shouldn't be far behind."

Toward the end of the afternoon they were in sight of Rock Harbor, a small port, where they spied a schooner at anchor in the distance. Rock Harbor was not a shipping point of great importance, but there were always a number of miscellaneous craft in evidence.

To enter the harbor they were obliged to pass within a short distance of the schooner, swinging about beneath the bows of the vessel. As the *Sleuth* plunged through the water, in the very shadow of the ship, Joe suddenly gave an exclamation of surprise.

"Frank! Look up on deck—quick!"

Frank glanced hurriedly upward. He was just in time to see the figure of a boy moving away from the rail, but there was something familiar about the young fellow that made him look incredulously at his brother.

"Chet!"

"I'm sure it's him," returned Joe hurriedly. "I didn't get a very good look at his face, because he only looked over the rail and then he drew back—but I'm almost positive it was Chet!"

"But what on earth can he be doing on that schooner?"

"Probably he's a prisoner. Let's give him a hail."

They shouted the name of their chum half a dozen times, but their only response was from a villainous looking sailor who glared over the side at them and bade them get away from the ship.

"No use causing trouble," said Frank, in a low voice. "We'll go now, but we'll come back later."

He steered the motorboat away from the vicinity of the schooner, but instead of going on into the harbor he put out to sea again.

"It won't be long until it gets darker. Then we'll go back. If Chet is on that ship we'll get word to him somehow."

"Well, if it isn't Chet Morton it's his double," declared Joe. "Even if I didn't get a very good look at him, I know he was just about the same height and build and the same general appearance. What puzzles me is why he didn't call out to us. And why did he draw back from the rail in such a hurry?"

"He mightn't have had time to call to us. Perhaps he managed to escape just for a minute or so and they dragged him back before he could give a shout."

"There's something in that. And of course he mightn't have recognized us."

"He would have recognized the boat, I'm sure."

"There's something strange about it. If we come back later on we may be able to see him again. Did you notice the name of the schooner?"

"Yes," answered Frank. "I watched for it. The *Persis*. I think what we'd better do is this: We'll go back down the coast and loaf around until it gets darker. Then we'll come back to the harbor and try to come up to the schooner quietly. If there's a rope ladder handy I'll go up over the side and see what I can find out."

"It looks like our only chance. You'll have to go easy. If Chet and Biff are held prisoners on that ship they'll be well guarded. You might be captured yourself."

"That's where you will come in. If you hear sounds of a struggle or if I don't come back, go right into the harbor and notify the police so they can have the schooner searched."

Joe nodded. "All right. I'll keep watch."

Frank steered the motorboat back along the coast again and for the next hour or more they cruised about, waiting for twilight. At length sunset came and gradually the shadows fell. Lights began to twinkle in the town. Lights glowed from the mysterious schooner, now but a rakish shadow at the entrance to the harbor. When the lads judged that it was sufficiently dark to cover their approach, they returned, then crept quietly up on the ship.

They drew up close to the schooner's stern without being noticed and to Frank's relief he saw that a rope was dangling over the side. From the boat he reached out and seized it. The rope held fast; it supported his weight.

There were vague sounds from the deck above. The shuffling of feet. A burst of laughter from forward. Most of the men, he judged, would be in port, but it behooved him to move with caution.

"All set," he whispered to Joe.

"Right."

Frank swung himself away from the motorboat and began to climb slowly to the deck. Water lapped against the schooner's hull. The night was very quiet. Complete darkness had fallen by now. In a few moments Joe could only distinguish his brother as an obscure shadow as he clambered slowly upward.

Anxiously, Joe Hardy watched. He saw his brother climb higher and higher until at last his head and shoulders were silhouetted above the side of the ship.

Then Frank scrambled quietly over onto the deck. He had removed his shoes so as to proceed with a minimum of sound, so that once he had disappeared over the side Joe could hear nothing. He crouched in the boat, waiting.

Finally he heard a low whistle from the deck above. He looked up. He could see Frank leaning over the side. His brother's face was only a grey blur. He motioned with his arm, indicating that Joe was to follow him.

The motorboat had been tied fast so, although Joe was somewhat puzzled, he was nothing loath to share the adventure. Seizing the rope, he swung himself free of the motorboat, then began to climb nimbly toward the deck.

The rope cut into his hands and the climb taxed his strength, but in a few minutes he was near the top. Frank had moved back from the side into the darkness again.

He scrambled over the side and dropped lightly onto the deck. Frank was crouched in the shadows waiting for him.

And at that moment a heavy hand fell on his shoulder and a gruff voice said in his ear:

"All right, young fellow. Now we've got you both!"

CHAPTER XI

THE ISLAND

Joe Hardy started violently. Then, realizing that he had been trapped, he dropped flat on the deck, wriggling to one side, wresting himself free of the clutching hand. He heard the man who had seized him give an angry grunt, then he saw the man lunging at him from the shadows. He dodged the outstretched arm and rolled over and over on the deck.

"Grab him, Mike!" roared another voice from near by, and then Joe was dimly aware that another struggle had started near the rail. He leaped to his feet and raced along the deck, the sailor in pursuit.

"Over the side, Joe!" shouted a voice that he recognized as being that of his brother.

He fled, hearing the pounding of feet on the deck close behind him. A dark figure stepped out of the shadows immediately ahead.

"Collar him!" roared the man at his back. The dark figure advanced with outstretched arms. Joe stepped neatly aside, dodged as the man swooped at him and blundered to the left. The two men collided violently, and by the time they had disengaged themselves Joe was a good five yards away.

The schooner was in an uproar.

A revolver roared from the shadows and the darkness was cleft by a crimson splash.

"Harbor thieves!" yelled a voice from behind. "Catch 'em."

Footsteps pounded on the deck. Shouts and muttered imprecations rang out. A light flared from somewhere ahead. Out of the shadows rose a man who lunged fiercely at Joe, grappled with him, and they fell to the deck together. Joe managed to wrench himself free and rolled to one side, scrambling to his feet.

He heard a splash near by and a shout. "Over the side!" he could hear Frank calling again. His brother's voice was far below and he knew that Frank must have dived from the rail.

He was not far from the side of the schooner, and he raced for the rail just as half a dozen figures came plunging out of the gloom, their heavy boots thudding tremendously on the deck. Again the revolver crashed out and again the tongue of crimson flame licked its way through the blackness. The bullet passed within a few inches of Joe's head, and he ducked instinctively.

He reached the rail. Desperately, he scrambled up. But just as he poised for the dive a great hand closed about his ankle and some one seized the back of his coat. He felt himself dragged back, but with his free foot he kicked out. The grasp of his pursuer relaxed and Joe heard him grunt from the impact. The man staggered back.

The moment he was free, Joe went over the side.

He struck the cold water of the bay with a splash and went far down into the depths. Then he found himself rising again and at last he bobbed up over the surface.

He did not know where the motorboat was, but he swam ahead, at the same time keeping a wary eye above. He could see dark figures silhouetted above the side of the vessel and he could hear voices.

"He's down there!" declared a gruff voice.

"I almost had him!" shouted another. "I grabbed him just as he was going over, but he kicked me in the jaw."

"How many were there?" asked another sailor.

"Two," declared the gruff voice. "Harbor thieves—both of 'em. Come sneakin' aboard, one at a time. I caught one of 'em peepin' down into the galley where the cabin boy was peelin' potatoes and I followed him till he went back to the side, so I figured he had the rest of his pals down below. I grabbed him and clapped my hand over his mouth and made him wave for 'em to come up. But there was only one come up and Bill here grabbed him, but he got away."

"Both of 'em get away?"

"Yeah! I hope they drown."

Then a thrill of fear ran through Joe as he heard one of the men say:

"Keep quiet! Listen! Don't you hear some one swimming down there?"

The voices died down. Joe could see the figures leaning over the side as the sailors intently peered down into the darkness. He ceased swimming to tread water quietly.

"Take a shot at him!" advised some one.

Joe let himself sink beneath the surface and hardly had he gone beneath the waves than he heard the muffled report of a revolver and a splash near by. He swam beneath the water until his lungs were almost bursting. Then, when he could stand it no longer, he came to the surface again. He was deep in the shadow of the ship and he had left the sailors behind, still watching the place where he had gone down.

"I don't believe there was any one there," muttered one of the men in a disappointed tone.

"No, I guess they both got away," agreed another. "We scared 'em off, anyway."

"Did they steal anything?"

"No. They didn't have time. I nailed the first one before he'd been on the ship long. I guess he just went on ahead to see if everything was clear."

"Aw, I'm goin' to bed. As long as we scared 'm off—"

The voices died away.

Relieved, Joe swam on. In a few minutes he caught sight of a dark shape ahead. It was the motorboat.

Silently, he swam toward it until he had reached the side. A voice whispered:

"Is that you, Joe?"

"Yes."

Frank had already gained the boat. He now leaned over the side and grasped Joe's hand, helping his brother on board. Dripping wet, they both crouched in the boat.

"Lucky they didn't see the *Sleuth* tied down here," whispered Frank. "I've been waiting here for you. I thought sure they had you."

"It was a close call. They mistook us for harbor thieves, eh?"

"Yes."

"Did you see Chet?"

"It wasn't Chet after all."

"No?"

"It was the cabin boy. I peeped into the galley and there he was, peeling potatoes. But it was another fellow altogether. He looked like Chet. So I started back and I had just reached the side when a sailor grabbed me. He kept his hand over my mouth so I couldn't call out. Then he grabbed my arm and made me wave over the side."

"I thought you were motioning for me to come on up."

"It was a bad mess. Oh, well, we're out of it, if we can only get away from here quick enough. I think we'd better wait for a while until the excitement dies down."

The boys waited in the darkness. Gradually the schooner became silent once more. The sailors had evidently returned to the fore-castle. At length Frank judged that they could escape without trouble.

Fortunately, the engine of the motorboat responded immediately, and although the noise of their departure was sufficient to arouse the ship, the *Sleuth* shot away into the gloom so swiftly that their escape was assured. When they were several hundred yards away they looked back and they could see the lights of lanterns moving about near the stern, but they knew that the sailors would not put out after them. Even if they had, the motorboat would not be overtaken.

They circled about in the bay for some time and eventually put back into the harbor for the night. At first they were afraid that the men on the schooner might have given word to the harbor police to be on the lookout for them but, as Frank said, their consciences were clear and they had no doubt of their ability to explain the situation satisfactorily.

However, they were not intercepted and, in Rock Harbor, they tied the motorboat up for the night, going to a near-by hotel, where a sleepy night clerk assigned them to a room.

Early next morning they were away again.

"Blacksnake Island isn't far away now," said Frank. "We should be there in a few hours at the most."

There was no sign of the other boys, but Frank and Joe decided that they would not wait, as the others would overtake them at the island or would meet them on their return. They had replenished their boat with oil and gasoline, they had again inspected their supply of provisions and were in every way in readiness for the last lap of their search.

It was mid-morning before they came within sight of Blacksnake Island. It lay not far from the coast, a low, lean, sinister stretch of swampy land, terminating in rocky bluffs on the seaward side. There was a dank, heavy growth of vegetation and the island seemed to steam in the summer heat.

"Ugly looking place, isn't it?" remarked Frank, as the motorboat sped on its way.

The craft drew closer to the island. There was no sign of life. As they came nearer the boys could distinguish the fetid swamp land facing the coast, the still, silent trees that seemed to droop beneath the scorching sun and they felt a qualm of repulsion. Blacksnake Island was not an inviting place. It lived up to its name. It was a fit abode for serpents—not for human beings.

When they were within half a mile of the island, they heard a vague but familiar sound.

"Motorboat!" exclaimed Frank.

They listened. They could hear the sound of a motorboat, apparently approaching from the far side of the island. Frank spun the wheel.

"We'll head down the channel. No use letting them think we're bound for the island," he said. "It's not likely to have anything to do with our search, but it's best to play safe."

The *Sleuth* changed its course, so that Blacksnake Island was now to one side, and the motorboat appeared to be heading on down the coast. The Hardy boys scanned the dark bank of land intently.

The other boat appeared in view at last. It emerged slowly around the lower point, poking its nose inquisitively out into the channel as though to assure itself that the way was clear. Then it picked up speed and came surging out toward the mainland. At that distance, Frank and Joe could not readily distinguish the features of the men in the craft, but they saw that there were two of them. Frank's eyes narrowed as he surveyed the boat.

"Seems to me I've seen it before," he remarked, picking up the binoculars. He raised them to his eyes and gazed long and earnestly at the speeding craft. Finally he handed the glasses to Joe. "What do you think?" he asked.

"Why, of course we've seen it before!" Joe exclaimed, after a brief inspection. "We saw that boat in Barmet Bay!"

Frank nodded.

"It's the same motorboat that chased us the afternoon of the storm!"

CHAPTER XII

INTO THE CAVE

Frank Hardy bent over the wheel.

"I'm going closer," he said. "We'll make absolutely sure of this."

He altered the course of the boat so that it would intercept the other craft, at the speed they were going. Then he turned up his coat collar and drew his cap lower over his eyes.

"If it's the same boat and if the same men are in it, we should be safe enough as long as they don't recognize us. They saw us that day, but they've never seen the *Sleuth*. We'll get as close to them as we can."

But the other craft had increased its speed. It was a powerful boat and a high curl of foam now rose from its bows as it plunged through the waves in a rapid flight toward the mainland in the distance. The roar of the engine was borne to the boys' ears on the breeze.

"We're going to lose them," muttered Frank. "They're too far ahead of us, unless we want to cut in and meet them right near the land."

"That will only make them suspicious."

"Yes, I guess we'd better let them go."

Still, he did not give up the attempt just then, opening the throttle so that the *Sleuth* was racing along at top speed. But the other boat had the advantage, and cut across their course with a quarter of a mile to spare. Joe gazed through the binoculars, striving to identify the two men.

"No use," he remarked, at last. "The fellow at the wheel is turned away from us, and the other man is bending down in the boat so I can't see his face."

"Is it the same boat?"

"I can't be positive. But I think so. It certainly looks very much like it."

"I'm almost sure. Of course, there might be lots of other motorboats just like it—but I've got a hunch that it's the same craft."

"What would it be doing at Blacksnake Island? There's no doubt that it came from there."

"That's for us to find out. We'll let them go on to the mainland. Then we'll circle back and go up the other side of the island."

In a short time the other craft disappeared from view, entering a small cove some distance down the coast, and Frank turned their boat about and headed toward Blacksnake Island again. They approached it from the seaward side and drew in as close to the island as they dared. The rocky bluffs were lonely and forbidding, seeming to offer no available landing place.

"We'll go right around it. If Chet and Biff are there we should be able to see their boat or a fire or some sign of them," said Frank, half questioningly, to his brother.

"After seeing that other motorboat, I'm pretty sure we won't see any sign of them at all. I'm pretty well satisfied that those men kidnapped them and brought them here. And if they did, you may be sure they'll be well hidden."

"We'll circle the island anyway, and if we don't see anything we'll land and make a search of the place."

But making a circuit of the island took longer than the boys expected. Blacksnake Island was bigger than it had first appeared. It was almost a mile in length, and correspondingly wide—a great, swampy tract of forbidding marsh at one end, rising to higher ground and desolate rocks at the other. On the swampy side there were sinister little creeks, dead bushes half inundated, logs floating about in the black water. Frank and Joe caught glimpses of triangular black heads forging slowly through the water here and there.

"The blacksnakes!" Frank exclaimed.

Once the motorboat passed within a few yards of one of these black reptiles. Fascinated, the boys watched the ugly black head that projected above the surface, and they could see the long, sinuous body writhing beneath the water as the snake swam toward the fetid marsh.

"There must be hundreds of them on that island."

"They're dangerous, too. I've read about them. A bite from one of them means your finish."

There were fewer snakes on the rocky side of the island and, after they had made the circuit without seeing any sign of human life, the boys decided to make a landing.

"Seeing that motorboat leaving here makes me believe some one is around," declared Frank. "I won't be satisfied until I find out for sure."

"We won't stay here all night?"

"It all depends. If we're satisfied that the island is deserted, we'll leave; but if we think we haven't searched thoroughly enough, we'll stay and hunt around again tomorrow. It'll take a few hours to give the place a thorough going-over."

"How about the snakes? Won't it be dangerous staying here all night?"

"Oh, we'll find some place where they can't get at us. If the worst comes to the worst we can anchor the boat and stay in it."

This decided, after some search they discovered a small cove, well protected from the sea, that appeared to offer a good landing place. The cove had a narrow entrance between the rocks, but widened out into a small lagoon, with water deep enough to enable the boys to bring their boat up close to a wide shelf of rock. They anchored the *Sleuth* then clambered up onto the rock.

"Feels good to stand on solid footing again," Joe commented.

"I'll say it does. Well, let's be starting. Which way shall we go? Is it to be north or south?"

"It doesn't matter much. To start with, we'll nose around among these rocks for a while."

The sun blazed on the bare crags as the boys picked their way over the rocks and boulders. Away in the interior they could see the waving tops of trees in the steaming marsh, but for the time being they contented themselves with exploring the rocky end of the island. It was quite barren and it appeared that no human being had ever set foot upon the place.

"You can't blame them, either," said Frank, when Joe had remarked on this fact. "It's certainly not a place where I'd care to build my happy home."

After about an hour of desultory search they came upon something that proved conclusively that human beings had indeed been there before them— and not long previously, at that. Charred embers and a crude fireplace built of rocks in a little hollow told the boys that someone had preceded them.

"We're on the track of something," declared Frank, as he examined the remains of the fire. "This blaze was built here not long ago. Some one has camped here." He circled the rock, which dipped toward a patch of undergrowth and luxuriant grass. "And here's a trail!" he exclaimed.

It was merely a faint depression in the deep grass, but it proved that more than one person had passed that way before. The trail wound along through the verdure, away from the shore, leading toward the interior of the island.

"Well, if some one else has gone this way, we can follow the path, too," Joe remarked. "Got your gun?"

"Yes." Frank patted his hip. Both boys had provided themselves with revolvers before leaving home. They were not adept with fire-arms, but the nature of their mission had prompted them to come prepared for any emergency. Fenton Hardy had a collection of weapons in his study, all trophies of his various cases, and the Hardy boys had each taken a small and efficient-looking automatic pistol for protection.

They struck out along the faint trail, the grass rustling about their feet. The green thicket loomed ominously before them and the heat became more intense.

Frank was striding along in advance, gazing at the thicket ahead, when he suddenly came aware of a disturbance in the grass almost at his feet. Some sixth sense warned him of danger. That strange tickling of the spine, man's instinctive reaction to the presence of a hidden peril, made him look down.

Immediately in front of him lay a huge blacksnake!

The reptile was easily five feet in length, and as the boy leaped back he could hear a prolonged hissing. The snake writhed and twisted, and its head came into view from amid the grass, the red tongue flickering wickedly.

Frank saw that the snake was coming directly at him. He leaped to one side, at the same time snatching his automatic from his hip pocket. He had not time to aim, but he pressed the trigger and pumped two shots in the direction of the reptile.

The snake stopped dead, then swiftly began to coil itself up in readiness to strike.

Not a word had been spoken. Frank had blundered back against Joe, who was unaware of the cause of his brother's sudden alarm. He quickly grasped the situation, however, and looked about him.

Close at hand, almost hidden by the grass, was a heavy stick. He bent and quickly snatched it up.

"Quick!" said Frank, taking it from him.

He brandished the stick and brought it down with terrific force upon the snake. The first blow did not kill the reptile, although it rendered it helpless. The hissing continued, the scarlet tongue flickered like flame. Then the boy brought the stick down again. It crushed in the evil black head. A few spasmodic wriggles, and the snake lay still.

"Whew!" breathed Frank, stepping back. "What a big brute he is!"

The boys inspected the reptile more closely, repressing a shiver of repulsion as they saw the sinuous, scaly body lying there in the grass.

"We'd better get away from here. Path or no path. Where there's one snake there are more. Its mate is probably close by."

The boys retreated until they gained the comparative safety of the rocks.

"It's lucky for me you saw that stick," declared Frank. "He was coming right for me, and the automatic wasn't much use. He was moving so quickly I couldn't have shot him. He was stirred up and angry, too. I guess I must have disturbed his morning nap."

"We'll stick to the rocks for a while, I guess. It's time enough to go nosing around the interior when we've finished with the outside of the island."

The boys descended a rocky slope that led into a small bay protected from the sea by a black reef. There were no snakes in sight as they skirted the shore, and then they came upon a well-beaten path leading up the side of a cliff.

"By the look of this path, the island isn't as deserted as it looks," Frank commented. "Perhaps we'll have better luck following it."

The path wound about among the rocks, seemingly in an aimless fashion, now diverging toward the shore, now bringing them farther inland. They followed it doggedly, however, convinced that it must have an ending somewhere, and that the termination would give them some clue as to the people who had used the trail before.

The trail at length brought them in front of a huge black opening in the rocks. It was a cave, over twelve feet in height, dark, gloomy and forbidding.

"Now what?" asked Joe.

Frank glanced at his brother.

"Shall we go in?"

"You can't scare me. If you'll go, I'll go."

"The trail leads here. Other people must have gone in here. If they can do it, so can we."

"Lead on!"

Frank picked up a heavy stick lying among the rocks near the entrance to the cave. "You never know when we'll run into snakes around here," he remarked. "It's just as well to be ready for them."

Joe hunted around until he, too, found a club that would be serviceable in the event of their encountering more of the reptiles. He patted his hip to make sure that the automatic was still in his pocket.

"All set?"

"All set."

Frank stepped forward and entered the mouth of the cave. Joe followed at his heels.

For several yards the cave was illuminated by the light from outside, but as they went on the gloom became deeper until at length they were faced by impenetrable darkness. Frank had brought with him a pocket flashlight and he switched it on. A wide ring of light shone before them, showing the damp rock walls ahead.

They stepped forward cautiously. The floor of the cave sloped upward, but the great opening in the rock was of such extent that the ceiling was scarcely visible above in the light of the flash.

"I don't know where we're going, but we're on our way," said Frank, as they toiled on up over the rough rocks. His voice awakened tumultuous echoes that were flung back and forth from the massive walls.

The flashlight showed him at length a place where the floor dipped abruptly to a steep slope, although there was still a wide ledge at the top, sufficiently wide for them to proceed. He turned the light down the slope but could see nothing save inky blackness.

The boys proceeded slowly along the ledge.

There were numerous pebbles and small rocks underfoot. It was difficult to see these, because Frank was obliged to keep the flashlight centered on the trail ahead, and they were obliged to proceed cautiously in order to keep their footing. This circumstance led to disaster.

Unwittingly, Frank stepped on a small rock that rolled suddenly beneath his foot. He staggered, stepped on another rock that slipped to one side and then he sprawled forward, the flashlight spinning from his hand.

The light clattered among the rocks ahead and darkness fell about them.

"What's the matter?" asked Joe, alarmed.

"It's all right. I just slipped." Frank got to his feet. "I lost the light. It fell down here somewhere. Hang onto the back of my coat and I'll go ahead and get it."

Joe caught at the back of his coat and Frank slowly felt his way forward in the deep blackness.

Suddenly he lurched ahead, his feet sinking in a treacherous mass of sand and gravel. Wildly, he strove to retain his footing, but the effort was in vain. He felt himself slipping and, as he uttered an instinctive cry of warning to Joe, he was flung into space.

Joe, who had been clinging to Frank's coat, was wrenched to one side. He stepped forward, grasping for his brother, then he, too, went hurtling into the darkness.

They pitched down amid a clattering of rocks and pebbles. Then, with an icy shock, they plunged into a deep pool of water!

CHAPTER XIII

THE FOUR MEN

Profound darkness enveloped the Hardy boys.

The blackness of the icy pool was no blacker than the darkness of the air above.

Frank rose spluttering to the surface, unharmed by his fall, and as he splashed about, his first thought was for his brother.

"Joe!" he shouted. "Joe!"

There was no answer except from the echoes, and the rocks shouted mockingly back at him. "Joe.... Joe.... Joe...." growing fainter and fainter until they died away to a mere whisper.

Then there was a splashing almost at his side, as his brother rose to the surface of the pool and struck out blindly.

"Are you all right?" called Frank.

"I'm all right!" gasped Joe.

"Keep beside me. We'll try to find the edge of this pool."

Frank swam forward, groping ahead, until at length his fingers touched the smooth rock at the water's edge. But the rock was almost vertical and it was so smooth and slippery that there was no hope of a handhold. He swam to one side, feeling the rock as he went. Despair seized him as he found that the rock still rose steeply above. If they had fallen into a circular pit they were doomed.

In pitch darkness, then, they battled their way about the border of the pool until at length Frank's searching fingers closed about a rocky projection that seemed to indicate a change in the surface of the cliff.

He was right. There was a small ledge at this point, and he was able to drag himself up on it. There was room enough for both of them, and he turned and grasped Joe's hand, dragging him up on the rock after him. They crouched there in dripping clothes, breathing heavily after their exertion. Presently Frank began to grope upward, still examining the surface of the cliff.

He found that it sloped gradually, and that the surface was rough, with a number of foot-holds.

"I think we can climb it," he told Joe. "It's mighty dark, but if we can ever get back on the main ledge again we'll be all right." He said this because he judged that the place that they had found was on the side of the pool that lay toward the entrance of the cave. If they had emerged on the other side and had regained the ledge they would have been in another dilemma, because they might not have been able to cross the treacherous breach in the trail that had proved Frank's downfall.

Frank groped his way up the face of the slope. He dug his foot against the first ledge and raised himself, clutching at a projection in the rock above. Then, scrambling for a further foothold, he managed to draw himself up. Here the slope became even more gradual and by pressing himself close against the rock, he was able to crawl on up, until at length he came to a flat shelf of rock that he recognized as the main ledge that they had followed from the entrance to the cave.

"I'm up!" he shouted back to Joe, and then he heard a scraping on the rocks, as his brother also began the ascent.

Joe made the climb without difficulty and in a short time rejoined his brother on the ledge.

"I guess we'd better go back," Frank said. "This cave seems to lead to nothing but trouble. We're better off out in the open."

"Is the flashlight lost?"

"Yes. I think it smashed when it fell against the rocks. Anyway, I'm not going back to look for it in the dark. That ledge was treacherous enough even when we had the light."

Step by step, proceeding cautiously, the Hardy boys made their way back toward the entrance to the cave. Their return journey was not so precarious because the entrance to the cave shone before them as a vague gray light and guided them on their way.

They reached the entrance at last and again stepped out into the bright sunlight. At first they were dazzled, after the blackness of the cave.

"First of all, we're going to dry our clothes," declared Frank, as he hunted around among the rocks for sticks that might serve for firewood. "I'm soaking wet."

"Me too. Thank goodness, it's warm out here."

"I'm glad I carried the matches in this waterproof case, or we'd have been out of luck."

They managed to find enough sticks and dry leaves to enable them to start a fire and soon they were standing about in various stages of undress, drying their soaked garments before the blaze. This occupied some time and it was mid-afternoon before they were able to proceed. They had taken some sandwiches with them from the boat and they made a lunch of these while their clothes were drying so that eventually, when they donned their garments again, they were warm, fed and contented.

"Where do we go from here?" inquired Joe.

"Anywhere but into caves," his brother replied. "I think we might as well follow along the shore again. One thing is certain—there have been people on this island, and not long ago at that. Why—"

Suddenly he stopped.

"Listen."

They remained quiet. Frank had heard what seemed to him like a distant shout, and as they listened he heard it again. It was a faint call that echoed among the rocks far ahead of them.

The boys looked at one another. Frank pressed his fingers against his lips as a caution to remain silent. Then, from among the rocks above them they heard another shout, clearer this time, evidently in response to the one they had first heard. The first shout was again repeated; then silence fell.

"That proves it," said Frank quietly. "There *are* people on this island."

"They're calling to each other."

"Sounded like that."

"We'll head down in the direction of the place that first shout came from. It was some one calling to some one else back up here among the rocks."

They went on in the direction from which the first call had been heard. For over ten minutes they proceeded carefully among the rocks until finally Frank caught sight of a curling column of smoke against the sky.

"Campfire," he said.

To approach this fire it was necessary for them to change their course and go up through the shrubbery toward higher ground. They moved slowly because they did not want to be seen until they had ascertained whether the strangers were friends or foes—and they were strongly suspicious that it might prove to be the latter.

A moving object ahead caught Frank's eye and he crouched down in the bushes, motioning to Joe. They peeped through the undergrowth and before them they could see a flat surface of rock in the center of which a fire had been built. Three men were about the fire. Two of these were sprawled in the grass at the verge of the rock while one was standing beside the fire stirring the contents of a pot that hung from a tripod above the blaze. It was this man that had first caught Frank's eye.

The strangers had not noticed the Hardy boys' approach.

"We'll crawl up closer," whispered Joe.

Frank nodded.

They began to make their way quietly forward through the bushes. Frank, who was in the lead, kept a wary eye for snakes and also kept watching the three men about the fire. The boys' approach demanded the utmost caution.

Foot by foot they made their way closer to the trio about the blaze until at last they were so close that they could distinguish what the men were saying. Also, they could distinguish the faces of the speakers.

They were the three men who had been in the motorboat the day of the storm in Barmet Bay!

Although the boys had expected this, they could scarcely restrain murmurs of astonishment. This proved definitely that the motorboat they had seen that morning was the same motorboat that had followed them in Barmet Bay.

The boys listened.

"No answer to that letter yet, is there?" one man was asking.

The fellow by the fire shook his head.

"No answer yet. Oh, well, we can wait."

"We can't wait forever," grumbled the other. "I'm not keen on staying on this confounded island much longer."

"There's lots worse places," remarked the man at his side significantly.

"What do you mean?"

"Jail."

"Oh, I suppose so. But I wish this business would get cleared up. I want to get back to the city and have a good time."

"We all want to get back. But there's no use rushing things," said the man standing by the fire. "We'll be well paid for our waiting."

"Do you think we've made a mistake? I tell you, it's been worrying me. If we've gummed up this job by doing a trick like that I'll never forgive myself."

"No—there's no mistake. Don't worry about that," scoffed the man at the fire. "Didn't we look things over mighty careful-like before we started?"

"Yes," admitted the other slowly. "But they keep harpin' on that tune all the time and I'm beginnin' to think there may be somethin' in it."

"Where's Red?" demanded the third man. "Didn't you call him?"

"Yeah, I called him. This is him now. He's comin' down from the grove."

Suddenly Frank clutched his brother by the arm and flattened himself against the ground. A footstep sounded immediately behind them. Twigs crackled.

Unobserved, a man had approached to within a few feet back of them, striding silently through the deep grass.

The boys remained motionless, wondering if they had been seen. For a breathless second they lay rigid in the bushes, then the footsteps passed by within a few inches of Frank's outstretched hand. They heard his deep voice:

"When did you all get back?"

"Just a few minutes ago," replied the man at the fire. "We left the boat in the bay. Anything new?"

"Nothing new," growled the deep voice. "The prisoners are still safe and sound." One of the other men chuckled.

"Have they quieted down yet?"

"No!" growled the newcomer. "They kicked up a big fuss all the time you were away. Still keep sayin' we've made a mistake."

"Mistake, nothin'!" the man by the fire declared. "There's been no mistake about this job! They can't fool me!"

CHAPTER XIV

THE STORM

The four men had dinner about the campfire and when the meal was over the man they called Red got up.

"May as well go back to the cave," he remarked. "It's cooler than out here."

"It's hot enough to put a man to sleep out on these rocks," said one of the others. "Yeah, let's go on up to the cave."

"I don't like the idea of stayin' too close to the cave," growled the man who had been by the fire. "If anybody comes around here and should find us they'll have to look some to find *them* as long as we're not near the cave, see?"

"That's all right, Pete," retorted Red. "If any one comes on this island we'll know of it in lots of time to clear away from the cave. We may as well keep cool."

There was a grumbled assent from Pete, and then the Hardy boys heard sounds of receding footsteps as the quartette strode off through the grass. They waited until the men were out of earshot, then peered through the undergrowth.

"Shall we follow them?" asked Joe eagerly.

"You bet we will! I want to know where this cave is that they're talking about. And I want to know who the prisoners are that they mentioned."

"Do you think it really could be Chet and Biff?"

"I'm almost sure it is. Didn't you hear the fellow saying that the prisoners kept insisting that there'd been a mistake? We've figured it out right all along. They captured Chet and Biff in mistake for us."

The Hardy boys began moving through the undergrowth on the trail of the four men. They crouched down and kept to the shelter of the bushes so that they were able to proceed at a good rate of speed without exposing themselves to view.

"If we can only get into the cave and get Chet and Biff free!" exclaimed Joe.

"It won't be any too easy. They seem to be guarding them pretty closely. First of all, we've got to be certain that it's them."

"I don't think there's any doubt of that. Everything hangs together too well. If we could get them out we could run for the boat and get them away to the mainland."

"That's what we'll have to plan on. But the main thing is to find this cave."

"Yes, of course."

The four men in the lead had entered the outskirts of a small grove toward the center of the island. Frank could just see the head and shoulders of the last man disappearing into the woods. He marked the spot where the fellow had entered the grove and the Hardy boys made toward it. They found it comparatively easy to follow the trail, for the others had beaten down the grass and twigs in passing, and in a few minutes they had reached the grove.

"Go slow," cautioned Frank, as they entered the shadow of the trees. "They may have seen us crossing the clearing."

They listened for a moment. They could hear the crashing of branches and the crackling of twigs, the distant hum of voices, as the quartette continued through the woods, so they went ahead.

The wood was steaming hot and the ground was dank underfoot. The grass was long and the leaves of the trees drooped of their own weight. Once Frank saw a blacksnake scurrying away through the grass, but none of the serpents molested them. The path the boys followed was beaten down by the feet of the men ahead and they made easy progress until at length the sight of a clearing ahead warned them to again exercise caution.

They crept along through the trees and underbrush until the clearing came fully into view. It was at that part of the interior of the island where the swamp gave way to the rocks, and the grassy clearing led in a gradual slope to a high wall of rock, at the base of which was the mouth of a cave. As the Hardy boys watched, they could see the four men at the opening. One of the fellows, a tall, dark man, was mopping his brow with a handkerchief, while another, a man with a shock of red hair, was just going into the cavern. The other two had flung themselves down on the rocks in the shadow of some overhanging bushes.

"So that's the cave!" exclaimed Frank.

"I wonder if Chet and Biff are inside."

"Most likely. I wish we could get a little closer."

"Too dangerous. They can see any one coming into the clearing."

This was true. The cave had evidently been chosen not only for its possibilities as a shelter but for its defensive virtues as well. It was plainly the hangout of the gang.

"We'll have our work cut out for us to get in there," muttered Frank. "The place is too much in the open. Our only chance is to wait until some of them go away."

"We might be able to sneak up closer when they're asleep."

"We'll try it. The only thing for us to do right now is wait until they're all asleep."

The boys settled themselves down in the bushes, prepared for a vigil until nightfall. It was now late in the afternoon, and when Frank glanced up at the sky he saw that clouds had gathered. The sunshine had gone, for a dense black cloud obscured the sun. The sultry and oppressive heat of the afternoon had evidently presaged a storm.

"Looks like rain."

"It sure does," agreed Joe, looking up.

As though in corroboration, there was an ominous rumble of thunder. The wind had died down. Every leaf, every blade of grass was still. The clouds were massing silently.

However, the storm held off, and although the sky was overcast and threatening, twilight fell without rain. Frank and Joe, from their hiding place in the bushes, watched the four men moving aimlessly about the cave that afternoon. Two of them had remained inside the cave for a long time while the other pair chatted on the rocks outside.

Night came at last. From the interior of the cave came the flicker of flames, and the Hardy boys knew that the gang was making a fire for the night.

The heat was still oppressive. Darkness fell without moon or stars.

"We'll soon be able to creep up on them now," said Frank. "If we can only get close enough to hear what they're saying we'll probably be able to make sure if they have Chet and Biff with them."

The boys waited until the fire had died down. The four men had all disappeared within the cave.

"Quiet, now," Frank whispered. He began to make his way out of the undergrowth. Joe followed close behind. They crept up toward the entrance to the cave.

They were about half-way across the open space when the whole scene about them was suddenly revealed with startling clarity in the livid glow of a flash of lightning. This was followed immediately by a crash of thunder that seemed to shake the very rocks on which they stood. As though this were but a prelude, rain began to fall, gently at first, then with increasing force. Other lightning flashes followed. Then the storm broke in all its fury.

A gradually rising wind began to rake the tree-tops and the swishing of leaves and creaking of limbs could be plainly heard. The dull booming of the waves on the distant shore, the moaning of the wind, the driving spatter of rain, the constant peals of thunder, continually rose in volume, and the rain poured furiously from the black skies above.

The storm had broken so suddenly that the Hardy boys were taken aback. Their first impulse was to race for the shelter of the cave, but second thought told them that this would be unwise, for the men in the cave might be aroused by the storm.

"We'd better go back to the boat," said Frank, turning about. "It's liable to be wrecked."

Joe had almost forgotten about their motorboat. It was on the seaward side of the island and the storm was coming in from the sea. Although the boat was partly protected by the little cove into which they had brought it, there was every danger that the storm might cast the craft up on the rocks and wreck it. The consequences, in that case, would be grave. They would be unable to escape from Blacksnake Island at all without giving themselves up to the gang.

The boys turned and fled back across the rocks. Rain streamed down upon them. Thunder crashed. Lightning flickered, illuminating for brief seconds the tossing trees and the tumbled rocks before them.

Joe, during the afternoon, had occupied himself ascertaining the position of the grove and the cave relative to the little bay in which they had left the motorboat and he had come to the conclusion that the grove was not far away from the end of the island and almost in a direct line with the cove. Now, in their mad race toward the shore, he took the lead, heading toward the rocky bluffs.

The Hardy boys stumbled through the grove, keeping somehow to the trail. They were aided by the lightning flashes that gave spasmodic illumination, revealing the soggy leaves, the black branches, the tossing tree-tops bowed in the wind.

The storm had become a din of furious sound. The gale shrieked its way across the island from the booming sea and the thunder rolled like a battery of cannon while the rain beat down on the forest in a drumming downpour.

The boys were soaked to the skin. They fled toward the shore, keeping their course more by instinct than judgment, and all the time there was the dread thought in their minds that they were lost if the *Sleuth* should be cast up on the rocks and wrecked.

CHAPTER XV

A STARTLING ANNOUNCEMENT

The Hardy boys reached the cove in the nick of time. Although the place was protected from the full fury of the sea, the high wind had lashed the waves to such an extent that the boat was pitching and tossing about, in imminent danger of running aground.

The beach was sandy, however, and after some maneuvering, the boys were able to run the boat up on the shore, where it was safe enough. The storm by this time was showing some signs of abating, although the rain was still pouring in undiminished vigor. Frank rummaged about in the boat until he located their oilskins, and these they donned, although their clothes were already drenched.

"I'd hate to be out at sea on a night like this," shouted Frank, as the lightning revealed the tossing inferno of waves under the black skies.

At that moment a light flashed away out to the right.

"A boat!" exclaimed Joe.

"Heading toward the island!"

They kept their eyes fixed on the place where they had seen the light. In a few moments a vivid splash of lightning cut the darkness and they had a momentary glimpse of a small motorboat tossing about in the black waves.

"He'll never make the shore in this storm," said Frank, shaking his head.

"Can it be Tony?"

"I hardly think so. He wouldn't come close in such a storm."

"That's true, too."

"I think it's some outsider."

"Do you think we can help him?"

"I don't think so. He'll probably pile up on the rocks."

"Perhaps he's one of the gang."

"That's so," agreed Frank. "I hadn't thought of that. Perhaps he knows where he's going, after all. Still, it won't hurt to go down the shore a bit and see if he makes his landing all right."

They went on down the shore in the darkness, picking their way among the rocks, feeling in their faces the salt spray blown in from the sea. The dull booming of the surf and the howling of the wind provided an almost deafening cacophony of sound. Every little while, a lightning flash would reveal the little boat, slowly heading in toward the shore.

Suddenly Frank stopped short, grasping his brother by the arm.

"I saw a light ahead."

"I thought I did too. Right on the shore."

They waited. In a moment the light reappeared. It bobbed slowly up and down and appeared to be moving down toward the beach.

"Somebody is going down to meet the boat. It must be one of the gang," declared Frank.

The boys went forward more cautiously. The next flash of lightning showed that Frank's assumption was correct. They could see four men in oilskins trudging down among the rocks. The man in the lead carried a powerful electric lantern that cast a vivid beam of light upon the rain-washed boulders.

They saw that the man in the motorboat was heading toward a small bay that afforded ideal protection from the storm. The entrance was very narrow and great waves dashed over the rocks with showers of white spray, but the man in the boat guided his craft skillfully into the channel. He was in difficulties for a few moments, but by good steering brought the craft around. Then it shot forward, making the channel neatly, and surged down toward the beach.

The men in oilskins were there to meet him. The boat was run up on the sand and the lone steersman sprang out and splashed through the water. For a few moments the five men conferred, standing there on the dark beach, with the wind whipping their oilskins about their legs, the lantern gleaming like a white eye, and the rain pouring down upon them. They looked like five sinister birds of prey as they stood there in the storm, and then they turned and began to walk back up over the rocks toward the center of the island.

"This must be their landing place," said Frank. "And that means they must have a good trail from here to the cave."

"Let's follow them," suggested Joe.

"Just what I was going to say. We know our boat is safe, and we can't get any wetter than we are now."

The boys therefore made their way down to the place where the five men had been standing. They could see the reflection of the lantern as it bobbed up and down while the quintette trudged back toward the trees, and they followed. True enough, there was a well-defined trail among the rocks and they made easy progress, considering the darkness and the fact that the trail was unknown to them.

The height of the storm had passed and the rain had settled down to a steady downpour. The roar of the thunder had diminished to an occasional distant rumble, and the lightning flashes were less frequent. The wind, too, had died down.

The light ahead guided them up the trail, across the rocks, then into the grove again, and in a short time they again emerged on the edge of the clearing and could see the dull mass of the granite slope before them. The fire still gleamed, and they could see the five men go into the cave, which was brilliantly illuminated for a moment in the light of the lantern which the first man held so that the others might pass.

"We may as well go right up," said Frank. "We've come this far. There isn't any use backing down now."

"I'm with you."

They crossed the rocks and crept up toward the entrance to the cave. They found tumbled boulders about the opening that afforded good protection and they were able to make their way up to within a few feet of the cave mouth without danger of being seen. The wind and the rain still created sufficient noise to drown out any sounds that they might have made in their approach.

Through an opening in the boulders, they peeped into the cave. As they were in darkness they knew there was little chance that they would be seen by the men within; as for the latter, they were in the full glare of the fire, which one of the men had replenished from a pile of wood near by. The boys, therefore, could see without being seen.

The men were divesting themselves of their oilskins, and one of them, the newcomer, had flung himself down on a pile of blankets, as though exhausted.

"I tell you it was a tough trip," he was saying. "I was sure I was going to be wrecked. I couldn't find the passage. If you hadn't come along with the lantern when you did I'd have been washed up on the rocks and the boat would have been smashed to pieces."

"Well, you're here, and that's all there is to it," declared the man they called Red. "You shouldn't have started out when you saw a storm was coming up."

"I didn't know it was going to be so bad. Anyway, I thought I'd get here before it broke."

"It must have been good news that brought you out here tonight," declared one of the others, sitting down.

"I'll say it was good news," said the newcomer. "Mighty good news."

"What is it?" they asked eagerly.

"I've found out why Fenton Hardy didn't pay any attention to that letter."

The boys listened eagerly. At the mention of their father they knew that all their suspicions had been verified. They waited tensely as the conversation went on.

"Why?" asked Red.

"He didn't get it."

"Why didn't he get it?"

The newcomer paused and smiled.

"The reason he didn't get it," he said, slowly and triumphantly, "is because we've got him."

"Got him?"

"We've got Fenton Hardy!"

"How?"

"Where?"

"How do you know?"

Questions were fired at the newcomer from all parts of the cave. He was enjoying the sensation he had caused. As for the hidden listeners, they experienced only a sickening amazement.

"The gang got him in Chicago last night. I just got word this afternoon. He went out there to catch Baldy; but the boys got wind of it and they laid a trap for him. He stepped right into it."

"Good!" exclaimed the red-headed man, rubbing his hands. "What could be sweeter? We've got Hardy and we've got his sons—"

"By the way, how are they acting?" asked the newcomer.

"Oh, still kicking up a fuss—the young brats," growled the man called Pete. "They say they ain't the Hardy boys at all."

"Don't worry about that. Bring 'em out here."

One of the men got up from beside the fire and disappeared into the rear of the cave. His footsteps died away and the Hardy boys judged that there must be some sort of inner chamber to the place. In a short time he returned, pushing ahead of him two boys. Frank and Joe peered forward, striving to catch a glimpse of the lads' features.

With a clanking of chains, the boys emerged into the firelight.

They were Chet Morton and Biff Hooper!

The lads were handcuffed and their ankles were bound by a gleaming length of chain, just long enough to enable them to walk. They appeared thin and tired, their shoulders drooped wearily, and as they stood before the fire they said nothing.

"Well, Hardys," said the red-haired man in a harsh voice, "we have some news for you."

"We've told you before," said Chet. "You've made a mistake. We're not the Hardy boys."

The man named Pete stepped suddenly forward from the shadows and cuffed Chet savagely on the side of the head.

"Shut up!" he snarled, and cuffed Biff Hooper as well. "No more of that. We're tired of listenin' to it. You're the Hardy boys, all right, and it won't do you no good to deny it."

"You've made a mistake!" insisted Chet stubbornly.

"We'll show you how much of a mistake we've made!" roared one of the men. "We brought you out here to tell you something. Our men have got your father at last."

"Mr. Hardy?" exclaimed Chet greatly taken aback.

"Yes, Mr. Hardy!" exclaimed Red, mimicking him. "That shot sunk home, didn't it? We've got him, and we've got you, and we'll starve you into making your mother come across with the money we want. If you have been holding out, hoping your father would come for you, it's no good now. We've got him and we've got you, so you may as well give up."

"There's no use asking us," declared Biff. "We're not the Hardy boys."

Red cuffed him viciously over the ears again. Biff staggered back from the blow.

"Oh, take them back and chain them up again," Red said, in disgust. "Let 'em starve for a while and they'll come around and tell the truth!"

"If I could get loose for about two minutes I'd show you—," declared Biff, clenching his fists.

But the red-haired man only laughed contemptuously. The Hardy boys, from their hiding place, saw Pete come forward and drag Chet and Biff back into the darkness at the rear of the cave, their chains clanking as they went.

CHAPTER XVI

THE ALARM

The Hardy boys were quivering with excitement. They had found the whereabouts of their chums; they had learned the dismaying news that Fenton Hardy had been captured by his enemies; they had discovered the hiding place of the gang. All this had taken place in a few fleeting hours.

Their first problem was to release Chet and Biff. But at first glance that seemed impossible. For when Pete came back into the cave he flung a bunch of keys into the sand beside the fire and laughed harshly.

"They'll get tired bein' chained up to a rock after a few more days," he said. "They'll come through yet."

"We can wait as long as they can," declared Red.

"If they'll only write a letter to their mother now and tell her we want that ransom we'll be sitting pretty. Fenton Hardy can't come after them—that's certain."

"Well, it's a good day's work. I'm goin' to sleep," said one of the other men. He pulled a blanket about him and curled up beside the fire.

"Good idea," remarked Red. "We might as well all turn in."

Shortly afterward, the various members of the gang were sprawled about in their blankets on the sand. Frank noticed that they all slept on the same side of the fire, and also noted that the reason for this was that on one side of the cave the floor was a ledge of rock.

"We'll wait till they go to sleep," he whispered to Joe.

His brother nodded. The two boys remained crouched among the rocks. The rain had died away to a mere drizzle.

Gradually the fire, untended, died down, and there was only a faint, rosy glow through the interior of the cave. Two or three of the men had talked together in low murmurs for a while, but gradually their voices died away and soon the boys could hear their snores. It was nearly an hour, however, before they were satisfied that all the men were asleep.

"I'm going in after Chet and Biff," whispered Frank, with determination.

"I'm with you."

"The keys are still lying beside the fire."

"Good."

Frank rose from his cramped position among the rocks. Joe followed his example. Quietly, they moved toward the entrance of the cave.

The snores of the slumbering men were unbroken. Frank took the lead and tiptoed slowly forward. Step by step, keeping a wary eye on the recumbent forms wrapped in the blankets, the boys made their way into the cave.

Frank remembered where the keys had been thrown, and now he saw them in the sand. The faint glow of the firelight gleamed on them.

The keys were on the side of the fire nearest the men. It would be a delicate job to get possession of them. He bent forward and crawled on hands and knees. Joe came silently behind.

Frank skirted the fire, then groped carefully forward.

There was a mutter from the shadows. One of the men stirred in his sleep.

The boys remained rigid.

The muttering died away. After a long pause, Frank again reached for the keys.

His hands closed over them. He gripped them tightly so that they would not jangle together. Then he moved slowly back onto the rock ledge, the keys safely in his grasp.

The Hardy boys continued their silent journey toward the darkness in the rear of the cave. The dying fire cast little light.

Little by little they edged forward into the depths of the cave, past the sleeping men. The slightest noise, they knew, might be sufficient to arouse one of the gang. They proceeded with the utmost caution toward the back of the cavern.

At length Frank found what he sought. It was a dark patch in the rear wall—the entrance to the inner chamber.

He reached it safely and groped his way through into the pitchy blackness beyond. He stopped and listened. The sound of deep breathing told him that his two chums were asleep within.

He reached back and laid a restraining hand on Joe's arm, indicating that he was to remain at the mouth of the inner chamber and keep watch. Joe realized his intention and remained where he was. Frank then continued.

Cautiously, he groped about in the darkness, moving slowly forward. At length his hand fell upon an outstretched arm, then a shoulder which stirred slightly.

He bent forward and shook the sleeper.

"Chet!" he whispered.

The other boy moved and began to sit up. The chains jangled.

"Quiet!" whispered Frank, fearing that his chum might be alarmed at this sudden and surprising awakening and make some sound.

"Who is it?" whispered the other.

"It's me—Frank. I've come to help you get free."

From the darkness he heard a gasp of surprise, but it was quickly silenced.

"I'll waken Biff," replied Chet. Frank had merely guessed at this being Chet Morton whom he had awakened, and found that his guess had been correct.

In a few minutes Biff had been aroused.

"The men are asleep," whispered Frank. "Don't ask questions. Keep quiet until we get outside. I have the keys. Where is the lock?"

"We're chained to the rock," Chet whispered in return. He grasped Frank's hand, guiding it to the wall of the cave until his fingers closed on a heavy padlock. "There you are!"

Frank tried several keys before he found the one that fitted, but at length the padlock snapped open. He grasped the chain with his other hand so that it did not fall to the floor with a clatter. He lowered it gently.

"Now for the handcuffs."

Chet extended his wrists and Frank finally located the small key that opened the handcuffs. He removed them, then released Chet's feet in a similar manner. Then he crawled over to Biff, releasing him from his chains.

All this work had been done with a minimum of noise, and as there had been no warning whisper from Joe, they assumed that the men in the outer cave had not been aroused.

Frank led the way out, the three crawling on hands and knees into the main cave. They could see Joe crawling ahead of them, past the ruby glow of the embers.

The snores of the men continued without interruption. Frank was jubilant. The most dangerous part of the affair was over. Could they but gain the entrance in safety and reach their motorboat in the cove before the gang should discover that their prisoners had escaped, all would be well.

Frank caught sight of a flashlight lying in the sand. His own light had been lost in the rock cave the previous day and he knew they would need a light to regain their boat.

He reached carefully over for it. His hands closed about the black cylinder and the light was his.

Chet and Biff nodded appreciatively when they saw what he had done. The flashlight would be a big factor in aiding their escape.

Joe had reached the entrance to the cave by now. They saw him get to his feet and glide silently out into the darkness.

Frank reached the end of the ledge. The flashlight was clutched in his hand. Slowly he rose to his feet. But a small pebble betrayed him. He lost his balance and staggered for a second.

Had it not been for the flashlight the emergency would have passed because he flung out his hand and supported himself against the wall of the cave. But the heavy flashlight struck a loose projection of rock.

There was a grinding clatter of stone as the rock came free.

In the dead silence of the cave the noise seemed magnified many times. Frank knew that the sleepers would be aroused. He threw caution to the winds.

He leaped forward, gaining the entrance at a bound. Chet Morton and Biff Hooper, seeing that nothing was to be gained by further caution, scrambled to their feet and raced in pursuit.

The noise of the dislodged rock had already wakened one of the men. He raised himself on elbow in alarm and peered about. Then he saw the fleeing figures in the mouth of the cave and heard the running footsteps.

He sprang at once to his feet.

"They're getting away!" he roared. "Wake up, men! They're getting away!"

Instantly pandemonium prevailed within the cave. The men hastily tumbled out of their blankets, bewildered at being aroused from slumber.

The Hardy boys and their chums, racing across the rocky stretch on the outskirts of the cave, heard the uproar and the cry:

"After them! Don't let them escape!"

CHAPTER XVII

CAPTURE

The men in the cave lost no time in taking up the pursuit. They had been sleeping in their clothes and, once aroused, hurried out of the cave in search of the fugitives.

The boys raced across the rocks. Behind them they could hear shouts as the gangsters called to each other. Then came the crash of a revolver as one of the men pumped shot after shot in their direction.

Biff sprawled full length on the rocks.

"Are you hurt?" asked Joe, stopping to help him rise.

"No, I'm all right," gasped Biff, scrambling to his feet. He had suffered bruises but seemed otherwise uninjured. However, when he began to run again Joe noticed that he was limping and his progress was slower than formerly.

Frank had the battered flashlight, but he did not dare switch it on for fear of revealing their whereabouts to the men. The latter, however, were stumbling along behind, following the trail by reason of the noise the boys made in their mad flight toward the trees.

The men had the advantage in that they knew every inch of the rocky ground. The boys had to proceed more cautiously because it was unfamiliar to them, especially to Chet and Biff.

Biff was limping along in the rear and Joe purposely slowed down his pace so as to remain with his chum. But the delay was fatal. Out of the darkness came one of their pursuers, and with a growl of triumph he flung himself at Biff.

His arms encircled the lad's legs in a perfect tackle and Biff went down with a crash. Joe wheeled about and plunged upon them, striking out desperately to fight off Biff's attacker. They struggled fiercely in the darkness. Joe felt his fist crash into the man's face and he heard a grunt of pain. Biff was wriggling out of his assailant's grasp, and the boys might indeed have made their escape had it not been that the other men came running up out of the shadows.

With a roar of fury, two of them plunged at the boys and hauled them away from their comrade.

"After the other two!" shouted a voice, which they recognized as that of Red, "They're heading for the bushes!"

Joe and Biff found themselves roughly hauled to their feet, their arms held tightly behind them. They heard the clatter of footsteps as two of the other men ran after Frank and Chet.

"Back to the cave with 'em." growled Red. "Looks like we've got one of the guys that helped 'em get away. I've been thinkin' all day that there was some one hangin' around here that we didn't know about."

The lads were shoved and pushed ahead of their captors, dragged and bundled across the rocks until they reached the cave. Then they were roughly shoved through the entrance into the light of the fire.

"Ah! I thought so!" declared Red. "One of the guys that tried to help them get away." He peered closer at Joe. "Blessed if it ain't one of those two boys that was in the boat with the Hardys that day."

One of the other men ordered the boys to sit down, and they crouched beside the stirred-up fire, sick at heart, wondering how it fared with Frank and Chet.

When Joe and Biff were captured it was Chet's first impulse to turn and go back, but a warning shout from Frank restrained him.

"Keep running!" he called. "If they're caught we'll have a chance to get help."

The wisdom of this course flashed through Chet's mind at once. If they went to the aid of their comrades they would probably all be captured and in a worse position than before. But if two, or even one, managed to escape, it would be possible to bring help to the island and effect the release of the others.

Chet heard Frank crash into the undergrowth. It was pitch dark, and although he tried to follow he knew he had left the trail. He did not call out because he was afraid of revealing his whereabouts to the men behind, but he blundered on, hoping to catch up with Frank. As for the latter, he was quite unaware of Chet's predicament.

Chet crashed into the bushes. Branches whipped his face. Roots gripped his feet. He struggled on through the dense growth, blindly, in the darkness. Far ahead of him he could hear Frank making his way through the underbrush, but when he tried to go toward the sound he found that his sense of direction was confused.

He struggled on for some time. Suddenly he saw a patch of gray light ahead. It was the open sky and he soon plunged out of the undergrowth into a rocky clearing. He breathed a sigh of relief.

But the relief was short-lived.

A dark figure loomed up before him. He dodged swiftly to one side, but a huge hand caught at his clothing. He was spun violently around and then he was caught by the collar, despite his struggles.

"Got you!" grunted the dark figure, with satisfaction. "Now if we can only get the other—"

He said no more, but shoved Chet before him across the rocks. Then it was that Chet found that, instead of fleeing farther away from the cave he had really made a circle in the wood and had emerged directly into the clearing again. He was sick with disappointment. He wriggled and twisted in the grasp of his captor, but the man was too strong for him and he shook Chet vigorously, tripping his feet from under him.

"None of that! You come along with me!" he rasped.

And in a few minutes Chet was shoved back into the cave, where he found Biff Hooper and Joe Hardy crouched silently beside the fire, with downcast faces.

Frank alone had escaped.

Frank knew that Chet had got lost but he did not dare call out, for he could also hear the running tramp of feet that told him their pursuers had not yet given up the chase. If he could only reach the cove and get the motorboat started he would be able to go over to the mainland for help. If only one escaped, it would be sufficient to save the others. He could not afford to risk his own capture in seeking Chet.

He crashed on through the bushes, trying to make as little noise as possible. But he was off the trail, and the tangled undergrowth was growing denser with every forward step he took.

He still clutched the flashlight that had been the cause of their undoing. He was glad he had found it, because in the pitch blackness he was unable to find his way. He could hear the roar of the waves, but they appeared to come from all sides and he was unable to judge accurately the route to the shore.

Frank decided that he would not make use of the flashlight until it was absolutely necessary. There was too much danger that its gleam might be seen by one of the searchers. And he knew that the gang would not give up the chase as long as they knew he was on the island.

"Perhaps they don't know there are two of us," he thought. "If Joe can convince them that he rescued Chet and Biff single-handed they won't know about me and they won't keep on searching."

In this lay his only hope—in this and in the chance that he would be able to reach the motorboat and make his escape before being seen. But if the gangsters knew he was still free they would leave no stone unturned to find him, as they would know that if he once left the island they were lost.

He blundered about in the deep thicket, turning vainly this way and that. Great vines trailed across his face; he brushed aside stubborn branches and soggy wet leaves; he stumbled over roots and little bushes; the deep grass rustled and hissed at his feet.

There was no other way. He would have to use the flashlight. The darkness was impenetrable. Trees and bushes enclosed him. He could not see where he was going.

He switched on the light and, to one side of him, descried a sort of passage among the bushes, so he headed in that direction. He managed to get free of the worst of the vines and the thick foliage and found himself in a forest aisle. He went down it, in the direction of the booming surf. His heart beat quickly at the thought that he was now free and that he would soon be back at the boat. What had happened to Chet? He judged that his chum was either captured now or lost in the grove. Frank knew that he could not wait to learn Chet's fate because any delay would be fatal to them all.

He had switched out the flashlight and was plunging along through the darkness when the forest aisle suddenly took a twist and he found himself again floundering in the midst of trees and trailing vines that entangled him.

Frank switched on the flashlight again.

And a second later he heard a grim voice from close by:

"Throw up your hands!"

He wheeled about and found himself suddenly bathed in a ring of light. Some one was standing only a few feet away with a flashlight leveled at him, and in the beam of the flashlight he could see a glittering revolver aimed directly toward him.

"Throw up your hands!" rasped the voice again, "or you'll be shot."

Slowly Frank raised his hands above his head.

"That's better. Now march back ahead of me. Back to the cave, young fellow. We've got you all now. Forward march!"

CHAPTER XVIII

BACK TO THE CAVE

"This is a piece of luck!" declared the red-headed man.

He squatted by the fire with his arms folded and surveyed the four prisoners. Frank and Joe had been dragged back to the cave with the others and were now bound and helpless, while the gangsters confronted them.

"Who are these two?" asked the man called Pete, indicating the Hardy boys.

Red shook his head.

"We've seen 'em before. They were in the boat the day we were looking these two birds over," he remarked, gesturing toward Chet and Biff.

"What's your names?" demanded Pete gruffly.

The Hardy boys glanced at one another. Their captors were not yet aware of their identity and they did not know whether to admit it or not. Frank resolved on silence as the best course.

"Find out!" he retorted.

An ugly look crept into Red's face.

"Is that so?" he snarled. "Won't talk, eh? I'll soon make you talk."

He leaned forward and wrenched open Frank's coat. Frank's wrists were handcuffed and he was helpless to resist. Red pulled him roughly to one side and groped in the inner pocket of the coat. There was a rustle of paper and he withdrew two or three letters. Frank bit his lip in exasperation. He had forgotten about the letters and he knew that any hope of concealing his identity was now lost.

The red-headed man brought the letters over to the fire and squinted at the addresses. His eyes opened wide; his jaw dropped.

"Frank Hardy!" he gasped.

"What?" demanded one of the other men.

"All these letters are addressed to Frank Hardy!" declared the astonished gangster. "What d'you know about that!"

With a sudden movement, Pete grasped Joe by the collar and held him while he turned his pockets inside out. Finally, with an air of triumph, he produced Joe's membership card in a Bayport athletic association, on which his name was written in full.

"Joe Hardy!" he read. "Why, these are the real Hardy boys!"

The gangsters looked at one another with crestfallen expressions, but their momentary astonishment at realization of their mistake was quickly changed to rejoicing.

"I told you we weren't the Hardys," put in Chet. "I told you all along that you were making a mistake."

"Shut up!" ordered Red. "Yes, men, we made a mistake, all right. We didn't have the Hardy boys after all. But now we have got 'em. I'll say this is a piece of luck! We've got the whole caboodle now."

Meanwhile one of the men had been going more thoroughly through the boys' pockets. Now he grunted.

"Armed! Would you believe it? Brats like these!"

"Take the guns away," came the order from Red.

"What'll we do with the others?" demanded one of the gangsters.

"With the two we caught in the first place? We'll hang right onto 'em. We'll hold the Hardy boys for ransom the way we intended to, and we'll make some money out of the other two as well. You two boys," he said, turning to Chet and Biff, "have your people got money?"

"Find out!" snapped Chet, following Frank's example.

"We'll find out, all right!" rasped Pete. "We'll find out. And if they haven't got money it'll be all the worse for the pack of you!" He chuckled suddenly. "We'll make a real haul out of this, men! Four ransoms!"

"Yes, and now that we have the real Hardy boys we'll give Fenton Hardy a few anxious minutes," laughed another of the men, from a dark corner of the cave.

"Where is our father?" asked Frank.

Red scratched his chin meditatively.

"You're gettin' curious, hey? Want to know where your father is? I'll tell you. He's in a safe place where he can't get out of. Our men out in the West got him."

"What are they going to do with him?"

"Ah!" said Red, with an air of mystery. "What are they goin' to do with him? That's the question. One thing is certain—they're goin' to let him live until we collect ransom for you two."

"And after that?"

"After that? Well, it's up to the boss. But I'm thinkin' he'll never let Fenton Hardy loose again. He's too dangerous. Maybe, now, my young friends—"

"Don't talk too much, Red," warned Pete, stirring the fire. "Put these kids all in the inner cave and let's go to sleep again."

"I guess you're right, Pete," agreed the red-headed man. "It don't pay to let 'em know too much."

With that, the Hardy boys and their two chums were bundled into the other cave, where a long chain was passed beneath the links of their handcuffs and passed through a staple embedded in the rock. The chain was fastened with a heavy padlock. Frank's heart sank as he heard the padlock snapped. There seemed to be no hope of escape now. They were securely chained together in the darkness of the inner cave.

Their captors left them.

"I guess you'll be safe enough in there until morning," grunted Pete as he departed, last of all. The gangsters returned to their fire and, after a brief discussion in low tones, they wrapped themselves up in their blankets once more.

The boys talked in whispers. Chet and Biff were anxious to know how the Hardy boys had followed them to the island and, in a few words, Frank told them of the alarm their disappearance had occasioned and of how they had decided to take a chance on searching Blacksnake Island.

"If only we could have got away!" muttered Joe. "We'd have been out toward the mainland in the boat by now!"

"If even one of us could have got away he could have gone for help," Frank whispered. "Oh, well—here we are, and we have to make the best of it!"

"I'm worried about what they said about dad."

"So am I. We've simply *got* to get out of here. If we can get word to the Chicago police they may be able to find him before it's too late!"

The boys were silent. The news that Fenton Hardy had been captured and that he was in the hands of a merciless gang cast a cloud of gloom over them all. They realized only too well their own helplessness in the situation.

"I'm going to try to smash the lock on this pair of handcuffs," Joe whispered finally. "It seemed rusty to me, when they put them on."

"We tried that with ours," whispered Chet. "It wasn't any use."

"I may have better luck."

"Wait until you're sure the gang are asleep," whispered Biff. "They might hear you."

The boys lapsed into silence. The darkness of the cave was impenetrable. Near the entrance they could see a faint glow of pink from the embers of the fire in the outer cavern, but that was all. They could not even see one another.

The fact that they were chained together made it impossible for them to rest comfortably. The gangsters had not even provided them with a blanket.

"We've been chained in here every night since they caught us," Chet whispered. "We've had to sleep on the bare rock."

Finally the silence was broken by the sound of steel against rock. Joe was trying to break the lock of his handcuffs. The effort was difficult, because his hands were cuffed behind him. But, as he had said, the handcuffs were rusty and of an antiquated type. Against the hard rock he could feel them gradually giving way.

For more than ten minutes he battered the lock, the steel digging into his wrists. He worked as quietly as possible, with long intervals between each attempt. For a while he was afraid the effort would be fruitless, as even the rusty steel seemed obdurate. Then, suddenly, he felt the lock give way. He eased his hands out of the cuffs with a sigh of relief.

"I'm free," he whispered to the others.

There were suppressed exclamations of delight.

"How are you going to get us out?" whispered Frank.

"I'll try to find the keys."

A low murmur from the other cave arrested his attention. Swiftly he leaned back against the wall. One of the gangsters was awake. The boys listened. They heard a movement in the outer cave, a jangling of keys, and then a heavy footstep.

Joe thrust his arms behind his back and feigned slumber. He could hear some one entering their cave.

Suddenly a bright light flashed in his face. The man on guard had come to inspect the captives and he brought with him a flashlight. Joe kept his eyes closed and breathed heavily. He hoped desperately that the man would not inspect their handcuffs.

The fellow appeared satisfied and in a few moments went away. Through narrowed eyelids Joe could see his dark form as he reached the passage between the two caves. He saw the round white circle of light shine for a moment on a small rock shelf in the passageway and he saw the guard reach up and toss a bundle of keys on the shelf. Then the man went on his way, switching out the light.

Joe's heart beat faster.

This was luck for which he had not dared hope. He now knew where the keys were kept. Could he but reach them without arousing the guard their chances of escape were multiplied tenfold.

He waited until it seemed that hours had passed. None of the boys dared so much as whisper. The silence was profound. From the outer cave they could hear snores, but whether the guard was asleep or not they could not tell.

Joe realized that they would have to make their attempt before dawn, but he also knew that he could afford to wait, because the hours just before the break of day are the hours in which the average person sleeps most soundly, and there was every chance that the guard might be asleep by then as well.

At last he decided that it was time to act.

He got up quietly and began to make his way across the cave. Inch by inch he crawled across the rocky floor. He scarcely dared breathe for fear of disturbing one of their captors.

He was at the passage at last. The fire in the outer cave had died down. There was scarcely a vestige of light. This gave him hope, for it seemed to indicate that the guard had fallen asleep, otherwise he would have replenished the fire to protect himself against the night chill.

Joe groped for the little rock shelf. At first it eluded him, but at last his hand closed upon the keys. Carefully, he raised them, his hand clutching them tightly to prevent a betraying jangle of sound.

He turned slowly to make his way back to the others. In silence he reached them and began to grope for the chain that bound them together. He found the chain at last, then the padlock, and felt in the darkness for the key to fit it.

The key at last! It was larger than the others, which he judged were the handcuff keys. The padlock snapped and he unhooked the chain.

"That's that," he whispered, quietly. "Now for the handcuffs."

One by one the other boys presented their shackled wrists to him in the darkness and he groped for the key that would set them free. In a tense silence he fumbled with the locks and the handcuffs but, one by one, the handcuffs opened, one by one the boys moved quietly aside, rubbing their chafed wrists.

At last the task was finished. They were free again.

But there still remained the outer cave!

CHAPTER XIX

SEPARATED

Frank Hardy led the way.

He paused in the passage for a few seconds, surveying the scene in the outer cave.

All the men were asleep. They were rolled up in their blankets and lay sprawled in the shadows. There was merely a faint crimson glow from the embers of the fire.

He did not go on all fours; he just crouched low as he moved across the cave among the sleepers. Quick, sure footsteps, as silent as those of a cat, brought him to the outer entrance.

So much depended on their escape that the lads were uncannily silent. They seemed like mere shadows as they progressed, one by one, to the mouth of the cave. There was not a sound. The snores of the sleeping gangsters were unbroken.

Frank waited at the entrance. Chet joined him in a few moments. Then came Biff, and finally Joe. Safely out of the cave, the boys halted for a second on the rocks.

"I'll take the lead," whispered Frank. "Join hands and follow me."

It was pitch dark and the rocky path to the outskirts of the wood, he knew, would be treacherous. He reached back and grasped Chet's hand. Then he moved forward, carefully testing every step. On him depended the success of their flight to the wood. One stumble, one dislodged rock, might ruin everything.

Step by step, he moved cautiously forward. He had a good idea of where the woods trail opened, and he made toward it. Once they reached the trail he felt sure they would be safe.

Frank had an idea. He stopped and turned to the others.

"If anything happens," he said, in a low voice, "don't stick together. Scatter and try to make for the boat. Even if only one of us makes it he'll be able to get to the mainland."

The others whispered assent. He turned and proceeded across the rocks.

This safeguard, he felt, was wise. In case the gangsters discovered their escape they would prevent a repetition of the previous occurrence. In the darkness it was entirely probable that at least one, if not more, would be able to evade recapture.

But as he went on, his hopes rose. There was still not a sound from the cave in the rock. The darkness was in heavy silence.

He could faintly discern the black mass of trees and bushes before him. If they could only reach the trail!

But when he eventually came to the undergrowth he found that he had somehow missed the path. The trees were densely massed before him. They would be certain to raise a commotion if they attempted to enter the thicket at that point, he knew. They would be certain of becoming lost as well. They must find the trail.

Every moment was precious. Frank moved to the left but the bushes were still dense in front of him.

Joe moved up beside him.

"I think the trail is farther over," he said quietly.

Frank turned in the direction indicated.

They found the trail at last. Joe and Frank were ahead. Chet and Biff followed. Here they were unable to avoid making some sound. Twigs and branches crackled underfoot. This was unavoidable, but every noise seemed deafening.

Suddenly, from behind them, arose a terrific uproar.

Shouts, yells, the crash of a revolver, heavy footfalls, rent the silence into shreds. The sounds came from the cave.

"They're gone!" roared a voice. "Wake up! They're gone!"

The boys remained stock-still for a moment in the gloom of the trail.

"They'll be after us," said Frank quickly. "Take it easy. Make for the cove. I'll take the lead. Make as little noise as you can."

He started off at a trot, and the others followed. Behind them the uproar increased in volume. They could hear the gangsters shouting to one another; they could hear rocks clattering as their pursuers came running down from the cave.

Their erstwhile captors were rushing directly for the trail. They assumed that the boys would attempt to regain their boat as quickly as possible.

A voice was shouting:

"Head them off at the shore! Don't let them get to their boat!"

The boys increased their speed. There was no attempt at concealment now. They could hear the branches crashing behind them as the gangsters hurried through the thicket.

In the pitch blackness of the grove they stumbled and fell, tripped and reeled as they rushed along.

Chet and Biff, being unused to the trail, were obliged to travel at a slower pace, and in this way they dropped behind. The Hardy boys did not notice. There was such a confusion of sound in the grove, what with the noise of their own flight and the uproar of the pursuit, that they did not know that their chums were straggling.

At a fork in the trail, Frank and Joe headed to the left, the path leading downhill at this point, and toward the cove. They could hear the boom of the surf not far away and they knew that they were nearing their goal.

When Chet and Biff hastened up they failed to notice, in the inky blackness, that the trail branched two ways. Chet was in the lead and his footsteps brought him to the right. He could not hear the footsteps of the Hardy boys ahead but he judged that they were so far in advance that he could not hear them.

Their pursuers had become scattered. Some were pursuing them down the trail. Others were skirting the grove, intending to watch the shore. In the distance they could see occasional flashes of light. Once or twice there was a revolver shot.

"It won't go so well with us if they see us this time," called Frank back to his brother.

"If we can only beat them to the boat we'll be all right," panted Joe.

They emerged from the grove. They could see the white line of the surf ahead and the gray shapes of the rocks along the shore. The cove lay below.

The Hardy boys raced down the rocky slope. Only then did they become aware of the fact that their chums were not following.

Frank stopped and turned.

"Where are Chet and Biff?" he asked, startled.

"I thought they were right behind," replied Joe blankly.

They listened. There were no sounds of running footsteps down the trail. Back in the grove they could hear a frenzied crackling of branches, but whether it was caused by their comrades or by their pursuers they could not tell.

"They must have taken the wrong turning in the dark," declared Frank, as the solution dawned on him. "Quick—we'll get to the boat first! If we can find them we'll bring them with us. If we can't we'll have to make for the mainland alone."

A flash of scarlet light showed against the blackness of the bush as a revolver crashed out, and a scattering of rock close by told them that the bullet had been meant for them. The gangsters were near at hand.

Without another word the Hardy boys turned and dashed down the rocky trail leading to the cove. The path was precipitous and rocky. Joe stumbled once and fell headlong, but he was up again in an instant, spurred on by the fear that they would be recaptured. Frank reached the shore first. The motorboat was just where they had left it, but it was drawn up on the sands.

Joe raced up and the boys placed themselves, one on either side of the bow.

"All right!" gritted Frank. "Ready!"

They shoved desperately at the motorboat, and it began to move slowly out into the water of the cove.

The gangsters were drawing closer. The boys heard heavy footfalls on the rocks at the outskirts of the grove.

Bang! Bang!

The revolver crashed out again. Bullets splashed into the water. Desperately, the Hardy boys struggled with their boat.

At last the keel left the sand, and the boat slid out swiftly into the cove waters. Frank and Joe splashed out into the waves and began to scramble over the side.

Frank had a glimpse of a dark figure racing down the rocky slope toward them. He leaped to the engine.

"Here they are!" roared a voice.

More footsteps came running along the shore. The gangsters were converging toward the cove. Frank worked hastily over the engine. There was a splutter and a roar as the motor responded. The boat began to back slowly out of the cove.

"Keep down," he cautioned his brother.

Joe ducked, and not a moment too soon, for a fusillade of shots suddenly crashed out from the shore. Bullets whistled overhead. Wood splintered as one of them struck the side of the boat. Frank heard a heavy splashing in the water and judged that one of the gangsters was wading out in pursuit.

The boat moved slowly out to the entrance of the cove. In the darkness it was a ticklish performance. Frank doubted if he could make it. At any time it demanded careful steersmanship, and now there was no time for caution. The cove entrance was merely a faint gray blur against the darkness of the rocks on either side. He guided the *Sleuth* toward it.

Shots crashed and echoed from the shore. A dark form suddenly rose up beside the boat, with revolver upraised, but Joe launched himself on the man with surprising suddenness. His fist shot out and crashed into the gangster's face. With a muffled cry, the fellow stumbled back and lost his balance, going beneath the waves. He rose again in a moment, waist-deep in water, spluttering and choking, but by that time the *Sleuth* was several yards away and the water was too deep to permit the fellow to wade out any farther. His revolver was useless, and he began to make his way back to shore, growling to himself.

The motorboat reached the cove entrance. The rocks loomed high on either side.

Frank held his breath. At any moment he expected to hear the dread sound of the scraping rocks, but the *Sleuth* glided through the narrow channel without mishap, then shot out to the open sea. He spun the wheel about, brought the boat forward, and a moment later the engine was roaring its staccato defiance to the gangsters in the cove.

Frank looked back. He could see flashlights bobbing up and down on the beach.

"They're going for their own boats!" he exclaimed.

Then, with a grim smile, he bent forward over the wheel. Instead of heading the motorboat out to the open sea, he directed it along the shore, toward the distant cove where the gangsters had hidden their own craft.

CHAPTER XX

SEIZING THE BOATS

"What are you going to do, Frank?" shouted Joe Hardy.

"They're going after their boats. We know the cove they're in, and if we can get there first I'll tow them out to sea. Then they can't follow us!"

Thus Frank briefly outlined his daring scheme to his brother. He knew that the gangsters would not expect any such intention and he knew as well that only by some action of this kind could he avoid danger of capture. If the gangsters followed in their own boats there was every chance that they might overtake or outmaneuver the *Sleuth*. Even if they did not, as long as they retained possession of their own motorboats they could make good their escape. But once marooned on the island, they would be at the mercy of the Hardy boys.

"We'll have to hurry!" said Joe anxiously.

He watched the progress of the flashlights on the shore. The *Sleuth* was well ahead, but the seizure of the boats would take some time. The gangsters were making their way slowly over the rocks on their way to the cove.

Frank increased the speed of the boat. It leaped through the waves, the motor roaring. The flashlights on the shore were left far behind.

"We'll make it!" he shouted gleefully to Joe, the spray dashing against his face. He could distinguish the jutting headland that told him the location of the coves.

The men on the shore finally seemed to realize his intention. The boys could now hear frantic shouts as the men called to one another and made desperate efforts to reach the boats. But the *Sleuth* had outstripped them and they were left stumbling among the rocks along the beach.

The motorboat swept around the headland and into the cove. Frank had switched on the searchlight above the bow, and in its glare he could see the two motorboats belonging to the gang.

It was the work of but a minute to bring the *Sleuth* alongside, for the craft were riding at anchor. Joe seized a length of rope from the stern, then stood in readiness while his brother brought the *Sleuth* close to the side of the first craft. He leaped lightly into the other motorboat, lashed one end of the rope to the bow, then returned to the *Sleuth* again, tying the loose end of the rope securely, so that the motorboat could be towed.

Swiftly, Frank brought his boat around to the bow of the remaining craft, where the process was repeated. Joe snubbed one end of a length of stout rope to the bow, the other to the stern of the next boat. The two craft were now ready to be towed away by the *Sleuth*.

There was a sharp clattering of rock from among the bluffs near the cove. Then a shout:

"Red! They're stealing the boats!"

"Head 'em off!" roared another voice frantically from behind. "Don't let them get away!"

But already the engine of the *Sleuth* was roaring its message of triumph to the pursuers. Slowly, the motorboat began to make its way out of the cove.

And slowly, the ropes tightened. The two motorboats began moving behind. Joe had raised the anchor in each case and the craft were free to follow the lead boat.

There was a yell of dismay from the shore.

"They're starting out! They've got the boats!"

This was followed by a fusillade of shots. The man on the beach opened fire, and his companion farther back among the rocks did likewise. Bullets whistled past the *Sleuth*. But, in the darkness, the men on shore could take but indifferent aim. Frank had switched out the headlight and the gangsters could see only a ghostly gray shadow on the water.

The *Sleuth* picked up speed and the two motorboats behind began to rock and sway as they surged forward. Frank knew that he could not go too fast, otherwise the boats that he was towing would run foul of one another or of his own craft and cause disaster. He contented himself by moving ahead at a moderate rate of speed, knowing well that once he cleared the cove he could afford to snap his fingers at the gangsters marooned on the island.

Shouts interspersed with revolver shots told him of their pursuers' wrath. The flashlights danced like fireflies. The full extent of the trick that had been played upon them was just beginning to dawn on the men marooned on the shore.

The headland loomed to the side, then slipped slowly by. The motorboat was throbbing its way out to open water.

"We've beaten 'em." declared Frank exultantly.

"I'll say we have! They'll never get off that island unless they swim."

"From the fuss they're making, they seem to know it, too."

"Where to now?"

"The mainland. If we can get to Rock Harbor we'll get help."

"How about Chet and Biff?" asked Joe soberly.

"We can't afford to take a chance on bringing them off the island just now. I hate to desert them, but we can't do anything else. If we went back for them we'd likely undo everything we've done so far. But I think they'll be safe enough. They'll hide in the bushes. Those fellows have been so busy chasing us that they haven't had any time to worry about them."

"Perhaps they think we all got away."

"If they do they won't be hunting around for Chet and Biff. In any case, we had the agreement that even if only one of us got away he would come back with help for the rest. They'll know we'll be back."

"So will the gangsters. I'll bet they're worrying about how they can clear away from this island before we get back."

Frank headed the boat for the mainland. It was his intention, as he had said, to make his way to Rock Harbor, where they could secure help—officers and men to come back with them to Blacksnake Island to aid in the rescue of their chums and in the capture of the gangsters.

There was the chance, of course, that the latter might have a canoe or a skiff hidden somewhere on the island, but he did not think they would trust themselves to the open water of the channel in any such frail craft. He felt convinced that by seizing the two motorboats they had effectually marooned their enemies.

They passed the last jutting point of the sinister island and the bow of the *Sleuth* was headed toward the coast.

"Perhaps we won't have to go all the way to Rock Harbor," suggested Joe. "If we could meet a ship we might get help."

"It seems to me I see a light now. Running low on the water. Do you see it?"

Joe peered into the darkness.

"I believe you're right," he said finally. "It seems to be coming this way, too."

"Perhaps some more of the gang."

"I hadn't thought of that. Better not go too close."

Frank eyed the approaching light warily. It was just a faint gleam in the darkness and he judged it was from a motorboat which was most certainly bound toward Blacksnake Island. Eventually he could hear the steady throb of the engine.

After a moment or so he started up excitedly.

"Joe! I'd know that engine anywhere."

"So would I! It's—"

"The *Napoli*!"

He spun the wheel about so that the *Sleuth* would cut across the bows of the approaching craft. Steadily, through the darkness, came the throbbing of the engine, and as the boat came closer the Hardy boys became more and more convinced that it was Tony Prito's craft.

"I've been wondering what became of him," Frank declared. "When he didn't show up earlier I began to think he must have had to call off the trip."

"It may not be him after all, but I'm sure it's his boat. If it isn't I'll never believe my ears again."

The two boats approached one another. Frank shut down the engine of the *Sleuth*, rose from his seat, and shouted:

"*Napoli*, ahoy!"

Almost immediately the roar of the other engine died to a murmur and a well-known voice replied:

"This is the *Napoli*. Who are you?"

It was the voice of Tony Prito. Joe gave a yell of delight.

"It's us!" shouted Frank. "The Hardy boys!"

They could hear sounds of excited talking in the other boat, and a suppressed cheer.

"Coming over!" Tony called out, and in a few minutes the two boats had drawn up alongside. In the glare of the headlight Frank and Joe could see Tony Prito, Jerry Gilroy and Phil Cohen.

Their greetings were cut short when the boys saw the two trailing boats and Frank tersely explained the situation.

"You couldn't have come at a better time. We found Chet and Biff on the island. They're still there. We tried to escape, but got separated and only Joe and I got away. Chet and Biff are in hiding somewhere and we stole the other motorboats."

"Whose motorboats?" asked Jerry.

"Chet and Biff were captured by a gang of crooks who mistook them for us. These fellows had a cave on the island and two motorboats of their own. When we made our get-away we towed their boats away with us so the men are all marooned there."

A chorus of excited questions broke forth as the newcomers demanded further details, but Frank went on:

"We're going to the mainland for help. What we want you to do is take charge of these two motorboats and keep cruising around the island to see that the gang doesn't get away."

"Good!" approved Phil. "And if we can pick up Chet and Biff we'll do it."

"If you can, without letting the gang get hold of those boats again."

"Fine!" Tony declared. "We'll take the boats. Throw over that rope."

He caught the rope deftly, and the captured motorboats were soon being towed by the *Napoli*, leaving the Hardy boys' craft free for its flight to the mainland.

"We'll be back as soon as we can," called out Frank.

"We'll be watching for you."

"Good. No use wasting any more time. Good luck!"

"Good luck!" shouted the others.

Frank bent over the wheel again. The engine of the *Sleuth* roared as the speedy craft turned toward the mainland. The *Napoli*, in its turn, began to forge ahead toward Blacksnake Island, its speed somewhat lessened now by the drag of the captured boats. Tony, Jerry and Phil were agog with excitement over this strange encounter in the darkness and the sensational news the Hardy boys had given them.

So the two motorboats went their separate ways in the darkness of the night—one to the mainland, the other toward the sinister island where Chet Morton and Biff Hooper were marooned with the gangsters.

CHAPTER XXI
AT THE ISLAND

In the meantime, what of Chet Morton and Biff Hooper?

When they took the wrong turn in the trail it was some time before they realized that the Hardy boys were not running along before them. They were blundering along through the undergrowth, in complete darkness, trusting to their chums to guide them through, when finally Chet stopped, panting.

"Frank and Joe must be running like deer," he muttered. "I can't hear them at all."

"We were all mighty close together a little while ago," returned Biff.

"I know. And they seem to have disappeared all of a sudden." The thought struck Chet that they might be on the wrong trail. "Do you think we could have taken a wrong turn?"

Biff listened. "There's no one ahead of us, that's sure," he said at last. "We must have got separated."

As this conviction forced itself upon them, the two lads were overwhelmed with disappointment. They knew that the Hardy boys would have little enough time to gain the boat and escape without waiting for them, and at the thought that they might be again left on the island at the mercy of their captors they were profoundly discouraged.

"We're up against it again, I guess," declared Chet. "Well, I think we'd better follow this trail anyway, wherever it leads to. Remember what Frank said—that if even one of us reached the boat safely he could get to the mainland and bring back help for the rest."

"Yes, that's right. It isn't as bad as it might be."

"I only hope the gang don't capture them before they make the boat safely. Listen!"

They stopped in their tracks and listened as the night wind bore to their ears the sound of gunfire from the beach. It was far over to one side of them. They could hear distant shouts, then the spasmodic firing of revolvers followed again.

"They must be having a sweet time. I guess the gang are trying to keep them from getting the boat," said Chet.

Then they heard the muffled roar of the motorboat in the cove.

"They're getting away!" declared Biff, in excitement. "You can hear the boat backing out."

More revolver shots—more shouts—the roar of the *Sleuth's* engine continued.

"As long as they get away safely I'm not worrying much," Chet said. "Just the same, I'd rather be with them. But they'll bring back help."

"In the meantime, the best thing we can do is to hide."

"The gang will be scouring the island for us now that they know we didn't get away with the others. And they won't be any too gentle with us either, if they get us."

Chet and Biff decided that it would be best to get as near the shore as possible before concealing themselves, so as to be ready for a rush to safety should the Hardy boys return with the promised assistance. By the sound of the motorboat and the shooting, they judged that the narrow trail led toward the shore, so they followed it as well as they could in the darkness. The wet branches slashed their faces and they stumbled over roots and slipped in the wet, deep grass, but gradually the sound of the breaking surf drew closer and they knew they were coming nearer to the beach.

The path suddenly dipped and they descended a slope, finally emerging from the trees to find themselves on a rocky hillside overlooking the gray shore. They could see the white foam of the breaking rollers, and the gray rocks below but there was no sign of motorboat or of any human being.

"We may as well stay right on this hillside, behind the rocks," Chet suggested. "If we go roaming about the shore we're likely to run into Red and his gang."

"Perhaps they've taken their own boats and gone after the Hardy boys."

"They may have. But we can't take a chance on it. If any of them are prowling around it would be just our luck to meet them."

The chums made themselves as comfortable as possible in the shelter of a huge rock, from which they had a good view of the shore and the sea beyond. It was still dark and they had little hope of rescue before morning.

"It'll take them quite a while to get to the mainland and rouse any one to come out here to help us," remarked Chet. "The big thing is for us to keep hidden until daylight and then lay low until we see a chance of rescue."

"You can trust me to lay low. I've no hankering to be dragged back to that cave again."

"Me neither."

The boys lapsed into silence. They realized that conversation was dangerous. At any moment some member of the gang might be venturing near and might hear their voices.

From a distant side of the island they suddenly heard more shots. They broke out in a perfect fusillade of gunfire, and the rocks flung back the echoes, mingled with yells of rage. At the same time, they again heard the sound of the *Sleuth's* engine, slower this time, as though the craft were but crawling along.

"I can't understand this," said Chet. "We heard them leave the cove a little while ago. Now they're away down the shore and going slow."

"Perhaps they're having engine trouble," said Biff mournfully.

"I can't figure it out at all. It's tough to be sitting here in the dark, not knowing whether they've got away or not."

"I don't dare let myself think they haven't got away," declared Biff, with determination.

An hour passed. The sounds of the motorboat had long since died away. Once in a while the chums heard voices back in the grove and they knew that at least some of the gangsters had been left on the island. Whether the others had left in pursuit of the Hardy boys, they could not tell. Had they known of the Hardys' *coup* in taking the gangsters' two boats they would have felt more relieved in mind. The chill of approaching morning had settled over the island, and they huddled together in the shelter of the rock, seeking warmth.

Suddenly, from the sea, they heard the steady chug-chug of a motorboat that seemed to be progressing slowly along in close proximity to the shore. They looked out and they could see a headlight slowly moving through the darkness.

"It's a motorboat, but it's traveling very slowly," said Chet.

"Let's take a chance and hail them."

"It might be some of the gang."

"That's right. But we can go down closer to the shore and see. It may be Frank and Joe looking for us."

The two lads left the shelter of the rocks and began moving cautiously toward the beach. They realized that there was every chance that the mysterious craft might be one of the gangsters' boats and that they would be risking recapture by making their presence known. But, on the other hand, it might be the Hardy boys returning in an effort to pick them up.

They had gone no more than a few yards when a loud voice only a short distance away made them jump with surprise:

"Is that one of our boats, Pete?"

"No. I don't know it at all. There's something funny about this."

A rock clattered down the slope. Chet looked back. Two dark figures appeared in sight at the top of the declivity.

The two parties saw one another at the same time.

"Here they are!" roared one of the men, and he plunged down the slope straight at the astonished boys.

The other man came running after him. The first impulse of the two chums was to run, but they saw that flight would be useless. They were midway on the hillside leading to the beach and the path was treacherous with rocks and loose gravel. They would be overtaken in a moment.

"Fight 'em," said Chet, gritting his teeth.

The boys stood their ground. The two gangsters, one of whom they recognized as Pete, came floundering down the slope. They had started out in such a rush that now they were not well able to stop, and as the pair came at them the two chums braced themselves for the shock.

Biff met the first man squarely. His passion for boxing now stood him in good stead. He judged his distance perfectly. As the fellow came at him, arms swinging, he drove a straight left to the fellow's midriff.

The gangster gasped and doubled up with pain. He wavered for a moment, then Biff swung. His right fist crashed against the man's jaw, and the gangster toppled over on his face. He rolled over in the gravel a few times, then came to a stop, sprawled senseless on the hillside.

As for Chet, he made use of strategy. When the second man rushed at him he sidestepped neatly.

His right foot went out. The gangster tripped over it and, so great had been the force of his rush and so sudden was his downfall, that he went ploughing forward on his face for several yards until he came to a ledge of rock. He made frantic efforts to save himself as he felt that he was going over the side, but his descent could not be checked. Chet had a glimpse of desperately waving arms and kicking legs; then his adversary disappeared with a crash. The ledge was only a few feet from the beach, but it was certain that the fall would knock the breath out of the gangster's body for several minutes at least.

Without another word the boys scrambled back up the hillside. They knew that the gangsters would recover quickly and that the alarm would soon be sounded. They must hide, and that quickly.

They gained the shelter of the bushes just as the gangster who had gone tumbling over the ledge began to find his breath again and shout for help. Desperately, the boys scrambled through the undergrowth, seeking no path, seeking only a hiding place.

At length, when they were in a dense thicket where the branches were so closely entwined that further progress seemed impossible, they halted.

"This is as far as we can go," panted Chet. "They'll be searching for us now, but they'll never find us in here."

"That was a narrow escape!"

"It sure was. But we gave them something to remember us by."

Biff Hooper doubled up his fist with satisfaction.

"I knocked my man colder than a sardine," he declared.

It was nearing dawn. The first faint streaks of light were appearing in the eastern sky.

"I wonder where that boat went," said Chet suddenly. "Perhaps it's still near the island."

"It wasn't one of the boats belonging to the gang, anyway, by the way those two fellows were talking. If we could get a hiding place a little nearer the shore we might be able to see it."

"Yes—let's get out of this thicket."

Quietly, the boys began to withdraw from the deep thicket in which they had become entangled. But the branches cracked underfoot and seemed to have the brittleness of matchwood. The chums were afraid they would be heard.

"Better stay where we are," muttered Chet.

They remained motionless for some time, and the swift dawn soon began to paint the sky. The darkness diminished and the boys could now see one another plainly, and could see the extent of the deep thicket in which they had become enmeshed.

"Now let's try to get out," said Chet.

Again they attempted to make their way out of the thicket, and this time, because they could see what they were doing, their efforts met with more success. But they could not avoid making considerable noise, and the crackling of branches seemed like the reports of rifles.

Then, to their horror, they heard a voice:

"I heard a noise in the bushes over there almost an hour ago, and now I hear it again."

"We'll go over and see," replied another voice.

The boys looked at one another, then froze into silence. They could hear heavy footfalls near by. Branches crackled.

"They're hiding around on this side of the island somewhere," said the first voice. "If I ever lay my hands on 'em."

Chet put his finger to his lips as a warning to silence, but there was no need. Biff was scarcely daring to breathe.

Just at that moment a sound broke forth that sent a thrill of fear through them both.

It was a sibilant, terrifying hiss, right at their feet.

Chet looked down and gave a low cry. A huge blacksnake was coiled in the grass, in readiness to strike.

CHAPTER XXII

THE CHASE

Chet Morton leaped back with such violence that he collided with his chum. He had seen the serpent in the nick of time, and his backward leap had been so instinctive and so involuntary that he somehow evaded the swift, whiplike thrust of the evil head that plunged at him.

The snake missed, although its body writhed against Chet's boot for a second and the fangs stabbed against the heavy leather. The boot saved the boy. Had the snake struck against his leg he would have been bitten.

The chums plunged blindly through the thicket.

There was no thought of caution now. They were filled with unreasoning terror of the blacksnake, the instinctive revulsion that fills most people at the sight of such a reptile, and they went crashing through the bushes. The noise of their flight did not escape the two rascals who had been searching for them.

"I see them!" shouted one of the men. He came plunging through the deep grass at the outskirts of the thicket to intercept the boys.

Chet saw him in time and veered to one side. He just managed to evade the outflung arm, then went running desperately to the top of the hillside overlooking the sea. Biff came thundering behind, outdistanced the second gangster, dodged the other man, and raced after Chet.

They went slipping and sliding down the slope. Chet had no clear idea of where they were bound, but he was determined to keep running either until he was captured or overcome with exhaustion.

But when he came over the brow of the hill and began the steep descent, he saw something in the sea below that made him give an exultant yell.

It was a motorboat, and one that he recognized immediately. The boat was none other than the *Napoli*, and in it were three figures. Even at that distance he knew them for Tony Prito, Phil Cohen and Jerry Gilroy. Behind the motorboat were two other craft, being towed.

He had not been seen as yet, for he saw that the *Napoli* was cruising leisurely around the island. He shouted hoarsely to attract attention.

He saw Tony look up, then speak excitedly to his comrades. They waved frantically in reply. Then the bow of the *Napoli* began to head in toward the shore.

Could they reach the boat in safety? Biff was thundering down the slope only a few feet behind Chet. Rocks and pebbles went bouncing and bounding along in front of them; sand and gravel flew from about their boots. And, coming in swift pursuit, were the two gangsters who had so nearly captured them in the thicket. These men were shouting hoarsely to them to stop.

But the two chums had no intention of stopping. They saw safety in sight. Could they reach the shore and gain the boat before the two gangsters overtook them?

Then, out from among the rocks along the beach emerged three figures. Chet's heart sank. They were the other gangsters and they were directly in the path. At the same time, he saw that Tony Prito was bringing the *Napoli* around, and away from the shore.

Spent and exhausted, he tried to dodge the three men ahead, but the effort was short-lived. One of the three leaped forward and grappled with him. They fell struggling into the sand. The other two leaped at Biff.

The boys fought bravely and desperately. Chet struck out and his fist crashed into the face of the man who had tackled him. The fellow sagged back for a second and Chet tried to free himself from the grasp around his waist, but as he did so one of the other two gangsters came rushing up and launched himself on him.

Biff battled with equal ferocity, but he was powerless against the three rascals. He kicked and struggled, but they had him down and they dragged him back behind the rocks, where the others soon brought Chet.

The red-headed man, with a bruise over one eye, produced a length of stout cord from his hip pocket.

"Tie 'em up!" he snapped. "We've got 'em this time for keeps."

Pete grabbed the cord, and in a few minutes Chet's wrists were bound tightly behind his back and his ankles were securely tied. Pete cut the cord and used the remainder for binding Biff. The two chums were helpless.

As for Tony Prito, in the *Napoli*, he had quickly seen that it would be impossible, even foolhardy, to attempt to rescue his two chums. In the first place, there were five boys against five men, the latter desperate and fully armed. The only result would be the capture of them all and the capture, as well, of the three motorboats by the gangsters.

"I hate to see them caught with us so close, but what can we do?" he said, turning to the others, as he slowly brought the *Napoli* around.

"If the men catch us and the motorboats, the boys will only be worse off than they were before."

"I guess you're right," agreed Jerry Gilroy. "I sure thought for a minute that we were going to be able to save them. Between the crowd of us we could have held off those other two toughs long enough to get Chet and Biff on board, but when the others showed up I knew it was all off."

"The fellows put up a good fight, anyway," declared Phil Cohen. "I hope those villains don't treat 'em too rough."

"We'll get them free yet," asserted Tony. "I don't know how it's going to be done, but we'll get 'em free. We've still got all the motorboats and the gang can't leave the island, that's sure."

When he had brought the *Napoli* out a safe distance from shore, Tony decided to drop anchor.

"We'll stick around," he decided. "They'll know that we aren't going to desert them anyway."

So the *Napoli*, with the two captured motorboats drifting behind, remained at anchor, while the three chums scanned the rocky shore. Once in a while they saw one or another of the gangsters emerging from behind the boulders to gaze at them, then return.

"We've got them guessing," chuckled Tony. "They don't know what to make of us. They know we have their boats, but they don't know who we are or how we got 'em."

Two hours passed. The sun rose higher in the sky. Blacksnake Island, in all its sinister ugliness, simmered in the morning heat. There was no further sign of life from the shore. Although the boys in the motorboat did not know it, the boulders behind which Chet and Biff had been carried hid the trail up to the grove and thence to the cave in the rocks. The gangsters had decided to return to this cave and Chet and Biff, with their ankle bonds untied, had been roughly ordered to their feet and bade proceed with the gangsters up the hidden trail. They had not been seen from the boat because a heavy veil of overhanging branches from the trees masked the trail where it wound up the hillside.

Toward mid-morning Tony chanced to look up and gaze out toward the mainland. He leaped up with a frantic yell.

"Here they come!" he shrieked. "Here they are!"

The others rose and stared. Then, as the meaning of what they saw dawned on them, they cheered hoarsely, and danced with delight until the motorboat rocked and swayed beneath their feet.

Cleaving the waves, came a low, rakish craft, speeding along with white wings of foam at her prow. It rushed silently toward them with the grace of an arrow. It was a United States revenue cutter, and when the boys in the boat witnessed its approach they knew that the Hardy boys had been successful in obtaining the aid they had gone to seek.

The boys cheered and waved their arms, trying to signal to the cutter that they had located Chet and Biff. Finally, Tony started up the engine and brought the *Napoli* alongside. The cutter slowly came to a stop, there was a clank and a clatter as the anchor was sent over.

A husky revenue officer with a revolver strapped to his waist leaned over the side and hailed them.

"Did you find them?" he roared.

"They were caught again, right on this shore!" shouted Tony. "The gang are still here."

"Fine! We'll be right over. Tie your craft alongside and come along in our boat!"

The lads needed no second urging. A ladder was flung over the side and, after securely tying the *Napoli*, they clambered up on the deck of the cutter where they found the Hardy boys awaiting them.

In a few swift words Tony acquainted them with the circumstances surrounding the recapture of Chet and Biff. The revenue officer who had first hailed them nodded with satisfaction.

"As long as we know that those rascals haven't left the island, it's all right," he declared. "We'll have them in hand before long."

He turned and gave a curt order to one of his men and in a remarkably short space of time there were a dozen broad-shouldered chaps in readiness, with rifles and revolvers. Another order, and a boat was lowered over the side.

"Away we go!" announced the officer. "It won't be long now."

CHAPTER XXIII

HOME AGAIN

Tony Prito and his chums guided the landing party to the boulders behind which the gangsters and their captives had disappeared, but when Frank Hardy saw that the prey had flown he assumed the rôle of guide.

"They've gone up to the cave," he said. "I know the way."

With Joe, he went in advance of the party. Tony, Phil and Jerry came behind, with the officer and his men, their faces alight with anticipation of a battle, clambering up the hillside in their wake. The sturdy, tanned men were alert and ready for the approaching fight.

Through the grove, down the leafy trail, the Hardy boys led them, and at last they came within sight of the clearing. The great rock and the dark entrance of the cave were in sight. There was no sign of any human being.

"Deploy!" ordered the officer.

The men scattered. The Hardy boys and their chums, being unarmed, were obliged to watch from the shelter of the grove, because they realized that there would probably be gunfire.

The men began to make their way across the open space, running from rock to rock, keeping well scattered, all eying the entrance to the cave.

Suddenly, a shot sounded from the cave entrance. Almost simultaneously one of the revenue men fired. The boys had seen no one in the cave but the keen eyes of the rifleman had, and when the body of a man slumped forward out of the cave, falling on the rocks, with a revolver clattering from his nerveless fingers, his judgment was verified.

And this, to the disappointment of the watchers, was the end of the fight. For the gangsters, like so many of their kind, were cowardly and they became unnerved at the fate of the first of their men who had shown fight.

Out of the cave entrance came a man bearing aloft a white handkerchief in token of surrender. He was followed by the others, with hands upraised, and behind them came Chet Morton and Biff Hooper, their wrists still bound, but their faces alight with joy, in contrast to the surly visages of the gangsters.

"Well, well!" declared the officer in charge, as he confronted the rascals, noting the frowning red-haired man. "If it isn't Red Hawkins and his gang! And you too, Pete! We've been looking for your hangout for the past three months—and for you as well. Put the cuffs on 'em. boys."

In a few moments the gang were securely handcuffed. The man who had been shot was attended to and it was found that he had been wounded, but after a brief examination and the rendering of first aid, the officer assured the victim that he would live to face trial with the rest for the abduction of Chet and Biff.

"And if that charge falls through—which it won't," he assured them all, "we have a list of other charges against you, as long as your arm."

But the Hardy boys and their chums were oblivious to this scene. They were too busy staging an impromptu reunion. Chet Morton and Biff Hooper, freed of their bonds, were busy shaking hands all round and trying to explain to their excited comrades some of the adventures they had gone through since leaving Bayport.

Then the Hardy boys were called on to explain how they had encountered the revenue cutter and how they had told their story and prevailed on the revenue men to come with them to Blacksnake Island to effect the rescue of their chums.

"But we can talk it over better on the way back," declared Frank.

"Coming back with us?" asked the officer. "We're taking these men to Rock Harbor, but you're welcome to come along."

"No thanks—we'll be going back in the motorboats."

"I see. Well, we'll take this gang back to the ship. Forward—march, you!" he shouted to the crestfallen gangsters.

So the party returned to the shore and Red Hawkins and his four men were herded into the boat. They had not said a word, but on their way back to the cutter Red turned to the Hardy boys and snarled:

"Well, you've got me, but our men in the West got your father. We've got that much satisfaction, anyway!"

With that he lapsed into silence, realizing that his words had the immediate effect of dampening the spirits of the Hardy boys and their chums.

Back at the revenue cutter, Frank and Joe said good-bye to the officer and his men, leaving Red and his gang in their charge. The motorboat had been towed behind the ship and they resumed their places in the *Sleuth* and cast away.

Tony Prito and the others took their places in the *Napoli* while Chet and Biff returned to the *Envoy*. One of the captured boats turned out to be none other than Biff's own craft, which the gangsters had been using while they were prisoners in the cave. Thus the journey home began.

Although there was rejoicing in the other boats and much good-natured badinage was passed about, the Hardy boys found it difficult to be cheerful. Red's words had brought back to them their fears concerning the safety of their father and they dreaded the news that might await them when they returned to Bayport.

"If there is no news from him, I think we should go to Chicago and search for him," said Frank gravely.

"I'm with you in that. But perhaps it won't be so bad. Red may have been only trying to frighten us."

"I hope so. If that was his object he sure succeeded."

"At any rate, we found the missing chums."

"Another feather in our cap, eh?" grinned Frank. "If dad does come back safely he won't have any reason to be ashamed of his sons."

"The Mortons and the Hoopers will be glad. The whole city will be in a fuss over what happened to Chet and Biff."

This proved to be the case. When the three motorboats returned to Barmet Bay and finally docked at Bayport they found a cheering throng awaiting them, for the news had been sent to the city by the revenue men from Rock Harbor, and the anxieties of the boys' families were set at rest. The Hoopers and Mortons, in particular, had been almost frantic with worry and Chet and Biff were given a welcome befitting heroes of an expedition given up for lost for many years.

Nor were the Hardy boys and their chums forgotten in the welcome. Chet and Biff gave full credit to the Hardys for the part they had played in the round-up of the gangsters. When Frank and Joe were finally able to break away from the crowd and make their way back home, the news of the exploit was beginning to spread rapidly through the city.

When they came within sight of the familiar house they broke into a run. They raced up the front steps. They flung open the front door and burst into the hallway, almost knocking over Aunt Gertrude, who was dusting.

"Lands sakes!" she exclaimed. "Can't you boys ever learn to come into a house properly? I never seen the like in all my born days! Go right back out that door and come in again like gentlemen!"

"Home again!" exclaimed Frank, with a grin. Then he turned anxiously to his aunt. "Any word yet from dad?"

"He's in the library!" sniffed Aunt Gertrude.

"In the library!" exclaimed the boys, in astonishment.

"Yes, in the library. And what of it? Where did you expect he'd be? Up in the attic?"

But the Hardy boys did not wait to reply. With a whoop of delight they rushed through the living room and into the library, where they found Fenton Hardy seated at the table. Their father got up quickly as they rushed at him, and in a moment all three were shaking hands and chattering in gladness and relief.

"We heard you'd been caught by the gang!" gasped Frank.

Fenton Hardy smiled. "It was the other way around," he corrected them. "The gang was caught by me."

"And we caught the rest of them!"

"Not Red Hawkins and his crew?"

The Hardy boys nodded. Their father gazed at them in incredulous astonishment for a moment. Then he slapped them heartily on the back and indicated the chairs near by.

"And I thought they'd clear out when they knew Baldy and the others were behind the bars! Why, this rounds up the entire pack! Tell me about it. But—first of all, have Chet and Biff been found?"

The boys nodded.

"We found them on Blacksnake Island. That's how we rounded up the gang. They captured Chet and Biff in mistake for us. They had 'em in a cave."

Then, in the seclusion of the study, the Hardy boys told of their search for the missing chums, of their deduction that the boys might have gone to Blacksnake Island, of their arrival on the island and the finding of the gangsters and their cave.

Fenton Hardy listened to the recital with sparkling eyes, for he realized that his sons had played a part that made him proud of them, and when the tale was finished his approval was evident by the manner in which he pounded the desk with his fist.

"Fine!" he declared. "It was real detective work in the first place and real grit and courage from then on. I'm very proud of my boys."

"But all the time," added Frank, "we were worried about you. The men said you had been captured in the West."

"It was a false report," said their father. "They thought they had captured me, but it wasn't for long. I played into their hands once, just to find out where they were all hiding. But I had another detective to shadow me and when I found out where the gang were gathered I gave the signal and we rounded them up."

"And now I hope the whole kit and bilin' of you will stay at home for a while!" declared a voice from the doorway. "I declare I never did see such a family for the men-folks to go gallivantin' around the country and never stayin' at home. It's a wonder to me, Laura, that you put up with it."

"Well," smilingly replied Mrs. Hardy, who had entered the room with Aunt Gertrude, "with three first-rate detectives in the family, I'm afraid I can't expect anything else. And they always come home again."

Aunt Gertrude sniffed.

"I'll guarantee that if I visit here much longer I'll see that those two boys haven't much chance for more detecting!" she announced. "I'll cure 'em. so I will. It's no business at all for boys."

Mrs. Hardy smiled serenely.

Fenton Hardy winked gravely at his sons, so Aunt Gertrude's threat did not greatly disturb them.

There were to be more exciting adventures in store for the Hardy boys, and what some of these were will be related in the next volume of this series, entitled "The Hardy Boys: Hunting for Hidden Gold," a strenuous story of the West.

"You're welcome to try, Aunt Gertrude," said Mr. Hardy; "but I'm afraid you'll never cure my sons of wanting to be detectives. I've set them the example, you see."

"More's the pity," sniffed Aunt Gertrude. "Why couldn't you have been a plumber? It's safer."

"But not as exciting," said Fenton Hardy, with a laugh.

HUNTING FOR HIDDEN GOLD

ORIGINALLY PUBLISHED IN 1928.

CHAPTER I

IN THE STORM

"A fortune in hidden gold! That certainly sounds mighty interesting."

Frank Hardy folded up the letter he had just been reading aloud to his brother.

"Dad has all the luck," replied Joe. "I'd give anything to be working with him on a case like that."

"Me, too. This case is a bit out of the ordinary."

"Where was the letter postmarked?"

"Somewhere in Montana. A gold-mining camp called Lucky Bottom."

"Montana! Gee, but I wish he could have taken us with him. We've never been more than two hundred miles from home."

"And I've never seen a mine in my life, much less a real mining camp."

The Hardy boys looked at one another regretfully. They had just received a letter from their father, Fenton Hardy, an internationally famous detective, who had been called West but a fortnight previous on a mysterious mission. The letter gave the boys their first inkling of the nature of the case that had summoned their father from Bayport, on the Atlantic coast, to the mining country of Montana.

"A fortune in hidden gold," repeated Frank. "I hope he finds it all right."

"It was stolen from one of the big companies, wasn't it?"

"Yes. He says that an entire shipment of bullion was stolen before it left the camp, so they believe it must have been hidden somewhere in the neighborhood."

"And his job is to find it."

"If he can. And the thieves as well."

Joe sighed. "I sure would like to be out there right now. We might be able to help him."

"Well, we've helped him in other cases, but I guess we're out of luck this time. Montana is too far away."

"Yes, and we have to keep on going to school. I'll be glad when we're through school and can be regular detectives like dad."

Frank grinned. "No use grouching about it," he said cheerfully. "Our time will come some day."

"Yes, but it seems a long time coming," replied Joe, smiling ruefully.

"Oh, in a few more years we'll be going all over the country just like dad, solving robberies and murders and having all sorts of excitement. We haven't done too badly so far, anyway."

"Yes, we had the fun of discovering the tower treasure."

"And running down the counterfeiters."

"Yes; and solving the mystery of the house on the cliff and finding out about Blacksnake Island."

The boys were referring to previous cases in which they had been involved and in which their ability had been proved. But it had been several months since any adventure or excitement had come their way and they were feeling restless, the more so now that they knew their father was at that moment in the remote mining camp in the West engaged on a mystery that seized their imagination.

"Hidden gold!" said Joe, half to himself. "That *would* be a case worth working on."

"Forget it," laughed his brother. "There's no use making yourself miserable wishing we were out there, because we're not and it doesn't look as if there's much chance that we shall be. Perhaps his old case isn't so exciting, anyway. You're not going to spend all Saturday wishing for something you can't have. Don't forget we're to go out with Chet and Jerry this afternoon."

"That's right," declared Joe. "I'd almost forgotten. We were to go skating, weren't we?"

"Yes; and it's about time we started or the others will be going without us."

This possibility moved Joe to action and in a few moments the Hardy boys had dismissed their father's letter from their minds and were rummaging in a cupboard beneath the stairs for their skates. They had planned to meet their chums at the mouth of Willow River, a stream that ran from the mountains down through the farm lands to Barmet Bay, on which Bayport was located. It was a brisk, clear winter afternoon, ideal for an outing, and their Saturday holiday from Bayport high school was much too precious to be spent indoors.

Their Aunt Gertrude, an elderly, crotchety maiden lady of certain temper and uncertain years, eyed them suspiciously as they came into the hallway with their skates and began donning sweaters and warm gloves.

"Skating, hey?" she sniffed. "You'll go through the ice, I'll be bound."

The boys knew from experience that it was always best to placate Aunt Gertrude.

"We'll try not to, Aunt Gertrude," Frank assured her.

"You'll try not to! A lot of good that will do. If the ice isn't strong, all the trying in the world won't keep you from going through it. And the ice *isn't* strong. I'm sure it isn't. It can't be."

"The fellows have been skating on Willow River for more than a week now."

"Maybe so. Maybe so. They've been lucky, that's all I can say. You mark my words, that ice will break one of these fine days. I only hope you boys aren't on it when it does."

"I hope so too," laughed Frank, drawing on his gloves.

"It's no laughing matter," persisted Aunt Gertrude gloomily. "Well, I suppose if you will court death and destruction, an old lady like me can't do anything to stop you. Although you'd be better off at home studying. Run along. Run along."

"Good-bye, Aunt Gertrude."

"Run along. Be home early. Don't skate too far out. Don't get lost. Don't get caught in a snowstorm. I'm sure there's one coming up. I know the signs. My lumbago is troubling me again today. Don't forget to come back in time for tea."

Aunt Gertrude's favorite word was "don't" and she persisted in treating her nephews as though they were but a grade advanced from kindergarten. Mrs. Hardy was out for the afternoon and in her absence the worthy spinster rejoiced in her opportunity to exercise her authority. When she had exhausted her store of admonitions, the boys departed, and she watched them from the door with gloomy forebodings as to the ultimate outcome of their skating trip. Aunt Gertrude was a pessimist of the first water.

When the Hardy boys reached the foot of the street they found Chet Morton, rotund and jovial, and Jerry Gilroy, tall and red-cheeked, awaiting them.

"Just going to start without you," declared Chet, swinging his skates.

"We had a letter from dad and we were so interested in reading it that we mighty near forgot about the trip," confessed Frank.

"Where is he?"

"Out in Montana, in a mining camp, working on a case."

"Gosh, he's lucky!" said Jerry enviously.

"I'll say he is," agreed Frank. "Joe and I have just been wishing we could be out there with him."

"Well, we can't have everything," Chet said cheerfully. "Come on—I'll race you to Willow River."

He dashed off down the snow-covered street, the others in close pursuit. The race was of short duration, for Willow River was some distance away, and the boys soon slowed down to a walk. At a more reasonable gait they continued their journey, and within half an hour had reached the river, now covered with a gleaming sheet of ice. In a few minutes the lads had donned their skates and were skimming off over the smooth surface.

The banks of the river were covered with snow and the trees along the shore were bare and black. Above the hills the sky was of a slaty gray.

"Looks like snow," Frank commented, as they skated on up the river.

"Oh, it'll blow over," answered Chet carelessly. "Let's go on up to Shallow Lake."

"We don't want to be away too long. It'll be dark before we get back."

"We can skate up there and back in a couple of hours. Come on."

It was a brisk, cold afternoon and the boys did not need much urging. Shallow Lake was back in the hills, but the boys made such good time over the glassy surface of the river that it was not long before they left the farm lands behind.

Frank Hardy cast an anxious glance at the sky every little while. He knew the signs of brooding storm and the peculiar haziness above the horizon indicated an approaching snowstorm. However, he said nothing, in the hope that they would be able to reach the mouth of the river again before the storm broke.

It was four o'clock before the Hardy boys and their chums reached Shallow Lake. It was a picturesque little body of water and the ice shone with a blue glare, smooth as glass and free of snow. It was a natural skating rink, and Chet Morton gave a whoop of delight as he went skimming out upon it.

The boys enjoyed skating on the lake so greatly that they scarcely noticed the first few flakes of snow that drifted down from the slaty sky, and it was not until the snowfall became so heavy that it almost blotted out the opposite hillsides that they thought of going back.

"Looks as if it's settling down for the night," Joe remarked. "We'd better start back before we get lost."

"Might as well," agreed Chet Morton, with a sigh. "I wish we'd come out here this morning. I'd like to skate here all day."

With Frank Hardy in the lead, the boys began to make their way toward Willow River, where it left the lake. They were about half a mile out on the open expanse of ice and the snow was now falling heavily. At first the soft white flakes had merely drifted down. Now they came scudding across the ice, whipped by a rising wind.

"It'll be harder getting back," Frank said. "The wind is against us."

The wind was indeed against them and it was rising in volume. It came in quick, violent gusts, storming sheets of snow down upon them, snow that stung their faces and erased the scene before them in a white cloud. Then it blew steadily, with increasing force. The storm moaned and whistled about them. They could scarcely see one another, save as dark, shadowy figures skating steadily on toward the gloomy line of hills that rose from the haze of storm.

"Why, this is a regular blizzard!" Chet Morton shouted.

As though in emphasis, the wind shrieked down upon them with re-doubled fury. The snow was swirling across the flat surface of the lake in great white sheets. The cold became more intense. It became apparent that in a few minutes even the near-by shores would be blotted from view.

"Let's make for the shore!" called out Frank. "We'll wait until it blows over."

There was a high cliff not far away, and Frank judged that it would provide shelter from the brunt of the storm until they should be able to continue their journey. Clearly, it was inadvisable to go on, for the wind was against them and they were making little headway. Also, in the fury of the sweeping snow it was possible that they might become separated. So they turned toward the cliff, that they could see dimly through the gray gloom.

The wind shrieked. The snow beat against them. The sharp flakes stung their faces, swept into their eyes. The hurricane seemed like a mighty wall, forcing them back. Doggedly, they skated on, into the face of the blizzard that seemed to be sapping their strength.

Chet Morton already was lagging behind. The snow was collecting on the ice in little heaps and banks that clogged their skates and made progress even more difficult.

The face of the cliff seemed a long distance away. And, with redoubled fury, the wind came howling down over the hills.

Frank was almost exhausted by the constant battle against the wind and snow, and he knew that the others, too, were tiring quickly. It would be death for them if they faltered now. They must reach the shelter of the cliff!

CHAPTER II

A CALL FOR HELP

Doggedly, the boys fought their way on through the blizzard.

Once Joe Hardy stumbled and fell prone in the snow. He was up again in a moment, but the incident testified to the difficulty of their progress. The cliff seemed no nearer. To add to their peril twilight was gathering and the gloom of the blizzard was intensified.

"We've *got* to make it," Frank muttered, gritting his teeth.

The boys were strung out in single file, Chet Morton in the rear. All were tiring. Frank skated more slowly to give the others an opportunity of catching up. When they were together again he waved his arm toward the gray mass that loomed through the storm ahead.

"Almost there!"

His words gave all of them new courage, and they redoubled their efforts. In a short while the force of the wind seemed to be decreasing. They were now gaining the shelter of the cliff. The snow had not collected so heavily on the surface of the ice, and they made better progress. In a few minutes they had skated into an area of comparative calm. They could still hear the screaming of the wind, and when they looked back the entire lake was an inferno of swirling snow, but in the shelter of the steep rocks they were protected from the full fury of the blizzard.

"Some storm!" grunted Chet, as he skated slowly to the base of the cliff and sat down on a frost-encrusted boulder.

"I'll say it is," agreed Jerry Gilroy, following Chet's example.

The Hardy boys leaned against the rocks. They were safe enough in this shelter unless the wind changed completely about, which was unlikely. With the approach of darkness it was growing colder, but all the boys were warmly clad and they had few fears on that score. Their chief worry was lest the storm should not die down in time to permit of their return to Bayport that night, because they knew their people would be worrying about them.

"I see where mother won't let *me* go skating again," declared Chet. "She's always afraid I'll get drowned or lost or something, and now she'll get such a scare that I'll never get out again."

"Aunt Gertrude will crow over this for a month," Joe put in. "She said before we started that we'd be sure to get into some kind of a mess."

"Well, we'll just have to wait here until the storm blows over, that's all," said Frank philosophically. "Even if it does get dark we can follow the river all right and get home easily enough. Perhaps the storm won't last very long."

The boys settled themselves down to wait in the lee of the high black rocks until the fury of the blizzard should have diminished. There seemed to be no indication that the storm was dying down and they resigned themselves to a wait of at least an hour. Frank scouted around in search of firewood, planning to light a blaze, but any wood there may have been along the shore had long since been snowed under and he had to give up the attempt.

While the boys are thus marooned by the storm in the shelter of the cliff it might be best to introduce them to new readers of this series.

Frank and Joe Hardy, sixteen and fifteen years old respectively, were the sons of Fenton Hardy, an internationally famous private detective, living in Bayport, on the Atlantic Coast. Although still in high school, both boys had inherited many of their father's deductive tendencies and his ability in his chosen profession and it was their ambition to some day become detectives themselves.

Their father had made an enviable name for himself. For many years he was with the New York Police Department, but had resigned to accept cases on his own account. He was known as one of the most astute detectives in the country and had solved many mysteries that had baffled city police and detective forces.

In the first volume of this series, "The Hardy Boys: The Tower Treasure," Frank and Joe Hardy solved their first mystery, tracing down a mysterious theft of jewels and bonds from a mansion on the outskirts of Bayport after their father had been called in on the case and had been forced to admit himself checkmated. The boys had received a substantial reward for their efforts and had convinced their parents that they had marked abilities in the work they desired to follow.

The second volume, "The Hardy Boys: The House on the Cliff," recounted the adventures of the boys in running down a criminal gang operating in Barmet Bay, and in the third volume, "The Hardy Boys: The Secret of the Old Mill," they aided their father materially in rounding up another gang.

The volume just previous to the present volume, "The Hardy Boys: The Missing Chums," told how they sought their chums, Chet Morton and Biff Hooper, who had been kidnapped by a gang of crooks and taken to a sinister island off the coast.

As the boys waited in the shelter of the rocks they talked of some of the adventures they had undergone.

"This is the first bit of excitement we've had since we left Blacksnake Island," declared Chet. "I thought we were never going to have any adventures again."

"This isn't much of an adventure," Frank said, smiling, "but perhaps it's better than nothing. Although I must say it's a mighty cold and uncomfortable one," he added. "I wonder if we'll ever have any adventures like the ones we've gone through already."

"I think you've had your fill," grumbled Jerry Gilroy. "You've had more excitement than any other two fellows in Bayport."

"I suppose we have. Like the time the smugglers caught dad and kept him in the cave in the cliff and then caught us when we went to rescue him."

"And the time we got into the old mill and found the gang at work," added Joe.

"Or the fight on Blacksnake Island when you came after Biff Hooper and me," Chet Morton put in. "You've had enough adventure to last you a lifetime. What are you kicking about?"

"I'm not kicking. Just wondering if we'll ever have anything else happen to us."

"If this blizzard keeps up all night you can chalk down another adventure in your little red book," declared Jerry. "That is, if we don't freeze to death."

"Cheerful!"

"It doesn't look as if the wind is dying down, anyway."

They looked out into the swirling screen of snow. The wind, instead of diminishing, seemed to be increasing in fury and the snow was even sweeping in little gusts and eddies into their refuge at the base of the rocks. The swirling snow hid the opposite shore of the lake completely and the howling of the wind was rising in volume.

Suddenly they heard a strange crashing noise that came from directly overhead.

All looked up, startled.

"What was that?" asked Chet.

The crashing noise continued for a moment or so, then died away, drowned out by the roar of the wind and the sweep of the snow.

"Perhaps it was a tree blown over," suggested Jerry.

"A tree wouldn't make that much noise," Frank objected. For the crash had been unusually loud and prolonged and it had seemed to be accompanied by the snapping of timbers.

The boys waited, listening, but the sound had died away.

"It was right above us," Joe said.

Hardly had he spoken the words than there came a second crash, louder than the first, and then, with a rush and a roar, a great avalanche of snow came hurtling down upon the boys from the side of the cliff. The snow engulfed them, swept over them, almost buried them as they struggled to avoid it. Then, in all the uproar, they heard another thundering crash close at hand.

Spluttering and struggling to extricate themselves from the avalanche of snow that had swept down from above, the boys could scarcely realize what had happened. As for the origin of the crashing sound they had heard, it was still a mystery.

Then, above the clamor of the gale that seemed to rage in redoubled volume, they heard a faint cry. It came from the fog of swirling snow close by. Then the shrieking wind drowned the sound out, but the boys knew that it had been a cry for help.

Frank struggled free and lent Joe a helping hand until they were both clear of the great heap of snow and ice. Chet Morton and Jerry Gilroy also fought their way clear without difficulty, for the snow was soft and the avalanche had not been of great proportions.

"I heard some one call," Frank shouted. "Listen."

Shivering with cold, the boys stood knee-deep in snow and listened intently.

There came a lull in the gale.

Then, faintly, they heard the shout again.

"Help!" came the cry. "Help! Help!"

It came from somewhere immediately before them, and as the wind shifted just then Frank caught sight of a dark object against the surface of the snow.

"Come on!" he shouted to the others, and began plunging through the snow over to the object he had spied.

The boys reached it in a few minutes. To their unbounded astonishment they found that they were confronted by the side of a small cottage!

CHAPTER III
JADBURY WILSON

In amazement, the Hardy boys and their chums stared at the cottage that had so strangely appeared in the snow.

"How did that get here?" shouted Chet Morton.

Frank waved his hand toward the top of the cliff.

"There was a little cottage up there," he told them. "It must have been blown off by the wind."

This, indeed, had been the case. Sheltered by the cliff, the boys had no adequate realization of the immense force of the hurricane. The little cottage at the top of the cliff had received the full brunt of the wind and had finally succumbed to the gale and to the force of a sudden avalanche of snow from farther up on the hillside. It had no foundation, and it had been swept away bodily.

The boys fought their way through the deep snow and inspected the little house. It had come through the terrific ordeal with surprisingly small damage. One side had crumpled under the force of the impact and the building was canted over at a precarious angle. But the roof and the other three sides were unbroken, thanks to the soft snow which had lessened the shock of the fall.

"There must be some one inside," Joe said. "Some one was shouting for help."

Frank found the door of the cottage and tried to open it, but it was jammed, as the house was not standing upright. Then he discovered a window, the glass of which was shattered, and with assistance from the others he made his way inside.

The interior of the place was wrecked. In the dim light Frank could see the broken boards and shattered timbers, the broken glass, the upturned stove, the smashed furniture—but there was no sign of any human being.

"Doesn't seem to be any one here," he called out to the others.

Just then he heard a sigh. It came from beneath an upturned cot at one side of the room. He investigated and saw a hand emerging from beneath the cot. In a few minutes he had raised the small bed and found an old man lying face downward on the floor.

"Help me out!" muttered the old man feebly.

Frank called to the others, and one by one they came scrambling through the window. Together, they raised the old man to his feet and set him down on the cot, which they turned to an upright position again. Painfully, the old fellow rubbed his aching joints.

"No bones broken," he said, at last. "I'm lucky I wasn't killed."

"You might have been crushed to death," Frank interposed.

"It's lucky you boys were near," he said. "I'd have frozen to death if I'd been left pinned under that cot. I mightn't have been found for days. But it takes a lot to kill Jadbury Wilson. I guess my time ain't come yet."

The old man looked around and smiled feebly at the lads. He was small but sturdy of frame, with kindly blue eyes and a gray beard.

"I've often thought it was dangerous to live in a place at the top of a cliff like that," he said. "There've been times when the wind was so strong I was afraid it would pick up my house and lift it clean out into the lake. But, somehow, it always stood up until today. It all came so suddenly I hardly knew what was happenin'. Mighty good thing the house landed right side up. How did you lads come to be near by?"

"We were on a skating trip and we got caught in the storm," Frank told him. "We took refuge at the foot of the cliff and we were standing there when we heard the crash. Then we heard some one call."

"That was me. I didn't think there was any use of hollerin', but I hollered just the same, although I didn't think there was a human soul within three miles."

Jadbury Wilson got up off the cot, but subsided back with a groan of pain.

"I got banged and bumped around too much," he said. "Thought I'd get busy and try to straighten things up around here."

"We'll do that," said Jerry Gilroy promptly.

"Everythin's pretty well smashed up," observed the old man. "But you could mebbe fix up the stove so it would work again. Looks as if we're all here to stay until the storm blows over."

The boys made Jadbury Wilson comfortable on his cot and then they set to work to restore some semblance of order to the interior of the little cabin. They managed to patch up openings in the walls through which the snow was drifting, and although one side of the cottage had collapsed completely there was still sufficient room in which to move about. They nailed a tarpaulin over the broken window, righted the table and chairs and picked up the tin dishes that were scattered about on the floor. The stove gave them most trouble, but they were able to set the stovepipe up again and light a fire so that before long a comfortable warmth began to pervade the interior of their shelter.

Jadbury Wilson, lying on the cot, approved of their efforts.

"We're in out of the storm, anyway," he said. "That's the main thing. And from the sound of that wind, it ain't as yet dyin' down any."

Frank Hardy drew aside the tarpaulin and looked out. It was dark now, and with nightfall the blizzard seemed to have increased in volume. The wind beat against the sides of the cabin, the snow swished madly against the roof.

"We're marooned here for the night," he told his chums.

"It could be worse," remarked Joe. "We're lucky to be under cover."

"I'll say we are," declared Chet. "Might as well make the best of it."

"How about eating?" demanded Jerry.

"You'll find tea and bread and bacon in the cupboard," said Jadbury Wilson. "I'm feelin' sort of hungry myself."

The boys rummaged about in the cupboard, which was undamaged, and found provisions. The water had been spilled, but Frank melted some snow on the stove and after a while had the kettle boiling. The fragrant smell of frying bacon pervaded the cabin and in due time supper was served, all doing full justice to the meal. Afterward, they washed the dishes and set about making themselves comfortable for the night.

Jadbury Wilson possessed but the one narrow cot, so the boys saw they would be obliged to sleep on the floor of the cabin. However, the old man had plenty of blankets, and it was decided to have each lad stand watch for two hours in order to keep the fire going. In spite of the fact that the bitter wind swept through chinks and crannies in the cabin walls, the place was comfortably warm, the fire radiating a good heat in the confined space.

Jadbury Wilson was disconsolate.

"Troubles never seem to come one at a time," he groaned, lying on the cot. "This is the finishin' touch."

"Have you been having bad luck, Mr. Wilson?" asked Frank, sympathetically.

"I've had nothin' but bad luck for more'n a year past now. This is the worst blow yet. I'll never be able to put this house back on the cliff again."

"Oh, perhaps it isn't as bad as that," said Joe cheerfully. "You might have been badly hurt. There's that to be thankful for."

"I suppose you're right, lad. I suppose you're right. I ought to be glad I'm still alive. But when you're gettin' old and poor and you ain't able to work like you've been used to and everythin' seems to be goin' against you, it ain't so easy to keep cheerful."

The old man seemed so down-hearted that the boys did their best to console him, but this final disaster to his humble cottage had proved a hard blow. He lacked the resiliency and optimism of youth.

"There was a time when I should have been worth lots of money," he told the boys. "And if I had my rights I ought to be worth lots of money today. But here I am, with not many years ahead of me, livin' away out here alone in a little two-by-twice cabin, and now the wind has to come along and blow it into the lake. It don't seem fair, somehow."

"What do you do for a living, Mr. Wilson?" asked Chet Morton.

"I've been doin' a bit of trappin' and huntin' lately," the old man replied. "Most of my life I've been a miner. I've traveled all over the country."

The boys were at once interested.

"A miner, were you?"

"Yep. I've been in Montana and Nevada in the early days."

At mention of Montana the Hardy boys glanced at one another. Jadbury Wilson did not seem to notice.

"I've been in the Klondike in the rush of ninety-eight and I've been up in Cobalt and the Porcupine, too. Made a little money here and there, but somehow somethin' always happened to keep me out of the big winnin's. If I had my rights I ought to be worth plenty. But it's too late now," he sighed. "It's too late for me to start out on the trails again. I ain't young enough now."

The boys were sorry for the old man, but after a while he was quiet and soon his heavy breathing indicated that he had fallen asleep.

"I hope Aunt Gertrude and mother aren't worrying too much," said Frank, as he prepared to undertake first watch.

"It can't be helped," said Joe, wrapping his blanket around him. "We'll be able to get back tomorrow."

"We might take the old man with us," Chet suggested sleepily. "He is pretty well bruised and battered, and he won't be able to live here until the cabin is fixed up again."

"That's a good idea." Frank put another stick of wood in the stove. "You have next watch, Chet. May as well get all the sleep you can."

In a few minutes there was scarcely a sound in the cottage save the crackling of the fire. The timbers of the building creaked and groaned as the night wind hurled itself against the fragile shelter. Snow slashed against the roof. Frank Hardy shivered. He was glad they had obtained even this refuge from the blizzard.

CHAPTER IV

A TALE OF THE WEST

Next morning the storm still raged, and although its fury had somewhat abated the snow was still falling so heavily and the wind was still blowing with such intensity that the boys decided to wait in the shelter of the wrecked cabin in the hope that the blizzard would die down. They were comfortable enough where they were and, after they had eaten breakfast, they even began to enjoy their predicament as an adventure which their school chums would envy.

"The worst of it is," commented Chet, "that today is Sunday and we're not getting out of one day of school. Unless," he added, hopefully, "the storm keeps up for another couple of days."

"I don't think it'll be that bad," Frank laughed.

Jadbury Wilson was feeling somewhat more cheerful, although it developed that his bruises and injuries sustained when his house was blown off the cliff were more serious than had been at first apparent. No bones were broken, but he was black and blue in many spots and unable to rise from his cot without pain. However, he was philosophic enough to regard the mishap as part of his lot in life and it was easily seen that the company of the boys cheered him up immensely.

"I've had so much bad luck already," he told them, "that it don't seem like much worse could ever happen to me."

"What kind of bad luck?" asked Joe, scenting a story.

"All kinds of it," the old man replied. "When I was out in the West in the early days it looked at one time as if I'd be a regular millionaire. And then my bad luck set in and it's follered me ever since."

"Did you find any mines?" asked Frank.

"In Nevada, we did. Me and my two partners—brothers they were, by the name of Coulson—prospected about for nigh on a year without findin' anything. Then, one day, just when our grub was runnin' low and it looked as if we'd have to give up, while I was cuttin' some firewood for the mornin' my axe-handle broke and the blade of it went flyin' about a dozen yards away. When I went over to pick it up I found it had gone smash against a rock and chipped some of the surface away."

"And you found gold?" asked Joe eagerly.

"That there little accident uncovered a fine vein of gold. So we started to work it and we staked our property and was gettin' along fine when some smooth strangers heard about it and come out to see what we had. Well, with half an eye they could see we'd made a real find. We was so joyful about it that we didn't try to hide it much. And that's where we made our mistake. You can't trust nobody where gold is concerned."

"What happened?"

"Those smooth chaps went back to town and got a slick lawyer to work with them and one night they come out and jumped our claims. Of course we laughed at 'em. for we knew we'd been there first, but we soon found out what we was up against. That lawyer made out that we hadn't registered our claims right, and he dragged out the case until all our money was gone and we couldn't afford to fight it any longer. And the judge gave a decision against us and we lost our mine."

"Gosh, that was crooked!" remarked Jerry audibly.

"Of course it was crooked! But what could we do? We had to pack up and get out. That there mine was later worth millions, although the joke was on the crooks after all, for their lawyer horned in on the property and worked it so that he got most of it in the long run."

"What did you and the Coulsons do then?"

"We was pretty well discouraged. We just hung around town for a while, but later on we packed up and got clean out of Nevada. We didn't want to be near anythin' that'd remind us of how near we'd been to bein' rich. So we went to Montana."

"Prospecting?"

"Prospectin'. And there we went through all the disappointments of huntin' for gold all over again. We managed to get a fellow to grubstake us and we went out into the mountains and spent almost a whole autumn searchin' high and low for some good ground, but nary a trace of gold did we find. But just as we was about to give up again, Bill Coulson struck it and we figgered that *this* time we would be able to hold on to it. We had a good block of claims and off one of them I got a nugget that prospectors told me was one of the biggest ever seen in that part of the country."

"Well," continued Wilson, "we took mighty good care that we registered our claims *right* that time, and we stayed there all winter and in the spring got down to business. We mined the place ourselves, the three of us. There was a syndicate made us an offer but it didn't seem high enough. A fellow named Dawson, who had been prospectin' with us for a while in Nevada, showed up at the camp one day, down and out. He had been havin' hard luck too and he was broke, so we took him in with us, for he was a good fellow and he had stood by us when things wasn't goin' well in Nevada."

"Our little mine was all right for a while, but after a time it began to peter out. We had four bags of gold by that time, some of it in big nuggets, but we didn't know whether to cash in and use the money to buy new machinery and sink a deep shaft or not. We were in our camp one night talkin' things over and wonderin' just what to do about it when we heard some one prowlin' around among the rocks.

"I went to the door and opened it, and just then I saw a flash in the dark and then I heard a gun go off. I jumped back into the cabin quick and I could hear the bullet go plunk into the wood at the side of the door. Next minute there was a regular gunfight under way. A gang of toughs from town had heard about our gold and had come up to rob us.

"Well, sir, they surrounded our camp half the night and it looked as if we was out of luck. There was the four bags of gold, everythin' we had in the world, and there was them bandits outside, ready to shoot us if we showed our noses out the door. And our ammunition was givin' out too. We knew we didn't have much chance.

"Finally, Dawson said the only thing to do was for one of us to try and get outside and hide the gold. There was no use hidin' it in the cabin, for they'd be sure to find it. He volunteered to try and reach the mine and hide it underground somewhere. So we figgered it out and decided that was our only chance. Mebbe the bandits might catch him and get the gold, but if we kept it in the cabin they'd be sure to get it anyway, so we figgered we'd better risk it.

"Dawson had lots of nerve. That's one thing I'll say for him although I'll never forgive him for what he done afterward. He had nerve, and somehow I could never believe he really meant to double-cross us at the time. We waited until the shootin' had died down, and along about three o'clock in the mornin', when everythin' was mighty dark, Dawson let himself out the back window. He got out all right, and nobody saw him, and how he ever got through the ring of bandits around the place I never could tell. He had the four bags of gold with him, and mighty heavy they were too. The last we knew, he was creepin' across the rocks toward the shaft. And that was the last we ever saw or heard of him."

"He ran away?" exclaimed the boys.

"He just cleared out. And he was a fellow any of us would have trusted right to the last. But it only goes to show you can't trust nobody when there's forty or fifty thousand dollars' worth of gold in his hands. We never heard of him again."

"But what about the bandits?"

"After we thought Dawson must have hidden the gold all right, we waited till mornin' and then hung a white handkerchief out the window and gave ourselves up. The bandits came swarmin' in—there was about ten of 'em. One of them was only a young chap, 'Black Pepper' they called him, for his real name was Pepperill. He was only a young chap, but a tougher and more cold-blooded fellow I never hope to meet. When they searched the cabin and found that Dawson was gone and the gold with him they was as mad as a nest of hornets. They raved and turned the whole cabin upside down huntin' for that gold, but it didn't do them no good. The gold was gone. So finally they went away, and we set out to hunt for Dawson. But he was gone.

"He wasn't in the mine, although we found footprints down on one of the levels that looked like his, but we couldn't find him anywhere. And there was no gold. Well, even then we couldn't imagine he'd cleared out on us and we waited around there for nearly a week tryin' to find him and hopin' he'd show up sometime. But he never showed up. He had just cleared out."

"That was a dirty trick!" exclaimed Joe indignantly.

"We didn't mind losin' the gold so much. It was thinkin' we'd trusted him so much. He was the last man on earth I'd have thought would do a thing like that. Bill and Jack Coulson, my pardners, they just *wouldn't* believe it of him. But after a while we knew we'd never see him, and although we tried to trace him it was no use. We heard from a prospector a few weeks later that he'd seen Dawson in a minin' camp up North, but that was the last we ever heard of him. He'd gone up and called him by name, but Dawson just looked at him kind o' funny and said he must be mistaken and that his name wasn't Dawson at all. So I guess that sort of proved he was crooked."

"And the mine?" asked Frank.

"It wasn't no good after that. We worked it a few months longer, but it had petered out and the syndicate wouldn't take a chance on it and we didn't have any money to work it any more. So we abandoned it and went away. We had to split up partnership. I prospected around Montana five or six years more but didn't make any more lucky strikes.

"The last I heard of Jack Coulson he was supposed to be dead, and as for Bill he sort of gave up prospectin' and left the mining camps for good. I've never seen either of them since. I went up on a couple of gold rushes in other parts, but I was always too late. I guess it was just my bad luck. I've never had any good luck since. So finally I come East and I've been livin' up here for the last few months, just makin' a living as best I could. And now look—" he gestured to the interior of the wrecked cabin. "Bad luck's still follerin' me."

The boys gazed at the old man in silence. His story of misfortune had made a profound impression upon them. Ill-luck had certainly pursued him relentlessly.

"The storm's dyin' down," said Jadbury Wilson at last. "You'll be goin' back to the city, I guess."

"But how about you?" asked Frank.

"I'll just have to stay here and make the best of it. I can build a new cabin, but I'm not goin' to build it on top of the cliff this time. I'll build it back in the wood where the worst that can happen is havin' a tree fall on it."

"But you won't be able to work for a few days yet," Joe pointed out.

"That's true," admitted the old man. "I can't even get up off this cot right now."

"You'll have to come to town with us. Have you got a sled here that we could draw you in on?"

"I got a sled all right. But what's the use? There's no place for me to go when I do get into town. I ain't got no money."

"You can stay at our place," declared Frank. "I know mother won't mind. You can stay there until you get on your feet again."

"I'm sure it's mighty good of you," said Wilson gratefully. "But I don't like to be intrudin' on people."

The old man's simple independence won the boys' admiration. But Frank and Joe knew it would be impossible to leave him alone in the wrecked cabin in his present condition. It was unthinkable.

"You'll come with us," Frank said, with determination. "Let's get the sled ready, fellows."

CHAPTER V

CON RILEY UNDER FIRE

The blizzard died down as suddenly as it began, and when the Hardy boys and their chums left the cabin they found that the snow had ceased falling and that the sun was shining brightly.

They found Jadbury Wilson's long sled tied to the outside of one of the cabin walls. It had been unharmed, and it did not take the boys long to place blankets upon it and make the old man comfortable. They had to assist him out of the cabin, so greatly did his injuries pain him. He had two pair of snowshoes, and Chet Morton and Jerry Gilroy donned them, the Hardy boys being content to trudge along in the deep snow of the lake.

In a short time they had left the cabin and were making their way toward Willow River, pausing frequently to rest because the deep snow soon wearied them. However, when they reached the river they found that they made better progress because the stream was protected by high wooded banks and the snow had not drifted as deeply as on the lake. But it was mid-afternoon before they reached the road leading into Bayport.

From there on their progress was easy, and, dragging the sled with Jadbury Wilson wrapped in his blankets, they at length reached the Hardy home on High Street. Here they were all welcomed by Mrs. Hardy and Aunt Gertrude, who had been frantic with anxiety concerning the boys' whereabouts.

"We were going to send out a searching party for you!" exclaimed Mrs. Hardy, as she kissed her sons and sent Chet and Jerry in to telephone to their parents the news of their arrival.

"I knew they'd get lost. I told them so!" declared Aunt Gertrude vigorously. But if she had a scolding in store for them she soon forgot it in her immediate concern over Jadbury Wilson, whom Chet and Jerry brought into the house.

When the Hardy boys explained the situation and told of their adventures and the reason for their delay, Mrs. Hardy was insistent that Jadbury Wilson should make his home with them until he could be on his feet again.

"You'll certainly have to stay with us!" she said. "There's plenty of room."

"I'm sure I'm most thankful to you, ma'am," said the old prospector humbly.

As for Aunt Gertrude, she was already scurrying about the kitchen making hot ginger for the new guest and when it was ready she stood over Jadbury Wilson until he had drunk the last drop.

Then the boys put him to bed, and as the old man relaxed into the warm blankets he sighed and remarked that it was the first time in five years that he had experienced the comforts of a soft mattress.

Jerry and Chet hastened home, wondering a little what would be said to them. But their people were so relieved at seeing them again that they forbore to lecture the lads, and, all in all, they came through the ordeal better than they had expected.

"Back to school tomorrow!" grumbled Joe, at supper that night.

"Oh, didn't I tell you?" said Mrs. Hardy.

"Tell us what?"

"There won't be any school tomorrow."

"What?" shouted the boys incredulously.

"You should say, 'I beg your pardon?'" corrected Aunt Gertrude acidly. Mrs. Hardy smiled.

"I thought you'd be surprised," she said. "And I suppose you'll be almost heartbroken. No, there's to be no school tomorrow. Last night's blizzard was one of the worst in the history of Bayport. The wind was so strong that it wrecked the high school roof."

Joe gave a whoop of delight and danced around his chair.

"There's nothing to cheer about that I can see," sniffed Aunt Gertrude. "They say the property damage was very bad and it will take about two weeks before the roof is fixed."

The news proved too much for the Hardy boys. Like most youths of their age, the unexpected prospect of a winter holiday filled them with delight. Mrs. Hardy smiled at them indulgently, for she had not forgotten her own schooldays.

Aunt Gertrude began laying down the law to the effect that the boys must pursue their studies at home quite as ardently as though the school had been undamaged, and on the following day she actually did insist that they do two hours' studying before they got out in the morning.

When the boys finally made their escape and raced to the nearest hillside with their bobsleds they found most of the students of the Bayport high school already there. Tony Prito, Phil Cohen, Biff Hooper, Chet Morton and Jerry Gilroy were on hand, as well as many of the girls.

Callie Shaw, of whom Frank Hardy was an ardent admirer, and Iola Morton, sister of Chet and the only girl who had ever won an approving glance from Joe Hardy, were hilariously bobsledding and looking unusually pretty in gaily colored sweaters and woollen toques, their eyes sparkling and their cheeks flushed with the cold.

For half an hour or more the sliding continued, the boys having the time of their lives, and then Nemesis appeared on the scene in the person of Officer Con Riley.

Now, as old readers know, Riley was the sworn enemy of the youth of Bayport. A stolid, thick-set individual with more dignity and self-importance than brains, he took the responsibilities of his position on the Bayport police force very seriously. He had the view, too common to the type of elderly people who have forgotten that they once were young, that all enjoyment is sinful and that all young people are continually up to mischief.

So, when Con Riley saw the merry party on the hillside he recollected an ancient and obsolete city ordinance forbidding bobsledding elsewhere than in the parks. This ordinance had originally been passed to prevent youngsters sliding down hills adjacent to the trolley tracks and thereby endangering their lives. The fact that there were no trolley tracks near this particular hill mattered nothing to Officer Riley.

Majestically he stood at the bottom of the hill and held up his hand. Sled after sled pulled to a stop and Officer Riley, the personification of the majesty of the law, ordered the fun to cease.

There was nothing to be done. Officer Riley had the authority, and he knew it.

"Well," said Chet Morton grimly, "we'll just have to have our fun some other way. Let's have a snowball fight."

Officer Riley looked dubious and produced a little notebook which he perused earnestly. He knew Chet Morton and his mischievous proclivities of old. But although he looked through the rules and regulations hopefully he could find nothing to prohibit snowballing. However, he withdrew to the street and paced slowly up and down in the faint hope that perhaps a stray snowball might break a near-by window, in which case he would have a delicious opportunity to interfere once more with the sport.

Chet gathered his cohorts and talked earnestly for a few minutes. Then, with many giggles, his followers set to work building two snow forts directly opposite one another. The forts were merely rude snow embankments, just sufficient to provide protection for the opposing sides. Then the young people began rolling snowballs.

So far, so good. Officer Riley was unable to detect anything wrong in this. Still, the fight had not started. There was still the hope of a shattered window pane.

Majestically, he paced to and fro, keeping a wary eye on the snow forts and the gaily clad figures behind the banks. Then, to his surprise, he saw Chet Morton walking slowly toward him.

Officer Riley eyed Chet suspiciously. The fact did not escape him that Chet had one hand behind his back.

"Aha!" he muttered. "A snowball."

He was right.

Hardly had the suspicion crossed his mind than it became a frigid reality.

Chet seemed to aim at one of the forts. But his foot appeared to slip and the snowball smacked Con Riley's helmet with deadly accuracy, knocking it off into the snow.

Riley emitted a roar of rage and astonishment. Snow was trickling down his neck. He stooped merely long enough to pick up his helmet and thrust it back on his head, where it rested at a ridiculous and rather precarious angle.

Then he gave chase to the rash youth who had thus tempted his wrath.

Chet went ploughing through the snow, directly in between the forts. Con Riley plunged recklessly in pursuit. Even yet he did not suspect the trick, did not suspect that Chet was merely luring him on to destruction.

Not until a second snowball whizzed past his head, not until a third smacked wetly against his ear, did he realize that he had plunged neatly into a trap.

He floundered about in snow up to his knees, and from either side came a volley of snowballs. They squashed against his helmet, knocking it off again, they thumped against his uniform on every side. No matter which way he turned, flying snowballs met him. And the boys took good care to keep their faces out of sight.

"Stop it!" he roared.

But the merciless bombardment continued.

He made a frantic rush toward one of the forts, but the snow was too deep to permit of rapid progress and the air seemed full of white missiles. One snowball caught him in the eye and stopped his rush momentarily. He wavered. More snowballs caught him in the rear. He turned around and a concerted bombardment opened up from each fort. Officer Riley decided that discretion was the better part of valor and he ignominiously retreated.

As for Chet Morton, he was safely ensconced behind a particularly heavy snowbank, laughing until the tears came to his eyes. When next he peeped out he saw that Officer Riley, having retrieved his precious helmet, was making great speed back toward the comparative safety of the sidewalk. With the greatest dignity that he could command under the circumstances, he brushed the snow off his uniform. Then, sadly, he resumed his beat, and headed toward the downtown part of Bayport, where citizens were more law-abiding and where snowballs were unknown.

The Hardy boys and their chums saw their enemy disappear around the block, and then Chet rose to the top of the ramparts and gave a cheer of victory.

"'We have met the enemy and they are ours!'" he quoted.

A snowball from the opposite fort struck him on the ear and he sat down abruptly.

Then the fight began in earnest. It was not until Chet had personally led his warriors out of their fortress and across the no man's land between to win a glorious victory over the other army and had personally washed the face of the marksman who had ruined his triumphant cheers that peace was restored. Then, the forts having been demolished, the bobsleds were pressed into service again, and the hill rang with shouts and laughter until nightfall. For Officer Con Riley made it his business to attend to duties downtown for the rest of the day.

CHAPTER VI

A MESSAGE FROM MONTANA

When the Hardy boys returned home that night after their afternoon's fun and sat down to an ample hot dinner of steak and onions, with mashed potatoes, thick gravy "and all the trimmings," as Jadbury Wilson expressed it, they found that the old miner had won a firm place in the household. He was able to be up and around again, although he hobbled painfully about, but his tales of the early days in the mining country of the West had won the interest of the women.

Mrs. Hardy was particularly interested when he talked of Montana, because of the fact that her husband was in that particular state at the time.

As for Aunt Gertrude, she was in a constant condition of solicitous excitement seeing that the old man was comfortable. And comfortable he was. It was a treat to see him relax in an easy chair after dinner, puffing contentedly at the pipe that he never allowed out of his sight.

In the evening Frank and Joe besought him to tell again the story of how he had been so basely cheated of his fortune in the West, and the women listened entranced to the strange tale.

"Do you mean to tell me that that wicked man actually ran away with all the gold you had worked for so hard?" exclaimed Aunt Gertrude indignantly.

"Looks that way, ma'am!"

"The scoundrel! I just wish I had him here for a minute. I'd tell him a few things!"

"I'd tell him a few things myself," said Wilson mildly. "Still, it was a great many years ago and there's no use thinkin' about it now. The gold's gone and I'm an old man."

"It's a shame!" said Mrs. Hardy.

"I guess I couldn't have been much use as a prospector, or I'd have been able to hold on to what I got," observed Wilson. "I've come to the conclusion that a man gets pretty much what he deserves in this world. If he ain't smart enough to hold on to what he's got, he deserves to lose it."

"Didn't you make anything out of your mining days at all?" put in Frank.

"Oh—a few dollars here and a few dollars there. Enough to keep me in grub and with a place to sleep. Once in a while I'd make some extra money, but it never lasted long somehow. I got a claim out in Montana yet, so far as that goes."

"Is it worth anything?"

Jadbury Wilson shrugged and stroked his beard.

"Maybe worth much—maybe worth nothing," he said.

"Can't you find out?"

"I haven't got enough money to work the property. It's the only claim I've been able to pay my dues on, all these years. But I kept payin' 'em. sort of hoping somethin' would turn up some day. I've always thought it *should* be a good claim. It's in a good location. But I've never had enough money ahead to do any more work on it."

"Can't you get any one to finance you?" asked Joe.

"Not me," sighed the old man. "All through Montana I got the reputation of bein' too unlucky. They're afraid to take a chance on me any more. They say, 'Why, that's Jad Wilson's claim. Even if it is good, he's always been so all-fired unlucky that we'll be bound to lose our money!' So they pass it up."

"Never mind. Perhaps you'll come into your own some day," said Mrs. Hardy comfortingly.

"It'll have to come mighty soon, then," replied the old man, with a wry smile. "I've waited so long now that it seems I'll be dead and gone before my luck starts to turn."

However, under the influence of the warm fire and the cheerful company his natural optimism manifested itself and he was soon entertaining his new-found friends with stories both humorous and tragic of his adventures in the early days of the rough-and-ready mining camps of the West.

"I'd love to go out there!" said Joe wistfully.

"It ain't all beer and skittles," said Jadbury Wilson. "There's quite a bit of adventure, but there's a lot of rough livin' and mighty skimpy eatin' at times. I've often seen the day when all my flour and beans would be gone and the grocer wouldn't trust me for another nickel's worth. And, of course, the West has changed a lot nowadays. It's got mighty civilized, they tell me."

"Our father is out in Montana now," Frank remarked.

"You don't say! And whereabouts in Montana is he?"

"He's at a mining camp. It's a place called Lucky Bottom."

Jad Wilson's eyes widened.

"Lucky Bottom!" he exclaimed. "Can you beat that?"

"Why?"

"Lucky Bottom is right near the place where Bart Dawson run away with all our gold."

"Isn't that a strange coincidence!" cried Mrs. Hardy.

"It shore is," agreed Jad Wilson. "Mighty strange. To think that he should be in the very place where we lost our fortune. It's a small world, ain't it?"

"What kind of place is Lucky Bottom?" asked Frank.

"It ain't very big. In the old days it was a real rough-and-ready minin' camp, with dance-halls and saloons. Then, as the mines got worked out and the miners went on up into the copper fields, the town sort of dwindled away. It's a sort of ghost camp nowadays, I guess. Nobody there but a couple of store-keepers and a few miners who keep pluggin' away still hopin' to find some gold that somebody else has missed."

Jadbury Wilson rubbed his eyes and smothered a yawn.

"You'll have to pardon me, ma'am," he said to Mrs. Hardy, "but I've always been used to goin' to bed at dark and it ain't often I sit up so late jawin'. If you don't mind, I think I'll turn in."

"'Early to bed and early to rise—,'" quoted Aunt Gertrude, with approval.

"'Makes a man healthy and wealthy and wise,'" finished Jadbury Wilson, with a wry smile. "Well, I been gettin' up early and goin' to bed early all my life and it's never made me wealthy and I'm mighty sure I ain't very wise. About all it's done is to make me healthy. You couldn't kill me if you belted me over the head with a church."

He bade them good-night and went upstairs to bed. Aunt Gertrude remarked that the Hardy boys would be well-advised to follow the old man's example in the matter of early retirement, but they sat up for almost an hour before the fire, talking over some of the yarns the old miner had recounted.

"He sure had some great experiences," said Frank, before they went to sleep that night.

"You bet he did. I wish we could get out there for a while."

"It probably wouldn't be the same now. He said the country has got pretty tame."

"It can't be so tame when they have to call dad out there in their gold-stealing cases. There must be some excitement left."

"Oh, well, there's not much chance of us getting out that far to find out. Go to sleep."

But in the morning a surprise awaited them. When they came down to breakfast they found Mrs. Hardy already at the table, perusing a yellow sheet of paper.

"Telegram?" said Frank.

Mrs. Hardy nodded.

"It's from your father."

"Is he coming back?"

"Not yet. As a matter of fact, he wants you boys to go out to him at once."

Frank and Joe looked at one another incredulously. The news seemed too good to be true. Mrs. Hardy handed over the telegram.

It read:

> Please let Frank and Joe come to me at once. Will send special word and instructions to Majestic Hotel, Chicago.
>
> Fenton Hardy.

"What on earth can this call mean?" exclaimed Frank, in complete amazement.

"I can't understand it at all," admitted their mother. She was frankly worried.

"I don't care whether I understand it or not," said Joe. "It means he wants us to go out West, and that's enough for me. When can we start?"

"The telegram says 'at once,'" Mrs. Hardy remarked. "It seems very strange. And so sudden, too. I wonder what on earth he can want you for?"

"Perhaps he needs our help on that case he's working on," Frank suggested.

Aunt Gertrude, who had hitherto taken no part in the discussion, sniffed audibly.

The Hardy boys were so excited that they could hardly eat their breakfast. All through the meal they jubilantly discussed details of the proposed trip and when Mrs. Hardy, although admittedly worried at the prospect of letting them go so far by themselves, agreed that they might go immediately, as the telegram suggested, they flung themselves into a feverish orgy of packing.

Jadbury Wilson was highly interested and gave them a number of excellent suggestions as to what they should take with them on the trip.

"Lots of good, heavy underclothes and plenty of woolen socks," he said. "You'll find it plenty colder out there than it is here."

The boys got their reservations on a train that would leave for Chicago late that afternoon. Their packing occupied more time than they had expected because they did not want to be burdened by too much luggage and had a difficult time eliminating the nonessentials. At last, however, they were ready. Aunt Gertrude, who had kept up a running fire of instructions and admonitions concerning their conduct on the journey, and who freely predicted disaster in the shape of train wrecks and robbers, gave them her final instructions. Mrs. Hardy, who merely kissed them good-bye and told them to write to her as soon as they reached Chicago, called a taxi to take them to the station, and Jadbury Wilson, warning them to be on the lookout for "them city slickers in Chicago" and advising them not to talk to strangers, told them not to worry inasmuch as he would look after their mother and Aunt Gertrude.

The taxi arrived. The luggage was tossed in. The boys scrambled into the back seat. Aunt Gertrude shrieked "Good-bye" a dozen times and sobbed audibly. Their mother waved a handkerchief. Jadbury Wilson brandished his cane. Then, with a roar, the taxi sped down the street and headed toward the station. Already the boys could hear the long-drawn whistle of the train.

"Off for Montana!" exclaimed Frank.

"I'm afraid of only one thing," remarked his brother.

"What's that?"

"I'm afraid I'll wake up and find I've been dreaming."

CHAPTER VII

IN THE WINDY CITY

The Hardy boys had never been on a long train journey before, and the trip, consequently, was replete with interest for them. As the train left Bayport behind and began speeding through the open country with its snow-covered fields, they felt a sense of elation and freedom.

"This is certainly better than school!" declared Joe, settling back in his seat with a sigh of contentment.

"Sure is. Chet Morton and the rest of the gang will be just about sick with envy when they hear where we've gone."

"I wish we could have them with us. When do we reach Chicago?"

"Some time tomorrow. Won't it be dandy to stay on the train all night!"

They watched the scenery that seemed to flash past as though on a moving scroll until gradually twilight fell and the lights in the Pullman were turned on. They went into the dining car, where they were served by a man with an air of elaborate courtesy. The novelty of eating an excellent and perfectly served dinner while speeding swiftly across country appealed to them, and when they had finally risen to their feet and left a tip for the waiter, Joe was of the opinion that he could imagine nothing better than living this way all the time.

"When I grow up, if I have money enough, I'll just live on the trains," he said solemnly.

"You'd soon get tired of it."

"Not me!" And not until the novelty of the long journey began to wear off did Joe admit to himself that possibly such an existence might be wearisome in the long run.

They slept the sound slumber of healthy youth and were up early next morning for the first breakfast call. There, at their table with its immaculate linen and gleaming silverware, they did justice to crisp bacon and golden eggs, the meanwhile looking out the wide windows at the murky chimneys and dark masses of factory buildings as the train entered the outskirts of a large city. The train roared across viaducts and they could see trolleys and automobiles speeding to and fro in the city streets in bewildering confusion. For the first time they began to have some appreciation of the real extent of their country.

"I guess Bayport isn't the only city in the States," said Frank, with a smile.

"It looks pretty small compared to some of these that we've gone through."

But as the morning passed they wearied at last of looking at the scenery, varied as it was, and toward mid-afternoon they began to be impatient for a sight of Chicago. When, at last, the train began to roar through the suburbs of the Windy City, as a friendly porter called it when they had failed to understand his reference to it as "Chi," they felt a mounting excitement. But the train rushed in past seemingly endless rows of houses, then past miles of industrial buildings overhung with a cloud of murky smoke, until they thought the center of the city would never be reached.

The journey came finally to an end. Their porter was on the platform with their grips, they tipped him for his services during the trip and made their way down the crowded pavement, through the gates into the concourse of the enormous station. Here they gazed about in frank wonderment at the bustling hordes of people, all intent on their own affairs, moving to and from the trains. The constant sound of shuffling feet, buzzing voices, clanging bells, all the varied noises of a great railway station, sounded like the roar of the ocean in their ears.

They made their way outside and clambered into a waiting taxi, directing the driver to take them to the hotel their father had mentioned in his telegram. In a short time the car drew up at the entrance, after a brief ride through crowded, noisy streets that made the main street of Bayport seem like a country lane on Sunday afternoon by comparison. A bellboy seized their grips and the boys presented themselves at the desk.

The clerk glanced at their names after they had signed.

"Ah, yes!" he said. "Frank and Joe Hardy. Your room has been reserved for you. And there is also a letter, I believe." He reached into a pigeon-hole in a compartment near by and produced a letter which he tossed over to them. He struck a bell smartly. "Front! Show these gentlemen to 845."

Feeling highly important at being referred to as "gentlemen" and at having a bedroom actually reserved for them in a hotel of such grandeur, the Hardy boys followed a military-looking bellboy to the elevators, whence followed a swift ascent to the eighth floor. Then down wide, silent corridors to their room, a substantial, bright and airy room with bath. It was all a revelation to the lads, who had never been in a big hotel before, and when they looked out the big windows down on the thronging life of the city streets below they were excited beyond measure.

"First of all, we'll read dad's letter," said Frank. "These are the instructions he promised, I suppose."

He opened the envelope and read:

My Dear Boys:

I could have given you all the instructions that were necessary in the telegram I sent to your mother, but I thought it best that you come to Chicago first and have a little rest before resuming your journey. This would also give me a chance to tell you more about the mission I have decided to send you on. The truth of the matter is, I have been hurt, and am now laid up in a miner's cabin and have been unable to continue my investigations in the case I have in hand. For this reason I am calling on you to help me, for I think I can trust to your abilities by now by reason of the assistance you have given me in other cases. I did not want to worry your mother needlessly, which is the reason I did not mention my injury. It is not serious but it will be some time before I am able to be on my feet again, and, in the meanwhile, time is precious.

In my investigations here I have discovered a secret concerning some stolen gold. It is this matter that I wish you to investigate for me. To do so it will be necessary for you to come to Lucky Bottom, Montana, at once. Have a good night's rest at the hotel and then come on here. I am under the care of a miner by the name of Hank Shale, and when you reach Lucky Bottom any one will be able to tell you where to find his place. I shall be expecting you, so do not fail me. I hope you have a pleasant trip. Do not worry about me, as I am in good hands and progressing favorably.

Your dad,
Fenton Hardy.

Frank put down the letter, with a low whistle.

"So that's the reason he called for us!" he said. "Dad's been hurt."

"He says it isn't very serious."

"It's serious enough when it means he's not able to be on his feet. Perhaps we ought to start out to him right away."

"Not much use of that," objected Joe. "We wouldn't gain much time and we'd be so tired when we got there that we wouldn't be of much use to him for a day or so. I think we'd better rest here tonight, as he suggests, and go on tomorrow."

Frank considered his brother's advice sound, and, after enjoying a good dinner, the boys went out and wandered about the busy streets for almost an hour, enjoying the sights of the Windy City. But it was a cold, bitter evening, and they soon sought the warmth and comfort of their hotel again, going to bed early, because they were tired after their long hours on the train.

They were told by the information clerk that their train would leave at eleven o'clock the following morning. This gave them plenty of time for a good sleep, a bath and a leisurely breakfast. When all their preparations for the continuation of the journey had been made they presented themselves at the desk in the lobby to check out. Frank paid the bill, and the boys were just about to move away from the desk when a neat, elderly man somewhat below medium height, came up to him.

"Are you the Hardy boys?" he asked, glancing quizzically at them.

"Yes."

"I was told to be on the lookout for you," said the elderly man. "My name is Hopkins."

"Who sent you, Mr. Hopkins?" asked Frank politely.

"I am your father's lawyer—that is, in Chicago," said the neat little man. "He sent me a telegram last night asking me to look you up here and do what I could for you. I have arranged for your transportation as far as Lucky Bottom. That's where you are bound, isn't it?"

"Yes, that's the place."

"Well, then," said Mr. Hopkins, "if you'll come with me I'll see that your accommodations are ready for you. I made the arrangements with the railway this morning."

Reflecting that they were certainly obtaining first-class service on their trip across country, the Hardy boys accompanied Mr. Hopkins across the lobby and out to the street, where a taxi was waiting. The porter put their luggage inside and Mr. Hopkins got in with them, directing the driver to the station.

"Your father is an old friend of mine," said the lawyer, "and I'm only too glad to be of service to his sons. I handle a great deal of his Chicago business for him."

Although the Hardy boys had not been aware that their father had a great deal of Chicago business, they were properly appreciative of Mr. Hopkins' kindness, and when they finally reached the station and he guided them through the gates to the train they expressed their thanks for what he had done for them.

"It's nothing—nothing," he said brusquely.

"We can hardly look at it that way," replied Frank.

Mr. Hopkins, absorbed in the details for the boys' comfort, did not answer. Instead he turned and said:

"Porter—how about Compartment B?"

"All ready, sah! All ready!" the porter assured him, leading them to the compartment. "All ready, sah, jes' as yoh asked."

"We're traveling in style," murmured Frank, nudging his brother.

CHAPTER VIII

THE SECOND STRANGER

Mr. Hopkins bustled about the compartment, making everything comfortable for the Hardy boys and chatting affably.

"You'll be looked after right until you reach Montana," he said. "You won't have to change trains. There'll be no bother."

"We're very grateful to you—" began Frank.

The little lawyer dismissed their thanks with a gesture.

"It's no trouble at all," he said. "No trouble at all. Your father would do as much for me any day."

From out on the platform they heard the stentorian cry, "All Aboard!" Mr. Hopkins glanced at his watch.

"I'll have to go," he said quickly. Then, without waiting to say good-bye, he dashed out of the compartment, slamming the door behind him in his haste.

The Hardy boys settled back in the comfortable seats as the train began to move. They looked out the window as they emerged from the great train-shed and then they were occupied gazing at the city streets as the locomotive picked up speed and roared on its way.

In due time the train passed through the outskirts of Chicago, then it rushed on through open stretches of country, past little towns and villages. It was an express that evidently stopped only at the larger cities.

"At this rate it won't take us long to reach Montana," Frank remarked.

"We're sure making good time."

"What do you say to going out and sitting in the observation car for a while?" Frank suggested. "It's roomier than this compartment."

"Suits me."

Frank went to the door. To his surprise he found that it would not open. He tried again, but the door refused to budge.

"That's funny," he remarked. "We're locked in."

Both the boys tried the door, but it was of no avail.

"The catch must have been on when Mr. Hopkins went out," Frank said. Even yet the real truth of the situation had not dawned on them.

They hammered on the door for a while, but no one heard them. At last Frank caught sight of the bell button.

"That's stupid of me," he said, with a smile. "I should have known there'd be a bell to call the porter."

He pressed the button and waited. No one came. There was no sound but the roar of the train as it rushed on its way. He pressed the button again and again.

"That porter must be either dead or asleep," he muttered, settling down to a prolonged ringing of the bell.

After what seemed an interminable length of time they heard a shuffling of feet in the corridor. The sound of the steps ceased, and some one rapped at the door.

"Something for you, gentlemen?"

"Yes—let us out of here!"

The porter tried the handle of the door.

"By golly," he observed, "you done locked yourselves in."

"We didn't lock ourselves in. Somebody locked *us* in. Haven't you got a key?"

"Just a minute."

They heard the porter shuffling away. After a while he returned with the sleeping car conductor, a key clicked in the lock, and then the door swung open.

"How on earth did that happen?" asked the conductor, mystified. He looked at the porter accusingly. "Did you lock these boys in there?"

"No, sir! No, sir!" protested the porter. "I had nothin' to do with it, sir! They come on at Chicago with an older man, and I showed 'em to the compartment and that's all I know about it."

"I don't think the porter had anything to do with our being locked in," explained Frank. "It was an accident. Our friend Mr. Hopkins slammed the door on his way out, and the catch must have been on without our knowing it. It's perfectly all right."

"I got their tickets all right," said the conductor.

"Yes, sir. I collected those tickets myself. The old gentleman with these boys gave 'em to me. Two tickets to Indianapolis, sir."

"To where?" asked Frank, in amazement.

"Indianapolis."

"But we're not going to Indianapolis."

"That's where your tickets read to."

The Hardy boys looked at one another in consternation.

"But we're going to Montana. Didn't Mr. Hopkins give you tickets to Lucky Bottom, Montana?"

The conductor produced some tickets from his pocket and glanced through them. "Even if he did," he remarked, "they wouldn't be any use on this train. We're bound south, not west. No," he concluded, "your tickets are here, Compartment B, and they read Indianapolis."

"We've been tricked!" declared Frank hotly. "Mr. Hopkins said he had been sent to look after us and that this train would take us right through to Montana."

"And then he locked the door on you so you wouldn't go around making inquiries until it was too late," added the conductor. "Your friend certainly put one over on you. But I'm afraid we can't do much for you now. We're quite a distance out of Chicago, and this train doesn't stop for another hour yet."

"Another hour!"

"That's the best we can do."

"Well," said Frank, disgusted, "I guess we'll just have to wait and get off at the first stop, and then take the next train back to Chicago. This will hold us up another day on our trip."

"Sorry," said the conductor sympathetically. "Of course it isn't our fault. We couldn't know you were supposed to be going West."

"No, of course not. It was Hopkins. He planned the whole thing from the start. Oh, well!" Frank shrugged. "We might as well wait."

He and Joe went back into the compartment and sat down again. This unexpected development left them silent and discouraged. Too late now, they saw that the astute Hopkins had deliberately sought to prevent them from joining their father in Montana. He had worked the trick very neatly, and it might easily have happened that the boys would not have discovered the deception until they reached Indianapolis had it not been for the chance remark of the porter. For that, at least, they were thankful.

"Dad's enemies mustn't be very anxious to have us reach Montana, if they'll go to these lengths to sidetrack us," said Joe, at last.

"We'll get there if we have to walk," Frank replied grimly.

They had no further enjoyment of the scenery. Each flitting telegraph pole meant that they were drawing farther away from Chicago and losing so much more time in resuming their journey to the West. At length the train began to slow down and, looking out, they saw that they were approaching a small railway town with an immense water tank.

The porter came to the door of the compartment.

"Here's the first stop," he told them. "You can get a train back to Chicago from here!"

He took their luggage and, when the train came to a stop, the boys got out onto the platform.

"Now I wonder how long we'll have to wait before we get a train back," remarked Frank.

His eye caught a bulletin board in front of the little station and he went over to it. At length he found what he sought, a late train bound for Chicago, and he almost groaned as he noted the time.

"There won't be a train along for five hours," he reported to Joe.

"Good night!"

"That means we've got to cool our heels around here until dark. Five solid hours."

Dolefully, they confronted the bulletin board. A young man in a heavy ulster and tweed cap was also studying it. He glanced toward them.

"What's the trouble?" he asked.

"Isn't there any earlier train to Chicago than that?"

The young man shook his head.

"I'm afraid not," he said. "I guess you're out of luck. In a hurry to get there?"

Frank nodded.

"That's too bad. But say—," the young man reflected a moment. "If you motored over to Greendale you'd be able to catch an earlier train. There's another railroad passes through there."

"If we can catch an earlier train, that's the train we want," said Frank decidedly. "How far away is Greendale and how do we get there?"

"It's about twenty miles across country. I'm motoring over there myself right now. You're welcome to come along with me if you wish. I'm just waiting until the line is clear so I can put through a telephone call."

"Do you think we can make the train at Greendale all right?"

"Oh, yes. I'm sure of it. There's a train leaves for Chicago in about an hour and we'll be there in plenty of time. There's my car beside the platform. Put your grips in it and I'll be along in a few minutes."

The young man went into the waiting room and the Hardy boys saw him go into a telephone booth to put through his call. Frank and Joe, congratulating themselves on this lucky turn of events that had saved them from a dreary five-hour wait, went over to the touring car the young man had indicated and put their grips in the back seat. In about five minutes their new-found friend emerged from the waiting room.

"All set?" he asked. "I made inquiries about your train and you'll be able to make it all right. Hop in."

He insisted that they sit in the front seat with him, as there was plenty of room. "I like company when I'm driving," he said cheerfully, and this removed the last vestige of reluctance in the Hardy boys' minds, as they had been slightly afraid that they might be proving themselves bothersome to the stranger.

He was a skilful driver and the roads were good. The big touring car sped along the highway and they left the village behind, racing out into the open country. The young man at the wheel said little, beyond an occasional remark about the weather or the condition of the roads.

Not until they were at least ten miles from the town did the boys have a suspicion that anything might be wrong. That was when the young man turned the car suddenly off the main highway down a lonely road. The car lurched heavily to and fro in the deep ruts.

"I thought you said the other town was on the main highway," said Frank.

"I know the way," retorted the man at the wheel gruffly.

Something in his tone made the Hardy boys suspicious. Frank glanced at his brother and he could tell by his expression that Joe did not like the situation either.

Some distance ahead they saw an object parked directly across the road. It was an automobile, and it effectually blocked their passage.

"Somebody wrecked, I guess," said their driver carelessly. He began to slow down. Frank, who was on the outside of the seat, groped under the flap in the door until his fingers encountered a heavy wrench. He was not going to be caught altogether unprepared.

The car came to a stop. From around the front of the other automobile came three unsavory individuals, unshaven, with peaked caps pulled low over their foreheads.

"Now," said the young man beside them, suddenly whipping out a pistol, "you'll just come along with us."

He leveled the weapon directly at the Hardy boys.

CHAPTER IX

THE ESCAPE

Frank Hardy wasted not a second.

Before the man with the automatic pistol could realize what he was doing, Frank had flung up his hands sharply, at the same time releasing his grip on the wrench. It spun straight and true, knocking the automatic out of the fellow's grasp, and the weapon clattered to the floor of the car.

When Joe saw that their antagonist was unarmed, he rose halfway up in the seat and launched himself upon the driver. Frank, in the meantime, reached for the pistol. He was unable to find it, but his fingers closed over the wrench again.

There was a yell of surprise and rage from the three men in the road, and they rushed toward the car. One of them came plunging along the side and attempted to grapple with Frank, but a sideways swing of the wrench caught him on the right of the head, and he staggered back with a yelp of pain.

Joe was still struggling with the driver of the car. The latter was at a disadvantage in that he had been caught unawares. The loss of his automatic had flustered him, and Joe's sudden onslaught had taken him completely by surprise. Penned in by the wheel, he was unable to use his superior weight to advantage, and Joe seemed all over him, pounding him unmercifully.

One of the other toughs leaned over the side and seized Joe by the back of the coat. The man who had been hit with the wrench was dancing about in pain and keeping at a respectful distance. The other fellow was attempting to close in on Frank. He sprang forward, just dodged a sweeping blow of the wrench, and then wrestled with the boy.

They swayed to and fro. The tough was of husky build and his gorilla-like arms were possessed of great strength. The door of the car flew open and the pair staggered from the running board into the roadway. They rolled about, fighting and struggling, while the man who had been hit with the wrench took occasion to deliver a vicious kick at Frank. A sudden twist, however, brought the other man into range at the moment and he received the kick that was intended for the boy.

But the Hardys were outnumbered. Joe was quickly overcome and the other pair would soon have beaten Frank into submission but for a surprising interruption.

Down the roadway came a clattering and roaring, and around the other car came plunging an ancient and decrepit Ford with an enormous black man at the wheel. Beside him sat another black man, and the pair gazed at the struggle before them, with mouths agape and eyes staring. Then the man driving the car brought it to a stop and clambered down, picking up the car crank as he went.

"You're the speeders what run over my chickens!" he roared, bearing down on the two toughs who were grappling with Frank. He dealt one of them a hearty rap on the back of the head with the crank, and the fellow bolted forthwith. Reinforcements had arrived, and he judged that the fight would soon be over. He raced for the car parked across the road and scrambled into the front seat.

The two black men rushed into the battle with enthusiasm. The three toughs in the other car had, it appeared, deliberately driven their automobile into a flock of chickens at the side of the road near the man's farm farther down the road. Revenge, therefore, was sweet.

In a very short time the fight was at an end. The toughs broke and fled, regained their car, and were soon careering down the road. As for the young man who had brought the Hardy boys into this trap, he managed to get his own car started, shook off his attackers, and his automobile plunged forward.

"Let them go," said Frank, picking himself up out of the ditch.

"If they run over any more of my chickens, I'll follow 'em from here till Doomsday," declared the big man.

"You certainly showed up in the nick of time," said Joe, brushing off his coat. "They had us beaten two to one."

"White trash!" declared the other man. "I know their kind. Just poolroom toughs."

"How come they were layin' for you way out here?" asked the big man curiously.

"The chap driving the touring car was going to drive us out to a town called Greendale so we could get a train back to Chicago," Frank explained, and telling the man where they had got into the automobile. "He turned down this road, and then we met the other three waiting for us. They all jumped us at once."

"No trains pass through Greendale!" declared their rescuer. "If you wait there for a train for Chicago, you'll wait years and years, and even then you won't get no train."

"We'll have to go back to that town then," said Joe.

"That's where we're goin'. Get in, and we'll drive you back to the railway."

Glad to have gotten out of the scrape thus easily, the Hardy boys clambered into the rickety Ford and the two men men resumed their seats in front.

"Soon's I see that car across the road, I knew it was the same car than run down my chickens!" declared the driver. "And when I saw them fightin' with you boys, I knew they wasn't up to no good, and I knew what side I was gonna take. And I took it."

"Yessir, we sure put the run on them!" chuckled his companion.

"A mighty good thing for us that you showed up when you did," Frank declared. "That gang was trying to kidnap us."

"How come?"

"They've been trying to keep us from catching a train to the West, and they nearly got away with it that time."

"Well, they won't harm you no more—not so long as you're in *this* car," the big man assured them. And, as the car bounded along onto the main highway, the Hardy boys discussed the trap into which they had been so cleverly led.

"It'll teach us to beware of strangers from now on," Frank said. "Evidently one lesson isn't enough."

"If a stranger says so much as 'Hello' to me after this, I'll yell for the police," Joe added.

"Perhaps not that bad," and Frank grinned. "But we know now that there is a plot on foot to keep us from reaching the West, and we'll have to be on our guard."

"I'm more anxious than ever to get to the West now. It looks as if we're heading into some real excitement."

"We've had more than we bargained for already."

* * * *

In a short time, the automobile came within sight of the town the boys had left but a little while before, and after warmly thanking their two rescuers and slipping a five-dollar bill into the hands of the big driver, who beamed with gratitude and delight, the Hardy boys settled down to wait for the night train back to Chicago. They were bothered by no more encounters with strangers, and after an almost interminable wait, the train arrived.

"One day lost on our journey," remarked Frank as the train pulled away from the station and headed northward.

"It could have been worse. If those fellows had captured us, we'd have likely been held prisoners in some out-of-the-way place for ever so long."

"That's true, too. Well, we won't take any more chances. When we get to Chicago, we'd better change our names and our appearance, too, if we can manage it. If these chaps are on the lookout for us, they won't stop now that we've escaped from them twice. We can't be too careful."

Joe agreed that his brother's idea was a good one, and for the rest of the tedious journey back to Chicago, they whiled away the time by discussing ways and means whereby they might journey to the West without being identified readily as the Hardy boys by the mysterious enemies who seemed determined to prevent them from joining their father.

CHAPTER X

ON GUARD

Back in Chicago, the Hardy boys went to a hotel. They were careful not to go to the place at which they had stayed on their first arrival.

"Hopkins has likely been told of our escape by now and he may be on the lookout for us," said Frank. "We'll just stay under cover."

"That should be easy enough in a big city like Chicago."

"It's not so easy if they know where to look for you, and I don't think they'll give up yet. For some reason, they're evidently mighty anxious to keep us from getting out to Montana."

In their hotel room that night they discussed the problem of changing their appearance. They had already changed their names, registering as Charles Norton and William Hill of Cleveland, Ohio, in case some prowling member of the gang that had evidently been assigned to see that they did not reach Montana should happen to drop into the hotel and glance over the register.

"I think," said Frank, "that the very simplest way for us to disguise ourselves would be to wear spectacles. If they chance to be looking for us they'll never think of looking for two boys wearing glasses."

"Good idea!" approved Joe. "Let's go out and get them now."

"Too late now. Shops will all be closed. We'll get them in the morning."

They left the hotel early and found a shop near by where Frank was fitted with a pair of horn-rimmed glasses that gave him a studious and benevolent expression. Joe bought a pair of cheap spectacles with plain rims. The transformation was remarkable. Instead of a pair of merry, bright-eyed lads, one saw two solemn, near-sighted boys who looked for all the world as though they had never had an unrestrained boyish impulse in all their lives.

"By all rights we ought to carry some books under our arms, too," Joe suggested.

So, to make the transformation complete, they stopped at a bookstore and purchased two weighty volumes. And, when it came time for them to catch their train, no one would have recognized in the two, sad-faced, bespectacled, earnest young students, the irrepressible Hardy boys of Bayport.

To allay suspicion, they decided to board the train separately. Frank went first, while Joe remained in the concourse of the station for a few minutes. Then he followed.

It was just as well that they did this. Near the gate leading to their train loitered a tall, sharp-featured youth who scrutinized every one who passed. He gave Frank but a fleeting glance as he went by and when Joe passed him later his gaze merely rested casually on the boy for a moment.

Had the Hardy boys but known it, the sharp-featured youth had been deputed by the mysterious Hopkins to report if the Hardy boys should attempt to leave Chicago. However, his instructions had been to keep on the lookout for two boys, aged sixteen and fifteen respectively, one dark, the other fair, who would board the train together. So the bespectacled students who had boarded the train separately did not arouse his suspicion and after the train pulled out he reported to Hopkins that the Hardy boys were certainly not on it.

Having left Chicago behind them at last and being assured that they were this time on the right train, Frank and Joe settled down to await with some little impatience their arrival in Lucky Bottom. The novelty of the cross-continent journey had worn off and the scenery had lost some of its earlier fascination. The unforeseen delay they had experienced left them all the more eager to join their father, and they wondered if he would worry because of their failure to arrive in Lucky Bottom at the expected time.

Gradually the scenery changed. The countryside altered in contour. The landscape became rockier and more mountainous, and on the second day they found themselves entering Montana. A suppressed excitement seized them as they realized that before long they would be at the end of their journey.

"I wonder how dad came to be hurt," Joe said, after reading over their father's letter again.

"I've been thinking about that, myself," said his brother. "From what we've gone through, I'd judge that he has enemies working against him in this case he is working on."

"Do you think they may have shot him?"

"They might have disabled him in some way. He was able to write to us, anyway. There's that much to be thankful for."

The Hardy boys realized that if a gang were arrayed against them, as seemed only too evident from their experience in Chicago, they must be very much on their guard from now on, as they drew closer to their destination. This was forcibly impressed upon them by an incident that happened at a small station in the mountains, where the train stopped to take on water.

"I think I'll take a walk up and down the platform," remarked Frank. "Coming?"

Joe looked up from his book.

"No, thanks. I think I'll stay here and read."

Frank left the coach and strode slowly up and down the platform. It was only a small, weatherbeaten station and there were few people in evidence. The town consisted of only one street, and it was built at the base of a huge mountain. The snow came sweeping down from the great crags in shifting sheets.

A rough-looking man in fur hat and mackinaw lounged down the platform, then swung himself up into the train. He appeared to be looking for some one. When Frank saw him next he was descending from one of the coaches far ahead. He came back to the platform again and there he was joined by another man, a villainous looking fellow with a black beard.

"Did you see anything of them Hardy boys?" asked the bearded man in a low tone of voice.

Frank, who was standing close by, could not help but overhear. He was electrified by astonishment.

The man who had gone through the train shook his head.

"Nary a sign of 'em on that train," he said.

"I can't figure out what happened," said the bearded man. "They ain't been on any train that's passed through here—we're sure of that."

"This here is the only way they can get to Lucky Bottom. If they did manage to sneak out of Chicago we'd be sure to see 'em goin' through here."

"Mebby they didn't get out of Chicago. The boys there might have picked up their trail again and caught 'em."

"They would have wired us if they had."

"That's true, too." The bearded man scratched the back of his head in perplexity. "I can't figger it out at all. Well, it ain't *our* fault. We've done the best we could."

"Yeah, they can't blame us."

"You're sure you went all through the train?"

"Right through. There was no two boys on it. There was one lad sittin' in the Pullman readin' a book, but he wasn't like the description of either one of 'em. Wore glasses. Looked like he was a regular little willy-boy."

"Wore glasses, eh? Well, he wasn't one of the Hardy boys, then. They don't wear glasses."

The pair moved off down the platform.

"You'd better go through the night train when it comes in. We'll keep on the lookout for 'em for a few days more until we get word one way or the other. The boss would be sore if they got through on us."

"Well, they haven't got through yet. That's one thing certain." The two men moved out of earshot.

Frank was tingling with excitement. He stepped toward the train, intending to go to Joe and tell him what he had heard. Then he hesitated. The rough-looking man who had searched the train might conceivably think he had been mistaken and might go through the train again. If he saw the two lads together he might be suspicious, spectacles or no spectacles. So Frank sauntered unobtrusively up and down the platform until it was time for the train to leave. Then he swung himself on board, but not until the train was actually pulling out did he rejoin his brother.

"What kept you?" asked Joe, looking up.

Frank sat down and, in a low voice, recounted the incident of the platform. Joe listened in almost incredulous surprise.

"So it looks as though we've run the gauntlet at last," concluded Frank.

"Boy! It was certainly a bright thought of yours that we wear spectacles on this trip. He would have spotted me in a minute."

"It was luckier still that we weren't together when he walked all through the train. If he had told that black-bearded man that there were two boys sitting together they might both have gone back for a second look at us."

"Well, we got out of it all right. I don't think there's anything more to be feared."

"Not until we reach Lucky Bottom."

"I wonder what we'll bump up against there."

"Plenty—by the looks of things so far."

The train continued on its laborious way through the mountains. It passed through little mining villages, abandoned camps, climbing on up to higher altitudes until, late in the afternoon, the Hardy boys heard the cry for which they had been waiting so long.

"Lucky Bottom! Lucky Bottom!"

CHAPTER XI

FENTON HARDY'S STORY

Lucky Bottom was a particularly desolate place in the winter time. It was not especially prepossessing at any season, but when the cold winds blew down from the rocky mountainsides and when snow drifted deep in the narrow street Lucky Bottom seemed like a deserted village. It had once been a prosperous mining camp, but one by one the mines had been worked out until now there was but one left. A few prospectors made the village their headquarters still, hanging on in the vain hope of some day making a lucky strike that would restore the town to its former grandeur, but the general impression prevailed that Lucky Bottom's days were numbered.

There were a few gaunt, hard-bitten individuals on the station platform when the Hardy boys got off the train. They were the only passengers that day and evidently it was unusual for any one to alight at Lucky Bottom, because the loungers stared at them as if they were beings from another world.

"Can you tell me where Hank Shale's cabin is?" asked Frank of one of the men leaning against the station.

The native shifted his chew of tobacco, spat into the snow, and reflected.

"Straight down Main Street," he said. "Then you start climbin' the hill. When you get to the top of the hill you'll find Hank's place. You can see it from here."

He conducted them to the end of the platform and pointed to the top of a hill back of the collection of shacks comprising the town. The boys could see a small log cabin, almost hidden by trees and almost buried in the snow. The distance was not great, so Frank and Joe, after thanking the man who had directed them, started off toward the cabin.

They went through Lucky Bottom, which was nothing more than a collection of shacks and cabins ranged on either side of a wide street, and struck out up the hill until the street came to an end. There they followed a narrow path through the snow until at length they reached Hank Shale's place.

Their approach had evidently been seen, because the door opened as they neared the cabin and an elderly man with heavy, drooping mustache stood awaiting them.

"You the Hardy lads?" he inquired, in a piping voice.

"Yes. This is Mr. Shale's place, isn't it?" returned Frank.

"Come in. Come in," invited Hank Shale, standing aside to let them enter. "We've been expecting you this last day."

The boys entered a small, two-roomed cabin, a typical bachelor's residence, which, however, was kept scrupulously neat. They had barely time to look around before Hank Shale led the way to the adjoining room.

"Your father's in here," he said. "Come along."

They followed the man into the bedroom, and there they saw Fenton Hardy lying on a small cot. He sat up in bed as they entered, and held out his hand.

"Hello, sons!" he greeted them, with his cheerful smile. "Glad to see you."

When greetings had been exchanged, Hank Shale took the boys' coats and hats and began setting the table for supper. Soon the cabin was redolent with the fragrant odor of coffee. While Hank was busy in the other room, the boys had a chance to talk with their father.

"But how did you get hurt, Dad?" asked Frank.

Fenton Hardy leaned back on his pillow with a sigh.

"I cracked two of my ribs," he told them. "Tumbled down off a big rock back in the mountains, and now I'm laid up until the ribs mend again. I'm thankful it wasn't a great deal worse."

"We thought perhaps some one had shot you."

"No, it wasn't that bad. I was chasing a fellow at the time, and if it hadn't been for falling off the rock I would have caught him. So my good friend Hank Shale insisted that I come to his cabin until my ribs set again. It isn't very serious, but it will keep me indoors for a while. That's why I sent for you."

"You want us to take up the case where you left off?"

Their father nodded.

"I'll be able to help you considerably, even if I am laid up," he said. "But what delayed you? We expected you here yesterday."

The Hardy boys glanced at one another.

"You must have enemies that knew we were coming, Dad," Frank said. "They tried to sidetrack us in Chicago. We were delayed a whole day there."

"How was that?"

The boys then told their father of their meeting with the man who called himself Hopkins, of being locked in the compartment on the wrong train, of their fight on the road and of their eventual return to Chicago. When they told him of their simple disguise on the trip westward he nodded approval. When they told him of the rough-looking man who had searched the train for them at the mining village he frowned.

"Just as I expected," he remarked. "Some one must have got their hands on a copy of that telegram I sent you."

"The operator wouldn't give it out."

"No. But they may have tapped the wires. They would know that if I sent a message it would be to bring some one out here to help me. And this gang I have been fighting are capable of anything."

"Who are they?"

"It's a long story, boys. But seeing that you're going to be working on the case, I may as well give you all the information I have. This case concerns a quantity of gold that was stolen from three miners. One of these men, called Bart Dawson—"

"Bart Dawson!" exclaimed Frank and Joe simultaneously.

Their father looked at them in surprise.

"Yes. Do you know him?"

"Why, that's the man Jadbury Wilson mentioned!" Frank exclaimed.

"And who, may I ask, is Jadbury Wilson?"

"We'll tell you later, Dad. It may not be the same fellow, but he mentioned a miner named Bart Dawson. Go on with the story, and then we can tell you about Wilson."

"Well, this chap Dawson called me out here on the case and told me that the gold was stolen from them by a gang of outlaws who have been terrorizing this district for years. The outlaws are known as Black Pepper's Gang."

"Black Pepper! And his real name is Jack Pepperill."

"You seem to know as much about these fellows as I do myself," said the detective, in surprise.

"We'll tell you how we happened to hear about him. It's the same man all right. Go ahead."

"Black Pepper's gang stole the gold from these miners. I discovered that before I'd been working on the case two days. We laid a trap for two members of the gang and managed to capture them. Then we threatened them with imprisonment if they didn't tell where the gold had gone to. They declared that one member of the gang had deserted and had taken the gold with him. The gold was in four bags, and although the outlaws gave chase and finally caught this man, the bags had disappeared. Try as they might, they could not get the fellow to admit where he had hidden it. He denied the theft utterly, said he had seen nothing of the gold, and that night he escaped.

"The outlaws were of the opinion that the gold had been hidden somewhere in a deserted mine shaft. That was the story the two rascals told us, and it was while I was checking up on this story that I was attacked by Black Pepper himself. I managed to fight him off and disarmed him, but he got away so I chased him and it was while I was chasing him that I fell off the rock and cracked my ribs."

"And that's how the case stands now?"

"That's how it stands now. I don't know whether to believe the two outlaws we captured or not. They may have been telling the truth. The gold may have really been stolen by the chap who deserted them. They said he later escaped from them and that they thought he had probably gone back to where he had hidden the gold and made away with it."

"In that case there wouldn't be much chance of getting it again."

"It's that circumstance that makes me suspicious of the story. If the deserter had recovered the gold and cleared out, the outlaws would likely give up hunting for it and they would certainly give up bothering me. But they are still in the vicinity and I have an idea they know just where the gold is and are waiting for a chance to get their hands on it. I think this story about the chap deserting from the gang and making away with the loot is false. They just wanted to throw me off the trail and probably thought I'd give up the case and go back East, leaving them a clear field."

"What is your theory about the gold?"

"I think they know where it is, all right. They have it hidden away safely but they don't dare remove it. They'll wait until the affair dies down and then they'll probably separate and leave this district, meeting somewhere else to divide the loot."

"Our problem is—"

"To find that gold." Fenton Hardy looked steadily at his sons as he said this. "I have a lot of confidence in you," he went on. "It just requires a lot of hard work and keeping your eyes open. Mainly, it will keep the gang on the jump. They'll know we haven't given up the case and they'll be afraid to do anything. And now," he said, "you might tell me how you happen to have heard the names of Bart Dawson and Black Pepper before."

Frank and Joe then told their father of their meeting with Jadbury Wilson, the old miner who said he had once lived in Lucky Bottom. They deemed it best not to mention the fact that Jadbury Wilson suspected Bart Dawson of stealing from him. If Bart Dawson were back in Lucky Bottom they felt safer in reserving this bit of information. They merely told their father that Wilson had mentioned the names of Dawson and Black Pepper, among others, as having lived in Lucky Bottom at the time he had been a miner there.

"What kind of chap is Dawson?" asked Frank.

"One of the finest!" declared their father promptly. "He is a real square-shooter, as the miners would say. The loss of the gold has broken him all up. He told me he had had hard luck all his life and now that he had a fortune within his grasp it was heart-breaking to lose it again."

Frank could not help thinking that life had evidently paid back Bart Dawson in his own coin. He had stolen a fortune from Jadbury Wilson after Wilson had endured hard luck for years. Now he was getting a taste of his own medicine. Still, it seemed strange that Fenton Hardy should be so convinced of Dawson's honesty if he were the type of man who would rob his own partners.

"Come and get it!" piped Hank Shale, from the next room.

"That's the supper call," laughed Mr. Hardy. "You must be hungry after your journey. Better go and eat. Hank will bring me mine in here."

Nothing loath, the two boys went into the combination living room and kitchen, where Hank Shale was already dishing out piping hot beans and stew from an enormous pot. What with huge slabs of bread, thickly buttered, and excellent coffee, the boys sat down to their supper with a will. They ate off tin plates and drank from tin cups, but they agreed that no meal could have tasted better. Even the food of the dining car on the train, exquisitely cooked and served though it had been, seemed somehow to lack the flavor of this meal in Hank Shale's mountain cabin.

Hank, like most men who have lived a solitary existence, was a silent man. He said nothing throughout the meal, but as he watched the boys eat and as he responded to their request for second helpings, a slow smile crept over his wrinkled face.

"That's the best meal I ever ate!" declared Frank emphatically, when he had cleared his plate for the second time.

"Me too," agreed Joe.

"Glad ye like it," said Hank Shale, deeply pleased.

CHAPTER XII

THE CAVE-IN

Next day, refreshed by their night's sleep, the Hardy boys set out on a systematic search for the hidden gold.

"There won't be much real detective work about this case," their father told them. "It will be just a plain case of plugging along and searching high and low for that gold. It is hidden somewhere, or the gang wouldn't be staying around. Hunt in all the abandoned mine diggings, in any place where it might possibly be hidden. You may follow that line or you may try to find where the outlaws are camping and possibly pick up some clues there."

With this to go on, Frank and Joe Hardy left the cabin in the morning. They decided to explore some of the abandoned diggings first.

"It's like hunting for a needle in a haystack," said Frank; "but we might have a bit of luck and stumble on the gold."

They did not go down into the town because they knew that their presence in the camp would cause considerable talk and, although they had little doubt but that news of their arrival had reached the outlaws by now, they preferred to remain under cover as much as possible.

Hank Shale had suggested searching the workings of an old mine just over the brow of the hill, and toward this place they went. There was a faint trail through the rocks, although it had long since been snowed over, but the boys managed to find the workings without difficulty. They felt the exhilaration of the clear, cold air and the excitement of at last being at work on the mystery of the hidden gold.

The abandoned mine did not look very much like a mine. It was just a large pocket in the earth, with a shaft that sank down into the darkness. The shaft was but a few yards across and a rickety ladder led down into the hard rock.

"We may as well try this one for a start," suggested Frank. "We can easily tell if any one has been around recently."

They had brought electric flashlights with them, and without further ado Frank began to descend the ladder. Joe followed. Their descent into the abandoned mine was precarious, as at various places the rungs of the ladder were broken, but after descending about forty feet they came to the first and only level. The mine had evidently been a failure.

In the light of the flashlights they saw that they were in a rocky cavern about two hundred feet in length. Not a great deal of work had been done in the mine and it had evidently been abandoned years before. The boys found the cavern extremely cold and damp and they made haste to explore it.

When they had almost completed the circuit of the place, hunting carefully for any sign of recent removal of rock, for any place where the stolen gold might possibly have been hidden, they were of the unanimous opinion that no one had been in the place since it was originally deserted. There was not the vestige of a hiding place. The abandoned working was but one of many in that locality, one lucky strike in the neighborhood having sent other miners into a frenzy of excavation on their respective claims. It had been worked for a short time and then left to its fate.

"I don't think there's anything here," said Joe.

"I'm sure of it. Oh, well, we couldn't expect to find the gold right off the bat. There are lots of other mines to search yet, and most of them plenty deeper than this."

"Think we should go back?"

"Just a minute. There seems to be a passage here."

Frank's light had revealed a narrow opening at the extreme end of the cavern. He bent down and examined it more carefully.

"This seems to lead somewhere," he said. "I think I'll follow it." He crouched down and made his way on hands and knees into the passage. Joe waited until he had disappeared and then called after him.

"I'll wait here."

"If it leads anywhere I'll call you."

Joe could hear his brother scrambling along through the little corridor in the rocks. After a while the sounds died away. It was dark and lonely in the cavern in which he stood. He waited for Frank's summons to follow.

After five minutes there was still not a sound from the opening into which his brother had disappeared. Joe began to get anxious. He knelt down and flashed his light into the interior of the passage. There was no sign of Frank.

"I wonder if anything has happened to him," he muttered.

When another five minutes passed and there was still no sign of his brother, Joe decided to invade the passage himself. Anything might have happened. Frank might have been overcome by poisonous gases in the depth of the mine. He might have tumbled down some unseen pit and hurt himself. Flashing the light ahead of him, Joe crawled into the narrow corridor in the face of the rock.

For several yards the passage extended directly ahead; then there was a turning. Examining the corridor, Joe saw that it was not a natural opening in the rock, but had been constructed by human hands, for the marks of pick and shovel were plainly visible. It had been blasted out of the rock, and for a short distance the dimensions of the passage were of good size, but gradually they narrowed.

He had just gone past the turn in the tunnel when he heard a faint shout.

"Joe! Joe!"

It seemed to come from a long distance, and there was a note of appeal in it that told the boy his brother was in danger.

Scrambling on through the tunnel that seemed to open before him in the vivid circle of light, he made his way toward Frank. He heard the cry again, and this time it was louder. He shouted back:

"I'm coming. What's the matter?"

"I'm trapped here. My foot is caught."

On through the gloomy tunnel Joe went.

At last the light revealed the form of his brother some distance ahead. Frank was lying flat on the rocky floor of the passage, with his foot caught in a crevice between two heavy boulders. He had tried to climb over them, and one rock had evidently become dislodged, pinning his foot against the other.

"Are you hurt?" asked Joe anxiously, as he reached Frank's side.

"No. I'm all right. But I can't move my foot."

Joe put down the flashlight so that its glare clearly illuminated the scene. Then he went over to the boulder and exerted all his strength to move it. But the boulder was heavy. Had it struck Frank's foot directly it would have shattered it to a pulp. Fortunately, it had merely slid into position above the other rock, pressing against the boy's ankle and imprisoning his foot in the crevice between.

Frank was unable to lend his brother any assistance. He was lying face downward and was unable to rise to a sitting position.

"It's—mighty—heavy!" panted Joe, as he strove to move the heavy boulder. It refused to budge.

"Rest a bit and then try it again."

Joe sat down, breathing heavily.

"How did it happen?" he asked.

"I was crawling along through the tunnel when I saw this pile of boulders ahead. At first I was going to turn back, but I thought that when I had come this far it was foolish to turn around, so I started to climb over the boulders. Just as I was almost over, that big boulder slid down against the other one—and there I was. Lucky I didn't break my leg."

"I'm afraid to move that boulder the wrong way, or it might roll over onto you. There's only one way to move it safely and that is to lift it straight up, just enough to release your foot. But I'm afraid I'm not strong enough."

"Try it again, anyway."

Again Joe applied himself to the heavy rock. Although he strained and gasped in his efforts to move it, the boulder defied his efforts and he was unable to budge it an inch. He made attempt after attempt, but it soon became evident that the effort was beyond his strength, and at last he was forced to sink back, exhausted, against the wall. He mopped his brow.

"Too heavy!" he declared, out of breath.

Frank was silent.

"If we only had a crowbar of some kind!" he suggested at last. "It wouldn't be hard to move it then."

Joe looked up.

"Why, I saw a crowbar back in the mine!" he exclaimed. "It will be the very thing."

"Go back and get it. You'll be able to move the boulder away without any trouble. Then we'll clear out of here."

Joe picked up his flashlight and turned to retrace his steps into the main working of the mine.

"I'll only be a few minutes," he promised.

"Don't worry about me. I won't go away," said Frank, with a laugh. He could be cheerful even in the dangerous position in which he found himself.

Back down the narrow tunnel crawled Joe, back toward the cavern into which they had first descended. He remembered having seen a long iron bar lying at the foot of the shaft and he realized that it would be an ideal lever for moving away the boulder that imprisoned his brother. He made haste, not wishing to leave his brother too long imprisoned, and in a few minutes he was back in the great cave.

At first he could not find the iron bar, and he hunted about, flashing the light here and there into dark corners. At last he found it, near the foot of the shaft. It was quite heavy and one end of it lay beneath a heap of rocks.

Joe tugged at the iron bar.

At first it resisted his efforts. He put all his strength into the attempt and the bar slowly moved. A final tug and it came free so suddenly that he staggered backward.

It was this circumstance that saved his life.

For, in extricating the bar, he had dislodged the mass of rocks. With a rush and a roar they came tumbling down across the bottom of the shaft. Had Joe been standing beneath he would have been crushed to death.

Then, before the clattering had died away, came a sullen, hollow roar from higher up in the shaft. Timbers snapped and crackled. The old boards, long since rotting away, suddenly gave beneath the pressure of rocks and earth. An avalanche of stones descended into the shaft on top of the first downfall of rock. More followed, showers of earth came rushing down and a cloud of dust pervaded the cavern.

Joe leaped back.

Then, with a roar like thunder, the entire shaft caved in. Rocks and timbers came tumbling down with a terrific crash. The air was filled with the noise of smashing timbers and falling rock. The faint light from the shaft that had given some vague illumination to the cave, was blotted out. The mine reverberated with echoes and shook with the force of the crash.

Silence reigned. It was broken by the sharp sounds of falling pebbles that descended in the wake of the avalanche. Then those noises too died away. The cavern was filled with a choking cloud of dust.

Joe was almost stupefied by horror. He realized to the full the peril of the situation.

"The shaft has caved in," he thought. "We're trapped in the mine! We'll never get out alive!"

He turned his flashlight on the place where the shaft had been. The light revealed only a high, sloping hill of rocks and shattered timbers. The shaft was completely blocked. It would take an army of men to clear away the débris.

Joe realized that he and Frank would never be able to accomplish the task. And he knew there was no hope of assistance from outside, for no one knew where they were. It might be days before they were traced to the mine.

CHAPTER XIII

IN THE DEPTHS OF THE EARTH

Joe Hardy still had the iron bar in his hand. He had not relinquished his grip on it.

"That's what caused all the trouble," he said to himself. The sight of the bar reminded him of Frank, still imprisoned back in the tunnel. He knew Frank would have heard the crash and would be wondering what had happened.

"I may as well set him free first and then we can reason out what we are going to do."

He turned and, dragging the heavy bar behind him, made his way to the opening of the tunnel. When he reached it he crouched down and proceeded into the passage.

With the flashlight illuminating the way, he went on toward the place where his brother was imprisoned. He found that the collapse of the shaft had shaken the entire mine. Bits of rock and heaps of earth and dirt along the floor of the tunnel testified to the shock of the cave-in. But when he came to the place where the tunnel turned to the right, he found, to his surprise, that the turning had vanished.

Instead, there was a solid wall of rocks and boulders ahead of him!

At first, Joe could not believe his eyes. Then realization dawned on him. The collapse of the shaft had shaken loose the boulders and rocks that lined the tunnel at this point and they had fallen down to block the passage.

He stared incredulously at the rocky wall ahead of him. He was cut off completely from his brother. Then he shouted:

"Frank!"

There was no answer. His shout echoed and re-echoed in the narrow space of the tunnel.

He shouted again and again, but the echoes were his only answers. Once he thought he heard a faint cry from beyond the wall, but he could not be sure. Communication had been cut off. He realized that his peril was doubled now. With the shaft blocked, with the passageway blocked, he was imprisoned underground in a small space, where the air would soon become foul and where suffocation would eventually end his life. He set his flashlight on the floor of the tunnel, seized the iron bar, and set to work to remove the blockade.

The task seemed hopeless. The rocks were piled up deeply and were so large and so tightly jammed together that it seemed impossible to remove them. Joe knew that if the roof of the tunnel had completely fallen in there would be little hope, as rock would continue to fall as fast as he removed the rock from underneath.

He pried away a huge boulder at the top of the heap and stood to one side as he exerted all the leverage of the iron bar. The great rock wavered, then rolled down the side of the heap into the open tunnel. Joe waited anxiously.

To his relief there was no crash of rock from the top of the tunnel. The removal of the boulder had left a small opening.

He shouted again:

"Frank! Can you hear me?"

A surge of gladness passed over him when he heard his brother's voice in reply:

"I hear you. What's happened?"

"The shaft caved in."

"The main shaft?"

"Yes."

"I heard the crash. I shouted to you but I didn't hear any answer. Are you hurt?"

"No. I'm all right. I jumped back just in time."

"Where are you now? Can't you reach me?"

"The tunnel caved in, too. I'm trying to dig my way through to you."

There was a moment of silence. Clearly, the news came as a surprise to Frank.

"That's bad," he said, at last. "Do you think you can get through?"

"I think so. I have the crowbar with me." Joe attacked another rock on the heap, edging the end of the crowbar into a crevice.

"How bad is the cave-in?"

"Very bad. The whole shaft went."

"That means we'll not be able to get out of here."

"We may find a way."

"Well, try to get through to me first. Then we'll see what we're to do."

Joe continued his labors at the rock pile. One by one he managed to dislodge heavy rocks and boulders until at last he had cleared away an aperture of sufficient extent to admit the passage of his body. He shoved the crowbar ahead of him and crawled over the remaining rocks.

Within a few minutes he had reached his brother, who was lying in the same position in which Joe had last seen him.

"How's the foot?"

"All right," Frank answered. "It isn't hurting any. See what you can do with that crowbar."

Joe inserted the end of the crowbar beneath the boulder, resting the middle of the bar on the boulder beneath. Then, exerting all his strength, he weighed down on the bar.

Slowly, gradually, the great rock began to move.

"It's giving way!" cried Frank. "Just a little more—a little more!"

By means of the bar and the principles of leverage Joe was able to apply much more strength to the removal of the boulder than if he had tried to move it with his bare hands. He shifted his grasp, bore down on the bar again, and the great boulder rose higher.

"Good," declared Frank, dragging himself forward. "I'm free."

He extricated his foot from the crevice and Joe lessened his weight on the bar. The boulder fell back into place again. But Frank was no longer a prisoner.

"That's that!" Frank said, scrambling to a sitting position and beginning to rub his ankle to restore circulation. "I'm out of that little jam, anyway, thanks to you and that crowbar."

Joe sat down on a near-by rock.

"We're up against a worse dilemma now," he said.

Frank looked grave.

"I know it. Still, there may be a way out. You say there's no use trying to get back up the shaft?"

"None at all. The whole place caved in with a crash."

"What caused it?"

"That crowbar had evidently been left there to prop up a weak place in the side of the shaft, and when I moved it, the whole thing gave way. Some of the rocks came tumbling out, and then the side of the shaft caved in. If I hadn't jumped back in the nick of time *my* goose would have been cooked. There must be a couple of tons of rock in the shaft now."

"We couldn't dig our way through?"

Joe shook his head. "We'd be wasting time trying. I guess the only thing we can hope for is that somebody heard the crash and comes to see what happened."

"But they don't know we're down here."

"That's true, too. And they won't be very likely to start clearing away the shaft unless they know we're here. This mine was abandoned a long time ago, by the looks of things."

"They might see our footprints up to the side of the shaft."

"It was snowing when we came here. They may be covered over by now."

The boys were silent. They realized that their plight was almost hopeless. In the cold, dark depths of the earth, with their air supply cut off, they were facing suffocation, exposure and starvation, and there seemed not the slightest possibility of escape.

"The only thing to do," said Frank, at last, "is to keep on following this tunnel. There's no use going back into the mine itself."

"No, there's no use going back. But to my mind I don't think there's any use going ahead, either. This tunnel probably ends in a blank wall."

"We might as well find out. We won't do ourselves any good by just sitting here and waiting to die." Frank got to his feet and picked up his flashlight. "Better turn out your light," he advised. "We need only one light at a time and we might as well be saving the batteries."

Joe got up and did as his brother had suggested.

Frank went on down the passage, followed by Joe. The boys felt in their hearts that there was very little hope that the passage would lead anywhere, but it seemed to be the only possible avenue of escape. They recognized that it was only a "drift" that the miners had dug and blasted away from the main workings in an effort to discover a vein of gold, and the fact that it had not been further developed seemed to indicate that the search had been unsuccessful and that the drift had been abandoned.

"I wish we had told dad exactly where we were going to go today," said Frank as they went slowly on down the tunnel.

"So do I. There'd be a chance for us then. They'd send some one out to look for us, and then they could start to work clearing away that shaft."

"Well, we can be thankful we weren't in the shaft when it collapsed."

"Yes, it could have been worse. If I had been caught in the cave-in you would be lying under that boulder yet."

"We still have a chance as long as we have that crowbar and can keep moving." Frank paused. "By the way, do you feel a draft?"

"Seems to me I *do* feel cold air!"

"Perhaps there is an opening to this tunnel. This seems promising."

The rush of cold air about their heads was soon quite evident. The boys' spirits rose forthwith and they proceeded through the tunnel more cheerfully.

"If air can get into this place we should be able to get out of it," said Frank. "Perhaps this tunnel is just another entrance to the mine."

"Let's hope so."

They continued, Frank flashing the light before him. The tunnel began to grow narrower. They had to crouch almost double in order to avoid bumping their heads on the rocky roof.

"Another minute or so and we'll know whether this place has an opening or not," called back Frank.

"It *must* have an opening! Where would that fresh air we feel be coming from if it hadn't one?"

"It might be coming through a small slit in the rocks. We can't depend on it too much. Ah! Here we are!"

His light had disclosed the fact that they were at the end of the tunnel. But his tones immediately changed to a murmur of disappointment when he saw that the tunnel ended in a sheer wall of cold, wet rock.

The boys crouched in silence gazing at the rock wall that seemed to crush all their hopes. The wall was a barrier that cut them off from all chance of reaching the sun-lit, outside world again.

"It's a blind alley!" said Joe, in a hushed voice.

Frank merely nodded. He had been buoying up his hopes by refusing to admit to himself that the tunnel could be anything else than an outlet to the mine. Now he was overwhelmed by disappointment.

"We're up against it," he said at last. "This tunnel leads nowhere and the shaft is blocked."

"I'm afraid so."

Joe tapped the crowbar tentatively against the wall of rock. It thudded dully. There was no hollow sound that might indicate another tunnel beyond. The dull ring of the iron bar seemed to sound their death-knell.

"I guess this is our finish, Frank," he said gravely.

CHAPTER XIV

ATTACKED BY THE OUTLAWS

The Hardy boys were so profoundly discouraged by the discovery that the tunnel, their sole hope of safety, ended in nothing but a blank wall of rock, that for a while they sat in the gloom, scarcely speaking. Their plight was perilous and there seemed not the slightest ray of hope.

At last Frank bestirred himself.

"I'm still thinking of that gust of fresh air we felt farther back in the tunnel!" he said.

"There is fresh air coming in somewhere. The air in here isn't getting foul."

"Let's go back and explore the tunnel again. We might find an opening of some kind."

"It won't be big enough for us to get through," predicted Joe, gloomily.

"Well, we'll go and see, anyway."

The boys turned back. Frank took the lead again and they moved on. The flashlight cast its bright circle of illumination on the dank rock walls of their prison as Frank explored every inch of the sides of the tunnel. For a while their scrutiny met with no reward. The tunnel was unbroken by crevice or cranny.

"We must have passed the place by now," said Joe.

"I don't think so. We'll keep on trying."

At last Frank gave an exclamation of satisfaction. He had felt a sudden rush of cold air against his face. It seemed to come from above and he stopped, flashing the light hither and thither.

"It's around here somewhere."

"I can feel the draft. There must be a big opening."

The circle of light ceased wavering and rested finally on a place at the side of the tunnel, toward the roof. It was just a dark patch, an indentation in the rock, but it was quite large and it seemed to indicate an opening of some kind. It was about five feet from the ground.

"I'll hold the light," Frank said. "See if you can clamber up and investigate that place, Joe."

He stepped back and directed the flashlight so that Joe was able to find a convenient foothold. Joe reached up and secured a grasp on the edge of the natural shelf of rock. Then he managed to scramble up the wall until he swung himself over the ledge. Frank stepped back farther and the light plainly revealed his brother kneeling on the rocky shelf.

"Find anything?" he asked.

"There's a powerful draft of air coming down through here," said Joe, in tones of suppressed excitement. "I think this is a sort of tunnel or air shaft through the rock. I'll turn on my own flashlight."

In a moment Frank could see the glow of his brother's light reflected from the rocks above. Then he heard Joe give a lusty shout of delight.

"It leads on up!" he called. "It is a tunnel running at an angle, and I think it goes to the surface."

"Can you see any light?"

"No. Nothing. But I think it won't hurt to explore it. By the force of the cold air rushing down through here I think it must lead to the top."

"I'm coming up."

Joe disappeared up into the tunnel and Frank, putting his flashlight into his pocket, scrambled up to the shelf of rock. There he knelt and turned on the light again.

He could see Joe ahead of him, crawling on up through the narrow passage. The tunnel in the rock was just as Joe had described it, a long, narrow shaft that led upward at a steep slope. It was not so steep that they would not be able to clamber on up to wherever it might lead.

"Go ahead," he called out. "I'll follow you."

"I hope it doesn't get narrower up ahead."

"We'll go as far as the tunnel lets us."

The two boys began crawling up the rocky shaft. Joe called back:

"It's widening out!"

And, truly, the shaft became gradually wider until the boys could almost stand upright in it. The draft of cold air blew against them with great force and roared and whistled down the tunnel. Suddenly Joe stopped and waved the flashlight back and forth.

"There's a drop here."

Frank joined him. There was room enough now for them to stand side by side, and the wavering flashlights showed them that they stood at the end of the tunnel and that it opened into a chamber of rock similar to the mine working they had first entered.

"Look, Joe! I think I see a glow of light away over there. Turn off your flash."

The flashlights were switched off and the brothers stood in total darkness. When their eyes became accustomed to the absence of the electric glow, they saw that almost directly across from them was a faint, bluish grey reflection of light.

"We've found our way into another mine," said Frank. "That must be the light from the shaft. There's a chance for us yet."

He switched on his light again and flashed it into the rocky chamber into which the tunnel led. They found that they stood but a few feet above the floor of the mine working, so they promptly leaped down and then began a cautious walk across the cavern. The floor was rough and strewn with chipped masses of rock which showed that mining had once gone on there, and once they stumbled over a pick that some one had left behind when the working was abandoned.

They drew closer to the light that emanated from the shaft, and at last their flashlights revealed a crude ladder leading up the wall. Here they were met by another rush of cold air. The draft created by the tunnel leading into the other mine was severe and the wind whistled about the cavern. At the bottom of the shaft the Hardy boys looked up.

The ladder led up a distance of about twenty feet, and they could see the blue sky above. The sight made them sigh with relief. It was as if a heavy weight had been lifted from them.

"Up you go," said Frank. "We'll be out of here in no time, now."

"I'll say we're lucky."

"I never thought we'd see daylight again. The old sky looks pretty good, doesn't it?"

"Never looked so good to me before."

Joe put his foot on the first rung of the ladder. Although the mine had evidently been deserted many years before, the ladder leading down into the shaft still held firm. Slowly he began to ascend.

Frank came behind. Each was filled with relief that they had escaped imprisonment in the abandoned mine, imprisonment that might easily have meant a wretched death. The cold wind about their faces was like the breath of life to them.

Suddenly Joe stopped.

"Listen!" he whispered.

They remained still. Then, from above, at the top of the shaft, they could hear voices.

"That cave-in must have finished them," some one was saying. "The whole shaft is gone."

"They might have found their way out," replied another voice. "These two mines lead into each other."

"I didn't know that."

"Yes—there's a tunnel leading down into their main drift."

"Oh, those kids would never find it. Probably they were crushed to death by the cave-in, anyway."

The voices died away as the men evidently moved back from the neighborhood of the shaft-head.

"Some one has been looking for us," said Joe, in a low voice.

"They've given us up for dead. They'll get a surprise when we pop up out of the ground. Evidently they weren't going to try to dig us out. Go on up."

Joe resumed his climb and in a few minutes he emerged above ground, stepping off the top of the ladder to a rickety platform covered with snow. Frank scrambled up beside him, and then the two brothers stared in amazement at what they saw.

Three rough-looking men were standing only a few yards away. One was a tall, surly chap in a short, fur coat. He was badly in need of a shave and his brutal chin and heavy jowls were black with a stubble of beard. The other two were short and husky of build. One was clean-shaven and thin-featured, the other had a reddish mustache. About the waist of one of the men, the thin-featured fellow, was a belt with a holster from which projected the butt of a revolver. The three were villainous in appearance.

As though some sixth sense warned the men that they were observed, they whirled about and confronted the Hardy boys.

The men were as surprised as the lads. Both Frank and Joe realized that there was something unsavory about the strange trio and when they saw the thin-featured man suddenly reach for his revolver they knew that they were confronting not friends, but enemies.

"That's them!" shouted the man in the fur coat excitedly. "Grab them!" And with that he began to run toward the two boys. "No shooting!" he shouted to the thin-featured fellow, who promptly shoved his revolver back into the holster.

"Run for it," muttered Frank.

He wheeled about and commenced to run down the hillside in the general direction of the town.

The snow was deep and it hampered their movements, but the pursuers also experienced this handicap. Frank and Joe were exhausted by their gruelling experience in the mine and they were unable to make good progress. The man in the fur coat came leaping after them, ploughing through the snow recklessly. He gained rapidly on them.

"Stop or we'll shoot," he roared.

This was but a bluff, and the Hardy boys recognized it as such. They raced madly on through the deep snow that clung to their limbs and held them back. Joe was lagging behind, unable to keep up the pace. The man in the fur coat was only a few feet back of him. The fellow leaped ahead and sprang at Joe in a football tackle that brought the boy down. The pair went rolling over and over in the snow, kicking and scrambling.

Frank stopped and turned back. He could not desert his brother and he was prepared to be captured with him at the expense of his own freedom. He met the thin-faced man, who led the other pair of pursuers, with a slashing blow in the face that knocked the man off his balance so that he tumbled backward into the snow with a grunt of pain and amazement. The short, stocky man came on with a growl. Frank swung and missed; then his attacker closed with him and they struggled to and fro in the snowbank.

His assailant twined one foot about Frank's leg and they toppled over into the snow. By that time the thin man had scrambled to his feet and again launched himself into the struggle. Frank Hardy was completely overpowered.

He was dragged roughly to his feet, his arms gripped behind his back. Joe had been no match for his more powerful antagonist and he too had been forced to submit to capture.

The trio held the boys in their power.

"What'll we do with 'em." asked the thin-faced man gruffly.

"Bring 'em back to the mine first," said the fellow in the fur coat. "I guess the boss will want to see these birds."

Frank and Joe were roughly bundled up the hillside again by their captors. All the time Frank's mind was in a whirl. Who were these three men? Why had they attacked them? Why had they been hunting for them in the first place? And who was "the boss" they spoke of?

In due time they reached the shaft-head again and there the man in the fur coat faced them.

"Who are you two boys?" he demanded.

"Who are you?" countered Frank.

"That doesn't matter. What's your names?"

"Tell us yours first."

"What were you doing in that mine?"

"What did you attack us for? Why are you keeping us here?"

The man in the fur coat became impatient at receiving questions instead of answers.

"Are you the Hardy boys?" he asked. "Sons of that detective?"

"Try and find out."

"We'll find out, all right," declared the man in the fur coat threateningly. "We'll take you to somebody that'll make you talk."

"You'd better let us go or the whole three of you will find yourselves in jail," said Frank.

The man laughed shortly.

"No fear," he said. "Not in Lucky Bottom, at any rate." He turned to the other two men. "Keep these boys here," he ordered. "I'll be back in a while. Don't let them get away!"

"Where are you going, Jack?" asked the thin-faced man.

"I'm going to get Black Pepper. He'll make these birds talk."

With that the fellow stalked away through the snow. Frank and Joe glanced quickly at one another. They knew now the explanation of their capture. They were in the hands of three members of the gang of the notorious Black Pepper, the outlaw.

CHAPTER XV

THE TRAP

The man of the thin features produced the revolver from its holster and sat down on a snow-covered rock near the top of the shaft. He held the weapon negligently, but there was no doubt that he could level it at the Hardy boys in a second if they attempted to escape.

"You can sit down if you want," he said. His partner still retained a tight grasp on Frank. "Let him go, Shorty. I've got this gun here and I guess they won't try to get away. We may as well be comfortable."

The fellow addressed as "Shorty" moved away from Frank and sat down by his companion. The Hardy boys found a heap of rocks near by and seated themselves. They knew there was no use of attempting to escape as long as that ugly-looking revolver was in the hand of their captor.

"Say, Slim," remarked Shorty, "do you think Black Pepper is at the camp?"

The other man nodded.

"Yeah! He came back this morning."

Slim looked up at the Hardy boys.

"What were you guys lookin' for in that mine, anyway?"

"Oysters," replied Frank, with a grin.

"None of your funny stuff," rapped out Slim. "We'll make you talk soon enough. We know what you're after."

"What did you ask us for, then?" asked Joe.

The outlaws were silent. They saw that nothing was to be gained by seeking information from the lads. They were content to await the return of Black Pepper and their companion Jack.

Frank and Joe Hardy sat on the snow-covered rocks in silence. Slowly Frank put his hand behind his back and began to grope about among the rocks. He knew that they were loose and that they were of various sizes. The idea had occurred to him that if he could but use one of them as a weapon he might be able to disarm Slim and perhaps effect his escape and that of his brother.

Bit by bit he groped about. One rock was too large for him to grasp. Another was too small to be of any use. Finally his hands closed about a good-sized stone that came from the rest of the pile without much difficulty.

He calculated the distance and eyed the revolver warily. Frank had been pitcher on the Bayport high school nine and the accuracy of his aim had often been the despair of opposing batsmen. Now he called on all his skill.

Without moving from his position he suddenly brought up the rock and flung it with all his strength directly at the revolver in Slim's hand. The outlaw's grip on the weapon had relaxed in his indifference, and when the stone struck its mark, full and true, the gun went flying into the deep snow.

"Come on, Joe!" shouted Frank scrambling to his feet. He had noticed a path leading through the snow in the direction of the road that went to Hank Shale's cabin and he ran toward this path with all the speed at his command. Joe had not been slow to grasp the situation, and he too came racing through the snow but a few paces behind.

The outlaws were taken off their guard. Slim instinctively reached for his revolver, but it had disappeared in the snow and he wasted many precious seconds hunting for it. Shorty had leaped after the boys, then, seeing that his companion did not follow, he hesitated, ran back, and then turned around again. He did not know what to do.

"After them!" roared Slim, and Shorty took up the pursuit. But his indecision had given the Hardy boys the opportunity they needed. They had a good start on their pursuer and Shorty was but a clumsy runner at best. Frank gained the path and there his progress was swifter because he was not handicapped by the impeding snow. Slim finally abandoned his search for the weapon and also took up the chase, but by this time he was far behind.

The boys gained the main road, with Shorty ploughing along in pursuit. Even yet they were not safe, but chance came to their aid in the shape of a stage that ran from Lucky Bottom to one of the neighboring camps. It rattled along, with sleighbells jingling, the driver muffled to the ears, and when Shorty and Slim caught sight of it they slowed up and abandoned the chase. The open road was a dangerous place. They did not wish any interference from the stage driver or his passengers.

When Frank and Joe saw that their pursuers had turned back they slowed down to a walk. Hank Shale's cabin was already in sight.

"We gave them the slip, all right," declared Frank jubilantly.

"I'll tell the world we did. Black Pepper and the other fellow will be hopping mad when they come back and find that we've escaped."

"We'll have to be on the lookout for them from now on. They won't stop until they do lay their hands on us."

"Perhaps it's just as well. We can be on our guard. If we weren't expecting anything wrong we'd be liable to walk right into their arms."

When the boys reached the cabin they found their father and Hank Shale greatly worried by their prolonged absence. They told of their descent into the abandoned mine, of the cave-in, and of their subsequent escape, of their capture by Black Pepper's men and of their get-away. Mr. Hardy looked grave.

"I think we'd better drop the case," he said finally. "It's too big a risk to take."

"Why?" asked the boys, in surprise.

"You might have been buried alive in that mine, in the first place. I would never have forgiven myself. And now that you have run up against Black Pepper's gang they'll be out to get you. I don't want to be responsible for making you run those risks."

"We won't drop the case," laughed Frank. "It's just getting interesting now. We'll find that gold for you, Dad."

"Don't worry about us," chimed in Joe. "We can look after ourselves. We probably won't be up against any worse dangers than the ones we faced today."

"Well," said Mr. Hardy, reluctantly, "you've come all the way out here, and I suppose you'll be disappointed if I don't let you go ahead; but I don't want you to take any unnecessary risks."

"I'm thinkin' they'll pull through all right," said Hank Shale solemnly. "Let the lads be, Mr. Hardy."

So, with this encouragement, Mr. Hardy consented to let his sons continue their activities on the case. Both Frank and Joe promised to take all due precautions and next morning they resumed their search for the missing gold.

During the days that followed they explored several abandoned workings, but the hunt was fruitless. They succeeded only in getting themselves well covered with dirt and grime and would return to the cabin hungry and weary. There had been no sign of any members of Black Pepper's gang. But finally Hank Shale, who had been down to the general store at Lucky Bottom one day, had news for them.

"They be sayin' down town," declared the old miner, "that Black Pepper and his gang have broke up camp."

"Have they left Lucky Bottom?" asked Mr. Hardy quickly.

Hank Shale shook his head. "Nobody knows. They had a camp somewheres back in the mountain, but they've all cleared away from it. Maybe the two lads here scared 'em."

"They've likely just moved to a new camping place," remarked Frank.

"I hope so," said Mr. Hardy. "If they've gone away it means that the gold has gone with them. If they're still around we have a chance yet."

Frank and Joe said nothing, but when they went to bed that night they talked in whispers in the darkness.

"What's the program for tomorrow?" asked Joe.

"We're going to find out if any of that gang are still around."

"Do you mean we'll go out looking for them?"

"Sure! It's just as dad says—if they've gone away the gold has gone with them. If they're still hanging around we'll know there's still a good chance of finding it ourselves."

"Where shall we look?"

"Up in the mountains. We can look around for trails in the snow."

"Suits me, as long as they don't catch us."

"That's a chance we have to take."

So next morning, without revealing their plans to any one, the boys started out into the mountains. It was a gloomy day and the sky was overcast. The lowering, snow-covered crags loomed high above them as they headed toward a narrow defile not far from the abandoned mine where they had been captured by Black Pepper's men some days previous. It was toward this defile that the man called Jack had gone on his way to summon Black Pepper, and the boys judged that the outlaws' abandoned camp was probably somewhere in that direction.

They discovered a narrow trail through the snow. It was a trail that had evidently been much used, for the snow was packed hard by the tramp of many feet.

"I think we're on the right track, all right," said Frank. "Even if we only find the deserted camp we may get some clues that will help us."

The boys went higher up into the mountain and at last they came to a protected spot beneath an overhanging crag, where the snow had not penetrated. Here the trail ended in a long platform of bare rock. They went across it, but were unable to pick up the trail again, although they searched about in every direction.

Suddenly Frank said to his brother in a low voice:

"Don't look around. Keep straight ahead."

"What's the matter?"

"There's some one following us. I just caught a glimpse of him out of the corner of my eye. He's hiding behind the rocks back there."

"Let's tackle him."

"There may be others with him. Let him follow, and if he's alone we'll grab him."

Without giving any indication that they had seen their pursuer, the Hardy boys cut down into a narrow ravine where huge masses of boulders made progress difficult. They came to a place where rocks rose on either side so close together that there was room for only one person to pass at a time. As soon as they had gone through the opening Frank leaped to one side, motioning to his brother to take the opposite side of the boulders. They were now completely hidden from the man who followed.

"We'll get him when he comes through," whispered Frank.

They waited expectantly.

At last they heard the crunch of snow that indicated the unsuspecting man was approaching. Cautiously he drew nearer, step by step. The boys prepared themselves.

The man drew nearer. He was just entering the passage between the boulders. Frank and Joe pressed themselves against the rocks. They saw a head appear in view, then the shoulders of the man. He stepped forward and, at the same moment, they sprang at him.

Frank launched himself full on the fellow's shoulders and he gave a cry of surprise. At the same time Joe flung his arms about the man's waist and all three came tumbling to the ground. There was a flurry of snow as they struggled, but the fight was short-lived. Taken completely by surprise, the man was quickly overcome. He had reached for a revolver at his waist, but Frank had seen it in the nick of time and had struck it from his grasp. He seized the weapon himself and pressed the barrel of it to the fellow's temple.

"All right! All right!" he gasped. "I give in."

There was something familiar about the voice. The man turned his head about and they saw that it was the man known as Slim, the thin-faced fellow who had been among their captors several days before.

CHAPTER XVI

INFORMATION

"So it's you!" said Frank.

"Just my luck," muttered the outlaw, in disgust. "I might have known better!"

Still leveling the revolver at Slim, Frank relinquished his grasp and stood back. Joe also withdrew. Slim, holding his hands above his head and keeping a wary eye on the weapon, got to a sitting position.

"This is luck," Frank remarked. "We hadn't expected to meet again so soon."

"If I'd had any brains I wouldn't have let myself step into a trap like this," growled Slim.

"What were you following us for?"

"What were you doing up here?"

"Trying to find you," said Joe cheerfully.

"Where's Shorty and Jack and Black Pepper?"

Something in the man's question made Frank think quickly. Was it possible that Slim had become separated from the rest of the gang?

"I suppose you know the camp's broken up?" he remarked.

A look of surprise leaped into Slim's face.

"No," he said, hoarsely. "I've been away. What happened? You don't mean to tell me—"

"We're telling you nothing."

"They caught the gang?" went on Slim.

"Wait until we take you down to Lucky Bottom. You'll find out all about it then," said Frank, evasively. If Slim thought the rest of the outlaws were captured he might be more disposed to talk.

"I might have known it," said Slim gloomily. "They were gettin' too careless. I told 'em a hundred times they'd be tripped up, especially after lettin' you two give us the slip."

"We might be able to make it easier for you," Frank suggested.

"How?"

"If you've got any information to give us we might be able to put in a word for you."

Slim looked at them steadily for a moment. Then he asked:

"What kind of information do you want?"

"You know what we're hunting for."

"The gold?"

"Of course."

Slim was silent for a moment.

"That gang has been tryin' to double-cross me all along," he said at last. "I don't owe 'em nothin'. They would have cleared out with the gold and left me here if they could."

"Did they know where it was hidden?" asked Joe.

"Of course some one knew. They didn't dare make a get-away with it as long as Fenton Hardy was watchin' them. I guess the game is all up now, though. If they've got Black Pepper in jail they'll make him come through and tell where it was hidden."

"Don't the others know?"

Slim shook his head. "He wouldn't tell any of us. He hid the gold himself and we couldn't find out where. He said he was afraid we'd be double-crossin' him and stealin' it on him. I think he planned to take it himself and ditch the whole bunch of us."

"What do you know about it?"

"I know everythin' about it," said Slim boastfully. "Everythin' except where it was hidden."

"Who owned it in the first place?"

"You ought to know that as well as me. Bart Dawson and one of the Coulsons had it. Dawson blew into camp a while ago with Coulson and they dug up this gold. Dawson had it hid away some place. It must be about twenty years ago since he's been here. At least that's what Black Pepper said. He was in Lucky Bottom when Dawson was here before."

The Hardy boys exchanged glances of surprise. The names of Bart Dawson and Coulson were familiar. These were Jadbury Wilson's partners and the gold must be the gold that Wilson presumed Dawson had stolen from them. There was a mystery here that they could not fathom. If Dawson had stolen the gold, why did he bring Coulson back with him? Why had he waited for twenty years before returning to dig up the loot?

"And Black Pepper's gang stole it from Dawson?" persisted Frank.

The outlaw nodded.

"Haven't you an idea where he hid it?"

"It was in one of the old mines somewhere around here. That's how we knew you fellows were after it when we found you were searching through the workings."

"Where was your camp?"

Slim looked up at them. "Don't you know?"

"We know it's deserted. We were on our way to try to find it."

"Don't kid me," sneered the outlaw. "You know where it is all right. You were headin' right for it when I began to follow you. You're not any too far away from it now."

This was a stroke of luck that they had not expected. Unwittingly, they had been on the right trail to the camp all the time.

"What are you going to do with me?" asked Slim.

"We're going to take you down to Lucky Bottom," said Frank.

"Aw, let me go," whined the outlaw. "I've told you all I know about it." Frank shook his head.

"I think you'll be safer in behind the bars."

"The sheriff's a good friend of our gang. He'll fix things for me."

"That's up to you and the sheriff. If he tries to fix anything this time he'll get into trouble. We'll see to that. You'd better come with us."

Frank gestured with the revolver and Slim got unwillingly to his feet. Then, making the outlaw lead the way, the boys started back down the trail toward Lucky Bottom. Both Frank and Joe were anxious to resume the search for the outlaw's camp, but they were confident that they could find it now, from the fact that Slim had admitted they were on the right trail.

They made the journey back to town without incident. Their arrival, with Slim marching ahead and Frank keeping the outlaw covered with the revolver, created a sensation. Word quickly sped about the mining camp that one of the members of Black Pepper's notorious gang had been captured and a crowd congregated about the jail as the little procession disappeared into the sheriff's office.

The sheriff was a shifty-eyed man of middle age, obviously weak and susceptible to public opinion. When he saw Slim led into the office he scratched his head dubiously.

"We want this fellow locked up," said Frank.

"What fer?" asked the sheriff reluctantly.

"For being mixed up in the gold robbery, for one thing. If that isn't enough you can hold him for carrying a revolver. If that isn't enough we'll charge him with assault, pointing a weapon, and half a dozen other things."

"I don't know," drawled the sheriff. "It ain't quite usual—"

Clearly he did not wish to put Slim in a cell. Frank became impatient.

"Look here," he said. "You're sheriff here and your duty is to lock up lawbreakers. We'll give you all the evidence you need against this chap, but we want him kept where he can't do any harm. If you're afraid of Black Pepper—"

"I'm not afraid of nobody," said the sheriff hastily.

Just then the door opened and a bearded old prospector strode in. He went right up to the desk and shook his fist beneath the sheriff's nose.

"Lock him up," he roared. "We've stood for about enough from you, and I don't care whether you're sheriff or not. If you're goin' to encourage outlaws and thieves, me and the boys will mighty soon see that there's a new sheriff in this here man's town."

Frank and Joe then saw that other miners were standing in the doorway, crowding against one another, muttering truculently.

The sheriff blinked, wavered, and finally gave in.

"I just wanted to make sure it was all right," he muttered. "Don't want to lock anybody up that don't deserve it."

"You know mighty well that Slim Briggs deserves it, if any one in this camp ever did," retorted the old miner. "Lock him up."

The sheriff took a ponderous bunch of keys from his pocket and unlocked a heavy door leading to the cells. "This way, Slim," he said regretfully.

Slim Briggs followed him into the cell. He looked around, plainly expecting to see the rest of the gang in jail as well. Suspicion dawned on him.

"Where's the others?" he demanded wrathfully.

"What others?" asked the sheriff mildly.

"Black Pepper—the rest of the boys."

"They ain't here."

Slim gaped in astonishment.

"They ain't here?" he shouted finally. "Why, those boys told me they'd all been rounded up! I spilled everything I knew, just so I'd get let off easy!"

"You're the only one that's been pinched," said the sheriff.

"So far," added Frank pointedly.

Then, as Slim Briggs burst into a wild outbreak of bitter recrimination against the way in which he had deceived himself, the boys withdrew and the cell door clanged.

The old miner laughed and slapped Frank on the shoulder.

"I guess Bart Dawson come along just in time!" he declared. "Sheriff would have let that bird go if I hadn't got the boys to back you up." He turned to the sheriff. "We've seen that Slim is in jail," he said. "You're responsible for keepin' him there. If he gets out—" he snapped his fingers ominously— "it means a new sheriff in Lucky Bottom."

CHAPTER XVII

THE OUTLAW'S NOTEBOOK

"Are you Bart Dawson?" asked Frank.

"That's me," said the old man. "I'm the fellow they stole that there gold from."

The Hardy boys looked curiously at the old miner. From what they had heard of Bart Dawson from Jadbury Wilson they had been prepared to dislike him. But he appeared so genial and friendly and his grizzled old face was apparently so honest that they could not help but feel drawn to him. He certainly did not look like the sort of man who would desert his partners and rob them in the way Jadbury Wilson had described. Still, the evidence seemed all against him. He had betrayed his comrades and decamped with their gold, according to Wilson's story.

But why, argued Frank, should he wait twenty years to return for the wealth he had hidden? Why should he return with one of the Coulsons? Could it be possible that the pair had been in league with one another against Jadbury Wilson? The mystery defied explanation, but the more Frank looked at the jovial, honest face of the old man before him the more he was convinced that Bart Dawson had none of the earmarks of either thief or traitor.

"We've got one of 'em behind the bars now," said Dawson, rubbing his hands with satisfaction. "I only wish we had 'em all."

"Perhaps we will have them all before long," remarked Frank. "We've run across a few clues that may lead to something."

"That's good! That's good!" declared the old man. "Do your best, lads, and you may be sure Bart Dawson won't forget you."

Frank and Joe forbore any mention of the name of Jadbury Wilson. It was best, they decided, to keep that information to themselves until they should learn more about the affair of the stolen gold. They had long since learned that one of the axioms of successful detective work is to listen much and say little. Accordingly, they bade good-bye to Bart Dawson and left the jail.

"Where to?" asked Joe.

"Back to where we caught Slim Briggs. We were on the right trail to the camp."

"But if the outlaws have left there isn't much use going up there now."

"We never know what we'll find."

The boys made their way up into the mountains again and, after about an hour of steady traveling, found themselves on the trail that led into the defile where they had trapped Slim so neatly. On the way they discussed their meeting with Bart Dawson.

"I can't imagine that old fellow being the kind of man who would desert his partners and steal their gold, the way Jadbury Wilson described," said Frank, for the tenth time. "I just can't figure it out at all! You can tell with half an eye that he isn't a crook."

"Yet Jadbury Wilson was absolutely convinced that he had left them all in the lurch."

"And he had the gold in his possession. We know that. He came back here to dig it up. That shows he must have hidden it, as Wilson said he did. The whole story hangs together mighty well."

"Yet why should he bring Coulson with him?" objected Joe.

"That's another strange angle. I can't figure it out at all. I think we should see Coulson and tell him what we know, tell him what Jadbury Wilson told us, and ask him about it."

"That's the best idea. But isn't it strange how Jadbury Wilson, away back in Bayport, should be connected with this case, away out here in Montana?"

"It's a coincidence, all right. We just seem to have blundered into the affair from both ends. Bart Dawson and Coulson know a lot that we don't know, but then we know a lot that Bart Dawson and Coulson don't know."

"I think we hold the advantage. Tomorrow we'll try to find Coulson."

The boys were going down the defile now and they passed between the overhanging rocks where they had captured the outlaw. The marks of the struggle were still plainly evident in the snow.

"Poor Slim!" remarked Frank, with a laugh. "He'll be kicking himself all around the cell for talking so much."

"He was nicely fooled. He was sure the rest of the gang were all in jail."

"We didn't tell any lies about it. He took it for granted that the outlaws were arrested. All we did was to look wise and let him keep on thinking so." The boys chuckled at the recollection of the ease with which the dull-witted Slim had been duped.

"If only the rest of them are that easy!" said Frank.

"No such luck. I'm thinking this Black Pepper will give us trouble before we are through. He seems to have Lucky Bottom pretty well under his thumb."

"He has the sheriff buffaloed, at any rate, by the looks of things. If Bart Dawson hadn't shown up when he did I don't think Slim Briggs would have been put in jail at all."

The trail now led toward a clump of trees, and here there were evidences of recent habitation. Some of the trees had been chopped down, presumably for firewood, and the stumps rose above the level of the snow. There were numerous footprints about the little grove and in some places the snow was closely packed down. As the boys drew closer they caught a glimpse of a small cabin in the midst of the grove.

"We'll go easy from now on," said Frank quietly. "Some of them may have come back."

The boys went cautiously forward, keeping to the shelter of the trees as much as possible. Every few moments they would stop and listen.

But they heard not a sound. There was not a voice from the cabin. The only noises were the rustling of the trees in the wind. Quietly, the Hardy boys stole up toward the cabin. It stood in a little clearing in the wood. At the edge of the clearing they waited, but still they heard nothing, and finally Frank was satisfied that the place was, in fact, deserted.

"No one here," he said, in a tone of relief. "We'll take a look around."

They advanced boldly across the clearing, directly toward the door of the cabin. It was half open. Frank peered inside.

The place was deserted. The cabin was sparsely furnished, with a rude table, two chairs, and bunks on either side. There was a small iron stove at the far end of the building and the place was dimly lighted by one window.

There was every evidence that the outlaws had left the place in a hurry. Papers, articles of clothing and rubbish of all kinds lay about the floor, scattered here and there in abandon. One of the chairs was lying overturned on the floor. The place was in confusion.

The boys entered.

"Looks as if they didn't waste much time in getting out," remarked Joe.

"I'll say they didn't. The cabin looks as if a cyclone had hit it."

"Wonder if there'd be any use looking through those papers." Joe indicated a scattered heap of old envelopes, letters, tattered magazines and torn sheets of paper lying on the floor.

"That's just what I was thinking." Frank scooped up a handful of the papers and sat down on a bunk. He began to sort them over. The magazines he flung to one side as worthless. Some of the sheets of paper contained nothing but crude attempts at drawing or penciled lists of figures presumably done by some of the outlaws while idling away their time in the cabin.

One or two of the letters, Frank put to one side, as liable to give some clue to the identity of members of the gang. When he had looked through the first handful of papers he picked up some more.

Suddenly he gave an exclamation of satisfaction.

"Find something?" asked Joe.

"This may be valuable." Frank held up a small black notebook and began flipping the pages. On the inside of the cover he read:

"Black Pepper—his book."

"This is the captain's own little record book. There should be some information here."

Frank began studying the book carefully. The first few pages gave him little satisfaction, the writing consisting largely of cryptic abbreviations evidently in an improvised code known only to the outlaw himself. There were the names of several men written on another page, and among them he recognized the names of Slim, Shorty and Jack, the trio who had captured them at the abandoned mine working. Across from their names had been marked various sums of money, evidently their shares of the gang's takings in some robbery.

Then, on the next page, he found a crude map.

He studied it curiously. It looked something like the ground floor plan of an extremely crude house. There was one large chamber with two passages leading from it. One of these passages was marked with an X, and each passage led to a small chamber. From one of these led still another passage which branched into a tiny room, in one corner of which was inscribed a small circle.

"That's the funniest plan of a house I ever saw!" said Joe, looking over his brother's shoulder.

Frank studied the plan for a few moments and then looked up.

"Why, it isn't a house at all. It's a mine!" he declared. "This is the plan of a mine. This big room is the main working at the bottom of the shaft, and these passages are tunnels leading out of it."

"Perhaps it's the mine where the gold is hidden!" cried Joe, in excitement.

"There may be something about it on another page." Frank turned the leaf of the notebook. There he found what he was so eagerly seeking.

At the top of the page was written, in a scrawling, unformed hand: "Lone Tree Mine." Beneath that he found the following:

"Follow passage X to second cave, then down tunnel to blue room. Gold at circle."

Frank looked up at his brother.

"This is what we wanted," he said jubilantly. "They've had the gold hidden there all the time. All we have to do now is find the Lone Tree Mine and we'll recover the stuff in no time."

"Unless the outlaws have taken it away by now," pointed out Joe.

"That's right, too. I hadn't thought of that. They may have taken it away right after they abandoned this camp. Well, we've just got to take our chances on that. If they've left it in the mine this long they may think it's safe enough there a while longer." Frank got up from the bunk and stuffed the notebook into his pocket. His eyes were sparkling with excitement. "Joe, I believe we're on the right track! We know just where the stuff has been hidden and I've a hunch it's there yet. We haven't any time to lose. Let's start right now, before those rascals get ahead of us, and hunt for the Lone Tree Mine."

"Why, I'll bet I know where that is!" declared Joe. "Don't you remember an old mine working near where they caught us the other day? There was a big pine right by the top of the shaft, standing all by itself."

"I'll bet that's the place! Come on! We'll try it, anyway!"

Hastily, they left the little cabin. They were sure now that they were on the trail of the hidden gold. Frank remembered the lone pine tree that Joe had mentioned; it seemed to identify the abandoned working as the place they sought.

It was snowing heavily as they started down the trail but the boys scarcely noticed it in their excitement. They even forgot that they had not had their lunch.

"If the outlaws haven't beaten us to it," declared Frank, "we'll have that gold before the day is out!"

CHAPTER XVIII

THE BLIZZARD

The Hardy boys set off down the trail at a good pace. The wind howled down from the crags and whistled through the trees. The entire mountain was veiled in a great mist of swirling snow and, as the wind rose, the snow stung their faces and slashed against them.

"Storm coming up," said Frank, burying his chin deeper into his coat collar.

"I hope it doesn't get any worse. We'll never find the place."

"We won't give up now. If we wait until tomorrow it may be too late."

The storm grew rapidly worse. The snowfall was so heavy that it obscured even the tops of the great masses of rock and it quickly drifted over the trail so that the boys were forced to follow the path by memory. This was difficult, as in some places the trail had wound about through tumbled masses of boulders and when it was hidden by snow they had to guess at its intricate windings. Several times Frank lost it altogether, but he was always able to pick up the trail again in some place that was sheltered from the storm.

The boys struggled on in silence. The wind was increasing in volume and the snow was so heavy that Joe could scarcely see the dim form of his brother but a few yards ahead. Suddenly he saw his brother stop.

"I've lost the trail!" shouted Frank, turning back.

They were standing ankle deep in snow. There was not the slightest vestige of a path. High above them they could discern the gloomy mass of a steep rock cliff and before them loomed a sloping declivity of rock that afforded not the slightest foothold.

"I lost the trail farther back, but I thought I was following it all right and could pick it up farther on. We'll have to turn back."

They retraced their steps. So furiously was it snowing that their own footprints were almost obliterated and they could scarcely find their way back to the place where they had left the trail. They found it again, however, and struck out in another direction.

It was growing bitterly cold, and although they were warmly clad they began to feel the effect of the chill wind that swept down from the icy mountain slopes. They pulled their caps down about their ears and made their way slowly forward against the terrific wind that buffeted them and flung sheets of snow against them.

Frank gave a shout of triumph when he finally picked up the trail again in the shelter of some huge rocks where the snow had not yet penetrated. They advanced with new courage.

At length they emerged through the defile where the trail to the outlaw's deserted camp led off the main trail up the mountain, and then they rested.

Far below them they could see the slope of the mountain, veiled in sweeping banners of snow that shifted and swirled madly in the blustering wind. The town was hidden from view, obscured by the white blizzard.

"Do you think we should try to make it?" asked Frank.

"The mine?"

"Yes."

"You're leading this procession. Whatever you want to do."

"If you think the storm is too bad, we'll start for the cabin."

"What would you rather do?"

"I hate to give up now," replied Frank, after a moment of hesitation.

"I feel the same way about it," Joe said. "I vote we try to find the mine. Once we get there we'll be able to get in out of the storm, anyway."

"I thought you'd say that," laughed Frank. "We'll head for the Lone Tree Mine then. As far as I can remember it is just below us, and then over to the right."

"We'll find it, I guess."

They started down the slope. But once they left the shelter of the rocks where they had rested they found that the fury of the storm was increased tenfold on the mountainside. The full force of the blizzard struck them.

The wind shrieked with a thousand voices. The snow came sweeping down on them as though lashed by invisible whips. The roar of the storm sounded in their ears and the fine snow almost blinded them.

"It's worse than I thought," muttered Frank.

The slope was steep and precipitous. They could not distinguish the details of the trail other than as a vaguely winding path that led steadily downward. Frank lost his footing on a slippery rock and went tumbling down the declivity for several yards before he came to a stop in a snowbank. He got to his feet slowly and limped on, suffering from a bruised ankle.

The trail wound about a steep cliff and he skirted the base of it, then disappeared between two high masses of rock. Joe could dimly see the figure of his brother, and he hastened on so as not to lose sight of him.

But when Joe came around the rocks he was confronted by an opaque cloud of snow, like a huge white screen that had dropped from the skies. He could not see Frank at all.

He followed the trail as well as he could, but in a few moments he came to a stop. He was out on the open mountainside and the winds at this point converged so that the snow seemed to be swirling about him from all sides. The faint trail had been wholly obliterated.

He shouted.

"Frank! Frank!"

But the wind flung the words back into his teeth. A feeling of panic seized him for a moment, but he quickly calmed himself, for he realized that when Frank looked behind and saw they were separated, he would retrace his steps.

He went on uncertainly a few paces, until it occurred to him that he might be wandering in the wrong direction and that if Frank did turn back he might not be able to find him. So he tried to return to the trail again. But the snow was falling so heavily by now that he seemed to be wandering in an enormous grey void, from which all direction had been erased.

He was hopelessly lost, so he stood where he was and shouted again and again. There was no answer. He could only hear the constant howling of the wind, the sweep and swish of snow.

Once he thought he heard a faint cry from far ahead, but he could not be sure, and although he listened intently he could hear it no more.

As he stood there on the rocks, with the snow sweeping down on him and with the wind howling about him, with only the gaunt, gloomy shapes of the boulders looming out of the heavy mist of storm, Joe felt the icy clutch of the cold and he began to beat his arms against his chest so as to keep warm. He knew the danger of inaction in such a blizzard.

Anything was better than remaining where he was. He struggled forward, slipped and fell on the rocks, regained his feet, and moved slowly on into the teeth of the wind. He did not know whether he was following the trail or not but, to the best of his judgment, he tried to descend the slope.

As for Frank, he had been plunging doggedly on through the storm, confident that Joe was close behind, and it was not until he had gone far down the trail that he became aware that his brother was not following. He turned, and when he could no longer discern the figure in the storm behind he retraced his steps, shouting at the top of his lungs.

There was no answer.

He searched about, going to left and right of the trail. He did not dare go far, being fearful of losing the trail himself. Frank was alarmed lest Joe had slipped and fallen on the rocks and injured himself. If he were unable to proceed he would freeze to death, lying helpless on the mountainside.

With this thought in his mind, he searched frantically. He tried to follow back up the trail, but the snow had swept over his footsteps and he soon found himself knee-deep in a heavy drift and he knew he had lost the path.

He tried to regain the trail, but the white screen of snow was like a shroud over the rocks and he had lost all sense of direction.

He floundered about in the snow aimlessly, but the trail constantly evaded him. Frank set his jaw grimly and went hither and thither, stopping every little while to shout. He knew that the wind drowned out his voice and he realized the futility of his cries, but still he hoped that there was just a chance that Joe might hear him.

Frank Hardy felt an overpowering sense of loneliness as he wandered about among the rocks and the deep drifts. He seemed to be alone in a world of swirling, shrieking winds and flailing snow that stormed down from a sky of leaden hue.

He shouted again and again, but to no avail.

It was mid-afternoon, but the sky was so dark that it seemed almost dusk. If darkness fell and they were lost out on the mountain there was little hope that they would survive until morning. They would perish from exposure.

"I'd better go back to Hank Shale's place and get a searching party to come up and look for Joe," he thought.

This seemed the only sensible solution. But when he turned and tried to find the trail down the mountain again he found that it eluded him. There was not the vestige of a trail, not the sign of a path.

"And I'm lost too!" he muttered.

The wind shrieked down from the rocks. The snow swirled furiously about him. The blizzard raged. The roaring of the storm drummed in his ears as he stumbled and floundered about among the rocks and snow.

The Hardy boys were lost, separated, in the storm.

CHAPTER XIX

THE LONE TREE

Suddenly, Frank Hardy had an inspiration.

In the shelter of some rocks he cleared away the snow, then began to search about for wood in order to build a fire. If he were lost the best plan was to build a fire which would serve the double purpose of keeping him warm and possibly guiding Joe toward him as well.

He found some small shrubs and stunted trees and managed to break off enough branches to serve as the basis of a fair-sized blaze. He had matches in a waterproof box in his pocket, and after several unsuccessful attempts he finally managed to get a fire going. The wood was damp, but the small twigs caught the blaze and within a few minutes the flames were leaping higher and higher and casting warmth and radiance.

Frank crouched beneath the rocks and warmed himself by the fire. Once in a while he got up and went away to search for more wood to cast on the blaze. Occasionally he peered through the screen of snow in the hope of seeing some sign of Joe. At intervals, he shouted until he was hoarse in the hope of attracting his brother's attention.

The flames leaped up in the wind and as he piled more wood on the blaze the fire grew brighter. It was in a sheltered spot where the gusts of snow could not quench the flames.

At last he thought he heard a faint shout.

Frank sprang to his feet. He gazed through the shifting veil of snow that swirled about his shelter, but he could see nothing. Then he called out:

"Joe!"

The fire roared. The wind shrieked. Snow slashed against the rocks above him.

Then, out of the inferno of wind and snow he heard the shout again, and a moment later he caught sight of a dim figure plunging toward him. He ran forward.

It was Joe. He was almost exhausted and he was blue with cold. He staggered over toward the blaze and collapsed in a heap beside the fire.

"Thank goodness I saw the flames!" he gasped. "I was almost all in. I couldn't have gone another step."

"I thought I'd never find you. I hunted all over."

"I got lost. I couldn't find the trail."

"We're both lost now. I got off the trail myself when I was looking for you."

"I don't much care where we are so long as we're together again and we have a fire."

Joe extended his trembling hands to the blaze. In a short while he ceased shivering, and as the warmth pervaded his chilled body his spirits rose.

"That fire was a lucky thought," remarked Frank. "I was cold and it just occurred to me that you might see a fire through the storm even if you couldn't see me."

"I just caught a faint glimpse of it—just like a little pink patch shining through the snow. I was just about to give up and lie down on the rocks when I saw it."

"You'd have died of exposure."

For a while the two lads were silent as they thought of how narrowly the blizzard had been cheated of its victim. Then, when Joe had become warmed by the fire, they began to consider their course of action. Frank looked out at the storm.

"The wind seems to be dying down a bit," he said. "I can see farther down the mountain now than I could a while ago."

"Think we ought to start home?"

"Do you feel well enough now?"

Joe got to his feet.

"Sure. I feel fine now. There's no use staying up here until nightfall. This storm may last a couple of days."

"All right. Let's go."

They stamped out the fire and resumed their journey down the mountain. They stayed close together this time, taking no chances on again being separated. As Frank had noticed, the wind had indeed lost much of its fury, although it still howled and blustered on the mountain slope, and the snow still fell steadily in a drifting cloud. The trail was almost obscured by the snowdrifts but Frank was able to find and follow it and they finally reached the place where they had turned off toward the abandoned mine workings several days before.

Here they hesitated.

"What do you think?" Frank asked.

"Now that we're so close to the mine I think we may as well go on with our search."

"I was hoping you'd say that. It shouldn't take us more than an hour or so and it isn't dark yet. Besides, we have our flashlights."

"I haven't mine. But one's enough. Go ahead. It shouldn't be hard to find the Lone Tree from here."

Frank turned off the trail. He headed directly toward the old mine workings they had previously visited and from which he remembered having seen the lone pine tree. The snow was deeper than they had expected and they ploughed through drifts up to the waist. They went on, however, and in a short while reached the abandoned mine of their harrowing experience underground. Here they paused.

"The lone tree was over to the right, I think," said Joe.

They peered through the storm. They could see nothing but drifting snow and the dull masses of the rocks. A shift in the wind raised the curtain of storm for a moment and then, like a gloomy sentinel, they saw the tall pine tree, solitary against the bleak background of grey.

"That's it!"

Now that their goal was definitely in sight they felt invigorated, and they hastened on through the snow toward the tree with new vitality. Forgotten for the moment was their weariness and exhaustion, the cold and the snow, in the lure of the gold that they felt sure lay somewhere in the neighborhood of that lonely tree.

Stumbling and plunging through the snow, they reached their goal at last. The tree creaked and swayed in the wind, and as they stood beneath it they saw that they were standing on the verge of a deep pit that seemed to have been scooped out of the earth by giant hands. There were a few ramshackle ruins of old mine buildings near by. The roofs had long since fallen in and the buildings sagged drunkenly. At the far side of the bottom of the pit, clearly discernible against the snow, they saw the wide mouth of a cave.

"That must be the shaft opening," said Frank. "We're on the track now."

The boys descended into the pit. The going was precarious, for the rocks were slippery and the snow concealed crevices and holes, so that they were obliged to proceed cautiously. But at length they reached the bottom and made their way across to the mouth of the cave.

Frank produced his flashlight as he prepared to enter.

"Stick close behind," he advised his brother. "We don't know what we're liable to run into here."

The snow flung itself upon them and the wind shrieked with renewed fury as they left the unsheltered pit and entered the half darkness of the cave mouth. It was as though they were entering a new world. They had become so accustomed to the roaring of the gale and the sweep of the storm that the interior of the passage seemed strangely peaceful and still.

The flashlight sliced a brilliant gleam of light from the blackness ahead.

Step by step they advanced across the hard rock. The dampness and cold became more pronounced. As they went on the passage widened and in a few minutes they found themselves in a huge chamber in the earth, a chamber that extended far on into darkness, and they could not see the opposite walls.

A curious rustling sound attracted their attention as soon as they entered the place, and Frank stood still.

"What was that?"

They remained motionless and silent. Away off in the darkness of this subterranean chamber they could hear a scuffling and rustling, and sounds that the boys judged were caused by pattering feet. Frank directed the beam of the flashlight toward them, but the light fell short and they could see nothing.

They advanced several paces. The rustling sounds became multiplied. Then, suddenly, Frank caught sight of two gleaming pinpoints of light glowing from the blackness.

"What's that light?" asked Joe.

"I don't know. I'm going closer."

Frank stepped forward again. As he did so, instead of two pinpoints of light, he saw two more, then two more, until at least a dozen of those strange glowing green spots shone from the darkness, reflected in the glow from the flashlight.

"Animals," he said quietly to Joe.

At the same instant he heard a low, menacing snarl.

The glowing greenish lights began to move rapidly to and fro. Into the radiance of the flashlight shot a lean, grey form that disappeared as swiftly as it came.

A prolonged and wicked snarling rose from the gloom. Frank glanced to one side and saw that two of the greenish lights had moved until they were circling behind him. He leaped back.

"We'd better get out of here!" he said. "Those are wolves."

But when the boys turned to retrace their steps they were confronted by a lean form that barred their way to the cave entrance, and in the glow of the flashlight they saw two greenish eyes that glowed fiendishly and two rows of sharp white teeth bared in defiance.

CHAPTER XX

DOWN THE SHAFT

Frank Hardy swung the flashlight, and the wolf before them sprang back, snarling ferociously, into the darkness. The pattering of feet at the back of the huge cavern became more insistent. The boys were conscious of those greenish eyes all about them. The wolves were circling around the cave.

Another wolf joined the animal that barred the entrance. By some animal cunning, they seemed to realize that by so doing they could entrap their prey. The Hardy boys knew that they had wandered into a veritable den of timber wolves who had found in this abandoned mine an ideal refuge and shelter, who had probably made the place their own for years.

The wolves drew closer. The circle was narrowing. The animals were beginning to pace about the cave in long strides, drawing in toward the boys as the circumference of the circle grew smaller.

"Keep the flashlight on," said Joe. "They're afraid of the light."

Frank kept turning slowly about, keeping the glare of the flash full on the circling wolves, and every time its radiance illuminated a gaunt grey form the animal would leap back, snarling, into the shadows.

But as quickly as the light was turned away from one side, the wolves on the other side of the circle would grow bolder and come closer. It was inevitable that in a few minutes the lads would be torn to pieces.

Suddenly Frank thought of the revolver they had seized from Slim Briggs. It was still in his pocket and he had forgotten all about it until this time. With his free hand he reached for the weapon.

Slowly he withdrew it. Then, turning the flashlight directly on one of the snarling beasts, he took aim and fired.

The animal dropped in his tracks with a yelp of pain, and instantly the ranks of the wolves were broken as they fled howling to the darkest corners of the cavern. The stricken wolf writhed and snarled wretchedly for a moment, then lay still.

The boys edged back toward the entrance, but before they could reach it a grey form shot across the circle of light and barred the way with a snarl of defiance. Again they were trapped. Frank fired at the animal. The shot went wide and the brute slunk back, but still remained in the passageway. Two or three of the other animals came rushing out of the darkness and pounced on the body of the dead wolf, tearing at the flesh with savage jaws. For a while the cave echoed with growls and snarls as the animals set about their hideous meal, and then the revolver crashed forth again and another wolf toppled over dead.

"Three shells left," said Frank.

"Save them. We'll take a chance on getting out."

But the chance appeared to be a slim one. More wolves had joined their leader at the entrance, and it seemed impossible that the boys could ever make their escape that way.

The wolves began to advance. The leader came forward, showing his teeth. His eyes glowed like spots of green flame.

Step by step, the boys retreated.

The animals appeared to have overcome their fear of the flashlight. They no longer slunk into the shadows when its fierce glare was turned on them. Instead, they came forward boldly, with dripping, gleaming jaws.

"I'm afraid we're trapped," declared Frank.

"We'll die fighting, anyway. I wish I had a gun."

"Wouldn't be much use against this pack."

"Turn your flash and see if there isn't any other way out of this place except the way we came in."

Frank turned the light swiftly about toward the walls back of them and in the radiant gleam the boys saw a narrow passage, like a dark splotch against the rock, just a few feet away.

"That looks like our only chance."

"We'll try it, anyway. It seems to lead back into the wall quite a distance."

"It may be all right—as long as we don't run into another wolf den."

"Those brutes will follow us."

"The whole pack can't get into that narrow tunnel, at any rate. We'll have a better chance of fighting them off." Frank turned the light swiftly on the dark passage again. "You try it first. They may try to rush us when they see us getting away."

They backed up as close to the opening in the rocks as they could. The wolves were very near now. Three of them had thrust their cruel heads directly into the circle of light from the flash. Their vicious snarling echoed throughout the cave. Frank sensed that they were preparing to spring.

"Quick!" he urged his brother.

Joe leaped and scrambled into the opening.

At the same instant the foremost wolf crouched for a spring. There was not a second to lose. Frank leveled the revolver and fired.

His aim was true. Halfway in the air the animal gave a convulsive twist of its body and crashed on to the rocks. It writhed in its death agony, snarling ferociously and snapping at everything within reach, until it finally lay still.

The respite was just what the boys needed. The other wolves slunk back, discouraged by the loss of their leader. Frank knew, however, that it would be but for a moment. He backed into the passage with Joe.

The tunnel was narrow, but high enough to permit them to move about without crouching. They were unable to light their way, as Frank needed the flashlight turned before him in order to frighten back the wolves. For a moment the animals seemed to hesitate, as though fearing a trap and then the foremost wolf cautiously entered the tunnel in pursuit of its prey.

The boys backed slowly down the tunnel, which descended on a slope. They did not know where it led, they could not see, but they knew they must keep backing away from the wolves.

"We're up against it if this is a blind alley," declared Joe, in a low voice.

"We're up against it if we stop and try to fight it out."

Step by step they moved backward, and step by step the foremost wolf pursued them.

The animal was more cowardly than the leader that had been killed. He did not advance boldly, but slunk along, pressing to the side of the tunnel as though trying to evade the dazzling gleam of light that shone in his eyes. Now and then he snarled viciously, showing his teeth.

"Are any of the wolves following him?" asked Joe, from the darkness.

"I can't see any. This brute seems to be alone."

"How about taking a shot at him?"

"What's the use? Even if I did kill him, we'd only run into the rest of them when we went out into the cave again. I'm not going to use this gun again unless I absolutely have to."

The brothers continued their weird journey. The tunnel was damp and chilly. The floor was rocky and uneven, and Frank was in constant dread lest he trip and fall. It would be all up with them then. The wolf would not lose a second in taking advantage of such an opportunity. So, stepping backward, they retreated farther and farther down the passage, watching the grey form that constantly followed, never gaining on them, but never falling back.

"I wonder how long this tunnel is?" Frank muttered.

"Can't last forever," said Joe, with an attempt at cheerfulness. "I think I feel a draft of cold air at my back."

"It doesn't lead outside, that's certain. If it did it would be sloping upward."

There was a low snarl from the wolf. It advanced farther into the circle of light. The brute had evidently decided that the light was not particularly dangerous, and was growing bolder.

Frank tightened his grip on the revolver. The animal was preparing for a rush.

The gaunt grey form gathered itself together and came directly at him.

Frank pressed the trigger.

The revolver crashed forth, awakening thunderous echoes in the narrow tunnel. The wolf gave vent to a howl of pain and fury, but although its onward course was checked for a moment and it swerved to one side it did not fall back. The bullet had not found a vital spot. Maddened by pain, the animal came on again.

The boys scrambled back. The wolf leaped. Frank flung himself to one side and the great body brushed against him. He struck out with the revolver and felt the weapon strike against flesh. Again he pulled the trigger, with the barrel of the weapon directly against the animal's hide, and then he sprang farther back into the tunnel.

Behind him he heard a shout. It seemed curiously far away. He retreated another step.

His foot did not find the solid rock. Instead, he stepped back into space. For an instant he wavered, clutching vainly at the air. Then he lost his balance, staggered backward, and then felt himself falling on downward into utter darkness.

CHAPTER XXI

UNDERGROUND

Frank Hardy could not have fallen more than ten or twelve feet, but he had the sensation of having dropped from an enormous height. The unexpectedness of it took his breath away, and when he finally crashed into a heap of earth and gravel with a jolt that jarred every bone in his body he could only lie there in the darkness and wonder that he was still alive.

Then, to his relief, came a voice from close at hand.

"Are you all right, Frank?"

"That you, Joe?"

"You didn't expect to find anybody else down here, did you?" asked Joe, with a chuckle.

"I'm all right. No bones broken. How about you?"

"I'm shaken up a bit, but I'm all right. Thank goodness I didn't land on my head."

"What on earth happened?"

"We must have stepped right back into the main shaft of the mine. That passage we were in was a drift that went right through to the cave. We're at the bottom of the shaft now, I guess."

Frank had still retained his grasp of the flashlight. Fortunately it had not been broken in the fall and when he switched it on the welcome glow of light again pervaded their prison.

High above them they could see a patch of snow-white sky, sharply outlined by the rectangular shaft-head. A crude ladder ascended the side of the shaft. They could see the black patch that marked the entrance to the drift from which they had fallen, and from it emanated growls and snarls of rage and pain.

"That beast won't follow us any farther. I guess that was why the wolves were so doubtful about chasing us in there. They steer clear of that tunnel," ventured Frank.

"Lucky for us we hit the shaft when we did. That wolf would have been all over us in two more seconds. He'd have made mincemeat out of both of us. I thought sure we were done for, and then I stepped back—wow! I thought I was falling clean through the earth."

"Me, too. I couldn't imagine what had happened. I thought the bottom of the tunnel had given way on us."

"Good thing the shaft isn't any deeper. We'd have saved our lives by escaping from the wolf and broken our necks by falling down the shaft."

"We're lucky. But now we're down here, what are we going to do about it?"

Joe pointed to the ladder.

"We can get to the surface easily enough now."

"But if this is the main shaft we ought to be able to find our way to the blue room mentioned on that map."

"No use backing out now that we've come this far. I'd almost forgotten what we'd come for."

Frank got to his feet. He was not seriously injured by the fall, although he had wrenched one knee. But he was able to walk without much difficulty. He explored the bottom of the shaft with the flashlight. Almost directly across from them he found the entrance to the tunnel indicated on the map he had discovered in the outlaw's notebook.

"Here we are!"

To refresh his memory he drew the notebook from his pocket again and the boys studied the map once more.

"This passage leads to the big chamber, by the looks of it. And when we get there we find two passages leading out of it. We follow this one," Frank indicated the tunnel marked X. "And from there we get to a smaller chamber. We follow a tunnel out of that until we get to what they call the blue room. And there we'll find the gold."

"If the outlaws haven't beaten us to it."

"Perhaps so. But perhaps they haven't."

Frank advanced toward the tunnel, flashing the light before him. It was a large passage and had evidently been frequently used. He examined the damp floor and found footprints that were plainly of recent origin.

"Some one has been here, and not so long ago either."

"Today?"

"It's hard to tell. Footprints would look fresh down here for weeks, as long as no one else stepped over them. What I mean is that there has been some one down here since the mine was abandoned. That's plain enough."

"Well, it means we're on the right track."

With rapidly growing excitement, the two Hardy boys made their way on into the tunnel. Frank, having the flashlight, took the lead. This tunnel, the main drift of the mine leading into the working level, was not of great length, and within the minute they had reached the first chamber indicated on the map.

In the glow of the flashlight they saw that it was of considerable extent and was bolstered up by timbers that were now rotting away. The marks of pickaxes were discernible on the walls and an overturned wheelbarrow bore mute testimony to the work that had once gone on here underground in the search for gold.

Frank turned the light this way and that. In one corner he found the entrance to a second corridor leading out of the working, but this was not the one he wanted. After a few minutes' search they discovered the tunnel indicated by the cross on the map.

"We're getting warmer," he said, as they advanced toward it.

The tunnel had heavy timbers at either side, to support the roof and to prevent a cave-in. They entered it and stumbled along across the uneven floor. Water dripped from the ceiling and from the rocky walls. The dampness and cold made them shiver.

The tunnel led into a second and smaller chamber.

"Now for the last passageway. Then to the blue room!"

They explored the little chamber. But of a tunnel leading from it there was no sign. A sloping heap of gravel and boulders lay in one corner, a broken pickax lay on the floor, and a rusty shovel stood against the wall. There were many footmarks on the damp floor, but there was not the slightest trace of an exit.

"That's funny," murmured Frank, as he turned the beam of the flashlight on the walls. "I'm sure we're in the right place."

He looked at the map again. They had followed the directions exactly, and if the map was correct they should find a tunnel leading from the rocky chamber in which they stood.

"Listen!" said Joe suddenly.

They stood stock-still, not saying a word. The silence of the mine was profound.

"What's the matter?" whispered Frank finally.

"I thought I heard a sound—like some one talking."

They listened again, but they could hear nothing save the occasional drip-drip of water from the walls.

"It must have been my imagination," said Joe, at last. "But I was sure I heard a voice."

"This mine is full of echoes. It was probably only the wind whistling down the shaft."

"I guess that was it. But this place is so creepy a fellow imagines almost anything."

"It would be a tough break for us if the outlaws marched in on us just now."

"I don't think there's much danger. They won't be roaming around in that storm outside."

The boys resumed their search of the cave. They turned the flashlight high and low in the hope of finding the tunnel that had been so plainly marked on the plan, but without success.

"We must have taken the wrong passage," Joe remarked.

"I'm positive we took the right one. I took special care—But say! Perhaps the tunnel has been covered up!"

"That's an idea. It may be hidden."

Frank turned the light on the heap of rocks and gravel in one corner of the cave. At the base of the pile he could see footprints, all of which led directly to or from the heap.

"Maybe this is where it is," he said, and, handing Joe the flashlight, he picked up the shovel. He attacked the gravel vigorously, casting shovelfuls of it to one side. In a few moments he gave an exclamation of satisfaction. For, back of the gravel he had shoveled away, he saw a wooden door.

"Now we're getting there!"

The gravel flew, and in a short time the door was revealed, back of a heap of boulders that the boys lost no time in rolling to one side. To their disappointment they found a rusty padlock on the door, but Joe remembered the broken pickax they had seen in the chamber a short while before and he seized it. A few sharp blows and the padlock lay broken and shattered. He wrenched at the door and it came slowly open, with a protesting creak of hinges.

Casting the shovel to one side, Frank once more took the lead and they passed through the doorway. The tunnel at this point was very rough and narrow. They made their way cautiously forward. Frank noticed a change in the color of the earth and rock at this juncture.

"It seems blue," he remarked to his brother. Some chemical constituent gave the underground passage that peculiar shade, discernible even in the dim light.

The tunnel narrowed and the boys squeezed their way through the passage, stepping directly into another chamber dug out of the earth. Here the blueness of the walls was intensified, the wet blue earth giving off a weird glow.

"No mistake about it this time!" declared Frank triumphantly. "We're in the blue room at last."

His words echoed and re-echoed in the confined space. The boys were trembling with excitement. The end of their search was at hand. Somewhere in that underground room lay the four bags of gold.

But where?

The floor of the chamber was unbroken. A few faint footprints could be seen, but there was nothing to indicate a secret hiding place. Frank again produced the map.

"Gold at circle," he said, reading from the instructions. "The map shows the circle to be in the far right hand corner." He went forward to the corner indicated. The earth here seemed unusually smooth and flat.

"I think it's buried here," declared Frank. "There's the mark of a shovel."

"I'll get that shovel we had in the other room. Lend me the light for a second."

Frank handed his brother the flashlight, and Joe disappeared from the blue chamber. His footsteps echoed in the narrow passage.

As Frank Hardy waited in the dank darkness, he felt a curious exultation possess him. They were on the verge of solving the mystery of the hidden gold—if only the outlaws had not removed it from its hiding place. He waited in suspense for his brother's return.

CHAPTER XXII
BLACK PEPPER

In a few minutes Frank Hardy saw the gleam of the light and heard his brother's footsteps as Joe returned. He was carrying the shovel that had served them to such good purpose in uncovering the secret door to the passageway of the blue room.

"I'll dig," he volunteered, handing the flashlight to Frank.

Then, with a will, he set to work.

The earth was soft, which showed that it had been dug up before and replaced. Frank held the light, directing its beam on the place where Joe was digging, and as a hole rapidly appeared in the ground he watched eagerly for some sign of the treasure which they sought.

In his mind was always the hated probability that they might have been forestalled and that the outlaws might have already visited the place and removed the gold. But, in that case, he argued to himself, it was not likely that they would have taken such precautions to bank up the locked door of the passage. There would have been no need for it.

"Nothing yet," panted Joe.

"It may be buried deep."

A far-off sound caught Frank's ear. He started violently, because his nerves were already tautened by suspense.

"Did you hear that?" he asked.

Joe rested on the shovel.

"I heard something," he said doubtfully.

They listened, but the sound was not repeated.

"It might have been a fall of rock," said Frank. "It sounded like rocks striking against the walls of the shaft."

"It's just like my thinking I heard voices a while ago. This place is so silent and creepy it gets your nerves all unstrung."

"Maybe."

Joe resumed his shoveling.

Another shovelful of earth and he bent forward.

"Something here!" he exclaimed. "My shovel struck something solid."

Frank brought the flashlight closer. Just above the earth he could see the top of a canvas sack.

"It's the gold! Dig, Joe. Dig!"

Joe Hardy needed no urging. He had seized the shovel again and the earth was flying furiously on all sides. Rapidly, he uncovered the top of the canvas sack, and then a second appeared in view. Frank bent down and seized one of the sacks, dragging it from the retaining earth. It came free. Joe flung aside his shovel and, in the illumination from the flashlight, Frank undid the heavy cord at the top of the sack and opened it.

He thrust his hand inside and withdrew it a moment later, clutching a handful of reddish brown objects that looked like pebbles.

"Nuggets!"

The boys gazed at the gold nuggets in silent delight. They were of good size, and the youths realized that they must be very valuable. Frank thrust his hand into the sack again and this time brought forth a handful of reddish sand that they recognized as gold dust.

"Gold dust and nuggets! We've found it at last!"

"There are more sacks yet. Didn't dad say there were four?"

Joe picked up his shovel again. After a few minutes' energetic digging he uncovered the rest of the sacks and in a short time all four were on the floor of the cave.

The Hardy boys examined each in turn, and found that each was identical with the first in that it contained gold dust and nuggets in large quantities. The sight of so much gold sent a thrill through them, just as it has sent a thrill through gold-seekers since the world began. Here was wealth, wealth in the raw, wealth for which men had fought and struggled, wealth that had been drawn from the depths of the earth.

"We've found it at last!" Frank declared, with a sigh of relief.

"Dad will be pleased."

"I don't think he ever really expected we'd find it."

"We've worked hard enough for it. Won't the outlaws be wild when they come here for it and find that it's gone!"

"Let them be wild. It isn't theirs."

"Four sacks of it," said Joe. "It must be worth thousands."

"It's the gold that Jadbury Wilson mentioned. I'm sure of that. And before we hand it over to Bart Dawson we'll have an explanation from him."

"Somehow, I can't believe he's dishonest. There must be a mistake in it somewhere, Frank."

"You can't always tell by looks in this world. Although, to tell the truth, I find it hard to believe that Dawson made away with this, myself. But we'll make him come across with the whole story, and if he did steal it, we'll see that Wilson gets his share."

"That's the ticket. And now—to get out of this mine with it."

"It'll be easy enough. We can go up the shaft. That's the way the outlaws got in here, I guess. We took the wrong entrance getting in here. We got into one of the side workings of the mine instead of coming down the main way."

"As long as we don't run into any more wolves I don't care how we get out," said Joe. "The sooner we get out though, the better. It must be night by now."

Frank bent and picked up two of the sacks of gold.

"I'll carry two and you carry two. Boy, but they're heavy! I never knew gold weighed so much."

"I shouldn't care if it weighed a ton. It won't seem like much, now that we've found it at last."

Frank hesitated.

"It might be as well to dig a little deeper there. They might have divided the gold up. I'd hate to overlook a sack of it."

"I was just thinking the same thing." Joe picked up the shovel again. "I'll dig down a little bit farther, just for luck."

He attacked the hole in the earth again, and for a while he shoveled industriously, but it soon became apparent that they had found all of the gold that had been buried in that place.

"I guess we got it all," he said, flinging the shovel to one side. "All the outlaws will find here will be a hole in the ground—a big one."

"I'd like to be listening in when they come to look for their treasure. They'll be as mad as hornets."

Joe picked up his two sacks of gold.

"Better let me carry one of yours," he suggested. "You have the flashlight to carry. It'll be awkward for you."

"I'd forgotten about the light," Frank agreed. "All right."

He passed over one of the sacks he had been carrying, and then bent down to pick up the flashlight that had been resting on the ground.

"And now," he said, "we'll leave the blue room. It isn't as blue as Black Pepper and his gang will be when they come to visit the place."

The boys looked at the hole in the ground and chuckled. They were just about to turn, ready to leave, when they heard a sound from the passage leading into the chamber.

This time they knew it was no trick of the imagination. They could sense plainly that some one was standing there. Some one had crept up through the tunnel, unheard, and was even then standing silently in the darkness.

Frank flung the flashlight about. Its circle of radiance illuminated the dark entrance to the chamber clearly. There, in the very center of the opening, stood a tall, swarthy man with villainous features. He had a heavy black beard and his dark eyebrows were knitted with wrath. And, leveled directly at the two boys, he held in each hand a wicked-looking black revolver.

"Hands up!" he rasped curtly, in a voice that vibrated with anger.

The Hardy boys knew without question that this man was none other than the notorious outlaw they had tried to circumvent—Black Pepper!

CHAPTER XXIII

THE CAPTURE

The Hardy boys were stunned by surprise. With victory in their grasp they had turned to confront this menacing figure that seemed to have risen like a ghost from the darkness. Black Pepper had captured them red-handed.

"Drop that gold!" growled the outlaw. "Drop that gold and put up your hands!"

They faced one another tensely. Suddenly Frank pointed to the tunnel directly behind Black Pepper.

"Grab him!" he shouted.

Almost instinctively, the outlaw wheeled about to face the enemy whom he judged was behind him. Before he realized the trick that had been played on him and while his revolvers were turned away from the two lads, the Hardy boys sprang into action.

Joe flung one of the sacks of gold with all his force. It struck against the outlaw's arm and knocked one of the weapons clattering to the floor. At the same instant Frank flung the sack that he was carrying, and it struck Black Pepper in the chest.

The outlaw reeled backward. The Hardy boys leaped toward him.

Frank was on him before he could raise his remaining weapon. Like a flash, he seized Black Pepper's arm, holding the revolver away from him. Then Joe joined the struggle and between the two of them they bore the outlaw to the ground by the sheer violence of their attack.

Grimly, Black Pepper struggled. The flashlight had gone out, and the battle raged in complete darkness. It was difficult to tell friend from foe. The outlaw was strong and powerful and he wrestled desperately to get free.

Frank clung grimly to the outlaw's arm, exerting all his strength to prevent Black Pepper from getting control of the revolver. The weapon exploded in the darkness, the shot sounding like a crash of thunder in that confined space.

Frank got his hands on the revolver and wrested sharply at it. Black Pepper's grasp relaxed. The revolver gave way and Frank wrenched it away from the outlaw. Quickly he reversed it and pressed the barrel against Black Pepper's body.

"Put up your hands!" he snapped. "I have you covered."

Black Pepper ceased his struggles and lay still.

"I give in," he said quickly. "I give in. Don't shoot."

"Get the flashlight, Joe."

Joe relinquished his grasp on the outlaw and searched for the flashlight, which had rolled to a distant corner of the cave. He found it at last and switched it on. The light revealed Black Pepper lying on his back, his hands upraised. His eyes were wide with fear.

"Get up!" ordered Frank.

The outlaw scrambled to his feet, arms still high.

"Get the other gun, Joe."

Joe found the other revolver on the floor and picked it up.

"Fine! Now we'll take you back with us."

"Let me go, boys," pleaded the desperado. "It was only a joke. I was only tryin' to scare you. Take the gold, if you want, but let me go."

"You have a funny idea of a joke. Well, just as a joke, we'll take you down to Lucky Bottom and clap you into jail. That's the kind of a sense of humor we have. Pick up the gold, Joe, and go ahead of him. I'll come behind."

Armed with the flashlight and two sacks of gold, Joe went to the entrance of the blue room. Frank picked up the other two sacks and, still keeping Black Pepper covered with a revolver, urged him ahead.

"Forward, march!" he ordered.

Reluctantly, the outlaw strode ahead, following Joe, who was silhouetted against the circle of light cast by the flash.

"My men will see that you pay up for this!" he growled savagely.

"Your men will be scattered so far you'll never be able to find them when they hear you've been taken in," replied Frank. "If they don't, they'll land in jail with you. How did you happen to be down in the mine without them? Trying to make away with the gold in the storm?"

The shot told. Black Pepper looked around sharply.

"I wasn't trying to double-cross them!" he shouted. "Don't tell them that! Don't say you found me down here. None of us was supposed to go in here alone."

Frank chuckled.

"So that was your game, was it? You thought you'd sneak down here and grab the gold, then make your escape under cover of the blizzard. If we hadn't got here first, you would have done it, too. Your men will be liable to take revenge on us after that, won't they? Why, they'll want to see you hanged!"

Black Pepper was silent. His bluff had failed, and he knew it. He knew that when the other outlaws heard he had been captured in the blue room they would realize that he had been trying to steal a march on them and make away with the gold without their knowledge.

Joe led the way down the passage into the next chamber, and from there they proceeded out into the main shaft.

"I guess we were right after all when he thought we heard noises," he called back to Frank. "It was our friend here making his way down into the mine."

"He came down quietly enough. I nearly jumped out of my shoes when I saw him standing there with those revolvers pointed at us. We'll say that much for you, Black Pepper—you took us completely by surprise."

The outlaw grunted, but it was not with satisfaction.

Joe began to ascend the ladder that led up the side of the shaft.

"Up you go," declared Frank, prodding the desperado in the ribs with the barrel of the revolver. Black Pepper scrambled up the rungs with alacrity.

They made the tedious climb without trouble, and when Joe emerged at the top of the shaft he took up his position and covered Black Pepper with the revolver until the outlaw was again on the surface and until Frank had joined him. The blizzard had died down to a mild snowfall, although darkness had fallen.

Far below, they could see the few twinkling lights of Lucky Bottom. A clearly defined trail led out toward the road. Joe took the lead once more.

So the odd procession made its way through the snow, the outlaw shambling despondently and dispiritedly between his captors. The weight of the gold was considerable, but Frank and Joe scarcely noticed it, so exultant were they over their double victory. They had not only recovered the gold for its rightful owners, but they had captured one of the most notorious outlaws of the West in the bargain.

When they reached Hank Shale's cabin they marched Black Pepper up to the door. Joe stepped inside and, still covering the outlaw, bade him enter.

Frank saw his father sitting up in bed, wide-eyed with astonishment, and Hank Shale and Bart Dawson by the fire, their mouths agape. Bart Dawson had just been in the act of putting his pipe in his mouth as they entered, and he held it suspended, staring at the trio as they came into the cabin.

Joe flung down his sacks of gold on the table.

"Here's the gold—part of it, anyway!"

"And here's the rest of it," said Frank as he closed the door and put down his two sacks. "And here," he said, indicating Black Pepper, "is the leader of the gang who stole it."

"Black Pepper!" said Hank Shale, starting up.

The outlaw was silent. He eyed Frank's revolver warily, as though even yet considering his chances of escape. But the weapon did not waver and he saw that he was trapped.

"Got a rope?" asked Frank of Hank Shale. "He must be tired keeping his hands up. We'll tie his wrists and then march him down to the jail."

"I'll say I have a rope!" shouted Hank, springing up, and within a few minutes Black Pepper's arms were firmly bound behind his back.

"But where on airth did ye find the gold?" demanded Bart Dawson, spluttering with excitement. "Tell us what happened! It's the very gold that was stolen!" He dug his hands into the sacks and sifted the gold dust and nuggets between his fingers. "It's all here—every bit of it! Tell us all about it, lads."

"Take him down to jail first," said Fenton Hardy quietly. "I'm as curious as any one to hear what happened, but the boys can tell us when they come back. The story will keep. But don't be long."

"I'll go with ye!" declared Dawson, picking up his hat and scrambling into his mackinaw coat. "This is too good to miss. I never thought I'd see the day when Black Pepper would be shoved into the calaboose!"

So, with Bart Dawson chattering excitedly by their sides, the Hardy boys left the cabin, where Fenton Hardy and Hank Shale were indulging in vain conjectures as to how the gold had been recovered and how the outlaw had been captured.

As they entered Lucky Bottom, although it was nightfall and people had long since retired indoors, the news quickly spread, by some mysterious system of telegraphy or mental telepathy, and by the time they reached the jail, husky miners and citizens were running down the street from every direction, anxious to witness the spectacle of Black Pepper being put behind the bars at last.

The sheriff was in his office and his jaw sagged with amazement when they entered.

"Here's Black Pepper for ye!" roared Bart Dawson. "Here's a prisoner for your jail, sheriff! Clap him in a good strong cell!"

"B—B—Black Pepper!" stammered the sheriff.

"This is him. And see that he don't get loose, neither. If he does, we'll string you up to a telygrapht pole."

"What's the charge?" asked the sheriff mechanically.

"There don't need to be no charge. You know as well as I do that there's been a reward of five hundred out for Black Pepper for the last three years. Put him in a cell, and no more of your foolish questions. If you must have a charge, put him down for stealin' four bags of gold that never belonged to him. Charge him with vagrancy and loiterin' and spittin' on the sidewalk. Charge him with mayhem and assault and battery and horse-stealin' and robbery and carryin' concealed weapons and parkin' his autymobile too close to a hydrant. Put him down for everythin' you've got on your book. He's been guilty of 'em all."

The sheriff wilted. He led Black Pepper to a cell, where Slim Briggs was sitting despondently. When Slim saw the leader of the gang being ushered in he shook his head in sympathy and groaned.

The door clanged.

"That fixes Black Pepper!" declared Bart Dawson, with satisfaction. "Now come on back to the cabin and tell us all about it. I'm just about dyin' of curiosity."

Dawson and the Hardy boys left the jail and had to fight their way through the crowd that surged about the doorway. Questions were hurled at them as they started up the street. Was it true that Black Pepper had been captured at last? Who caught him? What was he in for? How did it all happen, anyway?

"Tell ye all tomorrow," promised Bart Dawson, leading the boys on up the hill. "I'm not very clear about it just yet, myself."

So the Hardy boys returned to Hank Shale's cabin on the hill, there to tell the tale of their hazardous adventures and the successful outcome of their search for the hidden gold.

CHAPTER XXIV

BART DAWSON EXPLAINS

Sitting beside the fire in Hank Shale's cabin, the Hardy boys told their story. They were interrupted frequently by ejaculations of "Ye don't say!" and, "Well I'll be switched!" from the two old miners, and occasionally their father smiled in approval.

When they had finished, Bart Dawson slapped his knee.

"I never heard the beat of it!" he declared. "Ye went up on that there mountain and got lost and attacked by wolves and fell down the shaft and got held up by Black Pepper, and yet here ye are, and there's the gold. I never heard the beat!"

"Neither did I!" affirmed Hank Shale slowly.

"There's the gold," laughed Frank, indicating the four sacks on the table.

"Coulson will be tickled to death," declared Bart Dawson. "He never expected either of us to see it again."

"There's a question we wanted to ask you," put in Frank. "Are you sure there isn't anybody else but Mr. Coulson sharing the gold with you?"

Fenton Hardy looked up startled. He could not imagine what this was leading to. As for Bart Dawson, he looked blank.

"Not that I know of," he said.

"Are you quite sure?"

"I'm certain sure. There's Coulson's brother did own a share of it, but he's dead, and there's Jadbury Wilson, my old pardner, but he's dead, too. That leaves only me and Coulson."

"Are you sure Wilson is dead?"

"Last we heard of him he was. He went East, they say, and died out there. I sure wish he could be here tonight. Poor old Jad—he worked so hard for his share of that gold, and never got none of it."

"Jadbury Wilson isn't dead."

"What?" shouted Bart Dawson, leaping to his feet. "Say them words again, lad! Do ye know for sure? Is Jad Wilson still livin'?"

"He's staying at our house in Bayport right now," declared Joe.

Fenton Hardy looked more surprised than ever. The case was taking an angle he had never anticipated.

"If I'm sure Jad Wilson is still alive I'll be the happiest man in the world!" declared Bart Dawson. "But how do ye know? Tell me about him."

The Hardy boys thereupon told of their meeting with Jadbury Wilson and of the story he had told of his gold-mining days in the West.

"So he thinks that you stole the gold from him and went away with it," concluded Frank.

"I don't blame him for thinkin' that!" said Dawson heartily. "I don't blame him a bit! When I come back to Lucky Bottom I made it my business to trace up my old pardners, but the only one I could find was Coulson, and he told me his brother and Jad Wilson was dead."

"But what had happened to the gold?"

"I'm comin' to that. When the outlaws attacked our camp, the others sent me out to hide the gold. And I hid it. I was just gettin' away when a stray bullet hit me, and I'll be hanged if I didn't go clean off my head. I didn't remember nothin'. I must have wandered away from Lucky Bottom altogether, for when I come to myself I was miles and miles away, up in northern Montana, and I couldn't remember one thing of my life up to that time. It had been wiped clean out of my memory. I had papers on me that had my name written on them, but I didn't know where I had come from or nothin'."

"I have heard of such cases," said Fenton Hardy.

"I had clean lost my memory. I didn't even know I had ever been in Lucky Bottom. Everythin' was blank up to the time I come to myself. Then, a few months ago, a doctor told me he thought he could fix me up, and I had an operation and—click! I remembered everythin'. I remembered Lucky Bottom and our mine, and how I had hidden the gold. It all come back to me. So I came back to Lucky Bottom and dug up the gold again and tried to find my pardners, and Coulson and I was ready to split it up between us, seein' we thought his brother and Jad Wilson was dead, when the outlaws stole it on us. So that's how it happened."

Frank and Joe had listened entranced.

"Why, that explains everything!" Frank declared. "It clears it all up. We couldn't believe you had been crooked, although—" he stopped in confusion.

"Although it looked mighty like it, eh?" finished Bart Dawson, with a smile. "Well, I don't blame ye for bein' suspicious. And now, if you'll take me back East with ye, I'll meet my old pardner, Jad Wilson, again, and he'll get his share of the gold. It should be enough to keep him in comfort for all the rest of his life."

"He's been having a pretty tough time," said Frank. "He'll welcome it."

"And glad I'll be to see that he gets his share. As for you, Mr. Hardy," went on Dawson, turning to the detective. "I promised you a good fee if ye'd take this case for me and I promised you a reward if the gold was found. Two thousand dollars, I said, and two thousand dollars you'll get as soon as I can get these nuggets and the gold dust changed into real money."

"I won't take it all," said Fenton Hardy. "My boys did the real work."

"That's up to you. It was your case and you can do what you like with the money. But," Dawson declared with emphasis, "if ye don't divvy up with these two lads—!"

"Don't worry," laughed the detective. "I have no intention of letting them work for nothing. I want to share the reward with them."

"Well, that's fine, then. And they get five hundred dollars for capturin' Black Pepper—don't forget that." Bart Dawson turned to the Hardy boys. "Ye ought to have a nice fat bank account when you go back East."

"It begins to look that way," agreed Frank, with a pleased smile.

"You've done good work," said Fenton Hardy. "You've cleaned up this case in record time and, to tell the truth, I hardly expected you would be successful, because you were up against a mighty difficult undertaking and you didn't have very much to work on. You deserve everything that is coming to you in the way of reward. You've done me credit."

"Hearing you say that is reward enough," said Frank, and Joe nodded his head in agreement.

"Real detectives, both of 'em," said Hank Shale, puffing at his pipe.

THE SHORE ROAD MYSTERY

ORIGINALLY PUBLISHED IN 1928.

CHAPTER I

STOLEN CARS

"It certainly is a mystery how those autos disappeared," said Frank Hardy.

"I'll say it is," replied his brother Joe, raising his voice to be heard above the clatter of their motorcycles. "Just think of it! Two cars last week, two the week before, and one the week before that. Some thieving, I'll tell the world."

"And Martin's car was brand new," called back Chet Morton.

"Mighty tough," Frank affirmed. "It's bad enough to lose a car, but to have it stolen the day after you've bought it is a little too much."

"Must be a regular gang of car thieves at work."

The three boys, on their motorcycles, were speeding along the Shore Road that skirted Barmet Bay, just out of Bayport, on a sunny Saturday afternoon.

"A person takes a big risk leaving a car parked along this road," said Chet. "Every one of the five autos disappeared along the shore."

"What beats me," declared Frank, turning out to avoid a mud puddle, "is how the thieves got away with them. None of them were seen coming into Bayport and there was no trace of them at the other end of the Shore Road, either. Seems as if they just vanished into the thin air."

Chet slowed down so that the trio were riding abreast.

"If the cars were only ordinary flivvers it wouldn't be so bad. But they were all expensive, high-powered hacks. Martin's car would be spotted anywhere, and so would the others. It's funny that no one saw them."

"Some of these auto thieves are mighty smart," opined Joe. "They certainly have their nerve, working this road for three weeks, and with everybody on the lookout for them. It has certainly put a crimp in the bathing and fishing along the Shore Road." He gestured toward the beach below. "Why, usually on a Saturday afternoon like this you'll see a dozen cars parked along here. What with boating and fishing and swimming, lots of people used to come out from town. Now, if they come at all, they walk."

"And you can't blame 'em. Who wants to lose a high-priced car just for the sake of an hour's fishing?"

"It's certainly mighty strange," Frank reiterated. "After taking two cars from almost the same place, you'd imagine the thieves would be scared to come back."

"They have plenty of nerve, that's certain."

"It isn't as if the police haven't been busy. They've watched this road ever since the first car was lost, and the other autos were stolen just the same. They've kept an eye on both ends of the highway and there wasn't a sign of any of them."

"It's strange that they haven't turned up somewhere. Lots of times a stolen car will be recovered when the thief tries to get rid of it. The engine numbers alone often trip them up. Of course, I guess they'd clap on false license plates, but it's pretty hard to get away with a fine-looking car like Martin's unless it's been repainted and altered a bit."

"It's no fun to lose a car," declared Chet. "I remember how badly I felt when the crooks stole my roadster last year."

"You got it back, anyway."

"Yes, I got it back. But I was mighty blue until I did."

The motorcycles rounded a bend in the road and before the boys lay a wide stretch of open highway, descending in a gradual slope. To their right lay Barmet Bay, sparkling in the afternoon sun. At the bottom of the slope was a grassy expanse that opened out on the beach, the road at this point being only a few feet above the sea level. The little meadow was a favorite parking place for motorists, as their cars could regain the road easily, but today there was not an automobile in sight.

"Look at that," said Frank. "No one here on a nice afternoon like this."

At that moment, however, the appearance of a man who came running up from the beach and across the grass, belied his words.

"Some one's here all right," remarked Joe. "And he seems in a hurry about something."

As the boys rode down the slope they could see the man hastening out into the middle of the road, where he stood waving his arms.

"Looks like Isaac Fussy, doesn't it?" said Chet.

"The rich old fisherman?"

"Yes, it's Fussy all right. Look at him dancing around. Wonder what's the matter."

In a few moments the boys had drawn near enough to see that the old man who was waving at them so frantically was indeed the wealthy and eccentric old fisherman known as Isaac Fussy. He was an odd old fellow who lived by himself in a big house on the outskirts of Bayport, and who spent much of his time on the bay. Just now he was evidently in a state of great agitation, shouting and waving his arms as the boys approached.

The motorcycles came to a stop.

"Anything wrong?" asked Frank.

"After 'em. After 'em!" shouted the old man, his face crimson with wrath, as he shook his fist in the air. "Chase 'em. lads!"

"Who? What's the matter, Mr. Fussy?"

"Thieves! That's what's the matter! My automobile!"

"Stolen?"

"Stolen! Robbed! I left it here not ten minutes ago and was startin' out in my boat to fish. I just looked back in time to see somebody drivin' away in it. An outrage!" shouted Mr. Fussy. "After 'em."

"Why, it's been stolen just a few minutes ago, then?"

"They just went tearin' around the bend before you came in sight. If you look lively, you'll catch 'em. You know my car—it's a big blue Cadillac sedan. Paid twenty-eight hundred for it. Catch them thieves and I'll reward you. Don't waste time standin' here talkin' about it—"

The motorcycles roared and leaped forward.

"We'll do our best!" shouted Frank, as he crouched low over the handle bars.

A cloud of dust arose as the three powerful machines sped off down the road, leaving Isaac Fussy still muttering imprecations on the thieves who had stolen his Cadillac.

The boys were excited and elated. This was as close as any one had yet come to being on the trail of the auto thieves, and they knew that in their fast motorcycles they possessed a decided advantage. If, as Isaac Fussy said, the car had just disappeared around the bend a few minutes previously, they stood an excellent chance of overtaking it.

The motorcycles slanted far over to the side as they took the curve in a blinding screen of dust, then righted again as they sped down the next open stretch at terrific speed. There was no sign of the stolen car, but the open stretch was only about a quarter of a mile in length, skirting the shore, and the road then wound inland behind a bank of trees.

The clamor of the pounding motors filled the summer air as the boys raced in pursuit. Before them was a thin haze of dust, just settling in the road, which indicated that an automobile had passed that way only a few minutes before.

"We'll catch 'em." shouted Chet, jubilantly.

Without slackening speed, they took the next curve and then found themselves speeding through a cool grove, where the road wound about, cutting off the view ahead. When at length they emerged into an open section of farming land they gazed anxiously into the distance in hope of seeing their quarry, but they were disappointed. The fleeing car was not yet in sight.

Down the road, between the crooked fences, they raced, the engines raising a tremendous racket.

A few hundred yards ahead was the entrance to a lane that led into a farm. The lane was lined with dense trees.

Suddenly, Frank gasped and desperately began to cut down his speed. For, out of this lane, emerged a team of horses, drawing a huge wagonload of hay.

The dust raised by Frank's motorcycle obscured the view of the other boys, and for a moment they did not realize what was happening. The trees along the lane had hidden the hay wagon from sight and Frank was almost upon it before he realized the danger. It was impossible to stop in time.

The man on the hay wagon shouted and waved his arms. The horses reared. The clumsy vehicle presented a barrier directly across the road.

There was only one thing for it. The boys had to take to the ditch to avoid a collision. There was no time to stop.

Frank wheeled his speeding machine to the left, praying for the best. For a moment, he thought he would make it. The motorcycle bumped and lurched, and then it went over on its side and he was flung violently over the handle bars into the bushes ahead.

Behind him he heard shouts, the roar of the other machines, and then two crashes, which came almost simultaneously. Chet and Joe had also been spilled.

CHAPTER II

CIRCUMSTANTIAL EVIDENCE

For a moment Frank Hardy lay in the thicket, stunned by the shock of his fall, with the breath knocked out of him. Gradually, he recovered himself and managed to scramble to his feet. His first thought was for the other boys, but a quick glance showed that both Chet and Joe were unhurt, beyond a few bruises.

Joe was sitting in the ditch, looking around him in bewilderment, as though he had not yet realized exactly what had happened, while Chet Morton was picking himself up out of a clump of undergrowth near the fence. In the road, the driver of the hay wagon was trying to calm his startled horses, who were rearing and plunging in fright.

"Any bones broken?" asked Frank of his two companions.

Chet carefully counted his ribs.

"Guess not," he announced, cheerfully. "I think I'm all here, safe and sound. Wow! What a spill that was!"

Joe got to his feet.

"Good thing this is a soft ditch," he said. "It's lucky somebody didn't get a broken neck."

"Well, nobody did, and that's that. How about the bikes?"

Frank examined his own motorcycle, righted it, and found that the machine was not damaged beyond a bent mudguard. He had managed to slow down sufficiently before careering into the ditch, so that much of the shock had been averted and the motorcycle had simply turned over into the spongy turf.

"My bike's all right," announced Chet. "It's bent a little here and there, but it's good for a few more miles yet."

"Same here," said Joe Hardy, looking up. "I think we're mighty lucky to get off so easily."

"You mighta run me down!" roared the driver of the hay wagon, now that he had recovered from his fright. "Tearin' and snortin' down the road on them contraptions—"

"Why don't you watch the road?" asked Frank. "You heard us coming. We couldn't see you. You might have killed the three of us, driving out like that. You didn't have anything to worry about."

"I didn't, eh?"

"No."

"What if I'd been killed?"

"You could hear our bikes half a mile off—unless you are deaf," put in Joe.

"It ain't my business to listen for them contraptions," growled the man on the hay wagon. "I got my work to do."

"Well, don't blame us," said Frank. "And the next time you drive out of a side road like that, stop, look and listen."

"Say, who do you think you're givin' orders to?" and now the man reached for his whip and acted as if he meant to get down and thrash somebody.

"None of that—if you know when you are well off," cried Joe, his eyes blazing.

Chet stepped forward.

"If you say the word, we'll give you all that is coming to you," he put in.

All of the boys looked so determined that the man let his whip alone.

"Get out o' my way! I got to be goin'," he growled.

"Well, after this you be more careful," said Frank.

The driver grumbled, but the boys were not disposed to remain and argue the rights and wrongs of the matter. It had been an accident, pure and simple, with a certain amount of blame on both sides, so they mounted their motorcycles and drove on.

Because of the spill, the boys realized that their chances of overtaking the car thieves were correspondingly lessened, but they decided to continue the pursuit.

"At the rate they're going," said Chet, hopefully, "they may have an upset themselves."

While the Hardy boys and their chum are speeding along the Shore Road on the trail of the stolen sedan, it will not be out of place to introduce them more fully to new readers.

Frank and Joe Hardy were the sons of Fenton Hardy, a famous detective who had made a national reputation for himself while on the detective force of the New York Police Department and who had retired to set up a private practice of his own. Frank Hardy was a tall, dark lad, sixteen years old, while his brother Joe was a fair, curly-headed chap, a year younger. Both boys were students at the high school in Bayport.

When Fenton Hardy retired from the metropolitan force, owing to the great demand for his services in private investigations, he had moved with his family to Bayport, a thriving city of fifty thousand, on Barmet Bay, on the Atlantic seaboard. Here the two boys attended school and here it was that they met with the first adventures that strengthened their resolution to follow in their father's footsteps and themselves become detectives when they grew older.

Fenton Hardy was one of the greatest American criminologists, and his sons had inherited much of his ability. From their earliest boyhood it had been their united ambition to be detectives but in this they had been discouraged by their parents, who preferred to see them inclined toward medicine or the bar. However, these professions held little attraction for the lads, and when they eventually had an opportunity to display their ability as amateur detectives they felt that they had scored a point toward realizing their ambition.

In the first volume of this series, "The Hardy Boys: The Tower Treasure," the lads cleared up a mystery centering about a strange mansion on the outskirts of Bayport, recovering a quantity of stolen jewelry and bonds after the police and even Fenton Hardy had been forced to admit themselves baffled. Thereafter, their father had made but mild objections to the pursuit of their hobby and was, indeed, secretly proud of the ability displayed by his sons. Further mysteries were solved by the boys, the stories of which have been recounted in previous volumes of this series, the preceding book, "Hunting for Hidden Gold," relating their adventures in the far West, where they faced a bandit gang and went after a fortune in hidden gold in the depths of an abandoned mine.

Chet Morton, who was with the Hardy boys this afternoon, was one of their high school chums, a plump, good-natured lad with a weakness for food "and lots of it," as he frequently said. He lived on a farm about a mile outside Bayport and, like the Hardy boys, was the proud owner of a motorcycle. Frank and Joe also owned a motorboat, the *Sleuth*, which they had bought from the proceeds of a reward they had earned by their work in solving a mystery. Tony Prito, an Italian-American lad, and Biff Hooper, two other high school chums of the Hardy boys, also owned motorboats, in which the boys spent many happy hours on Barmet Bay and in which they had, incidentally, experienced a number of thrilling adventures.

"Often wished I owned a boat," said Chet, as they sped along, "but now I'm just as glad I have a motorcycle instead. I'd have missed all this fun this afternoon if I hadn't."

"You have a strange idea of fun," Joe remarked. "Getting dumped out on my head into a wet ditch doesn't make me laugh very hard."

"Better than studying algebra." Chet's aversion to school work was well known.

For a while they sped on without talking. There was no sign of the stolen automobile, but the boys did not entirely give up hope of catching up with it. When they had gone about three miles, however, even Frank was forced to admit that the fugitives had doubtless given them the slip.

"What's going on over there?" said Frank suddenly. "There's a state trooper and three men over in that farmyard."

"And a big car, too," said Chet.

"Why, I know this place," Joe declared. "This is Dodd's farm."

"Not Jack Dodd? The chap who goes to Bayport High."

"Sure. This is where he lives. I remember the place was pointed out to me once."

"I knew Jack Dodd lived on a farm but I didn't know it was this far out," said Chet. "Let's drop in and see what's up."

With Frank in the lead the three boys turned down the lane leading in to the Dodd place.

"I wonder what that trooper is here for," he said. "They all seem to be having an argument over something."

"Perhaps the trooper met the auto thieves!" conjectured Chet.

When they drove into the barnyard they saw a boy running toward them and they recognized him as Jack Dodd, a quiet, likable lad who was in their class at the Bayport high school.

"Hello, fellows!" he called to them, but they saw that there was a worried expression on his face. "What brings you away out here today?"

"Hunting trip," said Chet, with a curious glance toward the state trooper, who was standing over by the fence with Mr. Dodd and two burly strangers. Their voices were raised in a loud argument, in which Mr. Dodd appeared to be opposed to the others.

"Hunting trip?"

"Hunting for auto thieves," Frank explained. "Isaac Fussy's car was stolen a little while ago. When we saw that trooper here we had an idea that perhaps he might know something about it."

"What's that?" shouted the trooper, a broad-shouldered young chap. "A car stolen?"

"Yes, sir. We were chasing it. A big Cadillac."

"Didn't see it," replied the trooper. "It didn't pass this way, I'm sure of that. We've just found one stolen car, anyway."

"I tell you I didn't steal it!" declared Mr. Dodd heatedly. "I haven't the least idea how that car got there."

"That's all right," interposed one of the other men gruffly. "You can tell that to the judge. The fact is, we've found the car behind your barn and it's one of the cars that were stolen in the past couple of weeks."

The chums glanced questioningly at Jack Dodd.

"These men are detectives," he said, in a low voice. "They came out from the city with the trooper a little while ago."

"Did they really find a stolen car here?" asked Chet.

Jack nodded.

"They found one all right, but how on earth it got here, I don't know. It's a Packard and somebody must have driven it in and left it among the bushes behind the barn. We never noticed it."

"Well," the state trooper was saying, "I'm going to drive the car back to Bayport and return it to the owner. You don't claim it's yours, do you?" He gestured toward a splendid touring car near by.

"Of course it isn't mine," said Mr. Dodd. "I've never seen it before and I never want to see it again—"

"I guess you don't," growled one of the detectives.

"How it got here, I can't tell. I certainly had nothing to do with stealing it."

"People don't leave perfectly good cars hidden behind other people's barns," said the other detective. "You'd better tell us a straight story, Dodd. It'll be easier for you."

"I've told you all I know about it."

"Well, then, if you don't know any more about it, perhaps your son does."

"I don't know any more than Dad," declared Jack stoutly. "I've never seen the car before."

"Never?"

"No."

One of the detectives stepped swiftly over to the automobile and produced an object from the back seat. He held it out toward the boy.

"What's this?" he asked.

Jack gasped.

"My fishing rod!"

"It's yours, is it? How did it get there if you've never seen the car before?"

CHAPTER III

UNDER SUSPICION

For a moment after the detective's question there was dead silence. Jack Dodd stared at the fishing rod as though stupefied. Then, mechanically, he took it in his hands.

"Yes, it's mine, all right," he admitted. "I lost it."

"Oh, you lost it, did you?" said the detective unpleasantly. "That's very likely. You lost it in that car."

"I didn't! I've never seen the car. I left my fishing rod out by the front fence about a week ago and when I came to look for it the rod was gone."

The other detective snickered incredulously.

"It's true," protested Mr. Dodd. "Jack told me at the time that he had lost his rod."

"You'd back him up, of course. But that story won't go down. If he never saw the car before, how does his fishing rod happen to be in it?"

Jack and his father looked blankly at one another. Clearly, they were utterly astounded by this unexpected development, and at a loss to account for it.

"I think this pretty well clinches it," declared the trooper. "The rod couldn't have got there unless the boy was in the car—that's certain."

"But I wasn't in the car. I lost the rod a week ago."

"You'd say that, anyway," declared one of the detectives roughly. "Bring the car back to town, Jim." He turned to Mr. Dodd. "This isn't the end of the matter. There's not much doubt in my mind that you and your boy took that car. You certainly haven't been able to give us much of an explanation of how it came to be on your property, and the boy has told a pretty thin story to explain away that fishing rod."

"You're not going to arrest me!" exclaimed Mr. Dodd.

"No," said the detective reluctantly. "You don't have to come back with us. I guess you won't go very far away. But we're going to lay charges against you and your son."

"For what?"

"For stealing that car. What else do you think? And we're going to do a little more investigating about those other cars that were stolen, too."

Mr. Dodd said nothing. He realized the futility of objection. Nothing he might say would swerve the detectives from their determination to charge him and Jack with car stealing. On circumstantial evidence, they would be branded as thieves.

The state trooper turned to the Hardy boys and Chet, who had remained silent during this exchange of words.

"You boys said there was another car stolen?"

Frank nodded.

"A Cadillac sedan. It was stolen about half an hour ago, on the Shore Road."

"Describe it."

The trooper took out his notebook.

"We don't know the number. It was a blue sedan."

"Who did it belong to?"

"Isaac Fussy, the rich old fisherman."

"I've seen that car," said the trooper. "I'd recognize it anywhere. It didn't pass along this road. You've been following it?"

"We were right behind it until we had a spill a few miles back. That held us up for a while."

"I see. Well, the car has probably got away by a side road. I'll report it at headquarters, anyway."

He turned briskly away and went over to the Packard, getting into the front seat and taking his place at the wheel. The two detectives followed.

"You'll hear from us again in a day or so," said one gruffly to Mr. Dodd. "See that you stay here."

"I have nothing at all to fear. I didn't steal the car."

"You can tell that in court. Tell your boy to think up a better yarn about the fishing rod."

With this parting shot, the officers drove away.

Stunned by the misfortune that had befallen them, Mr. Dodd and Jack were silent. Frank Hardy was the first to speak.

"I'm sure it'll turn out all right, Jack. There's been a big mistake somewhere."

"Of course there's been a mistake," returned the boy heavily. "But it looks mighty bad for us."

"I've been living on this farm for more than thirty years," said Henry Dodd, "and there's never been any one could say anything against my good name or the name of any one in my family. I've no more idea how that automobile got here, than—" He shrugged his shoulders, and moved slowly away toward the house.

"We've told the truth," declared Jack. "We never saw the car before. We didn't know it was here. And I told them the truth about my fishing rod. I lost it last week and I didn't see it until that detective took it out of the automobile. How it got there, I don't know."

The chums were sympathetic. They tried, to the best of their ability, to cheer up Jack Dodd, although in their hearts they knew that the evidence against the boy would weigh heavily in a court of law.

"If you had known anything about the car and if you had left your fishing rod there you wouldn't have identified it so readily," said Frank shrewdly. "That was what made me certain you were telling the truth."

"I was so surprised at seeing the rod I couldn't help it! I told them just what they wanted to know. I suppose if I had lied about it they wouldn't have been so sure."

"It's always best to tell the truth in the long run," declared Frank. "It looks rather black for you just now, but after all they haven't very much to go on. The main thing is to find out who did hide that car behind the barn."

"And who put the fishing rod in it," added Joe Hardy.

"I don't suppose you suspect any one?"

Jack Dodd was thoughtful.

"I hadn't thought of it before," he said slowly; "but we had a hired man here up until last week who wouldn't be above playing a trick like that on us."

"Who was he?"

"His name was Gus Montrose. He worked here for about two months, but we had to let him go. He was lazy and he drank a lot and last week he had a quarrel with my father; so he was dismissed. I wouldn't say he stole the car and left it here, but he's the only person I can think of who might have cause to do anything like that."

"He might have had something to do with the fishing rod, at any rate," said Chet.

"He was a surly, bad-tempered fellow, and when he left he swore that he'd get even with us. But of course that may have been only talk."

"Talk or no talk, it's something to work on," Frank Hardy remarked. "Have you seen him around since?"

Jack shook his head.

"Haven't seen or heard of him."

"It's rather suspicious, having a thing like this happen so soon after he left. He might have found the stolen car himself and concluded that it was a good chance to pay off his grudge. Or he may have found the car hidden here and deliberately put the fishing rod in the seat so it would appear that you knew something about it. I wouldn't be at all surprised if Gus Montrose were mixed up in the affair in some way or another."

Jack's face flushed.

"I wish I had him here right now. I'd make him talk!"

"Just sit tight," advised Frank. "I know things look pretty bad, but something may turn up. We'll see if perhaps we can't do something for you."

Jack brightened up at this, for he knew that the help of the Hardy boys was not to be despised. The case looked black against him, but with Frank and Joe on his side he did not feel quite so disconsolate.

"Thanks, ever so much," he said gratefully. "I'm glad some one believes me."

"Those city detectives can't see any farther than the end of their noses," Chet Morton declared warmly. "Don't worry about them. If they put you in jail we'll dynamite the place to get you out." He grinned as he said this and his good humor alleviated the tension that had fallen over the group.

"Well, I guess we'll have to be going," said Frank, as he mounted his motorcycle. "Don't think too much about this, Jack. Something will turn up."

"I hope so," answered the boy.

Chet Morton and the Hardy lads said good-bye to their chum and rode out of the farmyard.

"No use chasing Mr. Fussy's car now," decided Joe.

"Gone but not forgotten," Chet said. "We might as well go home."

So, leaving Jack Dodd standing disconsolately in the yard, the three headed their motorcycles back toward Bayport.

CHAPTER IV

OUT ON BAIL

On the following Monday, Frank and Joe Hardy noticed that Jack Dodd was not at school. They had heard no more about the case, although the disappearance of Isaac Fussy's automobile had increased public interest in the car thefts and the local newspapers were making much of the failure of the police to bring the thieves to justice.

The Bayport Automobile Club had already taken action by offering a reward of $500 for information leading to the recovery of any of the stolen cars and the arrest of those responsible. Three of the victims had also posted rewards of varying amounts, comprising another $500 all told, for the return of their automobiles. The affairs had mystified Bayport, because of the fact that not a trace of any of the cars had been found, save in the case of Martin's Packard, and motorists were apprehensive. No one knew whose turn would come next.

As the Hardy boys were on their way to school on Tuesday morning Frank pointed out one of the Automobile Club posters in a window.

"I sure wish we could land those car thieves. That's a nice fat reward."

"If we caught the thieves we'd likely get the cars, too," replied Joe. "A thousand dollars is a nice little bit of money."

"It would come in handy. Added to the rewards we collected in the other cases, we'd have a good fat bank account."

"Reward or no reward, I'd like to catch the thieves just for the satisfaction of clearing up the affair. Most of all, so we could prove the Dodds haven't had anything to do with it."

"I wonder if the police have done anything about Jack yet. He surely was mighty blue on Saturday."

"Can't blame him," Joe said. "I'd be blue myself if I was accused of stealing a car I'd never even seen before."

As the Hardy boys entered the school they were met by Chet Morton, who called them over to one side.

"Have you heard?" he asked.

"About what?"

"About Jack Dodd and his father?"

"No. What's happened?"

"They were arrested last night for stealing Martin's car. They're both in the Bayport jail right now."

There was a low whistle of consternation from Frank.

"Isn't that a shame!" he declared indignantly. "They had no more to do with stealing that car than the man in the moon!"

"Of course, it was found on their farm," Chet pointed out. "I know they didn't do it, but you can't blame the police for taking action, when you come to think it over. The public are raising such an uproar about these missing cars that they have to do something to show they're awake."

"It's too bad Jack and his father should be made the goats."

"Sure is."

"They're in jail now?" asked Joe.

Chet nodded. "They're coming up for hearing this morning, but it's sure to be remanded. It's mighty tough, because they haven't much money and it will be hard for them to raise bail."

Chet's news disturbed the Hardy boys profoundly. For that matter, it had a depressing effect on all the boys in the class, for Jack Dodd was well liked and all his chums were quite convinced of his innocence of the charge against him. At recess they gathered in little groups, discussing the misfortune that had befallen him, and at noon a number of the lads stopped Officer Con Riley on the street and asked if he had heard the outcome of the morning's hearing.

"Remanded," said Riley briefly.

"For how long?"

"A week. They'll get about five years each, I guess. Been too much of this here car stealing goin' on."

"They're not convicted yet," Frank Hardy pointed out.

"They will be," declared Riley confidently. "We got the goods on 'em."

It was one of Mr. Riley's little eccentricities that he preferred to refer to the entire Bayport police force as "we," as though he had charge of most of its activities instead of being merely a patrolman on the beat adjacent to the high school.

"Got the goods on them—nothing!" snorted Chet Morton. "A car was found on the Dodd farm, that's all."

"It's enough," said the unruffled Con. "Men have been hung on less evidence than that."

"Are the Dodds out on bail?" Frank inquired.

The officer shook his head.

"Couldn't raise it," he said. "They've gotta stay in the coop."

"Even if they may be found innocent later on!" exclaimed Chet.

"That's the law," said Riley imperturbably. "If they can dig up five thousand dollars bail they'll be free until the case comes up."

"Five thousand! They'll never be able to raise that much money!"

"Then," said Officer Riley, as he stalked away, "they'll stay in the coop."

Frank and Joe Hardy went home thoughtfully. At lunch, their father noticed their pre-occupation and asked what the matter was. They told him the whole story, of the discovery of the automobile on the farm, the finding of the rod, Jack's repeated declarations of innocence.

"I'm sure he didn't do it," Frank declared. "He's just not that sort of fellow. And his father is as honest as—as you are."

"Thanks for the compliment," laughed Fenton Hardy. "And you say they're being held on five thousand dollars bail."

Joe nodded. "They'll never raise it. I wonder, Dad, if we could—if you'd help us fix it up."

The boys looked at their father hopefully.

"Joe and I can put up some of our reward money," interjected Frank. "We hate to see the Dodds kept in jail."

Mr. Hardy was thoughtful.

"You must have great faith in them."

"We have," Frank declared. "They had nothing to do with stealing the car, we're certain. It seems tough that they should have to stay in jail just because it was found on their property."

"It's the law of the land. However, as you say, it is rather hard on them. If you lads have enough confidence in the Dodds to put up some of your own money for their bail, I suppose I can do the same. I'll make up the rest of the five thousand."

"Hurray!" shouted Joe. "I knew you'd say that, Dad!"

Mrs. Hardy smiled indulgently from the end of the table. Aunt Gertrude, a peppery old lady who was visiting the Hardys at the time, sniffed in derision. Aunt Gertrude was a maiden lady of advancing years who had very little faith in human nature.

"Chances are they'll go out and steal another car and run away," she snapped. "Waste of money, I call it."

"I'll take my chances with the boys," laughed Mr. Hardy.

"Five thousand dollars gone!" Aunt Gertrude predicted.

"I don't think it'll be as bad as all that, Aunty," said Frank, winking at his brother.

"Wait and see, young man. Wait and see. I've lived in this world a good deal longer than you have—"

"Years longer," said Joe innocently.

This reference to her age drew a glare of wrath from over Aunt Gertrude's spectacles.

"I'm older than you are and I know the ways of the world. It seems you can't trust anybody nowadays."

However, in spite of Aunt Gertrude's doleful predictions, Fenton Hardy stood by his promise, and after lunch was over he went with the boys to the office of the District Attorney, where they put up bail to the amount of five thousand dollars for the release of Jack Dodd and his father, pending trial.

In a few minutes, father and son were free. When they learned the identity of their benefactors their gratitude was almost unbounded.

"We'd have been behind the bars right until the day of the trial," declared Mr. Dodd. "I don't know how to thank you. I give you my word you'll have no cause to regret it."

"We know that," Mr. Hardy assured him. "Don't worry."

"You're real chums!" declared Jack to the boys.

"Forget it," Joe said, embarrassed. "You'd do the same for us if it were the other way around."

"If you run across any information that might help us find who left the car on your farm let us know," put in Frank. "And, by the way, see if you can find out where Gus Montrose is now and what he is doing. I have an idea that fellow knows something."

"I haven't heard anything about him, but I'll try to find out," Jack promised.

"Are you going back home now?"

"I don't know. I hate to miss any more school, for I've been a bit behind in my work."

"Go on to school with the boys," advised Mr. Dodd. "I'll go back home alone. No use losing any more time than can be helped."

Fenton Hardy nodded his head in approval of this sensible advice and the boys went on to school together, where Jack Dodd received an enthusiastic welcome from his classmates, all of whom stoutly asserted their belief in his innocence and confidently predicted that he would come through his ordeal with flying colors.

"It's a crying shame ever to have arrested you," said one of the lads loyally.

"Oh, the police of this town are a lot of doughheads," said another.

"It's not the fault of the police, exactly," Frank pointed out. "It was also the state troopers and detectives."

"But Jack is innocent," came from several of the lads in unison.

"Of course he is—and so is his father," answered Joe.

"Gee, if only they round up the real thieves!" sighed one of the other boys. "Why, my dad won't let me park our car anywhere near the Shore Road any more!"

"My dad is getting so he won't hardly park anywhere," added another lad, and at this there was a general laugh.

"Those thieves are getting on everybody's nerves—they ought to be rounded up."

"Yes, and the sooner the better," declared Frank.

The kind words of his chums were very pleasing to Jack Dodd. Yet he was very sober as he entered the school building. He could not help but think of what might happen if he and his father could not clear their name.

"We may have to go to prison after all," he sighed dolefully.

CHAPTER V
MORE THIEVING

After school the following afternoon, the Hardy boys repaired to the boathouse at the end of the street, where they kept their fast motorboat, the *Sleuth*.

They had bought this boat out of money they had received as a reward for their work in clearing up the mystery of the Tower Treasure and in the capture of a band of smugglers. It was a speedy craft, and the boys had enjoyed many happy hours in it.

Tony Prito, one of their chums, an Italian-American lad, also owned a motorboat, the *Napoli*, as did Biff Hooper, the proud skipper of the *Envoy*. Tony's boat had been the fastest craft on Barmet Bay until the arrival of the *Sleuth*, and there was much friendly rivalry between the boys as to the speed of their respective boats.

Chet Morton was sitting in the *Sleuth*, awaiting Joe and Frank by appointment.

"Come on," he said. "Tony and Biff are out in the bay already."

The Hardy boys sprang into their craft, and in a few minutes the *Sleuth* was nosing its way out into Barmet Bay. The boys could see the other boats circling about, as Tony and Biff awaited their arrival. Tony waved to them and in a short time they drew alongside the *Napoli*.

"Where shall we go?" shouted Frank.

"Anywhere suits me. Might as well just cruise around."

There was a roar as the *Envoy* surged up, with Biff at the wheel, Jerry Gilroy and Phil Cohen were with him.

"I don't suppose you want to go to Blacksnake Island, do you, Biff?" called out Joe.

"I'll say I don't! Once is enough."

"Me, too," chimed in Chet, as the three boats, running abreast, headed in the direction of Barmet village.

Blacksnake Island, out in the open sea some distance down the coast, had been the scene of perilous adventures for the chums. Some time previous Chet Morton and Biff Hooper had gone out in Biff's launch and had been kidnaped by a gang of crooks who mistook them for the Hardy boys and who wished to revenge themselves upon Fenton Hardy. They had been taken to Blacksnake Island, as has already been told in the fourth volume of this series, "The Missing Chums."

"I never want to see the place again," shouted Biff. "I had enough of it to last me a lifetime."

"Between snakes and crooks, we had plenty of excitement," Frank said.

"Excitement!" declared Chet, settling back comfortably. "Why, I am sure that was nothing."

"What do you mean, nothing?" demanded Joe. "If anything more exciting ever happened to you, I'd like to hear of it."

"Haven't I ever told you of the time I was the only survivor of a shipwreck that cost ninety-four lives?"

His comrades looked at Chet suspiciously. Chet Morton's joking proclivities were well known. His jests were invariably harmless, but he dearly loved a laugh and some of his hair-raising fictions were famous among the boys.

"First time I've ever heard of it," Frank said. "When were you ever in a shipwreck that cost ninety-four lives?"

"Off Cape Cod in '23," declared Chet dramatically. "It was the night the good ship *Brannigan* went down with all on board. Ah, but that was a terrible night. As long as I live, I'll never forget it! Never!"

"I don't think you even remember it," sniffed Frank.

But Chet went on, getting up steam.

"The *Brannigan* left Boston harbor at four bells and there was a dirty sea running, with a stiff breeze from the north. I had booked my passage early in the morning, but as sailing time approached, my friends beseeched me not to go. 'It is death!' they told me. But I merely laughed. 'Chet Morton is not afraid of storms. I shall sail.' The *Brannigan* was not out of sight of shore before the storm broke in all its fury. Thunder and lightning and a roaring rain! It was the worst storm in twenty years, the captain said. The passengers huddled in their cabins, sick with fear. Some of them were seasick too. The storm grew worse."

"This sounds like a big whopper," declared Joe, interested in spite of himself.

Chet's face was solemn as he continued.

"Night fell. The waves rolled over the staunch little ship. The helmsman clung to the wheel. Down in the lee scuppers—whatever they are—the first mate lay with a broken leg. Down in the forecastle the crew talked mutiny. Then came a dreadful cry. 'A leak! The ship has sprung a leak!' And, by golly, it had. The skipper came down from the bridge. 'Take to the boats,' he cried. 'Women and children first.' But the *Brannigan* was sinking fast by the stern. Before they could launch a single boat the ship sank swiftly, and eighty-five people went to a watery grave."

He shook his head sadly, as though reflecting on this horrible tragedy.

"Eighty-five?" said Frank. "A little while ago you told us ninety-four."

"Ninety-four lives," Chet pointed out. "Eighty-five people, but ninety-four lives. The ship's cat was drowned too."

Joe snorted as he saw how neatly Frank had fallen into the trap. Frank looked foolish. Then Joe spoke, chuckling.

"And you were the only survivor!" he exclaimed. "How did you escape?"

Chet stood up and gazed out over the waves.

"I missed the boat," he explained gently.

Joe glared wrathfully at the jester, then jumped for the wheel. He bore down on it so suddenly that the nose of the *Sleuth* veered into the wind, and Chet was thrown off his balance, sitting down heavily in the bottom of the craft, with a yelp of surprise.

"That'll teach you!" said Joe grimly, struggling to suppress his laughter at Chet's melodramatic tale of the shipwreck. But the plump youth only grinned.

"Oh, boy, how you both bit!" he exploded. "How you gaped! You didn't know whether to believe it or not!" He roared with laughter. "Wait till I tell the others about this. 'How about the other nine lives?' 'How did *you* escape?' Wow!" He sat in the bottom of the boat and laughed until the tears came to his eyes. Frank and Joe joined in the laugh against themselves, for they were accustomed to Chet by now. Biff and Tony steered their boats over toward the *Sleuth* to learn the cause of all this mirth, but the boys refused to enlighten them as Chet wanted to reserve the yarn for a more convenient occasion when he might have some fresh victims.

For over an hour, the three motorboats raced about the bay, until the boys were aware that it was time to go home. The *Sleuth* reached the boathouse first, with the *Napoli* close behind, Biff Hooper's craft bringing up the rear. The launches safely in the slips, the six boys went up the street toward their homes.

"Going to try for the rewards?" asked Jerry Gilroy of the Hardy boys.

Frank smiled. "We won't turn them down if we happen to run into the auto thieves," he said. "A thousand dollars is a lot of money."

"Not to you," said Biff. "What do you two want with money after landing a fat reward in that gold case out West?"

He was referring to a case centering about some missing gold, in which the boys had gone all the way to Montana from their home on the Atlantic coast in order to help their father, who had fallen ill while tracking down the criminals.

Their good work in this case had netted them a handsome sum of money and they had the satisfaction of seeing their friend Jadbury Wilson, an old-time prospector who had come to Bayport to live, relieved from poverty. He had been one of the original owners of the gold and, following its disappearance, had fallen upon evil days.

"One can always use more money, you know," said Frank. "It'll come in handy if ever we go to college."

"I'll tell the world!" declared Chet. "Your father won't have to worry much about that. I wish my dad could say the same."

They had now reached the Hardy home and Frank and Joe said good-bye to their chums. When they went into the house they found that supper was almost ready. Aunt Gertrude sniffed, as they appeared, and expressed her amazement that they had managed to get home before mealtime. "For a wonder!" she said grimly.

Fenton Hardy emerged from his study. His face was serious.

"Well," he said, "I suppose you've heard the latest development?"

The boys looked at him blankly.

"Development in what?" asked Joe.

"In the car thefts."

"We haven't heard anything," Frank said. "Have they found the thieves?"

Mr. Hardy shook his head.

"No such luck. The thieves are still very much at large."

"You don't mean to say another car was stolen?" exclaimed Joe.

"Not only one. Two cars."

"Two more?"

Their father nodded.

"Two brand new autos, a Franklin and a Studebaker, were stolen last night," he told them. "Right in the city."

"Good night! And there's been no trace of them?"

"Not a sign. The police kept it quiet all day, hoping to recover them without any fuss, but they've had to admit themselves beaten. The cars have absolutely disappeared."

Aunt Gertrude spoke up.

"Mighty funny there were no cars stolen while those Dodds were in jail," she said pointedly. "The minute they get out—away go two new automobiles."

The boys glanced at one another uncomfortably. They were quite convinced that Jack Dodd and his father were innocent of any complicity in the car thefts, but they had to admit to themselves that their aunt had expressed a suspicion that might be commonly maintained throughout Bayport.

"The Dodds didn't have anything to do with it," said Fenton Hardy quietly. "I'm sure of that. Still—it looks bad."

"It certainly does!" declared Aunt Gertrude.

Frank turned to his brother.

"It's time for us to get busy," he said. "We'll go out on the Shore Road again tomorrow afternoon."

CHAPTER VI

ON THE SHORE ROAD

The Hardy boys were not the only investigators on the Shore Road the next afternoon.

The daring thefts of the two new cars from the very streets of Bayport had aroused public resentment to a high pitch and the police were thrown into a flurry of activity. Motorists were beginning to clamor for action; no one dared leave his car parked on the street without seeing that it was securely locked, even if only for a few minutes; the Automobile Club held a meeting at noon and passed a resolution urging Chief Collig to put all his available men on the case.

The Shore Road was patrolled by Bayport police and detectives, as well as by state troopers. All outgoing automobiles were stopped and credentials demanded of the drivers. It was a case, however, of locking the stable door after the horse was stolen, for no more cars disappeared that day.

Most of the people who were stopped took the matter good-naturedly, but some were exceedingly bitter.

"How dare you take me for a thief?" shrilled Miss Agatha Mitts, a rich and peppery maiden lady who lived in an ancient mansion down the coast. "It's outrageous! I won't show my license!"

"You'll have to or go to jail," answered the trooper who had halted her.

"The idea! How dare you talk to me like that? You know well enough who I am!"

"Sorry, but I don't know you from Adam. And, anyway, it doesn't make any difference. Show your license or I'll take you to the lock-up."

"I am Miss Agatha Middleton Mitts, of Oldham Towers," said the maiden lady heatedly. "And I—"

"Going to show your license or not? If you haven't one—"

"Oh, yes, I've got a license. But I want you to understand—"

"Let me see it, quick. You are holding up traffic."

"Well, it's outrageous, anyway," sighed Miss Mitts. But she had to rummage through her bag for the card and show it. Then she drove on, threatening all sorts of punishment to all the troopers in sight.

Drawn by the hope of earning the rewards offered for the apprehension of the thieves and recovery of the missing cars, a number of amateur detectives went scouting around the adjoining townships, harassing innocent farmers who had already been badgered and pestered into a state of exasperation by the officials. The Dodd family, in particular, suffered from these attentions. The Hardy boys and Chet Morton dropped in to see Jack Dodd and found him sitting disconsolately on top of the barnyard fence.

"It's bad enough to have detectives and troopers coming around and asking us to account for every minute of our time since we were let out on bail," said Jack; "but when nosey people come prying and prowling around, it's a little too much."

"You're not the only ones," consoled Frank. "Every farmer around Bayport has been chasing sleuths off the grounds all day."

"They keep popping up from behind the woodshed and under fences, like jack rabbits," said Jack, with a grin. "I suppose it would be funny if we hadn't gone through so much trouble already. One chap sat up in an apple tree half the morning watching the house. He thought we couldn't see him. I suppose he expects to catch us driving a stolen car into the barn."

"Is he there yet?" asked Chet.

Jack nodded.

"He went away for a while. I guess he went home for lunch, but he came back. He's patient. I'll say that much for him. He's up in the tree now, with a pair of field-glasses."

"The genuine detective!" said Chet approvingly. "Does he know you saw him?"

Jack shook his head.

"We didn't pay any attention. I suppose he thinks he's been very clever."

"Well, if he likes sitting in a tree so much, he'll have enough to suit him for a long while. You have a dog, haven't you, Jack?"

Jack nodded. "A bulldog. I'll call him." He whistled sharply, and in a few minutes an extremely ferocious looking bulldog came around the corner of the house, wagging his tail.

"Fine! Got a chain for him?"

The boys looked at Chet, puzzled, but Jack went away and returned with a long chain, which he attached to the dog's collar.

"I don't think you should let a dog run around loose," said Chet gravely. "It isn't good for him. I think he'd better be chained up. And if you'll show me just which apple tree contains our detective friend I'll show you the apple tree that should shelter Towser."

The others were beginning to see Chet's plan now. The Hardy boys grinned in anticipation.

"It's the tree right beside the orchard gate," said Jack. "You can see it from here."

"Come, Towser," said Chet, and stalked away. The bulldog waddled obediently behind, the chain clinking.

Chet went into the orchard and, without looking up, without giving any sign that he had noticed the man perched in the leafy branches above, he snapped the chain around the tree trunk, leaving Towser sitting in the shade. The bulldog looked puzzled, but he made no protest and settled down on his haunches.

"I guess that will hold our inquisitive friend for a while," said Chet cheerfully, as he came back with the air of one who had just accomplished a worthy deed. "If he wants to leave that tree, he'll have to argue the matter with Towser."

Hastily, the boys retired behind the stable so that the victim in the tree would not witness their mirth. They peeked around the corner every little while to see if there was any disturbance in the orchard, but the watcher stayed where he was, probably waiting for the dog to fall asleep.

"He'll get tired of that," predicted Chet, with a snicker. "I think we will see some action around that apple tree before long."

Just then the boys spied a familiar figure coming down the lane. A car was parked out in the main road and a bulky, stolid man was advancing toward them.

"Why, it's dear old Detective Smuff!" declared Chet.

Detective Smuff was one of the detectives on the Bayport police force. He was a worthy man, not over blessed with brains, and as a detective his successes had been mainly due to a dogged persistence rather than to any brilliant deductive abilities. Three of the cases on which he had been engaged had been solved by the Hardy boys, which had not tended to increase his liking for the lads, but he was cordial enough and bore no malice.

"Hello, Mr. Smuff," Frank called.

The detective nodded ponderously.

"More amatoors," he sighed. "What chance has a regular officer on a case like this when everybody else in town is puttin' their oar in?"

"Working on the car thefts?" asked Joe.

"I am." Smuff turned to Jack Dodd. "Just where were you, night before last, young man?"

"At home," replied Jack shortly. "There's no use asking me any more questions, Mr. Smuff. Chief Collig was out here yesterday morning and Dad and I were able to satisfy him that we hadn't been out of the house all evening."

"Oh," said Smuff, evidently disappointed. "The Chief was here, was he?"

"Yes."

"Well, I guess there ain't any use of me askin' questions, then," returned the detective.

"No sign of any of the cars, officer?" Frank asked.

"Not a trace."

"Any word from the other towns?"

Detective Smuff shook his head.

"There was three different ways they could have gone," he said. "The Shore Road branches off into three roads and we've sent men out along every one of 'em and every inch of the highway has been searched. Them cars have just plain vanished."

"The police in the other towns didn't see them?"

"No reports at all."

"Perhaps they were taken right through Bayport and out the other side," Joe suggested.

"They weren't taken through Bayport. The cars were missed within five minutes after they were stolen and all the patrolmen were told about 'em and kept a lookout. There was nobody on the Shore Road side, so this is the only way they could have come without bein' stopped. That's what makes it so odd," went on Detective Smuff. "The police in the other towns was given word and they were waitin' for the cars if they came through, but they never showed up."

"Then the cars must be hidden somewhere along the Shore Road!" Frank exclaimed.

"Looks like it. But we've searched every inch of the ground, and there's no place they *could* be hid." Detective Smuff shook his head sadly. "It's a deep case. A deep case. Well, I'll do my best on it," he said, with the air of a martyr.

"I'm sure you will," said Chet. He did not add that his private opinion of Detective Smuff's "best" was far from high.

A terrific barking from the direction of the orchard interrupted the conversation. The detective looked up, surprised. A loud howl and a protesting voice added to the uproar.

"The chap in the tree!" shouted Chet. He raced around the corner of the stable, and the others quickly followed. Detective Smuff, left alone, looked around in bewilderment, then jogged heavily after the boys.

Towser, beneath the apple tree, was doing his duty as guardian. The amateur detective in the tree had attempted to escape, perhaps lulled to a sense of false security because Towser had apparently gone into a doze. He was half way down the tree trunk now, and the bulldog was leaping and snapping at him from beneath. The chain was just long enough to hold the dog in check, and he fell short of the unfortunate victim by a few inches; but the frightened sleuth was unable to scramble back to safety and was clinging wretchedly to the tree, unable to retreat or descend. In the meantime he roared loudly for help.

Chet burst into peals of laughter, and the others, in spite of their sympathy for the inquisitive one in his plight, could restrain themselves no longer. The boys shrieked with merriment, Towser barked and leaped in renewed fury, and Detective Smuff came waddling up, audibly wondering what it was all about.

A whistle from Jack Dodd, as soon as he was able to stifle his laughter sufficiently, attracted Towser's attention. He stopped barking and looked inquiringly at his master.

"Down!" shouted Jack.

Obediently, the dog lay down.

"He won't hurt you."

The man in the tree, somewhat reassured, began to descend. The dog, beyond a low growl or two, paid no further attention. The moment the spy reached the ground he started for the fence at a run, scrambled over it and headed across the field toward the open road.

"What was he doing?" asked Detective Smuff suspiciously.

"Watching us," Jack returned. "Seems as if half the people in the county have their eye on us since those cars were stolen. I think that chap is cured."

"He should be," said Smuff, gazing respectfully at Towser. "If any one bothers you after this, let me know. Us regular detectives can't have any one buttin' into our work like that."

He glanced severely at the Hardy boys as he spoke.

"We certainly can't," said Joe innocently. Then, as Detective Smuff glared, he turned to his companions. "Come on, fellows. Let's take a look through the woods on the other side of the road. We might find some trace of the cars there."

CHAPTER VII

GUS MONTROSE

Detective Smuff walked back as far as the road with the boys, and then clambered into his car, where another detective on the Bayport force was waiting for him.

"You're just wastin' your time hunting through the woods," he told the boys heavily. "A car couldn't get down there, anyway, and we've hunted through there pretty thoroughly in the second place."

"It'll give us something to do," Frank said cheerfully.

"Keep you out of mischief, I guess," agreed Smuff, as though this were some consolation at any rate. He nodded to the boys and the car sped off toward Bayport.

"Dumb but good-hearted," said Chet.

"He isn't a bad sort," Joe remarked. "He's no great shakes as a detective, that's sure, but there are lots worse."

The boys crossed the road and struck off down a narrow trail that led through the undergrowth into the woods on the sloping land between the Shore Road and Barmet Bay. For the most part there were steep bluffs lining the bay, but at this point the declivity was more gradual.

"I think he's right about searching down through here," said Jack Dodd dubiously. "A car could never get down into this bush."

"A car mightn't but the car thieves might," Frank pointed out. "It seems mighty strange that none of the stolen cars have been traced at either end of the Shore Road. Those automobiles stolen the other night should have been picked up in one of the three towns on the branch roads. Smuff said the thefts were discovered in plenty of time to send out warning."

"It does seem strange. Out of so many cars, you'd imagine at least one or two would have been traced outside Bayport."

"I have a hunch that this whole mystery begins and ends right along the Shore Road," said Frank. "It won't hurt to scout around and see what we can find. Maybe there's a hidden machine shop where they alter the appearance of the autos."

"I was reading of a case in New York City not long ago," remarked Joe, as they pushed along. "The auto thieves got cars downtown and drove them to some place uptown. The police followed half a dozen gangsters for two weeks before they got on to their trick, which was to drive into an alleyway that looked as if it came to an end at the back of a barn. They found that a section of the side of the barn went up like a sliding door. The thieves would drive in with a stolen car. Inside the old barn was an elevator running down to a cellar. In the cellar was a machine and paint shop and five or six workmen down there could so alter a car in a few hours that the owner himself couldn't tell his own machine."

"Can you beat it!" exclaimed Chet. "Gee, it's a wonder they wouldn't work at something honest!"

Among the woods on the slope the boys wandered aimlessly. The sun cast great shafts of light through openings in the leaves above and once in a while they could catch glimpses of the blue waters of the bay in the distance.

Frank was in the lead. He was proceeding down a narrow defile in the forest when the others saw him suddenly stop and turn toward them with a finger on his lips, cautioning silence.

They remained stock-still until he beckoned to them, and then moved quietly forward, their feet making no noise in the heavy grass.

"I heard voices," Frank whispered as they came up to him.

"Ahead?" asked his brother.

Frank nodded.

"We'll go easy."

He moved on cautiously and the others followed. In a few moments they heard a dull murmur of voices and smelled the unmistakable odor of a wood fire. So far they could see no one, but soon the faint trail wound around in the direction of a clearing ahead and those in the rear saw Frank crouch among the bushes, peering through the leaves.

Quietly, the others came up. The four boys gazed through the under-growth at the scene in the grassy clearing.

Three men were seated about a small fire, over which one was holding a tin pail suspended from a green branch. They were unshaven, frowsy-head-ed, untidy fellows, and they sprawled on the ground in careless attitudes.

"Tramps," whispered Chet, but Frank pressed a restraining hand on his arm.

There was one thought in the minds of the four boys—that this trio might be the automobile thieves!

"Not far from Bayport, are we?" growled one of the men.

"Not many miles farther on," replied the man holding the branch.

"It's the first time I've ever been in these parts."

"It ain't so bad," volunteered the third man, lighting his pipe. "Easy pickin's around the farmhouses. It didn't take me ten minutes to rustle that grub tonight."

"You did well, Bill," said the man at the fire, glancing at a package of food near by.

"I wonder where that guy is that we met on our way in here? He gave us a funny look."

"He minded his own business, anyway."

"Good thing for him that he did. I don't hold with bein' asked questions."

"Me neither. A good rap over the dome for anybody that wants to know too much—that's my motto."

"Is that mulligan ready?"

"Not yet. We'll be eatin' in about five minutes."

Frank turned and gestured to the others, indicating that they might as well withdraw. It seemed clear to him that these men were simply tramps preparing their evening meal in the shelter of the woods, and nothing would be gained by making their presence known.

Jack Dodd and Joe turned and moved silently away, but the luckless Chet had not gone two paces before he tripped over a root and fell sprawling on the ground, with a grunt of pain and surprise.

One of the tramps looked up.

"What was that?"

"Somebody in the bushes," said another.

The two men scrambled to their feet and came directly toward the boys. Jack and Joe took to their heels, but Frank waited to help Chet up and the delay was fatal. The tramps came crashing through the bushes and caught sight of them.

"Kids, eh?" roared one. He sprang toward Frank and caught him by the shoulder. The other seized Chet. Joe and Jack were out of sight beyond the trees by now and the tramps were evidently unaware of their presence.

"Take your hands off me," said Frank coolly.

Somewhat taken aback, the tramp regarded him for a moment in a surly manner.

"What do you mean by spying on us?" he demanded.

"We weren't spying on you."

"What brings you around here, then?"

The other tramp had abandoned the pail of stew at the fire and came through the bushes toward them.

"What's the matter?" he asked. "What's goin' on here?"

"A couple of kids spyin' on us," said Frank's captor, and tightening his grip on the boy's shoulder.

"We oughta skin 'em alive," declared the newcomer. "How long have you been hiding in them bushes, boy?"

"We just came up a minute ago and when we heard voices we looked to see who was there. We were just going away."

"You were, eh? What were you going away for?"

"It wasn't any of our business if you wanted to cook your supper in the woods."

This answer seemed to placate the tramps, for they glanced from one to the other, seemingly reassured.

"You weren't going for the police?" asked one suspiciously.

Both boys shook their heads.

"Did somebody send you here?"

"No. We were just wandering through the wood and we came on your fire."

"That fellow we met a little while ago didn't send you here, did he?"

"We haven't seen anybody," said Frank. "What did he look like?"

"Thin, hard-lookin' guy with a hook nose."

"We haven't seen any one like that."

"He was prowling around here a little while ago," said the tramp, in a more friendly tone. "I guess you boys are all right. If we let you go will you promise not to run and tell the police?"

"Oh, sure!" piped Chet, in vast relief.

"We're not doin' any harm here. We're just three poor chaps that's out of work and we're on our way to Bayport to look for a job," whined one of the others. "You wouldn't set the police on us, would you?"

"It's none of our business who you are or what you're doing," Frank assured them. "We won't mention seeing you."

"All right, then." His captor released his grip on Frank's shoulder. "Beat it away from here and don't bother us again."

The two boys lost no time in making their way out of that vicinity. The three tramps stood watching until they disappeared beyond the trees at the bend in the trail, then went back to their fire.

Some distance away, Frank and Chet came upon the other boys, who had halted and were devising ways and means of rescue.

"Golly!" said Joe, "we thought you were in for it. We were just going to toss up and see who would go back to find out what had happened to you."

"Why couldn't you both come back?" Chet asked.

"We thought if one of us went back he might be caught too, and that would still leave somebody to go for help."

"Good idea. They were only tramps. Gave us a bit of a scare," said Chet airily. He had been almost frightened out of his wits. "We just talked right up to them and they let us go."

"I wonder who is this hook-nosed man they were talking about," said Frank. "They seemed to be worrying more about him than about us."

"A hook-nosed man?" exclaimed Jack Dodd. "What about him?"

"You remember when they were talking by the fire, they mentioned meeting somebody on their way into the wood. They asked us about him, and seemed to think he may have sent us in to spy on them."

"Thin, hard-looking chap," Chet remarked, remembering the description the tramp had given.

"Why, that must be—but it couldn't be *him*!" exclaimed Jack.

"Who?"

"Gus Montrose. The hired man that Dad discharged a little while ago. I was telling you about him. The description fits him exactly."

"I thought he went away," said Joe.

"We haven't seen him since he left the farm, but I've always had an idea he was prowling around."

Just then Frank clutched Chet's arm.

"Listen!"

The boys halted. They could plainly hear the sound of snapping twigs and a scuffing that indicated the approach of some one on the trail ahead. A moment later, a man came into view.

He stepped out from among the trees and came to a stop, staring at the lads, plainly astonished at seeing them. Then he wheeled about and sprang into the bushes. They could hear him plunging through the undergrowth as he disappeared.

Although they had only a momentary glance, the boys readily identified him as the man the tramps had mentioned. Disreputably clad, he was a thin man with a cruel mouth and a hooked nose.

"Gus Montrose!" exclaimed Jack Dodd.

CHAPTER VIII

THE MISSING TRUCK

"Let's tackle that fellow!" exclaimed Frank Hardy. "We can ask him about your fishing rod, Jack."

Frank scrambled into the bushes, where Gus Montrose had disappeared, and in a moment his companions were hurrying after him. But although Frank had lost little time making up his mind to question the former hired man, Montrose had been too quick for him. The fellow was nowhere to be seen.

"Shall I call to him?" asked Jack Dodd.

"You can if you want to," answered Frank. "I doubt if he'll answer."

"Might scare him into running faster," suggested Joe.

"I reckon he's running about as fast as he can now."

"Gus! Gus Montrose!" yelled Jack. "Come back here! We want to talk to you!"

All listened, but no reply came to this call.

"Silence fills the air profound," came soberly from Joe.

"So much noise it would wake a tombstone," added Chet.

Again Jack called, and with no better results.

"Let's all yell together," suggested Joe.

This was done, but no answer came back.

"Sorry, but I've got a date elsewhere," mimicked Joe. "Be back next month at three o'clock."

"That fellow is no good, and I know it," murmured Frank. "An honest man would come back and face us."

"Listen!" cried Jack, putting up his hand.

All listened with strained ears.

"Don't hear a thing—" began Chet.

"I hear it," interrupted Frank.

A snapping and crackling sound among the bushes ahead lured the boys on and they went plunging through the woods. They failed to catch sight of the quarry, however. Evidently Montrose was well acquainted with this part of the country, for after a while the sounds of his retreat died away.

Frank, who was in the lead, came to a stop, realizing that further pursuit was useless. In a few minutes the others came up, panting.

"Did he get away?" asked Joe.

Frank nodded. "He was too quick for us. When he knew we were after him he didn't lose any time."

"I wish we had been able to talk to the rascal," said Jack Dodd. "I would have had a few things to tell him."

"Probably we wouldn't have got much satisfaction out of him, anyway," Frank remarked. "Still, you could have asked him what he knew about that fishing rod."

"It's something to know that he's still hanging around this part of the country," pointed out Chet. "He has evidently been lying low since he left your farm."

"He's up to some mischief, I'm sure of that."

"Probably built himself a shack somewhere in the woods," suggested Joe.

"Well, we may run across him some other time. It's getting late and I think we'd better be starting home," said Frank.

Chet and Joe agreed that it was about time, and as there seemed little to be gained by continuing the search for Gus Montrose or for any evidence of the stolen cars, the boys retraced their steps back through the woods until they reached the Shore Road. Their motorcycles had been parked in the shelter of the trees.

"About time for my supper, too," said Jack Dodd. "If you're out this way again, look me up and we'll make another search through the woods."

His friends promised to do this and, bidding Jack good-bye, they mounted their motorcycles and were soon roaring off in the direction of Bayport. They had spent more time in the wood than they had been aware of, and were anxious to get back to the city without being too late for the evening meal. Mrs. Hardy seldom scolded, but the boys had vivid recollections of Aunt Gertrude's acid remarks on similar occasions.

They emerged on an open stretch of road where a sand embankment sloped steeply down to Barmet Bay. The beach lay beneath them at the foot of the sheer declivity and the waters of the bay sparkled in the rays of the late afternoon sun.

A movement on the beach caught Frank's eye and he brought his motorcycle to a sudden stop.

"What's the matter?" asked Joe, swerving wildly to avoid piling headlong into Frank's machine.

"Run out of gas?" inquired Chet, putting on the brakes.

But Frank had dismounted and was walking over to the side of the road, out on to the top of the embankment.

"There's somebody down on the beach."

"What of it? Somebody swimming or fishing. Do you mean to say you stopped just because of that?"

But Frank was gazing down the steep, sandy slope.

"There's something odd about this," he said slowly. "There are two men down there, lying on the sand."

Joe and Chet, immediately interested, came running over. The three boys looked down at the two figures on the beach far below.

"They're not asleep," said Joe. "One of them seems to be rolling around."

"They're tied!" shouted Frank. "Look! You can see the ropes! I was wondering what was so strange about them. Those men are tied hand and foot!"

Joe was examining the embankment at their feet.

"Why, they've been rolled down the side!" he exclaimed. "Look where the sand has been disturbed!"

True enough, sand and gravel at the top of the slope showed a distinct depression, and all the way down the embankment this depression continued, as though a heavy object had slid to the bottom.

From the beach below came a faint shout.

"Help! Help!"

The men on the shore had seen them.

"We'd better go down," said Frank. "I wonder if there isn't a path of some kind around here."

"Let's slide!" Chet suggested.

"We're liable to break our necks tobogganing down this slope. No, there should be a path."

Frank ran along the top of the embankment toward a clump of trees a few yards away, where the slope was not so steep, and there he found a foot-path that led a winding course down the side of the hill toward the beach. It wound about across the face of the slope and covered twice the distance they would have had to go if they had adopted Chet's suggestion, though it was a great deal surer. They emerged on the open shore eventually and saw the two bound figures lying on the beach not fifty yards off.

In a short time the boys were bending over the prostrate victims. The men, who were clad in overalls, were bound hand and foot with heavy rope, at which the lads slashed vigorously with their pocketknives.

The strands fell apart and the two men were able to sit up, rubbing their limbs, which had been chafed by the ropes in their efforts to free themselves.

"I thought we'd be here all night!" declared one of the men, a plump, grimy young fellow about twenty years of age.

"Mighty lucky thing for us that you saw us," said the other, who was older in appearance. "We shouted and shouted. At least a dozen cars must have passed along the road and no one saw us."

They got to their feet.

"What happened?" asked Frank. "How on earth do you come to be down here, tied up like this?"

"Hold-up!" said the older man briefly. He looked up toward the road, an anxious expression on his face. "I don't suppose you met a truck along the road anywhere?"

The boys shook their heads.

"It's gone, then," said the younger man with a gesture of resignation. "Six thousand dollars' worth of goods!"

"We'll have to get back to town and report this."

"We can take you back," said Frank quickly. "We have motorcycles up on the road."

"Fine. Let's hurry!"

The two men started back toward the path at a rapid gait and the three boys hurried along. As they ascended the slope, the plump young chap explained what had happened.

"We're truck drivers for the Eastern Importing Company, and we were bringing a load of silk into Bayport," he said. "Right at the top of the embankment we were held up by those two men."

"How long ago?" Joe asked.

"A little over an hour ago. They stepped out of the bushes, each man masked and carrying a revolver. Bill was at the wheel and I was on the seat beside him. They made him stop the truck and then they made us get down into the road. When we did that, one of the hold-up men covered us with his revolver while the other tied us up. He made a good job of it, too, I'll tell the world. We couldn't move hand or foot."

"How did they get you down onto the beach?"

"They rolled us down the embankment! Don't we look it?"

The clothes of both men had been badly tattered and torn, while their arms and faces also gave evidence of the bruises and lacerations they had suffered in their descent.

"I thought we'd roll clean into the bay," said the other man. "If we had, it would have been all up with us."

"We'd have been drowned, without a chance to save ourselves," his companion agreed. "As it was, we came pretty close to the water's edge, banged and battered from that toboggan slide, and then we just had to lie there until somebody came along and set us free. At first we thought some one would surely see us from the road, but as car after car went by we began to lose hope. I was afraid it would get dark and then no one would be able to see us, even if they did chance to look down this way. It wouldn't have been very pleasant, staying out on that beach all night."

"Did you see where the truck went to?" asked Frank.

The men shook their heads.

"The hold-up men drove away in it—that's all we know," said one.

"It took us a few minutes to recover our senses after the slide down the embankment, and by that time the truck was gone. Whether it went on toward Bayport, or turned around, we can't tell," added the other.

"It certainly didn't pass in the other direction," said Chet.

But Frank was dubious.

"We were down in the woods quite a while, remember," he pointed out. "It might have gone by during that time."

They regained the road.

"Perhaps we can find the marks of the tires," suggested Joe.

Assisted by the two men, the lads searched about in the dust of the roadway, but so many cars had passed in the intervening time that all trace of the truck had been obliterated.

"No use searching now," said the driver. "If you lads will get us into Bayport we'll report the case to the police."

They abandoned the quest and in a short time the party had arrived in the city, Frank and Joe taking the two men as passengers on their motorcycles. At the police station, the hold-up was duly reported and immediately word was flashed to the police in other cities and to officers out in the country.

But to no avail.

By nine o'clock that night there had been no report on the missing truck. It had not passed through any of the three cities at the other end of the Shore

Road, and Bayport police were positive it had never entered the city. The truck, with its six thousand dollar cargo, had utterly disappeared.

CHAPTER IX

FOLLOWING CLUES

This new sensation soon had Bayport by the ears.

Although the owners of private cars had been content to leave the matter of their stolen property in the hands of the police, the Eastern Importing Company went a step farther. They not only demanded the fullest official investigation, but they retained Fenton Hardy to take up the case, as well. They were by no means resigned to losing a valuable load of silk without a struggle.

In his study, next day, Mr. Hardy called in his sons and told them the importing company had asked him to do what he could toward recovering the stolen goods.

"Aside from my fee," he said, "they are offering a reward of five hundred dollars if the silk is returned to them. What I want to ask you is this—do you think there is any chance that the truck driver and his assistant may have been lying?"

The boys scouted this theory.

"I don't think so, Dad," returned Frank. "They told a perfectly straight story. As a matter of fact, they were so anxious to get to Bayport and report the robbery that it was some time before we could get them to tell us what actually happened."

"And they could never have tied themselves up as thoroughly as they were tied," Joe declared.

"Men have been known to rob their employers before this," said Mr. Hardy. "We can't afford to overlook any possibilities."

"I think you can afford to overlook that one, sir. These men were honest, I'm sure of that."

"Well, Frank, I'll trust your judgment. I've investigated the records of the two men and they have never had anything against them, so I suppose it was an honest-to-goodness hold-up."

"It was real enough. We could see the marks in the embankment where they had been rolled down from the road," put in Joe.

"I'm sorry they couldn't give a better description of the hold-up men. All they could say was that they were both of medium height and that they wore masks. It isn't very much to go on. However, I may be able to get a line on the case when they try to get rid of the silk. The stuff is bound to turn up sooner or later and I may be able to trace it back to the thieves."

However, although Fenton Hardy devoted the next two days to the case, he made little progress toward locating either the missing truck or its cargo. As in the case of the other stolen cars, the truck seemed to have vanished into thin air, and although its description was broadcast all through the state, and police officials and garage mechanics were asked to be on the lookout for it, the mystery remained unsolved.

One evening toward the latter part of the week, the Hardy boys mounted their motorcycles and rode down High Street in the direction of the Shore Road. This was in accordance with a plan made earlier in the day.

"It stands to reason that if any of the cars ever got out into the state, at least one or two of them would be found," said Frank. "I have a mighty strong hunch that the whole mystery begins and ends right along that road."

"Perhaps those tramps we saw in the woods might have something to do with it."

"They may have had something to do with the hold-up, although it's not very probable. They looked as if they'd been sitting around that fire for quite a while, and it was a good distance from the place where the truck was robbed. However, it won't hurt us to do a little sentry duty and keep an eye on the Shore Road. We may have our trouble for nothing, but you never know what will turn up."

The lads drove out the road to a point mid-way between the scene of the truck hold-up and the Dodd farm. It was growing dark by the time they drew their motorcycles beneath the shelter of some trees.

"We might as well wait right here," said Frank, making himself comfortable on the grass. "If we see anything suspicious we can follow it up."

In the heavy shade, the boys could not be seen from the road. They talked in whispers. They had no clear idea of what they expected to find, but they were convinced that the Shore Road hid the mystery of the stolen automobiles, and their experience in previous cases had taught them that patience was often rewarded.

A few cars passed by, some bound toward Bayport, others in the opposite direction, but they were obviously pleasure cars and there was nothing about them to arouse suspicion. Once in a while, through the trees on top of the bluff, the boys could see the twinkling lights of a boat out on Barmet Bay. In the summer night, the silence was only broken by the trilling of frogs in the ditches along the road.

Presently they heard voices.

There was no one approaching along the highway, but as the voices grew louder they appeared to come from a field beyond the fence. At that moment the moon appeared from behind a cloud, and in its ghostly light, the Hardy boys distinguished two figures moving toward them in the meadow.

Silently, the lads crouched in the shadow of the trees, watching.

"This is a good night for it," growled one of the men.

"It's a good night if we don't get caught."

Joe's hand tightened about Frank's arm.

"What are you worrying about? We won't get caught. It isn't the first time we've got away with it."

"Yes, I know. But, somehow, I'm nervous tonight. I'm afraid we'll land up in the police court some of these fine days."

"If you're scared, go on home. I'll go on alone," said the first man scornfully.

"I'm not scared! Who says I'm scared?"

"Well, if you're not scared, shut up. I know we're breakin' the law, but we've never been caught yet."

The men scrambled over the fence. The boys saw that the first fellow was carrying two long poles and that the other carried a bag over his shoulder.

"Have you got all the stuff?"

"Yes."

"We'd better not walk along the road. Somebody's liable to spot us. Keep to the shadow and then we'll cut down into the woods."

The men hastily crossed the road in the moonlight. They were only a few yards away from the boys but, fortunately, did not see them. In the dim light, the watchers could not distinguish the features of the pair.

"There's a path here somewhere, isn't there?" asked one.

"Don't you remember it? If it hadn't been for that path the other night we'd have been nabbed."

"That's right. You know this country pretty well."

"I should. I've lived around here long enough."

About fifty yards away, the men turned down toward the woods and vanished in the darkness of the trees. Their voices receded. Frank and Joe scrambled to their feet.

"Come on," said Frank, in excitement. "We'll follow them."

"Do you think they're the thieves?"

"I'm sure of it. They're up to some kind of monkey-business, anyway. We'll find out where they're going."

In the soft grass the boys made not a sound as they sped along in the shade of the trees toward the path the two men had taken. They found it without difficulty, a fairly well defined trail that was quite visible in the moonlight. The lads plunged into the depths of the woods and there the moonlight did not penetrate. They had to feel their way forward, moving slowly in order to keep their progress silent.

After a while they could hear the voices of the two men again, not far ahead.

"Go easy," one was saying. "You never know who's likely to be prowling around here these nights."

"Too many police been nosing around these parts to suit me."

"We've got to take those chances."

The boys emerged into a clearing on the slope just in time to see the two men disappearing into the heavy wood on the opposite side. The clearing lay wide and deserted in the bright moonlight.

"They're up to some mischief," said Frank. "We'll have to be careful they don't see us."

"I wonder what those long poles are for!"

"They're not fishing poles. Too short and straight for that."

"Well, we'll soon find out. I think we're on the trail of something big."

"I'm sure of it."

The boys sped across the clearing and went on down the trail through the dark wood beyond. They were drawing closer to a brook now and they could plainly hear the lapping of the water against the rocks in the distance. In this vicinity there were several brooks flowing down into Barmet Bay.

Frank suddenly came to a stop.

"Look!" he said.

The boys peered through the gloom.

Beyond the branches of the trees they saw a glimmer of light. It disappeared, then shone again, steadily.

CHAPTER X

THE GREAT DISCOVERY

"I'll bet that light's a signal light," whispered Joe Hardy to his brother.

The boys watched the yellow gleam among the trees. Then, slowly, the light began to move. It swung to and fro, as though it was being carried by some one, and finally vanished.

Frank led the way down the path. In a few minutes they heard a snapping of twigs that indicated that the two men were not far ahead. The path dipped sharply, down a rocky slope, sparsely covered with underbrush. Then the brook came into view.

They could see the pair clearly now. One of the men was carrying a lantern; the other bore the long poles and the bag. Drawn up on the side of the brook, below the rocks and just above its mouth, the boys distinguished a small boat.

They crouched in the shelter of the bushes, and watched as the man who carried the lantern put the light down and strode over to a clump of trees from which he presently emerged, carrying a pair of oars. He dumped them into the boat with a clatter, which aroused the wrath of his companion.

"What do you think you're doing?" he demanded fiercely. "Want to rouse up everybody from here to Bayport?"

"I forgot," the other answered apologetically.

"Don't forget again."

"There's nobody around, anyway."

"Don't be too sure."

He fitted the oars in the rowlocks quietly, and the pair pushed the boat out into the brook.

"What shall we do?" whispered Joe. "Tackle them?"

"Wait a minute."

Hardly were the words out of Frank's mouth before he heard a rustling in the bushes almost immediately behind him. He looked around, startled, and saw a shadowy figure flit among the bushes, then another and another. He was so astonished that he almost cried out. Where had these newcomers appeared from? Who were they?

The Hardy boys pressed close to the ground as the three figures passed so close by them that they could almost have reached out and touched them. Not a word was said. The three men made their way silently past, in the direction of the brook.

"All right," said one of the men at the boat. "I guess we can start out now."

At that instant, the three newcomers sprang out from the depth of the brush.

There was a wild yell from the man bent over the boat.

"Come on, boys!" shouted one of the attackers. "We got 'em."

Trembling with excitement, the Hardy boys looked on. They saw the three men close in. One of the fellows at the boat made a dash for liberty but he was tripped up and flung heavily into the brook. The other fought back, but he was quickly overpowered. The struggle was sharp but brief, and in a few minutes the two men were prisoners and were taken out into the moonlight.

"You came once too often, Jed," said one of their captors. "We've been watchin' for you."

"You ain't got anythin' on us," said Jed.

"Oh, yes we have! Caught you red-handed. Any of your pals around?"

"Just the two of us."

"Boat, lantern and everything, eh? You were too sharp for us most of the time, Jed, but we were bound to catch you sooner or later."

Greatly puzzled by this dialogue, wondering who the newcomers were and wondering why Jed and his companion had thus been captured, the Hardy boys rose slightly from their hiding place to get a better view of proceedings.

Just then they heard a heavy footstep in the bushes immediately behind them.

They dropped again to the earth, but it was too late. They had been seen.

"Who's there?" growled a husky voice, and some one came plunging in through the bushes toward them.

Frank got to his feet and scrambled wildly for safety. Joe did likewise. The man behind them gave a loud shout.

"Here's some more of 'em." he called.

Joe tripped over a root and went sprawling. In the darkness it was almost impossible to see a clear way to safety. Frank paused to help his brother to his feet, and their pursuer was upon them. He seized Frank by the coat collar.

One of the other men came crashing through the underbrush.

"I've caught 'em." announced their captor. "Two more."

The newcomer emerged from a thicket and pounced on Joe.

"Good work!" he said exultantly.

The Hardy boys were hauled roughly out of the bushes and down into the moonlight, where the two captives were being held.

"Caught 'em hiding right in the bushes," said the man who had discovered them, tightening his grip on Frank's collar.

"Boys, eh?" said the leader, coming forward and peering closely at them. "Since when have you had boys helping you, Jed?"

The prisoner called Jed looked at the Hardy boys suspiciously.

"I never saw 'em in my life before," he growled.

"What are they doing here, then?"

"How should I know?" asked Jed. "I tell you I don't know anything about them."

"Why were you hiding in those bushes?" demanded the leader, of Frank.

"We were watching those two men," Frank returned promptly, indicating Jed and his companion.

"Watching them? Helping them, you mean."

"We don't know yet what they were up to. We were watching the Shore Road for automobile thieves and we saw those men going down into the woods, so we followed them."

The boys were still completely mystified. Just what errand had brought Jed and the other man to this lonely place at that hour of night, and just who were their captors, remained a puzzle to them.

"You didn't come here to spear fish?"

"Spear fish?" exclaimed Frank.

"Don't be so innocent. You know Jed and this fellow were coming down to spear fish by night-light, and it's against the law!"

The whole situation was now clear. Frank and Joe felt supremely foolish. Instead of trailing two automobile thieves, they had merely been following two farmers of the neighborhood who had been engaged in the lawless activity of spearing fish by night. This explained the mysterious conversation and their allusions to fearing capture. The other men were nothing more or less than game wardens.

"We didn't know," said Frank. "We thought perhaps they were the auto thieves."

The game wardens began to laugh.

"You were on the wrong track that time, son," said one. "I guess they're all right, Dan. Let them go."

The man who had stumbled on them in the bush released Frank reluctantly.

"They gave me a start," he said. "Hidin' there so quiet. I was sure they were with this other pair."

"Never saw either one of them before," repeated Jed.

"Well, if you stand up for them, I guess they're telling the truth. You boys beat it out of here and don't go interfering with our work again. You might have scared these two away if they'd caught sight of you."

"I wish we had seen 'em," said Jed. "We wouldn't be in this mess now."

"You'd have been caught sooner or later. You've been spearing fish in the brooks and ponds around here for the past three weeks, and you know it. You'll stand a fine in police court tomorrow."

The Hardy boys did not wait to hear the rest of the argument. Sheepishly, they left the group, thankful to be at liberty again, and retraced their steps up the trail through the wood until they again reached the road. Neither said a word. This inglorious end to the adventure had left them crestfallen.

They mounted their motorcycles and drove back to Bayport. The house was in darkness. Quietly, they went up the back stairs and gained their bedroom.

"Spearing fish!" said Frank in a disgusted voice, as he began to unlace his boots.

He glanced at Joe, who was grinning broadly. Then, as they thought of their cautious pursuit of the two fishermen and of their certainty that they had found the automobile thieves at last, they began to laugh.

"The joke is on us," snickered Joe.

"It sure is. I hope the game wardens don't tell any one about this."

"If Chet Morton ever gets hold of it we'll never hear the end of the affair."

But Chet, who had a way of picking up information in the most unexpected quarters, did hear of it.

CHAPTER XI

FISH

One of the game wardens chanced to live near the Morton farm, and as he was on his way into Bayport next morning to give evidence against the two men arrested, he fell in with Chet and in the course of their conversation chanced to mention the two boys who had so neatly blundered into the trap the previous night.

"Said they were lookin' for auto thieves," he chuckled.

"What did they look like?" asked Chet, interested.

"One was dark and tall. The other was about a year younger. A fair-haired chap."

Chet snorted. The Hardy boys! No one else.

"What are you laughin' about?" asked the game warden.

"Nothing. I just happened to think of something."

On his way to school, Chet stopped off at a butcher's shop long enough to purchase a small fish, which he carefully wrapped in paper. He was one of the first students in the classroom and he watched his opportunity, putting the parcel in Frank Hardy's desk. Then, before the Hardy boys arrived, he put in the time acquainting his chums with the events of the previous night, so that by the time Frank and Joe came in sight there was scarcely a student in the school who did not know of their blunder.

"It sure is one on the Hardy boys," remarked Tony Prito.

"I'll say it is," returned Biff Hooper. "They don't usually trip up like that."

"Trip up? They never do—that is, hardly ever," put in another pupil.

"They are the cleverest fellows in this burg," came from one of the other students. "Of course, everybody falls down once in a while."

"Just the same, it must gall them to think of how they were fooled."

"You bet."

Frank and Joe did not at first notice the air of mystery and the grinning faces, as they entered the school yard, but they were soon enlightened. A freshman, apparently very much frightened, came over to them at Chet's bidding.

"Please," he said, "my mother wants to know if you'll call at our house after school."

"What for?" asked Joe.

"She wants to know if you have any fish to sell."

Whereupon the freshman took to his heels. There was a roar of laughter from a group of boys who were within hearing. The Hardy boys flushed. Then Chet approached.

"Hello, boys," he said innocently. "You look sleepy."

"Do we?"

"What's the matter? Been up all night?"

"No. We got lots of sleep."

"Fine. Little boys shouldn't stay out late at night. It's bad for 'em. By the way," continued Chet airily, "I'm going out fishing tonight. I wonder if you'd like to come and sit on the shore and watch me."

Frank took careful aim with an algebra and hurled it at the jester, but Chet dodged and took to flight, chuckling heartily.

"Fish!" shrieked Jerry Gilroy, from a point of vantage on the steps.

"Fresh fish!" roared Phil Cohen.

"Whales for sale—ten cents a pound," chimed in Biff Hooper.

"How on earth did they hear about it?" gasped Joe. "We're in for it now."

"Just have to grin and bear it. Let's get into the classroom."

Pursued by cries of "Fish!" the Hardy boys hastened into the schoolroom and sat down at their desks, where they took refuge in study, although the bell had not yet rung.

Chet came in.

"Not in police court this morning?" he asked politely. "I heard you had been arrested for spearing fish last night."

"Just you wait," retorted Frank darkly.

He thrust his hand into his desk for a book and encountered the package. In another moment he would have withdrawn it, but a suspicion of the truth dawned on him. He knew that Chet was a practical joker and, with a chance like this, almost anything might be expected. So, thinking quickly, he left the package where it was and took out a history. By the expression of disappointment on Chet's face he knew his suspicions had been correct.

There were still a few minutes before school opened.

"Get him out of the room," whispered Frank to his brother, as Chet went over to his own desk.

Mystified, Joe obeyed.

"Well," he said to their chum, "we can stand a bit of kidding. Come on out and I'll tell you all about it."

They went out into the hall. Frank took the package from his desk. The odor was enough. If ever a fish smelled fishy, it was that fish. One stride, and he was over at Chet's desk. In a moment the package was nestling among Chet's books and Frank was back at his own desk, working busily.

The bell rang.

The students came into the classroom, Chet among them. He sat down, chuckling at some private jest, and began opening his school bag. Mr. Dowd, the mathematics teacher, entered for the first class of the day. Mr. Dowd was a tall, lean man with very little sense of humor, and Chet Morton was one of his pet aversions.

He went up to his desk and looked around, peering through his glasses.

"First exercise," he announced. Most of the students had their textbooks in readiness, but Chet usually took his time. Mr. Dowd frowned. "Morton, where is your book?"

"Right here, sir," replied Chet cheerfully. He groped in the desk and took out the textbook. With a sickening thud, the package dropped to the floor.

Chet's eyes bulged. He recognized it in an instant. A guilty flush spread over his face.

"What have you there, Morton?"

"N-n-nothing, sir."

"Don't leave it lying there on the floor. Pick it up."

Chet gingerly picked up the package.

"Your lunch?" suggested Mr. Dowd.

"N-no, sir. I mean, yes, sir."

"Just what *do* you mean? Why are you looking at it with that idiotic expression on your face?"

"I—I didn't expect to find it there, sir."

"Morton, is this another of your jokes? If so, I wish you'd let us all enjoy it. Do you mind telling us what's in that package?"

"I—I'd rather not, sir. It's just a—a little present."

"A little present!" Mr. Dowd was convinced, by Chet's guilty expression, that there was more behind this than appeared on the surface. "Open it this instant."

"Please, sir—"

"Morton!"

Miserably, Chet obeyed. Before the eyes of his grinning schoolmates, he untied the string, removed the paper, and produced the fish. There was a gasp of amazement from Mr. Dowd and a smothered chuckle from every one else.

"A fish!" exclaimed the master.

"Y-yes, sir."

"What do you mean, Morton, by having a fish in your desk?"

"I—I don't know, sir."

"You don't know? Don't you know where the fish came from?"

Chet Morton, for all his jokes, always told the truth. He did know where the fish came from.

"Yes, sir," he answered feebly.

"Where?"

"Hogan's butcher shop."

"Did you buy it?"

"Yes, sir."

"And you brought it to school with you?"

"Yes, sir."

The master shook his head in resignation.

"You're quite beyond me, Morton," he said. "You have done a great many odd things since you've been in this school, but this is the oddest. Bringing a fish to school. Your lunch, indeed! Stay in for half an hour after school." Mr. Dowd sniffed. "And throw that fish out."

"Yes, sir."

Chet departed in disgrace, carrying the fish gingerly by the tail, while his classmates tried to stifle their laughter. Half way across the hall the unfortunate Chet met the principal, who spied the fish and demanded explanations. These not being satisfactory, he ordered Chet to write two hundred lines of Latin prose. By the time the jester returned to the classroom, after consigning the fish to the janitor, who put it carefully away with a view to taking it home so his wife could fry it for dinner, he was heartily regretting the impulse that had made him stop at the butcher shop.

For the rest of the morning he was conscious of the smothered snickers of the Hardy boys and his chums.

Just before the recess period a note flicked onto his desk. He opened it and read:

"He laughs best who laughs last."

Chet glared and looked back at Frank Hardy. But that youth was innocently engaged in his studies. There was a twinkle in his eye, however, that told better than words just who had written the note.

CHAPTER XII

THE NEW CAR

As days passed and the Shore Road mystery was no nearer solution, police activity was redoubled. Motorists became caustic in their comments and Chief Collig felt it as a reflection on his force that no clues had been unearthed.

The matter, however, was not wholly in the hands of the Bayport force, inasmuch as the Shore Road was beyond Chief Collig's jurisdiction, and the state troopers were also made aware of their responsibility. So, with local police, detectives and troopers on the case, it seemed that the auto thieves could scarcely hope to evade capture.

However, the search was in vain. Not a trace of the missing cars could be found. Even Fenton Hardy had to confess himself baffled.

"Looks as if there's a chance for us yet," said Frank Hardy.

"Looks to me as if there isn't. How can we hope to catch the auto thieves when every one else has fallen down on the job?" demanded his brother.

"We might be lucky. And, anyway, I've had an idea that might be worked out."

"What is it?"

"Come with me and I'll show you."

Mystified, Joe followed his brother out of the house and they went down the street in the direction of a well-known local automobile agency.

As they walked, Frank explained his plan. At first Joe was dubious.

"It couldn't be done."

"Why not? All we need is a little capital, and we have that. Then if we have nerve enough to go through with the rest of it, we may be lucky enough to trap the thieves."

"Too many 'ifs' and 'may bes' to suit me," demurred Joe. "Still, if you think we could get away with it, I'm with you."

"We may fail, but our money won't be altogether wasted. We've always wanted a car, anyway."

"That's true. We'll go and look this one over."

Arriving at the automobile agency, they were greeted by the manager, who knew them well.

"What is it this morning, boys?" he asked, with a smile. "Can I sell you a car today?"

He meant it as a joke, and he was greatly surprised when Frank answered:

"It all depends. We'll buy one if you can make us a good price."

"Why, that's fine," said the manager, immediately becoming business-like. "What would you like to see? One of the new sport models?"

"No," replied Joe. "We're in the market for a used car."

"We heard you had Judge Keene's old car here," added Frank.

"Why, yes, we have. He turned it in and bought a new model. But you wouldn't want that car, boys. It looks like a million dollars, but it's all on the surface. I'll be frank with you—Judge Keene said the engine was no good, and I agree with him. It was put out by a new company that went bankrupt about a year later. They put all their money into the bodies of the cars and not very much into the engines. You would be wasting your money."

"We want a good-looking car, cheap," insisted Frank. "I don't care so much about the engine. It's the looks that count this time."

The manager shook his head.

"Well," he said, "I suppose you lads like to have a car that'll knock everybody's eye out, and I'm not denying this is a dandy-looking boat. But I won't guarantee its performance."

"We don't care, if the price is right. Where is it?"

The manager led the boys to the back of the showrooms, where they found a luxurious-looking auto. It looked, so Joe afterward said, "like a million dollars." With a fresh coat of paint it would have seemed like a model straight from the factory.

"What do you think of it?" Frank asked his brother.

"A peach."

"Boys, I hate to see you buy this car," the manager protested. "Take the money and put it into a good, standard car that you can depend on. You'll have more trouble running this automobile than the looks are worth. If you weren't friends of mine I wouldn't waste my time telling you this, for I'm anxious to get this mass of junk off my hands. But your father would never forgive me if he thought I'd stung you boys with a cement mixer like this one."

"It's the looks that count with us," said Frank. "How much do you want for it?"

"I'll sell it to you for four hundred dollars."

"Four hundred!" exclaimed Joe. "Why, that looks like a three-thousand-dollar car!"

"It looks like one, but it isn't," said the Manager. "You'll be lucky to drive a thousand miles in it before the engine gives out."

"We won't drive any thousand miles in it," Joe remarked mysteriously.

"Don't let any one else have the car, and we'll go and get the money," Frank told the man.

They left the manager smoothing his hair and pondering on the folly of boys in general, although he was secretly relieved at having got rid of the imposing looking car, which he had regarded as a dead loss.

Going directly to the bank, the boys withdrew four hundred dollars from their account, after cautioning the teller not to mention the matter to their father.

"We're going to give him a little surprise," said Frank.

"All right," said the teller, wondering what the boys wanted with such a large sum, "I won't tell him."

Back to the agency they went, handed over the money, and drove out in state, Frank at the wheel of their new possession. The car was indeed a splendid-looking vehicle, having excellent lines, good fittings, and a quantity of nickel trimmings that enhanced its luxurious appearance. Frank soon found that the manager had spoken correctly when he said that the value was all on the surface, for the engine began giving trouble before they had driven two blocks.

"However," he said to his brother, "this old boat may earn us a lot more than the money we paid for it, and if it doesn't we'll have plenty of fun tinkering around and putting a real engine in it."

They drove into the yard of their home. Aunt Gertrude spied them first and uttered a squawk of astonishment, then fled into the house to inform Mrs. Hardy of this latest evidence of imbecility on the part of the lads. Their mother came out, and the boys admitted that the car was theirs.

"We're not extravagant, Mother," they protested. "We got it for a certain reason, and we'll tell you all about it later. The old boat isn't as expensive as it looks. We picked it up cheap."

Mrs. Hardy had implicit confidence in her sons and when they said there was a reason behind the purchase she was content to bide her time and await their explanations. She was curious to know why they had made this extraordinary move, but was too discreet to ask any questions.

With the car in the garage, the boys went downtown again and bought several cans of automobile paint. And, for the rest of the week, they busied themselves transforming the automobile into "a thing of beauty and a joy forever."

Their parents were puzzled, but said nothing. Aunt Gertrude was frankly indignant and at mealtimes made many veiled references to the luxury-loving tendencies of modern youth.

"It's not enough for them to have motorcycles and a motorboat, but now they must have an automobile!" she sniffed. "And it's not enough for them to buy an ordinary flivver—they must have a car that a millionaire would be proud to own."

Secretly, the boys considered this a compliment. They felt that their aunt would be vastly surprised if she knew the low price they had paid.

"Wait till she sees it when we have it painted," said Frank.

Their chums, too, were unable to imagine what had possessed the Hardy boys to purchase a so large and expensive-looking car. Frank and Joe did not enlighten them. They had bought the car for a certain purpose and they were afraid that if they confided in any one, their plans might leak out. So they busied themselves with painting the new car, and said nothing of their intentions to any one, not even to Chet Morton.

At last the work was finished.

On Friday night after school Frank applied the last dab of paint, and the brothers stood back to survey their handiwork.

"She's a beauty!" declared Joe.

"I'll tell the world!"

The automobile was resplendent in its fresh coat of paint. The nickel glittered.

"Looks like a Rolls-Royce."

"A car like that would tempt any auto thief in the world."

"I hope it does."

"Well, we're all set for Act Two," said Frank. "I think we'll go out tonight. Our bait is ready."

"I hope we catch something."

With this mysterious dialogue, the boys went into the house for supper.

They were so excited over their impending journey that they could scarcely take time to eat.

"Some mischief on foot," commented Aunt Gertrude.

CHAPTER XIII

IN THE LOCKER

The massive roadster rolled smoothly out of the garage that evening and the Hardy boys drove down High Street, greatly enjoying the attention their new car attracted. Freshly painted, the automobile had not the slightest evidence of being a second-hand car. It was long and low-slung, with a high hood, and there was a big locker at the back.

The upholstery was in good condition and the fittings were ornate and handsome. All in all, it was a car to arouse the envy of all their chums, and one that would arouse the covetousness of any auto thief.

This was precisely what the Hardy boys were counting on.

They drove about the streets until it was almost dark. They met Biff Hooper and Tony Prito, who exclaimed over the luxurious appearance of the roadster and immediately wanted a ride, but the boys were obliged to refuse.

"Sorry," said Frank. "We'll take you out any other time but tonight. We have business in hand."

"I'd like to know what it's all about," remarked Biff. "You two have been mighty mysterious about something lately."

"Some time you'll understand," sang out Joe, as they drove off.

They headed out the Shore Road.

It was getting dark and the headlights cut a brilliant slash through the gloom. Leaving Bayport behind, the boys drove about two miles out until they came to a place where a grassy meadow beside the road provided a favorite parking place for motorists who wished to descend the path leading down through the woods to the beach below.

"This is about as good a place as any," said Frank.

"Suits me."

He drove the car off the road onto the grass. It came to a stop.

"Any one around, Joe?"

Joe looked back.

"No other cars in sight," he reported a moment later.

"Then make it snappy."

Any one observing the roadster at that moment would have seen the two boys clamber out, but in the gloom they would not have seen what followed. For the boys suddenly disappeared.

The roadster remained where it was, parked by the road, in solitary magnificence.

A few minutes later an automobile passed by. It belonged to a Bayport merchant, out for an evening drive. He saw the splendid car by the roadside and said to his wife:

"Somebody is taking an awful chance. I wouldn't leave a fine-looking automobile like that out here without some one to watch it. I guess the owner is down on the beach. If one of those auto thieves happens along there'll be another good car listed among the missing."

"Well, it's their own lookout," returned his wife.

They drove past.

But the roadster was not deserted, as it seemed. So quickly had the Hardy boys concealed themselves that, even had any one been watching, it would have been difficult to follow their movements.

The roadster, having been built for show, had a large and roomy locker at the back. By experimenting in the privacy of the garage and by clearing this locker of all odds and ends, the boys found it was just large enough to accommodate them both.

Here they were hidden. They were not uncomfortable, and the darkness did not bother them, for each was equipped with a small flashlight.

"You didn't forget your revolver, did you?" whispered Frank.

"No. I have it here," answered his brother. "Have you got yours?"

"Ready in case I need it."

Although there would seem to be no purpose in spending an evening crouched in the locker of a parked roadster, the Hardy boys had laid definite plans. From the morning they had bought the car they had perfected the various details of their scheme to capture the auto thieves on the Shore Road.

"Most of the cars have been stolen while they were parked on the Shore Road," Frank had argued. "It stands to reason that the auto thieves are operating along there. Since the first few scares, not many people have been parking their cars along there, so the thieves have taken to stealing cars in town and to hold-ups. If we park the roadster, it's ten chances to one the thieves won't be able to resist the temptation."

"And we lose a perfectly good car," objected Joe.

"We won't lose it, because we'll be right in it all the time."

"The thieves won't be likely to steal it if we're in it."

"They won't see us. We'll be hiding in the locker."

Joe saw the merits of the plan at once.

"And they'll kidnap us without knowing it?" he chuckled.

"That's the idea. They'll drive the car to wherever they are in the habit of hiding the stolen autos, and then we can watch our chance to either round them up then and there or else steal away and come back with the police."

This, then, was the explanation of their mysterious behavior, and as they crouched in the locker they were agog with expectation.

"We'll just have to be patient," whispered Frank, when they had been in hiding for more than half an hour. "Can't expect the fish to bite the minute we put out the bait."

Joe settled himself into a more comfortable position.

"This is the weirdest fishing I've ever done," he mused.

It was very quiet. They had no difficulty in breathing, as the locker had a number of air spaces that they had bored in the top and sides, invisible to a casual glance.

Once in a while they could hear a car speeding past on the Shore Road.

Minute after minute went by. They were becoming cramped. Presently Joe yawned loud and long.

"I guess it's no use," said Frank, at last. "We're out of luck tonight."

"Can't expect to be lucky the first time," replied his brother philosophically.

"We might as well go home."

Frank raised the lid of the locker and peeped out. It was quite dark. The Shore Road was deserted.

"Coast is clear," he said.

They got quickly out of the locker. They lost no time, for there was a possibility that one of the auto thieves might be in the neighborhood, watching the roadster, and if their trap was discovered it would be useless to make a second attempt.

They got back into the car, Joe taking the wheel this time. He drove the roadster back onto the highway, turned it around, and they set out back for Bayport.

Both lads were disappointed, although they had not yet given up hope. They had been so confident that their plan would be successful that this failure took some of the wind out of their sails, so to speak.

"We'll just try again tomorrow night," said Frank.

"Perhaps the auto thieves have quit."

"Not them! They'll fall for our trap yet."

"I'm glad we didn't tell any of the fellows. We'll look mighty foolish if it doesn't work."

The car sped along the Shore Road, the headlights casting a brilliant beam of illumination. As they rounded a curve they caught a glimpse of a dark figure trudging along in the shadow of the trees bordering the ditch.

"Wonder who that is," Frank remarked, peering at the man.

Joe bore down on the wheel, swinging the car around so that the headlights fell full on the man beside the road. Then he swung the car back into its course again.

The fellow had flung up his arm to shield his face from the glare, but he had not been quick enough to hide his features altogether. Frank had recognized him at once.

"So!" he remarked thoughtfully. "Our friend again."

"I didn't get a good look at him," Joe said. "Somehow, he seemed familiar."

"He was. I'd recognize that face anywhere now."

"Who was it?"

"Gus Montrose."

Joe whistled.

"I wonder what he's doing, skulking along here at this time of night."

"I have an idea that we'll find out before long."

"Do you think he has anything to do with the car thefts?"

"Shouldn't be surprised. He seems a rather suspicious sort of character."

They sped past the dark figure, who went on, head down, hands thrust deep in his coat pockets.

"I'd like to know more about that chap," mused Frank. "I'll bet he's not hanging around here for any good reason."

CHAPTER XIV

MONTROSE AGAIN

The Hardy boys were not discouraged by this failure. They realized that it was too much to hope for success in their venture at the first trial and resolved to lay their trap again.

If their parents were curious as to why they had remained out so late, they gave no sign of it, and the following night Frank and Joe again drove out along the Shore Road in their new car. This time they went to another parking place, not far from the spot where Isaac Fussy's automobile had been stolen.

Again they turned out the lights, again they crawled into the locker at the back, and again they remained in hiding, while car after car went by on the Shore Road.

An hour passed.

"Looks as if we're out of luck again," whispered Joe.

"We'll stay with it a while longer."

Frank switched on his flashlight and glanced at his watch. It was almost ten o'clock. They heard an automobile roar past at tremendous speed, and a few moments later there was the heavy rumble of a truck.

"Funny time of night for a truck to be out," Frank remarked.

"That first car was sure breaking all speed laws."

After a long time, Frank again looked at his watch.

"Half-past ten."

"Another evening wasted."

"Are you getting tired?"

"My legs are so cramped I don't think I'll ever be able to walk straight again."

Joe had inadvertently raised his voice. Suddenly Frank gripped his arm.

"Shh!"

They listened. They heard footsteps coming along the road. The steps sounded clear and distinct on the hard highway. Then they became soft and muffled as the pedestrian turned out onto the grassy slope.

"Coming this way," whispered Frank.

Some one approached the roadster cautiously. The boys could hear him moving around the car. After a moment or so, one of the doors was opened and some one clambered into the seat.

The boys were breathless with excitement. Was this one of the auto thieves?

But the intruder made no move to drive the car away. Instead, when he had snapped the lights on and off, he got out, closed the door behind him and strode off through the grass.

The first impulse of the two brothers was to clamber out, but they realized that this would be folly. They remained quiet, as the footsteps receded into the distance. The man gained the road again and walked slowly away. Finally, they heard the footsteps no more.

Frank sighed with disappointment.

"I thought sure we had a bite that time," he said.

"It was only a nibble."

When the lads were quite sure their unknown visitor had gone, Frank raised the lid of the locker and the boys got out.

"I guess it was only some farmer on the way home. He probably just got into the car out of curiosity."

"He wasn't an auto thief, that's certain, or he would have driven off with it."

"Not much use staying around any longer."

They got back into the seat. Nothing had been disturbed. Beyond turning the lights on and off, the stranger had tampered with nothing.

Frank started up the engine, and drove the car back onto the Shore Road. There was not much room in which to turn around, so he drove on down the road for about a quarter of a mile until he came to a lane which offered sufficient space.

Just as he was bringing the car around to head back toward Bayport, the headlights shone on two figures coming up the road. In the glare, the men were clearly revealed.

"There's our friend Gus again," remarked Frank quietly.

He was right. There was no mistaking the surly visage of the ex-farmhand. The man with him was unknown to the boys, but he was no more prepossessing than his companion. Broad of build, unshaven of face, he was not the sort of fellow one would care to meet alone on a dark night.

"Handsome-looking pair," Joe commented.

The car swung out into the road and the two men stepped out into the ditch, turning their faces away. Frank stepped on the accelerator, and the roadster shot ahead.

"This seems to be Gus Montrose's beat," he said, when they had driven beyond hearing distance.

"Wonder what takes him out along here every night."

"Perhaps he was the chap who got into the roadster."

But Frank shook his head.

"That fellow went away in the direction Montrose is coming from," he pointed out. "And, besides, he was alone."

"That's true, too."

Wondering what brought Montrose and his villainous-looking companion out the Shore Road on foot at that hour, the Hardy boys drove back into Bayport.

"Better luck next time," said Frank, cheering up.

"We won't give up yet. Third time's luck, you know."

"Let's hope so. Tomorrow night may tell."

They drove back into the city without incident, and when they reached their home they saw that there was a light in their father's study. Frank's face lengthened.

"I'll bet we're in for it now. He doesn't often stay up this late."

"He's likely sitting up to lecture us."

They put the car into the garage. The light in the study seemed ominous just then.

"Well," said Joe, "I guess we might as well go in and face the music. If the worst comes to the worst we'll tell him just what we were up to."

They went into the house. It would have been easy for them to have gained their room by the back stairs, but the boys had too much principle to dodge any unpleasantness in this manner, so they made a point of passing by their father's study. The door was open and they saw Fenton Hardy sitting at his desk.

He was not writing, but was gazing in front of him with a fixed expression on his face. A telephone was at his elbow.

To their relief, he smiled when he saw them.

"Come in," he invited.

Frank and Joe entered the study.

"Did you catch any auto thieves?" asked their father.

The boys were astonished.

"How did you know we were after auto thieves, Dad?" asked Frank.

"It doesn't take a great deal of perception to find that out," their father answered. "All these mysterious doings can have only one reason."

"Well, we didn't catch any," Joe admitted.

"I didn't think so. They've been busy tonight."

"Again!"

Fenton Hardy nodded.

"I've just been talking to the secretary of the Automobile Club. He telephoned me a short time ago. The thieves cut loose in earnest this evening."

"Did they steal another car?"

"Two. They made off with a new Buick that was parked down on Oak Street, and then they stole a truck from one of the wholesale companies."

"Can you beat that!" breathed Joe. "Two more gone!"

"They were taken within a few minutes of each other, evidently. The reports reached the police station almost at the same time. The truck mightn't have been missed until morning, but one of the wholesale company employees was coming home and he recognized it as it was driven away. He thought it rather suspicious, so he went on up to the company garage and found the truck had disappeared."

The brothers looked at one another.

"A truck and a pleasure car!" exclaimed Frank. "Why, that must have been—"

The same thought had struck Joe.

"The two cars that passed us on the Shore Road! What time were they stolen, Dad?"

"Some time between half-past nine and ten o'clock. Why? Did you see them?"

"Two cars went out the Shore Road a little before ten o'clock. They were both going at a fast clip. I remember we remarked at the time that it was a funny hour of the night for a truck to be out."

"The Shore Road, eh? Did you get a good look at them?"

The boys were embarrassed.

"Well, to tell the truth," said Frank hesitatingly, "we didn't exactly see them. We heard them."

"Hm! You didn't see them, but you heard them, and you were on the Shore Road. That's a little mystery in itself," remarked their father, with a smile.

He reached for the telephone and asked for a number. In a short time his party answered.

"Hello, Chief. This is Fenton Hardy speaking.... Yes.... I've just had information that the big car and the truck went out the Shore Road way a few minutes before ten o'clock.... Yes.... You've made inquiries?... I see.... That's strange, isn't it?... Yes, my information is quite reliable.... All right.... Let me know if you hear anything.... Don't mention it.... Thank you, Chief.... Good-bye."

He put down the telephone.

"I was talking to Chief Collig. He says the three towns at the other end of the Shore Road were notified immediately after the thefts were discovered and that they had officers watching the roads from ten o'clock on."

"And they didn't see the cars?"

Fenton Hardy shook his head.

"Not the slightest trace of either of them."

Frank and Joe looked at one another blankly.

"Well, if that don't beat the Dutch!" Frank exclaimed.

"You're quite sure of the time?"

"Positive. I had just looked at my watch."

"Well," said Fenton Hardy, "since the cars haven't been seen in any of the other towns and since there aren't any other roads, the Shore Road must hold the solution. I think I'll do a little prospecting around the farms out that way tomorrow."

"We've been doing a little prospecting ourselves," admitted Joe, "but we haven't been very successful so far."

"Keep at it," their father said encouragingly. "And good luck to you both!"

CHAPTER XV

THE SUSPECT

It was late before the Hardy boys got to sleep that night.

The events of the evening, culminating in the discovery that the auto thieves had been at work in Bayport while they were lying in wait for them on the Shore Road, gave the lads plenty to talk about before they were finally claimed by slumber.

In the morning, it required two calls to arouse them. They dressed sleepily and had to hurry downstairs in order to be in time for breakfast. This did not escape the notice of ever-watchful Aunt Gertrude.

"When *I* was a girl," she said pointedly, "young people went to bed at a reasonable hour and didn't go gallivanting all over the country half the night. Every growing boy and girl needs eight or nine hours' sleep. I'd be ashamed to come down to breakfast rubbing my eyes and gaping."

"It isn't very often they get up late," said Mrs. Hardy. "We can overlook it once in a while, I suppose."

"Overlook it!" snorted Aunt Gertrude. "Mark my words, Laura, those boys will come to no good end if you encourage them in coming in at all hours of the night. Goodness knows what mischief they were up to." She glared severely at them.

Frank and Joe realized that their aunt was curious as to where they had been the past two evenings and was using this roundabout method of tempting them into an explanation. However, as Joe expressed it later, they "refused to bite."

Instead, they hastily consumed their breakfast, drawing from the good lady a lecture on the dreadful consequences of eating in a hurry, illustrated by an anecdote concerning a little boy named Hector, who met a lamentable and untimely death by choking himself on a piece of steak and passed away surrounded by weeping relatives.

The boys, however, were evidently not impressed by the fate of the unfortunate Hector, for they gulped down their meal, snatched up their books, and rushed off to school without waiting for Aunt Gertrude's account of the funeral. They were crossing the school yard when the bell rang and they reached the classroom just in time.

"I feel like a stewed owl," was Joe's comment.

"Never ate stewed owl," returned his brother promptly. "How does it taste?"

"I said I felt, I didn't say I ate," retorted Joe. "Gee, but your eyes do look bunged up."

"What about your own?"

"Oh, if only I had had just one more hour's sleep!"

"I could go two or three."

"Aunt Gertrude was onto us."

"Yes, but she didn't get anywhere with it."

"Hope I don't fall asleep over my desk."

"Same here."

The morning dragged. They were very sleepy. Once or twice, Joe yawned openly and Miss Petty, who taught history, accused him of lack of interest in the proceedings.

"You may keep yourself awake by telling us what you know of the Roman system of government under Julius Cæsar," she said.

Joe got to his feet. He floundered through a more or less acceptable account of Roman government. It was dreary stuff, and Frank, listening to the droning voice, became drowsier and drowsier. His head nodded, and finally he went to sleep altogether and had a vivid dream in which he chased Julius Cæsar, attired in a toga and with a laurel wreath on his head, along the Shore Road in a steam-roller.

Miss Petty left the Romans and began comparing ancient and modern systems of government, which led her into a discourse on the life of Abraham Lincoln. She was just reaching Lincoln's death when there was a loud snore.

Miss Petty looked up.

"Who made that noise?"

Another snore.

Joe dug his brother in the ribs with a ruler and Frank looked up, with an expression of surprise on his face.

"Frank Hardy, are you paying attention?"

"Yes, ma'am," replied Frank, now wide awake. In his dream he imagined Julius Cæsar had turned on him and had poked him in the ribs with a spear.

"Do you know who we were talking about?"

"Oh, yes, ma'am."

"Do you know anything about his death?"

"Yes, ma'am," said Frank, under the impression that the lesson still dealt with Cæsar.

"How did he die?"

"He was stabbed."

"He was stabbed, was he? Where?"

"In—in the Forum. He was murdered by some of the senators, led by Cassius and Brutus, and Marc Antony made a speech."

The class could contain itself no longer. Snickers burst out, and these welled into a wave of laughter in which even Miss Petty was forced to join. Frank looked around in vast surprise.

"This," said the teacher, "is an interesting fact about Lincoln. I don't remember having heard of it before. So he was stabbed to death by the senators and Marc Antony made a speech?"

"I—I was talking about Cæsar, Miss Petty."

"And *I* was talking about Abraham Lincoln. Will you be good enough to stay awake for the remainder of the lesson, Hardy?"

Frank looked sheepishly at his book, while Chet Morton doubled up in his seat and gave vent to a series of explosive chuckles that soon brought the teacher's attention to him and he was required to recite the Gettysburg Address, stalling completely before he had gone a dozen words. By the time the teacher had finished her comments on his poor memory, Chet had other things to occupy his mind.

Frank and Joe Hardy were wide awake for the rest of the morning.

After lunch, they were on their way back to school, resolving to cut out the late hours, so as not to risk a repetition of the ridicule they had suffered that morning, when Frank suddenly caught sight of a familiar figure not far ahead.

"Why, there's Gus Montrose again," he said. "Wonder what he's doing in town?"

"Let's trail him," Joe suggested.

"Good idea. We'll find out what he does with his time."

The former hired man of the Dodds was shambling down the street at a lazy gait, apparently wrapped up in his own concerns. Frank and Joe followed, at a respectful distance. When Montrose reached a busy corner he turned down a side street and here his demeanor changed. His shoulders were straighter and his step more purposeful.

Taking the opposite side of the street, the boys strolled along, keeping well behind Montrose but not letting him out of sight. They followed him for about two blocks and then, leaning against a telegraph pole at the next corner, they saw Montrose's companion of the previous night. He looked up as Montrose approached, and then the pair met and joined in earnest conversation.

There was something peculiarly furtive about the two men. Not wishing to be observed, the Hardy boys stepped into a soft drink place near by and bought some ginger ale, which they drank in the store, keeping an eye on the pair across the street, through the window.

Finally, Montrose's companion moved slowly away, and Montrose himself shambled across the road. He was lost to sight for a moment.

"We'll trail him a little while longer," said Frank. "We have about a quarter of an hour before school opens."

They paid for the ginger ale and stepped out of the shop. To their astonishment, Gus Montrose was coming directly toward them. They had lost sight of him in the window and had assumed that he had gone on down the street. Instead he had turned back.

They affected not to notice him, and were starting back up the street when Montrose overtook them and brushed against Frank rudely.

"Look here," he said, in a gruff voice. "What's the idea of followin' me, hey?"

"Following you!" said Frank, in tones of simulated surprise.

"Yes—followin' me. I saw you. What do you mean by it?"

"Can't we walk down the same street?" inquired Joe.

"You didn't walk down here by accident. You followed me here."

"You must have something on your conscience if you think that," Frank told him. "This is a free country. We can walk where we like."

"Is that so? Well, I'm not goin' to put up with havin' a pair of young whippersnappers trailin' *me* around town," snarled Gus Montrose. "Hear that?"

"We hear you."

"Well, remember it, then. You just mind your own business after this, see?"

"If you think we were following you, that's your own affair," returned Frank. "We're on our way to school, if you'd like to know."

"Well, see that you go there. You're better off in school than monkeyin' in my affairs, let me tell you. And a sight safer, too."

The man's tone was truculent.

"Oh, I think you're pretty harmless," laughed Joe.

"You'll find out how harmless I am if I catch you followin' me around again. Just mind your own business after this and keep goin' in the opposite direction when you see me comin'."

The man's insulting tone annoyed Frank.

"Look here," he said, sharply, facing Montrose. "If you don't start off in the opposite direction right now, I'll call a policeman. Now, get out of here."

Somewhat taken aback, Gus Montrose halted.

"You were followin' me—" he growled.

"You heard what I said. Clear out of here and stop annoying us."

If Montrose had hoped to frighten the lads, he was disappointed. Like most cowardly men, he backed down readily when confronted with opposition. Grumbling to himself, he turned away and crossed the street.

The Hardy boys went on toward school.

"That'll give him something to think about," remarked Frank.

"You hit the right note when you said he must have something on his conscience or he wouldn't have thought we were following him."

"I'm sure he has. A man with a clear conscience would never suspect he was being trailed. There's something mighty fishy about Gus Montrose and his odd-looking friend."

"Too bad he saw us. He'll be on his guard against us now."

"That doesn't matter. We can keep an eye on him just the same. I'd give a farm to know what the pair of them were talking about."

"And I'd give a five-dollar bill just to know if he put that fishing pole in the car up at the Dodds' and got Jack into trouble."

"So would I."

The boys were greatly puzzled. They were convinced that Gus Montrose was up to no good and this conviction had only been strengthened by their encounter. They reasoned that a law-abiding man would scarcely have shown such resentment as Montrose had evidenced.

"Well, whether he's one of the thieving party or not, we'll take another whirl at the Shore Road tonight," said Frank, as the two brothers entered the school yard.

Joe glanced at the sky. Massed clouds were gathering and the air was close.

"Looks as if we'll have to call it off. There's going to be a storm."

"Storm or no storm, I have a hunch that we'll get some action before the day is out."

Both Frank and Joe were right.

There was a storm, and before midnight they had more action than they had ever bargained for.

CHAPTER XVI

KIDNAPED

Rain threatened throughout the afternoon, but although the sky darkened and there was an ominous calm, the storm held off. After supper the Hardy boys went outside and looked at the clouds.

"It's sure going to be a jim-dandy," declared Joe. "Do you think we really should go out tonight?"

"A little thing like a storm won't hold the car thieves back. They'll operate in any weather."

"Won't they think it strange to see a car parked out in the rain?"

"They'll probably think it was stalled and that the owner went to get help."

"That's right, too," Joe agreed. "I guess we can chance it."

"We'll put the top up to protect ourselves. And, anyway, it's dry in the locker."

"The rain will be the least of our worries in there," said Joe, with a grin. "Let's be going."

They went out to the garage and put up the top of the roadster, then got in. As they drove down High Street there was a low rumble of thunder and a splash of rain against the windshield.

"Storm's coming, right enough," Frank said. "Still, I have a hunch."

Ever since the previous night he had been possessed by a feeling that their next venture would be crowned with success. He could not explain it, but the feeling was there nevertheless.

They spied Con Riley, in oilskins against the approaching downpour, patrolling his beat, and drew up at the curb.

"New car, eh?" said Riley, surveying the roadster grimly. "I'll be runnin' you in for speeding some of these days, I'll be bound."

"Not in this boat," Frank assured him. "If we ever hit higher than thirty the engine would fly out."

"Thirty!" scoffed the constable. "That looks like a real racin' car. You mean ninety."

"We'll take you for a drive some time when you're off duty. We just stopped to ask if there was anything new about the auto thieves."

Riley looked very grave, as he always did when any one asked him questions pertaining to police matters.

"Well," he said, "there is and there isn't."

"That means there isn't."

"We ain't found 'em yet. But that don't mean they won't be found," said the officer darkly. "We're followin' up clues."

"What kind of clues?"

"Oh, just clues," said the officer vaguely. "We'll have 'em behind the bars before long. But you'd better keep an eye on that car of yours. It's just the kind somebody would steal."

"Trust us. There's been no trace of the other cars, then?"

Riley shook his head.

"Not a sign. But them thieves will go too far some of these fine days, and then we'll catch 'em."

"Well, we hope you're the man who lands them," said Frank cheerfully, as he edged the car out from the curb again. "So long."

The boys drove away, and Con Riley patiently resumed his beat.

"The game is still open," remarked Joe. "If the police had learned anything new, Riley would have heard about it."

"Whenever he says they're following up clues, you can be certain that they're up against it. The thieves are just as much at large as they ever were."

It was beginning to rain heavily before they reached the outskirts of Bayport and by the time they were well out on the Shore Road the storm was upon them. Thunder rolled and rumbled in the blackening sky and jagged streaks of lightning flickered through the clouds. Rain streamed down in the glare of the headlights.

As the downpour grew in violence, the road became more treacherous. Without chains, the rear wheels of the car skidded and slithered on the greasy surface.

One of the numerous defects of the roadster's mechanism was a loose steering wheel. Under ordinary circumstances it gave little trouble, but on this treacherous road, Frank experienced difficulty in keeping the car on its course.

Just outside Bayport was a steep hill, dipping to the bluffs that overhung the bay. Under the influence of the rain, the sloping road had become wet and sticky, and as the roadster began the descent Frank knew he was in for trouble.

The car skidded wildly, and the faulty brakes did not readily respond. Once, the nose of the roadster appeared to be heading directly toward the steep bluff, where only a narrow ledge separated the boys from a terrible plunge onto the rocks of the beach below. Joe gave a gasp of apprehension, but Frank bore down on the wheel and managed to swing the car back onto the road again in the nick of time.

But the danger was not yet over.

The car was tobogganing down the slope as though entirely out of control. The rear wheels skidded crazily and several times the car was almost directly across the road, sliding sideways, and when it did regain the ruts it shot ahead with breath-taking speed.

Almost any second the boys expected the roadster would leave the slippery clay and either shoot across the ledge into space or crash into the rocky wall at the left.

Somehow, luck was with them. Luck and Frank's quick work at the unreliable wheel saved them from disaster.

The car gained the level ground, settled into the ruts, and went speeding on at a more reasonable rate. The lads now breathed more easily.

"Looked like our finish, that time," observed Joe.

"I'll say it did! I wouldn't have given a nickel for our chances when we were about half way down the hill."

"Well, a miss is as good as a mile. We're still alive."

"And the old boat is still rolling along. When we get back I'm going to have that steering wheel fixed. It very nearly cost us our lives."

On through the storm the Hardy boys drove, until at last they reached the place where they had parked on the previous night. There was no one in sight as they drove out onto the grass, and Frank turned off the engine and switched out the lights. Quickly, they scrambled out, raised the lid of the locker, and got inside.

The locker was warm and dry. The boys were comfortable enough, aside from being somewhat cramped, and they could hear the rain roaring down on the top of the roadster as the storm grew in violence.

Warned by their former experience, the boys had made themselves more comfortable than they had previously been. On the floor of the locker they had spread a soft rug and they had also supplied themselves with two small but comfortable pillows.

"I am not going to wear out my knees and elbows," Frank had said. "The last time we were out my left elbow was black and blue."

"We'll fix it up as comfortable as a bed," Joe had answered.

In addition to the rug and pillows the boys had brought along a small box of fancy crackers and also a bottle of cold water, for hiding in the locker for hours had made them both hungry and thirsty.

"I could eat a few crackers right now," remarked Joe, shortly after they had settled down to their vigil.

"Same here," answered his brother. "Pass the box over."

Each lad had several crackers and followed them with a swallow of water. As they munched the crackers the thunder rolled and rolled in the distance and they could see an occasional flash of lightning through a crack of the locker door.

"It sure is a dirty night," Frank whispered, as they crouched in the darkness of their voluntary prison.

"Even for auto thieves."

Thunder rolled and grumbled and the rain poured down in drenching torrents. They could hear the beating of the surf on the distant shore of Barmet Bay, far below.

Minutes passed, with only the monotonous roar of the storm.

"What's the time?" asked Joe finally.

Frank switched on the flashlight and glanced at his watch.

"Half-past nine."

"Time enough yet."

They settled down to wait. Scarcely five minutes had passed before they heard a new sound above the clamor of the rain and wind.

Some one stepped up on the running board of the roadster, flung open the door, and sat down behind the wheel. The boys had not heard the intruder's approach, owing to the noise of the storm, and they sat up, startled.

The newcomer lost no time.

In a moment, the engine roared, and then the car started forward with a jerk.

It lurched across the grassy ground, then climbed up onto the Shore Road. Back in the locker, the lads were bounced and jolted against one another. They did not mind this, for there was wild joy in their hearts. At last their patient vigil had been rewarded.

"Kidnaped!" whispered Frank exultantly.

Once on the road, the car set off at rapidly increasing speed through the storm. The man at the wheel was evidently an expert driver, for he got every ounce of power the engine was capable of, and held the roadster to the highway. The roar of the motor could be heard high above the drumming of the rain.

In the darkness of the locker, the boys sat tight, not knowing where the car was going, not knowing how long this wild journey might last. They kept alert for any turns from the Shore Road, realizing that they might have to find their way back by memory.

For above five minutes, the car held to the Shore Road, and then suddenly swerved to the right.

Neither of the boys had any recollection of a side road in this part of the country, and they were immediately surprised. However, by the violent lurching and jolting of the roadster they were soon aware that they were on no traveled thoroughfare and that they were descending a slope over rough ground. There was a loud swishing of branches and the sharp snapping of twigs, that indicated the roadster was passing through the woods.

The man at the wheel was driving more carefully now that he was off the Shore Road and comparatively safe from observation. He was evidently following a road of sorts, although the car swerved and jolted unmercifully, but at length he came to even more precarious ground.

The rear of the roadster went high in the air and came down with a crash. Frank and Joe were flung violently to the bottom of the locker, and Frank felt a most stunning blow on the head.

Thud!

Another terrific jolt. The car pitched and tossed like a ship in a storm.

Bang!

A tire had blown out.

But this did not appear to worry the driver. The car canted far over on one side, lurched forward, and then came down on all four wheels with a terrific impact.

The boys were badly shaken up. They tried to brace themselves against the sides of the locker, but this was of little use as the roadster's bumpy and erratic progress inevitably dislodged them. They were thrown against one another, bounced from side to side, bruised and battered.

It was apparent to them that the roadster was being driven over some rocks—not the boulders of the beach, but over a rocky section of ground where there was no road.

They shielded their heads with their arms as well as they could, to prevent themselves from being knocked senseless against the sides of the locker.

The speed of the car slackened. Then they felt a long series of short, sharp bumps, as though the car were being driven over pebbles. Stones banged against the mudguards.

"We're on the beach," reflected Frank.

They did not suffer the jouncing and jolting that had given them such discomfort a short time previously. The car traveled along the beach for a short distance, then turned to the left and ran quietly and smoothly over what the boys judged to be a stretch of sand. It then began to climb. The ascent flung the lads against the back of the locker.

It was of short duration, however.

The roadster came to level ground again, then rattled and rumbled on over an uneven surface.

The boys noticed a peculiar, hollow sound. The roar of the motor seemed to be echoing from all sides. The car had slowed down, and at last it came to a stop.

Battered and bruised, the lads crouched in their hiding place, wondering what would happen next. They could hear the driver scrambling out of the front seat. Then there was a voice:

"That, you, Alex?"

"Yep."

"What have you got?"

"Big roadster."

"The one we were talking about?"

"You bet."

Other voices followed, voices that echoed and re-echoed, and then footsteps clattered on rock.

"A beauty!" exclaimed some one. "Have any trouble?"

"None at all," said the voice of the man who had been addressed as Alex. "Nobody in sight, so I just hopped in and drove it out."

"Swell boat!" declared some one else. "Fine night to leave it out in the rain."

"That's what I thought," said Alex. "So I drove it in out of the wet."

There was a general laugh. From the number of voices, the lads judged that there were at least three or four men standing near the big car.

"Wonder who owns it," said one of the several men.

"I don't know who *did* own it, but I know that *we* own it now," answered Alex promptly.

"What'll we do? Leave it here?"

"There isn't room inside. Might as well leave it."

"I guess nobody will come along and steal it," remarked Alex, who was evidently the wit of the party, for another burst of laughter greeted his words. "Want to look the car over?" he asked.

"Oh, it looks good enough from here."

"What's in that locker?" said one of the men. "There might be something valuable."

A thrill of fear went through the two boys.

One of the men approached the back of the car. Frank gripped his revolver firmly.

CHAPTER XVII

THE CAVE

In a moment the lid of the locker would have been raised.

Then came an interruption.

"The boss wants us," said one of the men.

The man approaching the back of the car halted.

"All right," he growled. "We'll leave this."

He turned away. The Hardy boys sighed with relief.

"I guess he's waitin' for a report," observed a voice, as the men began to move off. Their footsteps sounded sharp and clear on the rocks.

The sounds died away.

Complete silence prevailed. Not even a murmur broke the stillness. The lads remained quiet in the darkness of their hiding place.

Finally Frank stirred.

"They've gone," he whispered.

"What shall we do now?" asked Joe.

"Let's get out of here first. They may come back at any minute."

Frank raised the lid cautiously. The blackness without was as utter and complete as the darkness within. He could see nothing.

He listened for a moment, thinking possibly some of the gang had remained behind, but he heard nothing. Quickly, he got out of the locker and leaped to the ground. Joe followed. They closed the lid.

"Boy! I thought it was all up with us," whispered Joe. "When he came over to open the locker my heart was thumping so loudly I was sure he could hear it."

"Me, too. Well, we can thank their boss—whoever he is. I wonder what kind of place we're in, anyway."

Frank switched on his flashlight.

By its brilliant gleam, he saw that they were in a rocky passageway, a large tunnel evidently in the bluffs along Barmet Bay. It was wide enough to accommodate the roadster, but did not offer a great deal of leeway on either side. It appeared to be a natural tunnel, although there was evidence that human toil had been responsible for widening it and clearing it out.

Frank stepped forward and cast the ray of light before him.

It revealed a blank wall of rock. Then, as he moved the flashlight to one side he saw that the tunnel slanted toward the left.

"What'll we do?" asked Joe. "Follow it up along?"

He spoke in a whisper, but the walls magnified his voice and he awakened uncanny echoes.

"Sure. We'll have to be careful, though, or we might meet them on the way back."

Frank took the lead. He stepped forward very carefully, making no move that might dislodge a loose fragment of rock and start a tumult of echoes that would bring the gang upon them.

Cautiously, they advanced. Joe took his revolver from his pocket and gripped it tightly.

They realized that they were dealing with a band of desperate men, who would stop at nothing if they were discovered.

The Hardy boys rounded the corner of the passageway, and Frank's flashlight revealed a number of large boxes, stacked up against the side of the tunnel. They halted and Frank scrutinized some lettering on the boxes.

"The Eastern Importing Company," he read.

"Why, that's the name of the company that lost the truck!" Joe exclaimed. "Remember? The two men who were held up and rolled down the bluff."

"It's the same name, all right. I'll bet this is some of the truck cargo."

The boxes were seven in number, and on each was inscribed the name of the Eastern Importing Company.

There was no doubt in the minds of the Hardy boys now that they had made a momentous discovery. This was plainly the hiding place of the auto thieves, and although none of the stolen cars were in evidence, the big packing boxes spoke for themselves.

"We'll see what's farther on," Frank decided.

He went ahead. Joe tiptoed close behind. The flashlight illuminated the rocky floor of the tunnel.

It began to widen out. Stacked against the wall they came upon more packing boxes, some of which had been torn open.

"More loot," Joe commented, in a whisper.

Every few steps, Frank halted and switched out the light. Then they stood in the darkness, listening. They had no desire to stumble on the auto thieves or reveal their own presence.

However, the boys heard not a sound. There was not a glimmer of light in the impenetrable gloom that lay before them.

A few yards farther, the tunnel widened out into a veritable cave. Here, as Frank turned the flashlight to and fro, and the boys were confronted by a sight that made them gasp for the moment.

In the great rocky chamber, they saw three large pleasure cars and a small truck, parked close by the clammy walls.

"The stolen autos!" breathed Joe.

There stood four of the missing cars, undamaged, in this secret cavern in the bluffs. They had been driven in along the tunnel from the beach. It was an ideal hiding place and as the entrance to the tunnel was doubtless well masked, the cars were as safe from discovery as though they had been driven into the ocean. At least, so the thieves probably thought.

"We've found them!" Frank exclaimed.

All the missing cars were not hidden here, but the boys judged that the rest were probably stored farther on. For the flashlight revealed a dark opening in the rock at the other end of the cavern, an opening to a tunnel that no doubt led to other caves farther on.

The Hardy boys knew that the Shore Road bluffs, in certain places, contained caves and passages, some of which had never been entered. Although like most Bayport boys, they had done a certain amount of exploring along the beach, they had never heard of the existence of this underground labyrinth. It seemed strange to them that so elaborate a series of caves had never been explored and their existence was comparatively unknown.

"Wait until Bayport hears of this!" Joe said. "Let's get out of here and hurry back to town."

"I suppose we should," Frank admitted. "I'd like to know where those men went."

"If we go any farther they may catch us, and then we'd be out of luck."

"But if we start back to town we'll have to walk, and they might all clear out in the meantime. It would be a few hours before we could get back here with the police."

"We'd have the satisfaction of recovering the cars, anyway," Joe pointed out. "I believe in playing safe."

"I'd like the satisfaction of rounding up this gang as well."

Frank advanced toward the opening at the far side of the cave.

"I think I'll just poke along in here a little way and see where it leads," he said.

Joe was dubious. He was of a more cautious nature than his brother, and was satisfied to let well enough alone. They had found the missing cars. This alone was sufficient, he reasoned. Having come this far without mishap he did not like to risk spoiling their success. However, he followed Frank into the tunnel.

It was narrower than the one which had led them to the cave, and its sides were rocky and uneven, while the roof was low. It was quite evident that none of the cars could have been driven through this narrow space, and as the boys went on they found that the roof was lower and the walls even closer together.

Finally, the flashlight showed them that it was almost impossible to continue, as projecting rocks jutted out and there was just enough space to admit passage of one person. Beyond that, the tunnel seemed to close altogether.

"Guess this is a blind alley," said Frank. "We may as well turn back."

He handed the flashlight to Joe, who led the way on the return trip through the tunnel.

Suddenly there was an uproar immediately ahead, a clamorous, deafening crash. The boys jumped with astonishment. In the darkness of the subterranean cavern their nerves had been keyed up to a high pitch, and this tremendous clatter was so unexpected in the dead silence that had surrounded them that they were almost paralyzed with momentary fright.

There followed a rattling and bumping of rocks, and then silence once more.

"What was that?" exclaimed Joe, recovering from his scare.

"Sounded to me like a fall of rock." Frank's voice was shaky, for he had a suspicion of what had actually happened.

"It seemed mighty close."

"That's what I'm afraid of. It may have blocked up this tunnel."

Hastily, the boys went forward. In a few moments the flashlight revealed a sight at which their hearts sank.

The passage before them was completely closed up!

Great boulders, ledges of rock, and a heavy downpouring of earth formed an apparently impenetrable barrier ahead. A loose stone, no doubt dislodged when they went by a short time before, had given way and had brought down this miniature avalanche from the roof and sides of the tunnel.

"We're trapped!" Frank exclaimed.

CHAPTER XVIII

THE AUTO THIEVES

The cave-in had imprisoned the Hardy boys.

The flashlight revealed not a single opening. The tunnel was blocked up, and for all the boys knew the barrier continued right to the outer cave.

"Now we're in for it," remarked Joe dubiously.

The boys realized that there was nothing to be gained by shouting for help. Even if their cries were heard, which would be unlikely with that solid mass of rock before them, it would only bring the auto thieves upon them.

"We'll have to work fast," said Frank. "There isn't any too much air in this place now, and if we don't get that rock cleared out of the way we'll be smothered."

"Do you mean to say we'll have to move all that rock aside?"

"What else is there to do?"

"It might take hours."

"That's better than dying in here," returned Frank philosophically. "You hold the light and I'll get busy."

He flung off his coat and attacked the formidable barrier.

Starting at the top, he moved rock after rock aside, placing them on the floor of the tunnel. The work was slow, and he seemed to make little progress. For, as the rocks were taken away, they showed only more rocks behind. It was evident that the cave-in had been of considerable extent.

Joe became impatient.

"I feel useless," he said. "You hold the light for a while and let me work."

"Put it in a ledge some place and we can both work."

Joe hunted around and managed to find a convenient ledge of rock on which to rest the flashlight. Its beam was directed at the barrier and, rid of the encumbrance, Joe was then able to lend a hand to the work of removing the débris.

Patiently, the brothers toiled, lifting aside the rocks and putting them back on the floor. Every little while a fresh shower of dirt and stones would come rattling down from the roof. The task seemed hopeless.

"Looks as if this goes on for yards," panted Joe wearily.

"We might get out in a couple of years," Frank said, resting for a moment. "Still, if we can only clear a small opening it'll be enough to let us out."

He attacked the barricade again with renewed vigor.

Wrenching at a large rock, he tugged and pulled until it became dislodged from the surrounding débris. Frank was just dragging the huge stone away when there came a warning rumble, a cry of alarm from Joe, and he leaped back.

He was just in time.

With a crash, a large section of the roof caved in, a flat ledge of rock just missing his head by inches. A mass of rubbish descended with a roar.

"Get out of the way!"

"Get out yourself!"

"Gee, it looks as if the whole roof might come down!"

"I got some dust in my eyes."

"Same here. Say, this is the worst yet."

"Humph! We'll be lucky if we are not buried alive."

Much crestfallen, the boys bumped into each other, rubbing their eyes and clearing their throats of the dry dust that had come down with the rocks.

Then they gazed at each other in dismay, and not without reason.

All the boys' work was undone. The barrier was now larger than it had ever been.

"That fixes it!" said Frank gloomily.

The ledge of rock that had given way was of such extent that it was impossible for any one to move it. Their path was completely blocked.

"No use working at *that* any more!"

Frank sat down on a rock, regarding the impassable heap.

"Buried alive," he remarked, at last.

"No one will ever find us here."

The boys realized the gravity of their plight. No one knew they were in the tunnel. No one had seen them enter. If they perished here, their bodies might never be recovered.

"Think we ought to start calling?" asked Joe hopefully.

"Looks as if we'll have to do something. Perhaps if we do call, the men won't hear us."

"How about going back along the tunnel? There was still a sort of opening, you remember."

"It's our only chance."

Frank had little hope that the tunnel had another outlet. However, he grabbed up the flashlight and the boys picked their way back along the rocky passage.

When they came to the place where the tunnel had seemed to end, they surveyed it dubiously.

"I'll go ahead," said Frank. "Like as not, I'll get stuck in here and you'll have to come in and pull me out."

He wedged himself into the opening between the rocks, holding the flashlight before him.

To his surprise he found that although there was a blank wall immediately ahead, the tunnel turned sharply to one side and in the glow of the light he saw that it continued for some little distance, a very narrow passage, but one that offered sufficient space for him to continue.

"It doesn't end here after all," he called back to Joe. "Perhaps it does lead outside."

He went on. Joe scrambled through the opening and followed close behind.

With growing elation Frank found that the tunnel continued. When he had gone about fifteen yards he rounded a sharp corner, and gave a cry of delight.

Here, on the wet floor, he spied the imprint of a man's shoe!

"There's been some one here before us," he said to Joe, in excitement. "A footprint!"

"Which way does it lead?"

"The way we're going. This isn't so hopeless after all."

This evidence that another human being had been in the tunnel gave the boys new courage.

"We'd better go quietly. Chances are that the auto thieves are somewhere around."

A few steps farther, and Frank spied a light in the distance. At first he thought it was only a reflection from his own flashlight, but when he switched it out, the light still glowed steadily through the darkness ahead.

They moved cautiously. Frank did not turn on the flashlight again. He was afraid it might be seen. Step by step, they moved forward, and the glow of the mysterious light became brighter. It was soon so strong that it even cast a certain amount of illumination into the tunnel and the boys saw that the passage was almost at an end.

Then they heard a voice.

They could not distinguish the words, but they could hear some one talking in a quick, rasping tone. Then another voice interrupted.

Frank laid a warning hand on his brother's sleeve.

"Quiet does it," he warned.

They crept forward.

The tunnel evidently opened into another cave. Edging ahead as close to the entrance of the passage as they dared, the boys saw that the light was from a huge lamp. It was not turned toward them, or the tunnel would have been bathed in a strong glare and they would have been seen, but it cast a strong radiance over a small cave-in which half a dozen men were sitting.

The cavern was bare, but there were boxes scattered about on the rocky floor, and these provided makeshift seats. The lads caught only a glimpse of the eerie scene, the shadowy figures, and then they drew back, for two of the men were facing them and for a moment they thought the fellows could not have failed to see them.

However, the glare of the immense lamp evidently blinded them to anything beyond, for they did not move.

A gruff voice spoke.

"Well, we can run that big touring car out tonight. Clancy says he can do the repainting tomorrow and we can get rid of it in a day or so if everything goes well."

"He took his time about selling that coupé."

"There was a hitch somewhere. He thought the dicks were watching his place, so he had to lay low for a few days."

"Well, I guess it's all right. I don't blame him for not taking any more chances than he has to."

"Rats!" said some one else. "He's takin' no chances! We've got away with everything fine so far and the cops haven't suspected any of us yet."

"Clancy's different," said the man with the gruff voice. "He's at the selling end, and that's where the danger lies. It's no trouble to steal these boats. The dicks don't try to trace 'em from that end, for they know there isn't much use. They watch until we try to get rid of 'em."

"Clancy's smart. He even burns out the engine numbers. When one of those cars leaves his hands, even the owner wouldn't recognize it if you took him for a ride in it."

"We've been making out all right so far, but we can't get too bold. The whole countryside is stirred up, and the farther we go the more chances we're taking."

"That's true. Just the same, we're about as safe here as any one can be. Nobody knows about these caves."

"Lucky break for us that they don't. If I didn't know about them I could walk up and down that beach for a month of Sundays and never spot an opening."

"That's a nice-lookin' roadster you landed tonight."

"It's been parked out on the Shore Road for two nights past. It seemed a shame to neglect a nice boat that way, so I took it in."

"What would anybody park a car out there for on a night like this? Wasn't there anybody around?"

"Not a soul. Mebbe the driver was out fishin' and got caught in the rain and didn't get back. Or he might have had engine trouble."

"It ran for you, didn't it?"

"Sure. But I can make 'em run when nobody else can."

"You sure know how to handle a car. I'll say that for you."

There was a stir in the cave.

"Here he comes now," announced some one.

Then the boys heard a familiar voice, a voice that sent a thrill of excitement through them.

"Coast is clear. You can run that car out now, Dan."

It was the voice of Gus Montrose!

CHAPTER XIX

CAPTURED

Tensely, the Hardy boys crouched in the tunnel, as they heard the voice of the Dodds' former hired man.

"It's a dirty night out," he was saying. "You're welcome to the trip, Dan."

"Still raining?"

"Pouring. I'm soaked to the skin," grumbled Montrose. "It's no fun, ploughing down through that gully."

"Well, you won't have much more to do tonight," said one of the men placatingly. "We landed a fine roadster while you were out."

"The one I was telling you about?"

"The same."

"Seems funny about that car being parked on the Shore Road three nights in a row. I saw it there the other evening and passed it up. Then last night I got in and would have driven it away, only I couldn't get it started. Different kind of car than any I've ever been in. I went out and found Sam and we were going back when we ran right into the car turning around in a lane."

"Didn't see who was in it, did you?"

"No. The headlights shone right in our eyes. Seemed like a couple of young fellows. If they had been a little slower we'd have had the car."

"Well, we have it now. They'll wish they wasn't so smart, leavin' it out in the rain that way."

"Nice wet walk they'll have if they live in Bayport," laughed Gus Montrose shortly. "I know who I *wish* owned it."

"Your little friends?"

"Those brats of Hardy boys," returned Gus. "Followed me for about three blocks today when I went uptown to meet Sam."

"What was the big idea?"

"Aw, they kid themselves that they're a couple of amateur detectives," rasped Montrose. "Just because they've been lucky in a couple of cases they think they gotta go spyin' on everybody."

"What made 'em spy on you?"

"How should I know? I guess Dodd must have put them up to it."

"They don't figger you're mixed up with these missin' cars, do they?"

"How could they? Nobody has anythin' on me," bragged Gus. "But I told them a few things, anyway. I told 'em to lay off followin' me or they'd get somethin' they wasn't lookin' for."

"What'd they say?"

"They backed down. Got scared and beat it."

"That's the way to talk to them," approved the man called Dan. "Scare the daylights out of them."

"Speakin' of daylight—it'll be daylight before you reach Atlantic City with that car if you don't hurry up."

"All right. All right. I'll start movin'," Dan growled.

"You might as well take some of that junk we got from the Importing Company's truck, and ask Clancy to sell it for us. And don't you forget to collect the money from him for the last car we turned over to him."

"I won't forget. Some of you guys had better come along and load a couple of those boxes for me."

There was a heavy tramping of feet, that indicated the men were leaving the cave. The Hardy boys could hear their receding footsteps and the diminishing voices. Finally the cave was in silence.

Frank peeped out of the tunnel.

"They've gone," he whispered.

"Are you going in?" questioned Joe.

"Sure. There's no one around."

He stepped out onto the rocky floor, with Joe at his heels.

The cave was not as large as the one in which the cars were stored, but from the boxes scattered around and from a litter of empty cigarette packages, burnt matches, old clothes, and other things lying about, it was clearly the meeting place of the gang.

"Well, we've found the auto thieves, all right. The next thing is to trap them."

"We can't do it alone, that's certain," said Joe. "I think we ought to get out of here as quickly as we can."

"There's probably only one opening to this place," answered Frank, flashing the light about the walls.

It fell on a dark opening through which the thieves had departed. There was no other passage apparent, beyond the one through which the boys had entered.

"Not much use going after them. They're probably all out in the cave where the cars are kept," remarked Joe.

"We'll just have to watch our chance."

"Let's take a look around here," remarked Frank, after a minute of silence.

"We'll have to be careful. They may come back and catch us," answered his brother.

"We'll watch out for that."

With caution the boys began to look around them.

"Look!" cried Frank in a low tone.

He bent down and from the rocky floor picked up a big bunch of keys.

"Auto keys," came from Joe.

"Yes, and all different. I suppose they have all the keys necessary to unlock any car."

"More than likely."

Near the keys they found a dark coat and a cap.

"I guess the keys dropped out of that coat," remarked Frank.

"Looks like it." Joe's gaze traveled to a spot back of the coat. "Look, a wig!" he exclaimed.

"That shows they go out disguised."

"It sure does. Say, we're getting to the bottom of this mystery!"

"I hope so."

The boys explored the underground chamber, but found nothing of further interest.

"So we were right, after all," Frank said. "Gus Montrose is mixed up with the auto thieves."

"He probably discovered these caves in the first place, and saw how they could be used for concealing stolen goods. Perhaps this place was used by smugglers long ago."

"Probably. They are natural caves, and it's easily seen that they've been used for a long time. Some of the tunnels look as if they'd been blasted out to widen them. We're certainly lucky to have found their hiding place, for we'd never have found it unless we'd been brought here."

"From their talk, they evidently drive the cars to Atlantic City from here."

"Must have a secret road of some kind, or they'd never get through."

"Montrose spoke of coming through a gully."

"There is a gully near the Dodd farm. Now that I come to think of it, I believe there is an abandoned road through it. The place has been overgrown with brush for the past five years, though."

"Perhaps they cleared it out."

"The road used to lead out to one of the private, right-of-way roads in the back township. Since the Shore Road was extended, it's never been used. I'll bet that's what they're doing—using that old road and bringing the cars out the back way. The police haven't been watching the private roads at all."

"It's a smart scheme. Well, it won't last much longer."

Suddenly, a voice rang out, clear and sharp:

"I'll get the lantern. It's right here."

Startled, the boys wheeled about. The voice seemed to be right beside them. Instantly, they realized that it was only a trick of the echoes, and that the voice came from the passage leading into the cave.

Some one was approaching. They could hear his heavy boots clumping on the rocky floor.

"Quick! The tunnel!" whispered Frank.

He sped across the cave toward the opening in the wall. But they had moved farther away from their hiding place than they imagined. By the time the brothers reached the passage, they heard a cry of alarm behind them.

"Who's that?"

They scrambled into the tunnel.

Another shout, footsteps across the floor, and then the lantern cast its beam directly on the entrance of the passage. It was a powerful light and the boys knew they had been seen.

The man in the cave began shouting for help:

"Gus! Sam! Come here! Quick!"

His voice echoed from the walls.

The Hardy boys heard a faint shout from outside the cave.

"What's the matter?"

"Some one in here. Hurry up!"

The uproar out in the cave grew in volume as other members of the gang joined their comrade. There was a hasty gabble of voices.

"There was some one in the cave when I came back for the light," shouted the man who had discovered the boys. "They beat it into that tunnel. I just saw them."

"Sam, go around and watch the other side!" ordered some one sharply. "That tunnel goes out into the big cave."

The thieves were evidently unaware of the cave-in that had blocked the passage. Frank and Joe retreated beyond the first bend. They were trapped. The barricade cut off their flight, and they knew they were facing certain capture.

"The guns!" snapped Frank.

He drew his revolver from his pocket and fired into the darkness, around the corner.

There was a shout of alarm.

"Get back! Get back, Gus! They've got guns!"

Then followed a wild scrambling, as the man who had pursued them into the tunnel hustled back to safety.

Frank pressed himself against the rocky wall, in case any of the gang should enter and open fire on them. But the thieves had been frightened by his shot.

"That'll hold them for a while!"

"How long?" Joe reminded him. "They have us trapped, Frank. We can't go back. They'll starve us out."

"We won't give up without a fight."

There was a tremendous uproar out in the cave. The men were talking loudly and their voices were intensified by the tumultuous echoes of the place.

"Follow them in!" some one shouted. But Gus snarled:

"We can't. They're armed."

"Well," said Frank quietly, "we have enough bullets to keep them back for a while, at any rate."

"They'll get us, in the long run."

"I suppose so."

Then the Hardy boys heard the voice of the man called Sam. He came into the cave, shouting:

"They can't get out! There's been a cave-in and the tunnel is jammed up with rock."

"Good!" exclaimed Gus exultantly. "Here! Hand me that light."

There was a moment of silence. Then the powerful lantern was evidently turned toward the mouth of the tunnel, for the light gleamed on the walls. As they were just around the bend in the passage, the boys could not be seen, but the glaring light was reflected from the rocks.

"They're out of sight," muttered some one. "Try a shot!"

Instantly, there was an explosion, as a revolver roared. The echoes were deafening in that confined space.

Something whizzed past Frank's head and smacked against the rock.

The bullet, aimed for the rock wall, had ricochetted across the bend and had missed him by a hairbreadth.

This was too close for comfort. The revolver crashed again, and there was a cry from Joe.

"Are you hurt?" asked Frank anxiously.

"No. But the bullet glanced off the rocks. I think it went through my sleeve. It sure was close."

Their voices had been heard by the men in the cave.

"That's got 'em scared!" yelled Gus.

The boys retreated out of range of the glancing bullets.

"We're up against it," Frank admitted. "If we stay here they'll starve us out. If we try to rush them, we'll get shot."

"I guess we'll have to surrender."

"Looks as if there's nothing else for it. We'll give ourselves up and take our chances on escape. The way things are, we're liable to be shot."

He edged back toward the bend in the passage. There was a lull in the firing.

"We give up!" he shouted.

A yell of triumph followed.

"Now you're talkin' sense!" shouted Gus. "Throw your gun out here."

Frank hurled his revolver around the corner and it clattered on the rocks. Some one crawled into the passage and retrieved it.

"Now come out with your hands up."

Bitter though their defeat was, the Hardy boys had to acknowledge that the odds were against them. With their arms in the air, they came around the corner, into the glare of the big lamp. Step by step, they advanced until, at the junction of cave and tunnel, they were seized by their captors.

CHAPTER XX
TABLES TURNED

The dazzling glare of the big lamp was turned full in the faces of the Hardy boys.

They heard a gasp of astonishment.

"Why, it's a couple of kids!" exclaimed one of the men.

"Couple of kids!" rasped Gus Montrose, in astonishment. "Do you know who we've got here?"

"Who?"

"Them Hardy boys. The pair that followed me yesterday."

"What?"

"It's them. The very same spyin' pair of brats." A rough hand seized Frank's shoulder and swung him around. "I'd know them anywhere. Fenton Hardy's kids."

The name of Fenton Hardy made a distinct impression on the gang. There were mutterings of anger and fear.

"The detective's boys, eh?" growled one. "What are you doin' here, boys?"

"That's for you to find out," replied Frank shortly.

"Is that so? Well, you've got no business here. You know that, don't you?"

"Your own business here doesn't seem any too lawful."

"Never mind about us. You come spyin' around here and you've got to expect to take the consequences. What'll we do with 'em. Gus?"

"They're not goin' out of here, that's certain. We're not goin' to let them go back home and tell what they've seen."

"Or what they heard. How long were you two boys hidin' in that tunnel?"

"You can try to find that out, too," retorted Frank.

"Smart, ain't you?" snarled Montrose. "You won't be so smart when we get through with you. Anybody got a rope?"

"Here's some," said a man in the background.

"Give it here, then. We'll tie these brats up and keep 'em until we figure out what to do with 'em."

"You let us alone," said Frank.

"You have no right to make us prisoners," added Joe.

"We'll take the right."

"You are mighty high-handed."

"Rats! You'll be lucky if you don't get worse," growled one of the auto thieves.

"We ought to throw 'em into the bay," added another.

"Yes, with a few big stones in each pocket to hold 'em down," came the response from a third.

"Shut up, you all talk too much," commanded Montrose. "Where is that rope you spoke of?"

He snatched a length of heavy cord from the man who handed it to him. Frank was turned roughly around and his arms thrust behind his back. In a moment his wrists were firmly tied. Joe received the same treatment. The boys were bound and helpless.

"Put 'em over in the corner," ordered Montrose.

The boys were pushed and jostled across the rocky floor and were made to sit down against the wall at the back of the cave. The big lamp was turned on them all this time and they could see the faces of none of their captors.

"This is a fine mess!" grumbled one of the men. "It ruins the whole game."

Montrose turned on him.

"We were going to clear out tomorrow anyway, weren't we?" he said. "We'll just have to work a little quicker, that's all. Instead of sending one car out tonight and the rest tomorrow night, we'll get busy and drive 'em all out right now."

"What about these kids?"

"Leave 'em here."

"They'll starve," said one man dubiously.

"What of that?" demanded Gus Montrose. "They'd have had us all landed in jail if they could."

"Well—I don't hold—"

"They brought it on themselves. Who'll ever find 'em here, anyway?"

"I'd rather take 'em out to the railway and dump 'em into an empty box car. They might be five hundred miles away before anybody found 'em. That would give us plenty of time to scatter."

Murmurs of approval from the other men greeted this plan.

"Do as you like," growled Montrose. "I figger we ought to clear out and leave 'em here."

Suddenly the big lamp, which one of the gang was holding, dimmed and went out.

"What's the matter now? Turn on that light, Joe."

"It's gone out."

"D'you think we're blind? Of course it's out. Turn it on."

"The lamp's gone dead, I think. There's somethin' wrong with it. It won't light again." They could hear the man tinkering at the lamp. "No use," he said at last.

The cave was in pitch blackness. One of the men struck a match, and it cast a faint illumination.

"There's candles around here somewhere, ain't there?" asked Gus Montrose.

"Whole box of 'em around if I can find them."

The man with the match moved off into another part of the cave. He fumbled around for a while, then announced with a grunt of satisfaction:

"Here they are." He lit one of the candles, brought it over and stood it on a box.

"Light some more," ordered Gus.

The man did as he was told. In a few moments half a dozen candles provided a fair amount of light in the gloom of the cave.

"That's better."

Just then there was a shout from the passage leading into the main cave. Gus Montrose wheeled about.

"Who's that?"

The men crouched tensely.

"I don't know," whispered one. "We're all here but Dan."

In a moment footsteps could be heard in the passage. Then a voice:

"Hey—come out and help me. My car got stuck!"

"It's Dan," said Montrose, in a tone of relief.

A man entered the cave. He stopped short, in surprise.

"For the love of Pete!" he exclaimed. "What's this? Prayer meetin'?"

"The lamp went out," explained Gus. "We caught a couple of kids spyin' on us."

The newcomer whistled.

"Spies, eh? Where are they?"

"We got 'em tied up. In the corner, there."

Dan, who was evidently the man who had driven the roadster down from the Shore Road, came over and regarded the Hardy boys.

"This don't look so good," he said. "What are we goin' to do?"

"We'll attend to 'em." growled Montrose. "Your job is to drive that car in to Clancy's place. The rest of us are bringin' the other cars in tonight."

"Clearin' out a day earlier, eh?"

"That's the idea."

"Well, you'll have to come out and help me get my car out of the mud or none of us will get away."

"You're bogged?"

"Up to the hubs. There's been so much rain that the gully road is now knee-deep in mud."

"All right. We'll come and get you out. How many men do you want?"

"It'll take the whole crowd of us."

"No, it won't. We're not goin' to leave these kids here alone. Joe, here, can stay and watch 'em."

"They're tied, ain't they?"

"What of it? I'm not trustin' to no ropes. Somebody's got to stay and keep an eye on them."

"I'll stay," grumbled the man addressed as Joe.

"I don't care who stays," snapped Dan. "If you don't come out and help drag that car out of the mud it'll be in so deep we'll never get it out. Come on."

The men trooped out of the cave. Joe, who was left behind, sat down on a box and regarded the lads balefully. However, he said nothing. Gus came back through the passage.

"You might as well be loadin' some of those boxes into the other cars, while we're away," he said. "Take a look in every little while and see that those kids are still tied up."

The man grumbled assent, and followed Gus back down the passage.

The Hardy boys were left alone in the light of the flickering candles ranged about the gloomy cave.

"Well, we've lost out, I guess," remarked Frank bitterly. "If we ever do get back to Bayport it won't be until the auto thieves have all cleared out of here with the cars."

"It doesn't look very bright," sighed Joe.

Suddenly, Frank sat up.

"Say!" he exclaimed. "Did they take your revolver?"

"No. I guess they didn't know I had one."

"They took mine and missed yours. You still have it?"

"Right in my pocket."

"Good!"

"What good is it when I can't get at it?"

"If you can, we have only this chap Joe to deal with." The flame of the candle caught Frank's eye. He had an inspiration. "If only I could just get these ropes off my wrists!" he said.

Frank edged over toward the candle. Then, with his back to the flame, he lowered his arms until the cord that bound his wrists was within an inch of the wick.

A candle does not throw out much heat, but that little flame seared Frank's wrists and he had to clench his teeth to keep from crying out with the pain.

He could hold the rope in the flame for a few moments only, and then he withdrew it. When the scorching pain had somewhat subsided, he tried again. The flame licked at the heavy cord, weakening it strand by strand.

"Look out, Frank," warned Joe.

Frank scrambled back to the corner.

He was just in time. Heavy footsteps in the passage announced the approach of their guard, who came to the entrance, looked at them sullenly for a moment, then turned away again. He went back to the outer cave.

Hardly had he disappeared when Frank was back at the candle. He thrust the rope into the flame again.

When he could stand the burning heat no longer he withdrew and tried to break his bonds by sheer force. But, although the ropes had been weakened, they refused to break. He returned to the flame again, and on the next attempt he was successful. So many strands had been burned through that the cords snapped, and his hands were free.

Quickly, Frank went over to his brother. First of all, he took the revolver from Joe's pocket and put it on the rock beside him, in readiness. Then he knelt down and tugged at the strong ropes that bound Joe's wrists so tightly.

The knots were stubborn, but he finally undid them. The ropes fell apart and Joe was free.

"Now!" gritted Frank, picking up the revolver. "We'll go and attend to our friend in the cave."

"Hadn't we better wait here for him? There may be some one with him."

"I guess you're right. We'll take him by surprise the next time he comes back."

Frank went over to the side of the tunnel that led out into the main cave.

"Bring those ropes with you, Joe. Take the other side."

Joe picked up the cords that had bound his own wrists, and took up his position at the other side of the entrance. There the boys waited.

In a short time they heard heavy footsteps in the tunnel. Their guard was returning.

Frank gripped the revolver. The lads pressed themselves against the wall. The footsteps drew closer. Then a dark figure emerged from the opening.

Frank stepped swiftly out behind the rascal and pressed the revolver against his back.

"Hands up!" he ordered sharply.

Their victim gave a cry of fright. He had been startled almost out of his wits. His hands shot up.

"Stand where you are!"

Frank still pressed the muzzle of the revolver against their erstwhile captor while Joe searched the man for weapons and found a small automatic in the fellow's hip pocket. This he took.

"Put your hands behind your back!" ordered Frank.

Their prisoner obeyed.

Quickly, Joe tied the man's wrists.

"Go over and sit on that box!"

Muttering and grumbling with rage, the fellow did so. Joe hunted around until he found another length of rope, and with this he bound the man's feet.

"I guess you'll be all right here until the others come back," Frank told the captive.

"If ever I get free of these ropes—"

"Keep quiet," ordered Frank, brandishing the revolver menacingly. Their prisoner was silenced abruptly.

"Blow out the candles, Joe. He might think of the same idea."

The candles were blown out. The boys were in complete darkness.

"Hey!" roared their prisoner. "You're not goin' to leave me here alone in the dark, are you?"

"Exactly. Where's our flashlight, Joe?"

"I have it here. It was in my pocket." Joe turned on the light. In its glow they saw their prisoner, bound hand and foot, sitting disconsolately on the box.

"Fine. We'll go now."

They left the cave, unmindful of the appeals of the auto thief, and made their way down a passage that led into the outer cavern where the stolen cars were stored. The light showed them a large opening that they had not seen when they were in the place on the first occasion.

"I guess this is the way they drive the cars out," remarked Frank. "We'll go out the way we came in. We won't be so likely to meet the others."

The boys hastened down the far passage. They hurried past their roadster, on through the tunnel. At last they saw a gleam of light ahead, shining faintly in the distance.

CHAPTER XXI

AT THE FARMHOUSE

In a few moments, the Hardy boys had emerged from the passage and stood in a heavy clump of bushes that obscured the entrance to the tunnel in the bluff. Brushing aside the trees, they stepped out onto the beach.

The light they had seen was from a ship, steaming into Bayport Harbor, and in the distance they could see a dim yellow haze—the lights of the city.

Above them towered the rocky bluff. Farther down the beach they saw the break in the cliffs where the gully ran back toward the Shore Road.

"We can't go that way," Frank decided quickly. "The thieves are up in the gully helping get that car out of the mud."

Joe looked up at the steep cliff.

"We certainly can't climb up here."

"We can go out the way we came in. The roadster came down the beach, you remember. We may find the trail back."

The storm had spent its force and a fine drizzle of rain was now falling. The boys went back down the beach, the flashlight illuminating the way.

By the smoothness of the beach they knew that this was the route the car had followed on the way in. Later on they came to an open stretch of sand. Beyond that lay rocks.

There was a break in the cliff, and by the flashlight, the boys picked out an automobile track in a patch of sand, leading toward low bushes that masked the entrance to a gully.

"This is the place we're looking for," said Frank. "I'll bet the roadster came down through here."

He pushed aside the wet bushes. In the damp grass, the track was still plainly visible. The gully was dank with undergrowth, but there were evidences of a wide trail.

"We're getting there, anyway. From the direction, this ought to take us up to the Shore Road."

"What shall we do then?" asked Joe. "Walk to Bayport?"

"We shouldn't have to. There are farms along the road. We ought to be able to telephone to town."

"To the police?"

"Sure! Police and state troopers. We can't round up this gang by our-selves, and we haven't any too much time to get help, as it is."

"Well, we at least know where they can trace the stolen cars. That's one consolation."

"You mean Clancy?"

"In Atlantic City. The police ought to be able to catch him without any trouble."

The boys struggled on up the gully, along the trail that led through the wet woods toward the Shore Road. The underbrush had been cleared away for the passage of the stolen cars, and they found no difficulty following this strange road.

Finally, Frank gave a cry of delight.

"We're at the road!"

He emerged from the bushes, raced across a grassy stretch, and scram-bled up onto the highway. It was, indeed, the Shore Road at last.

The boys looked about them. Some distance away they saw a gleam of light.

"A farmhouse! We'll try it."

They hurried down the road, and at length the flashlight revealed the en-trance to a lane. Splashing through the water-filled ruts, the boys made their way between the crooked fences toward the dim mass of farm buildings.

"This place seems sort of familiar," remarked Joe.

"I was thinking the same thing."

"I know now! It's the Dodd farm!"

Joe was right. When the boys entered the barnyard, in spite of the fact that darkness obscured their surroundings, they knew from the size and posi-tion of the buildings that they had reached the Dodd place.

"This makes it easier. They have a telephone," said Frank.

"And that light in the window shows that some one is up."

They hurried to the door of the farmhouse and knocked. In a little while the door was flung open and Jack Dodd confronted them.

"Who's there?" he asked, peering out into the darkness. Then he ex-claimed with astonishment: "The Hardy boys! What on earth are you doing here at this hour? Come in!"

Frank and Joe entered. They were wet and bedraggled, and Jack Dodd looked at them curiously.

"I was working late at my studies," he explained. "What happened? Did your car get stalled?"

"We've found the auto thieves—and the stolen cars!" Frank told him quickly.

"They're not far from here, either. We want to use your telephone," add-ed Joe.

"The auto thieves!" gasped Jack incredulously. "You've found them?"

"The whole gang. And if we move fast we'll be able to land the outfit," answered Frank.

Jack quickly realized the situation. There was no time to be lost. He led the way into a hallway and pointed to the telephone.

"There you are!"

As it was a rural telephone line, he had to explain to the Hardy boys the proper number of rings necessary to arouse Central.

It took Frank some little time to get Central, as calls at that hour were infrequent out the Shore Road. The boys waited impatiently, but at last a sleepy voice answered the ring, and Frank hurriedly demanded the Bayport police headquarters.

He was soon in touch with the desk sergeant. He outlined the situation quickly.

"The gang were all up in the gully hauling a car out of the mud when we left. They'll be clearing out as soon as they discover their man in the cave, so you'll have to hurry," said Frank.

"I'll put every man available on it right away," the sergeant promised. "I'll call up Chief Collig at his house and tell him, too."

"Fine! Will you notify the state troopers? It's outside the city limits, you know."

"I'll call them up."

"You'll need a strong force of men, for this crowd are armed, and they'll have a hundred hiding places in the woods and along that beach. We'll keep a watch on the gully roads until you get here, and we'll wait for you."

"Good work! Are you sure it's the gang we've been after?"

"Certain. We found most of the stolen cars."

The sergeant was astonished.

"Found 'em. Where?"

"We'll tell you all about it later. In the meantime, get as many men out here as you can."

The sergeant disconnected abruptly. Frank had a mental picture of the activity that would follow in Bayport police circles on receipt of the news.

Jack Dodd was eagerly waiting for information.

"You mean to say you've actually found the thieves!" he exclaimed joyfully. "Then that means Dad and I will be cleared!"

"I hope so," Frank told his chum.

Briefly, the Hardy lads explained how they had hidden in the locker of the roadster, how the car had been driven away by one of the thieves, how they had overheard the conversation of the gang in the cave, how they had been captured and how they had escaped.

The Dodd household had been aroused, and Mr. Dodd came hurrying downstairs, half dressed. When he learned what had happened he hustled into the rest of his clothes and produced an ancient rifle from the back shed.

"I want to be in on this," he said grimly. "Those thieves have caused us more trouble than enough, and I'd like to get some of my own back."

Jack snatched up a flashlight.

"We'd better go out and watch the gully roads," Frank said.

"I know the road they drive out!" exclaimed Jack. "It's just a little below the end of our lane. There's an abandoned road that used to lead back to that old right of way, but I don't see how they reach it, for there's a fence to cross."

"Probably they take down the bars and drive through the field," said Mr. Dodd. "Now that you mention it, I always did think part of that fence looked pretty rickety."

They left the house and hurried down the lane toward the main road.

"We'd better split up," Frank suggested. "I have a revolver—it's Joe's, by the way—and Mr. Dodd has a rifle. Jack has a flashlight and so has Joe. Two of us can watch the first gully."

"You and Joe know the place where you came out onto the Shore Road," said Jack. "You'd better watch there. Dad and I will take the upper gully."

"Good! We'll just keep watch until the police arrive."

They separated at the end of the lane. Frank and Joe hurried off down the road, while the Dodds went in the opposite direction. When the boys reached the gully that led down to the beach they settled down to wait.

Because they were impatient and because they realized that the gang would doubtless scatter to points of safety as soon as their escape was discovered, it seemed to them that the police were a long time in coming. In reality it was not long, because the desk sergeant had lost no time in sending out the alarm.

The roar of approaching motorcycles and the drone of a speeding motor car were the first intimations of the arrival of the police and the state troopers. Even before the machines came into view their clamor could be heard.

Then dazzling headlights flashed over the rise. Frank ran out into the road, waving the flashlight, and in a few moments the first motorcycle skidded to a stop.

"Where are they?" shouted a trooper.

"There are two ways in. We have two men watching the other gully. If you'll put some of your men up there on guard, we can take you down to the beach from here."

The other motorcycles came up, and finally an automobile which was crowded with police officers. Everybody talked at once. The first trooper, however, quickly took charge of the impending raid, and in decisive tones he gave his orders.

"Johnson, take three policemen and go on up to the other gully. These lads say you'll find a farmer and his son on guard. They have a flashlight, so you can't miss them. Watch that gully and grab any one who comes out."

One of the troopers got back onto his motorcycle. All but three of the policemen scrambled out of their car. The motorcycle leaped forward with a roar, and the automobile followed close behind.

"All right," said the trooper. "We'll leave one man here to watch the road in case any of them slip through our fingers. The rest of us will go on down this gully."

"Callahan, stay on duty here," ordered the sergeant in charge of the police officers.

Callahan, a burly policeman, saluted. His face, revealed for a moment in the glare of a flashlight, showed that he did not relish the assignment, evidently preferring to go where there was promise of some excitement.

"All right, boys. Lead the way!"

Frank and Joe went across the grass beside the road and plunged into the undergrowth at the entrance of the gully. Their hearts were pounding with excitement. The moment of success was at hand.

Behind them trooped nine stalwart officers, heavily armed.

Down the sloping gully they went. The trooper in charge fell in step beside Frank and the boy explained the situation that lay ahead.

"Two openings to the caves, eh?" said the trooper. "Well, we have them cornered. That is, if the birds haven't flown."

They came to the beach. Their boots clattered on the rocks as the men hurried forward.

At length the bushes that concealed the entrance to the first tunnel were in sight.

CHAPTER XXII

THE ROUND-UP

"This is the place!" Frank Hardy excitedly told the officer in charge of the party. "The tunnel is right behind those bushes."

"Mighty well hidden," the trooper commented. "Do you think you can find the other opening?"

"It's farther down the beach."

"I think I could find it," volunteered Joe.

"Take three of these men and watch that part of the beach, at any rate." The trooper detailed three men to accompany Joe. "I'll wait until I see your flashlight signal," he said. "When you find the place where they drive the cars out, turn the light on and off. Then wait for my whistle."

Joe and the men with him hurried on down the beach. The others waited in silence near the entrance to the tunnel.

Eventually they saw the blinking light that plainly told them that the outer passage was guarded.

"Fine," said the trooper. He raised the whistle to his lips. "All ready, men?"

"All set," answered one of the constables, in a low voice.

The shrill blast of the whistle sounded through the night. With one accord, the men leaped forward, plunged into the bushes, and crowded into the tunnel. Their flashlights made the dark passage as bright as day.

As they entered they could hear a confused uproar ahead. The roar of an automobile, the sound magnified tenfold in the subterranean passages, crashed out. There were shouts, cries of warning and alarm.

"We've got them trapped!" shouted the trooper.

They stumbled down the rocky passage. A man came blundering around a corner, right into the arms of the foremost officer. He was seized, there was a gleam of metal, a click, and the auto thief was handcuffed before he fully realized what had happened.

"One!" counted the sergeant. "Now for the others!"

They passed the Hardy boys' roadster and caught a glimpse of a man fleeing before them into the main cave. The trooper drew his revolver and sent a shot over the fellow's head.

The man came to an abrupt stop and raised his arms. He surrendered without a fight.

"Two!" yelled the sergeant gleefully, pouncing on his prisoner. Another pair of handcuffs was produced, the chain was slipped through the chain of the other thief's shackles, and the pair were swiftly manacled together.

The officers plunged on into the main cave.

In the glare of the flashlights they saw the truck and one of the pleasure cars standing by the wall. The two other cars that had been in the cave had disappeared. No men were in sight.

The raiding party heard the roar of a racing engine, a grinding of brakes, and a confusion of shouts.

"They're getting out!" Frank Hardy shouted. He pointed to the huge opening in the wall, through which the car had disappeared.

With the police at his heels, he headed down the passage. It was wider than the one through which they had entered, and the rocky floor gave way to earth, in which ruts were clearly visible.

Ahead of them they heard a shot, then more yells.

"Joe and his men are on the job," Frank reflected.

He was right. They reached the mouth of the passage, and there they came upon a large touring car. Two men were standing up in the front seat, arms upraised, and in the glare of the headlights they could see Joe and the three officers pointing their weapons at the pair.

The round-up was soon over. One of the policemen scrambled into the automobile and clapped handcuffs on the two men. The trooper, standing on the running board, turned a flashlight upon them.

The surly features of Gus Montrose were revealed. The other man was his companion, Sam.

"All out!" snapped the officer, urging the crestfallen thieves out of the car.

They stepped out sullenly.

"Well, here's four of 'em. anyway!" declared the trooper. He turned to Frank. "Do you think there are any more?"

"There's still another. He was the chap who got stuck in the mud up in the gully. Perhaps he's up there yet, if the Dodds haven't caught him on the way out."

The trooper despatched two of his men up the gully road at once, to see if they could locate the other member of the gang.

"Well, Montrose," he said, turning to the former hired man, "so we've landed you at last."

Gus looked down at the handcuffs.

"I'd have been clear away if it wasn't for them brats of boys!" he said viciously.

"They were a little too smart for you and your gang."

The four auto thieves were herded together and an officer with drawn revolver was put on guard.

"I guess we'll go back into the cave and see what we can find," decided the trooper.

Leaving the prisoners under guard, he and some of his men, together with the Hardy boys, went back into the main cavern, where the officers inspected the remaining cars and the loot that they found stored there. The sergeant rubbed his hands gleefully.

"Everything's here," he said. "At least, everything we need to make an airtight case against that gang. And we'll recover the rest of the stuff without much trouble, I imagine."

He turned to Joe Hardy.

"You said you learned where they were sending the cars?" he inquired.

"They spoke of a man named Clancy in Atlantic City. They drove the stolen cars out through the gully, across the Shore Road onto one of those old private roads, and then down the coast."

"That's all we want to know. We'll wire the Atlantic City police as soon as we get back to headquarters."

"We might as well bring back as much of this stuff as we can," said the trooper. "Make a triumphal procession of it."

Some of the loot they found already loaded into the small truck, in preparation for the get-away, and in a short time they had cleared the cave and the passage of the other packing boxes. One of the officers was assigned to the wheel of the truck and another was detailed to drive the other car. Frank and Joe announced their intention of driving their own roadster back to Bayport.

Before long, the little cavalcade was in readiness to start.

In the lead was the touring car, with four sullen and defeated auto thieves huddled in the back seat, a trooper and a constable in front.

Next came the truck, loaded with stolen goods. It was followed by the other pleasure car, with the sergeant and the other officers sitting at their ease. Behind it came the roadster, with the Hardy boys.

The foremost car followed the gully road without difficulty. The headlights illuminated the way clearly, and the automobiles lumbered up toward the Shore Road. They had no trouble in the muddy section where Dan had come to grief, for the thieves had covered the spot with branches and the cars crossed without becoming stalled.

The road led through the woods and finally ended in a seemingly impenetrable screen of trees.

Gus Montrose jeered.

"Try and get through there!" he said.

Puzzled, the driver got out and advanced toward the heavy thickets. It seemed impossible to go any farther, and yet the tire marks of other cars were visible right up to the undergrowth. He gave one of the trees a kick, and it fell back. The secret was revealed. A cunningly contrived platform held the trees in place, and it swung back, in the manner of a gate. When a car passed through, it was drawn shut again and gave the appearance of an unbroken mass of foliage.

This explained why the secret road had never been discovered and why the thieves were able to drive their cars out through the gully without great risk of detection. The loose trees formed a perfect screen.

At last the Shore Road was in sight. The foremost car lumbered up onto the highway. In its headlights a strange group stood revealed.

There, in front of a fine sedan, stood Mr. Dodd, rifle in hand, confronting the remaining auto thief. With him were Jack Dodd and the officer who had been despatched to their assistance.

The thief, presumably the man called Dan, was sitting disconsolately on the bumper of the car, handcuffs about his wrists.

"We got him!" shouted Jack, in excitement, as the cars lumbered out of the bush. "Held him up just as he came out onto the road."

"Fine work!" applauded the sergeant, scrambling out. "This just about cleans up the gang—all except Clancy."

Dan looked up sharply.

"How do you know about Clancy?"

"Never mind. We know all about him. And he'll be behind the bars with the rest of you before long, if I'm not mistaken."

The trooper who had been in charge of the round-up came up at this juncture.

"Another, eh?" he said cheerfully. "Well, the little procession is growing. Better join the parade, boys."

He assigned one of the men to replace Dan at the wheel of the stolen car.

"We'll let you be a passenger, for a change," he said, motioning the thief to the back seat. "Guest of honor."

From Dan's expression, as he took his seat, he did not appreciate the compliment.

"You'd better come to town with us for the finish," called Frank to the Dodds.

"I wouldn't miss it for a farm," Jack said, as he scrambled into the roadster with them.

So, with police, auto thieves, troopers, the Dodds and the Hardy boys duly seated in the various cars, the procession started for Bayport. One of the officers drove back the police car, with the motorcycles securely lashed in place on the running boards, and one piled in the back seat.

In the Hardy boys' roadster, jubilation prevailed. Jack Dodd was loud in his praises of the work the lads had done, and beneath it all was the undercurrent of intense relief because he knew the capture of the gang would clear himself and his father from suspicion.

"That's the best part of it, for us," said Joe Hardy, when their chum mentioned this.

CHAPTER XXIII

THE MYSTERY SOLVED

The capture and subsequent trial of the automobile thieves provided Bayport with one of its biggest sensations in many a day. Although some of the gang stubbornly insisted on their innocence, the evidence against them was so complete that the state had no trouble in securing prosecutions against them all, and they were sentenced to long terms of imprisonment in the state penitentiary.

The man, Clancy, was arrested in Atlantic City and was convicted with the rest of the gang, on charges of receiving and disposing of stolen property. The Bayport police notified Atlantic City detectives, and Clancy's arrest was accomplished within an hour after the other members of the gang were lodged in the cells.

Gus Montrose was questioned by detectives shortly after the triumphant procession reached the city. This was done at the request of Mr. Dodd, who was anxious that he and Jack should be cleared of all suspicion in connection with the thefts as quickly as possible.

Montrose saw that the game was up. He admitted that his former employer knew nothing of the stolen cars.

"It was while I was working for Mr. Dodd that I found the caves in the bluffs," he confessed. "I used to go down to the beach a lot to fish, and one day I found the opening into the tunnel and explored the big cave. I thought at the time that it would be a good place to hide stolen goods. Then one day I met Sam. He had just been released from the pen and we got to talking together and he said he thought there would be good money to be picked up stealin' cars."

"Where did you pick up the rest of the crowd?"

"Sam's friends, mostly. When I told Sam about the caves in the bluffs, he said it was just what we needed and he asked me if there was any roads in. I said there wasn't, but we could make roads in and out through the gullies, and cover 'em up. Then I told him about the old private road through to the back townships. He come with me and we looked the place over and he said it was just right. He wrote to some of his friends and they come on here and we started to work."

"That was when you quit your job at the Dodd place?"

"I didn't want to quit, for I figgered people wouldn't be so likely to think I was mixed up with the car stealin' if I kept on workin', but it took up so much of my time that Mr. Dodd let me go."

"Who did the actual car stealing?"

"The rest of the fellows. My job was to keep my eyes open for good chances. People would see me goin' along the Shore Road and think nothin' of it, but if any of the other boys went out, somebody might see 'em and take note because they was strangers. Mostly I stayed down on the beach fishin', and kept watchin' the road for places people parked their cars. Then I'd signal to Dan or one of the others and they'd come and drive the car away."

"Fishing!" exclaimed Jack Dodd. "I'll bet that's how my rod disappeared."

"I took it after your father fired me," Montrose admitted.

"How did it come to get into the car found behind Dodd's barn?" one of the detectives demanded.

"That was a car Dan had stolen; but the owner chased him in another car and he couldn't get down the gully without bein' seen. Dan had picked me up and I had the rod with me. He drove the car up behind the barn and hid it there and we got back to the cave on foot. I left the rod in the car."

"Well, that explains everything," the detective remarked. He turned to Mr. Dodd. "There shouldn't be any difficulty withdrawing the charges against you and your son."

"It takes a big load off my mind," declared the farmer. "It was a terrible worry to have that hangin' over our heads when we knew we were innocent."

"You must admit that the circumstances looked bad. We only did what we thought was our duty."

"I suppose so. Well, if the charges are withdrawn we won't say anything more about it."

Withdrawal of the charges was a formality that was soon executed.

In the week following, both Mr. Dodd and Jack were congratulated by scores of people on having been cleared of all suspicion in connection with the Shore Road mystery. The bail money was returned to Mr. Hardy and the boys.

Frank and Joe Hardy were the real heroes of the case. Their good work in discovering the hiding place of the auto thieves and in notifying the police in time to capture the gang, earned them praise from all quarters. The Bayport newspaper gave much space to the affair and the story of the lads' adventures in the cave provided thrilling reading.

"Some detectives, Frank and Joe!" commented Biff.

"Headliners—right on the front page," came from Chet.

"Well, they deserve it, don't they?" put in another high school student.

"They certainly do," answered Chet.

"And to think Jack Dodd and his dad are cleared," went on Biff. "That's the best yet."

"Jack's smiling like a basket of chips," said Tony. "Mouth all on a broad grin."

So the talk ran on among the boys.

The girls were equally enthusiastic.

"Oh, I think Frank and Joe are too wonderful for anything," remarked Callie Shaw, who had always been looked on with favor by Frank.

"I never thought Joe could be so brave," breathed Iola Morton.

"They are sure a pair of heroes," said Paula Robinson.

"I really think they ought to be in a book," added Tessie, her twin.

Even the Applegates, for whom the Hardy boys had solved the mystery of the tower treasure, had their word of commendation.

"As brave as the knights of old," said Miss Adelia.

"If I had my say, I'd print a stamp in their honor," said Hurd Applegate, who was an expert on stamp collecting.

The new roadster became famous in Bayport as the car that had lured the auto thieves to their downfall. Motorists in general were able to breathe easier when they learned that the gang had been rounded up. A little to their embarrassment and much to their delight, at a banquet of the Automobile Club, Frank and Joe were the guests of honor.

"I am sure," said the president of the club, in a speech, "that the automobile owners of the city are grateful to these two boys for the courage and ingenuity they displayed in running down the gang when even the organized police had failed. They ran grave risks, for they were dealing with desperate and experienced criminals. If the hiding place had not been discovered, it seems likely that the thefts might have continued for some time and it is certain that none of the cars would have been recovered. As it is, all the automobiles have been located and returned to their owners, as well as all the stolen goods. As you all know, various rewards were offered by this association and by a number of the car owners, and to these rewards the Hardy boys are justly entitled. I have great pleasure, then, in presenting them with the sum of fifteen hundred dollars, comprising the three separate rewards of five hundred dollars each."

Amid cheers, two checks for $750 were presented to Frank and Joe.

Mr. Hardy, who was present at the banquet, beamed with pleasure. But when he returned home with the lads he invited them into his study and closed the door.

Wondering what was coming, the boys faced their father.

"I think you've had enough congratulations for one week," he said to his sons. "Don't let it turn your heads."

"We won't, Dad," they promised.

"It was a good idea, hiding in that locker," their father remarked. "It was a good idea and it worked out very well. There was only one thing wrong with it."

"What was that?" asked Frank.

"It was too dangerous."

"Too dangerous?"

"You took too many chances, dealing with a gang like that. Don't try anything like that again or I may have to hunt up my old shaving strop."

But Fenton Hardy smiled indulgently as he spoke.

"He wasn't real mad," whispered Joe, as he and his brother left their father. "He was only a little bit provoked."

"Well, it really was dangerous—hiding in that locker," admitted Frank. "Those thieves might have caught us like rats in a trap."

"I wonder if we'll have any more such thrilling adventures," mused Joe.

Additional thrilling adventures were still in store for the brothers, and what some of them were will be related in another volume, to be entitled, "The Hardy Boys: The Secret of the Caves."

In that volume we shall meet all our old friends again and learn how a peculiar accident led up to a most unlooked-for climax.

The reception Frank and Joe received at the Automobile Club was tame in comparison to the way they were greeted by their chums.

"The biggest little detectives in the world," was the way Chet expressed himself.

"They can't be beat!" came from Tony Prito.

"But it's nothing to what I expect them to do in the future," was Biff Hooper's comment.

The recognition Frank and Joe received at the automobile Club was due in comparison to the way they were greeted by their friends. Joe spoke of the detectives in the series. It was the way that enjoyed himself.
Joe's comments...

THE SECRET OF THE CAVES

ORIGINALLY PUBLISHED IN 1929.

CHAPTER I

OVERBOARD

"Well, the stealing of autos in this neighborhood has come to an end, Frank. Wonder if anybody will ever take to stealing motorboats."

"Perhaps, Joe. But there isn't the chance to steal a boat that there was to steal cars."

"Gee, now that the excitement is over I wonder what will come up next."

"Don't know; but something is bound to happen sooner or later—it always does."

"Hope it comes soon—I don't want to get rusty."

It was a Saturday afternoon in June, one of those warm, drowsy days when even the leaves of the trees seem too indolent to stir. There was scarcely a ripple on the surface of the water, no movement but the flow of the incoming tide.

Three motorboats circled lazily about in Barmet Bay within sight of the city of Bayport. The lazy spirit of the afternoon seemed to have spread to the occupants of the boats, for they lounged about in comfortable attitudes.

Biff Hooper, in his craft, the *Envoy*, had devised a way of steering with his foot while sprawled on the side cushions.

In a motorboat close by, the *Napoli*, sat Tony Prito, whose dark hair, olive skin, and sparkling eyes indicated his Italian parentage even more emphatically than his name. In the third craft were two lads who need no introduction to readers of previous volumes in this series.

The boy at the wheel, a tall, dark, handsome lad of about sixteen, was Frank Hardy, and the other, a fair, curly-headed fellow about a year his junior, was his brother Joe. These boys were the sons of Fenton Hardy, an internationally famous private detective who lived in Bayport.

"I didn't expect to see you fellows out on the bay this afternoon," shouted Biff Hooper, raising his head over the side of his boat.

"Where did you think we'd be?" called back Frank. "Up in the attic, studying?"

"Thought you'd be out in your car," and Biff grinned widely.

There was a laugh from Tony Prito, and the Hardy boys also laughed with great good-humor. Their car was a standing joke among their chums, and, as Chet Morton put it, "standing" joke described it exactly, for it seldom moved.

"Never mind," returned Joe. "That old car served its purpose, anyway. We used it only as bait."

"It was mighty good bait," said Tony. "You caught some big fish with that old crate."

"It has earned its keep," Frank called back. "We're going to put it on a pension and let it stay in our garage for the rest of its life, without charge."

The boys were referring to a roadster that the Hardy lads had purchased out of their savings some time previous. It was a car that proved the old axiom that beauty is only skin deep, for although it glittered with nickel and paint and although its lines were trim and smooth, its inner workings were utterly beyond the comprehension of Bayport mechanics. For a few weeks after its purchase the car ran, eccentrically enough, but still it ran. Then, one day, for no apparent reason, it gave up the ghost and no amount of tinkering would prompt it even to move out of the garage.

However, as Joe had said, the car had served its purpose. The boys had picked it up cheaply, with a definite object in view. As told in the preceding volume of this series, "The Hardy Boys: The Shore Road Mystery," there had been a series of mysterious automobile thefts on the Shore Road leading out of Bayport, numerous pleasure cars and trucks having been stolen, and no amount of investigation on the part of the police had succeeded in revealing their whereabouts or the identity of the thieves.

Frank and Joe Hardy, who had earned considerable local fame by their activities as amateur detectives, in emulation of their famous father, had decided to lay a trap for the automobile thieves and, buying the gorgeous rattletrap, parked it on the Shore Road for several nights, concealing themselves in the rear. After many adventures, the Hardy boys captured the thieves and recovered the stolen cars. They collected several handsome rewards for their work, so their investment in the roadster proved exceedingly profitable after all.

"The car owners around Bayport have sure been breathing easier since that affair was cleared up," said Biff.

"I don't think there'll be any more car thieving for a long time," Tony declared. "The two sleuths here put a stop to that."

"We had a good time doing it," Frank admitted. "I'm rather sorry it's all over."

"Never satisfied!" commented Biff.

He prodded the wheel with his foot and the *Envoy* swung about with its nose pointing down the bay. Barmet Bay, three miles long, opened on the Atlantic, and in the distance the boys could see a motor yacht that ran daily between Bayport and one of the towns on the coast, a trim little passenger craft that was proceeding toward them at a fast clip.

"Where are you going?" shouted Tony.

"Out to meet the passenger boat."

"Race you!"

"So will we!" called Frank.

Biff abandoned his indolent posture and settled down to take advantage of his head start. His boat leaped ahead with a roar. Tony Prito had to make a half turn before he could get under way.

The Hardy boys were similarly unprepared, but they had no doubt of the ability of the *Sleuth* to overhaul Biff's boat quickly. Their craft was one of the speediest in the bay, with smooth lines and a powerful engine.

They had trouble on the turn, for the swells of the other boats caught the *Sleuth* and put it off its course, and by the time the craft was nosing in pursuit, Biff Hooper had a good lead and Tony Prito was also ahead of them.

"Step on it!" said Joe.

Frank "stepped on it," and the *Sleuth* began eating up the intervening distance. Rocking and swaying, prow well out of the water, the boat overhauled the *Napoli* and Frank grinned at Tony as they crept by. The Italian lad was getting every ounce of speed of which his engine was capable and although he jockeyed to try to put the Hardy boys off the course, they sped on and soon left him behind.

Biff had been tinkering with the engine of his craft and had evidently made a few improvements, for the *Envoy* was going along at a clip it had never before achieved.

"Looks as if he intends to put one over on us," muttered Frank, as he opened up the engine to the last notch. "He'll beat us to the boat at this rate."

The motor yacht was about a mile away.

On through the water plunged the *Sleuth*, gaining slowly but surely on the craft ahead.

Once in a while Biff cast a hasty glance backward to wave mockingly at them. He misjudged an approaching wave on one of these occasions and the *Envoy* swerved; he lost valuable seconds righting the craft into its course again and the *Sleuth* gained.

The yacht was about a quarter of a mile distant when the *Sleuth* at last pulled up beside the other boat. Inch by inch it forged ahead until the bow of each boat was on a line with the other. Then the *Sleuth's* greater speed became manifest as it pulled away, leaving Biff shaking his head in exasperation.

Suddenly Joe, who had been looking at the passenger yacht in the distance, gave a shout of alarm.

"Look!" he cried.

Frank glanced up just in time to see an immense puff of black smoke bursting from above the deck of the yacht. Then, across the waves, was borne to their ears the roar of an explosion.

They could see figures running about on the deck of the boat. One of them, a woman, ran directly to the rail and began to clamber up on it.

"What on earth—" gasped Joe.

"She's going overboard!"

Another figure ran out, making a frantic grab at the woman who was balanced perilously on top of the rail. Then, her arms outspread, the woman jumped. The boys saw her plunge down the side of the yacht, and there was a splash as she hurtled into the water.

A moment later she emerged and they could see her swimming about and waving her arms. The *Sleuth* had drawn closer to the yacht in the meantime and now the boys could hear a faint cry for help.

Tensely, Frank leaned over the wheel. Great clouds of smoke were pouring from the yacht.

"We'll have to rescue her!" he said. "It's her only chance."

The yacht had passed the woman by now, and although a life-buoy had been flung out it was some distance away from her. Hampered by her wet clothes, the woman was making no progress toward it. Slowly, the yacht began to circle, but the lads saw that it would never reach her in time.

The *Sleuth* ploughed on through the waves.

The boys saw the woman throw up her hands with a despairing gesture and disappear beneath the surface.

CHAPTER II

THE RESCUE

As the Hardy boys sped toward the woman, who appeared above the surface again in a moment and began to struggle wildly, they saw that confusion prevailed on board the yacht.

Great clouds of smoke were pouring from amidship. People were running frantically about the deck. Efforts were being made to lower a lifeboat, but apparently something went wrong, for it sagged perilously and then stuck, with two sailors working hastily to release it.

But the boys' immediate concern was the woman. She disappeared beneath the water again and they were fearful that she had gone under for the last time. Then, as the *Sleuth* surged forward, they saw her emerge once more. They were close enough now to see her frightened face, and, as the *Sleuth* sped within a few yards of her, Joe poised himself and dived.

He plunged into the water just as the woman was going down for the third time. He kept cool and, remembering the first aid instruction he had received, took care not to come within reach of the wildly clutching hands. He grasped the woman by the hair and then, keeping behind her, managed to get a grip that did not endanger himself. Had she been able to throw her arms about him, he would have been dragged beneath the surface with her.

Joe struggled toward the *Sleuth*. It had sped past when he dived, but Frank had quickly brought the craft around and Joe had to swim but a few strokes. Frank throttled down the engine and he was able to give a hand in assisting the woman on board. She was dragged into the boat, dripping and almost unconscious, and Joe clung to the gunwale until Frank grasped his shoulders and hauled him over the side.

In the meantime, the Hardy boys' chums were speeding toward the yacht. The race was forgotten.

Frank and Joe did their best to revive the half-conscious woman. Her immersion in the water and the shock of being face to face with death had left her weakened, and she was moaning and murmuring as she lay on the cushions. Joe gave what first aid he could, moving her arms back and forth to restore circulation, while Frank set the course of the *Sleuth* in the direction of the yacht.

Biff Hooper had already reached the passenger boat. He drew up alongside, with Tony Prito, in the *Envoy*, not far behind. Passengers were crowding to the rail, some shouting and screaming with fright, some pleading to be taken off.

Biff and Tony were ready to offer their boats for this purpose, but they noticed that the cloud of smoke had diminished in volume. A uniformed man was bellowing through a megaphone.

"No danger!" he roared. "The fire is under control!"

But it was plain that many in the crowd were afraid there would be another explosion.

"Take us off!" screeched a wild-eyed woman. "Take us off before the boat blows up!"

She scrambled up on the rail, but the uniformed man seized her and prevented her from trying to leap overboard.

"Need any help?" shouted Biff.

"Stand by for a while," returned the officer. "We're getting this fire under control but we don't know how bad it is."

Biff and Tony, in their motorboats, cruised in the neighborhood of the yacht, as the ship's officer asked. The passengers were milling about on deck, badly frightened, but gradually they became calmer as a steward assured them that there was no danger. The heavy cloud of smoke decreased in volume. The boat's crew was small and the fire-fighting equipment was limited, but in a little while it became evident that the blaze was not as bad as it had seemed and that it had indeed been checked in time.

Soon the smoke cloud ceased rolling up from below.

The uniformed man came on deck again with a megaphone. He raised it to his lips and bellowed:

"Thanks, boys, but we won't need you."

"That's fine!" shouted Tony, in reply. "Fire all out?"

"Tin of gasoline exploded. It didn't spread much. We'll be able to make Bayport under our own power."

"Righto!" called Biff. "We're going in now, anyway. If you need us, give us a hail."

"We'll do that."

The motorboats circled away. In the distance, Biff and Tony could see the Hardy boys in the *Sleuth*, with the woman they had rescued.

"Your passenger is all right!" shouted Biff, to the captain. "Our chums will bring her back with them."

He turned the nose of his craft toward the *Sleuth*.

The Hardy boys were doing their best to revive the woman they had rescued from the waves.

She was not unconscious but she seemed very weak and scarcely appeared to realize where she was.

She was an elderly woman, dressed in black, and although her immersion in the water had undoubtedly been a tremendous shock, the boys could see that she was of an exceedingly nervous temperament and evidently not in the best of health, for she was worn and pale.

"Where am I?" she moaned. "Where am I now?"

"You're quite safe," Frank assured her. "You're in a motorboat."

"You saved me?"

"We got you out of the water just in time."

"I want to go to Bayport," said the woman weakly.

"We'll take you there," promised Joe. "It isn't very far away. We will take you there at once."

"I want to go to Bayport," she repeated. "It's important. I have to see some one there."

"Head the boat around, Frank," said Joe quietly. He had seen their chums returning from the neighborhood of the yacht, so he realized that there was no further danger from the fire.

"I must be in Bayport tonight," gasped the woman. "I must go there to see Fenton Hardy—the detective."

Then she collapsed weakly, her eyes closed, and she was a dead weight in Joe's arms. She had fainted.

The Hardy boys looked at one another in astonishment.

"She wants to see Dad!" exclaimed Frank incredulously.

It was a strange coincidence that they, of all people, should have rescued her when she was on her way to see their father.

Fenton Hardy had many clients, some of whom came long distances to consult him. He was one of the greatest private detectives in the country and his fame was widespread. He had been for many years on the New York force and had finally achieved his ambition of setting up an agency of his own. He had moved to Bayport, on the Atlantic coast, with his family and his success had been immediate. He had successfully handled many difficult cases and his services were much in demand.

Frank and Joe Hardy, his sons, were anxious to follow in their father's footsteps, in spite of his objections and in spite of their mother's desire that they prepare themselves for medicine and law respectively. But the boys had a natural deductive bent and they had taken several local cases on their own initiative, succeeding so well that Fenton Hardy had finally withdrawn his objections and agreed that if, when they were of age, they still desired to become private investigators, he would not stand in their way.

The Hardy boys were introduced in the first volume of this series entitled, "The Hardy Boys: The Tower Treasure," wherein they handled their first case of any consequence. A large quantity of bonds and jewels had been stolen from an old mansion on the outskirts of Bayport and after numerous adventures the lads traced the loot and ran the criminal to earth. Other volumes of the series have recounted their adventures in handling other cases that came their way, all of which they successfully solved.

In the volume immediately preceding the present book, entitled, "The Hardy Boys: The Shore Road Mystery," the lads, as already mentioned, rounded up a gang of automobile thieves who had stolen a number of cars and trucks from points along the Shore Road above Barmet Bay. After that, things had been quiet around Bayport and the boys were beginning to think that mysteries were at a discount.

"We'd better get her back to Bayport right away," said Joe, as he looked down at the unconscious woman. "She may be dying."

"Splash some water on her face. She's just fainted, I think."

Joe rendered impromptu aid, but the woman was in a dead faint and he could not revive her at all.

In the meantime, the motorboat was heading back in the direction of the city. Frank had "let her out" to the utmost and the speedy craft was eating up the distance. He crouched tensely at the wheel, and sheets of spray splashed over the bow.

"I wonder what on earth she wants to see Dad about," he said to himself. Then he chuckled. "Dad will have to thank us for saving one of his clients."

CHAPTER III

MISS TODD

Frank Hardy lost no time on the run back to Bayport. Instead of proceeding directly to the boathouse, he docked the *Sleuth* at one of the city wharves. There the lads were fortunate enough to find a taxi. The woman was still unconscious when they arrived, so with the assistance of the taxi driver they lifted her out of the boat and into the car.

Frank instructed the man to drive to the office of a doctor they knew well, and there the woman received attention.

"She has evidently been under a great strain," the doctor told them. "The shock of the explosion and her struggle in the water were just the finishing touches."

Under his expert administrations the woman was soon revived sufficiently to sit up. She looked about her.

"What happened?" she asked weakly.

"You are in good hands, madam," the doctor assured her. "Just be quiet for a while and you will be all right."

In a few minutes, the woman had recovered. First of all, she insisted on thanking the boys for rescuing her.

"If it hadn't been for these brave lads I would have been drowned. It was foolish of me to jump off that yacht, but I've been very nervous lately, and when I heard the explosion and saw all that smoke I lost my head completely."

"Well," said the doctor genially, "there's been no harm done. You were on your way to Bayport, weren't you, and here you are."

"Am I in Bayport now?"

"Yes."

"You must take me to Fenton Hardy at once, please," said the woman, sitting up. "I must see him."

"There'll be no trouble about that. These boys are Fenton Hardy's sons."

The woman gazed at the Hardy boys in surprise.

"His sons!" she exclaimed.

"Fenton Hardy is our father," stated Frank.

The woman was evidently astonished.

"Isn't that strange! To think that your father should be the very man I was coming to see."

"He's at home now," said Joe. "As soon as you're feeling well enough we'll take you there."

"That will be good of you. I came to Bayport for the sole purpose of seeing your father."

"Are you coming to visit us?" asked Joe.

The woman shook her head.

"No. I want to see your father on business. Important business. It is private, so I'm afraid I can't tell you any more about it."

The boys forbore to question her.

"I suppose I should tell you my name. I am Miss Evangeline Todd."

They bowed in acknowledgement.

"Will you take me to your father now? I feel much better. I'm very anxious to see him at once. There is no time to lose."

Miss Todd seemed quite agitated, and although the lads felt that a few minutes more or less would make no particular difference, they decided that it would be best to humor her. Miss Todd got to her feet, and although she was still physically weak, she evidently had a mind of her own for she was determined to remain no longer in the doctor's office when she was so near her goal.

Accordingly, the Hardy boys helped her out of the office to the waiting taxi.

During the brief drive she repeatedly expressed her astonishment at having been rescued by the Hardy boys "of all people."

"I've often heard of you boys," she said. "You often help your father, don't you?"

"Whenever we can," laughed Frank.

"Well, I hope you can help him now. I want to learn the truth about poor Todham."

The lads waited expectantly, but the elderly lady said no more about the object of her call. She seemed somewhat eccentric, and muttered to herself a great deal.

"Poor Todham," she repeated, over and over again. "I do hope Mr. Hardy can help me. It's all very strange."

The car drew up at the door of the Hardy home and the boys helped Miss Todd alight. They brought her into the house and their father met them at the door, evidently surprised.

"A client for you, Dad," explained Frank. "We picked her up just a little while ago."

He did not tell his father just how they had "picked up" the elderly woman.

"And is this Fenton Hardy?" said Miss Todd. She grasped the noted detective by the hand. "I've come a long distance to see you. These fine boys of yours saved my life."

"You've been in the water!" exclaimed Mr. Hardy. He called to his wife. "Laura, will you look after this lady and make her comfortable?"

Miss Todd's clothing was not entirely dry, owing to her immersion in the waters of Barmet Bay, and when Mrs. Hardy appeared she insisted on taking the guest upstairs and providing her with a complete change of garments. Miss Todd insisted that her business could not wait, even for such an important detail as dry clothes, but the better counsel of Mrs. Hardy prevailed.

When Miss Todd came downstairs some time later she was still very weak and nervous but in a more settled frame of mind.

"If you'll come into my office," suggested Fenton Hardy, courteously, "I'll be glad to hear your story."

Miss Todd looked around.

"I had intended to keep it private," she said; "but you've all been so kind to me that I'm sure it will do no harm if you all know. That is, if you would care to listen," she added, turning to Mrs. Hardy and the boys.

Both Frank and Joe were very curious to know the nature of the mysterious affair that had brought Miss Todd to Bayport and it did not require any persuasion for them to remain.

Miss Todd sat down in an armchair, and after she was duly settled began a long, rambling narrative.

"It's about my brother," she said. "My twin brother, Todham. He's a very clever man—a professor. Perhaps you've heard of him. Professor Todham Todd, Ph.D. It all started when Todham and I went on that railway journey to visit Cousin Albert. At the time I said that I had a strange feeling that something was going to happen, and perhaps we had better not go, but Todham said I was foolish, so we went. And I was right. It turned out that I was right after all."

"Yes?" said Mr. Hardy encouragingly, wondering to what all this was leading.

"I was quite right," declared Miss Todd emphatically. "Because something *did* happen. There was a wreck. The train jumped off the track. It was a terrible wreck. There were five people killed and it was a blessing Todham and I weren't killed too. But we were hurt. We were badly hurt. I've never felt the same since. My nerves have never been right. As for Todham, he always had been a nervous sort of man, and after that wreck he went all to pieces. The doctor said he would be all right after a while, that all he needed was rest and quiet, and I believed he was right. But we sued the railway for damages."

"Did you win the suit?" asked Mr. Hardy.

"It has not come to trial. The lawyers delayed everything. In the meantime, poor Todham was acting strangely. You wouldn't think he was the same man. He was very odd. I used to wonder if the railway wreck had affected his mind. Instead of getting better, he became worse. Then one night, just before the trial was to come off, he disappeared."

"Disappeared!"

"He walked out of the house one night and from that minute to this we haven't seen hide nor hair of him," declared Evangeline Todd. "We have heard of him, but he's like a will-o'-the-wisp. We have heard of him in different places, but when we come to look for him, he's gone. He has never written to us. There hasn't been any real trace of him. The shock was too much for me, and I collapsed and I haven't been well since. Not a bit well. My nerves have been completely shattered."

"When did your brother disappear?" asked the detective.

"Months ago. This happened four months back."

Fenton Hardy frowned.

"Four months ago! That makes it more difficult. If you had come to me earlier I would have had a better chance of helping you."

"Don't say you won't help me, Mr. Hardy," entreated the woman. "Please don't say you won't take the case."

"I didn't mean it that way," said the detective kindly. "I meant that the chances of tracing your brother are not as good now as they would have been four months ago. I'll do what I can, of course, but I'm afraid it will be a hard task."

"We searched for him everywhere, Mr. Hardy. I'm sure he is still alive, for we've had reports of him from different places. But I have no idea what can have happened to him."

"It's just possible that he has had a mental breakdown," said the detective. "You say he was acting strangely after the wreck. He may be in a hospital somewhere, and unable to communicate with you."

"I'm quite sure he didn't deliberately run away. Todham has always been so quiet and studious and so anxious to give no trouble to any one. Something dreadful must have happened to him. If it weren't for hearing that he has been seen in these different places, I would believe that he is dead. As it is, I'm sure he is still alive."

"Perhaps we can find some trace of him," said Mr. Hardy. "I'll take the case, Miss Todd, and, although I can't promise to find your brother, you may be sure that I'll do the best I can."

"Thank you. Thank you, Mr. Hardy. I knew you wouldn't refuse. I wish now I had come to you in the first place, instead of wasting so much precious time."

"Perhaps we can recover the lost ground. With a bit of luck, we may be able to pick up his trail."

Miss Todd sank back in her chair.

"Oh, I hope so. I hope so. I have been so worried." She clasped her hands nervously. "Find him for me, Mr. Hardy, and I'll pay you well. I must know what has become of Todham."

Her face suddenly became pale. The strain of the narrative had been too much for her. She relaxed limply.

Mrs. Hardy hurried forward.

"Get me a glass of water, Frank," she said quickly. "She has fainted."

CHAPTER IV

CONCERNING TODHAM TODD

It was quite evident that Miss Todd was in no condition to go to any of the city hotels. She needed rest and quiet more than anything else, and when she had been revived a few minutes later, Mrs. Hardy insisted that she remain in the Hardy home for a few days as a guest. Her sympathy had gone out to the distracted woman, and although at first Evangeline Todd would not consider the proposal, being afraid of imposing on their hospitality, Mr. Hardy insisted that she remain.

"Your story interests me very much," he said. "I'll be very glad to take the case, on one condition."

"What condition is that?"

"On condition that you accept our invitation to stay here for a while until you are feeling better."

So Evangeline Todd was prevailed upon to stay and Fenton Hardy at once prepared to take up the trail of the missing professor. He had no important cases in hand at the time, so he was able to spare a few days for preliminary investigation work and he decided that his best plan was to go directly to the college town where the Todds had their home.

"Sometimes a professional, and a stranger, can pick up clues that wouldn't fall in the way of a police detective who is known in the town," he said. "I'll run up there and see what I can discover."

Mr. Hardy was accustomed to being called out of town suddenly and the family were used to his abrupt departures. The detective was a man who acted quickly, once he had made a decision, and Miss Todd was surprised to see him leaving immediately.

"No use wasting any time," he explained cheerfully, having paused only long enough to pack a bag with a few essentials. "I'll get busy at once."

Although Frank and Joe Hardy were curious to learn further details of the latest mystery on which their father was working, and in which they had taken a small part, Miss Todd had evidently suffered more from her adventure in Barmet Bay than they had at first thought. She was obliged to keep to her room over Sunday and the lads had no chance to talk to her, as Mrs. Hardy decided that their guest should not be disturbed. Wisely, Mrs. Hardy wanted to keep the woman's mind off the matter of her brother's disappearance and she knew that if the boys besieged her with questions her state of anxiety would be only rendered worse.

On Monday, when the boys returned to school, they were met at the gate by Chet Morton, heading a group of grinning chums. Chet, a plump, jovial youth, equally fond of food and fun, held up a restraining hand.

"We would fain talk with thee, noble youths," he said. "Humble varlets though we are, we would crave your indulgence for a time."

"You sound like Shakespeare or somebody," said Joe.

"Probably somebody," Chet agreed. "Young masters, we have gathered here today to do honor to two brave and bright young men whom we are proud to call our chums. Perhaps," he went on, in the manner of an orator, "in the years to come, when we are poor and unnoticed people, we may be able to say to our grandchildren that once upon a time we went to school with the Hardy boys, that we went swimming with them, and that they often gave us rides in their motorboat. However, that is not getting to the point—"

"What's it all about?" asked Frank. "What's all this speech for?"

"Patience. Patience. Our little committee has waited patiently for your arrival and now we wish to show you our esteem and regard. It has come to our notice that on Saturday, the fourteenth instant, you did bravely, heroically, and nobly perform the humane act of hauling an old lady out of the water when she had swallowed several gallons of Barmet Bay and was in grave danger of drowning. As a slight token of our appreciation we wish you to accept these little tokens—" here Chet gestured to Biff Hooper, who grinned and stepped forward with two shiny objects on an old cushion—"not so much for their intrinsic value, which is considerable, but for the spirit in which they are meant."

Chet took a deep breath.

"I don't know whether that's all quite correct," he said, "but I learned some of it from a book."

Then, very gravely, he picked up the shiny objects, which proved to be impromptu medals carved from the tops of tin biscuit boxes, dangling from red ribbons, and pinned one on the chest of each of the Hardy boys.

There were loud cheers and shrieks of laughter from the boys at this mock ceremony, and the Hardy boys joined in the laugh as well. However, behind all the nonsense, the lads realized that their chums were proud of them. The tin medals were embarrassing, and the boys watched for their first opportunity to take them off.

"Seriously," said Chet, some time later when he was alone with the brothers, "the fellows think you did some mighty smart work fishing that lady out of the water. The captain of the boat told people about it when the yacht docked."

"We couldn't very well stand by and watch her drown," said Frank. "If Biff and Tony could have got there first they'd have done the same."

"Sure! But the point is, you chaps got there first and saved her life. If you hadn't been there, Biff and Tony couldn't have done very much, for their boats aren't fast enough. Where is the lady now? Did she give you her name?"

Frank and Joe then told Chet about Miss Evangeline Todd and about the coincidence that her visit to Bayport had been with the object of seeing Fenton Hardy. Chet was greatly interested when they told him about her search for the missing professor.

"A professor missing, eh? That's something new. If one of the professor's students had disappeared there wouldn't be much mystery about it. I know one student of this high school who would like to drop out of sight for a while—until after these exams are over, at any rate."

"You're hopeless," laughed Frank, and just then the opening bell rang, cutting off further conversation.

When the boys returned home at noon they found that Miss Todd had recovered sufficiently to come downstairs. She seemed in much better spirits and the rest had evidently done her a great deal of good, because she was not in the highly nervous state of the previous Saturday.

"It's such a relief to know that the case is in good hands," she said. "If Fenton Hardy can't find poor Todham, I'm sure no one can. Though he may turn up of his own accord," she added.

"We'll hope for the best," said Mrs. Hardy quietly.

"Dad didn't like to question you too much on Saturday," Frank remarked. "He didn't want to bother you more than he could help."

"I'm afraid I wasn't in any condition to tell him many details."

"Perhaps if you would tell us anything you overlooked, we might be able to help out a little, too."

Miss Todd was thoughtful for a moment.

"There were a few things about Todham that would identify him almost anywhere," she said. "For instance, he was very careless about his shoes."

"His shoes?" echoed the boys.

"He *would* not keep them laced. It was simply impossible to keep an eye on that man, and if I didn't watch him he was just as likely as not to go out to classes in the morning with his shoelaces dragging on the ground, and he wouldn't notice them unless he tripped over them. He was very absent-minded."

"That's a pretty good clue to go on. What did your brother look like, Miss Todd?"

"He was tall and rather thin. His hair was white and he was clean-shaven. His eyes and his teeth were very good. Even in spite of his age and all the reading and studying, he never had to wear glasses. Oh, yes—there's something else. He had an expression he often used, about as near swearing as he ever went. 'By jing!' it was. Whenever he was excited about anything or wanted to emphasize something he had said, he would always exclaim 'by jing!' I remember that he forgot himself in a lecture one day and said that. The dean spoke to him about it."

"'By jing!'" remarked Frank thoughtfully. "It isn't an expression one hears every day."

"It was the only expression I can remember that was quite characteristic of Todham."

Miss Todd had little of further value to tell them, and when the Hardy boys were by themselves later on they discussed the peculiarities of the missing professor.

"He forgets to tie his shoelaces and he says 'by jing!'" observed Joe. "It should be easy enough to pick him out with a description like that. It's strange he hasn't turned up long ago."

"Unless he met somebody who knew he was missing and who had heard of those little habits, he wouldn't be noticed. And it's just about a thousand chances to one that we would ever run across him."

"Well, we can at least make a note of it and tell Dad when he comes back. Chances are, he will never hear about those things, and Miss Todd may forget to tell him. It might help him a lot."

"I guess this is one mystery where we won't have much chance to help," said Frank ruefully. "Still, we'll do what we can."

But the Hardy boys were destined to take an even more active part in the mystery of Todham Todd than Fenton Hardy himself.

CHAPTER V

PLANS FOR A TRIP

Vacation time came, as it always does, although the days dragged, and when the last examination was written and the Hardy boys and their chums faced the long summer holidays, the boys had more exciting concerns than the affair of Todham Todd.

Miss Todd had left the Hardy home, after profuse thanks for the hospitality the family had shown her, and had returned to the college town. Mr. Hardy, after spending a day or so there, had gone on to parts unknown and it was assumed that he was following clues that he hoped would lead to the discovery of the missing professor.

"What are you going to do now?" asked Chet, on the first day of the holidays, when a number of the boys were sitting in the barn back of the Hardy home.

"Joe and I were figuring on a motorboat trip," said Frank.

"Good idea," Tony Prito remarked. "Where are you going?"

Frank shrugged.

"No place in particular. We hadn't come to that."

"As long as you go *somewhere*, it's all right with you, eh?" suggested Chet.

"That's about the size of it."

"I'd like to go on a motorboat trip myself," said Biff Hooper slowly. "As a matter of fact, I know of a place to go, but I don't know whether we can reach it in a boat."

"Where's that?"

"I was talking to an old sailor the other day in one of the villages down the shore and he was telling me a story about some caves that are said to be down on the main shore. We were talking about buried treasure, and that's how he brought the matter up. He said that there were old rumors of treasure in these caves."

"Treasure!" exclaimed Chet, brightening up. "That's our meat!"

"Of course, I'm not saying there is treasure in these caves. But the old chap said he had heard the story and he thought there might be something in it."

"In the caves, you mean," said the irrepressible Chet.

"Sure! These caves are out on the coast, south from the mouth of Barmet Bay."

"It wouldn't take us very long to go down and look the place over," Frank remarked.

"They're not easy to reach. I'm not sure that we can get to them by motorboat. But I believe there's a road that runs down the coast in that neighborhood and we might be able to get there by land."

"We have the motorbikes," said Joe promptly.

"I'll find out more about it from the old chap and let you know," Biff promised.

"Find out more about the treasure," advised Chet. "Find out if it is in gold or silver and if we have to dig for it, and if there's enough to divide up among the crowd of us."

"So far as treasure is concerned, I don't hold much stock in these stories usually," said Biff. "But this old chap said that a gang of wreckers at one time lived in these caves. They had a pleasant little habit of changing the lights on the buoys along the reefs and wrecking ships. Then they would rob the vessels and store the loot in the caves."

"Good night!" exclaimed Tony. "Regular pirates."

"I'll say they were. Of course, all this was years ago. The gang was wiped out eventually and some of the leaders were hanged, but this old chap I was talking to said that very little of the loot was recovered. Of course, it may have been sold or shipped away, but he believes a lot of it is still hidden in the caves!"

"Hasn't any one ever hunted for it?"

"Oh, yes. But they've never found anything."

"Why should we?" asked Chet.

"Why shouldn't we? And what does it matter if we don't? We might have some fun making the trip."

"I think it's a good idea!" approved Frank Hardy. "We can take the motorcycles, run down there and poke around, and then come back. Of course I don't think we'll find any treasure, but it'll give us some sort of an objective, anyway."

"Suits me," declared Chet. "My motorbike is hereby enlisted. I can take Biff along in the side car."

"And we have our machines," Joe said. "Tony can ride with one of us."

"We ought to have a mighty good trip," said Frank. "How long do you think we should be away, Biff?"

"It will take about a day and a half to reach that part of the coast, for the roads aren't very good, and then it will take another day or so finding these caves. If we want to do any exploring I guess we could stick around for the rest of the summer and still have lots left to do."

"Well, we won't stay for the rest of the summer. But about a week or ten days should give us a good outing."

"That suits me," said Chet. "I have other things to do in the holidays besides crawling around in caves."

It was decided that the lads should inform their parents of the projected trip and make ready immediately. They planned to leave Bayport in two days, as they wanted a day in which to overhaul their motorcycles and get everything in readiness. Tony Prito was dubious about getting permission, as his father had been talking of putting him to work in the wholesale fruit depot for a few weeks during the summer season.

When the Hardy boys went into the house to tell their mother about the trip to the caves, they found that their father had just returned. He was unpacking his bag as they entered the hall.

"Hello, Dad!" they greeted him. "What luck?"

Fenton Hardy shook hands with his sons and returned to the bag.

"What kind of luck do you mean?" he asked.

"In the Todd case? Did you find the professor?"

"No," said the detective, "I didn't find the professor."

"Didn't you get any trace of him at all?"

"I found traces of him, all right. He's still alive, which is the main thing I learned."

"And yet you couldn't find him?" asked Joe.

"I followed him through half a dozen towns and cities, but I must say he is mighty elusive. He was always about three jumps ahead of me."

"He knew you were looking for him?"

"I don't think so. He wasn't running away from me. But he keeps on the move and he jumps around from one place to another without any rhyme or reason, so he was hard to follow. I finally lost track of him."

"That's tough," said Frank. "Where did you lose the trail?"

"At a little place called Claymore, about fifty miles south of here. He had been seen there last week, but he went away and no one knew where I could find him. So I gave up the search and came home."

"Have you dropped the case?"

Fenton Hardy laughed.

"Did you ever hear of me dropping a case before it was cleared up in one way or another?"

"No," admitted Frank. "But I thought you may have considered it a waste of time."

"It was a waste of time to keep following him about and never catching up with him. I decided to try another angle. Oh, we'll pick up Todham Todd yet."

"Joe and I have some information for you. But perhaps you know it already. Miss Todd gave us a few facts about her brother's appearance—"

"I have all that. I have a pretty good description of him, and I managed to get hold of a photograph at the college."

"Did you hear about his shoelaces?" asked Joe, excitedly.

"His shoelaces?"

"Miss Todd said her brother was mighty absent-minded and that quite often he forgot to tie up his shoelaces."

Mr. Hardy was interested.

"I didn't hear that one," he said. "It might be valuable. I'll make a note of it. A clue like that might mean a great deal in a case like this."

"And about 'by jing?'" asked Frank.

"By jing?"

"It's an expression he used. He never swears, but once in a while he says 'by jing!' if he is excited."

"That's something new, too. In all the information I picked up about Todham Todd I didn't hear anything about that expression or about the shoelaces, and they are two of the most important clues I could ask."

The boys were gratified that they had gained this much information for their father's benefit. They knew that although Fenton Hardy had given up the direct search for the missing professor, he would never abandon the case until there was a definite solution one way or the other.

"Have you found why he disappeared from home?" asked Joe.

"I imagine he simply lost his memory," said Mr. Hardy. "At the present time, from what information I could pick up, he has no idea that his real name is Todham Todd. His memory is completely gone and he isn't able to remember anything of his past life. Probably if he met his sister again or some old acquaintance, it might all come back to him. He is wandering around, trying to find out who he is and where he comes from."

"Poor old chap!" said the boys sympathetically.

"He evidently had some money on his person when he disappeared, because he hasn't been in want, and the reason it was so hard to follow him was because he didn't stay in any one town more than a day or so. Just long enough to know that it wasn't his own town and that he could learn nothing about himself there. Then he would go on to the next place. But he'll turn up, I'm sure. I have a number of places being watched, where he's likely to put in an appearance some time, and I'll be notified at once."

"In the meantime," promised Frank, "we'll keep our eyes peeled for him. But we'll not be able to help much for a couple of weeks yet."

"Why?"

"We're going on a motorbike jaunt down the coast to look over some caves."

"Hidden treasure?" asked their father, his eyes twinkling.

"Perhaps."

"I hope you make a million," laughed Mr. Hardy. "I'll try to find Todham Todd before you come back."

CHAPTER VI

THE MISSING MOTORCYCLE

"I wish I were a boy," sighed Callie Shaw.

Iola Morton looked up from her ice-cream soda.

"Me, too."

"It's tough luck that you're not," said Joe Hardy. "We'd like to have you along on the trip with us."

"Boys have all the luck. Girls have to stay at home."

The Hardy boys, Chet Morton, and Biff Hooper were celebrating their departure by treating Callie Shaw and Iola Morton—and incidentally, themselves—to ice-cream at the Bon Ton Confectionery Shop. Iola, a plump, dark girl, was Chet's sister, and fully as fun-loving as her brother. Of all the girls at Bayport High she was the special favorite of Joe, as Callie Shaw, brown-haired and brown-eyed, was above all other girls in Frank's opinion.

"This one is my treat," Joe announced. "Another soda won't hurt any one."

It was a warm afternoon and the others promptly accepted. Six tall, frosted glasses of soda, pink and white and orange in color, were placed before them and imbibed with many gurgles of satisfaction.

"Well, sis," remarked Chet, "I don't know but that I'd trade places with you."

"Yes, you would!" said Iola ironically. "You wouldn't give up that trip for a million dollars."

"I've just been thinking that you're lucky to be staying in town. You'll be able to have ice-cream sodas and we shan't."

"That's true, too," said Joe reflectively. He was very fond of sodas, and he had not considered the matter in this light before.

"Yes, but think of all the fun you'll have. And if you find any treasure in those caves you'll be able to eat ice-cream sodas for the rest of your lives."

"Our lives wouldn't last very long if we did nothing but eat sodas after we came back," laughed Frank. "How about another?"

The girls shook their heads. Chet groaned.

"This is my fifth today," he said. "I *could* take another but I wouldn't have any room left for supper. Guess we'd better quit."

"We'd better," agreed Biff. "If you're sick tomorrow morning we'll start without you."

The thought of this possibility drove all desire for another ice-cream soda from Chet Morton's mind and the boys and girls left the Bon Ton. As they would not be seeing one another again before the start of the trip, Callie and Iola said good-bye to Biff and the Hardy boys.

"We'll miss you," Callie assured them. "The town won't seem the same without you."

"It won't be, either," grinned Chet. "It'll be a lot quieter when we clear out."

"Our house will be quieter, at any rate," Iola agreed. "It'll be a relief when you're gone, Chet."

"That's a sister for you! Frank, you and Joe are lucky. You have no sisters."

"I don't know about that," replied Frank. "If we had sisters like Callie and Iola we wouldn't have any kick."

Chet and his sister, in spite of all their good-natured banter, got along very well together. So, with much laughter and good wishes, the friends parted, and the Hardy boys went home to finish their packing.

Next morning found the four boys bowling along a country road leading out of Bayport, on the first stage of their journey to the caves on the coast. Greatly to their disappointment, Tony Prito had been unable to come with them, as his father needed him. Biff Hooper and Chet rode together. Frank and Joe, of course, had each his own motorcycle.

It was an ideal summer morning, cool and bright. The boys carried their blankets and cooking utensils, but they had agreed it would be best not to carry too many provisions, as food could be purchased along the way as it was needed.

"This won't be our first experience searching through caves," called out Frank, who was in the lead of the little procession.

"It will be old stuff to you chaps," answered Biff. "I sure wish I had been with you when you were going through the caves below the Shore Road."

He referred to the experience of the Hardy boys when they were in search of the automobiles that thieves had hidden in secret caves beneath the cliffs along the Shore Road above Barmet Bay.

"By the way," said Chet, "did you know that one of that gang of rascals escaped from jail the other day?"

This was news to the others. When the Hardy boys discovered the stolen cars they also aided in the round-up of the gang of automobile thieves, some of whom had been sentenced to long terms of imprisonment. Others, who had been merely tools of the ring-leaders of the outfit, were given lighter sentences in the local jail.

"Who was that?" asked Joe.

"Carl Schaum. He made a getaway the day before yesterday. The police were keeping quiet about it because they thought they might catch him again before the news leaked out. But he's clear away."

"Carl Schaum!" exclaimed Frank. "He was one of the chaps who got off lightly."

"And to my mind he was one of the worst rascals of the lot," added Joe.

"Well, he's at large now. They haven't been able to trace him. He's a tough bird, all right."

"Carl Schaum used to live around here, didn't he?" asked Biff.

"Sure. He used to live just outside the city. He's been in and out of plenty of scrapes. A real bad egg."

"Oh, probably the police will pick him up again," Biff said. "He won't get very far. It's a cinch he won't hang around Bayport."

"Not if he knows what's good for him," remarked Frank.

The road the boys had taken went south and then east toward the coast, through a beautiful countryside. The boys had been on their way a little over two hours, but already they were hot and dusty. Just at that moment, Joe spied a flash of blue among the trees beyond an inviting shady lane.

"Looks like a lake down there," he said. "What say we investigate?"

"I'm game," said Chet. "Maybe we can have a swim."

As time was not pressing and the boys were traveling leisurely, in no hurry to reach the caves, they at once fell in with the suggestion. Frank headed down the lane and in a few minutes the lads were riding beneath shady trees down toward the banks of a small lake that lay calm and clear among the woods. There was a wide, sandy beach, and with whoops of delight the boys at once brought their motorcycles to a stop, parked them beneath the trees by the road, and raced gayly down through the grass.

It was one of the finest natural swimming places they had ever seen and the boys lost no time flinging off their clothes and splashing out into the cool water. For about half an hour they enjoyed themselves as only boys can, swimming and diving, until at last, refreshed, they came up onto the beach and donned their garments again.

Their motorcycles had been parked just out of sight of the beach, because the road ran past the lake, about a hundred yards distant. However, the boys had given little thought to the safety of the machines because the lake was in a secluded spot and there was no sign of human habitation near by.

"I'll race you back!" shouted Frank, as they began to dress.

There was a mad scramble for clothes. Chet adroitly hurled one of Biff's shoes into a thicket, thinking thereby to get a head start on his chum, but Joe sat on Chet's trousers as he drew on his own socks, and Chet hunted in vain for the essential garments, losing more time than Biff did. All this byplay took time, and Frank, in the meanwhile, was dressing hastily but calmly, and was ready before any of the others. With a yell of triumph, he darted up the grassy slope.

Joe was next. Shoelaces dragging, he set out in pursuit. Chet did not even bother to put on his shoes but hastened after, his shirt open, and hanging onto his trousers with one hand while he fastened his belt. Biff, plunging about in the bush in search of the missing shoe, was last.

"First up!" shouted Frank. Then the others heard him give a sudden exclamation of surprise.

"What's the matter?" called Joe.

He ran up in time to see Frank standing in the roadway, an expression of consternation on his face.

"The bikes!" he exclaimed. "There are only two here!"

"What?" yelled Joe.

"One of our bikes is missing! What do you know about that!"

As Chet and Joe hastened up they saw that he was right. Where three motorcycles had been parked beside the road, there were only two left.

Frank's motorcycle was gone!

CHAPTER VII

CARL SCHAUM

Frank Hardy wasted no time.

The motorcycle had been stolen. There was no doubt of that. That it had been stolen within that past five minutes, he knew. When the boys were coming out of the water he thought he had heard the clatter of a machine, but at the time he had paid no attention to the sound, thinking it came from the main road.

"Come on!" he shouted. "We'll chase him."

"Which way has he gone?" gasped Chet.

Frank looked at the road. It was not a traveled thoroughfare and weeds and grass were in the ruts. It was impossible to see any sign of the tire tread.

"Joe and I will go ahead," he decided. "Chet, you and Biff go on back to the main road on your bike. If you don't get any trace of him, wait for us."

He sprang onto Joe's motorcycle and his brother leaped up behind. Biff Hooper was just emerging from the bushes and Chet quickly told him what had happened.

In a moment the two machines were roaring off along the road in opposite directions, Chet and Biff returning to the highway and the Hardy boys going on down the country lane.

Once past the lake, Joe and Frank found the going was rough. Presumably, it was just a lane connecting with the highway, and there was little traffic over it. The motorcycle bumped along, Frank letting the machine out as much as he dared.

They came to a dusty spot in the lane and Frank gave a cry of exultation.

"This is the way he went! There's the tire marks!"

Clearly defined in the dust was the imprint of the tread. The boys knew they were on the right track, but they knew that the thief was undoubtedly proceeding as quickly as they were, if not faster.

Could they overtake him?

Coming to a more level stretch of road, Frank risked a greater speed and the motorcycle leaped forward in a cloud of dust. There were many curves and the high trees obscured a view of the road ahead so they had no idea how close they were to the fugitive.

Owing to the roar of their own machine they could not have heard the clatter of the other motorcycle even if it had been only a short distance ahead. They could only trust to their own speed and to the chance that the thief had not obtained too much of a start.

Suddenly, as they swerved around a bend in the road, Joe gave a cry of delight.

In the distance, on an open stretch, half hidden by a heavy cloud of dust, a motorcycle was hurtling toward an expanse of paved highway that lay like a white ribbon far beyond the trees.

"That's him!" Joe shouted.

But Frank had already seen the dark object ahead.

He let the machine out to its fullest speed. He knew that if the fugitive once gained the highway it would be impossible to overtake him. It was now or never.

But the country road was deceptive.

Just a few yards away, he spied a culvert. It had been poorly constructed and a bad bump was inevitable. It was suicidal to take it at their present speed.

He desperately tried to slacken pace, but the machine reached the rise in the road in a moment, lurched over it, seemed to leap through the air, and then hit the road again with a crash. There was a tremendous jolt.

Frank's grip was almost torn from the handlebars, but he held on tightly. Joe had grasped him tightly around the waist and still retained his seat.

The motorcycle swerved, skidded wildly, and headed toward the ditch.

But Frank had set himself for the shock of going over the culvert and he acted almost instinctively.

Had he been unprepared he would certainly have lost control of the motorcycle and both he and Joe might have been killed. He swung the hurtling machine back into mid-road again just when it seemed that it was about to crash into the deep ditch. He did not slacken speed, for that would have meant a dangerous skid.

By skillful handling, he settled the machine on the smoothest part of the road again and it roared on down the stretch.

The fugitive, too, seemed to be having trouble. The motorcycle ahead was lurching and bouncing in an alarming manner and its speed had slackened. Frank's experienced eye saw that the thief had encountered a rough and treacherous piece of road that ran for about half a mile before it met the main highway.

Suddenly they saw the machine swerve wildly and go completely over on its side. The driver was thrown into the middle of the road.

"He's done for!" Frank shouted.

But his joy was short-lived. The thief had not given up yet. He scrambled to his feet and returned to the motorcycle, righted it, and leaped into the saddle. The machine, evidently undamaged, bounded forward again.

However, the accident had given the Hardy boys a chance to make up ground and they had gained considerably. In a few moments they reached the beginning of the rough section of the road and the fugitive was no more than two hundred yards ahead.

The two motorcycles lurched and bounded over the bumpy surface. Frank saw that the thief was not a first-class driver. He seemed to be having a great deal of trouble keeping the stolen machine on the road and did not dare travel at high speed.

As for himself, he saw that he would have to take chances. He shouted to Joe, "Hang on!" and let the motorcycle out as much as he dared.

It was a rough ride. More than once it seemed as though they would crash, but they steadily gained on the fugitive.

The man looked behind. He saw that he had no hope of reaching the highway.

The stolen motorcycle came to a stop. The rider leaped out into the road and ran toward the ditch. Beyond it there was a fence and a high bank of trees. Through the ditch and over the fence scrambled the fugitive. He looked back again just as the Hardy boys drew up beside the abandoned machine and then disappeared among the trees.

The boys were at first inclined to follow, and Joe dashed toward the ditch in pursuit. But Frank's better counsel prevailed.

"Let him go," he said. "We'd never find him in that underbrush, and he might just double back to the road again and clear out on the motorcycle. We've got the machine back. That's the main thing."

Reluctantly, Joe came back.

"Yes, we've got the machine. But I'd like to lay my hands on that crook."

"Didn't you recognize him?"

Joe shook his head.

"I only caught a glimpse of his face but it seems to me I've seen him before."

"We've both seen him before."

"Where?"

"The Shore Road gang."

"The auto thieves?"

Frank nodded his head in assent.

"Then," exclaimed Joe, "that must be Carl Schaum! All the others are in jail."

"That's who it is, all right. I recognized him the moment he looked back."

"I wish I had chased him!" declared Joe.

"He's likely putting a lot of distance between himself and us just now. I guess the reason he stole the motorcycle was to help him in his getaway, for the police are looking for him since he escaped from jail."

"If we had caught him we would have had to take him back to Bayport anyway," Joe remarked philosophically. "It would have interrupted our trip. Perhaps it's just as well."

"He'll be picked up somewhere else. I'm glad he didn't get my motorcycle. That would have upset the trip even worse."

Frank examined the machine. It had been slightly damaged by the upset on the rough road and there were a few dents and scrapes, but there was nothing seriously wrong with it. He mounted the motorcycle and its staccato roar soon filled the air.

"Running as good as ever," he said, with satisfaction.

"Good! Shall we go back now?"

"We may as well. There's no use chasing Carl Schaum, and the others will be wondering what has happened."

The brothers rode back toward the swimming pool and then out to the highway, where they found Chet and Biff waiting for them. Not having found any trace of the machine on the highway the chums had waited according to instructions. When they saw the brothers coming in view, each on his own machine, they raised a cheer.

"Good work!" shouted Chet. "Did you have to battle for it?"

"No battle at all," returned Frank, bringing the motorcycle to a stop. "An old friend of ours had just borrowed it for a little ride."

Chet looked at him incredulously. Frank laughed at the expression on his chum's face.

"An old friend!" exclaimed Biff. "I didn't know you had any friends around this part of the country."

"He wasn't exactly a friend. An acquaintance, I should say. Carl Schaum swiped the machine."

Chet and Biff whistled simultaneously.

"Schaum was the thief!" Biff exclaimed. "Are you sure?"

"Where is he?" demanded Chet. "Did you tie him up?"

"We didn't catch him," confessed Joe. "He left the bike in the road when he saw we were gaining on him. Then he cleared out over the fence and into the woods."

"That was too bad!" exclaimed Chet.

"Are you sure it was Carl Schaum?" asked Biff Hooper, for the second time.

"I got a good look at him," Frank said. "It was Carl Schaum, all right. When we get to the next town we'll tell the police. If they know he's around here at all they'll probably land him without much trouble."

Chet went over to his motorcycle.

"Well, the sooner we get to the next town, the better. We've lost quite a bit of time already. What say we start on again?"

The chums agreed that the discovery of the swimming hole had cost them considerably more time than they had expected, so accordingly they mounted their machines again and set out on the highway once more.

CHAPTER VIII

STRANGE DOINGS

The Hardy boys and their chums spent the night at a hotel in a small village. They were up bright and early next morning, eager to reach the end of their journey. Had it not been for the delay consequent on the attempted theft of Frank's motorcycle, they might have reached the neighborhood of the caves that evening, but, as it was, they had a two hours' trip before them when they set out shortly after six o'clock.

Their immediate destination was a fishing village by the name of Glencove. It was a sleepy little place, quite picturesque but redolent of fishy odors, a typical hamlet of the kind. The boys were aware that Glencove was some distance north of the caves, but as they did not know the precise location of the "Honeycomb Cliffs," as they were called, they preferred to stop off at the village and get what information they could.

The general store, a ramshackle building where one could buy anything from safety pins to grindstones, where one could mail a letter, put through a telephone call, or obtain garage service, appeared to be the most likely spot. Parking their machines by the wooden sidewalk, the lads went into the store, where they found a venerable man with white whiskers patiently scrutinizing his newspaper.

"I guess we'd better stock up on a few supplies, eh, fellows?" Frank suggested.

This had been their plan. Instead of burdening their machines with provisions all the way from Bayport, they had decided to get supplies at the village nearest to the caves.

"Perhaps we won't have to stock up very heavily," said Joe. "If the caves aren't far away we may be able to drive up here when we run short of grub."

"That," said the hungry Chet, "would be terrible."

Frank turned to the old gentleman, who had put aside his paper and was regarding them through his thick-lensed spectacles with grave curiosity, as though they were some new specimen of humanity entirely.

"How far is it to the place they call Honeycomb Cliffs?" he asked.

The old gentleman's eyes widened.

"Honeycomb Cliffs!" he said, in a high, cracked voice. "Be ye goin' to pass by there?"

"We want to camp around there for a few days and we were figuring on buying some supplies. If it's far away we'll buy all we need right now and carry the stuff with us."

The old man leaned farther over the counter.

"Ye're agoin' to *camp* at Honeycomb Cliffs!" he exclaimed incredulously.

"Why, yes."

"For three or four days!"

"Perhaps longer."

The old gentleman shook his head solemnly.

"Ye're strange to these parts, ain't ye?"

"This is the first time we've ever been down this way."

"I thought so," returned the old man with a great air of satisfaction, as though his judgment had been verified.

"Well," said Frank, becoming a trifle impatient, "we'd still like to know how much farther we have to go."

"It's a matter of about ten mile by the road. Then ye'll have to walk a ways."

"Ten miles. Why, that isn't very far. We'll just buy enough food to last us a day or so and then if we need more one of us can come back here. There's no use packing along too much."

"And ye say ye're goin' to camp there?" persisted the old man, as though he could not quite grasp the fact.

"Yes. What's wrong about that? Aren't there any places we can pitch a tent?"

"Oh, yes, there's places ye can pitch a tent and I've no doubt but there's fishermen's cottages that you could find a room at. But if I was you I wouldn't do no campin' near Honeycomb Cliffs. That is," said the old man, "unless ye stay away from the caves."

"Why, that's what we came for," put in Biff. "We intend to explore the caves!"

The old man gave a perceptible gasp at this.

"Explore 'em. Lads, ye're crazy."

The old gentleman's attitude puzzled the boys extremely.

"Is it against the law?" Chet inquired.

"No, it ain't agin the law, but it's agin common sense."

"Why?"

"It just is—that's all," retorted the storekeeper, as though that explained everything.

"You don't mean to say it's dangerous!"

"Maybe. Maybe," returned their informant mysteriously. "It may not be dangerous, but it would be foolish. If ye'll take my advice ye'll stay away from them caves."

"Why?"

"There's some strange things been goin' on down there lately. Folks tell me the fishermen down that way are scared nigh to death."

"What are they afraid of?" asked Biff.

The old man shrugged eloquently.

"That's just it. Nobody knows. But there's been strange lights seen down around them caves. And shootin'."

"Shooting!"

"Guns goin' off," explained the storekeeper, as if they had failed to understand the word. "Mighty weird doin's, they say. Two men a'ready that tried to find out what was goin' on—they got shot at."

Chet whistled softly.

"This sounds good," he observed. "We may stay longer than we had intended."

"Ye may stay forever," growled the old man gloomily.

Frank smiled at this thrust.

"Has anybody any idea what's wrong?" he asked.

The storekeeper leaned across the counter and lowered his voice, in the manner of one imparting a deep secret.

"They do say," he declared, "that there's smugglin' of liquor in them parts."

"I suppose that's only natural. There's a lot of it along the coast, and the caves would make that an ideal spot."

"Well, whether there is or there ain't, the caves ain't healthy for strangers. If I was you lads, I'd stay away from there."

"Well, we've planned this trip and I think we'll go through with it," Frank said. "If you'll fix us up with some supplies, we'll be on our way. We're not afraid of bootleggers."

"Do as ye like," the old man returned, as though washing his hands of any further responsibility. "But I'm warnin' ye. It ain't no place if ye're lookin' for a quiet outing."

"The one thing we're afraid of, is a *quiet* outing," Joe assured him. "Excitement," he added slangily, "is our meat."

"Ye'll get lots of it if ye go pokin' around them caves," the old gentleman predicted. "Mebbe a lot more than ye bargain for."

However, he was prevailed upon to sell the lads a quantity of provisions for their trip, although he accompanied the transaction by a running fire of dismal comments on the unlikelihood that they would ever be seen alive again. When he saw that they were determined to go to the caves, in spite of his admonitions, he wagged his head sadly and mumbled a few caustic remarks on the stubborness of boys in general who would never listen to their elders.

The Hardy boys and their chums, far from being frightened at the prospect of danger at Honeycomb Cliffs, were elated. They were disposed to disregard much of what the old man had said—the perils were most probably exaggerated in the re-telling—but there was no mistaking the old man's sincerity and they knew that undoubtedly there was a mystery of some kind concerning the neighborhood of the caves.

"What that mystery is, we're going to find out," said Joe, as they mounted their motorcycles again, duly laden with supplies. He expressed the determination of all.

"It looks a lot brighter," Chet agreed. "There's a chance of a bit of excitement now."

"Oh, probably there's nothing to it," scoffed Biff. "Somebody has seen a tramp's campfire on the cliffs and heard some one shooting at a rabbit, and started a big yarn out of it."

"Well, we are going to have our own fun exploring those caves, and if there's a mystery on foot, so much the better," said Joe.

The boys followed the directions given them by the old storekeeper and in due time left the coast road and turned down a rutty, tortuous lane that ended on the open seashore, near a fisherman's cottage. The little house was built at the base of a hill and the beach ended at this point in towering cliffs. The lads could see a faint, winding path leading up the side of the hill back of the cottage.

"I know what they call this place," said Chet gravely.

"I don't think it has a name," said Biff.

"Oh, yes, they call this place Fish-hook."

"Fish-hook? Why?" asked Biff, neatly falling into the trap.

"Because it's at the end of the line."

With that, Chet brought his motorcycle to a stop. The Hardy boys also stopped, joining Chet in his laughter at the foolish look on Biff's face when he saw how he had been duped.

The storekeeper had told them that the fisherman's cottage was the last human habitation on the way to the caves and that they could very likely get permission to leave their machines there for safe-keeping. To reach the caves they had to climb the path up the hillside until they reached the top of the cliffs, then proceed for a considerable distance until they came to a deep ravine, where they could descend to the shore. They would then find themselves on a beach whereby they could reach the caves to right and to left. The cliffs themselves cut off access to the caves by any other route than the ravines, several of which were to be encountered in the three miles of steep coast, as at the northern and southern extremities the cliffs were sheer to the deep water and could not be skirted even at low tide.

The boys had scarcely dismounted from their motorcycles when the door of the cottage opened and a stocky, leathern-faced man of middle age emerged. He was plainly a fisherman and he came over to them, a look of surprise on his broad, good-natured countenance.

"What can I do for you, my lads?" he inquired. "It ain't often I see strangers here."

"We want to know if we could leave our motorcycles here for safe-keeping?" asked Frank.

"Certainly. Most certainly, you can. There's a shed back of the house, where you can put 'em. Is it just for an hour or so? Goin' up on the cliffs?"

"Perhaps for a few days. We were planning to go exploring among the caves."

The fisherman's expression changed instantly.

"Explorin' the caves!" he exclaimed. "You'd best go back home. There's strange doin's in the caves these days. It's no place for boys."

CHAPTER IX

THE STORM

Chet Morton laughed.

"We heard there were some strange things happening around here, but that doesn't frighten us."

"There's nothing to laugh at, young man," returned the fisherman tartly. "I've lived here for twenty years and I'm no fool. The caves ain't healthy just now."

"Rum-runners, I suppose," said Frank.

But the fisherman scorned this suggestion.

"If it's rum-runners, they'd be bringin' their cargoes out to the road, wouldn't they? Not much sense in 'em hidin' the liquor in the caves and leavin' it there, is there?"

"I wouldn't think so. But perhaps they bring it out to the road quietly."

"Nothin' of the sort. It's been investigated. There's been no unusual doin's on the road at all. All the strange doin's are right in the caves. If it was rum-runners, they'd be bringin' the stuff in by boat, and there ain't been any boats seen around here that can't be accounted for."

"Just what are the strange doings?"

"Lights, mostly. And shootin'."

"But has no person been seen?"

"Not a livin' soul."

"That's strange."

"Strange ain't the word for it!" declared the fisherman. "It's downright spooky. Like ghosts or somethin'."

"Do you believe in ghosts?" asked Joe.

"I don't. If I did believe in ghosts, though, I'd say there was ghosts down in them caves lately and that's all I'd think about it. But not believin' in ghosts, I don't know what to think."

"Have you gone down to the caves yourself?"

"I went down there a couple of weeks ago, but I didn't see anything until just when I was comin' back that night. Then I saw a light away down in one of the caves I'd been in just a couple of hours before. Next I heard two or three shots, and then a yell."

"A yell!"

"The most awful screech I ever heard."

"Well, that proves that there's *somebody* down there," remarked Biff.

"Maybe it does and maybe it don't. I wouldn't say it was a human voice I heard. More like an animal."

"But an animal couldn't make a light."

"And there ain't many human bein's could make that yell. So there you are."

"Yells or no yells, we're going to explore the caves," declared Frank, with finality. "What say, fellows?"

"I'll tell the world we are!" exclaimed Chet. "You couldn't drive me away now with a squad of marines."

The fisherman shrugged.

"It's your funeral," he said. "I'm thinkin' you'll come away from there a lot faster than you go in."

"Perhaps," agreed Joe, with a grin. "And perhaps we'll find out just who or what is causing all the disturbance. We'll go prepared for anything that may happen to turn up, at any rate."

"You'll need to," said the fisherman gloomily. "Don't say that I didn't warn you. You're welcome to put your machines in the shed, and if you'd like a bite to eat, I guess my wife can fix up a bit of a snack for you."

This hospitality was appreciated by the boys and they saw that the fisherman's bark was worse than his bite, as the saying is, but they politely declined, as they had eaten just a short time before. Chet, who could—and would—eat at any time, was not very emphatic in his refusal; he would willingly have accepted the invitation. But the other lads were anxious to be going on.

"It's very good of you," said Frank, "and I hope you don't think we're rude in going ahead to the caves after your warning. But there are four of us, you see, and we think we can look after ourselves pretty well. So, if you'll just let us leave the motorcycles in the shed while we're around here we won't bother you any further."

"You're welcome to do that. And I suppose if you're bound to go on to the caves, nothin' I can say will stop you."

The fisherman led the way to the shed, where the motorcycles were safely stored. The machines would be under cover in the event of rain, and there was a stout padlock on the door that ensured their safety against being stolen. The lads unloaded their supplies and each filled his pack with provisions.

"Have we got everything?" asked Frank finally. "Matches, flashlights, revolver, bullets, bread, salt, coffee—"

"Everything needed for an expedition to the South Pole," said Chet, shifting his pack to a more comfortable position on his shoulders.

A complete check-up showed that they had everything they needed; so, after bidding good-bye to the fisherman, who drew them a rough map showing the route they should follow in order to reach the caves, they set out up the path just back of the cottage.

"Nobody seems very encouraging about this trip," said Biff, as they ascended the hillside.

"What do you think *can* be the trouble down in the caves?" asked Joe.

"Rum-runners, I'll bet! In spite of what the fisherman says, I can't think of any other explanation," Frank replied. "They probably have some way of getting the stuff out to the road without being seen. Underground passages, or something of the sort."

"It seems likely. The shots and the yells were just to frighten people away."

"Well, we should soon find out."

Although the hillside path had not seemed very formidable from the shore, the boys found that it was steeper than it looked, and it was more than an hour before they finally reached the top of the cliffs. Here a magnificent view awaited them. Far below, the fisherman's cottage seemed to lie at their very feet, like a toy house. The ocean lay like a flat blue floor, far to the east, north, and south, and back of them was a great, barren expanse of tumbled rock, without sign of path or road. Venturing close to the edge of the cliff, the lads saw a sheer wall of rock, many feet in height, at the bottom of which the waves were lapping.

"No wonder we couldn't reach the caves by skirting the shore!" said Frank. "The only way along the base of that cliff is by boat."

"We'll have to go ahead and search for the ravine the fisherman told us about," suggested Joe.

Chet looked up at the sky.

"Yes, and we can't afford to lose any time about it either. We're in for a storm."

Although the lads had noticed that the sun had gone behind a cloud, they had not seen the heavy black cloud banks massing above them, so intent had they been on their climb up the steep, winding path. Now, when they looked up, they saw that a storm was indeed imminent. The breeze bore to their ears a rumble of distant thunder.

"It looks like a bad one," said Biff. "We'd better hurry."

Without further ado, the boys hastened off along the faint trail that led among the rocks. They could see no sign of the ravine, but judged that it would be almost invisible until they came almost on it. Their progress was slow, as it was difficult to make haste over the rocks and boulders.

The storm came up swiftly. Within ten minutes the clouds were banked blackly in the sky above. A streak of livid lightning rent the gloom and there was a peal of thunder.

"We're out of luck if we can't find shelter before this storm breaks," panted Chet. The air was insufferably close. A few scattered raindrops warned the lads that they had no time to lose.

They plodded on, mentally wishing that they had remained at the fisherman's cottage but realizing that it was too late to turn back now.

Another flash of lightning, a terrific thunder-clap, and the storm broke.

Rain began falling heavily. It streamed down from the black skies as though the clouds had opened. The wind rose. Far below them the surf boomed and the waves crashed against the base of the cliff. Rain poured in a veritable deluge. The lads had neglected to provide themselves with slickers, as they were already burdened by the weight of their supplies, and they were soon drenched to the skin.

They stumbled on, scarcely able to follow the faint path in the gloom. Lightning flickered, thunder crashed constantly, the wind rose to a howl. There was not the slightest vestige of shelter, not even a tree, out on this rocky waste. Frank looked in vain for a boulder large enough to offer some protection.

They plunged forward into a streaming wall of rain.

Frank was in the lead. Chet and Biff were next, and Joe brought up the rear. They could scarcely see one another in the gathering gloom. On and on they went, heads bent to the storm, and, to Chet especially, time seemed to stand still in a gray world.

Suddenly Frank looked behind, then came to a stop.

"Where is Joe?" he shouted, above the clamor of the gale.

The others looked back.

Joe had vanished.

CHAPTER X

THE CAVE

The boys gazed at one another in surprise.

"Where on earth did Joe disappear to?" exclaimed Biff Hooper.

They peered into the gray oblivion of the storm, but the rain was teeming down in such heavy torrents and the gloom was so intense that it was impossible to see more than twenty yards away.

"We'll have to go back," decided Frank quickly. "He probably sat down to rest and got lost when he tried to catch up with us again."

They retraced their steps over the rocks, keeping close together. They shouted again and again, but in the roar of wind, rain, and thunder they knew there was little chance that Joe would hear them.

"I never thought to look back," said Chet. "I thought he was right behind us."

"Same here," declared Biff. "He might have dropped back five or ten minutes ago and we didn't know it."

The search seemed hopeless. It was late in the afternoon and already getting dark. Once in a while they stopped and listened, hoping to hear some faint cry from Joe, but there was nothing.

"Perhaps he fell down and hurt himself," suggested Frank, "He may be lying behind some of these big rocks and we can't see him."

The boys searched patiently.

Joe Hardy was nowhere to be found.

They did not dare scatter, for fear of losing one another, but they hunted among the rocks, realizing the hopeless nature of their quest. At last they halted, standing in a little group, with rain pouring down on them.

Frank expressed the fear they had all held for the past few minutes.

"I wonder if he could have fallen over the cliff!"

They had been going along within a few yards of the uneven edge of the cliff and they realized that, in the rain and the dim light, it would have been easy for Joe to have stumbled into the abyss. They turned sick at the thought of the frightful plunge, ending in certain death, had he tumbled over the verge.

Suddenly, above the roar of the storm, they heard a faint cry.

"Listen!" cried Frank.

Breathlessly, they waited.

Again came the cry.

"Help! Help!"

It was from almost at their feet.

Frank ran quickly forward. At the very edge of the cliff, he stopped and peered down.

Over to one side, a few feet below the top of the sheer wall of rock, he spied a dark figure.

It was Joe!

He seemed to be clinging directly to the side of the cliff.

Hastily shouting to the others, Frank ran across the rocks until he came to a place immediately above where he had seen his brother. He flung himself flat and peered over into the dizzy depths.

Just beneath, he could see Joe's white face. His brother was clinging to a small bush growing out of the side of the cliff. Had the bush been his only support, he would not have been able to maintain his hold, but fortunately there was a ledge of rock, a few inches wide, in which he had managed to implant his feet. Thus he had clung to the face of the cliff.

"Quick!" shouted Frank, to the others. He realized the need for haste. "He's here!"

"I can't hold on much longer!" called Joe, in a strained voice.

"We'll get you out of this," Frank assured him. But his heart sank when he saw that Joe was beyond his reach.

Biff and Chet came running up, and Frank tersely explained the situation to them.

"There's only one thing to do," he said. "Both of you hang on to me while I lower myself over."

Biff peeped over the edge of the cliff.

"You'll never make it," he said. "You'll both be killed."

"We're not going to stand idle until he gets exhausted and lets go his hold," declared Frank. "It's the only chance, and I'm going to take it."

He flung himself down and began to edge forward until he was leaning far over the verge. Biff and Chet seized his ankles and set themselves by digging their heels against the rocks. Bit by bit, Frank lowered himself, head-first, over the side. His outstretched hands were but a few inches away from Joe's wrists. Joe still clung to the bush that had saved his life.

Frank dared not look down, for he was hanging at a dizzy height. He closed his eyes.

"A little more," he called out.

He swung lower and gripped Joe's wrists. He secured a tight hold. There was no time to lose, as he knew it would take every ounce of strength he possessed to drag his brother back to safety, and he was growing weaker all the time.

"Ready, Joe?"

"All right," gasped Joe.

"Haul away!"

Chet and Biff began dragging Frank back. There was a double weight now, for Joe relaxed his grip on the root to which he had been clinging and was now dangling in space, supported only by Frank's firm grip on his wrists. Frank had no idea that his brother weighed so much; the strain was terrific.

Gradually, however, he was drawn back to safety. For one horrible moment he thought he was losing his hold on Joe's wrists, as their locked hands reached the edge of the precipice. But Chet, leaning forward, seized the back of Joe's shirt, clung to him while Biff scrambled over, and together they hauled him up onto the rocks.

For a moment, neither of the Hardy boys could say a word, they were so exhausted by the ordeal. Above them the storm still raged, the rain still poured from the black skies, the lightning still flickered, and the thunder still boomed and rumbled.

"Boy, that was a narrow squeak!" said Chet solemnly, at last.

"Don't talk about it," said Joe, closing his eyes, as though to shut out the memory of the sight. "I can still see the waves away down beneath me. I was never so near death in my life."

"We'll stick closer together after this. How did it happen?" Frank asked.

"I stopped to tie my shoelace. When I looked up again I couldn't see you chaps at all, so I began to run to catch up. I didn't realize I was so near the edge of the cliff. Then some of the rock must have broken off under my feet, because everything gave way and I felt myself falling."

"You're mighty lucky you're here to tell us about it," said Biff.

"I'll say I am! I just managed to grab that root growing out of the side of the cliff and I hung there until I thought my arms would be pulled out of their sockets. I thought I'd never be able to hold on until you found me."

"It was quite a while before we missed you."

"At any rate, I *couldn't* have held on, but I managed to find that ledge and got my feet on it. That rested me. I was certainly glad when I heard you fellows shouting for me."

Recovering somewhat from their grueling experience, Frank and Joe Hardy got to their feet.

"Let's run for it," suggested Chet. "We're drenched to the skin, as it is, but I don't want to stay out in this storm any longer than I have to."

With one accord, the boys resumed their journey over the rocks. This time no one lagged behind. For safety's sake they stayed close together and well away from the verge of the cliff.

In a short time Frank gave a cry of delight.

"The ravine!" he yelled.

Through the pouring rain, just a few yards ahead, they discerned a deep cut in the rocks.

They scrambled toward it. The ravine was deep and the slope was steep, but they had been fortunate in reaching it just at a point where a path led down among the rocks.

Far below, they could see the beach and the breaking rollers.

Slipping and stumbling, the boys made their way down the steep, winding path in the down-pour. The storm was unabated. Its violence, on the contrary, seemed to have increased. The rain came down in sheets.

Halfway down the path, Joe gave a cry of excitement.

"A cave!"

He pointed down toward the base of the cliff, just visible from the path.

There, but a short distance from the breaking waves, was a dark hole in the steep wall of rock.

CHAPTER XI

FOOTSTEPS IN THE NIGHT

With the goal in sight, the Hardy boys and their chums hastened down the treacherous path, along the steep side of the ravine. The path was slippery and little rivulets of water ran at their feet. Chet Morton slipped and went sprawling in the mud, getting to his feet with exclamations of disgust.

"Oh, well," he said philosophically, "I can't be any wetter than I am already."

Frank consoled him.

"When we get to that cave we'll light a fire and dry ourselves out a bit."

They at length reached the floor of the ravine where little streams of water were coursing from the upper levels to the sea and splashing across to the beach. It was only a few yards from there to the black entrance of the cave, which was well above the reach of high tide.

Frank led the way.

He took a flashlight from his pack as the boys hastened into the dark mouth of the cavern. They were in shelter, at any rate, and they could look out at the streaming rain and feel thankful that they had a roof over their heads, although that roof was a rocky one.

Frank directed the beam of the flashlight into the gloomy interior and in its gleam he saw that their shelter was no mere niche in the face of the cliff, but a cave that led to dark and unknown depths.

"Looks as if we can start our exploring right here and now," he said.

"Explore my neck!" grumbled Chet. "Let's have a fire."

"How about firewood?" inquired the practical Biff.

This had not occurred to the others. They glanced at one another in dismay.

"That's right too," said Joe. "There's not much wood around these rocks and it's all wet by now, anyway."

"Nothing but driftwood," Frank observed disconsolately. "The rain has drenched it." He glanced out, and along the shore he spied a few bits of wood tossed up by the waves, but they were sodden and useless.

"This is going to be fine," said Chet. "We'll have to shiver here all night without a fire. A great beginning to our visit!"

To tell the truth, the boys were feeling none too cheerful over the prospect, for they were all cold, wet, and hungry and they had been looking forward to dry clothes and a hot meal by a roaring fire. Now it seemed that they were doomed to spend the night in the cheerless shelter of a damp, cold cave, without the vestige of a blaze.

"Thank goodness our blankets are dry, at any rate," Joe said philosophically.

Frank moved farther back into the cave, with the flashlight illuminating the way. Suddenly he gave an exclamation of mingled astonishment and delight.

"Well! Can you beat this, fellows?"

"What have you found?"

"Firewood."

"Where?"

The others came hastening over to Frank Hardy.

"Look!" Frank cast the beam of the flashlight against the black wall near by.

Full in the center of the circle of radiance, they saw a neat pile of wood. It had not been placed there by accident; that much was certain. It had been stacked carefully by human hands.

Frank stepped over and picked up one of the sticks.

"Good dry driftwood. We don't have to worry about a fire now."

"I wonder who on earth piled it in here?" remarked Biff.

Chet shrugged.

"Why worry about that? The main thing is that some thoughtful soul has been kind enough to put it here, and we're the boys who are going to use it. Where shall we light the fire, Frank?"

"Right here, I guess. This is far enough back from the entrance so that we won't have to worry about the rain beating in. It's certainly odd how that wood comes to be here, though."

"Probably the mysterious chaps who are doing all the yelling and shooting," said Biff. "We'll be out of luck if this is *their* cave we've stumbled on."

"It's ours now. I don't see any 'No Trespassing' signs." Frank began carrying wood over to the center of the cave. Then he set down the flashlight, took out his pocketknife, and whittled at a particularly dry stick until he had a small heap of shavings. Carefully stacking a few of the smaller sticks over the shavings and the larger sticks above, crosswise so that there were plenty of air spaces, he took a match from his waterproof case and ignited it, putting it to the shavings. They flared up brightly.

Anxiously, the boys watched the little blaze. The flames caught the small sticks, which snapped and crackled. Then, as the fire rose higher, the heavier wood was ignited, and in a short time the boys had a roaring fire. Never had a campfire been so welcome. Frank had been afraid that lack of a draught in the cave might cause so much smoke that they would be almost smothered, but evidently there was some opening in the roof, some overhead passage that acted in the nature of a chimney, for the smoke was carried off above.

As the warmth of the fire penetrated the cave, the boys took off their drenched clothes and spread them about the blaze, in the meantime wrapping themselves in the heavy blankets they had brought with them. Chet produced the frying pan, and the fragrant odor of sizzling bacon soon permeated their refuge. He improvised a tripod from which was suspended a tin pail, duly filled with rain water that coursed in a gushing stream just beside the mouth of the cave, and in a short time the coffee was boiling.

The boys never enjoyed a meal more than they enjoyed their supper in the cave. The driftwood blazed and crackled, casting a cheerful glow, illuminating the rocky ceiling and walls of the underground chamber. With crisp bacon, bread toasted brown before the fire, hot coffee and jam, they ate ravenously, and at last sat back with deep sighs of sheer content.

"This old cave isn't so bad after all," said Chet, wrapping his blanket around him like a cocoon and wriggling his toes toward the flames.

The others glanced toward the entrance of the cavern.

It was pitch dark outside, and still raining. They could hear the constant beat of the down-pour, the incessant roar of the surf, the splash of the waves, the moaning of the cold wind out in the blackness of the night, and the cave seemed the most comfortable place in the world.

"We owe a vote of thanks to the chap who stacked this driftwood in here," said Biff.

"I'll tell the world!" declared Joe. "We'd have been shivering and hungry yet if it hadn't been for him."

"I wonder who he could have been," mused Frank.

"Perhaps somebody who was down here searching for the smugglers or bootleggers or whoever has been raising all the fuss around here," his brother suggested.

"He hasn't shown up yet," Chet remarked cheerfully. He looked out into the storm and shivered. "Somehow, I have an idea he won't be along tonight, either," he added, edging nearer the fire.

"I guess we'd better have a good night's sleep and then start our exploring tomorrow," Frank said. "We can start right on this cave, for that matter. It seems to lead back for quite a distance."

"Sleep sounds good to me." Biff yawned.

Although part of the floor of the cave was rocky, much of it was sand, which provided a fairly comfortable resting place. The boys were tired after their long journey, so they wrapped themselves up in their blankets and were soon drowsily chatting, while the fire died lower and lower.

At last only the embers glowed crimson in the darkness. Chet Morton was already snoring. Soon, all were asleep.

The fire was a scarlet eye in the blackness of the cave. Beyond the entrance, rain still poured in a seemingly endless torrent and the surf roared dully.

An hour passed. Two hours.

Joe, who had been sleeping soundly, was awakened. At first he did not realize where he was, could not imagine why he was sleeping on the ground, wrapped in a heavy blanket, and then it gradually came back to him and he remembered about the cave.

He was just about to turn over and go to sleep again, wondering vaguely what had aroused him, when he heard a footstep.

It came from close by.

He listened, and then he heard it again. Some one was moving cautiously about in the darkness.

Joe raised himself on one elbow and peered into the gloom. But he could see nothing. However, he reasoned that it was probably only one of his chums.

When he heard a rustle, he spoke.

"Is that you, Frank?"

The words rang out clearly in the silence of the cave.

But the consequence was surprising. Instead of the reassuring voice of his brother, Joe heard a muffled exclamation, quick footsteps as some one ran across the floor of the cave, and then the crash of a fallen rock.

CHAPTER XII

A DISAPPEARANCE

"Who is that?" demanded Joe Hardy, scrambling to his feet.

There was no answer. He heard the sound of running footsteps gradually growing fainter.

"Hey, there!" he shouted, now thoroughly aroused. "Fellows! Wake up!"

He stumbled about in the darkness, trying to find his flashlight and his chums. Then he heard Chet's sleepy voice:

"What's the matter? It isn't morning yet. Lemme sleep."

"Wake up! There's some one prowling around here."

"What's that?" called out Frank, from the darkness.

"There was some one else in the cave just now. He woke me up."

"Perhaps it was only Biff. Hey, Biff!"

A deep sigh. Then Biff mumbled:

"Whaddaya want?"

"Wake up." Frank switched on his flashlight and he turned it on each member of the startled group. "Everybody here?"

"Sure!" replied Biff, sitting up in his blanket. "What's wrong?"

"Joe says somebody was prowling around the cave."

"It wasn't me. I've been sleeping like a log."

"It wasn't me either," spoke up Chet.

"I guess I was right, then," declared Joe. "There really *was* somebody. I thought for a minute it might be one of you playing a trick on the rest of us."

"We're all accounted for," said Frank. He got up and tossed a stick of wood on the embers of the fire. In a few minutes it began flaming up brightly, casting a circle of illumination through the cave. "Tell us about it, Joe."

Joe thereupon told of hearing the mysterious footsteps in the cave, of calling out and of hearing the exclamation, the crash of the rock, and the running footsteps as the intruder fled.

"Did he go out the front way?"

Joe shook his head.

"No. He seemed to go farther into the cave, toward the back."

"Well, then," said Frank decisively, "we'll just go and look for him. If he went that way, he's in the cave yet."

"Aw, let's look for him in the morning," protested Chet, as he rubbed his eyes. "I think Joe was dreaming."

"It was no dream. I *heard* him walking around. It wasn't any of us, so it must have been a burglar—or somebody."

"What would a burglar come around here for?"

"Perhaps it's the chap who piled up all that wood," said Frank. "Maybe this is his cave and when he came in and heard Joe call out he got frightened and ran."

"That sounds more reasonable. Anyway, we'll take a look around for him. He can't be far away."

The boys hurriedly dressed. They were soon wide awake, excitement having banished all desire for further sleep.

"We were going to explore in here, anyway," said Frank, as he took his flashlight and led the way toward the back of the cave.

The boys confronted an arch in the rock, an opening that seemed to lead into a tunnel. They approached it cautiously, and Frank often turned the light on the floor to make sure that no pitfalls lay before them.

Frank went into the tunnel first. In single file, the others followed.

It was about fifteen feet in length and about six feet high. As the floor was of solid rock, they were unable to find any foot-prints that would serve to prove that the intruder had passed that way.

The tunnel led to another cave.

"Why, there's a regular chain of caves in here!" exclaimed Joe, as the boys stepped out into a massive underground chamber.

"Our cave was only the beginning," said Chet.

In the glow of their flashlights they saw that the cave in which they now stood had a number of dark openings in the walls. These were, presumably, tunnels leading into further caves beyond.

"There are a dozen different passages out of here. Our friend might have taken any of them," said Frank.

"We'll tackle the biggest," suggested Biff.

"Good idea. If we don't get anywhere, we'll try the others."

The largest tunnel was immediately ahead. Frank, accordingly, stepped into the gloomy passage. The others followed.

"When I was going to sleep tonight, I never thought I'd wake up and take part in an exploring trip underground before morning," observed Chet.

Frank gave an exclamation.

"Here's what we were looking for!" he cried.

"What?"

"A footprint."

The others crowded around him.

Clearly discernible in the radiance of Frank's flashlight, the lads could see the imprint of a boot in a patch of wet sand on the floor of the tunnel.

"Looks like a fresh track, too," said Joe.

"We're on the right trail. Let's keep moving."

With increasing excitement, the chums pressed forward and in a few moments Frank stepped out of the passage into another cave. This was the largest cave of all, an enormous underground vault, and even the flashlight beams failed to reveal the rocky walls and ceiling.

The floor was rough and broken fragments of rock were strewn about.

"Watch your step," warned Frank, as he made his way across the cave.

The others had flashlights and the floor was well illuminated as the boys slowly picked their way among the rocks. The far wall of the huge cavern was still invisible.

"This is a whopper!" said Joe, in an awed whisper.

Frank stopped, with a murmur of annoyance.

"What's the matter?" asked Chet.

"My flashlight. It's on the blink."

Vainly, Frank tried to coax a gleam from the refractory instrument. It was no use. He put the light in his pocket.

"I'll have to fix it tomorrow," he said. "It won't work any more tonight by the looks of things."

"Here's mine," offered Biff.

But Frank declined.

"No thanks. One of you chaps take the lead for a while. I can follow easily enough."

Joe took the lead, as Frank suggested, and the little party moved on again.

It was rough going. The floor of the cave became piled high with rocks, evidently from cave-ins that had occurred in times past; in other parts it was pitted with little gullies and holes. In trying to avoid these, the chums gradually became separated.

Frank stumbled along behind. He felt the loss of his flashlight, but said nothing, relying on finding his way by the radiance provided by the lights carried by the others.

Soon, however, the three lights became scattered. Joe had gone to one side to avoid a huge boulder; Chet had gone to the other side and encountered a pit that prevented him from returning to Joe's trail; Biff had tried to follow Chet and had blundered into a labyrinth of rocks.

Frank stood uncertainly for a moment, then called out.

"We're getting separated. Wait for me."

The walls of the great cave flung back the echoes time and again.

He heard Joe shout:

"Where are you?"

Had it not been for the glow of Joe's light he would never have known where the voice came from because the echoes confused him, and the tones seemed to come from all parts of the cave.

Frank realized that his own shouts would cause the same confusion to the others.

"Don't move around!" he called, "I'll head toward one of the lights."

But evidently his order was misunderstood, for one of the lights began to move erratically through the darkness.

Frank went forward. He blundered against a rock and fell, bruising his knees. He got to his feet and went on, still in the direction of the nearest glow.

He was confused by the moving lights. Had his own flashlight not failed him this would not have happened.

Suddenly, he stumbled.

He lurched forward. His foot groped wildly for the firm rock, but there was nothing to stop his plunge. He had fallen into a pit.

Straight down through the blackness he hurtled, with a wild cry of terror.

The others heard that cry. They heard a far-off crash, and then the clatter of falling rock.

Joe was the first to shout.

"Frank!" he called.

There was no answer. The echoes rang back.

Although the other boys shouted time and again there was no answer from Frank Hardy. They searched frantically, casting the beams of their lights here and there, but they found no trace of him.

CHAPTER XIII

STOLEN SUPPLIES

The other boys searched for nearly an hour, but Frank Hardy seemed to have disappeared literally into the bowels of the earth.

With only their flashlights to illuminate the huge cave, they found it difficult to conduct the search with any degree of satisfaction. They blundered here and there, not at all certain that they were anywhere near the place where their companion had disappeared.

They found several deep pits in the floor of the cave, natural crevices and holes in the rock, but although they shouted at the top of their lungs they heard no answering cry from below.

"He must have fallen down one of these holes, that's certain," Joe declared. "I'm sure we haven't missed any."

"Why doesn't he call back then?" said Biff.

In the glow of the flashlights the boys glanced at one another anxiously. Joe expressed the thought that the others were afraid to put into words.

"Perhaps he can't."

"Do you think he may be dead?" asked Chet quietly.

"We'll hope not," sighed Joe. "But when he doesn't answer, things don't look any too bright. Any of these crevices may be hundreds of feet deep, for all we know."

"It will be a terrible end to our trip if anything like that has happened."

"Not much use waiting for morning," declared Biff. "This cave is just as dark in the daytime as it is right now. I sure wish we had a few more flashlights."

"Or more powerful ones. We can't see very far down the crevices in the rocks, with these lights."

The boys talked in low tones. They were awed by the thought of what might have happened to Frank Hardy. In their ears still rang that last dreadful cry and they could still hear the crashing of rocks as their companion hurtled into the depths. Even now his mangled body might be lying in some subterranean pit from which it would be impossible to recover it. Joe shuddered.

They listened in vain for some faint cry. But there was nothing but the echoes of their own voices.

"We won't give up for a while yet," said Joe, with as much steadiness of voice as he could muster. "We'll search around every pit and hole we can find. I *can't* believe he was killed!"

Keeping close together, the lads slowly crossed the floor of the cave. When they reached an opening in the rocks they directed the beams of their three flashlights into the shadowy depths, thus gaining more radiance than had they been searching singly. Then they yelled and shouted.

There was no reply. The flashlights revealed only jagged walls of rock. There was no sign of Frank.

On to the next crevice. This, fortunately, was not deep, but although the lights revealed the bottom and although they played the triple beams along every inch of the floor of the subterranean ravine, there was no sight of a crumpled figure.

Patiently, they searched the cave, but at last they were forced to admit that they were at a standstill.

"Not much use going any farther just now," sighed Joe. "We need more light." He sat down moodily on a rock and buried his face in his hands.

"I wish we had never followed that fellow who was in the cave," said Chet. "Chances are, it has cost Frank his life."

"I'm not giving up hope yet," Joe declared. "There's a chance that he might have been knocked unconscious by his fall, and if we can only reach him in time we may be able to save him. But these flashlights aren't much help. We're just groping around in the dark."

"I have an idea," offered Biff.

"What is it?"

"Let's build a fire. It might light up the cave enough to show us what we are doing."

"How can we light a fire?" asked Chet. Then he looked up sharply. "You're right, Biff. I forgot that we have lots of wood in the outside cave."

"That's not a bad stunt!" declared Joe hopefully. "With a roaring bonfire in here we'll be able to light up the whole place and see what we're about."

"Let's get at it."

Biff's plan seemed valuable, but before leaving the cave in search of wood, the boys made a last attempt to locate their missing comrade, by shouting loudly. However, as before, there was not the faintest reply.

They made their way out into the next cave, and from there into the outer cavern where they had originally taken refuge from the storm. They were harassed by the thought that death might have overtaken their missing companion, and they said scarcely a word as they went about the business of gathering driftwood for the proposed bonfire.

Each of them took an armful of the wood and they were just about to return through the caves again when Joe noticed something that caused him to drop his wood on the floor with a clatter.

"What's wrong now?" asked Chet, in surprise.

"That's funny," Joe returned. "I was sure we left our supplies right near this woodpile."

"So we did," Biff assured him.

"They're not here now."

"They must be. I piled them there myself, all except a few that I put over by the other wall."

"Come and see for yourself."

Joe turned the beam of his flashlight on the place where Biff had stacked the greater part of their supplies. A loaf of bread and a tin of sardines lay on the rock, but that was all.

Biff's astonishment was so great that he could scarcely speak for a moment.

Then he gasped:

"They've been stolen!"

"All of 'em." demanded Chet, in alarm. The loss of their provisions would be a serious matter to him.

"Where did you put the rest of the stuff, Biff?" asked Joe.

Biff turned his flashlight on the opposite wall. There the light revealed a few bundles and tins, the rest of the supplies.

"Well, they're safe, at any rate."

"But where are the others? They *can't* be stolen. They were here when we went to sleep."

"Must have been stolen while we were in the other caves," declared Chet.

"But who could have taken them?" exclaimed Joe.

"The chap who woke us up. I'll bet he didn't go into the other caves at all, or if he did he just hid himself until we passed. Then he came out and stole our food."

"Perhaps that's what he came for in the first place," suggested Biff.

Solemnly, the lads looked from the loaf of bread and the tin of sardines on the floor of the cave to the few things on the other side.

"He sure didn't leave much. This means we'll have to go back to the village," said Chet, a bit impatiently.

"We can't take time to worry about that now," Joe reminded him. "We have to keep up our search for Frank."

"That's right," agreed Biff. "It's tough to lose our food; but we have enough to last us another day, anyway, and it's more important to get Frank back than our supplies."

"Of course it is," agreed Chet soberly.

The boys picked up their firewood again and, with Joe in the lead, went into the second cave, then on into the cavern where their chum had vanished. As they trudged on through the darkness, following the gleam of the flashlights, Chet and Biff wondered vainly about the thief who had disturbed them and robbed them. Joe's agonized thoughts circled about his vanished brother.

CHAPTER XIV

CAPTAIN ROYAL

When the three boys reached the cave where they had last seen Frank Hardy they piled the driftwood in a heap close by one of the pits in the floor.

They were surprised at the number of holes and crevices they had discovered.

"It's a wonder we weren't all killed," said Chet. "We were all prowling around this cave without any idea of the danger."

"It's a good place to stay out of," Joe remarked. "But first of all we'll try to get Frank out of it too."

He was trying to be hopeful, but it was difficult. The ominous silence since his brother's disappearance had been none too encouraging.

They lit the fire. In a short time, the flames flared high and a flickering radiance illuminated the cave, revealing the damp ceiling high above, the clammy walls in the distance, and the rough floor, seamed and pitted with cracks and holes in the rock.

Methodically, they resumed their search, investigating each of these gigantic crevices. But in spite of all their shouts, in spite of the fact that they were enabled to make a more thorough search now that the cave was not as dark as it had been, in spite of the fact that Joe even descended one of the shallower pits on the chance that Frank might be lying unconscious at the bottom, their search was in vain.

"I'm afraid it's no use," said Biff finally.

"I hate to give up!" declared Joe. "And yet—we've done all we can."

"Better have some sleep and try again tomorrow," Chet suggested. "Frank is either unconscious or—or dead. Some of these pits seem terribly deep."

Joe realized that the advice was reasonable. They were all very tired and in no condition to continue the search. As Chet said, if Frank were alive or conscious, he would have shouted to them.

"All right," agreed Joe. "We'll go back to the other cave. But I'm afraid I'll never be able to sleep."

"We'll have a rest, anyway. Then we'll come back. If we still can't find him we'll go back to the village and get some men to help us with ropes and big searchlights. We'll never go back to Bayport until we find out what has happened to him."

Disconsolately, the boys turned away.

They were almost at the entrance of the second cave when they heard a faint sound.

Joe wheeled about.

"What was that?"

They listened. The sound was repeated. It was like a distant cry.

"Somebody calling!" declared Biff excitedly.

"It must be Frank!"

The boys stood quite still and listened for a repetition of the call. It came again, muffled and far away, but unmistakably a human voice.

With one accord, they turned and ran back into the cave.

"It's Frank!"

They hurried across the treacherous floor in the direction of the sound. It was clearer now.

"Joe! Joe!"

They recognized Frank's voice.

The call came from a part of the cave that they had not searched carefully. Joe shouted back excitedly:

"We hear you, Frank! Call again, so we'll know where to find you!"

Again came the faint shout. It guided them toward a pit that was almost hidden from view by a huge boulder. It was one of the few pits that they had overlooked.

Evidently Frank had seen the reflection of their searchlights, for he shouted weakly:

"Right over here."

At the edge of the pit, they looked down.

There, just a blur in the gloom, they distinguished a figure. Frank was standing up, leaning against the side of the rocky shaft, just a few yards below.

Chet had brought with him a length of stout rope and he quickly flung one end of this down into the pit.

"We'll have you out of there in no time. Boy, but it's good to hear your voice again!" There was heartfelt relief in his tones.

Frank explained that the sides of the pit were too steep to enable him to make his way to the surface without assistance. However, with the aid of the rope, and with Joe and his chums pulling lustily, he was soon hauled to the top.

As he scrambled up out of the pit, the others noticed, in the glow of the fire, that he had a nasty gash across his temple.

"You're hurt!" said Joe, when the first exclamations of enthusiasm and delight had died down.

"I'm all right now," Frank assured them. "I'm a little dizzy yet, and weak, but it isn't serious."

"What happened?"

"I fell down the pit, and I struck my head against the rocks. It must have knocked me out for a few minutes but when I came to, I began to shout."

"A few minutes!" exclaimed Chet. "We've been hunting for you over an hour."

Frank looked incredulous.

"An hour! Why, I thought I had been unconscious only a little while."

The others then told him of the search they had made and of their anxiety on his account. However, they were so relieved at seeing him safe and sound again that they soon forgot the serious side of the affair and Chet remarked that Frank had been lucky in having an hour's sleep while the rest had been shouting their lungs out. They trooped out of the cavern back toward their own cave, and Joe told his brother about the missing supplies.

"That's weird," said Frank. "Were they stolen while we were in the big cave?"

"It looks like that."

"But the man who woke us up went into the big cave ahead of us."

"He may have hidden and we might have passed him."

"That's possible. Perhaps it wasn't a man at all. The thief might have been an animal."

The others had not considered this explanation.

"No use crying over spilled milk now," declared Frank. "We'd just better go back to sleep and hunt for our supplies in the morning."

When morning came, a diligent search of the cave failed to reveal any clues that would help the boys trace the thief, whether man or animal.

"We're out of luck, that's all," concluded Frank finally. "Our friend must have fooled us nicely. Perhaps he came into the cave to steal supplies in the first place, then slipped past us in the darkness when we went to look for him."

"And helped himself," said Chet gloomily.

"He left something, at any rate. We won't starve today, and if our grub runs out we can go back to the village for more. We'll make the best of it. Let's start exploring the shore-line. That's what we came for."

The matter of the stolen supplies was thus dismissed, although Chet was very gloomy for some time as he thought of the food that had been taken, notably a tin of strawberry jam, of which he was inordinately fond.

The storm was over, and from the cave they could see the sun shining on the blue waters of the sea. They lost no time in eating breakfast and then hastening down to the beach. Although they were dubious as to the advisability of leaving their remaining supplies in the cave, they reasoned that as it was impossible to take the provisions everywhere with them, they would have to run the risk of further theft.

Out on the beach, beneath the lowering black cliffs, they forgot the unfortunate beginning of their quest in the delight of the keen, salty air and the cool breeze from the sea. The sandy shore wound about the face of a great bluff of black rock and when the lads had skirted this precipice they were confronted by a dark opening at the base of the cliff just a few yards away.

"Another cave!" exclaimed Frank.

Chet gave a cheer.

"Let's investigate."

They advanced on the cave, but when they were just in front of the entrance they halted with exclamations of surprise.

Tacked on a board stuck in the sand beside the cave-mouth was a tattered fragment of paper. On it, in black letters scrawled with a heavy pencil, they read:

NO TRESPASSING.

The boys looked at this sign in astonishment.

"By order of the chief of police," murmured Chet, with a grin.

"Looks as if somebody has been here before," Biff observed.

"Perhaps somebody just put up the sign for a joke. Let's take a peep inside."

Frank advanced toward the cave.

But at the entrance he paused. He peered into the gloomy beyond and then turned back to his companions.

"The sign isn't a joke," he said quietly. "Somebody lives here!"

"*Lives* there!" said Chet incredulously.

"Come and see for yourself."

Curiously, the lads crowded into the entrance of the cave. They saw at a glance that Frank was right. In the gloomy interior of the cave they could see a crude table, a mattress with blankets, and on a ledge of rock was an improvised cupboard consisting of an old soap box. That the cave had only been recently tenanted they saw by the fact that the box held some canned goods and some other provisions that had certainly not been there long.

"Well, I'll be switched!" declared Joe. "We have a neighbor."

"We certainly have. And if I'm not mistaken, here he comes now."

Frank was looking down the beach. The others turned.

"What an odd duck he is!" exclaimed Biff.

"I'll say he is!" cried Chet Morton. "Where do they get 'em like that?"

Coming around a jutting promontory of rock was a strange old man, clad in fisherman's garb, with a huge straw hat on his head. He had not seen them as yet. He was singing, in a high-pitched voice, and even at that distance they could make out the words:

*"I'm Captain Royal, of the King's Navee,
And I want two lumps of sugar in my tea."*

CHAPTER XV

THE OLD SAILOR

Having concluded this verse, the strange old man elevated one arm above his head and danced a couple of steps of a sailor's hornpipe. In the middle of this he caught sight of the boys, and came to an abrupt stop.

"Ahoy!" he shouted.

"Ahoy!" cried Chet promptly.

The man in the straw hat advanced.

"When did you come ashore?"

"Just this morning."

The old man drew closer. He was an odd figure, in the flopping straw hat, with oilskins much too big for him, and as he came up to the mouth of the cave he looked closely at the lads, then smiled and extended his hand.

"I'm Captain Royal," he announced. "You should have saluted, but I guess you didn't know."

To make up for this breach of etiquette, the boys saluted, and this appeared to gratify the old gentleman immensely.

"You're landlubbers, eh?"

"I suppose so," admitted Frank, with a smile.

"Well, we can't all be sailors. It isn't often people come to see me."

"Do you live here?" asked Joe, indicating the cave.

"This is where I live when I'm ashore. I'm resting up between cruises just now."

The old man sat down on the sand and fanned himself with the straw hat, for it was a warm morning and the sun was strong. The boys looked at him curiously. In spite of his garb, he did not look like a sea-faring man; his skin was tanned, it is true, but it was not the deep, mahogany tan of one who has lived for years in many climes. His voice was high-pitched and his expression was mild. But the boys were old enough to know that one cannot always judge by appearances.

"What are your names?" asked the old man.

The lads introduced themselves.

"Glad to meet you," returned Captain Royal. "It ain't often I have visitors. I get used to being alone."

"It's lonely enough here," agreed Frank.

"It isn't bad. Not half as lonely as the time I got marooned in the South Seas."

The boys looked at him with new interest.

"You were marooned?"

"Aye. It was when I was in charge of a destroyer cruising the South Seas a good many years ago. We landed for water on a little island that you won't find on any of the maps. It was a hot day—very hot. Must have been over a hundred degrees in the shade. So while my men were loading the water on my boat I sat down in the shade of a cactus tree. Before I knew it, I was asleep."

"And they went away and left you?"

"They did."

"But you were the captain!"

"I guess they thought I was in my cabin, and of course none of 'em dared disturb me. When I woke up, the ship was gone."

"Gosh!" exclaimed Biff.

"Well, sir, I didn't know what to do. I was like this here fellow Robinson Crusoe, that you read about. But I had to make the best of it, so I fixed myself up a little house and I lived there for nearly six months, all by myself."

"Didn't the boat come back for you?"

"They couldn't find the island again. It wasn't marked on the maps. The engineer couldn't set a course back to the island. Anyway, the quartermaster who took charge of the schooner after they found I was gone, didn't want to find me, I guess. He wanted my job."

"How did you find anything to eat when you were on the island?"

"Oh, there was lots to eat. Cocoanuts and prunes and bananas and grapefruit and figs and all sorts of fruit. There was plenty of mud-turtles on the island, so I had mock turtle soup whenever I wanted it. I tell you, I lived high. Once in a while I had my little troubles, of course, and two or three times I had some mighty narrow escapes. There was a rhinoceros came after me once."

"A rhinoceros!"

"Aye! He swam up to the island one day. I was just in for my morning swim when I saw his big ears flapping and heard him give a roar. I tell you, I was scared. He came surging through the waves and up on the beach and he chased me clean up a pineapple tree. I had to stay there for three days until he went away, and I had nothing but pineapples to eat. I was never so sick of pineapples in my life. I've never been able to eat one since."

Frank glanced at his brother. He was beginning to suspect that Captain Royal was having some fun at their expense. The old man rattled on.

"The rhinoceros finally swam out to sea again and I was able to come down. I lived on that island for half a year, hoping that my warship would come back, but it never did. So I made myself a raft and loaded it up with water and fruit and finally sailed away. It took me more than a month of steady sailing before I finally reached land off the coast of South America. By jing, I was glad when I saw the Andes Mountains again. I landed at a port where there was a ship, and I'm swizzled if it wasn't my own boat."

"Your own boat!"

"Yes sir. I could hardly believe my eyes. So I come on board, and they were going to throw me off."

"Why?" asked Chet, in surprise.

"They didn't know me. You see, I hadn't been able to shave when I was on the island, and I'd grown a beard. So nobody knew me and they wouldn't believe me when I said I was their captain. But I told them to lend me a pair of scissors and a razor and I took off that beard and stepped out on deck, and by jing they all saluted me then, I can tell you. I made the quartermaster walk the plank and we all sailed back to San Francisco."

"That was quite an adventure," said Frank politely.

"Oh, I've had many things happen to me. I've been in a lot of battles, too. Of course, I've retired from the navy now, for there isn't the excitement nowadays."

"Were you in the Spanish-American war?" asked Chet.

"I was all through it from start to finish. I had a narrow escape during that war. I took my ship out one night off the Philippines to see if I could catch a Spanish warship that I'd heard was in the neighborhood, and we sighted her just about midnight, not half a mile away. So we pumped a couple of shots over her keel and she turned and went steaming away to the north. Well, I gave chase, but the Spaniard was fast and it was three hours before we came alongside. We were just going to board the ship when the steward came up to me and said some other boats were coming up. There was. Five of 'em. All Spanish."

"What did you do?"

"What could I do? I couldn't run away. I told my men to get on board the Spaniard and I took all the sailors from that boat and made 'em surrender and put 'em on my ship. So the other boats didn't dare fire at my ship for fear of killing their own men and they didn't dare fire at the boat I was on for fear of sinking their own ship. So we opened fire on them and they didn't dare fire a shot back."

"That was mighty clever."

"Wasn't it? I sunk two of the Spaniards and the others surrendered and I brought 'em back to Manila Bay. I was given a medal for that."

Captain Royal looked very pleased with himself, and he dug into a capacious pocket and produced a plug of tobacco, taking a huge bite.

"Oh, I've had experiences," he said, wagging his head. "Are you going to be around here long?"

"Just a few days."

"I'd invite you to come and live in my cave, only there ain't much room."

"We have a cave of our own, farther down the shore."

"That's fine. I'll call and see you some time."

"We'll be glad to have you do that," said Joe cordially.

The old man got up and walked toward the entrance of his own cave.

"Come on inside," he urged. "You'd better stay and have some dinner with me. I was out fishing this morning and I caught quite a few fish. As soon as they're ready, we'll sit down and eat."

The boys accepted the invitation eagerly, and trooped into the cave of Captain Royal. Chet looked around hungrily for the fish, but there was none in sight. The old man invited them to sit down, and they squatted in the sand, there being no chairs or boxes.

"Are you the only person living around here, Captain Royal?" asked Frank.

"The only one. I thought I was the only person who knew about these caves until I saw you lads here."

"There was some one visited us last night—" began Frank. Then he hesitated in surprise, for Captain Royal leaped to his feet, a look of fear on his face.

"What's that?" he exclaimed. "Some one visited you! Don't tell me there's some one else around here!"

CHAPTER XVI

"GO AWAY!"

"Some one came into our cave last night and stole most of our supplies," said Frank.

"A man?"

"We didn't see him, but it could scarcely have been an animal of any kind, for he carried off a whole box of food."

"You don't say!" exclaimed Captain Royal.

"And we found a footprint too," added Joe.

Captain Royal shook his head in amazement.

"This is very strange. I had no idea there was any one else around this part of the coast. You can see for yourself that it is hard to get here, and if there were any one else around I would be sure to see him."

"And you've seen no one?"

"Not a living soul, besides yourselves. And he stole your supplies?"

"Nearly all of them. He left us some canned beans, a loaf of bread, some butter and some coffee; but that's about all."

"Canned beans! It's a long time since I've had any canned beans. Perhaps we could trade."

"That's not a bad idea," said Chet. "There are other things we need."

"I have some dried fish here," said the captain. "I have fish and a case of eggs and some other things. Go get those beans and we'll trade."

Chet hastened back to the other cave and returned in due time with the cans of beans, which the captain accepted with considerable delight. In exchange, the boys received some fish and two dozen eggs.

"I got the eggs off a boat yesterday," explained Captain Royal, "and I've been thinking ever since that it was foolish of me to buy a whole case, because they mightn't keep. I'd rather have canned beans any day."

When the exchange was effected, their host suddenly became silent and sat for a long time looking gloomily at the sand. The boys were wondering when the promised fish dinner was to put in its appearance. Apparently, Captain Royal had forgotten all about his invitation. Suddenly he looked up.

"Well," he demanded curtly, "what are you hanging around for, boys?"

They gazed at the man in surprise.

"Why—you asked us to stay," stammered Frank.

"Yes," returned the old man tartly, "but I didn't ask you to stay all day."

The boys were so astonished at this sudden change of front that for a moment they thought the captain was joking. But they soon learned that he was in earnest, for he got to his feet with a mutter.

"Must I order you out?"

"Why, what's the matter?" inquired Joe, "Have we offended you in any way?"

"Be off with you! Go away! Get out of here."

The boys got to their feet, vastly surprised.

"Go away!" repeated Captain Royal, advancing on them with a threatening gesture. "Clear out. I prefer to be alone."

"Why, certainly," said Frank. "We had no idea we were disturbing you, Captain."

"Don't argue. Get out. By jing, I've had enough people bothering me lately and I'm not going to stand for it any longer. I thought when I found this cave that people would leave me alone, and now I am annoyed by a pack of meddlesome boys. Go away!"

Without further ado, the lads retreated from the cave. Captain Royal stood in the entrance, shaking his fist at them angrily.

"Clear out of here!" he stormed. "Don't let me catch you around this cave again or it will be the worse for you."

Then he wheeled about abruptly and disappeared into the darkness of the cave.

The boys looked at one another in amazement.

"Can you beat that!" exclaimed Chet.

"What's wrong with the old coot, anyway?" demanded Biff. "Has he gone crazy?"

"I can't understand it," said Frank. "One minute he invites us to stay for dinner, and in the next breath he orders us away."

Joe tapped his head significantly.

"I think he's a little bit off his head."

"Perhaps it's the heat," volunteered Chet.

"He is certainly a character," Biff declared. "I don't know what to make of him."

The boys went back down the beach toward their own cave. Fortunately, before he started, Chet had had enough presence of mind to pick up the provisions they had obtained from the old man, so the boys were so much to the good, at any rate.

"He's crazy," insisted Joe. "Those stories he told us were the wildest yarns I ever heard in my life. I wonder if he thought we were simple enough to believe them."

"As if anybody didn't know that a rhinoceros couldn't swim the ocean!" scoffed Chet.

"And pineapples that grow on a tree!"

"I don't think he's ever been a sailor at all," Frank declared. "His naval terms were certainly mixed. He called his ship a destroyer and a warship and a schooner and didn't seem to notice the difference. And he said the quarter-master was in charge after he left the ship."

"And everybody knows they don't make people walk the plank nowadays."

"His stories were as full of holes as a sieve. But I don't know whether he told them just for the fun of stuffing us or just because he is clean crazy and doesn't know any better."

The boys discussed Captain Royal and his eccentric behavior all the way back to their cave, and agreed that if the old gentleman was not a lunatic he was at least slightly unbalanced.

"The very fact that he lives away off here all by himself proves it," insisted Joe. "No man in his right mind would live in a cave down in this lonely spot. I wonder if he was the man who came and stole our supplies last night."

Frank shook his head.

"I thought of that and I took a look around his cave, but there was no sign of any of our stuff. Besides, he seemed much surprised when we told him there was some one else hanging around."

"He might have been smart enough to act as though he were surprised. Perhaps he had our provisions hidden away."

"But why would he want to trade with us?"

"Because he's crazy."

The lads went back to their own cave and then went for a swim in the surf, forgetting Captain Royal in their enjoyment of the stimulating salt water. In spite of the generally rocky nature of the coast the beach in front of their cave was sandy and sloped gently into the water, providing an ideal bathing place.

When the swim was over they prepared lunch from what limited food they had on hand, and in the afternoon they went back down the shore again to resume their tour of exploration.

They did not see the captain again, although they passed his cave, keeping at a respectful distance so as not to incur his wrath. Farther down the shore they found a series of large caves, and some of these they explored. However, they found nothing of interest, although they spent the entire afternoon prowling about the caverns. At sundown they returned, footsore and weary, to their own headquarters.

After supper they sat about their campfire chatting, but Chet and Biff were so tired that their heads soon began to nod and they decided to retire for the night. Joe would have done likewise, but Frank asked him to sit up a while longer.

Biff and Chet were soon snoring, and not until then did Frank broach the subject on his mind.

"Did you notice an expression Captain Royal used several times when he was talking to us?" he asked his brother.

Joe reflected.

"I can't say that I noticed anything in particular," he confessed.

"Don't you remember that he said 'by jing' now and then?"

Joe looked up, startled.

"Now I remember! Yes, he did say that. And 'by jing' is the very expression—"

"The very expression Evangeline Todd said her missing brother used so often!"

"That's a fact!" exclaimed Joe. "And now that I come to think of it, I remember his shoelaces."

"They were untied."

"And Todham Todd had a habit of going about with his shoelaces untied too!"

CHAPTER XVII

THE MAN ON THE SHORE

The Hardy boys looked at one another solemnly in the glow of the campfire.

"Do you think Captain Royal and Todham Todd are one and the same man?" asked Joe.

"What do you think of it yourself?"

"It certainly looks strange. But how *could* this strange old chap be Todham Todd? How would the college professor get away down among these caves, and what would be his idea in passing himself off as a sea captain?"

Frank was thoughtful.

"Stranger things have happened. You remember that Evangeline Todd suggested that her brother might have lost his memory. He was always more or less eccentric, no doubt, and if he was suffering from amnesia there is no telling where he might go or what he might do."

"It's mighty strange if we have run across him in this place. Perhaps it's just a coincidence that Captain Royal says 'by jing' once in a while. As for having his shoelaces untied, he seems pretty sloppy anyway, and that would be only natural."

"Oh, yes, there's every chance in the world that Captain Royal is simply an eccentric old tar. I agree with you there. Just the same, we can't afford to overlook the chance that he *might* be Todham Todd."

"How are we going to find out?"

"If we asked him, he would deny it, certainly. But perhaps if we could talk to him and ask a few questions he might give himself away."

"If he has lost his memory he would not remember anything to give away."

"I hadn't thought of that," admitted Frank. "Still, my plan is worth trying, don't you think?"

"It certainly is. But do you think he'll talk to us at all, after what happened today?"

"Perhaps he's forgotten all about it by now. He might be as nice as pie if we went back."

"Yes, he seems a rather changeable old boy," laughed Joe. "And perhaps if he isn't around we might find some clue in that cave of his."

"Good idea. We'll make a try at it tomorrow."

"Do you think we should tell Chet and Biff?" asked Joe.

"I don't think so. Not just yet. After all, they don't know about the Todd affair, and if we find out that our suspicions are all wrong there'll be no harm done and they'll be none the wiser."

"But how can we question him if they're with us?"

"We'll make some excuse to get away by ourselves. Of course, we may be disappointed. The more I think of it the more impossible it seems that Todham Todd should actually be living here. But it is strange that he hasn't been found before this if he is living in any town or city where people would meet him and talk about him."

"Dad said he was traced as far as Claymore and there the trail vanished. Claymore isn't very far from this coast."

"That's right. He may have wandered down to these caves."

"How about the shooting and the mysterious lights we were warned about?"

Frank laughed.

"Oh, as to that," he said, "I think Captain Royal has just been having a little fun at the expense of the people around here. Perhaps he is trying to keep people from finding out too much about him."

"Well, we'll find out all we can, anyway. He can't scare us."

Having decided to investigate the eccentric old gentleman further, the Hardy boys rolled themselves up in their blankets and went to sleep. Frank hardly dared hope that his surmise was correct and that in Captain Royal they had discovered the missing college professor, but he was convinced that the old man was not a sailor, in spite of his claims, and the circumstances of the exclamation "by jing" and the untied shoelaces, slender as the clues were, led him to believe that they were at least on a trail worth following.

When the boys awakened next morning they found the sea hidden by a dense fog. It was damp and cold and the weather put all idea of further exploration of the coast out of their heads.

"I'm not going to wander among the rocks in this fog," declared Chet emphatically. "If it got worse we'd have a fine time finding our way back here."

"Looks to me like a good morning for fishing," said Biff.

Chet greeted this suggestion with enthusiasm.

"That's the brightest idea you've had in years. We brought lots of tackle with us, thank goodness, and there's a high rock over there that hangs over deep water. Perhaps we could catch a whale or so for lunch."

Frank and Joe saw their opportunity. They encouraged their two chums to go fishing. As for themselves, they said they would go down to Captain Royal's cave and see if the old gentleman was in a better humor than he had been the previous day.

"You're welcome," said Chet. "I've had enough of that old lad's society to last me the rest of my life. He'll probably set his dog on you, if he has one."

"I didn't see any dog there yesterday," grinned Joe.

"Well, he'll likely have a dogfish then. You want to be careful. Better come fishing with us."

But the Hardy boys persisted in their determination to beard the lion in his den again, as Frank put it, so Biff and Chet unpacked the fishing tackle and made their plans for a morning's sport.

After breakfast they set out for the high rock, Chet ironically asking the Hardy boys to give his love to Captain Royal, and Frank and Joe started off down the beach, delighted that they had escaped so easily.

They proceeded along the beach. The fog hung low over the sea and it was so dense that they could scarcely distinguish the outline of the dark cliffs above.

"Not much chance of catching Captain Royal away from home today, I'm thinking," said Frank.

"No, he's likely sitting in his cosy little cave beside a good fire. Well, he may feel more like talking."

There was no breeze blowing, and the sea lay calm and slatey beneath the fog. It was a damp, clammy morning and the chill penetrated to the bone. The boys felt rather guilty at having left Chet and Biff, to set out on this expedition of their own, but as Frank had pointed out it was, after all, private business. They well knew that if their suspicions were incorrect, Chet would joke about the affair unmercifully. It was better to keep it to themselves until they were certain of their ground.

They were just approaching the cliff that hid Captain Royal's cave from view when Frank halted and peered through the fog at the base of the rocks some distance ahead.

"Do you see somebody lying there, Joe?"

Joe looked in the direction he indicated.

"Looks like an old log—no, it moved!"

"Seems like a man sprawled on the sand."

"Perhaps it's Captain Royal. Maybe he fell and hurt himself."

The boys hastened across the rocks in the direction of the figure on the shore.

As they drew nearer they saw that it was indeed a man who lay sprawled at the base of the rocks, apparently asleep. However, they soon saw that it was not Captain Royal.

"Perhaps somebody fell off the cliffs from above," ventured Joe, as they hastened up to the recumbent figure.

Frank looked up. The cliff loomed high above.

"If he did, we can't help him now. He would be dead."

They came up to the man sprawled on the sand. He was not dead. An empty bottle lying by his side told the reason for his slumber.

"He's drunk!"

The man's face was turned away from them and the boys could not distinguish his features. He was roughly dressed and his clothes were wet with fog.

Just then the fellow stirred restlessly in his drunken sleep. He slowly turned his head.

When the boys saw his face they gasped with surprise.

"It's Carl Schaum!" exclaimed Frank.

It was indeed the escaped automobile thief, the man who had stolen Frank's motorcycle the day the boys left Bayport.

CHAPTER XVIII

THE PRISONER

Carl Schaum did not awaken. His slumber was too deep. He was quite senseless from the effects of the liquor he had drunk.

"This is luck!" exclaimed Frank. "I wonder how he got here!"

"I suppose he's hiding down in these caves away from the police."

Something beside the bottle near the slumbering man caught Frank's eye. He bent forward and examined it.

It was a small package containing several tins of meat, of the same variety the Hardy boys and their chums had brought with them on their expedition to the caves.

"There's our thief!" Frank declared, with conviction. "It was Carl Schaum who stole the provisions from our cave."

There seemed little doubt that this was the case. The evidence of the package of food was conclusive.

"What shall we do with him?" asked Joe.

Frank groped in his pocket and produced a length of stout cord.

"We'll tie him up first. He's an escaped criminal and it's our duty to turn him over to the police."

"What if he puts up a fight?"

"He's too drunk. Anyway, we should be more than a match for him."

They looked at the man sprawled on the ground. He was snoring loudly, quite oblivious of his danger. Quietly, the Hardy boys took up their positions, one on each side of the fellow, and then with a quick movement they turned him over on his back and pinned his arms behind him.

To their surprise, Carl Schaum did not struggle. He merely groaned in his sleep.

"He's dead drunk," said Frank. "We won't have any trouble with him."

Quickly he flipped the cord about Carl Schaum's wrists, and they bound the unconscious man. Still he did not awaken. When the boys were satisfied that their captive was firmly trussed up they stood back to await further developments.

Carl Schaum snored on.

"I guess we'd better wake him up," said Frank, with a mischievous grin.

"It would take a cannon to waken him, by the looks of things."

"Good cold water should do the trick."

Frank went down to the shore, took off his hat and dipped it in the sea. He hastened back, the hat half full of water, and dashed it in Carl Schaum's face.

There was a splutter. Then Joe, anxious to be in on the fun, filled his hat and flung a copious supply of cold water at their captive.

Carl Schaum blinked, groaned, spluttered again, and tried to sit up.

"This will make us even for stealing my motorcycle," said Frank, as he dashed more water into the fellow's face.

"And this," said Joe, hastening up with another hatful.

Carl Schaum was literally drenched. He opened his eyes, then gave vent to a strangled yell. Frank managed to fling another hatful of water into his face before the boys decided that their captive was sufficiently awake.

"Hey! What's this?" roared Schaum indignantly. He had just discovered that his wrists were bound.

"Just a little joke," said Frank.

Water was streaming down the man's face. He was thoroughly aroused by now.

He was still too dazed to recognize the Hardy boys. As he sat on the beach, with his wet hair down over his eyes, his clothes completely soaked, he was a ridiculous object, and his expression of mingled wrath and surprise made it difficult for the lads to restrain their laughter.

"Lemme go!" demanded Schaum, struggling to release his wrists, without success.

Frank shook his head.

"Nothing doing. You're wanted back in Bayport, Schaum, and that is where you're going."

Schaum gasped.

"Bayport!" he said, after a moment. "Where's that? I never heard of the place."

"Oh, yes you have. You escaped from the Bayport jail, Schaum, and they'll be glad to see you back again."

"You're crazy!" the rascal stormed. "I was never in any jail!"

"How about the stolen automobiles on the Shore Road?"

"And Gus Montrose and the others in the gang?"

Carl Schaum saw that his bluff had failed. Then he looked more closely at the brothers. He turned pale.

"The Hardy boys!" he exclaimed.

"At your service," returned Joe, with a bow.

"You see, we know what we're talking about. Get up, Schaum."

"What are you going to do with me?"

"Get up!" repeated Frank. "We're going to take you out to the road and see that you're turned over to the authorities."

"Don't do that," whined Schaum. "Honest, I never had anything to do with stealing them cars. Let me go."

"You were in the gang, and if they've been punished, it isn't fair that you should get off," insisted Frank. "You escaped from the jail and if you are innocent you had nothing to fear. You'd better get up and come with us."

He prodded the prisoner firmly with the toe of his heavy tramping shoe, and Schaum struggled to his feet. He made many whining pleas for mercy, but the Hardy boys were determined that he should be sent back to Bayport to answer for his participation in the Shore Road automobile thefts.

"I've reformed," sniveled Schaum. "I've gone straight ever since I got out of jail."

"Yes, you have!" laughed Frank. "How about stealing my motorcycle while we were in swimming?"

Schaum looked confused.

"I didn't know it was your motorcycle."

"It doesn't matter whose motorcycle it was. You meant to steal it. That doesn't look as if you've reformed very much. No, you must come along with us."

Unwillingly, Carl Schaum stumbled along the beach with his two captors.

Frank and Joe did not have a very clear idea of what they were to do with Schaum, now that they had captured him. At first they thought of keeping him in the cave, but Joe pointed out that he might get away again and that it would mean too much trouble keeping guard over him.

"And he'd eat too much," added Frank. "That's another little score we have to settle with you, Schaum. You were in the cave the other night and stole most of our provisions."

"I was hungry," whined the prisoner. "I only meant to borrow a little bit of food."

"Borrowers don't come sneaking around when every one is asleep. Where are our provisions now?"

"They're in my own cave," said Schaum sullenly.

"Where is that?"

"Try to find it."

"All right," returned Frank. "When you go back to Bayport you will find yourself facing an extra charge of robbery. We'll lay a complaint against you for stealing our provisions. You've already admitted that you took them, so it will go hard with you."

Schaum wilted at this threat.

"Aw, don't tell on me," he begged. "Your grub is all right. It's in the cave that you'll find not ten feet from where I was lying on the beach. I got to drinking last night and I wandered out of the cave and fell down."

"I'm glad you've decided to be sensible," observed Frank. "We'll go to the cave and get our food when we come back. We didn't know you had a cave."

"I came here just a little while before you boys came."

"Did you bring your trunk?" asked Frank, with a grin. "Anything in your cave you'd like to take back to jail with you?"

Schaum shook his head.

"No," he answered shortly. "Just a pair of blankets. You can have 'em."

"They'll give you blankets in jail."

The boys soon reached their own cave. There was no sign of Chet and Biff, and they realized that the fishermen might be far off down the shore by now, so they decided to take Carl Schaum out to the road themselves.

They clambered up the trail through the ravine until they reached the top of the cliff, and then they made their way over the rocks and down the hillside back to the fisherman's cottage. The fisherman was at home, and when he saw the little procession coming down the path he rushed out, anxious to learn what had happened. He was greatly excited when he saw that the villainous-looking Carl Schaum was bound.

"Have you cotched the man who was firin' off all the guns?" he asked.

Frank shook his head.

"I don't think this is he," he said, remembering that Schaum had reached the caves only a short time in advance of their own arrival. "But he's almost as bad."

"What's he been doin'?"

The Hardy boys explained why they had captured Carl Schaum, and when the fisherman learned that they were going to take their captive out to the main road he promptly volunteered the use of his car, an ancient and decrepit flivver. The boys had been wondering how they would get Schaum out to the road by motorcycle, and the fisherman's offer solved this difficulty.

Accordingly, they all wedged themselves into the ramshackle car and set out for the main road, which they reached in due time. Frank and Joe did not want to waste too much time with Schaum, and they decided to wait in hope that some passing motorist would take the fellow in to the nearest police station.

In a short time a car came into sight and when it came near, Frank stepped out into the road and signaled the driver to stop. The automobile slowed down.

The man at the wheel looked at them curiously.

Then Frank gave an exclamation of delight.

"Why, he's from Bayport!" he shouted to Joe. "It's Mr. Simms."

At the same moment, the driver recognized Frank.

"Hello there, Hardy!" he exclaimed. "What are you doing so far away from home?"

Frank and Joe knew Mr. Simms, having met him at the time of the solving of the Shore Road mystery, because he was one of the automobile owners who had suffered at the hands of the car thieves. The very car Mr. Simms was driving just then had been recovered by the Hardy boys when they had found the automobiles stolen by Gus Montrose, Carl Schaum and the other members of the gang.

"This is luck!" exclaimed Frank. "How would you like to take a passenger back to Bayport with you?"

"Do you want a ride?" asked Mr. Simms. "Hop in."

"I'm not asking for myself. But our friend here is wanted back in Bayport. Perhaps you could take him in."

Mr. Simms looked doubtfully at Carl Schaum.

"Well," he said slowly, "if he's a friend of yours, I suppose it's all right—"

He had noticed that Schaum's wrists were tied.

Frank laughed.

"I was just joking. This is one of the fellows who stole your car last month. Carl Schaum—"

"Oh! The thief that escaped, eh?"

"Yes. We ran across him down along the shore, and we were anxious to turn him over to the police again."

"Put him in the car," said Simms grimly. "I'll put the rascal where he belongs."

Rejoiced at having the prisoner taken off their hands so readily, the Hardy boys bundled Schaum into the rear seat of the automobile. They apologized to Mr. Simms for troubling him, but the man assured them that it was no trouble at all.

"It's a pleasure," he said. "I'll see that he doesn't get away." He glared at Carl Schaum. "So you're one of the scoundrels who stole my car, are you? And you thought you were going to escape a term in jail! You'll have to be mighty smart to do it then, for I'm going to break a few speed records getting you back to Bayport. I'm going to enjoy this trip."

He waved good-bye to the Hardy boys.

"I don't know how you caught him," he said; "but I'll tell the Bayport police to give you the credit. I'm certainly glad I came along in time to drive this guy back to jail, where he belongs."

With that, he drove off and in a few minutes he was carrying out his promise to break speed records on the way back to Bayport, while the helpless prisoner in the back seat was jounced and bounced until his teeth rattled.

Frank and Joe grinned.

"I guess Carl Schaum won't forget that ride for a while."

"Serves the rogue right!" declared the fisherman.

"Well, let's be getting back," said Frank. "The morning is almost gone and we haven't called on Captain Royal yet."

CHAPTER XIX
CLIPPINGS

Their friend, the fisherman, was greatly interested in the Hardy boys' adventure with Carl Schaum and wanted to know all the details of the affair. Frank and Joe told him why they had captured Schaum, and also told him of the Shore Road automobile thefts, although they modestly omitted any mention of their own part in bringing the car thieves to justice.

When they arrived back at the cottage the fisherman was anxious that they go in and continue the chat, but the Hardy boys wanted to return to the caves.

"Some other time," they promised.

"Well," said the fisherman reluctantly, "if you won't come in, I suppose you won't; but you must come back and see me before you leave these parts. You're smart lads, cotchin' that jailbird, and I'm sure he's the fellow that's been performin' all the monkeyshines down around Honeycomb Caves."

Frank and Joe said nothing. It occurred to them that possibly the fisher folk did not know of Captain Royal's presence in the vicinity and they preferred to keep the secret to themselves.

"Yes," said the man, wagging his head, "I guess he was the chap, all right, even if you don't seem to think so."

"He was a thief, at any rate," said Joe.

"He stole your grub, you was sayin'. If you need more, you're welcome to anything I've got here. It ain't much, but you're more'n welcome," said their hospitable friend.

The boys thanked him, but assured him that Carl Schaum had been forced to divulge the hiding place of the provisions. With great glee they told how they had frightened him into telling.

"We're all set for a few days' stay now," said Frank. "I guess we won't be bothered any more."

The boys parted from the fisherman and ascended the path up the hillside again. Up over the rocks, along the cliff edge until they came to the ravine, down the steep slope, and after an arduous hour they were again at their cave.

Chet and Biff were nowhere to be seen, so the Hardy boys assumed that they were still fishing.

"When we tell them all the adventures we've had, they'll be as mad as hops," laughed Frank.

"We've sure covered a lot of territory since they last saw us."

"And the day isn't over yet. We still have Captain Royal to attend to."

It was still damp and foggy as they went on down the beach, and although it was midday the mist hung so heavily over the sea that they could see only a short distance ahead. It was almost as dark as at dusk.

"I believe the fog is growing worse," remarked Frank.

"It certainly seems worse since we've got down on the shore again."

"I hope Chet and Biff don't get lost."

"Not much danger of getting lost around here. It's pretty hard to get far from the ocean, and once you're on the beach you just have to keep walking until you find the caves."

The boys came to the place where they had spied Carl Schaum in his drunken slumber.

"Let's see if he was telling us the truth about that cave of his," Joe suggested. "We might as well make sure that our provisions are safe."

"There's a cave here, all right. Look, I can see it over by those big boulders."

"So there is. Queer that we didn't notice it before. The rocks hide it from view unless you stand right in front of it."

"Trust Carl to pick a good hiding place. If he hadn't made the mistake of getting drunk and wandering beyond his own front door, he might be a free man yet."

"It isn't the first time that liquor has landed a man in jail."

The boys approached the entrance of the cave. It was, as Joe had pointed out, almost invisible from the beach, unless one happened to look up when standing directly in front of the opening, because a number of huge boulders obscured it.

Inside, they found unmistakable evidences of human habitation.

"There are our provisions!" exclaimed Frank.

He pointed to a box that stood beside a few blankets in a corner of the little cave. It was filled with the food that Schaum had stolen from them. Very little of it had been touched; the robber had been given no time to dispose of his loot.

"Well, I never expected to see *that* again," said Joe.

"I guess it's safe enough where it is. We can pick it up on our way back from Captain Royal's."

"How about these blankets? Schaum said we could have them."

Frank picked up one of the blankets. It was heavy and of excellent quality.

"I'll say he was mighty generous, letting us have good blankets like these," he declared. "They seem brand new, too."

"If they are, there must be a catch in it somewhere."

"There is. Look!"

Frank held out the blanket. Stamped into the fabric was the name, "Hotel Bayport." The reason for Schaum's sudden burst of generosity was now clear.

"No wonder he didn't want to take them with him. He knew that if the police laid eyes on those blankets he'd have another charge laid against him. He must have stolen them from the hotel after he escaped from jail."

"I think he would take anything that wasn't nailed down," said Joe. "Well, we can take the blankets back with us and return them to the hotel, at any rate."

"Sure. We'll leave 'em here with the grub until we're ready to go back to our own cave."

The boys found nothing else worthy of attention in Carl Schaum's crude abode except a revolver hidden beneath a rock near the blankets. They appropriated this, to turn over to the police when they should return to Bayport.

They departed, well satisfied with their visit.

"Chet will give three cheers when he sees the grub again. I don't think he was very cheerful about the thought of going on short rations until we got new supplies," said Frank.

"I wasn't very cheerful about it myself," Joe admitted. "It makes me sore when I think of Schaum stealing all that stuff. Why, one man couldn't eat it all in a month."

"Perhaps he intended to stay a month, or even longer, if he could get away with it."

"Well, he might have left us more than he did. I'm glad I was able to douse some water in his face."

The Hardy boys were soon in sight of Captain Royal's cave. The gloomy opening was barely visible through the lowering mist.

"I wonder if the old gentleman could be at home, Joe."

"No sign of life around, anyway."

"Perhaps he's asleep."

They made their way to the cave-mouth, cautiously. Still there was no sign of the captain.

"Better call him," suggested Frank.

They halted.

"Captain Royal!" shouted Joe.

There was no answer.

"I guess he's not at home."

They called out Captain Royal's name again, but still there was no reply, so they ventured close to the cave-mouth and peeped inside. The place was deserted.

"Shall we go in?" said Joe.

"Sure. We'll take a look around."

They stepped inside the cave. Captain Royal had evidently spent the night there, for his bed was even untidier than it had been the previous day.

"Perhaps he's gone fishing," said Frank.

He was looking about the cave and suddenly his gaze fell on a small cupboard, consisting of a box on a ledge of rock, in which he could see a number of books. He gave a low whistle of surprise.

"The worthy captain has a library," remarked Joe.

"Let's see what his taste in reading matter is like."

Frank went over to the improvised cupboard and picked up one of the books. It fell open and a number of strips of paper fluttered to the floor of the cave.

Frank bent to pick up the papers. He looked at them curiously.

"Newspaper clippings!"

"We might get a clue about him from them," Joe suggested.

In the dim light, Frank scrutinized one of the clippings. It was a despatch from Boston, dated several months previous, and consisted of an address on Egyptian civilization given by a world-famous traveler who had spoken in that city.

"This is uncommonly dull, if you ask me," said Frank at last, putting the clipping aside and picking up another.

"No mention of Todham Todd?"

"Not that I can find."

Joe took one of the other clippings and the boys perused them diligently, seeking some mention of the missing college professor.

All the clippings were devoted to various lectures that had been given by various speakers in different parts of the country within recent months.

"Looks as if he was a lecturer, or had some interest in lectures, at any rate," Joe commented.

Patiently, they examined clipping after clipping, but in none of them did they find any mention of Todham Todd. A further search of the cupboard, however, revealed a veritable mass of papers, and the boys settled down to a thorough study of them.

"He's a strange kind of sailor, that's sure," declared Frank. "I never heard of a sailor who collected clippings about lectures."

The other papers were similar clippings, as well as typewritten documents. When the boys examined these documents in the hope of finding some clue to the former activities of Captain Royal, they found that they were manuscripts of lectures on philosophy and other topics. But still they found no mention of the name of Todham Todd.

"Well, whether he's mentioned in these papers or not, I'm sure that Captain Royal and Todham Todd are the same man," observed Joe. "No sailor would ever carry all this stuff around with him."

"It certainly looks peculiar," his brother agreed. "But there are some more papers yet. We'll look through them all. If he is Todham Todd it's hardly likely that he would carry clippings about other men's lectures and none of his own."

Sheet after sheet, they perused. There were lectures by visiting authors, lectures by big-game hunters, lectures by Arctic explorers, lectures by college professors, photographs of lecturers.

"He is certainly interested in lecturing. Perhaps it's just a coincidence. Crazy men will do crazy things. Perhaps Captain Royal just has a sort of lunatic streak that way," said Joe finally, when it seemed evident that none of the clippings or documents bore any mention of Todham Todd.

"Perhaps you're right. I hate to admit it, though. I was sure we had stumbled on a red-hot clue."

Frank scrutinized the last of the clippings.

"Nothing about him in this one either. I can't figure it out. Beyond the fact that all these stories deal with lectures, there is no connection between them. They're all by different men and all on different subjects."

At that moment Joe espied a small box close by. He opened it, and out tumbled a second mass of clippings.

"Gee, look at this!" he exclaimed.

"More lectures?" questioned his brother, with a sigh.

"Lectures? No!" shouted the younger Hardy boy. "It's a murder case! Look, Frank!"

"You're fooling!"

But even as he spoke Frank Hardy scanned the sheet of newspaper his brother held towards him. There, in glaring headlines, were the words

BARTON BIXBY SHOT DOWN
Former Naval Officer Kills Old Friend
With a Shotgun
Police Follow Clues in Vain

There followed a long account of a killing that had taken place in Richmond three weeks before. A certain Lieutenant Patwick had murdered a former friend who had spoken ill of him at a club. Patwick had then fled to parts unknown. The lieutenant was said to be of a nervous, high-strung temperament.

"Gosh! He may not be Todham Todd after all," remarked Frank. "He may be this Lieutenant Patwick simply trying to conceal his true identity."

"Or else gone crazy because of his crime," added Joe.

There were several other clippings concerning the crime. Evidently the perpetrator had outwitted both police and detectives.

"We'll have to look into this," said Frank soberly.

"You bet. For all we know—"

Joe stopped speaking and thrust all the clippings behind him. A shadow had darkened the mouth of the cave.

"Who is in there?" an angry voice bellowed.

CHAPTER XX

THE SHOTGUN

So quietly had the man approached the cave-mouth that the Hardy boys were taken completely by surprise. They wheeled about.

There, in the entrance, stood Captain Royal.

Evidently, it took him some time to become accustomed to the dim light of the cave, for he was peering intently at the boys, but with no sign of recognition on his face.

"Who's that?" he shouted impatiently. "Answer me!"

Frank gulped. Then, trying to achieve a confident tone of voice, he said: "Why, hello, Captain. We just dropped in for a visit."

But Captain Royal was not appeased.

With a roar of wrath, he advanced into the cave.

"I know you now!" he bellowed. "I know you. It's those boys who were here yesterday. Don't deny it!"

"Sure!" said Joe. "It's only us."

The captain came closer.

"What are you doing in my place?" he demanded. "Stealing, eh?"

"We're not stealing," returned Frank indignantly.

"Yes, you are!" Captain Royal was plainly angry. "You came here to steal all my money and my jewels. I know it! You waited until I went out and then you sneaked in here to rob me."

"Now, Captain, be reasonable," pleaded Frank. "We just came here to have a little talk with you. If we wanted to steal we would have cleared out long ago."

"You came to steal!" insisted the old man. "Don't tell me anything different. Why can't you leave an old man alone? I've never done you any harm."

"Certainly not. We had no intention of disturbing you—"

Just then Captain Royal caught sight of the mass of clippings and papers. His face was suddenly distorted with fury.

"My papers!" he shrieked. "You've been at my papers!"

He made a sudden lunge toward the boys. So quickly did he rush at them that neither Frank nor Joe had a chance to escape. Captain Royal grasped each lad by the collar.

"You've been at my papers! My precious papers! I knew you came here to steal something!"

He shook them roughly.

"I'll teach you to come prowling around my cave!" he roared. "I will teach you to look at my papers."

The Hardy boys struggled to free themselves, but Captain Royal was stronger than he looked, and he kept a tight grip on their collars. Frank almost wriggled free, but the captain tightened his grasp. As for Joe, he told his chums later that "the old lad shook me until my back teeth rattled."

The captain was raging and roaring almost incoherently in a terrible outburst of wrath. There was now little doubt in the minds of the Hardy boys that the man was a lunatic. What would happen to them at the hands of this madman?

At first they had not taken Captain Royal's outburst seriously, but now Frank realized that they might be in genuine danger.

He lashed out with his fists and dealt the captain a blow in the ribs that brought a startled grunt. At the same time, Joe wriggled to one side and tried to trip the old gentleman. But Captain Royal was alert and wary. He would not let go, and although he lost his balance and tumbled to the floor of the cave, he dragged the boys with him.

"Break loose, Joe!" shouted Frank. "He means business."

But this was more easily said than done.

The trio sprawled on the floor of the cave, Frank and Joe fighting desperately to get out of the clutches of their captor, but the old man clung to their collars like grim death.

"I'll teach you!" he panted. "I'll shoot both of you."

His words sent a thrill of fear through the boys. They knew now that they were dealing with a maniac and they realized that in his present frame of mind, he was quite capable of carrying out the threat.

Joe had fallen in such a way that his collar had become twisted, and with Captain Royal still grasping it, he was almost choked. He could not turn without increasing the throttling pressure, so he was quite helpless. As for Frank, in spite of his struggles, he was unable to break the captain's hold.

"I have the better of you!" chuckled the old man fiendishly. "You can't get away from me. Try to kill me, would you! I'm going to shoot you both."

He began to struggle to his feet.

Captain Royal was eying something on the wall at the back of the cave. Following the direction of his gaze, Frank saw something that terrified him.

It was a double-barreled shotgun!

"I've got it loaded to the muzzle!" roared Captain Royal, as he floundered about in his efforts to get to his feet without losing his grip on the boys. "I've always kept it loaded just for prying thieves that come to steal my papers."

He stood up and lurched across the cave, dragging the boys with him. His intention was clear. He meant to get the shotgun.

The lads redoubled their efforts to escape. By a concerted effort, they turned on him, striking at him with their fists. Frank heard a ripping, tearing sound and then he was suddenly free. He staggered back, and the captain was left holding a small fragment of his shirt in his hand.

Frank thought quickly. He must reach the gun first. He leaped across the cave.

But Captain Royal was too quick for him. Flinging Joe to one side so that he went stumbling and then sprawled in the sand, the captain reached the shotgun at a bound.

He was just reaching for it when Frank came at him from behind. Captain Royal tried to fend the boy off, but Frank grappled with him and dragged him away from the wall.

"Get the gun, Joe!" he panted.

Joe was just getting to his feet. Captain Royal whirled about. His fist struck Frank against the side of the head, and it caught Frank off balance. He was knocked off his feet. Captain Royal gave a yell of triumph, and seized the shotgun.

It had been resting on a rocky ledge. Frank was sprawled on the sand, entirely at the man's mercy. Joe was equally helpless. In another moment they expected to hear the explosive roar of the weapon.

"Now, I'll teach you!" roared the captain, dancing about in fury. "I'm going to shoot the pair of you."

Frank had a sudden idea.

"I'll keep him occupied, Joe," he said in a low voice. "Keep edging back until you get to the cave-mouth."

A daring plan had formed in his mind. It meant, as he thought, risking his own life, but he was prepared to do this for the sake of his younger brother.

If he could but distract Captain Royal's attention by taunts and jeers, even if it meant arousing the man to a pitch of murderous madness, Joe might make good his escape.

"You wouldn't have the nerve to shoot," he shouted.

Captain Royal brandished the shotgun and glared at Frank.

"I wouldn't have the nerve, hey? You think I haven't?"

Joe was moving back, step by step, toward the opening.

"No, you wouldn't shoot me," scoffed Frank. "I don't believe your old gun is loaded anyway."

Captain Royal had forgotten all about Joe by now.

"Not loaded?" he screeched. "It's loaded to the muzzle, I tell you. It's always loaded. You'll find out if it's loaded or not."

Frank was preparing to spring to his feet.

"Listen, Captain Royal," he said placatingly. "Let me go this time and I promise I won't bother you again."

But the captain shook his head.

"You're a spy!" he screeched. "You're a spy! You were sent here to look through all my papers. I'm an old sailor, I am, and in the navy we have only one cure for spies."

"And what's that?"

"We shoot 'em." Captain Royal brandished the shotgun viciously. "We shoot 'em when we can't make 'em walk the plank."

"You haven't the nerve to shoot me. You wouldn't dare. You know you'd be hanged."

Frank glanced toward the mouth of the cave. Joe was almost safe by now.

"I'm not afraid!" bragged Captain Royal. "They'd never catch me to hang me. Death for the spies. I'll shoot both of you—"

Only then did he become aware that Joe had disappeared. With a growl of alarm, he swung about, just in time to see Joe vanishing beyond the cave-mouth.

"He's gone!" roared the captain. "Come back here, you young scoundrel! Come back!"

He ran across the cave. Frank seized the opportunity to leap to his feet again. Captain Royal heard him and turned, raising the shotgun to his shoulder.

"You won't escape me!" he yelled.

The shotgun was leveled directly at the boy. Frank thought that the next moment would be his last. He could see Captain Royal's finger tightening about the trigger.

But there came an interruption from the mouth of the cave. Joe had heard the uproar and had realized his brother's danger. He had not fled. He had returned to the entrance, and there he gave vent to a shrill, blood-curdling shriek.

Captain Royal gave a shout of surprise.

"Who's that?" he exclaimed.

He whirled hastily about, but Joe had disappeared.

"Who's there?" he roared.

Joe, hidden beyond the rocks, shrieked again.

"Just wait!" yelled the captain. "I'll come out there and fix you. I'll fix you!"

Frank, in the meantime, had been circling about the side of the cave, trying to gain the entrance unobserved. His heart sank as Captain Royal turned around just when he was about to make a dash for liberty.

"So!" yelled Captain Royal. "You thought you could get away from me, eh?"

The shotgun was aimed directly at Frank.

Captain Royal fired. There was a loud explosion.

CHAPTER XXI

OVER THE CLIFF

To Frank Hardy's unbounded astonishment, the explosion was followed by a white cloud that rose from the barrel of the shotgun. It was not smoke, and although Captain Royal had aimed the gun directly at him, he found that he was uninjured.

The white cloud was flour!

"A hit!" roared Captain Royal. "A hit! I've wounded him!"

Frank wasted no further time.

He raced toward the mouth of the cave and scrambled out onto the beach. Behind him he could hear Captain Royal screeching wildly.

Frank almost collided with Joe.

His brother's face was white. He had heard the shot and was sure Frank had been a victim of the maniac's wrath.

"Are you all right, Frank?"

"Sure. Come on—let's beat it out of here."

They stumbled across the rocks toward a great heap of boulders that offered shelter. Frank glanced back in time to see Captain Royal emerge from the cave, still carrying the shotgun.

"Did he miss you?" panted Joe.

Frank chuckled.

"If that gun had been loaded, my goose would have been cooked by now."

"But I heard the shot."

"It was loaded to the muzzle with flour. That's all. Just plain, ordinary flour."

They dropped down behind the boulders.

When they peeped out again they could see Captain Royal at the mouth of the cave, dancing with rage. Evidently he saw them, for he yelled:

"You can't hide from me. I can see you."

He raised the shotgun to his shoulder again and pressed the trigger. Once more there was a shower of flour distributed in every direction.

"Whether he's Todham Todd or Captain Royal, he's a lunatic," declared Joe.

"There's no question of that."

The boys crouched behind the boulder and watched the antics of the captain. He was yelling and shrieking like a wild Indian, waving the shotgun on high. Both barrels had been discharged.

"My ammunition is gone!" he roared. "My ammunition is gone!"

He hurled the gun away from him. It fell with a clatter among the rocks.

Hatless and coatless, he was a weird figure in the fog. He made no move toward the Hardy boys, however, but contented himself with dancing about at the mouth of the cave.

"The battle is lost!" shrieked Captain Royal finally. "On to the execution!"

"What on earth does he mean?" said Joe.

"Oh, he's crazy, that's all. He doesn't mean anything."

"All is lost! My enemies are upon me! On to the execution! On to the execution!"

Captain Royal whirled about and ran down the beach through the lowering mist.

"Where is he going?"

"Let's wait and watch him," advised Frank.

They saw the odd old man running and stumbling among the rocks along the shore. Then he turned to his right and began to clamber up among the boulders until he came to a scarcely visible path that led up toward the top of the cliff.

From the boulders among which the Hardy boys were standing they could scarcely see the man now, so they emerged and went down toward the cave. Captain Royal, yelling at the top of his lungs, was climbing on up the path.

"What's his idea, anyway?"

Frank shook his head.

"He's certainly running amuck! I hope he doesn't fall and hurt himself."

The path the captain had taken wound about in precarious fashion and at one point crossed a ledge of rock that overhung the beach, immediately over the rocks that sloped down into the deep water.

Captain Royal stumbled and fell, but he got to his feet again and went on.

"If he ever slips when he comes to that ledge, he'll go over the cliff!" Joe declared.

"I wonder if we should follow him."

At that moment, the Hardy boys saw two figures come into view from beyond the rocks. At that distance and through the mist it was impossible to distinguish their features, but as they drew closer the Hardy boys saw that they were none other than Chet and Biff.

"What's going on here?" shouted Chet, as they hastened up.

"Lots of excitement," Frank replied. "Captain Royal has just had a brainstorm."

"What happened?"

When their chums came near, the Hardy boys told them of their adventures of the morning, how they had captured Carl Schaum, and how Captain Royal had come upon them while they were in the cave.

"And he shot at you?" cried Biff.

"With his gun loaded with flour."

"Flour?"

"Yes."

"He must be crazy."

"Absolutely."

"Where is he going now?"

Joe pointed to the captain, scrambling on up the path toward the cliff.

"There he is. And if he doesn't watch out he's going to tumble off into the sea."

"I'll say he is," declared Chet. "We ought to go after him."

In the distance, they could hear the wild shrieks of Captain Royal as he went stumbling among the rocks. He was drawing nearer to the ledge, and as the path at this point was extremely narrow, the boys could see that he was indeed in danger.

"Stop!" shouted Joe. "Stop, Captain!"

But Captain Royal, if he heard at all, paid no attention to the warning. He continued his ascent of the rocky path.

"We'd better follow him up," said Frank. "He can't hurt us—we know that—and he's sure to hurt himself if we don't get him down off those rocks."

With one accord, the boys hurried across the beach until they came to the trail leading up the steep incline toward the top of the cliff. Then, with Frank Hardy in the lead, they began the climb.

Captain Royal turned and saw them. He stopped and shook his fist at them.

"Go back!" he shouted wildly. "Go back, I tell you!"

"Come down!" called Frank. "Come down, Captain Royal, or you'll be killed."

"The battle is lost!" howled the madman. "My enemies are upon me! But they'll never capture me alive!"

He bent down and lifted a heavy stone, which he hurled down the path. It came rolling and bouncing down the slope, gathering momentum every second. It was headed directly for the Hardy boys and their chums.

"Scatter!" shouted Joe.

The boys had little protection. The path was so narrow that they could go neither to right nor left for more than a few inches.

On came the heavy stone.

The boys crouched, listening to the crash and clatter of the great missile as it bounded toward them. There was no use attempting to escape. If they ran back down the path they could never hope to reach the shore in time. The rock was plunging down the path at terrific speed. It seemed that the deadly object would crash among them in another moment.

Frank closed his eyes. Just then the rock bounded high in the air, shot forward in a wide arc, lit in the path just a few yards above the boys, and struck a projecting stone. It flew off at a tangent, the impact diverting it from its course so that it plunged wide of the boys who were crouched in the path. A moment later there was a tremendous crash as the heavy rock struck the beach.

Captain Royal, on the cliff above, was yelling with glee.

"You won't chase me now!" he shrieked. "That will teach you a lesson! That will teach you something!"

Frank scrambled to his feet. He was white with anger. The maniac's action had endangered their lives.

"We'll teach *you*!" he shouted. "Don't do a trick like that again. Come down off those rocks before you fall and break your neck."

"I won't come down."

Captain Royal shook his fist at them again, wheeled about and then continued his perilous climb. The boys hastened in pursuit. They knew that the old man might turn and cast another rock down the path, but they were determined to save him from the consequences of his own folly if they could.

The fog had left the rocks and the path slippery and treacherous. At almost every step the boys stumbled. It was almost impossible to maintain one's footing as the path grew steeper. As for Captain Royal, he was no better off, and more than once he went sprawling on all fours, only to pick himself up again and resume his hazardous progress.

At last he reached the top of the cliff.

The boys were still many yards from the summit. Captain Royal made no attempt at caution as he ran along the narrow path. The rocks were slippery under foot.

"He'll go over, as sure as fate!" exclaimed Frank.

Scarcely were the words out of his mouth when the boys saw Captain Royal stumble. He lurched sideways, his arms thrashed the air as he vainly grabbed for support, he gave a desperate yell. The boys gave a simultaneous cry of terror as they saw the man plunge through the air, over the side of the cliff, down toward the water far below!

CHAPTER XXII

IN SWIRLING WATERS

The boys looked at one another in awe.

Their ears still rang with Captain Royal's last dreadful cry as he went hurtling over the cliff toward the watery depths.

"He's gone!" gasped Chet. "I knew something like that would happen. He slipped on the rocks."

Frank, however, was already slipping and stumbling back down the path toward the beach.

"There's still a chance," he shouted to the others. "He may be alive yet. If we hurry we may be able to get him out of the water before he drowns. The tide's coming in, so he may be washed ashore."

It was a slim chance, he knew. Captain Royal had fallen from a great height and perhaps the impact of his collision with the water had rendered him unconscious. From the path, the boys could not see where the old man had struck the water, so they could not know if he had come to the surface as yet.

The boys scrambled down the path, almost risking their necks in the pellmell descent. Rocks and pebbles went skittering before them as they plunged toward the beach.

All their resentment against Captain Royal because he had hurled the rock at them and because he had threatened them, had vanished in their concern for his safety. They realized that he was not responsible for his actions and that his eccentricities were the fruits of a disordered mind. They had done their best to save him from going over the cliff. This was some consolation. But the very thought of such a horrible death made them shudder.

"He'll be battered to pieces on the rocks!" panted Joe.

"If we get there in time we may be able to save him," returned Frank. "Of course, it's ten chances to one that he was killed by the fall."

They reached the rocks of the shore at last, Frank and Joe in front, Chet and Biff stumbling breathlessly along behind. The boys raced down the beach toward the base of the cliff from which Captain Royal had fallen. It was invisible to them from where they were, but as they skirted a ledge of rock they saw the steep wall of the precipice.

It descended to a raging foam of angry waters, where the surf beat among the black pinnacles of rock projecting from the sea at the base of the cliff.

"He hasn't a chance in the world," declared Chet, when he viewed the gloomy scene.

Fog hung over the shore, and through it loomed the black cliff and the cruel rocks. They could see no sign of Captain Royal in the waves.

However, the boys hastened on toward the base of the cliff, approaching as near as they dared. Frank scanned the water in vain for a glimpse of a bobbing figure being cast in toward the shore.

"He wouldn't live ten seconds in that sea!" declared Biff, with conviction.

"I'm afraid you're right, Biff," replied Frank sadly. "I guess we'll never see the poor old chap again."

"Pretty tough," said Chet. "After all, he didn't know what he was doing. He was just crazy. He should have been somewhere in a place where his friends could look after him."

"And now," put in Joe, "we'll probably never know if he was Todham Todd or not."

Chet looked up, interested.

"What's that?" he asked.

But before Joe could explain further, Frank gave a shout of excitement. "I see him! Look!"

He pointed toward the black rocks at the base of the cliff. There, in the midst of the tossing waves, they had a momentary glimpse of a limp figure, an upturned face among the dark waters. There was no doubt that this was Captain Royal, but whether he was alive or dead they could not tell.

A gigantic wave picked up the body and hurled it toward the dark rocks again. Somehow, the limp form was thrown clear, otherwise it would have been battered to pieces, and it tumbled into a quiet pool beyond the jagged pinnacles. There the body lay, face upward, arms flung helplessly out.

"We've got to get him out of that," declared Frank, taking off his coat.

"How can we?"

"You'll be smashed to pieces against the rocks!" exclaimed Biff.

"I'm going to risk it anyway."

"You'd better wait for low tide."

"Too late then."

"Frank, don't be foolish!" cried Joe, in alarm. "You'll never be able to make it."

But Frank was obdurate.

"I can reach him if I'm careful," he said. "Perhaps he isn't dead. He may be only stunned and unconscious. If we leave him there he will be killed."

"But if he's dead already there's no sense in your risking your life."

"But he may not be dead. I'm going to try it, anyway."

Without another word, Frank handed his coat to Chet and then made his way along the rocks at the base of the cliff. For a few yards his progress was uneventful, but as he reached the deep water and the great waves pounded against him he was obliged to exert all his strength to breast the angry surf.

Once he was knocked off his feet and the watchers had a glimpse of his head and outflung arms in a smother of foam, then he disappeared from sight. A moment later, however, they saw him emerge, dripping, beside a rock that jutted out of the water and pull himself up to safety.

He still had a perilous journey before he could reach the limp form at the base of the rocky wall. He rested for a moment, with waves breaking over him as he clung to the rock. Then the watching boys saw him slip down into the water again and flounder on.

"He'll be battered to pieces!" exclaimed Biff.

"I wouldn't give a nickel for his chances, myself," said Chet.

Joe shook his head.

"He may get there all right, but if he tries to bring Captain Royal's body back with him, he hasn't a Chinaman's chance."

Frank was now but a few yards away from the shallow pool where the old man lay. He vanished for a moment, emerged from the waves, staggered a few paces, then a huge roller swept over him and sent him against the side of the cliff. But he was evidently unhurt, for the others saw him wave toward them. Then he plunged along the base of the wall, flattened himself against the cliff as another wave rolled down upon him, and then splashed into the little pool.

"He made it!"

"Yes. But can he get back?"

Frank was bending over the body of Captain Royal. The other boys saw him straighten up suddenly and wave to them. He shouted something but the roar of the waves drowned his voice.

"Perhaps he's trying to tell us the captain is alive," suggested Joe.

They saw Frank tugging at the limp form, trying to get a convenient grip on Captain Royal's body.

"He's too heavy for Frank. It's hard enough for one person to get back through those waves alone, without dragging some one else along."

But evidently Frank was going to try it.

Going to the pool, his danger had been that a wave would pick him up and dash him to pieces against the rocks. Returning, his danger was that he would be unable to pit his strength against the force of the waves at all, that he would become exhausted before he reached the open shore again.

He had hoisted Captain Royal's body up until the old man's arms were over his shoulders, and he gripped the wrists over his chest. The body was thus across his back.

Head down, Frank plunged forward out of the sheltered pool, directly into the waves.

The first breaker smashed against him with terrific force. He lost his balance, staggered and fell. The watchers groaned. They saw the two figures in the foam, saw that Frank had lost his grip on Captain Royal.

But Frank managed to get to his feet. Then he reached out and seized the captain by the back of the shirt. He was not beaten yet.

He dragged the unconscious form into the very heart of the raging waves, where they surged against the sharp rocks. Each time a mighty roller came toward them, its crest tipped with foam, he lowered his head and set himself for the shock. So, inch by inch, he forged his way forward until he was among the rocks.

Here his danger was at its worst.

The water was not deep but a misstep would have grave consequences for if he once fell the waves would batter him against the rocks and his chances of regaining a foothold would be slim.

He rested a while in the shelter of the largest rock, waited until a huge wave went by with a crashing roar, then, as the water receded, plunged on again. Once he seemed to stagger, but he kept his balance, somehow, and clung to another rock.

Another wave came rolling in. Frank lowered his head and waited for it. Crash!

It broke over him in a cloud of flying spray. He was completely hidden for a moment, and the watchers on the beach were breathless with suspense.

Then, through the mist, they saw that he was still clinging to the rock.

Frank was almost exhausted now. His burden, a dead weight, was very heavy. The beach seemed very far away. There were more rocks to pass. He rested for a short while, then plunged on.

By a miracle, he kept his footing among the treacherous rocks, and by good judgment he managed to get set in time to resist the shock of the breaking waves. At last he felt the sand beneath his feet.

He had only a short distance to go now, but his knees gave way beneath him. He stumbled and fell. He lost his grip on the body of Captain Royal. A great wave broke over them.

But Joe and Chet and Biff were already wading toward them. In a moment, Frank felt strong hands seizing him. Half-conscious, he was dragged out of the water onto the sands.

"Captain Royal!" he stammered. "Get him! He's all right!"

"Chet is bringing him in," said Joe assuringly.

"He's unconscious," gasped Frank, "but he's alive."

Then he collapsed, gasping and exhausted, on the sand. Chet came up, carrying the limp body of Captain Royal.

"He's breathing!" declared Chet excitedly. "Frank saved him."

CHAPTER XXIII

BACK TO BAYPORT

Captain Royal was unconscious, but he was still breathing. There was a bad cut on his head and it had bled profusely.

"We'd better get him to a doctor right away!" said Joe.

"I don't think he's been badly hurt." Chet began feeling the unconscious man's ribs. "There are no bones broken, at any rate. He hit his head against a rock, I guess."

"The blow on the head knocked him cold," Biff remarked.

"Perhaps he's got concussion of the brain."

"In that case, he needs a doctor," Joe said.

"How about Frank?"

But Frank was already sitting up.

"I'm all right," he told them. "I'm just about all in, but I'll be as right as rain in a few minutes. Whew, those waves sure battered me about, I'll tell the world!"

"We never expected to see you come back alive," Chet told him.

"It was pretty bad coming back," Frank admitted. "The captain is heavier than he looks!"

"He's still alive, at any rate."

"Isn't he conscious yet?"

"Not a bit of it. He's breathing, but he's still dead to the world, and there's no sign that he's coming to."

"Well, we've got to get him to a doctor, that's all," declared Frank decisively.

He got to his feet, exhausted though he was.

"Do you mean that we'll carry him back to the road?" asked Joe.

"We'll take him right back to Bayport. That's where the nearest hospital is that we know anything about." Frank looked down at the unconscious man. "He's in bad shape. If he were just stunned, he'd be awake by now. Chances are, his skull is fractured. That's a bad cut."

The boys looked down at the unconscious Captain Royal, sprawled limply on the sand.

"It's a long haul," demurred Biff.

"We can't leave him here. We can't do anything for him ourselves, you know that."

"You're right." Biff bent over and grasped the unconscious man's feet. "Give me a hand with him, some one."

Chet and Joe helped him. They raised Captain Royal from the ground and began carrying him up the beach. Frank went on ahead, still weak from the effects of his grueling ordeal in rescuing the eccentric old man from the sea.

Captain Royal showed no signs of returning consciousness. He was a dead weight as the boys carried him on past his own cave, past the place where Carl Schaum had been hiding, past the boys' cave. There the lads rested, before undertaking the hard climb up the path to the top of the cliff.

They tried all the first aid measures they had ever heard of, but Captain Royal still remained unconscious. The cut on his head was not bleeding any more; his breathing was heavy, and the lads saw that it was no ordinary case of being rendered senseless by a blow on the head.

"A doctor is the only thing," declared Frank. "His lungs are clear of water, so he's all right in that respect. He must have struck his head when he was washed in among those rocks."

"Well, let's get busy then," said Biff, who was no laggard. "We had better get him to the hospital as quickly as we can."

They took turns carrying Captain Royal up the path that led to the top of the cliff. It was an arduous climb, and it was late in the afternoon before they finally reached the rocks above. Then they rested once more before starting the journey to the fisherman's cottage.

"Thank goodness, he has a car," said Joe. "He'll help us take him in to the city. We would never be able to carry him on the motorcycles."

"A strange end to our exploration trip," grunted Chet.

Puffing and panting, they carried the unconscious man on over the rocks until they came to the path leading down to the fisherman's cottage. There they rested again.

Finally, after a halting descent, they came to the cottage. Their friend, the fisherman, was fortunately at home. Accompanied by his wife, he came running out when the boys appeared in sight with their burden.

"First it's a prisoner and now it's a sick man!" he exclaimed, as he drew near. "I declare, you chaps seem to scare up more excitement than anybody that ever came to Honeycomb Caves."

"This is an old man who was living in one of the caves," explained Frank. "He fell off a cliff and hurt himself. Do you think you could help us get him to a doctor?"

The fisherman glanced inquiringly at his wife.

"Go ahead, John," she said. "You wouldn't let the poor man die, would you?"

"I wondered if you'd mind bein' left alone."

"Go on. I'm not a baby. Drive the poor fellow out to a doctor. It's easy to be seen he needs attention."

The fisherman quickly brought out his car and they carefully put Captain Royal in the back seat. The boys brought out their motorcycles and, with Biff riding in company of the fisherman, the little party set out for the main road.

"I don't know whether we can find a doctor at the village or not," said the fisherman. "If we can't, there's nothing for it but to drive on into Bayport."

"We'll fix the expenses," Frank assured him.

"That's all right. I don't want any money for my trouble. The poor old chap seems to have got a terrible wallop on the head. How did it happen?"

"He fell off a cliff."

"Did it have anything to do with the fellow you brought out this morning?" asked the fisherman shrewdly.

"No. Nothing to do with him."

They reached the main road and drove on toward the village. There they found that the one and only doctor had been called out on a case and would not be back until the following morning.

"Bayport it is, then," said Joe.

It was plain that the fisherman did not relish the idea of the long trip to Bayport. It was equally plain that he felt it his duty to bring the unconscious man to a doctor. On the other hand, the chums did not like the idea of using his battered car, not only because of the trouble it would give the fisherman but because the car would not go more than thirty or thirty-five miles an hour. The motorcycles were invariably far ahead.

The difficulty was soon solved, however. A heavy touring car pulled up in front of the village general store and when the driver stepped out the Hardy boys gave a cry of delight.

"Mr. Jacobson!" exclaimed Frank.

"Why, hello there, Frank Hardy!" said the man. "What brings you away out here? Hello, Joe. And who have you with you? Chet and Biff, or I'm a Dutchman. What's up now?"

The man was a Bayport merchant, a close friend of Fenton Hardy.

Swiftly, the boys explained the situation to him. Jacobson soon realized the importance of the matter, and readily consented to take Captain Royal to Bayport with him.

"Absolutely!" he said. "It's no trouble to me. I was going to Bayport, anyway, and it won't hurt if I put on a little extra speed. How about you chaps?"

"Joe and Chet and I have our motorcycles," said Frank. "Biff will go with you, and look after the captain."

"Righto! We'll make it in good time, I fancy."

The Hardy boys and their chums thereupon thanked the fisherman for his trouble. He seemed relieved that he was not called on to make the long journey into Bayport.

"Write and let me know how the old gentleman gets along," he requested before he left the boys. "I hope he recovers all right."

The boys promised that they would do so. Then the Hardy boys and Chet mounted their motorcycles, Biff got into the automobile with Mr. Jacobson to look after Captain Royal in the back seat, and they started off.

Frank and Joe often talked of that wild ride back to the city. Jacobson's car was big and powerful and he wasted no time on the road. They realized that the matter was urgent and that it was necessary for Captain Royal to receive medical attention as soon as possible, so they paid little attention to the speed laws. The big car roared along the Shore Road, and the motorcycles clattered on behind.

"We should be there by midnight, at this rate," grunted Joe, as they sped around a curve.

"We're going back a lot quicker than we left," replied his brother.

At length they came within sight of the twinkling lights of Bayport. The roar of the big automobile did not diminish. At breakneck speed they clattered into the city limits.

In the back seat of the car, Biff turned frequently to look at the unconscious form beside him. To his relief, Captain Royal was still breathing.

"I think the old chap will pull through all right," he said to himself.

Up a dark, quiet street sped the car, then came to a stop before a massive stone house with a neat gilt plate beside the door. The motorcycles roared up and the boys dismounted.

"We'll take him in and let the doctor have a look at him," said Mr. Jacobson. "If he is in bad shape, the doc will put him in his own private hospital. He'll get the best of care here."

Carefully, they carried Captain Royal up the steps. Their ring was answered by a servant, and they took the old man into a waiting room. The doctor, who had been in bed, soon came downstairs in pyjamas and dressing gown.

"An accident case, Doctor," explained Frank. "This old man fell off a cliff into the sea and he's been unconscious for eight or nine hours."

The doctor made a swift examination. His frown deepened as he inspected the cut on Captain Royal's temple.

"Queer!" he said. "It isn't a very bad cut, and there seems to be no sign of a fracture. It looks like concussion of the brain, to me, but he doesn't appear to have had a very hard blow."

"The waves washed him up against the rocks," said Joe.

The doctor shook his head.

"He seems in a bad way. Eight hours, you said?"

"Yes."

"I'll have to give him a more detailed examination. I'll admit him as a patient to my own hospital if you people will be responsible for him."

"That's all right, Doctor. Do what you can for him and send the bill to us," said Frank promptly.

The doctor rang a bell. An attendant appeared, wheeling a long, white table. Captain Royal was placed upon it and wheeled away.

"I'll let you know in the morning," promised the doctor. "Frankly, I don't mind telling you he's in bad shape. He may never regain consciousness again."

The boys were sobered by the thought that Captain Royal, for all his eccentricities, might be dying as a result of his wild dash over the rocks. Slowly they filed out into the street, bade good-bye to Mr. Jacobson and thanked him for his assistance, then went home. As Chet Morton lived out in the country, the Hardy boys invited him to spend the rest of the night with them. He accepted the invitation gladly, for the prospect of a long trip out of the city had not appealed to him. Biff Hooper, who lived near by, went to his own home.

The house was in darkness when they arrived, so the Hardy boys and Chet quietly parked their motorcycles, slipped up the back stairs and were soon in bed. They were so tired after their adventures of the day that in spite of the temptation to discuss matters, sleep soon overcame them.

CHAPTER XXIV

AT THE HOSPITAL

Next morning, refreshed by their sleep, Frank, Joe and Chet were downstairs early, but not earlier than Fenton Hardy, who was already busy in his office clearing up some work before breakfast. He welcomed them cheerily.

"Back so soon!" he exclaimed. "I thought this trip would keep you away at least a week. What's the matter? Did you get frightened by the sea serpent?"

"We didn't get frightened, Dad. We had to come back with a man who got hurt."

"Oh." Fenton Hardy's expression changed to one of concern. "Who is he?"

"We think he's Todham Todd."

"Todham Todd!" exclaimed the detective. "Are you sure?"

"We're not sure. But we have an idea that's who he is. And he may be a murderer too."

Mr. Hardy motioned the three boys to chairs. "Sit down and tell me all about it. A murderer! That sounds bad."

With Frank as spokesman, and Chet and Joe prompting him once in a while, they told Mr. Hardy about their meeting with Captain Royal, about the eccentric behavior of the old man and of his actions on finding the brothers looking over the clippings in the cave, culminating in his fall from the cliff.

"And he's at the private hospital now," concluded Frank.

"Well," said Mr. Hardy, "we'll have breakfast now and then we can soon settle the matter once and for all. Evangeline Todd is staying at the summer hotel and we can ask her to come over to the hospital and have a look at this Captain Royal."

"Do you think he can be this Lieutenant Patwick, Dad?" asked Joe.

"Possibly. If so, the crime may have turned his mind. Such things have happened."

"Well, if he's Patwick then we'll have cleared up something anyway," remarked Frank.

Breakfast was announced a few minutes later, and after the Hardy boys had been warmly greeted by their mother they sat down to fruit, bacon and eggs, toast and coffee and jam, to which they did full justice. They were anxious, however, to call on Miss Todd.

Mr. Hardy called up the private hospital and inquired about Captain Royal. He came back, his face serious.

"The old chap is still unconscious. The doctor seems to think he has only a slim chance."

"It will be tough if he turns out to be Todham Todd after all," said Joe. "Too bad if we've found him, only to have him die."

"Everything may turn out all right," said Mr. Hardy. "Of course he may not be Todham Todd. You have only your suspicions to go on, although I must say it's very strange that the old man should have had all those lecture clippings in the cave. I've been thinking that Todham Todd may have lost his memory and forgotten his identity. He may have had a dim recollection of once having been a lecturer of some kind so he took to collecting all the newspaper stories he could, in an effort to awaken his memory again."

"I'll bet you're right!" exclaimed Chet. "That sounds mighty reasonable to me."

"It's just a theory. Still, it may be true. We'll call on Miss Todd."

They left the house and went on down to the hotel at which Miss Evangeline Todd was staying. She had just concluded her breakfast when they arrived.

"Have you any news?" she asked quickly, when she recognized her visitors.

"We have news, of a sort," admitted Fenton Hardy.

"Tell me. What is it? Has Todham been found? Is he well?" Miss Todd sank back in a chair and fanned herself with a magazine. "Don't keep me in suspense."

"We have found a man who may or may not be your brother."

"Where is he?" demanded Miss Todd, getting up quickly. "Take me to him at once?"

Mr. Hardy laid a restraining hand upon her arm.

"Don't count on this too much, Miss Todd," he advised. "This man may not be your brother at all. As a matter of fact, we have nothing definite to go on, but we'd like to have you come with us and identify him if you can."

"Identify him? Is he dead?"

"No. But he's in a local hospital."

"Todham in a hospital? Where? I must go to him at once."

"Now, as I've already said, we're not at all certain that this man is your brother. If you will come with us we will show you this man and you will be able to see for yourself if he is your brother or not."

"Just a minute, until I put on my hat. I'll go with you right away. My goodness, if it's really Todham—"

Talking to herself in her excitement, Miss Todd bustled away upstairs and returned in a few minutes, her hat awry.

"Hurry!" she said. "Where is the hospital? We'll take a taxi and get there more quickly."

Fenton Hardy smiled sympathetically. Miss Todd was tremendously agitated at the prospect of again seeing her long-lost brother. The hospital was less than three blocks away, so they did not hail a taxi after all, but walked the short distance, and in a little while they found themselves in the doctor's waiting room.

A uniformed nurse entered.

"You want to see the patient called Captain Royal?"

"If you please."

"The doctor is with him now, but he says you may go up. I will show you to his room."

"Captain Royal!" exclaimed Evangeline Todd. "That isn't his name! I thought you said he might be my brother."

"That is the name he has been using," explained Frank. "How is he this morning, nurse?"

"There isn't much change in his condition. The doctor says it is a strange case. But, I'm afraid—"

"Isn't he going to live?" asked Miss Todd sharply.

Fenton Hardy soothed her anxiety.

"Now, Miss Todd, try to calm yourself. We must be very quiet, you know. This man is very, very sick."

The lady heeded his advice. During the rest of their journey down the long corridor she talked only in whispers. At length they reached the door of a private room. The nurse knocked. The boys heard the doctor's voice, saying, "Come!"

The nurse held open the door and they entered a spacious private room, spotlessly clean and well-lighted. Lying on the bed was Captain Royal, with a white bandage around his head.

Evangeline Todd looked at the man wildly, then rushed to the bedside.

"My brother!" she cried. "It's my brother, Todham!"

She leaned over the unconscious figure.

"Speak to me, Todham! Speak to me! Don't you recognize me? It's you're sister. I've hunted everywhere for you, and now I've found you at last."

Then, overcome with emotion, she sank beside the bed and burst into tears.

"It's the missing professor, after all!" exclaimed Chet, in awe.

The Hardy boys, while they had expected that Evangeline Todd would identify Captain Royal as her brother, were electrified with delight.

"We were right!" said Frank, "He was Todham Todd all along."

Mr. Hardy and the doctor tried to calm the weeping woman, who was almost hysterical with relief, now that her long search was ended.

"It's Todham!" she said, over and over again. "It's my brother. I would know him anywhere."

But the man in the bed knew nothing of what was going on. His eyes were closed. His face was white and calm. Had it not been for an occasional slight twitching of the nostrils one might have thought that he was dead.

The doctor, who knew nothing of the reason for Miss Todd's outburst, was astonished, but in a few words Fenton Hardy explained the situation to him. He shook his head sadly.

"And this is where she has found her brother, at last?"

"Yes. He has been missing for months."

"I'm afraid," said the doctor, "that she has found him only to lose him."

"Is it that serious?"

"It's concussion of the brain, and there seem to have been complications. He has only a slim chance to live."

CHAPTER XXV

THE LAST OF CAPTAIN ROYAL

Todham Todd hovered between life and death for almost two weeks. For days he lay unconscious, knowing nothing of the efforts that were being made to save him. He had the best of care, and the doctor gave him every attention, but admitted that the case was one in which he could do little.

"We simply have to wait," he told the Hardy boys and Miss Todd. "He may be restored to consciousness at any moment. On the other hand, he may die just as quickly. He has a good constitution, so we may at least hope for the best."

They were anxious days. Every morning, the Hardy boys called at the hospital to inquire about the strange patient, and every morning the answer was the same.

"Mr. Todd's condition is unchanged."

One morning Fenton Hardy came to his sons with a newspaper in his hand. He was smiling broadly.

"I think the mystery is explained," he said. "Read this."

In the newspaper was an account of the capture of Lieutenant Patwick. The man had been shot down on the seacoast by detectives. Thinking he was going to die, he had admitted the murder of Barton Bixby. He also spoke of hiding in a cave with a strange old man, a lunatic.

"Todham Todd," murmured Frank.

"That makes everything as clear as day," added Joe.

"He must have left his clippings with Captain Royal," said Mr. Hardy. "Murderers usually like to read all that is printed about their crimes."

The boys told Evangeline Todd the entire story of their meeting with Captain Royal, although in deference to the good lady's feelings they refrained from mentioning the fight in the cave or the incident of the shotgun. How Todham Todd had found his way down to the coast and what had prompted him to call himself Captain Royal and take up his hermit existence in the cave, were mysteries.

"If he recovers, he may remember nothing about that phase," the doctor had said. "You may use your own judgment whether to tell him of it or not."

"We shan't tell him," declared Evangeline Todd decisively. "Let him take up the threads of his old life anew."

Then her face clouded.

"That is—if he recovers," she added, with a catch in her voice.

There came a morning when the nurse in charge saw the eyelids of the sick man flutter, and then he spoke.

"Where am I?" he asked, in a puzzled tone.

"You are quite safe," the nurse told him. "You have met with an accident. You are in the hospital."

"Ah, yes," he said. "I remember now. There was a railroad accident. Something must have struck me on the head. I can remember a sudden blow, and that is all."

"You have been unconscious for a long time, Captain. You must be quiet."

"Captain?" he said. "I'm not a captain. My name is Todd. My name is Todham Todd. I'm a professor at the university."

The doctor was called. He questioned the patient carefully and it was soon evident that Todham Todd had recovered his memory with the exception of the time following the first accident that had resulted in amnesia. From that time, everything was a blank. He knew nothing of his wanderings, knew nothing of what had happened in the caves, knew nothing of the accident that had restored his memory again.

"He will live," the doctor told Evangeline Todd a short time later. "His memory is completely restored. Unless complications set in, he should be able to leave the hospital within a few days."

The doctor's prediction was correct.

Todham Todd, completely restored in memory, was able to leave the hospital before the week was out. The reunion between the man and his sister was an affectionate one. The professor had not the slightest inkling of all the strange events that had transpired from the time of the first accident until he woke up in the hospital at Bayport. He was deeply puzzled when he learned where he was, but the doctor covered up his bewilderment by explaining that his case had been so unusual that he had been brought there for special treatment when the doctors of his home city had failed to bring him back to consciousness.

He was introduced to the Hardy boys by Miss Todd, who was pathetically grateful to the lads for restoring her brother to her, safe and sound again. But there was no sign of recognition. Seeing the boys struck no responsive chord in Professor Todd's memory. He knew nothing of the days when he had played at being Captain Royal. To all intents and purposes, he was seeing the Hardy boys for the first time.

They were content to let it remain at that and were careful to say nothing that might indicate they had known him previously. And when Todham Todd finally left the hospital and went to the hotel where his sister was staying, to rest there a few days before going back home, the Hardy boys were his firm friends.

"We must never let him know," said Evangeline Todd to the boys that evening.

"You may rely on us, Miss Todd," they assured her.

"I can't tell you how grateful I am," she said. "If you boys had not been shrewd enough to think that Captain Royal might be Todham Todd after all, things might not have turned out as they have. You might not have concerned yourselves with him any more, and he might still be living that wretched life in the caves. I want to reward your father and yourselves for finding him."

But Fenton Hardy had already expressed himself on the subject of the reward.

"I want nothing," he said. "You have already paid any expenses I incurred in trying to trace Mr. Todd. As for finding him, the credit belongs to the boys."

But the Hardy boys were insistent in their refusal.

"We're only too glad that we helped find him," they told Miss Todd. "We couldn't accept a reward for what we did. In a way, it was chance that threw him in our path."

Although Miss Todd pleaded with them to alter their decision, they were firm.

"Our greatest reward is in seeing your brother with you again, with his memory restored," declared Frank. "We want nothing more than that."

But Miss Todd expressed her appreciation in tangible form before she left Bayport. She invited the Hardy boys and some of their chums, Chet Morton, Biff Hooper, Phil Cohen, Tony Prito, Jack Dodd and Jerry Gilroy, to a banquet at the hotel, and there the lads sat down to a "spread" the like of which they had not seen before. There was everything dear to the heart of a boy, from fried chicken, fluffy mashed potatoes and sweet pickles, to ice-cream and five different kinds of pie.

Professor Todham Todd, white-haired, kindly-faced, looking quite different from the wild-eyed Captain Royal of Honeycomb Caves, presided at the banquet and made a little speech in which he thanked them all for their interest in his welfare and their kindness to him. Although he had no idea of the real part the Hardy boys and their chums had played in his recovery, he had taken a genuine liking to them and it is probable that he enjoyed the banquet as much as any one.

When the lads had eaten of chicken and ice-cream until they could eat no more, Miss Todd stood up and said she had an announcement to make.

"You all know something of the circumstances under which we have gathered here tonight. You all know the debt of gratitude I owe to the Hardy boys, in particular, and to Chet Morton and Biff Hooper. So if they will stand up, I have something for them."

Blushing, the four lads got to their feet.

"All I can say," continued Miss Todd, "is that my brother and I thank you very, very much."

Todham Todd looked a bit bewildered, but he smiled quite as though he knew what it was all about. It was probable that the good man was mildly puzzled until the end of his life as to the reason for the presentations.

For Miss Todd thereupon handed Frank and Joe an order for a handsome motion picture camera, something they had long wished to own. To Chet and Biff she gave each a gold watch and chain.

"Speech! Speech!" shouted the other boys, as the recipients of the gifts stammered their thanks.

After considerable pressure, Frank was at last prevailed upon to say a few words.

"I'm not a very good orator," he said.

"You're a better detective," shouted one of the lads at the table.

"I'm not a very good orator," he repeated, "but I certainly want to thank Miss Todd very much indeed, although we don't deserve such a beautiful present. I'm sure we're going to have a lot of fun with it. But we're mighty glad Professor Todd is better and—I guess that's all."

There were loud cheers for this effort, and Frank sat down blushing.

"Speech from Chet Morton!"

"Say, listen—" protested the bashful Chet.

But he was shoved to his feet.

"Speech! Chet Morton's going to make a speech!"

"Gosh, I can't say anything except that I thank Miss Todd very much and I'm glad Professor Todd is well again and—and I wonder if there's to be a second helping of ice-cream."

There was.

THE MYSTERY OF CABIN ISLAND

ORIGINALLY PUBLISHED IN 1929.

CHAPTER I

ICE-BOATING ON THE BAY

Driven by a stiff breeze from the west, a trim little ice-boat went scudding over the frozen surface of Barmet Bay. The winter air was cold and clear, the hills rising from the shores were blanketed in snow, and although a patch of black water away off toward the east gave evidence that King Frost had been balked at the Atlantic, the bay itself was a gleaming sheet of ice.

The long cold snap had caused rejoicing in the hearts of the young folk of Bayport. Although the ice in mid-bay was not solid, along the shore and in the numerous coves of the indented bay it was frozen to a safe depth. The dark figures of skaters sped like swallows in flight on the miniature natural rinks close to shore, and farther out the speeding ice-boats with their billowing sails resembled huge sea gulls as they raced before the wind.

Frank Hardy, a dark, handsome boy of sixteen, was at the tiller of the craft that represented several weeks' hard work on the part of himself and his brother Joe. Although it was homemade, the ice-boat was staunch and stoutly built and as it sped over the gleaming surface the boys were justifiably proud of their handiwork.

"This is great!" shouted Frank. "Ice-boating beats motorboating all to pieces."

Joe, a fair, curly-haired youngster who was a year Frank's junior, was sitting forward with their chum, Chet Morton.

"I'll say it is!" he agreed. "I don't think there's a faster boat on the bay."

Chet, plump and good-natured, his round face red with cold and shining like a full moon, kicked up his heels in ecstasy and nearly went overboard as the boat swerved to avoid an ice hummock ahead.

"This is real speed!" he declared, scrambling back to safety. "No traffic cops out here, either."

"Glad tomorrow is Saturday," said Frank. "We can spend the whole day out here."

"And the holidays!" exclaimed Joe. "Don't forget the Christmas holidays. Only another week."

"I'm glad you reminded me," Chet called out. "I had clean forgotten about them."

The others laughed. In his desk at school, Chet had a small calendar, and as each day passed he carefully stroked out the date and hopefully counted the days that remained before vacation.

"What say we go camping when the holidays come?" he suggested.

"Camping!" Frank exclaimed. "Camping is for summer time."

"Just as much fun in winter. There are lots of shacks and cottages along shore. We could rent one for a couple of weeks. One with a fireplace and a stove. With lots of firewood and blankets and grub we'd be as comfortable as we could wish—and think of the fun we'd have ice-boating."

"Say, that's a mighty good idea," ventured Joe. "Sometimes you do use your head for something besides putting your hat on it. What do you think, Frank?"

"I think that Chet has had a real idea—for once in his life."

Chet grinned good-naturedly at this chaff of his comrades.

"Well, if it's a good idea, let's carry it through."

Further discussion of the proposal was interrupted just then by the appearance of two large ice-boats racing out of one of the coves almost even with each other.

"A race!" shouted Frank. "Let's go."

He maneuvered the boat around and waited until the other boats were abreast, jockeying to get the full benefit of the wind. Then, when all three boats were on a line, they shot forward.

The boys in the other craft waved to the Hardy boys and shouted. On down the bay, over the smooth surface, sped the trio. The lad at the tiller of the biggest boat, over to the left, became excited and his craft swung around broadside. By the time he got around with the wind again his rivals had forged steadily ahead and he saw that it was almost hopeless to attempt to overtake them.

The remaining craft had an advantage over the Hardy boys' boat in that it had been constructed by a professional builder in Bayport. Its lines were trim and graceful and it had a wider spread of canvas. But the boy at the tiller found that he could not shake off the homemade boat that scudded persistently alongside.

Frank was taking advantage of every changing gust of wind. The breeze was changing and he tacked to starboard, allowing his rival a momentary burst of speed that left the Hardy boys trailing in the rear.

"Too bad!" muttered Chet. "Can't beat *that* boat."

"Just wait and see," advised Frank.

The changing breeze filled the sail and again the ice-boat sprang forward. The other craft was slowing down, and the steersman was desperately trying to bring it about with the wind again. But he was too late. The Hardy boys' boat swept triumphantly across his bow and Chet gave a shout of delight. On down the bay sped the little craft and by the time the other boat's sails were billowing again the lads were far in the lead. Looking back, they saw the beaten rival slowly turning about into the wind, heading back up the bay.

"That's real seamanship!" declared Joe.

"Oh, well, we have a good boat," returned Frank, refusing to claim any credit for the victory. "We were lucky the wind changed."

Ahead of them loomed a high, gloomy cliff, rising sheer from the ice. Beyond that, they knew, was one of the largest coves on Barmet Bay, known as Cabin Cove.

"Let's go on and take a look at Cabin Island," suggested Chet. "Seeing we're so close to the place we might as well pay it a visit."

"Sure thing," approved the others.

Cabin Island, in Cabin Cove, was a lonely spot, even more desolate now that the bay was locked in ice. It was seldom visited, even in the summer months, because it was an inhospitable place, with high cliffs rising almost directly from the water, with only a few landing places that were difficult of access.

The Hardy boys had often wanted to visit the island in the summer, but their motorboat, the *Sleuth*, was too large to be maneuvered among the rocks that skirted the lonely shore, without running danger of being dashed to pieces by the angry waves.

"We won't have any trouble making a landing now," said Frank. "We can bring the ice-boat right up to the base of the cliffs until we find a place where it is possible to climb to the top."

The island was heavily covered with timber, and at one time it had been inhabited, for a big log cabin had been constructed on an eminence overlooking the bay. From this cabin, the island had derived its name. The cabin was deserted now, and to the boys' knowledge no one had lived there for the past five years, either in summer or winter.

The ice-boat swung around the point, the cliffs lowering bleakly overhead, and they sped down into the great cove.

Cabin Island, dark and austere, lay before them, the ice gleaming on every side. The evergreen timber rose above the white snow, and at the southern end of the island the cabin could be plainly seen.

Within a few minutes, the ice-boat was speeding along in the lee of the island, close to the steep walls of rock. The boys eagerly scanned the cliffs in the hope of finding a landing place.

At last Frank gave a murmur of satisfaction and steered the craft toward a break in the cliff. Here there was a small ravine and against the background of snow the boys distinctly saw a path that wound up the sloping side of the ravine toward the cabin above.

"Thought there'd be a landing place here somewhere," he said.

"Queer," said Chet, eyeing the path. "Must be some one on that island."

"There are footprints, sure enough."

"It snowed three days ago. There must have been some one here since then," Joe observed.

"Probably some other chaps came out here in an ice-boat," said Frank carelessly. "If that's the case, they've been kind enough to break trail for us."

He guided the ice-boat into the little bay and its sail flapped idly as it came to a stop just a few feet from shore. The boys hopped out on to the ice and stretched their legs, then anchored the craft and made it secure. The little bay was sheltered from the wind. It was a natural harbor, and evidently the owner of the island had built his cabin where he did because of this ideal landing place that in summer was almost hidden from view by the overhanging trees.

Frank was examining the footprints leading toward the upper level.

"Only one set of footprints here," he said. "They seem quite fresh, too. I wonder if any one is up there now."

"Must be," returned Joe. "The footprints lead up the hill, but there is none leading back."

"Perhaps he went down the other side," Chet suggested. "Well, we can't let that scare us away. Let's go."

With Frank in the lead, the boys began to ascend the winding path, following those mysterious footprints in the snow.

They were about halfway up the side of the ravine when suddenly a dark figure appeared from behind a clump of trees a few yards ahead. A surly-looking man, black-browed and swarthy, advanced toward them, striding through the snow.

"What are you doing here?" he demanded in a rasping voice.

"Just thought we'd explore the island, sir," answered Frank. "We hope you don't mind."

"I do mind!" retorted the stranger curtly. "Get away from here and stay away. I don't allow visitors."

"But—"

"No argument!" he snapped. "You're trespassing here. Get away, now. Make tracks."

"We won't damage anything," piped Chet.

"Do you hear me? Get off this island at once! Clear out, and be quick about it!"

The stranger glared at them angrily. Frank saw that nothing would be gained by arguing the matter. He shrugged.

"All right, sir."

"Thanks for the hospitality!" sang out Chet, as the boys turned about and retraced their steps down the path.

CHAPTER II

HEADING FOR TROUBLE

"Something odd about this business," said Frank Hardy, as the three boys went back toward their ice-boat. "I don't see why he should be so anxious to keep visitors off his old island. We weren't doing any harm."

"He's a crab!" declared Chet. "Who is he, anyway?"

"I think his name is Jefferson," said Joe. "Elroy Jefferson. I've heard that he owns Cabin Island."

"Jefferson," said Frank reflectively. "I've heard that name before."

"Of course you have. He's an antique dealer. Sort of strange old codger, from all accounts. We saved his automobile for him, don't you remember?"

"Oh, now I know where I heard his name!" exclaimed Frank. "You're right. He lives in a big house up the Shore Road."

"Sure. His car was one of those stolen when the auto thieves were busy on the Shore Road. We found it in the cave when we rounded up the gang."

The incident to which Joe referred was the climax of one of the numerous mysteries solved by the Hardy boys. The brothers, who were introduced to our readers in the first volume of this series, entitled: "The Hardy Boys: The Tower Treasure," were the sons of a celebrated American detective, Fenton Hardy by name, and had already won considerable fame for themselves in and about their home city of Bayport by reason of their success in solving a number of mysteries that had baffled the local police.

Frank and Joe, although still in high school, were anxious to follow in their father's footsteps. Fenton Hardy was a hero to them. For many years he had been connected with the detective bureau of the New York police department, where he had earned such distinction that he was able to resign and move to Bayport, there to accept cases as a private investigator. Internationally famous, he was frequently called in to solve mysteries that had been given up by the police in all parts of the country, as well as accepting other assignments in which police action was not desired.

Already the two boys showed that they had inherited much of their father's ability. They were sharp, observant and intelligent enough to draw shrewd deductions from small clues.

In the volume immediately preceding the present story, "The Hardy Boys: The Secret of the Caves," the lads tackled a mystery that even Fenton Hardy had not been able to solve, the disappearance of an aged college professor, and had eventually found the old man after a series of thrilling adventures on a lonely part of the Atlantic coast.

"So that's Elroy Jefferson, is it?" said Frank. "Pleasant sort of customer, isn't he? He didn't treat us very well, considering we saved his automobile for him."

"Perhaps he doesn't know you," suggested Chet.

"That's possible. I remember now. He was in Europe at the time of the car-stealing affair."

"Perhaps this chap isn't Mr. Jefferson at all," put in Joe. "He may have sold the island."

"Well, whoever he is, I don't think much of him. What did he think we were going to do? Burn down his cabin?"

Chet laughed. "I guess he doesn't want his nice, pretty island all tracked up. Well, I suppose there's nothing for us but to go home. It's getting late, anyway."

The boys scrambled into the ice-boat. Before they started off, however, Frank looked back up against the lonely cabin, silhouetted at the top of the cliff against the dreary winter sky. The man who had driven them away was nowhere in sight.

"I can't get it out of my head that there's something strange about this business," he said. "I'd like to know why he was so anxious to chase us away."

"Aw, you see a mystery in everything," scoffed Chet. "He's just a cranky old chap who likes to show his authority. I'll bet he even tries to boss the rabbits and the snowbirds on the island. Let's go!"

The ice-boat moved slowly away from Cabin Island and the boys soon forgot their disappointment in the exhilaration of swift flight across the ice.

They swept out of the cove, around the rocky point, out into the bay. Far ahead of them lay Bayport, its towers and spires shining in the sunset. It was getting colder, and the wind stung their faces to a rosy glow.

"If we go camping in the holidays!" shouted Frank, "I guess Cabin Island is off our list, at any rate."

"It would be a mighty fine place to camp," said Joe regretfully. "It's too bad Mr. Jefferson is such a crank. A good-hearted chap would let us live in his old cabin during the holidays."

"Well," remarked Chet, "this particular chap isn't at all good-hearted, so I suppose we'll just have to hunt up another camping spot."

The boys were silent. Cabin Island would have been an ideal place for their outing. It would be difficult to find another cabin as well constructed and so near Bayport.

Suddenly, Chet pointed ahead.

"Look at that ice-boat!" he exclaimed. "Must be a crazy man steering it."

Away in the distance they could see a large craft, twisting and turning in an erratic fashion. It would speed in a straight course for a hundred yards or so, then it would commence to zigzag crazily, at times veering over until the sail was almost level with the ice.

"He'll break his mast or his rudder," opined Frank. "Then he won't be so smart, when he finds himself stranded about three miles from town. A chap who will handle a boat like that doesn't deserve to have one."

However, the other craft seemed to be standing up under the senseless strain being imposed on it. It was a larger boat than that of the Hardy boys, and it was able to withstand mishandling that would have wrecked a smaller craft.

The boys did not alter their course, for they were some distance to leeward and under ordinary circumstances would not pass within shouting distance of the big boat. However, as they sped on, Frank saw that the other craft had ceased zigzagging and was now bearing toward them. Its huge sail was full and it was gathering speed.

"That big boat can certainly travel!" exclaimed Chet.

"I'll say it can. If he doesn't change his course that chap will travel right into us."

As the big boat drew nearer the boys saw that there were two men on board. Frank mentally checked over the various ice-boats he had seen on the bay and thought he recognized the approaching boat as belonging to Tad Carson and Ike Nash, two young men of unsavory repute in the city. They were loud-mouthed, insolent fellows who had never been known to do a day's work, and it was a mystery how they had managed to raise sufficient money to buy the ice-boat in which they were now amusing themselves.

"He'd better change his course," said Joe nervously. "He's heading right toward us."

"Not if I know it," said Frank. "If he won't change, then I will."

He bore down on the tiller and their ice-boat swung around out of the path of the other.

Then, to their amazement and consternation, the lads saw that the big craft had also swung around and that it was still hurtling forward at terrific speed.

"They're going to run us down!" shouted Chet, in alarm.

The big boat was only fifty yards away. The lads could see Ike Nash at the tiller, his mouth open in an ugly grin.

In another moment, the big craft would crash broadside into the small boat, and so great was its speed that the Hardy boys' boat would certainly be wrecked beyond repair and it was possible that the boys themselves might be seriously injured.

Then they saw Ike bear down on the tiller again, evidently trying to avert the catastrophe at the last minute. It had been a crude practical joke on his part, to frighten the lads.

Then he looked up, his face frightened, and shouted.

The tiller had not responded!

The big ice-boat did not change course. It was booming down on the smaller craft at terrific speed!

CHAPTER III

A STRANGE NOTE

Had it not been for Frank Hardy's coolness and presence of mind, there would have been a disastrous collision.

His quick hand at the tiller averted the crash by a hairbreadth. How he did it, he could not later explain. At the time, Chet and Joe could see no possible chance of escape. But, just as the collision seemed imminent, their craft veered off to one side and the other boat went booming past at terrific speed, the two ice-boats so close together that their sides almost touched.

It was a narrow escape. Frank had swung the nose of his boat around just in the nick of time.

He brought the craft around in a circle, for the boys were in no mind to let the affront pass. Then they saw that the other boat had overturned. The boy at the helm, frightened by the imminence of peril, had lost his nerve, had swung the boat too far over, and it had gone on its side. The mast had snapped. The boat was wrecked.

The Hardy boys and Chet Morton went back to the scene. Tad Carson and Ike Nash were just crawling out from under their capsized craft.

"What's the big idea?" roared Nash, in an ugly humor. "Now see what you've done. You might have killed us!"

"Take some of that for yourself," rejoined Frank, walking over. "It was your own fault. You tried to run us down."

"Run you down! I like that! You head straight for us and then say we tried to run you down. You've smashed our boat, so you have, and you'll pay for it."

"Try to collect!" advised Chet airily. "By rights, we ought to have you up in court. Trying to be smart, weren't you?"

Both the other boys were bigger than Chet, but this never bothered that boy—as long as some one was with him.

"Absolutely deliberate, wasn't it, Tad?"

"You bet!" said Carson. "The young brats drove right at us. If they had hit us we might have been killed."

Their cool effrontery amazed the Hardy boys.

"You've got a lot of nerve," snapped Joe. "Trying to lay the blame on us. It serves you right to have your boat smashed up. You would have smashed ours if we hadn't been lucky. After this, watch where you're going."

"Look here!" said Ike Nash truculently, doubling his fists and stepping forward. "I won't stand talk like that from you."

"No?" said Frank, edging over to Joe's side, and doubling his fists as well. "What are you going to do about it?"

"Yes," added Chet, trying to achieve a threatening expression, "what are you going to do about it?"

Ike and Tad surveyed the three lads who stood facing them, with fists ready. Like most bullies, they were cowards, and now that their bluff had been called they were not anxious to risk a battle that might prove the worse for them.

"You'll find out what we'll do about it," growled Ike. "As for me, I wouldn't waste my time thrashing you, although you need it mighty bad—"

"Sure," agreed Tad Carson quickly. "I wouldn't lower myself to lick you. Just a pack of babies, that's all. You oughtn't to be allowed out on the bay when you can't handle a boat."

"It's your boat that got smashed," Chet reminded them cheerfully. "How was that for handling?"

"Come on," said Ike. "Don't talk to the brats, Tad. What's the use wasting time on them?"

"That's what I say," agreed his companion, and they returned loftily to their smashed boat, trying to conceal their chagrin.

"Want a ride back?" chirped Chet.

"You clear out of here, or we'll smash your boat too."

"Let's go," advised Frank. "They're in a bad humor. It wasn't our fault. I think we were lucky to escape so easily. If our boat had been smashed they would have just laughed at us."

The lads scrambled back into their ice-boat and in a few minutes they were sailing up the bay again, past the wreckage of the other craft. Ike Nash and Tad Carson were clumsily trying to put it to rights.

"That'll teach 'em to go around scaring people," observed Chet Morton virtuously, as they flashed by. He waved ironically at the marooned sportsmen, and was rewarded only by a shake of the fist from Ike Nash.

In a short time, the lads were back at Bayport, and, having placed the ice-boat in its berth, they walked up the snow-covered street toward the Hardy home. This was a fine brick residence on High Street, with a garage where the boys kept their motorcycles and the decrepit auto they had bought with their savings and which had been of so much value in solving the Shore Road mystery of the stolen automobiles, as recounted in the volume of that title. At the rear was a barn, which had been fitted up as a gymnasium, where the Hardy boys and their chums spent many happy hours on rainy and stormy Saturdays.

When the Hardy boys said good-bye to Chet Morton and entered the house they were greeted by Aunt Gertrude, a peppery, dictatorial lady of certain temper and uncertain years, who was again with the Hardys for a visit of indeterminate length. Aunt Gertrude could never reconcile herself to the idea that the boys were growing up and persisted in treating them as though they were still infants, or, as Joe expressed it, "as if we were half-witted."

"Go back and stamp the snow off your shoes!" she ordered, as they tramped into the hall. "It's a disgrace, the way you two boys track up this house just as soon as I've got everything all cleaned up."

There was very little snow on the boys' boots, and Aunt Gertrude never, under any circumstances, assisted in the house cleaning, but it was her nature to give orders. The boys knew better than to disobey, so they meekly returned to the vestibule and stamped their shoes, then came back into the hall.

"That's better," said their aunt grudgingly. "Now go into the library. Your father is waiting for you. You should have been home hours ago. I declare I don't know where you spend your time. Just gallivanting around when you should be at home doing your studies."

The boys went on into the library. The door was open and when they entered they found their father, Fenton Hardy, the noted detective, perusing an imposing grist of legal documents at his desk. He glanced up and smiled at them.

"Hello, sons! Been out on the bay?"

"Yes, sir," returned Frank. "Out in the ice-boat."

"Good, healthy sport. Have a good time?"

"Oh, yes. We went away down as far as Cabin Island."

"Cabin Island, eh? That's strange. I've had Cabin Island in my mind for the past hour or more. There has been a message here, waiting for you."

"A message?"

Mr. Hardy reached into his desk and produced an envelope.

"A man called here this afternoon and left this message for you boys."

"But why should it remind you of Cabin Island, Dad?" asked Joe.

"Because the man who left the message here was Elroy Jefferson's chauffeur."

"Elroy Jefferson!" exclaimed Frank. "Why, he is the man who owns Cabin Island."

"So I believe. Well, there's the note, at any rate. Better read it and find out what he has to say."

Frank tore open the envelope and removed a folded slip of paper. There were a few type-written words. He and Joe read them with growing amazement.

"Well, what do you know about that?" exclaimed Frank finally.

"I wonder what's the idea?" said his brother.

Frank handed the note over to their father.

"What do you make of it, Dad?"

Fenton Hardy read the note. He looked puzzled. Then he handed it back to the boys.

"I can't say, I'm sure," he said. "It's a strange note. Still, I suppose you had better do as he asks, and then you'll know more about it later."

"We certainly will!" said Frank.

Then he read the note over again.

CHAPTER IV

HOLIDAY PLANS

The note which puzzled the Hardy boys was as follows:

Messrs. Frank and Joseph Hardy,
Bayport.

Dear Sirs:

If it is convenient for you to call upon me at my residence tomorrow I should like to talk to you about a matter that has been in my mind since my return from Europe. If you will be good enough to call early tomorrow afternoon I will explain further.

Yours very truly,

Elroy Jefferson.

"A matter that has been in his mind ever since his return from Europe," said Frank. "I wonder what it can be."

"Well, we recovered his automobile for him from the Shore Road thieves," ventured Joe.

"What has that to do with it?" asked Fenton Hardy, smiling.

"Mr. Jefferson wasn't in Bayport at the time. You remember, we got a big reward for clearing up that case and the owners of the stolen cars contributed to it. But as Mr. Jefferson was away, he wasn't in on that. Perhaps he wants to add to it," said Joe hopefully.

Fenton Hardy shook his head in amusement.

"I thought you did very well. Surely you aren't looking for more money."

"Oh, we're not *looking* for more. Still, if Mr. Jefferson feels hurt because he couldn't show his appreciation, why, we wouldn't turn down any offer," and Joe grinned.

"I don't know Mr. Jefferson," said Frank. "What's he like, Dad?"

"He is an antique dealer," returned Mr. Hardy. "He is quite well known in his own field. He travels in Europe a great deal, buying antiques. Of late years he has kept very much to himself. I believe he has made a great deal of money, and in his time he was one of the leading experts in antique furniture in the country."

"Isn't he still an expert?"

"Oh, yes. But he isn't as prominent as he once was. Something happened to him a few years ago that made the old fellow very strange. I don't remember exactly what it was; but since that time he has been something of a character."

"Sounds interesting," commented Joe. "Well, I guess we'd better go and see him tomorrow, hadn't we, Frank?"

"Sure thing. We can ask him why he keeps such a tough-looking watchman on Cabin Island."

"A watchman?" exclaimed Fenton Hardy.

"Yes. We landed there this afternoon and a man told us to clear out. Said we were trespassing."

"That doesn't sound like Elroy Jefferson," said Mr. Hardy. "I'm sure he wouldn't give any such orders. As far as I remember him, he has always been a rather kindly old chap."

"We thought perhaps he had sold the island."

"I haven't heard of its changing hands. I can't imagine why he would have a watchman there in the winter, anyway. Ask him about it when you see him tomorrow."

The next morning, although the boys had discussed the note from Mr. Jefferson many times, they had still failed to arrive at any satisfactory conclusion as to the reason why he should want them to call on him; so they were awaiting the interview with curiosity and expectation.

That morning, while on an errand downtown for their mother, the brothers met Callie Shaw and Iola Morton. Both girls attended the Bayport high school and were in the same grade as the Hardy boys. Callie, a brown-eyed, brown-haired girl, was Frank's particular favorite among the girls at school, while Iola, plump and dark, Chet Morton's sister, was the only girl who had ever won even a reluctant admiration from the bashful Joe, who had even gone so far as to admit that she was "all right—as a girl." Which, from Joe, was high praise.

"Well, it's good to see you alive!" exclaimed Callie. "From what we've been hearing, it's lucky you're able to come downtown at all today."

"Yes," chimed in Iola, "Chet has been telling me all about it. I should think you'd have been patting yourself on the back ever since."

The boys looked at one another blankly.

"What yarn has Chet been springing now?" asked Frank.

"No yarn. He was telling us how narrowly you all escaped being killed out on the bay yesterday afternoon."

"Oh, that!" laughed Frank. "It wasn't so bad. We might have got bumped about a bit, but we were lucky."

"That's letting *you* tell it!" exclaimed Iola. "Chet says that if it hadn't been for the way you handled that ice-boat, Frank, there would have been a terrible smash-up."

"Oh, Chet usually exaggerates," said Frank uncomfortably.

"You're too modest," put in Callie quickly. "He told us all about it. I think you deserve a lot of credit, Frank."

"You bet he does!" cried Joe warmly, oblivious of his brother's embarrassment. "He saved our lives."

"And as for those other boys!" continued Callie. "If that Ike Nash or Tad Carson ever dare speak to me again I'll go past them with my nose in the air. Won't you, Iola?"

"I certainly will. And I'm going to tell the other girls about it, too. I think it was mean of them, and I'm glad their old boat got smashed."

"Oh, I guess they've suffered enough," said Frank. "No use rubbing it in."

"If they had smashed your boat they would have told the story all over Bayport. I'm certainly glad it turned out the way it did," said Callie.

"Drat that Chet," muttered Frank, after the girls had gone on down the street. "Why can't he keep quiet? He'll be making me out a hero if he keeps up. I didn't want anything said about that affair."

"Well, only two girls know about it now," returned Joe, comfortingly.

"*Only* two girls!" snorted Frank. "He might as well have published it in the newspaper."

Nevertheless he was inwardly pleased by Callie's evident concern over his narrow escape and by her admiration of the way he had acquitted himself in the emergency.

That afternoon, immediately after lunch, the Hardy boys set out for the handsome Jefferson home on the Shore Road. The place was not far away, and as the snow was too deep to permit of using their motorcycles, the boys went on foot. Before they had come within sight of the place they met a chum, Biff Hooper, who frequently accompanied the Hardy boys on their adventures.

They found Biff, who was pugilistically inclined, dancing about in the snow, making wild dashes and lunges at an imaginary sparring partner. He did not see Frank and Joe at first and when they came up to him he had evidently just put the finishing touches to the invisible antagonist, for he was breathing heavily and, as he looked down into the snow, he was counting! "Seven—eight—nine—ten—Out!"

"Hurrah for the new champion!" shouted Joe. "Did you knock him out, Biff?"

Biff swung around quickly and looked very foolish.

"Just doing a little shadow-boxing," he explained, very red in the face. "I didn't hear you coming."

"Practising to clean up on the championship?" asked Frank pleasantly. "Whoever he was, you knocked him right off the map."

"Say," said Biff, anxious to change the subject, "I've been wanting to see you fellows."

"Looking for a fight?" asked Joe. "Sorry, but we've decided not to do any fighting until after Christmas because Santa Claus mightn't like it and then he wouldn't put anything in our stockings. You want to be careful, Biff. If Santa hears you've been shadow-boxing out in the main road you mightn't get any lollipops on Christmas Eve."

"Aw, dry up," grumbled Biff. "I've been wanting to see you—no kidding."

"What about?"

"What are you going to do in the Christmas holidays?"

"Don't know," replied Frank. "We haven't made any plans yet. I guess we'll just hang around town. We've got the ice-boat, and there'll be some skating."

"How about an outing of some kind? I've had that in my mind for the past two or three days. Don't you think we could all get away somewhere and go camping."

"Sounds good," approved Joe. "Where shall we camp?"

"I don't know. I thought you chaps could look after that end of it."

"It isn't so easy to go camping in winter. In summer there are lots of places."

"Well, think it over," said Biff. "If you think of a good place and decide to go, be sure and let me know. I'd like to be in on it."

"Sure thing. We wouldn't leave you out, Biff."

"If we could get away right after school closes we could have a good long holiday in camp."

"How about Christmas?" inquired Joe doubtfully. "We shouldn't want to miss Christmas, should we?"

"Worrying about your presents?"

"I'd hate to miss them."

"Maybe we could get them before we went."

"In that case," said Joe, relieved, "I wouldn't care when we went to camp."

"Well, think it over." Biff made a vicious left swing at his imaginary sparring partner. "Be sure and let me know."

Then he chased the invisible enemy down the road and was soon lost to sight around the bend.

"He's going to miss one of those wild swings of his some day and knock himself out," prophesied Joe. "I never did see a fellow so crazy about boxing."

"He's good at it. Still, that's not a bad idea he has about camping during the Christmas holidays. We'll talk it over with Chet."

"Sure."

The boys went on and in a short time they came to the Jefferson house. It was a large, gloomy mansion, set back some distance from the road, and when the boys went up the walk, which had been swept and shoveled clear of snow, it was with a quickening sense of anticipation.

They rang the bell.

"We'll soon know what Mr. Jefferson wants to see us about," said Frank.

The door opened.

The housekeeper, a prim, angular woman, regarded them silently for a moment.

"Mr. Jefferson asked us to call," explained Frank.

"He is expecting you," said the woman. "You will please come in."

They stepped into a gloomy hall and the housekeeper ushered them toward a reception room.

"Please be good enough to wait," she said stiffly. "Mr. Jefferson is engaged at present."

Then she went away, her skirts swishing.

Frank and Joe Hardy sat uncomfortably on the extreme edges of their chairs and looked at the enormous family portraits on the walls. They could hear voices from a living room beyond. At first they could not distinguish anything that was being said—not that they listened—there being a mere hum of conversation, but suddenly one of the men in the next room raised his voice, sharply:

"I don't see why you won't sell, Mr. Jefferson! I offer a good price."

It was evident that the speaker was angry and perturbed.

Then, in another voice, also raised, came the reply:

"The island is not for sale at any price, Mr. Hanleigh, and that settles it."

This, presumably was Elroy Jefferson, the antique dealer. The other man expostulated.

"But you know very well I'm offering more money than—"

"I do not care to discuss it!" returned Mr. Jefferson. "The island is not for sale. That's final! No! No! I don't care to talk about it any more. You are only wasting your time. Good-day to you, sir."

CHAPTER V

MR. HANLEIGH

The Hardy boys heard the door of the living room open and saw two figures pass out into the hall. A moment later the front door closed with a bang. There were footsteps, and then a small, kindly, gray-haired gentleman stood in the entrance of the reception room.

Frank and Joe, in the meantime, were looking at one another in astonishment. They had recognized the voice of Mr. Jefferson's caller, and they had recognized the man himself as he passed in the hall. It was none other than the man who had ordered them away from Cabin Island!

Elroy Jefferson was advancing toward them, his hand outstretched.

"I'm sorry to keep you waiting, boys. You are Fenton Hardy's sons, I presume. Well, well. I'm glad to make your acquaintance. I didn't mean to make you wait, but my caller seemed insistent." He seemed rather disturbed and glanced back toward the door, shaking his head. "That fool can't take no for an answer," he muttered.

Then, smiling, he turned toward the boys again.

"I asked you to call here this morning because I wanted to thank you for getting my Pierce-Arrow back for me. I was traveling in Europe at the time and I didn't know anything about the affair until I came back. I'm afraid you must have thought me very ungrateful."

"Not at all, sir," said the boys politely.

"Well, if I had been here at the time you may be sure I would have expressed my appreciation at once. However, better late than never. I was away when the Automobile Club passed the hat for that reward."

Elroy Jefferson referred to a reward which had been subscribed by various owners of cars which the Hardy boys had recovered from the Shore Road thieves.

"That's all right, sir," said Frank. "We weren't looking for any reward."

"I know. I know. But you deserved one. And, if you will allow me, I should like to give you a reward of my own."

With that, he produced a wallet from his pocket and withdrew two crisp, new bills which he handed to the boys. The lads glanced at the money with surprise, for Elroy Jefferson had handed each a hundred-dollar bill.

"Oh, we can't take this, Mr. Jefferson," protested Joe. "We've been very handsomely rewarded already, much more than we deserved—"

"I want you to take this money. My car was not insured and was worth a great deal more than that to me, and if it hadn't been for you two boys I would have lost it."

The boys protested, but Elroy Jefferson insisted, and finally they were forced to accept the reward.

"Now," said Mr. Jefferson, "if there is anything else I can do for you at any time, don't hesitate to ask me."

The boys looked at one another.

"There is something we'd like to ask you," hesitated Frank. "That is, if we're not intruding—"

"What is it?" asked the antique dealer agreeably.

"It's about the man who just left here."

"Hanleigh? What about him?"

"If you don't object to the question—does Mr. Hanleigh own Cabin Island?"

Mr. Jefferson shook his head.

"Certainly not. Why do you ask?"

Frank then told him about the adventure of the previous day, and related how Hanleigh had driven the three boys away from the island.

"We thought it was strange at the time, for we didn't think that the island had changed hands. Then, when we recognized Mr. Hanleigh as the chap who ordered us away, we thought we'd ask you about it."

Elroy Jefferson was indignant.

"Why, I never heard the like!" he said testily. "He had no authority to order you away. None whatever. In fact, he had no right to be on the island himself. The whole place belongs to me."

"He had no right to order us away, then?"

"No right at all. The island is mine. Mr. Hanleigh, it seems, is anxious to buy it, but he hasn't bought it yet and he won't buy it, as long as the matter is in my hands. He came to me a few weeks ago and offered me five thousand dollars for the place."

"That is a large sum for an island, isn't it?" said Frank.

"More than the place is worth. He came back this morning and raised his offer. Wanted to give me eight thousand dollars if I would sell. But I won't sell. I won't sell him the island at any price, and I told him so. You see, when my wife and son were alive they loved to go there in winter and summer, so Cabin Island has certain associations for me that cannot be estimated in terms of money. They are dead now, and I cannot bear to part with the place. The cabin was erected for the use of my family, and my wife and boy used to go there and watch the workmen building it. So I'm not at all inclined to turn the place over to strangers."

"I see, sir," remarked Frank sympathetically.

"I'm sorry if Mr. Hanleigh drove you away. He had no right to do that."

"Of course, we had no right there, in the first place," ventured Joe.

"Just as much right as Hanleigh. Now, boys, I have no objection to letting you visit the island from time to time, if the place appeals to you, providing you don't disturb things."

"We would be very careful."

"I'm sure of that. Any time you want to visit Cabin Island, go right ahead. And if Mr. Hanleigh is there and has anything to say about it you can tell him he has no authority and no right to be on the property. I can't imagine why he was prowling around there at all."

"We were thinking of having an outing during the Christmas holidays," said Frank. "Our big difficulty was in finding a good camping place. Why couldn't we stay on Cabin Island, Mr. Jefferson? We could have our outing there, and at the same time we could look after your property."

Elroy Jefferson nodded agreeably.

"An outing, eh? Just you two boys?"

"We have two or three of our chums along with us."

"That would be fine. I envy you. A winter outing. I think Cabin Island would be ideal for that. And, if Mr. Hanleigh is busying himself ordering people away from there, I imagine it wouldn't be a bad idea to have some one on the ground to look after things. You have my permission, boys. Go ahead, and have your outing at Cabin Island."

"That's mighty good of you, Mr. Jefferson!" exclaimed Frank impulsively, and Joe echoed:

"You bet!"

"Not at all. I know you can be depended on to leave things as you find them. I'll tell you what I'll do. I'll put the whole matter in your charge and I'll turn over the keys of the cabin to you. I think you'll find it a very comfortable place."

That was how the Hardy boys and their chums received permission to hold their winter outing on Cabin Island.

CHAPTER VI

PREPARATIONS

When the Hardy boys returned home after their visit to Elroy Jefferson they hastened to tell their father about the munificent reward the antique dealer had given them for recovering his automobile. Then came the momentous matter of securing permission for the vacation outing.

Fenton Hardy listened with a smile.

"So you want to leave us during the Christmas holidays," he said. "You don't mind missing Christmas dinner, with the turkey and the pudding and the nuts and raisins and candy. You don't mind going without your presents this Christmas. You'd rather go camping."

"Would we *have* to miss our presents?" asked Joe anxiously.

"Well, you know that Christmas presents are usually given out on Christmas morning in this house. If you're not here—"

"Couldn't we get them before we go away?"

Mr. Hardy laughed. "You want presents and outing both, I see. Well, I suppose it can be arranged. I have no objections to letting you go camping, seeing Mr. Jefferson has been good enough to allow you the use of Cabin Island. If you take proper equipment with you, plenty of food and blankets, you should be comfortable enough. As a matter of fact," he murmured, "I wouldn't mind going with you myself."

"Will you come, Dad?" shouted Frank.

"I'm afraid I wouldn't be able to get away. Go ahead with your outing— if your mother agrees."

Mrs. Hardy, it appeared, had no objections, although at first she was reluctant in view of the fact that the boys would be absent from the family circle over Christmas Day. "It won't seem like Christmas without my lads," she said.

Aunt Gertrude, of course, insisted on contributing her "two cents' worth," as Joe expressed it.

"Camping in the winter time!" she sniffed. "I never heard the like of it. They'll freeze to death."

"We'll be just as comfortable as if we were in town, Aunt Gertrude," said Frank. "The cabin is well built and warm, and we'll have plenty of heavy blankets with us."

"You'll need 'em. As for being comfortable, I'll warrant you'll be glad to come humping back home where everything is nice and cosy. You'll find a big change, my fine young men, when you get away down in that rickety shack, with the wind blowing through the chinks and the snow drifting in on the floor. If you stay there longer than one night, it will be a big surprise to me."

"Of course," put in Joe, "if you think you will miss us so very much—if you really think it would spoil your Christmas not to have us here, why we won't go."

Aunt Gertrude laughed mirthlessly.

"Spoil my Christmas! The idea! It will be a real merry Christmas again, without two noisy boys making life a botheration to me."

"In that case, then, we'll go camping," said Frank.

When they told Chet Morton of their interview with Elroy Jefferson, that youth was loud in his delight. He insisted promptly on being included in the proposed outing.

"The family is going to Boston for the holidays," he said. "They were going to leave me at home alone. It looked like a fine Christmas! But now— oh, boy! When do we start?"

"Three days before Christmas."

"Great! Who else is coming?"

"We promised Biff Hooper."

"Sure! Biff's a good scout. But don't make the party too large. That cabin won't hold very many."

"We figured on just the four of us," said Frank. "The ice-boat won't hold any more, anyway."

"Fine. We'd better get together tomorrow and decide how much grub we should take along. We've got to eat, you know."

"You *would* bring that up," laughed Joe. "No fear of going short of supplies when you're in the party. You'll see that we take enough."

"I must keep up my strength," returned Chet, unabashed.

When the boys met Biff Hooper and told him that the outing was assured and that Cabin Island was available, the pugilistic lad turned several handsprings in the snow by way of expressing his delight.

"Yeah!" he shouted. "That let's me out. My Uncle Oscar and his five kids are coming to spend Christmas at our place, and it would have been up to me to entertain the little pests. Now I'm out of *that*! Hurray!"

"This trip seems to be popular," remarked Frank. "Well, you'd better start figuring out what you can contribute in the way of grub. We each carry our own blankets."

"Suits me. I'll take *all* the grub, if you want."

Next day, the four gathered at Biff Hooper's home and, in a very businesslike manner, drew up a list of requirements for the trip, and apportioned what would be required of each. Inasmuch as Frank and Joe had secured the privilege of Cabin Island and were also giving the use of the ice-boat, Chet and Biff insisted on looking after the matter of food. Each boy was to take along whatever cooking utensils he could beg or borrow from home.

In this manner, with conferences after school and during the noon hours, the boys made their preparations for the outing, and the last days of the autumn term slowly dragged past. They had decided to leave Bayport three days before Christmas, almost immediately after school closed, and the intervening time was occupied by putting the ice-boat in readiness and accumulating everything they would need.

"We don't want to keep trotting back to the city every day for something we've forgotten," Chet pointed out.

At last, everything was in readiness. The food supplies were packed, the blankets were stowed away, the ice-boat had been overhauled, the boys had loaded skates, skis, and snowshoes on their craft, and everything had been checked over so that nothing would be forgotten. News of the proposed outing had circulated among the other boys at the Bayport high school and the Hardy boys were besieged with requests from many of their chums who wanted to accompany them. But they were obliged to refuse. The cabin was large, but it would not accommodate everybody.

Finally, school closed. There were the usual closing exercises, which the lads sat through impatiently, and then they raced toward home, for the trip to Cabin Island was definitely scheduled for the morrow.

Mrs. Hardy had taken liberties with the calendar, and when the boys came home that night they found, to their unbounded delight and astonishment, that the Christmas dinner had been set ahead. There was a turkey in the oven and the kitchen was redolent with the savory odors of a Christmas feast.

"Whoopee!" cried Joe. "We shan't miss our Christmas after all!"

The dinner, being in the nature of a surprise, surpassed all previous Christmas dinners. Somehow, the turkey was more succulent, the mince pie had a better flavor, simply because the boys had been resigning themselves to missing the good things that year. The mere fact that the calendar indicated Christmas Day as being actually four days off seemed to matter little.

Mr. Hardy had even ordered a Christmas tree and, after dinner, when the boys went into the library and found that even this crowning touch had not been omitted, they felt that life had little more to offer. The tree glittered with lights and there were certain mysterious packages in tissue paper that aroused speculations. Frank and Joe immediately dashed upstairs and returned with the presents they had bought for their parents and for Aunt Gertrude, which they distributed at the base of the tree.

"I think we're lucky," said Frank, when they went to bed that night.

"Lucky! I never expected to have Christmas and our outing too," returned his brother.

"Christmas dinner, a tree, and our presents!"

"I hope Chet and Biff get off as well."

They fell asleep, happy.

In the morning, the usual Christmas ceremony of opening the presents was observed. Frank and Joe were unusually fortunate. The usual gifts of clothing, which included neckties, scarfs, socks and shirts came first, then for each of the lads came a complete outing costume of breeches, mackinaw shirts and short coats. To top it all came two small calibre rifles, each with a box of ammunition.

"Don't kill too many rabbits," laughed their father.

Christmas was complete. Frank and Joe had given their parents one of the newest and finest radio sets and to Aunt Gertrude they gave several volumes of poems, as that lady was very fond of reading. For once in her life, their aunt did not sniff.

"Just what I wanted!" she beamed. "I have always adored Longfellow!"

At that moment the telephone rang. Chet was calling.

"All set!" he reported. "Biff and I are down here waiting."

"We'll be with you in a minute," said Frank.

So the Hardy boys set out on their vacation outing to Cabin Island. Little did they dream of the many strange happenings in store for them.

CHAPTER VII

THE OTHER ICE-BOAT

Chet Morton and Biff Hooper, it appeared, had not missed Christmas either. Their parents had surprised them just as Mr. and Mrs. Hardy had surprised Frank and Joe, and when the lads met at the boathouse half an hour later their preparations for an immediate departure were somewhat hindered by joyous discussion of the presents each boy had received. Among Biff's gifts was an ice-boat from his father, over which the lad was ecstatic.

"Well, let's go!" shouted Chet finally. "We can talk it all over when we get to Cabin Island."

They clambered into the ice-boats, Chet getting into Biff's new craft with the proud owner.

"Ready!" cried Frank.

"Ready!"

"We're off!"

The boats glided out onto the ice of the bay. There was a stiff breeze blowing and the boys anticipated a quick run to the island. The wind was strong and the sky was clear. The two boats sped alongside one another, their sails billowing.

The city was swiftly left behind and the open bay lay ahead. The winter air brought the flush of health to the boys' cheeks. Once in a while they waved to one another. The shores sped past.

Frank, at the tiller of the Hardy boys' craft, swung the boat around so that it got the full benefit of the breeze, and it forged ahead, leaving the other behind. This meant a race, so Biff brought his boat around with the wind and soon managed to overhaul his rivals. A vagrant breeze gave him the advantage for a while and he gained steadily while the Hardy boys, to their chagrin, lagged behind, but the breeze soon changed. Biff found himself running against the wind before he realized it. The Hardy boys' craft scudded swiftly across the ice, overtook him, then shot across his bows.

Frank and Joe maintained their lead from then on, taking advantage of every change in the wind, and in due time they came within sight of the dark bulk of Cabin Island, looming against the distant line of the shore.

Joe stood up and waved his arms in excitement. There was an answering wave from Chet, in the speeding craft to the rear.

Frank swung the boat toward the south, down into the cove. They drew closer to the island.

"Our friend Hanleigh can't bother us now," laughed Frank.

"We have full authority. It was a mighty lucky thing for us that we mentioned Cabin Island to Mr. Jefferson."

"I wonder what Hanleigh was doing on the island, anyway."

"I'll bet he was up to no good," said Joe. "Well, we won't worry about him. He won't trouble us."

However, Joe was destined to be mistaken.

The ice-boat sped across the glassy surface, drawing closer and closer to Cabin Island. Frank, peering ahead, suddenly gave an exclamation of surprise.

"Looks as if some one is here ahead of us."

"Where?"

Frank pointed to the little bay where they had landed on their previous visit. A white-sailed object was clearly outlined against the dark background of trees.

"Another ice-boat!"

Joe gazed at the strange craft in consternation.

"I wonder what that means."

"We'll soon find out. Somehow, that boat looks familiar to me," said Frank, as he steered toward the bay.

As they came closer, they saw that the other boat was deserted. Frank could not escape the conviction that he had seen the boat before. Slowly, he veered around until they ran alongside, within a hundred yards of the bay. Then he nodded.

"I knew it," he said quietly.

"That's the boat Tad Carson and Ike Nash were in the other day!" exclaimed Joe.

"There's something odd about this business. I wondered why they were so close to Cabin Island when we met them. I'll bet they were coming here to get Hanleigh."

"Perhaps you're right. What shall we do now, Joe?"

"Scout around a bit. We may learn something."

Frank did not go toward the bay. Instead, he guided the boat around the arm of the island. The boys signaled back to Biff and Chet, indicating that they were to follow.

"It beats me why Tad and Ike should be here, unless they have some connection with this fellow Hanleigh," said Frank.

"And I don't see why Hanleigh should be here at all. He hasn't bought the island yet. According to Mr. Jefferson, he has no business here."

"We'll run around the island once, and see what's what."

The Hardy boys did not have long to wait. Circling the end of the island, they came to a sheltered nook where they decided to land.

"We can leave the boats here and go up toward the cabin on foot," decided Frank. "If there is anybody here, we'll have a better chance of taking them by surprise."

They put in to the little bay and then waited until Chet and Biff, in the other boat, came up.

"What's the matter?" asked Chet, when their craft came to rest. "Who owns that other boat?"

"That's what we want to find out. We figured it would be best to lie low until we find what's going on around here," Frank told him.

"Good idea," approved Biff.

"That boat belongs to Tad Carson and Ike Nash. I thought the best plan would be to land here on the quiet and then go up to the cabin. They have no right here, and I'd like to know what they're up to."

The boys alighted from the boats. There was a sloping hillside before them, leading to a clump of evergreens. The snow was unbroken.

Frank took the lead and advanced up the slope. The others followed. When Frank reached the evergreens he paused and looked about. To his right he could see another bay farther down the shore, and there he spied a small boathouse.

The boathouse itself would not have attracted his attention so greatly had it not been for the fact that he saw a distinct line of footprints in the snow leading toward the rear door. Frank had his wits about him sufficiently to notice that the footprints were those of two people and that they led toward the boathouse—not away from it.

"Somebody there now," he commented briefly.

He led the way toward the boathouse. The others trudged silently after him.

Near the little building, Frank suddenly stopped and raised his finger to his lips. He had heard voices. With renewed caution, the boys stole forward. In the lee of the boathouse, they halted. Frank listened. He had heard the murmur of voices from some distance back. He pressed close to the boards.

"Well," he heard a voice saying, "it's none of my business, so I'm not going to worry about it."

Then there was a second voice.

"I'm not worrying. I'm just wondering."

"We have our money. That's all that should concern us."

"Nothing wrong in wondering what he's up to, is there?" said the other. "I think there must be something important around that old cabin."

Frank turned to the others. "Tad Carson and Ike Nash!" he whispered.

He turned to the wall of the boathouse again.

"I tell you, he wouldn't pay us for bringing him out to Cabin Island so often unless there was something behind it," Ike Nash was saying.

"That's all right. What if there is something behind it?" returned Carson. "It's none of our affair. He pays us. That's all we want. If Hanleigh cares to spend his time prowling around this island, why should we worry, as long as we get our money?"

The Hardy boys and their chums glanced at one another in surprise.

Hanleigh!

The man who had ordered them away from Cabin Island on their previous visit! The man whom Elroy Jefferson had said wanted to buy the place!

"I don't see why he won't let us go up to the cabin with him," grumbled Nash. "What does he want to keep secret from us?"

"That's his business," snapped Tad Carson. "If you go asking questions, then you'll just spoil everything. Leave well enough alone."

"Well, what are we going to do now? That's what I want to know."

"Stay where we are. He told us to leave the ice-boat and wait here until he came down from the cabin. Those are his orders. We get paid for obeying orders."

"Fine place to stay in!"

"What did you expect? A palace? We'll stay where we are. He said he wouldn't be long."

"He's been up in that cabin for half an hour already. What's keeping him?"

"I don't know and I don't care," snapped Tad Carson. "He's paying us to wait here for him, and we'll wait."

Without a word, Frank Hardy turned away and motioned to the other boys. In the deep snow they moved silently from the boathouse.

"Hanleigh's up at the cabin now," said Frank, when they were beyond earshot. "I think we'd better go up and find out what he's doing."

"Right!" approved Chet.

In single file, the boys went back up the slope in the direction of the cabin at the north end of the island.

CHAPTER VIII

SUSPICIOUS ACTIONS

"Well, I guess that explains why Tad Carson and Ike Nash were heading in this direction the day Hanleigh ordered us off the island," Frank Hardy said, when the boys were out of earshot.

"They were on their way to bring Hanleigh back to town," agreed Joe.

"He's been using their ice-boat to get back and forth to Cabin Island."

"Wonder what's the big idea," remarked Chet. "They don't seem to know what he's up to."

"No, but we will—and mighty soon. We're responsible for the cabin now, so it's up to us to find out what Hanleigh is doing there."

Biff looked dubious.

"He won't tell us, you can depend on that. Probably he'll tell us to clear out of here."

"What if he does? We now know he hasn't any authority. I'll tell you what we ought to do, fellows," said Frank. "We should try and catch our friend Hanleigh off his guard. If we detour around through the woods, we can come out at the back of the cabin. He'll never hear us coming through the snow. We'll take a peep through one of the windows and see what it's all about."

"That's a long way around," grumbled Chet.

"It won't take us far out of our way. The snow isn't very deep. We can make it easily enough. Come on."

Under Frank's leadership, the boys set out into the woods, trudging through the snow, detouring in order that they would not emerge at the front of the cabin. At last they were within sight of the little building. It seemed utterly deserted, but the boys were quite convinced, from what they had overheard at the boathouse, that Hanleigh was somewhere in the immediate neighborhood. They advanced cautiously.

At the rear of the cabin was a small window. They made this their objective. In the light snow their footfalls made no sound.

Frank took the lead. The others stood back for a moment while he went ahead, pressing close to the cabin wall. When he was at the window, he peeped in carefully. Frank gazed into the interior of the building for a short time. Then he turned and beckoned to his companions.

They came forward. Together, the boys looked into the cabin.

The interior design of the building was simple. One long room, with a huge stone fireplace, ran the length of the cabin. Bedrooms and a kitchen led off to the side. From the rear window the boys could see every detail of the main room, and as they now looked they could see a man standing before the fireplace.

Although the man had his back turned to them, they had little doubt but that he was Hanleigh. Frank and Joe nudged one another in excitement.

Hanleigh was quite unconscious that he was being watched. He stood before the fireplace, a long, slender stick in his hand. He stepped forward, measured a section of the stone chimney, stepped back and regarded the measured part, got down on his hands and knees and measured the base. Once in a while he shook his head in disgust and muttered something that the boys could not overhear.

The boys were puzzled. Why should Hanleigh be measuring the fireplace in this abandoned cabin?

In their eagerness, they forgot caution and gradually crowded closer and closer together until all four faces were pressed full against the windowpane. Had Hanleigh chanced to turn their way he would have seen them in a moment.

However, the man seemed too greatly occupied. He was concerned just then with the fireplace and evidently he considered himself quite safe from observation. Back and forth he went, examining the interior and exterior of the fireplace and the chimney, measuring it from every possible angle, even counting the number of stones. He took an envelope from his pocket and jotted down figures on the back of it.

Suddenly, there was a gust of wind.

The side door of the cabin, through which Hanleigh had evidently entered, blew wide open.

With a mutter of astonishment, the man swung around. He looked toward the door.

The Hardy boys and their chums ducked beneath the level of the window sill. But they were too late.

Hanleigh had seen them. They heard a shout of consternation. Then they heard heavy footsteps on the cabin floor. The door slammed. Hanleigh came running around the side of the building.

"Hold your ground!" advised Frank quietly to his companions. "Don't let him bluff us."

Hanleigh, red with wrath, confronted them. He recognized the Hardy boys at once.

"Spying on me, are you?" he shouted. "I thought I told you boys to stay away from this island."

"You told us," returned Frank coolly.

"Then what do you mean by this?" roared Hanleigh. "What do you mean by coming back here again? I've a good mind to horsewhip the whole crowd of you. A bunch of meddling youngsters! Now get out of here and stay away. If I catch you fellows on this island again, I'll—I'll—"

"You'll do nothing, Mr. Hanleigh," said Frank.

The man looked at them suspiciously.

"How do you know my name?" he demanded.

"It doesn't matter how we come to know your name. But we're here to tell you this, Mr. Hanleigh—you have no right to order us off the island. As a matter of fact, it works the other way."

"What?"

"We're not trespassing. You are. You have no right to be on this island at all. And you certainly have no right to be in this cabin."

"Why, you young whippersnapper!" choked Hanleigh. "I'll show you if I have any right to be here!"

"You can't show us. What are you doing here, anyway?"

"None of your business!"

"It *is* our business." Frank reached in his pocket and produced the key to the cabin. "See this key. Mr. Jefferson gave it to us. We're in charge of Cabin Island from now on. I'd advise you to clear out unless you want us to report the matter to Mr. Jefferson. He can very easily have you prosecuted for trespassing on the island. He told us you had been given no permission to come here."

Hanleigh was at a loss for words. This development came as a complete surprise to him.

"It's a—a lie!" he gasped finally.

"There's the key!" piped Chet. "Laugh that off."

"I don't believe Jefferson gave you that key at all."

"Oh, yes, he did. We know more about you than you think, Mr. Hanleigh. We know you've been trying to buy this place and we know Mr. Jefferson refused your offer. We were at his house the day you offered him eight thousand dollars for the place and he turned you down. Does that look as if we don't know what we're talking about?"

"What do you know about this place?" demanded Hanleigh.

"Nothing except what we've told you," Frank continued. "We would like to know, though, just why it is so interesting to you."

The shot went home. Hanleigh licked his lips nervously, then stared at the boys in silence for a while before replying:

"It isn't interesting to me," he said lamely. "That is—except as a cabin I'd like to buy."

"Was that why you were measuring the fireplace so carefully?" put in Biff dryly.

"I'm not going to argue about it. I'm going back to town and take up this matter with Jefferson. He gave me to understand that he wanted to sell the island, but he wants too much money for it. That's why I came out here to look the place over."

"You seem to come out quite often," remarked Frank. "Well, you'll find us in charge here from now on. Any time you can bring us a note signed by Mr. Jefferson, stating that you have permission to visit the place, we'll let you in. Just now, though, I think you'd better clear out."

Hanleigh clenched his fists, glared at the boys for a moment, and then turned on his heel. Without another word, he went away. The boys followed him around the side of the cabin and watched him as he strode heavily down the slope, muttering to himself.

"We'll see that he does go away," declared Frank.

The boys followed.

Near the edge of the cliff they saw Hanleigh turn and look back. He seemed surprised to find that they had followed him. Then, evidently deciding that further opposition was useless, he went on down the path that led toward the boathouse at the base of the cliff.

The boys stood watching until he reached the boathouse, and they watched until he emerged again with Tad Carson and Ike Nash. The trio stood looking up for a moment, and Hanleigh shook his fist in their direction.

"Merry Christmas!" shouted Chet.

If Hanleigh heard the greeting, he did not return it in kind.

The interlopers went on down the shore toward the place where they had left their ice-boat. They vanished around the bend. After a while, the boys saw the ice-boat emerge into the open bay and recede swiftly in the direction of Bayport.

"That's that!" exclaimed Biff cheerfully.

"He didn't have a leg to stand on, did he?" added Chet.

"I don't think we're through with Hanleigh yet," said Frank thoughtfully. "He isn't the sort to back down so easily at the first sign of fight. I have an idea that we'll see him on Cabin Island again before very long."

"Let him come," said Chet. "We have the authority. All he has is nerve. Let's put the ice-boats up in the bay and get our stuff unloaded."

The boys turned and went back toward their ice-boats.

"Just the same," muttered Joe, "I'd like to know what he was up to, measuring that fireplace so carefully."

Joe's thought was echoed in the minds of all. There was some mystery about Hanleigh's visits to Cabin Island.

CHAPTER IX

NIGHT ON CABIN ISLAND

It took the boys the greater part of the day installing themselves in the cabin on the island and "getting everything shipshape," as Chet expressed it, by nightfall. After they had made the boats secure they were obliged to make numerous trips from the shore to the cabin, bringing up supplies, but by the time the early winter twilight fell they had managed to make the place very cosy and habitable.

They were too busy to discuss the strange affair of Hanleigh. Mid-afternoon had brought a rising wind that sent sheets of snow scurrying across the frozen surface of Barmet Bay and they saw that a storm was approaching, which made them more anxious to get settled by night.

They drew lots for the position of cook, the agreement being that each boy should alternate, a day at a time. Chet, to his relief, won the first appointment. As he did not relish the business of tramping back and forth to the ice-boats in the snow, the arrangement was to his entire satisfaction and he was soon busying himself at the warm stove endeavoring to prepare a savory stew for their evening meal.

"Looks like a dirty night," commented Frank, as he gazed out over the bay. "I'm glad we'll be all snug and settled."

Blankets had been brought up, the beds had been made, the cupboard had been stocked and the main food supplies had been stored in a little room just off the kitchen. The lamps had been filled with oil, and Biff had even tacked a few highly colored pictures on the walls, "to take away the bare look of the place."

By nightfall one would have thought the adventurers had been living in the cabin for months.

The rising wind soon became a storm. As darkness fell, the snow began beating against the cabin windows and the gale howled down the great chimney. The boys had decided against using the fireplace for cooking purposes, the kitchen stove being more adaptable, but a roaring fire had been built and it cast a ruddy glow throughout the main room of the cabin.

Chet, with an apron tied about his corpulent waist, emerged from the kitchen from time to time, reporting the supper as "nearly ready," and each announcement was greeted with groans, for the fragrant odors were whetting the boys' appetites. At last, however, the table was laid, the steaming plates of stew were brought forth, and the boys fell to. Second helpings were in order, for the stew was excellent and the lads were hungry. Bread and butter, canned peas and corn, an immense mince pie and tin cups of hot coffee went the way of the stew, and in due time the boys sat back, sighing that they could not manage another bite.

Chet beamed with satisfaction when the others complimented him on the meal. The boys sat about the table for a while, laying plans for the forthcoming week, and then they washed the dishes. After that, they explored the rambling old cabin and finally sprawled on rugs before the roaring fire.

"Listen to that wind!" exclaimed Joe. "It sure makes me glad to be indoors by a warm blaze."

"With a full stomach," amended Chet.

"You *would* think of that."

"The place wouldn't seem half as cosy without that fireplace," said Biff. Frank regarded the great stone chimney.

"It certainly is a whopper. I wonder what Hanleigh was so interested in it for."

"Let's forget about Hanleigh," said Chet. "He won't bother us any more."

"Let's hope not. But, just the same, I'd like to know why he was making all those measurements."

"If he comes back, we'll heave him into a snowdrift and teach him a lesson," suggested Biff. "We won't let him spoil our holiday."

Outside, the storm had become a blizzard. Joe went to the window. He could see nothing but driving snow, and the wind was howling down upon the island. The cabin, staunchly built, scarcely trembled before the impact of the winter gale. The activities of the day had left the boys tired and they decided to go to bed early.

In due time, after much scuffling about and after Biff had chastised Chet for trying to hide his socks in the woodpile, the boys retired for the night and blew out the lamps. The fire glowed red and the night wind howled down the chimney. Under the heavy blankets, the lads were warm and comfortable.

Silence descended upon the cabin.

The boys were just snuggling down to sleep when a terrifying sound rose above the clamor of the wind.

"Owoooooo!"

It was like the wail of some anguished spirit.

With one accord, the boys felt their hair rising upon their scalps. No one said a word. The dreadful wail died away, then broke out again.

"Owoooooo!"

Then came Chet's voice, from between chattering teeth.

"Wh—wh—what was that?"

"Some of you chaps playing a joke on us?" demanded Frank suspiciously.

"N-not m-me," declared Chet.

"Me neither," said Joe.

"It wasn't me," Biff clamored.

Just then the sound broke out afresh.

"Owoooooo!"

It was a long-drawn-out, moaning sound that rose in volume to a veritable shriek, indescribably terrifying.

"Ghosts!" clamored Chet.

"There aren't any such things!" snorted Joe. "It must be the wind."

"You n-never heard the w-wind make a n-noise like that before, d-did you?" stammered Chet.

The other boys were forced to admit that they never had. The sound had a quality that was almost human. Besides, they had been listening to the howling of the wind all evening and at no time had it approached that mournful wail they had just heard.

"Maybe somebody is lost out in the snow and crying for help," suggested Biff.

"How could anybody get out to this island on a night like this?"

"Wait till we hear it again."

They listened. For a long time they did not hear the mysterious sound. Then, with a suddenness that made them all jump convulsively, the wailing was resumed.

"Owoooooo!"

This time, the noise lasted a good ten seconds, rising to a shriek of terror, then dying away to a dismal moaning.

"It's right in this cabin!" Chet said, in a muffled voice which indicated that he had hidden his head beneath the blankets. "It's ghosts—I know it."

"Ghosts, my foot!" exclaimed Frank, scrambling out of bed. "I'm going to find out what is making that racket."

"Be careful," warned Joe nervously.

"I'll help you," declared Biff. He, too, got out of bed, and then there was a yelp of pain, followed by a crash.

"Ow!" yelled Biff.

"What happened?" demanded the others in chorus.

"I barged into a chair. Stubbed my big toe. Ow!"

This relieved the tension a trifle. The others snickered at Biff's predicament. Frank lit the lamp and in its glow the boys were revealed, shivering in their pajamas. Chet's round face peeped out above a heap of blankets.

"Owooooooo!"

The dreadful sound broke out again. Chet dived beneath the blankets.

"That's the strangest howl I ever heard," declared Biff, rubbing his injured toe. "It certainly isn't the wind."

"It certainly isn't a human being," said Frank.

"It can't be a dog," volunteered Joe.

"Nor a cat."

"Then what is it?"

"Ghosts!" bellowed Chet, from beneath the blankets. "Put out that lamp."

Frank, however, raised the lamp on high and began to prowl about the cabin.

"The noise seemed to come from over this way," he said, moving toward one of the big windows near the front.

Even as he spoke, the sound broke out afresh, immediately above his head.

Frank looked up. He could see nothing, yet that mournful wailing continued, and at last died away again.

"There's certainly nothing up there," he announced, peering into the shadows.

"There must be!" exclaimed Biff, close at his heels.

"Hold the lamp. I'll soon find out."

Biff took the lamp, and Frank dragged a chair over to the wall. He stood on the chair and began examining the surface of the logs. At last, just when the sound broke out again, he gave vent to a howl of laughter.

"I've found it!"

"What was it?"

Biff raised the lamp.

"Here's your ghost. Come and see it, Chet. A glass ghost."

Frank was pointing to an object embedded between two logs. Chet, his fears laid at rest, emerged from beneath the blankets and came over.

There was a small hole between the logs where the plaster had fallen away. Some one, for some unknown reason, had placed the neck of a bottle in this hole in order to plug it up. On the floor below lay the cork, which had somehow worked its way loose from the bottle neck. The wind, whistling through the glass tube, had created the doleful, fearful sounds the boys had heard.

"Ghosts!" said Frank significantly, as he stepped down, picked up the cork and replaced it in the neck of the bottle.

"I didn't *really* think it was a ghost," murmured Chet lamely.

Then the boys began to laugh. Although they had refused to admit it, all had been puzzled and more or less frightened by the uncanny wailings, and their relief was now expended in shrieks of laughter at their own expense. But the brave Chet, who had even refused to search for the cause of the sound, came in for his full share of ridicule.

The ghost was not heard again that night. But it was another hour before the boys finally fell asleep, snickering to themselves.

CHAPTER X

STOLEN SUPPLIES

A complete recital of the boys' doings on Cabin Island during their first two days would be of small interest to any but themselves. Suffice it to say that they enjoyed themselves just as any other group of boys of the same age would in similar circumstances.

Cabin Island was located in a lonely cove, and, as it was some distance away from Bayport, few ice-boats ever ventured so far down the bay. However, this isolation did not mar the holiday. On the contrary, as Joe expressed it, they could easily imagine that they were having their outing in the remote Canadian wilderness, instead of but a few miles from their own homes.

The storm that had welcomed them to the island, died down during the night and when they awakened the next morning they found that there had been a heavy snowfall, with deep drifts. To get down to the ice-boats they had to break trail in real Northern fashion.

"This will spoil the ice-boating," predicted Joe. But, to their delight, they found that the high wind had swept clear great expanses of the bay, and although there were certain areas where the snow was piled high, by dexterous steering they could skirt these patches and keep to the open ice.

The first morning, they spent clearing a path from the cabin to the ice-boats in the little cove. In the afternoon, they went out in the boats for a while, then returned to the cabin for a piping hot supper. That evening, they sat about the fire, telling stories and chaffing one another. They found that the keen winter air and the wholesome outdoor exercise rendered them sleepy long before their accustomed bedtime and they were glad to turn in shortly after nine o'clock.

"At home I'd raise a rare kick if any one tried to get me to go to bed at this hour," said Biff. "Now I'm mighty glad to hit the hay. Boy, I'm tired!"

The next morning they explored the lower reaches of Barmet Bay, going as far as a little village that nestled in a cove on the southern shore, about three miles to the east of the island. After lunch, they decided to make an exploration of the country along the shore. Leaving the island, they went inshore by ice-boat, then donned snowshoes and went up on to the mainland.

This country was heavily wooded in spots, and they spent an enjoyable afternoon snow-shoeing far up on the hills, from where they could look down and view the entire expanse of the bay, with Cabin Island looking very small in the distance. To the west, however, they saw that clouds were gathering, and although there was no wind, Frank remarked that he was sure a storm was rising.

"I guess we'd better get back before we get caught in any blizzard," he decided.

Joe had been peering at Cabin Island, an intent expression on his face.

"Do any of you chaps see any one on the island?" he said.

All looked. The island seemed deserted.

"You must be dreaming," scoffed Chet. "There's no one there."

"I can't see any one now, but I'm sure I saw some one moving against the snow down by the northern end of the island."

"Perhaps it was some animal," Biff suggested.

"It looked like a man. Of course, he was so far away that I can't be sure. I just caught a glimpse of him."

"Well, we will find out when we get back."

By the time they reached the boats again, Frank's prediction of a storm seemed to be in a fair way of being verified. The whole western sky was black and a light breeze sent the snow skimming across the surface of the ice.

"We'll just about make it. Thank goodness, the wind is in our favor," said Frank, as he clambered into his boat.

They started off and made a quick run across the intervening stretch of ice. It was already growing dark when they reached the island. The boys could see the snowstorm approaching down the bay, sweeping toward them like a gigantic gray veil. It was beginning to snow and the air was filled with swirling white flakes.

"Just in time!" shouted Chet.

They put their boats in shelter for the night, then scrambled up the path toward the cabin. Frank unlocked the door and they dashed inside.

"We'll get a fire started and have a feed."

"Feed!" declared Chet. "We'll have a banquet. I'm as hungry as a bear. I could eat my own boots, without salt and pepper."

"You won't have to. There's plenty of grub."

Frank began making up the fire. Chet went out into the kitchen to look over the food supplies with a hungry eye.

A moment later he emerged, his eyes almost popping out of his head.

"It's gone!" he gasped.

"What's gone?" demanded Joe.

"The grub!"

"What?"

"Every speck!" Chet was almost tearful. "There isn't a bit of food in the kitchen."

"There was plenty there this morning," said Biff. "What happened to it?"

"Stolen. Come and see for yourselves."

They all trooped into the kitchen.

Chet had spoken only too truly. All their food supplies had disappeared. The shelves had been swept clear. The lads gazed at the empty kitchen in consternation.

"Well, what do you know about that?" breathed Joe.

"Old Mother Hubbard had nothing on us," muttered Biff.

Frank's face was serious.

"I guess you were right, Joe, when you said you saw some one on the island. Some thief has been here while we were away. That's a mighty mean trick. He hasn't left us even a loaf of bread."

"And a fine chance we have of getting any tonight, either," Biff pointed out. "We can't get back to town in this storm."

The boys were disconsolate. The prospect was cheerless. After an entire afternoon in the open their appetites had been whetted to razor edge.

"Take off your boots, Chet," said Joe, with a feeble attempt at a joke. "You can have your chance at eating them now."

This effort fell flat. The boys were in no mood for jesting now. The loss of their food supplies was a serious matter.

"I wonder who could have done it," said Chet.

Frank shrugged.

"Looks like some of Hanleigh's work."

"But why would he try to steal our supplies? What good would that do him? Perhaps it was only some sneak thief who chanced in here and saw a chance to make a good haul."

"Perhaps. But I imagine it was Hanleigh. He knew we were here."

"Wants to get us off the island," remarked Joe. "Perhaps he figured that if he stole our food, we'd have to clear out."

"We'll show him."

"But in the meantime," moaned Chet, "I'm hungry."

"Looks as if you'll have to go without eating until morning. We can go down to that little village and buy some more food then."

Chet patted his empty stomach.

"But I can't wait until then."

"You still have your boots," Joe reminded him again.

Then a thoughtful look crossed Chet's face.

"Just a minute!" he shouted, and ran out of the room.

"What's he up to now?" demanded Biff.

They soon found out. Chet returned with one of the packsacks from under his bed.

"I just remembered. When we were unpacking the grub I forgot to take everything out of this packsack. Look!" He delved into it and produced half a loaf of bread, three tins of sardines, a can of salmon and a small quantity of tea in a canister.

The others raised a cheer of delight.

"Hurray!" shouted Biff. "We won't starve after all."

"You *forgot* to unpack it, did you?" said Frank pointedly. "I'll bet you didn't forget. You just cached that grub away in case you might get hungry some time during the night."

"Now what good would a can of sardines do me in the middle of the night?" asked Chet.

"I know you. Never knew of you taking any chances on running out of food yet," Frank told him. "Well, this time it worked out all right. We'll help you get rid of your little supper, Chet."

"There isn't very much."

"Enough to keep us from starving, at any rate."

Soon, with a blazing fire casting a glow through the cabin, with the lamps lighted and with the table spread, the lads felt more cheerful. The meal was not at all what they had anticipated as a conclusion to their day, but their appetites were too keen to admit of any fault-finding.

"I suppose this means we go without breakfast," groaned Chet, as soon as he had finished the last sardine.

"That's right! Start worrying about breakfast the moment you've finished your supper," said Biff. "I never saw such a hungry wolf in all my life."

"I'm not hungry now, but I'll be hungry in the morning."

"Then wait until morning before you start talking about it." Frank got up and went over to the window. "Another wild night. If it weren't for this storm we could have made the run to the village and back tonight, with more food."

"I hope the storm dies down by morning," muttered Chet gloomily.

"If it doesn't, you'll probably die of starvation."

"Just wait until I lay my hands on the fellow who played this dirty trick on us, that's all. Just wait!"

"It was Hanleigh, I'm sure of that," Frank said. "I'd give a lot to know why he's so anxious to get us away from this island!"

"He won't freeze us out now. We'll stay here to the last minute," said Joe firmly. "And after this, believe me, we'll keep an eye on the supplies."

"You bet we will!" declared Chet. "From now on, I appoint myself guard of the food supply—providing we get some more food for me to guard."

The lads finally went to bed, although Chet had to be silenced on a number of occasions when he persisted in inquiring as to the probability of reaching the village and returning next morning before their usual breakfast time. Before slumber claimed them all, however, Frank expressed the common thought when he observed:

"Just wait until we meet Mr. Hanleigh again!"

CHAPTER XI

POSTAGE STAMPS

Next morning, the snowstorm having abated, the boys went outside in a futile search for footprints. The snow had obliterated any tracks the thief might have made in the immediate vicinity of the cabin, but down by the boathouse, on the side sheltered from the wind, they found several footprints. Frank took measurements of them.

"Might come in useful some day," he commented. "I should say they were made by a fairly big man."

"How about food?" asked Chet, who had gone without breakfast.

"Right away. Joe and I will take our ice-boat and go down to the village. You and Biff had better stay here."

"Can't I go with you? Perhaps I could get something to eat at the village, and I wouldn't have to wait so long."

"You'll eat with the rest of us," laughed Frank.

"Why do you want Biff and me to stay?"

"I'm thinking the thief may not have taken those supplies away with him. If Hanleigh did it, his purpose would be served by merely hiding the food. You and Biff can spend your time hunting around the island. You may find where the grub has been hidden."

Chet's face lighted up at this probability.

"Come on, Biff!"

The Hardy boys got into their ice-boat and started off, leaving their two chums hopefully searching for the lost supplies.

The wind was favorable, and the Hardy boys reached the little village down on the mainland in a short time. It was a summer resort, and at this season of the year most of the houses were closed and boarded up, but a few permanent residents stayed on the year round, among them being the general storekeeper. His name, as it appeared from a weatherbeaten sign hanging above the store, was Amos Grice.

The boys left their boat by a little wharf which was almost covered with snow and made their way toward the store.

An elderly man with chin whiskers peered at them through his glasses as they entered. He was sitting behind the stove, reading a newspaper and munching at an apple, and he was evidently surprised to see any customers so early in the morning, particularly strangers.

"How do, boys! Where you from?" he asked.

"We're camping on an island farther up the bay," Frank explained. "We came here in our ice-boat."

"Camping, hey? Well, it ain't many that camps in the winter time. As fer me, I think I'd rather set behind the stove when the colder weather comes on. It's more comfortable. What can I do for you?"

"Some one raided our cabin last night and stole all our food. We want to get some more supplies."

"Stole all your food!" exclaimed Amos Grice, clucking sympathetically. "Well, now, that's too bad. Fust time I ever heard of any thievin' in these parts. Was it a tramp, do you think?"

"We don't know who it was, but we have an idea. I don't think it was a tramp. Just somebody trying to do us a bad turn."

"A mean thing to do," commented Mr. Grice, wagging his head. "Well, I guess I can fix you up all right. What do you want to buy?"

The boys spent some time giving the storekeeper an order, and when the goods had been wrapped up, Amos Grice invited them to sit down beside the cracker barrel and "chat for a while."

"It ain't often I see strangers in the winter time," he explained.

Frank and Joe told him that they could not stay very long, because their chums were back at the island, awaiting their return with the supplies.

"Back at the island, hey? What island?" insisted Amos Grice.

"Cabin Island, it's called."

"Cabin Island, hey? Why, ain't that Elroy Jefferson's place? Little island with a big log cabin on it?"

"That's the place."

"Why, I know Elroy Jefferson very well. When he was living on the island in the summer months he used to come down here for his supplies." Mr. Grice cackled with delight at having found a common topic of conversation. "Yes, I know Elroy Jefferson real well. He's a fine fellow, too, but very odd."

"He's a bit eccentric," agreed Frank.

"Yes, he's a odd old chap, but a better man never wore shoe leather. How was he when you was last talkin' to him?"

The boys decided to humor the lonely old storekeeper. Frank reflected that possibly they might learn something about Hanleigh.

"He was quite well. He let us have the cabin for our outing."

"Yes, that's just like Mr. Jefferson. Got a heart of gold, specially where boys is concerned. But strange—mighty strange in some ways," said Amos Grice, again wagging his head. "Do you know"—and he leaned forward very confidentially—"I really think he married Mary Bender because of her postage stamp collection."

This amazing announcement left the Hardy boys rather at a loss for words.

"He married his wife because of her postage stamp collection!" exclaimed Joe.

"That's what I said. You've heard of the Bender stamp collection, haven't you?" he demanded.

The boys shook their heads.

"Well, I ain't a stamp collector and *I've* heard of it. The Bender collection is supposed to be one of the greatest collections of postage stamps in the world. Why, I've heard tell that it's worth thousands and thousands of dollars."

"And Mrs. Jefferson owned it?"

"Yep. Her name was Mary Bender then, and she inherited it from her father. I got parts of the story from people who knew Mr. Jefferson well. It seems he has always been a collector of antiques and old coins and stamps and things, but one thing he had set his heart on was the Bender stamp collection. But he couldn't buy it. Either Mr. Bender wouldn't sell or Elroy Jefferson couldn't raise the money—but somehow he could never buy them stamps he had set his heart on."

"So he married Mary Bender?"

"Well, now—maybe he didn't marry her *entirely* on account of the stamps. You see, he used to call at the Bender house quite often, trying to get Mr. Bender to sell the stamps, so in that way he met Mary Bender. I've no doubt he fell in love with her, but, anyway, they got married, and after Mr. Bender died his daughter got the stamps. So, of course, then Mr. Jefferson got 'em. His wife turned 'em over to him as soon as she inherited them."

"And then what?" asked Joe, interested.

"Then," said Amos Grice, with great effect, "the stamps disappeared."

"Disappeared?"

"They went."

"Stolen?"

"Nobody knows. They just went."

"Haven't they been found?"

"Never been found from that day to this. Not hide nor hair of them stamps has been seen since."

"Didn't they have any clues?" asked Frank. "Were the stamps simply lost?"

"They disappeared," insisted Amos Grice. "And not only the stamps disappeared. There was one of the Jefferson servants dropped out of sight at the same time."

"He probably stole the stamps and cleared out," Frank suggested.

"If he stole 'em, why didn't he sell 'em? The stamps have never been heard of since they left the Jefferson home. This servant—his name was John Sparewell—could have raised a lot of money by sellin' the stamps, but the stamps would have turned up sooner or later, because only other stamp collectors would have bought 'em. But of all the rare stamps in that collection, not one has ever been found."

"That's a strange yarn," said Frank.

"You bet it's a strange yarn. The stamps were all kept on sheets, in a rosewood box. The day John Sparewell walked out of the Jefferson home, the rosewood box disappeared from the safe it was always kept in."

"Has no one ever heard of Sparewell? Didn't Mr. Jefferson get the police to look for him?"

"Certainly. But the police never found him. They sent descriptions of this man Sparewell all over the world, but he never turned up. Queerest story I ever did hear. Mary Bender died just a short time after. And ever since the stamps were lost, Elroy Jefferson ain't been the same."

Amos Grice wagged his head sadly.

"How many years ago did this happen?" Frank asked.

"Oh, it must be nigh on fifteen or twenty years ago. Guess that explains why you lads never heard of the Bender stamp case, because there was a lot about it in the newspapers at the time. It was a mighty famous case, I can tell you. It seemed to break Elroy Jefferson all up, because that collection was the pride of his heart, and when it disappeared so strangely, he just didn't seem to take any more interest in anything. What *I've* always said was that if the police could only find this man John Sparewell, they'd find what happened to the stamps."

"That seems reasonable."

"Yep. That's the way I figgered it out. The only trouble was, they never were able to find Sparewell."

"I wonder why he stole the stamps if he never sold them," said Joe.

"I guess he was up against it when he tried to sell 'em. He knew that nobody but stamp collectors would buy the collection, and any stamp collector would recognize the Bender collection right away and tell the police. So perhaps he's never been able to sell them and is waitin' until Elroy Jefferson dies before he tries to make any money out of it."

Frank and Joe got up.

"Perhaps that's what happened," Frank agreed. "Well, Mr. Grice, we've been very much interested in the story, but we must be getting back to the cabin or our chums will think something has happened to us."

The boys paid for their supplies and then left the store, after saying good-bye to the garrulous old man.

"Come again!" he called after them. "Drop in and have a chat any time you want."

The Hardy boys went down to their ice-boat, packed away the supplies of food they had purchased, and headed back toward the island.

"So that's the mystery in Elroy Jefferson's life," mused Joe.

"Wouldn't it be wonderful if we could find the Bender stamp collection for him?" returned Frank.

CHAPTER XII

THE NOTEBOOK

When the Hardy boys returned to Cabin Island they found Chet and Biff awaiting them hungrily.

"We thought you would never come!" moaned Chet. "Quick—where's the grub? We have a fire all ready. Now for some breakfast!"

"You didn't find the stolen supplies, then," said Frank, bringing in a side of bacon they had bought from Amos Grice.

"No sign of the food at all," admitted Biff ruefully. "No, I think the chap who stole that food took it away with him."

"And ate it," growled Chet, as he poured some ground coffee into the pot.

"We hunted every place we could think of—down in the boathouse, under the trees, all around the cabin—but we didn't find the grub."

"All I can say is that he must have been a mighty strong man to pack all that stuff away with him in one trip," remarked Joe.

"That's right, too," agreed Biff. "I never thought of that. Perhaps the supplies *are* around this island yet. We'll take another look this afternoon."

For the present, however, their immediate interest was the long-delayed breakfast which Chet was enthusiastically preparing. He soon had bacon and eggs, bread, coffee and jam on the table, and the lads attacked the meal with gusto. Eventually their hearty appetites were appeased.

"What now?" asked Joe.

"I think we ought to spend the rest of the day exploring the island," Frank suggested. "We haven't really looked the place over yet and we might just chance to run across those supplies."

The others agreed that his plan was good, so they donned their coats and caps and set about a systematic search of the island.

Frank, in charge of the hunt, outlined a plan of procedure.

"We'll figure it this way," he said. "Suppose we were coming to this cabin to steal those supplies, with the idea of hiding them. Where could we go? There are only certain directions we could go without ending up at a cliff or without finding ourselves in the deep snow at the top of the island. We'll try to put ourselves in the thief's place."

"If it were I," said Joe, "I'd make right for that clump of trees over to the left. Those supplies were heavy. The thief wouldn't want to carry them very far, yet he would want a good hiding place."

"That's right," agreed the others.

"Well, let's tackle the trees, then."

The boys made their way across the snow-covered rocks until they reached the clump of bushes Joe had pointed out, and there they searched carefully, kicking away the snow at the base of the trees, in the hope of uncovering the missing supplies.

But their efforts met with no success. They hunted through the entire grove and the only result of their search was that Chet stubbed his toe when he dealt a vicious kick at a rock hidden beneath the snow.

"We're out of luck here," said Frank finally. "Has any one else any good suggestions?"

"Well," said Biff, "if I stole those supplies I'd hide them down by the shore some place, among the rocks."

"We'll give it a try. What's the nearest way to the shore from the cabin?"

"Down that little path at the back."

"Away we go, then!"

They left the clump of trees and ploughed through the snow toward the defile that led down from the rear of the cabin to the rocks along the ice-bound shore. The rocks were covered with snow, but their round masses rose irregularly against the background of the ice.

"We have a job ahead of us if we start moving all these rocks," objected Chet, with misgivings.

"We're not going to move 'em," said Frank, "That would take us about five years of steady work. We're just going to kick the snow loose."

They attacked the heaps of rocks, prowling about, kicking gingerly at the snow, dislodging it from the hollows. For some time their efforts met with no success. But at last Biff, who had edged a considerable distance away from his companions, gave a sharp cry.

"I believe there's something here, fellows!"

The others went running over to him.

"What have you found?"

Biff held up an object he had picked up from the snow.

"My foot bumped against this," he explained. "It looks like a can of coffee from our supplies."

"It's the same brand!" declared Chet excitedly.

"We'll hunt carefully all around here," Frank decided. "Perhaps the thief just happened to drop that can of coffee as he was going toward the ice, but perhaps he didn't. It's worth making a good search."

With this clue to guide them, the boys plunged into the search with feverish activity. The snow flew in clouds as they rolled away the rocks. After a while, Frank and Joe, dislodging a particularly large boulder, gave a yell of triumph.

"We've found it!"

The large rock had been placed carefully on top of two others, protecting a big hollow underneath. And in this hollow the boys found the two boxes containing all of the missing supplies. They had been well sheltered from the snow, and were dry and unharmed.

Chet gave a howl of relief.

"Hidden treasure!" he gloated. "So that's where the supplies went! Come on, fellows! Back to the cabin with them!"

As the lads loaded themselves with boxes, cans, and packages, Frank nodded his head with satisfaction.

"I didn't think they had really been stolen. I guess this pretty well proves that some one hid them here just to get rid of us."

"A mighty mean trick!" snorted Biff.

"If that can of coffee hadn't rolled out, we'd never have found the supplies," observed Joe. "I'd have thought twice before I'd have tackled that big rock."

"Well, we've found the grub, and that's all that matters," came from Chet.

Joe was emptying one of the boxes when he came across an object that he knew had not been among the supplies originally.

"I wonder what this is," he remarked, picking it up.

The object was a small notebook. He glanced through its pages and found that most of them were blank, although there was a certain amount of writing on the opening sheets.

"What's this you've found?" asked his brother, coming over.

Joe handed him the notebook.

"I'm sure none of us had a notebook like this."

"It isn't mine," said Biff.

"Nor mine," added Chet.

Frank's expression brightened.

"Say, I wonder if it belongs to the chap who stole our supplies. Perhaps it dropped out of his pocket into the box as he was bending over."

"Perhaps the fellow's name is in it," suggested Biff. "Look through it and see."

Frank skimmed the pages.

"Here's where we get the goods on Hanleigh, I'll bet. If this is his notebook, we have positive proof that he stole our supplies."

On the fly leaf of the notebook he came across an inscription. It was a man's name.

But the name was not that of their enemy, Hanleigh.

Written across the page, in a bold, flowing script, they saw the name, "J. Sparewell."

"Well, can you beat that!" exclaimed Chet. "It wasn't Hanleigh, after all."

"Sparewell," mused Frank. "Where have I heard that name before?"

"Nobody around Bayport by the name, that I know of," remarked Biff.

"Nor I," added Chet.

They looked at one another, puzzled. Then Joe made a suggestion.

"Perhaps Sparewell and Hanleigh are the same man."

"Perhaps you've hit it," said Frank. "Sparewell—I'm *sure* I've heard that name before. Oh, now I know! Don't you remember, Joe? Remember what Amos Grice was telling us this very morning? Remember the story he told us about the missing postage stamp collection? Sparewell was the man who disappeared from Elroy Jefferson's home the day the collection was stolen."

"John Sparewell! That was the name. I remember now!" Joe exclaimed. "The very same!"

"What are you fellows talking about?" demanded Chet. "I don't get this at all."

Biff was equally in the dark.

"Who is Amos Grice? What did he tell you? What's all this about postage stamps?"

"The Bender collection! John Sparewell's disappearance!" exclaimed Joe excitedly.

"Hey! Talk sense!" admonished Biff.

"Come on back up to the cabin," said Frank. "We'll tell you all about it. This is sure strange!"

CHAPTER XIII

THE CIPHER

Back at the cabin, with the precious supplies again safely stored away in the kitchen, the Hardy boys and their chums settled down before the fire while Frank and Joe told Chet and Biff about the conversation with Amos Grice. They told the tale of Elroy Jefferson's missing postage stamp collection and about the strange disappearance of the servant, John Sparewell, who had never been heard of since.

"And now we find his notebook among our supplies!" exclaimed Chet. "That's the strangest thing I ever heard of."

"There's an explanation somewhere," said Frank, puzzled.

"How about my idea?" remarked Joe. "Perhaps Hanleigh and Sparewell are the same man."

But Frank shook his head.

"You forget," he said, "that Sparewell was a servant in Elroy Jefferson's home for many years. If Jefferson saw him again he would certainly recognize him, don't you think?"

"That's right. And he has seen Hanleigh. The man was at his house the day we visited Mr. Jefferson."

"Then how did Hanleigh get the notebook?" asked Biff.

"We're not sure that Hanleigh was the man who stole our supplies," replied Joe. "We think so, but we're not sure."

"It couldn't be any one else," scoffed Chet.

"I don't know," observed Frank. "For all we're aware, there may be more than Hanleigh interested in this island. Perhaps we have a bigger fight on our hands than we imagine."

"It's certainly a mighty deep mystery," Joe said.

"Well, we may find out more about it if we examine the notebook."

Frank began going over the pages.

First of all, were several sheets of accounts, evidently notes of receipts and expenditures. On one page was listed: "Suit, $35. Necktie, $1. Shirts, $6. Postage, 40 cents." A long list of items indicating that the owner of the notebook was a careful and methodical man who kept track of every cent he spent. At the top of the page was written: "October, 1917."

"Why, that's eleven years ago!" Frank exclaimed.

"And Sparewell disappeared fifteen years ago."

"It shows that he was alive for at least four years after he left the Jefferson place, at any rate."

On the opposite page was a record of receipts, showing money Sparewell had received from various people. These sums were small, showing that Sparewell had not been enjoying a luxurious existence by any means.

On the page following the boys came across a puzzling item.

"Appointment with Jordan on Saturday. My condition is worse. Doubt if I will be able to last out the year. Would appeal to J. but am afraid."

"Wonder what he meant by that," said Chet.

"Perhaps it means he was going to die," Joe suggested.

The boys puzzled over the item for some time, then went on to the next page. It had a number of items concerning the stock market, of little interest. Other pages were filled with equally ambiguous and uninteresting notes. Then another page was filled with a crude drawing in the shape of an irregular oval, with a cross marked at one side.

"Looks like a warped egg," commented Chet.

"Looks to me like a map of some kind," Frank said. "Well, perhaps we'll learn some more about it." He turned the page.

There he found a number of other entries with dates.

"Nov. 3—hire of boat—$3."

"Nov. 4—hire of boat—$3."

"Nov. 6—boat—$5."

"Finished, Nov. 6."

The boys looked at one another, unable to understand.

"He was certainly doing a lot of boating that week," said Frank. Then on the next page he found two words.

"Cabin Island."

"Ah, now we're getting somewhere. 'Cabin Island.' Sparewell had something to do with this place."

"Perhaps that's why he was making so many boat trips," Joe suggested. "He may have been coming here."

On a sudden inspiration, Frank flipped back the pages until he found the mysterious map.

"This much is clear, at any rate. Take a look at that map, fellows. What does it remind you of?"

"Cabin Island!" they shouted.

They had not noticed the resemblance before. Now, it was perfectly clear. Cabin Island was oval-shaped, and in general contour it resembled the crude drawing in the notebook.

"Well, we know now that this man Sparewell was alive for at least four years after his disappearance from the Jefferson place, and that he was interested in Cabin Island for some reason, and that he probably made several trips here by boat."

"Next page!" said Chet, eagerly.

But the next page puzzled them more than ever. There were several lines written, but, so far as the boys could see, they were simply gibberish.

This was what Sparewell had written:

XZYRM. RHOZMW. XSRNMVB. OVUG.
UILMG. MRMV. UVVG. SRTS.

And that was all.

"A cipher message!" Joe exclaimed.

Chet sniffed.

"A lot of good that does us. We can't make any sense out of that!"

"I'd give my shirt to know what that message means," remarked Biff. "I'll bet it is something mighty important."

"He wouldn't have put it in cipher if it wasn't important," Frank agreed. "Well, this is certainly pretty deep. I wonder if Sparewell really was the man who came here and hid our supplies. The more I think of it, the more it seems to me that he did come here. There's absolutely nothing in this book to connect it with Hanleigh. His name isn't mentioned from beginning to end." Frank had flipped over the rest of the pages and found that they were blank.

"Why should Sparewell pop up here at this time?" pondered Joe. "Do you think he and Hanleigh may be working together?"

"Perhaps. And still, if Sparewell is still alive, I can't see why this notebook ends where it does. Eleven years have passed since he made these entries."

"He may have kept other notebooks," Joe suggested. "Perhaps he merely kept this one because of the cipher. There was some secret he didn't want others to know, and he kept that notebook in his possession at all times, for fear some one might find it and solve the cipher."

"That sounds reasonable. But I'm afraid we can't do much more unless we can learn the secret of that message."

"It's a tough one," Chet commented.

"Ciphers have been solved before this. Have you ever read Edgar Allan Poe's story called 'The Gold Bug?' In that yarn, he had a cipher to solve and he went on the idea that the letter 'e' was the letter most frequently used in the English language," said Frank. "Suppose we apply it to this case. Looking it over, the letter most often used in the cipher is the letter 'm.' If we take 'm' to mean 'e'—"

"You've got it!" shouted Chet. "I'll bet we'll solve this riddle yet."

Frank marked down the letter "e" above each place in the cipher where the letter "m" occurred. But he was no farther ahead than he was before.

Presuming that "m" should really be "e" he found that it occurred once in the first word—for he took it for granted that each dot in the message represented a division between two words—once in the second word, once in the third, once in the fifth and twice in the sixth. This simply rendered the cipher more confusing than ever, for there was no clue as to what the other letters might be.

"If there was a three-letter word in the message," he said, "we might get somewhere. That's how the fellow in the story worked it. He found a lot of three-letter words, each of the same combination of letters, so he gathered that they would mean 'the' because the letter he thought meant 'e' was at the end of each. That gave him two more letters, 't' and 'h,' to work on, and from there he found the cipher easy."

"Mr. Sparewell was too smart for us," said Joe. "He didn't use 'the' in this message at all, from the looks of things."

"I guess that scheme isn't so good. Well, we have the notebook, and whoever lost it is sure to miss it and come back for it. I think it wouldn't be a bad idea if we kept an eye on that place where the stores were hidden."

"Catch him in the act!" said Biff.

"If the man is Sparewell, I guess Mr. Jefferson will be mighty glad to know where he is. The police have been searching for the man for fifteen years now. If it isn't Sparewell, he'll have a lot of explaining to do concerning this little book and how it came into his hands."

"From now on, then, we keep a weather eye on those rocks," Chet declared. "We ought to stand guard."

"I don't think that will be necessary," said Frank. "It would only frighten him away. The best plan is to watch the place from here. We can easily see any one approaching the island and we can watch to see where he goes. If he heads for those rocks, we'll know we have our man."

"That means that some one has to stay on the island all the time."

"I think it would be best. We can take turns at that, so it shouldn't spoil our outing. Somehow, I don't think we'll have very long to wait. The moment that man finds his notebook is gone, he'll hurry back for it."

The other boys agreed that Frank's plan was about the best that could be devised toward laying the mysterious thief by the heels. They were tingling with excitement because their outing on Cabin Island had plunged them into the depths of a first-rate mystery.

That afternoon they remained on the island. The next day was Christmas and they were preparing to celebrate it accordingly.

But the intruder did not return that day.

CHAPTER XIV

CHRISTMAS DAY

"I think we ought to make this outing an annual affair," said Chet Morton the next morning after the boys had wished one another "Merry Christmas."

"Why?"

"We get two Christmases out of it. It suits me fine."

"If you expect to get any presents around here, you're badly mistaken," sniffed Joe, putting on his shoes.

"I didn't. If I had expected any I would have hung up my stocking. But we'll have a Christmas dinner, anyway. That'll be the second Christmas dinner this week."

"If we hadn't found those supplies, you'd be out of luck for your Christmas dinner today. The chicken and the pudding and the Christmas cake were all in those two boxes," Frank said.

"Didn't I know it? But everything is all right now."

"Take a look out the window and see if Hanleigh is snooping around the rocks," advised Biff.

Chet sped to the window.

"A glorious day!" he reported. "A beautiful, sunshiny Christmas day. The only cloud on the whole horizon is that there is no sign of Mr. Hanleigh. The ice is clear and it looks as if we'll have some splendid ice-boating this afternoon. But Mr. Hanleigh is not ice-boating this morning. There is snow on the hillside—but our dear friend Hanleigh is not snow-shoeing. But let us not lose hope. He may yet emerge from his hiding place and proceed forth to enjoy the keen Christmas air in the vicinity of Cabin Island, that clear atmosphere that he doesn't want us to breathe."

Chet's rhapsody came to an abrupt halt when Joe hurled a wet towel that caught him squarely on the back of the neck. Frank, who had been appointed cook for the day, put a stop to hostilities by announcing breakfast just then and the lads sat down to piping hot plates of ham and eggs, accompanied by fragrant coffee.

The big surprise came when Frank, with a flourish, drew aside a curtain that had been screening a mysterious table in one corner of the big room. Here, the Hardy boys had put their presents to each other and to their chums. There was a handsome pair of boxing gloves for Biff and a glittering, nickel-plated flashlight for Chet. Frank had given his brother a new watch-chain and Joe, in turn, had given Frank a pair of cuff-links with his initials engraved thereon.

"Well," said Chet, admiring the flashlight and switching it on and off to see that it was in good working order, after the boys had exchanged thanks for the gifts, "Biff and I thought we were putting something across, too, but you got ahead of us."

And, going into the kitchen, he emerged with some mysterious-looking parcels which he promptly distributed. These were the presents Biff and Chet had arranged to give the Hardy boys and to each other. Frank received a pair of ski-boots and Joe the same. Biff's enthusiasm over a punching bag was long and loud, while Chet himself was delighted with a little book of tickets to the best motion picture house in Bayport.

"I see where I won't do much homework until these tickets are used up," he said, with a wink.

Their presents having been duly examined and admired, the lads donned their outing clothes, with the exception of Frank. As cook, it was his duty to stay and prepare the Christmas dinner, at the same time keeping an eye on the rocks where the supplies had been hidden. The base of the cliff was in plain view of the big cabin window so there was little danger that the owner of the mysterious notebook would approach unobserved.

"What if he should chance along while you're all away?"

"We never thought of that," said Biff, in dismay. "You couldn't very well handle him alone."

"How about your rifle?" Joe suggested.

"The very thing! Even if you chaps go as far as the mainland, you will be able to hear a rifle shot. I'll fire one shot into the air and that will be the signal to come back as quickly as you can. If he tries to get away, you can easily head him off in the ice-boat."

This arrangement seemed to preclude any possibility of the stranger's escape if he chanced to show up, so Joe, Chet and Biff trooped out. For the morning, they had decided to stay close to the cabin, "so there won't be any risk of missing dinner," as Chet explained, and amuse themselves by fishing through the ice. So, with lines ready and hooks baited with pieces of salt pork, they made their way down the slope and out on the ice.

There they set to work with their hatchets and soon had three holes chopped in the ice. They dropped in their lines and from then on it was a game to see who would catch the first fish. Chet, of course, raised a clamor every few minutes, claiming that he had a bite, but somehow the fish always managed to get away.

"No wonder," grumbled Biff. "You scare 'em away, with all that racket. Try being quiet for a while and see how it works."

To the astonishment of the others, Chet actually did manage to refrain from noise for the space of five minutes and the plan evidently had good results—but not for Chet. Joe suddenly gave his line a yank. A silvery body flashed through the air and flopped wildly on the ice.

He had caught a good-sized fish and when it has been despatched, the others returned to the ice-holes with renewed enthusiasm. Within a few minutes, Biff was the fortunate one, and a second fish was laid to rest on the ice beside the first. Chet endured the chaffing of the others, who elaborately complimented him on his skill. A moment later, he gave a yell of delight.

"I've got one! I've got one!"

He began to haul and tug at the line.

"A whopper!" gasped Chet. "I can hardly pull him in."

The other boys watched his efforts, their eyes bulging. Chet was struggling with all his might and although he was gradually drawing in his line, there seemed to be a tremendous weight on the end of it.

"Must be a whale!" grunted Chet. "Ah—here he comes!"

He drew in his prize. It rose above the surface of the water. Chet stared at it in disgust.

The "fish" was nothing more than a very battered pail. Chet's hook had somehow caught the handle. Full of water and mud, the pail had almost broken the stout line by its weight.

Joe and Biff whooped with laughter. Joe gave the pail a kick that sent it back into the water again.

"Some fish!" yelled Joe.

"It wasn't a whale. It was a pail!"

Chet glared at his companions.

"I'll show you!" he said.

He baited his hook and again cast in his line. Immediately there was a lively wrench. Chet gave the line a twitch, and this time he did catch a fish. The only drawback to his enjoyment lay in the fact that it was only about four, inches long.

"A sardine!" grinned Joe.

However, Chet placed his capture beside the other fish, just as proudly as though it were a ten-pounder.

"It isn't any fault that I caught it before it had time to grow a little more. It might just as easily have been a big one," he said.

The fishing became cold sport after a while, inasmuch as the boys were obliged to stay in the one place and could not move around enough to get exercise. They soon began to feel the cold and before long began to await the sound of the dinner bell. This, as Frank had warned them, would be achieved by banging the poker against a tin pan.

"Well, if our supplies are stolen again, we can live on fish," remarked Joe cheerfully.

"Not if we depend on Chet to catch them for us," said Biff. "I'm sure we wouldn't make much of a meal out of that whale he caught. A little bit tough for my taste."

Chet was just thinking up a retort in kind when they heard the welcome clatter of the tin pan. With one accord, they hauled in their lines, seized the fish they had caught, and raced madly back to the shore, scrambled headlong up the slope and breathlessly plunged into the cabin.

"What's the matter?" asked Frank, as they made their hurried entry. "Somebody chasing you?"

"Hunger is chasing us!" declared Chet.

"Dinner is ready. Wash up and hop to it."

They needed no second invitation. Frank opened the oven door and a delicious odor of browned chicken permeated the cabin. The Christmas pudding, which Mrs. Hardy had prepared before the boys left Bayport, was already steaming, and the table was loaded high with good things, pickles, potatoes, "and all the trimmings."

The boys later vowed that of all the Christmas dinners they had ever eaten, with all due respect to the dinners they had sat down to at home, the one that would remain longest in their memories would be the Christmas feast they devoured during their outing on Cabin Island.

The afternoon they spent quietly, trying out their skis on the sloping hillsides on the eastern side of the island. This exhilarating sport made the hours pass quickly, and when the winter twilight fell the boys returned to the cabin, weary and happy.

"The best Christmas ever!" they voted it.

"Well," said Frank, as they sat about the fireplace that evening, "the man who lost the notebook didn't show up today."

"He'll be back," said Joe.

"And we'll be ready for him."

"Perhaps he hasn't missed it yet," suggested Biff.

"Perhaps not. What I'm afraid of," Frank said, "is that he won't consider it important enough to come back for."

"Important! Why, the cipher is in it!" exclaimed Joe.

"Yes, but he knows the cipher by heart, no doubt. And the very fact that the message is in cipher will protect him. He knows that if we do chance to find the notebook, it will be a hundred chances to one that we'll never be able to find out what it means. He may not worry about losing the notebook after all."

The boys were thoughtful.

"We may never catch him, then?"

"I hope so," said Frank. "But we can't count on it too strongly."

"We'll get him," Joe declared. "That message had something to do with Cabin Island. The man will be back here anyway, notebook or no notebook, I'm dead sure."

CHAPTER XV

CHICKEN THIEVES

Next morning, although the boys kept a sharp lookout, there was no sign of the marauder.

"We're not going to let him spoil our holiday," declared Frank. "If he decides to come back for his notebook we'll be ready for him, but we don't have to sit around waiting."

"What say we go back and call on Amos Grice?" suggested Joe. "He may be able to tell us some more about Elroy Jefferson and the stamp collection."

"Good idea!" declared Biff. "I'd like to meet the old chap."

Chet said nothing. He was already struggling into his coat. The prospect of a jaunt in the ice-boats appealed to the boys strongly, for it was a bright, sunny morning and the air was keen.

In a short time, the lads were ready, and went scrambling down the slope toward the little cove where the ice-boats were sheltered. Chet, who was anxious to learn how to manage the craft, seated himself at the tiller of Biff's boat.

"Guess I'd better take out some insurance, if you're going to steer," said Biff.

"Don't worry about me, my lad," Chet advised. "Hang on to your cap, for you're in for a swift ride, with plenty of fancy twists and curves."

The Hardy boys got into their own boat, the sails flapped in the wind, then filled out, and the boats sped out of the cove into the open bay.

Chet soon found that steering was not the simple thing it had seemed. He was in difficulties before he was more than a few hundred yards away from the island. Then, essaying a sharp turn, he almost upset the boat.

Frank and Joe could see Biff remonstrating with him, but Chet evidently refused to give up the tiller.

"He means to learn how!" laughed Frank. "I'll bet Biff is sweating. He's afraid Chet will wreck the boat."

"I'm just as glad I'm not riding with them, myself," returned Joe.

At that moment they saw the other boat veer sharply around. The sails bellied in the stiff breeze and the ice-boat came plunging across the bay toward them.

"What's the matter now?" exclaimed Frank. "Is he trying to run us down?"

The boat boomed on, without changing its course. They had a glimpse of Biff Hooper standing up and waving his arms wildly.

"Guess we had better get out of the way." Frank, who was at the tiller, swung the boat to leeward, and at the same instant the other craft changed its course and was still heading directly down upon them.

Then, to their astonishment, the oncoming boat swerved again, this time with such violence that Biff Hooper lost his balance, staggered, and tumbled out on to the ice. Chet, the amateur, was left alone at the tiller of an ice-boat which was out of his control.

Then ensued a weird game of tag. Chet's boat was at the mercy of the shifting winds. It dodged to and fro, plunged from side to side. No one could tell where it was going next. Most of the time, it seemed to be plunging directly at the Hardy boys' boat, and Frank was kept busy steering out of the way.

Once it seemed that a collision was inevitable. The runaway boat swung sharply about, seemed to gather speed as the wind caught it, and then came on with a rush. Frank desperately tried to maneuver his craft out of its course. The other boat was rushing down on him.

"Jump!" shouted Joe.

"Stay where you are!" Frank yelled. There was still a chance. He bore down on the tiller. The ice-boat swung into the wind just as the other craft went flashing past. They could see Chet, a look of comical fear and amazement on his face, frantically trying to get the boat under control.

Out on the open ice, Biff had scrambled to his feet and was madly pursuing the fleeing craft. Chet managed to get the boat back against the wind, it turned wildly and raced directly at Biff. Then Biff turned and fled. He might have been run down had he not leaped to one side just in time. As the boat was speeding past he watched his chance and jumped.

Biff clambered over the side and crawled over Chet, who gladly moved over to allow him to take the tiller. In a few moments the boat slackened speed. Shortly afterward, Biff had the situation well in hand, turned the boat about, and drove alongside the Hardy boys.

"Are you satisfied?" said Biff, glaring at Chet.

"Must have been something wrong with the steering gear," Chet explained weakly.

"Steering gear, nothing!" snorted Biff. "Something wrong with the fellow who was steering, that's all. After this, I'll take charge of the boat myself."

"You're welcome. I've had plenty."

"Thank goodness!"

"What was the big idea?" shouted Frank "Trying to wreck us all, Chet?"

"No harm done. We'd better forget it," muttered Chet sheepishly. "I can't seem to get the hang of this steering business. I'd rather be just a passenger, anyway."

"That suits everybody," growled Biff. "When I go out ice-boating I don't care to spend half of my time chasing the boat."

Joe snickered. The recollection of Biff slipping and sliding across the ice in pursuit of the runaway craft, and then slipping and sliding with the boat in pursuit of him, appealed to Joe's sense of humor. That snicker was like a match touched to gunpowder, for Frank also laughed, then Chet, and finally Biff himself had to grin. So, in high good humor again, the lads got back into the boats and resumed their journey toward the village.

They reached the little place about ten o'clock and made their way up through the snow to Amos Grice's store, where they found the proprietor sitting beside the stove, munching crackers from the barrel, just as they had last seen him.

"Howdy, boys!" he greeted them. "Come to pay me a call? Sit down and make yourselves at home. Help yourselves to the crackers. I keep 'em here to sell, but somehow it seems I never sell any, although the barrel keeps gettin' empty all the time just the same. I've been always intendin' to put a cover on that there barrel but I just can't seem to get around to it."

"We found our supplies, Mr. Grice," Frank told him.

"You found 'em, eh? Where were they?"

"Somebody had hidden them on us, as a joke."

"Just this mornin' I was thinkin' about you lads," said Amos Grice. "There's been a couple of thieves around here, too, and I was wonderin' if it was the same ones that swiped your supplies."

"Thieves!" exclaimed Chet.

"Yep. They paid me a visit last night. Stole a lot of my chickens."

The boys looked at one another. Amos Grice laughed. "Not the kind of thieves you're thinkin' about," he remarked. "These ain't two-legged thieves. Four-legged ones. They mighty near cleaned out my hen-house. Seven fine fat chickens I lost."

"Foxes?" ventured Joe.

Amos Grice nodded.

"Foxes! A couple of 'em raided the hen roost last night and made off with seven chickens and I never even caught a sight of 'em at it. If I only had time to leave the store I'd certainly set out after 'em. Still, they may come back, and if they do they'll find me settin' up waitin' for 'em with a shotgun."

"Perhaps they have a den just outside the village," Biff said.

"I know they have. I ain't the first man to lose chickens here this winter."

"Did they leave any tracks?" asked Frank.

"Plenty of 'em. Come with me and I'll show you."

Amos Grice led the way out of the store toward the hen-house in the back yard. A few chickens, the only ones remaining of the flock, were pecking at some grain. The old storekeeper showed the boys two distinct trails in the snow, leading away from the hen-house, up toward the hill at the back of the store.

"That's the way they went," he said. "With my chickens. I tell you, I had a mighty good mind to close up the store and start after 'em right away. I'd like to get a shot at the rascals."

"Joe and I have a couple of small rifles down in the ice-boats," Frank said. "Perhaps we could try our hand at shooting the foxes."

"Good idea!" approved Chet. "I wish I had a rifle."

"You can have mine," declared Amos Grice. "I have a couple of guns up in the store that I'll let you have. And if you can drill them two foxes I'll be mighty grateful to you."

The Hardy boys and their chums were at once enthusiastic over the idea of a fox-hunt. Amos Grice provided Chet and Biff with rifles while Frank and Joe hastened to get their own weapons. Amos Grice even insisted on lending them his dog.

"If there's any foxes within five miles, that dog will dig 'em out," he said. "Only be sure and not shoot my dog."

"We'll be careful," promised the boys.

"Just follow those tracks in the snow and you'll come right to the den, I'll bet a cookie," declared the old man.

"Let's go!" shouted Joe. "We'll bring back your foxes, Mr. Grice."

"Sure will," added Chet jubilantly.

The boys started off through the deep snow, following the double trail up the hillside.

The dog was a lanky, mournful looking brute who seemed too lazy, as Chet expressed it, "to wag his own tail," but he lived up to his master's recommendation. The moment the boys started following the trail, the dog seemed to have a new interest in life, and he plodded on ahead, sniffing at the trail left by the marauding foxes.

The snow was deep but the boys thoroughly enjoyed the excitement of the chase.

"We didn't expect to blunder into a fox-hunt when we left the cabin this morning, did we?" said Joe, when the village was out of sight behind them.

"I'll say we didn't," returned his brother. "This beats ice-boating all hollow."

"It will, if Chet will keep from pointing that gun in my direction," said Biff. "He has already tried to kill me once this morning."

Chet, blushing, reversed the weapon, which he had been carrying in a highly dangerous position, with the barrel pointing toward the other members of the party.

They went down into a gully extending several hundred yards to the west, following the tracks that led along the bottom of the ravine, then turned sharply up the slope again toward a thicket of trees. Here and there they could see flecks of blood on the snow.

"That's from the chickens," Frank said, as they strode along.

Suddenly the dog became very active. Reaching the top of the slope, he plunged along in a swift run and soon disappeared among the trees. Then they heard him howling with excitement.

"He's found them!" shouted Chet.

The boys hastened on. When they overtook the dog they found him frantically raising clouds of snow as he dug among some rocks in the depth of the thicket. He had found the den.

The boys knew little or nothing about the habits of foxes, but they reflected that the dog would be scarcely making such a clamor unless the animals were at home. They waited, rifles in readiness.

"Shoot 'em when they come out!" advised Biff, capering about.

The dog suddenly disappeared into the mouth of the den. The lads heard a yelp of pain, and the dog emerged again, his tail between his legs. He scuttled between their legs and headed down the home trail, howling. A moment later he was lost from view.

The lads looked at one another blankly.

"What happened to him?" demanded Biff.

"One of the foxes must have bitten him," Joe said.

A shout from Chet interrupted him.

"Look!"

He was pointing over among the trees. The boys saw a tawny object flash against the snow, then another. The foxes had emerged from their den by the back entrance, evidently alarmed by the intrusion of the dog, and were fleeing for their lives back toward the ravine.

Chet flung his rifle to his shoulder. He was trembling with excitement, but he managed to aim at the foremost fox, and pressed the trigger.

There was only a dull click!

Chet had forgotten to load the weapon.

The others were too excited to notice his discomfiture. They were running about wildly, each seeking a good view of the fugitives. Frank and Biff, noticing the direction the foxes were taking, went plunging through the snow, back toward the rim of the ravine, with the intention of heading the animals off.

Frank tripped over a hidden tree-trunk and went sprawling headlong. He lost his rifle, and while he was searching for it Biff passed him and ran on toward the gully. Chet and Joe, in the meantime, were heading toward the gully in the opposite direction.

Biff emerged at the top of the slope. He looked down into the gully, just as Frank came racing up.

"See them?" demanded Frank.

"Not yet. They must have doubled back."

The boys looked down into the gully. The snow was white and unbroken. Suddenly, at the far end of the gully they saw a movement among the bushes. A moment later, a fox came streaking out of the thicket, followed by its mate. The animals did not see the lads watching at the top of the slope.

"Take your time, Biff," advised Frank, as he raised the rifle to his shoulder.

The foxes were hampered by the deep snow, but even at that they were racing down the gully so quickly that the boys had to take swift aim.

Bang!

Biff's rifle spoke. The lead fox stopped short, whirled in his tracks and darted back. The other animal did likewise. But Frank's aim was more accurate.

Bang!

The lead fox dropped into the snow, threshed about for a moment and lay still.

The other animal raced madly away, seeking cover. But by this time Biff had ejected the empty shell and had taken aim again. He pressed the trigger, sighting at the fleeing fox.

This time his aim was sure. The animal leaped high in the air, turned completely over and fell motionless in the snow.

"We got 'em!" yelled Biff joyfully. He began scrambling down the slope, anxious to inspect the prize. Frank followed him. At the bottom of the gully they came upon the dead animals, lying only a few yards apart. Each had been killed almost instantly.

"Amos Grice won't lose any more hens after this," declared Frank, with satisfaction.

"Just got them in the nick of time!" said Biff. "In another two seconds they would have been back among the trees and we'd have never seen them again."

Chet and Joe, attracted by the sounds of the shots, now appeared at the top of the slope. They were astonished when they found that the hunt was already ended and that Frank and Biff had slain the marauders.

"You're lucky, that's all," said Chet solemnly. "Just lucky. It was just by chance that the foxes headed this way instead of going down toward where we were waiting for them."

"Well, *we* had our rifles loaded," said Biff pointedly.

This silenced Chet, as he did not care to start any discussion concerning his failure to load the rifle when he started out on a fox-hunt.

The boys started back toward the village, carrying the dead bodies of the four-legged chicken thieves with them. When Amos Grice saw them enter the store he was almost speechless with amazement.

"Back already?" he exclaimed. "What did you do to that dog of mine? He come back here howlin' his head off and he went and hid under the wood-shed and I ain't been able to get him out."

"He found the foxes," explained Frank gravely.

"One of them nipped his nose," added Joe.

"And why are you lads back so soon? Can't catch foxes by just goin' out for half an hour or so," declared Amos, wagging his head. "It's an all-day job, often."

"Come on outside," invited Chet proudly, as though he had been person-ally responsible for the success of the hunt.

Amos Grice went outside and when he saw the two foxes lying in the snow, he rubbed his spectacles, as though he thought his eyes were playing him false.

"I wouldn't have believed it!" he said, at last. "I wouldn't have believed it! And yet I can see 'em lyin' there, with my own eyes. If this don't beat the Dutch!"

"We were just lucky enough to catch them at home," explained Frank.

"And smart enough to shoot 'em on the run," declared Amos Grice. "It takes some shootin' to get a fox, lads, for they're mighty tricky rascals. Well, now I can sleep in peace at night and I'll know that my chickens are safe. I can sure breathe easier now that I know them two thieves are through with chicken stealing."

He took the boys back to the store and, by way of showing his gratitude, insisted on filling their pockets with crackers and apples.

"You're welcome at my store any time, lads," he told them. "If ever you need any more supplies, come right to me and—and I'll sell 'em to you at wholesale price."

Seeing that this, to Amos Grice, was the height of generosity, the boys thanked him warmly.

"We've had a rare good morning," declared Frank, "and we're much obliged to you, Mr. Grice, for telling us about the foxes. We wouldn't have missed that chase for anything."

"I'm more'n obliged to *you*," said the old man.

"I guess we'd better be getting back to the island. It's lunch time now," said Chet.

Before they left, the boys cut the brushes from the two foxes and when they returned to Cabin Island that afternoon they placed the prizes in a place of honor above the fireplace.

CHAPTER XVI

THE CHIMNEY

In spite of Joe Hardy's predictions that the marauder would be back for his notebook, that afternoon and the next day passed uneventfully on Cabin Island. No one had appeared in the vicinity of the rocks, for the boys examined the place carefully in search of footprints and the snow was still unbroken.

The mystery surrounding Hanleigh, John Sparewell, and the Bender postage stamp collection was gradually receding into the background. But to the Hardy boys it still remained a matter of great concern, especially to Frank. Each evening he sat down and puzzled over the strange cipher, vainly trying to solve the mystery it presented.

"Can't you figure it out?" asked Joe.

"It beats me," said Frank, flinging down his pencil. "Once in a while I think I'm on the right track, then something always happens and I find I'm farther away than ever."

"Let the cipher look after itself. Something will turn up, I'm sure," put in Chet.

"But if we could only find the message of the cipher, we wouldn't have to wait for something to turn up."

Chet looked at the message again. He shook his head.

"It's too much for me. Don't let it spoil your holiday, Frank."

"You know what I'm like when there's a mystery in the wind. And this is one of the most mysterious puzzles we've ever tackled."

"We'll get to the bottom of it yet. I'm sure of that. Just wait. Something will turn up," said Joe.

The next day, the boys were outdoors from morning until night, skimming over the surface of the bay in their ice-boats, skating on an improvised rink down by the shore, and enjoying themselves on the ski slide. Frank, for the time being, seemed to have dismissed the mystery of the notebook from his mind. That evening, as the boys sat in front of the fireplace, the Sparewell case was not even mentioned. It was a windy, stormy night and the cabin creaked in the gale.

"Must be a good, strong chimney to hold up in a wind like that," remarked Chet.

"Why shouldn't it?" said Biff. "It's made of solid stone."

"I know; but the wind gets a terrific sweep when it hits this island. That chimney isn't so new, either."

"Stone chimneys will last a hundred years," scoffed Joe.

Chet pointed to the big fireplace.

"This one won't. Look. You can see where it is cracked already."

The boys inspected the chimney. They saw that Chet had noticed something that none of them had observed before. There was a distinct crack across the surface of the stone near the ceiling.

"It doesn't look any too secure at that," remarked Frank. "A crack like that might easily cause a fire."

"It sure could!" exclaimed Biff.

"I don't worry about fire so much as the danger that the chimney might come tumbling down in a high wind," Chet said. "If there is one crack like that, there may be others, higher up. And if the chimney ever gave way—wow!"

"We would certainly have a nice little shower of stone," Biff said. "Well, why go looking for trouble? Wait until it happens."

Chet insisted that he was not looking for trouble, but that he was merely pointing out what *might* happen. Just then there was a particularly violent gust of wind. The cabin shook. The chimney was staunch.

"I think it's good for a few years yet," Joe said. "Why worry?"

Their conversation about the chimney, however, was to be recalled to the boys very forcibly later on.

The next day it was Joe's turn to remain at the cabin as "chief cook and bottle-washer." The others went out in one of the ice-boats and made a trip as far as the village. They did not stop at the little place, being in no mind to incur any of Amos Grice's long-winded conversation, and turned about, sending the fleet little boat swooping down into the wind. They were about a quarter of a mile from the cabin and just debating the advisability of making a trip down into the cove when they heard a sound that aroused them to a high pitch of excitement.

Crack!

Sharp and clear, the sound carried through the winter air.

"The rifle!" exclaimed Frank.

"Somebody down at the rocks!"

Frank swung the boat around toward the island. The wind, however, was against them and he could make little speed. He was obliged to tack about for some time, while the others speculated impatiently on the reason for Joe's signal.

"Just when we need speed, the wind is against us!" groaned Biff.

"Perhaps the fellow will clear out before we can get back."

"Not if I know it," said Frank grimly. "We'll come around on the other side of the island, and if he is making a getaway we can head him off."

The boat seemed to labor slowly forward at a snail's pace. Anxiously, the boys peered toward the island.

They could see no one.

"Perhaps the shot didn't scare him away," said Chet hopefully.

They circled around until at last they had a full view of the side of the island on which the stolen supplies had been hidden. The ice was bare. The hillside was bleak. There was no sign of any human being.

The boys brought their craft around until they were close to the rocks. They could see footprints in the snow.

"There was somebody here, all right," said Frank, in excitement.

"I wonder if it was Hanleigh!"

"We'll mighty soon find out."

They brought the boat inshore and took in the sails. Then they scrambled out, made their way up over the rocks, and examined the footprints. They did not lead up toward the cabin, but instead they led along the shore around the bend.

"Follow him!" said Chet.

"Not yet," Frank advised. "I think we'd better go up to the cabin first and find out what Joe knows about it. Perhaps he recognized the fellow and saw where he went."

They ploughed through the snow up to the top of the slope. They found Joe awaiting them in the door of the cabin.

"Did you see him?" shouted Frank.

"Just caught a glimpse of him," returned Joe, as the boys came running up to him. "I happened to look out the window and caught sight of somebody down among the rocks."

"Who was he?"

"I don't know. His back was turned to me, and he was crouching over. He was looking for that notebook, all right. I waited for a while, but I still couldn't get a good look at him, so I went and got the rifle. By the time I got back to the window he was gone."

"Before you fired the signal shot?"

"Yes. I could hardly believe my eyes. He just seemed to disappear into thin air. Well, I didn't lose any time firing the shot, I can tell you. I could see your boat away up the bay."

"The wind was against us," said Frank. "We tried to get here quickly, but we didn't have any luck."

"He's still on the island," said Joe quickly. "I'm pretty sure of that."

"Wonder how he got here," remarked Chet. "There isn't any other ice-boat around, that we saw."

"Probably walked over from the mainland," Frank remarked. "Well, I guess we had better explore a bit and see if we can't get a sight of him. You're sure you didn't recognize him, Joe?"

"No. I couldn't say if the man was Hanleigh or not. I didn't get a good look at him at all."

"We'll get a good look at him," growled Biff. "And mighty soon, too."

"I suggest that two of us take the north side of the island and the other two take the south," said Joe.

Frank shook his head.

"Some one must stay here," he decided. "We don't want to run the risk of losing our supplies again. If this fellow managed to draw us far enough away from the cabin, there's no telling what damage he might do. Joe, I think you had better stay here. If you see the man coming this way, fire another shot, and we'll come a-running."

"Good idea!" approved Chet. "I think we all ought to separate. Each go in a different direction. If we catch sight of him, whistle!"

Frank quickly directed the search. Joe was to stay at the cabin, Chet was to go to the northern side of the island, Biff was to explore the south. Frank himself was to cut through the trees in the center of the island, emerging on the other side.

They separated.

Frank ploughed through the snow, heading toward the heavy growth of trees at the top of Cabin Island. He soon reached a point from where he could get a good view of the entire island. He could see Biff and Chet industriously exploring the shore lines.

A little distance away, in the snow beneath the trees, he caught sight of a line of fresh footprints.

He picked up the trail at once, and followed the marks in the snow.

They led him in and out among the trees, then veered and seemed to be directed toward the rocks.

"What am I thinking of?" said Frank, to himself. "I'm not following the man's trail at all. I'm going back on it."

He turned, and retraced his steps, after a while reaching the place where he had first found the footprints. He went on from there, deeper into the thicket, proceeding cautiously.

At last he stood still for a moment, listening. Then he slipped in behind a tree.

He heard a crackle of branches. Some one was moving about among the trees, only a few yards ahead.

Frank peeped out.

He saw a dark figure emerge from behind a clump of evergreens. The man stepped out, looked cautiously about, then moved up the slope in the direction of the cabin.

"Hanleigh!" said Frank, under his breath.

Frank Hardy's first impulse was to whistle, in order to bring the others to his assistance. Then he paused.

What did Hanleigh want? What did he plan to do?

CHAPTER XVII

THE ESCAPE

Frank was so close to the man that he recognized him readily. He knew now that Hanleigh was the man who had stolen their supplies and hidden them, evidently to get the boys to leave the island. He knew that Hanleigh was the man who had lost the mysterious Sparewell notebook. He wanted to know more. If he raised the alarm now, the man would simply refuse to talk.

Frank waited until the fellow had vanished among the trees. Then he turned and made his way toward the cabin by a short-cut. He wanted to reach the place first and warn Joe, so that they could better observe the man's actions without raising an immediate alarm.

"If he thinks we don't see him, he may give himself away," Frank reasoned.

He reached the cabin unobserved. Hanleigh had not yet emerged from the trees.

Frank found Joe standing at the window, looking down toward the rocks.

"I saw him! He's coming this way."

"Who is he?" demanded Joe eagerly.

"Hanleigh."

"I thought so all along. Is he coming here?"

"I think so. Look, Joe—here's my plan. I think he intends to come here. He imagines we're all out hunting for him. Let's hide and find out what he wants."

"How about Chet and Biff?"

"They're away down at the far ends of the island. We can capture Hanleigh any time we want."

"Where shall we hide?"

They looked around hastily. If Hanleigh came to the cabin, they knew the man would probably search the place high and low for the notebook which was his probable objective in returning to the island.

"We'll have to stay outside. No use running any risks. We'd better hide in the bushes until we see him come in here. Then we can creep up and watch him through the back window," Frank decided.

They left the cabin and ran across to a heavy clump of bushes only a few yards away. There they crouched, waiting.

For a while, nothing happened. Then they heard a snapping and crackling of branches far over to one side. In a few moments, Hanleigh came into view. He looked cautiously from side to side, then advanced swiftly toward the door of the cabin. There was a smile of satisfaction upon his swarthy face. It was quite evident that he believed the lads had departed to search for him. Swiftly, he stepped into the cabin.

Frank and Joe came out of their hiding place. They sped quickly over to the window and peeped inside.

Hanleigh had paused uncertainly in the middle of the room. He was looking at the fireplace. He stepped toward it, then apparently changed his mind, for he paused, shook his head, and turned toward the kitchen. They heard him rummaging about there for a few minutes, and in a little while he returned.

That he was searching for something, soon became evident. He went over to the beds and flung blankets, pillows and even mattresses on the floor. With an expression of disgust, he began going through the boys' packsacks.

"If he's looking for the notebook he might as well quit now," whispered Frank.

"Where is it?"

"In my pocket."

Hanleigh made a thorough search of the cabin. He rummaged through the bureau and the desk, and as his search went on, with no success, he apparently lost his temper for he flung things on the floor and stamped angrily about.

"Let's rush him before he wrecks the cabin," whispered Joe.

But Frank restrained his brother.

"Wait!"

Hanleigh came over toward the window.

The boys ducked out of sight. They could hear the man talking to himself. They listened, and they heard him mutter:

"Well, they won't be able to read that cipher, anyway, so I guess it's all right."

Frank and Joe nudged one another. Hanleigh was certainly searching for the Sparewell notebook. The man went away from the window. They heard a crash as, in a fit of vicious temper, the man swept off a few of the little ornaments some one had placed above the fireplace.

"If he's going to start smashing things, I guess we'd better take a hand," remarked Frank.

The boys stole around the side of the cabin. Then they stepped suddenly across the threshold.

With an exclamation of surprise, Hanleigh swung around, facing them.

"Good-day, Mr. Hanleigh," said Frank. "I see that you have decided to pay us a little call."

The man said nothing. He merely glared at the boys. They could see that he was estimating his chances of escape, but they barred the doorway.

"Why don't you wait until we're all at home?" asked Joe.

"You boys have no right here, anyway," growled the intruder.

"Did you ask Mr. Jefferson about it?" inquired Frank sweetly.

"I came back here to look for something I lost the other day."

"What other day? The day you came and stole all our supplies?"

"I don't know anything about your supplies. I mean the day I was here when you fellows first arrived."

"Haven't you been here since?"

"No."

"I'm pretty sure you have, Mr. Hanleigh. What was the idea of hiding our food supplies?"

"I don't know anything about your food supplies, I tell you!" shouted the man, in exasperation. "I haven't been here since the last time you saw me."

"Well, I suppose we'll have to take your word for it," said Frank, with a shrug. "Although I don't believe you for a minute. What was it you lost? Perhaps we can help you."

"My pocketbook," growled Hanleigh, after a moment's silence.

"Your pocketbook? Was there much money in it?"

"About fifty dollars. You don't blame me for coming back to look for it, do you?" sneered Hanleigh.

"Not at all. Where did you lose it?"

"I don't know. Somewhere on the island."

"Not down among the rocks, by chance?"

"I wasn't down there."

"Are you sure it wasn't a notebook?" asked Frank quietly.

The shot told. Hanleigh's fists clenched.

"No, it wasn't a notebook," he said thickly.

"Well, if it wasn't a notebook, I guess we can't help you. Quite sure, you didn't lose a notebook?"

"I don't know anything about a notebook."

"That's too bad. If it had been a notebook you lost, instead of a pocketbook, we'd be able to help you. We did find a notebook and we have been wondering whom it belonged to."

"What kind of notebook?"

"Why should you ask?" said Frank. "If you didn't lose one, you shouldn't be concerned. I think you'd better sit down, Mr. Hanleigh. We have a few things to talk over with you before we turn you over to the police."

Hanleigh went pale.

"The police?" he gasped.

"Why, of course. You don't suppose we're going to let you get away with this, do you? You have no right here, you are trespassing on the island, you break into our cabin and go through all our belongings, just like a common burglar. What did you expect?"

"You won't turn me over to the police," declared Hanleigh.

"No?"

Hanleigh advanced toward them.

"Get out of my way!" he ordered.

The boys stood their ground.

"Just a minute," said Frank. "We have rifles here. If you try to make a getaway, we won't be afraid to shoot."

Hanleigh hesitated.

"That's just a bluff," he said weakly.

"Try it, and see."

"I'll try it!" roared Hanleigh.

He made a sudden lunge. Frank reached out to seize him and grabbed the man's arm. But Hanleigh shook himself free, plunged forward and collided with Joe. The boys were taken by surprise. Joe struggled desperately, but Hanleigh was a grown man and much stronger. He sent Joe reeling back against the wall.

Frank flung himself upon the man and tried to trip him up.

Hanleigh struck out viciously with his fist. It caught Frank full in the face. He was obliged to relinquish his hold. Before he knew it, Hanleigh had dashed toward the door. The man leaped across the threshold and out into the snow.

Frank recovered himself quickly. He ran toward the wall and took down the little rifle. Joe, in the meantime, raced out of the cabin in pursuit of the fugitive.

"Stop, or I'll shoot!" Frank shouted.

But the man evidently realized that Frank would not make use of the rifle. He turned and shook his fist in their direction. With a yell of defiance, he disappeared among the trees.

Frank raised the rifle and fired two shots into the air. His aim was partly to frighten Hanleigh and partly to warn Chet and Biff.

Joe turned.

Pursuit was futile. The heavy snow hampered his footsteps.

"No use chasing him!" shouted Frank. "Perhaps Chet and Biff will catch him. It doesn't matter. We know that he is the fellow who had the notebook, and that's the main thing."

CHAPTER XVIII

THE CIPHER SOLVED

Hanleigh made good his escape.

Chet Morton and Biff Hooper, who were widely separated at the time, heard the rifle shots and returned posthaste to the cabin, but they did not meet the fugitive. By the time they reached the cabin, further pursuit was out of the question. Looking out the window, Frank pointed to a dark figure hastening across the ice toward the mainland.

"By the time we got one of the ice-boats out, he would be on the shore, and we'd never find him there," he said. "Let him go. We learned something, at any rate."

"What happened?" clamored Chet. "All we know is that Hanleigh was here. What did he do?"

Frank then told them of seeing Hanleigh among the trees, and of returning to the cabin to warn Joe.

"We watched him searching the place high and low. He was looking for the notebook—there's no doubt of that. As a matter of fact, we heard him say that it didn't really matter, because we wouldn't be able to solve the cipher, anyway. So then Joe and I came in and asked him what he was doing. He tried to fool us with some cock-and-bull story about hunting for his pocketbook. He denied that he stole our supplies, but he was lying, of course. I threatened to turn him over to the police if he didn't tell us what he knew about the notebook, and I guess that frightened him for he made a dash for the door."

"We weren't ready for him," said Joe mournfully.

"I'll bet he thinks twice before he comes here again," declared Chet.

"I don't think we've seen the last of him," Frank remarked. "There is something mighty important about that notebook, and I'm sure he is not the man to give up as easily as all that."

Chet shook his head.

"He'll just wait until we leave the island for good."

"I don't think so. He knows that we're apt to stumble on the secret of that cipher at any time. I'm going to tackle that message again. It can't be so very difficult."

Frank immediately sat down at the desk, the cipher message before him, and began figuring on a pad of notepaper, while the other boys set about restoring the damage their visitor had created.

First of all, he set down all the letters of the alphabet in order, and studied them intently, with reference to the cipher.

"If I were writing a cipher," he mused. "How would I go about it? Perhaps this thing is really a lot simpler than it looks."

The easiest thing to do, he thought, would be merely to reverse the alphabet. Instead of the letter "a" he would use the letter "z." Instead of the letter "b" he would use "y," and so on.

With this in mind, he jotted down the alphabet backward, so that he had two rows of letters. Then he picked up the cipher again.

The first word was "XZYRM."

By replacing these letters with the corresponding letters in the other column he discovered that he had the word "CABIN."

Frank leaped to his feet with a shout of delight.

"I've got it!"

The others came running over to the desk.

"Have you solved it?" demanded Joe excitedly. "How did you do it? What does it say?"

"It's as simple as a-b-c. It was so easy that it looked hard. The man just turned the alphabet backward. Look! The first word is 'cabin.'"

"The rest of it! The rest of it!" exclaimed Biff.

"I haven't tackled the other words yet. Wait a minute. I'll have them in a jiffy."

Frank turned to the cipher again. For a few minutes he worked industriously. Little by little, the complete message took shape on the sheet of paper.

At last he sat back with a sigh of satisfaction.

"All serene! The cipher is solved."

"Read it."

Frank picked up the paper and read aloud:

CABIN ISLAND CHIMNEY LEFT FRONT
NINE FEET HIGH.

Chet groaned with disappointment.

"And what good does that do?"

"What good does it do? Don't you understand? This message refers to the chimney right in this very cabin. All we have to do now is examine a part of the chimney on the left hand side, in front, nine feet from the floor."

The boys were immediately plunged into excitement. Everything else was forgotten. The chimney became the center of interest.

"Now we know why Hanleigh was measuring the chimney! Something is hidden there!" exclaimed Chet.

"Well, well!" said Joe approvingly. "And you actually figured it out all by yourself."

"Nine feet high," mused Frank. "We'll have to get something to measure by."

A stick was obtained and the boys roughly estimated its length as being about three feet. Then Joe went over to the chimney. Measuring from the floor, he marked off its length three times until he reached a spot which he judged would be nine feet high.

"It doesn't look any different from any other part of the chimney," said Chet.

Frank got up on a chair and carefully examined the chimney stone at the place to which Joe had measured. He felt the mortar, tapped the stone, ran his hands over the surface, but he found nothing to indicate anything amiss.

"Solid rocks and mortar," he said, with disappointment. "All but those few cracks."

"That's odd," said Joe. "Why should the cipher mention that part of the chimney so particularly?"

"We're on the wrong track, for some reason or other." Frank repeated the cipher message again: "'Cabin Island chimney left front nine feet high.'"

"I can't understand it," remarked Biff. "The message must mean *something*."

Frank's face suddenly lighted up.

"Perhaps it means inside the chimney. If there is anything hidden, that would be the logical place. It couldn't be from the outside, for we'd have to tear the whole chimney down to get at it."

"How are we going to get at it if it is hidden inside the chimney?" Chet inquired.

"One of us will just have to turn Santa Claus for a while."

"You mean, climb up nine feet into the chimney?"

"Sure. Why not?"

"Somebody else can do it."

"Who volunteers?"

Biff and Joe regarded the chimney doubtfully.

"I'll bet there's a lot of soot in there," muttered Biff.

"Besides, there's a fire on."

"We'll put the fire out first, of course," Frank said. "Well, if nobody else wants to go, I'll do it."

"You will certainly need a bath when you come out," Chet told him.

"Listen." Biff seemed a trifle ashamed because of his reluctance to enter the chimney, "It's a sort of messy job, and Frank shouldn't have to do it just because the rest of us don't like the idea. Suppose we draw lots for it."

"That's fair enough," Joe agreed. "The fellow who draws the short straw goes up the chimney."

There were no straws available but the boys broke up some small sticks, leaving one considerably shorter than the others. Frank held the four sticks between the palms of his hands so that only the tops were visible. Biff drew first—one of the long sticks. Joe was next, and the drawing was abruptly terminated, for he held the short one.

"It's up to me, I guess," he said, with a grimace. "Oh, well. It won't be so bad. Perhaps I'll find a fortune in diamonds hidden inside that chimney."

"We'll all take turns at scrubbing you when you come out," Chet consoled him.

"We'll have to wait until the fire dies down, first of all."

Frank took the poker and broke up the burning log in the fireplace.

"In the meantime, you'd better get into some old clothes, Joe," he said.

While they waited for the fire to burn itself out, Joe changed into some garments found in a shed that were so old and disreputable that the soot would make no appreciable difference. Much as the boys wanted to learn the secret of the chimney, none of them envied Joe his task, and, to tell the truth, he regarded it with some misgivings himself.

At last the fire had burned so low that a dipperful of water quenched the embers, and when the smoke had cleared away, Joe stepped into the big fireplace. He glanced up.

"Dark as a cellar!" he observed.

Chet came forward with his flashlight.

"I didn't think it would be useful so soon," he said, as he handed it over. "Away you go!"

Joe seized the flashlight and began his ascent into the chimney.

The stones were large and rough, affording a good foothold. No sooner had Joe begun his climb than a shower of soot descended into the fireplace. The lads heard a smothered gurgle.

"I'll bet that chimney hasn't been cleaned out since the cabin was built," said Biff.

"I'm sure of it!" gasped Joe, from inside. Then there was another gurgle and Joe said no more because he had received a mouthful of soot.

Those below could hear him scrambling about inside, and, by peering up into the fireplace, they could see the reflection of the flashlight. More soot continued to pour down the chimney. Joe was evidently having a bad time of it.

"Wonder what he'll find," speculated Biff.

"Soot," said Chet.

They waited. Then they heard a muffled cry of dismay.

"What's the matter?" they shouted.

"I'm stuck! I got up here, but now I can't get back." Joe evidently gave a violent lunge for freedom, because an unusually heavy shower of soot followed.

"Come on, fellows! Don't stand down there doing nothing!" he clamored. "Get me out of this before I smother!"

CHAPTER XIX

DISAPPOINTMENT

Frank Hardy sprang forward.

He crouched down in the fireplace and looked up. He could see Joe's wildly plunging feet a short distance above.

"Kick yourself free!" advised Chet helpfully.

"That's all I can do—kick!" replied the prisoner. "My elbows are wedged in against these rocks and I can't get loose."

"Hold steady a second," Frank said. "I'll try to drag you out."

He reached up and seized one of Joe's feet. He tugged, but Joe was evidently firmly wedged in the chimney.

"Keep on climbing and come out at the top," called Chet.

"Wait till I get you!" answered Joe. "This isn't funny."

"Come on, you chaps," said Frank, to the others. "Lend a hand. We'll just have to drag him out by main force."

Gingerly, Biff and Chet entered the fire place. The three boys were crowded together. They reached up to grab Joe by the feet just as the prisoner made another struggle and sent more soot pouring down on his rescuers. Within a few seconds, the three were liberally covered with the black substance.

"All together, now," said Frank, when they had grabbed Joe by the ankles. "Pull!"

They pulled.

With surprising quickness, Joe came loose. He came plunging down into the fireplace on top of the others, each of whom lost his balance and sat down heavily. There was more soot.

The four lads were piled in a heap in the fireplace, so blackened and dirty as to be unrecognizable. Joe, of course, had the worst of it. His face was as black as coal. He was a bedraggled, sooty object, but not much sorrier sight than his companions.

As they sat up and looked at one another, the humor of the situation suddenly struck them.

"Oh, boy! You chaps look funny!" yelled Chet, and burst into a howl of laughter.

"No funnier than you!" roared Biff. "You look like a chimney sweep."

They scrambled out of the fireplace, laughing in spite of themselves.

"If somebody could have seen us all when Joe came down out of that chimney!" laughed Frank. "I'll bet we looked funny. What a glorious tumble!"

"I vote we all take a bath," said Chet mournfully.

"We certainly need it. And the fire is out and we have no hot water."

They looked glumly at each other, black and wretched, and then they began to laugh again.

"What did you find, Joe?"

"Soot!" returned the victim.

"We know you did. But what else did you find? Or didn't you have a chance to explore the chimney?"

"I explored it, all right. And I can tell you this—there's nothing hidden up there."

This announcement was a shock to them all.

"Didn't you find anything?" demanded Frank.

Joe shook his head.

"I turned on the flashlight and examined the inside of the chimney very carefully. The rocks and mortar are just as solid inside as they are on the outside. I didn't find a trace of anything unusual."

"You looked on the left hand side, at the front?"

"Exactly as the cipher said. And I tried to figure it out at about nine feet from the floor. Just to be sure, I examined every inch of the chimney on that side. I was just going higher when I got stuck."

Even the grime could not hide the disappointment expressed in the boys' faces just then.

"I guess that message was just a fake," said Biff finally.

But the Hardy boys would not agree with this.

"If it is a fake, why was Hanleigh so frightened lest we would be able to read it?" asked Frank.

"Well," shrugged Biff, "if it isn't a fake, why isn't there something in the chimney? We've examined it from the front, and Joe has examined it from the inside, and there is certainly nothing hidden there."

"I can't understand it," Frank admitted. "Just the same, I believe that message means something. It is certainly disappointing to find ourselves up against a blank wall just when we thought we were going to solve the whole mystery."

The boys lighted the fire again and after they had heated water they scrubbed themselves thoroughly and had a good cleaning-up. Within an hour they were presentable again, the soot had been swept up from the floor, and all evidences of their adventure in the chimney had been removed.

"I wonder," suggested Joe, "if there is another Cabin Island."

"Not in Barmet Bay," said Frank.

"Perhaps somewhere else. Perhaps this message refers to an island in some other part of the country altogether. Perhaps Hanleigh merely guessed that this was the place."

"There may be something in that. It's just possible that Hanleigh is in the same boat as we are, and that we are all being fooled."

"Well," said Chet, "we've done the best we could, and there is something wrong somewhere, so why should we worry about it any longer? We came here for an outing—not to solve puzzles."

"That's right," declared Biff. "If this chap Hanleigh comes back we'll try to get the truth out of him, but we won't do ourselves any good by racking our brains over this business. Forget it!"

So the subject of the cipher message was officially dropped.

To Frank, however, their failure to discover anything of importance in the big chimney had been very disappointing. He had been elated by his success in solving the mystery of the cipher message and he had looked upon the entire riddle as being near solution. The setback was a hard pill to swallow. In spite of the fact that Biff thought the message was a fake, Frank clung stubbornly to the belief that it was genuine and important.

"Hanleigh wouldn't have made such a fuss about it," he argued, "unless there was something important behind it all."

He regretted Hanleigh's escape now. Frank longed to meet the man again. He wanted another chance to force the fellow into an explanation of how he came to be in possession of Sparewell's notebook. And, above all, he wanted to know what the cipher message referred to. What was hidden in the chimney?

"We'll find out," he insisted. "Perhaps, in the long run, it will all turn out to be just as simple as that cipher."

He looked gloomily at the big chimney.

What mystery did it hide? Was there any mystery? Was the whole message just a hoax?

He could not believe this. In any case, Hanleigh knew something about the mysterious Sparewell—else how did he get possession of the notebook? And in this respect alone the mystery was worth following up.

That evening, the Hardy boys and their chums were gathered around the fire. Chet and Joe were playing checkers. Biff had rigged up the punching bag, had donned his boxing gloves, and was making the bag drum in a lively manner. Frank was still studying the cipher, wondering if there might not be some little clue he had missed. Once in a while he referred to the pages of the notebook again.

It was growing colder outside and the boys had to keep a roaring fire in order that the cabin should be warm enough. The wind was rising and there were fitful slashes of snow against the windows.

"More dirty weather!" growled Biff, dealing a particularly vicious blow at the punching bag.

"Seems it's done nothing but snow since we came here," said Chet.

"It's your move," Joe reminded him.

Chet moved his checker and Joe promptly captured it, with a king as well.

The scene was peaceful. The boys would have been interested if they had known of what was happening in a little house in Bayport just then.

Hanleigh was preparing to return to Cabin Island.

CHAPTER XX

WHEN ROGUES FALL OUT

Hanleigh, who had taken up his quarters in a small bungalow at the eastern limits of Bayport, had made an appointment for that evening with Tad Carson and Ike Nash, the two youths who had taken him to Cabin Island in their ice-boat on the occasion of his first meeting with the Hardy boys.

An alarm clock ticking on the kitchen table showed the hour as eight o'clock. Hanleigh, listening to the rising wind, made a gesture of impatience.

"What's the matter with them?" he growled. "Can't they ever get here when I tell them?"

He was obliged to wait another ten minutes before the door of the bungalow opened, and Ike Nash slouched in, followed by his companion.

They tossed their caps on the table and nodded coolly to Hanleigh.

"I thought I told you to be here at half-past seven!"

Tad Carson shrugged.

"That's the time you told us, all right. We just couldn't make it."

"Keep me cooling my heels while you shoot another game of pool, I suppose!" snapped the man.

"You haven't anything else to do," replied Nash. He sat down and put his feet on the table. "Well, what's it all about?"

"I want to go over to the island tomorrow."

"What island?" asked Tad Carson.

"What island do you think? *The* island, of course. Cabin Island. I want to go there early tomorrow morning."

"What's stopping you?" asked Nash insolently.

"Well, you know why I sent for you? I can't walk there."

The two youths glanced at one another.

"I suppose you want us to take you over in the ice-boat again, eh?"

"Of course. I want you to call here for me at seven o'clock in the morning. Have the ice-boat ready so we can make a quick start."

"You're giving orders tonight, ain't you, Hanleigh?" said Ike. "What if it doesn't suit us to go?"

"Why shouldn't it suit you? Neither of you is working."

"That's all right. Tad and I were just talking it over as we came up here tonight. We'd like to know more about this business. Hanleigh. We have an idea there may be something crooked about it."

Hanleigh stared at them incredulously. That these allies should be inclined to back out had never entered his calculations.

"Crooked!" he exclaimed. "Of course not. I'm thinking of buying the island and naturally I want to look the place over before I make an offer."

"Yes? Why don't you wait until summer? The winter is no time of year to inspect an island."

Hanleigh became angry.

"Will you two mind your own business!" he blustered. "Is it any concern of yours why I want to go to the island. I pay you well for carrying me there, and all you have to do is keep your mouths shut."

"We won't keep 'em shut," remarked Nash, "unless we get more money than you have been giving us."

"I've been paying you very well, I think. Ten dollars each is very good money for a trip that most boys would be glad to take just for the fun of it."

"We don't run the ice-boat just for our health," said Carson. "Every time we go there we have to hang around and freeze until you are ready to come back. You won't even let us go up to the cabin with you. I'd like to know what there is about that place that interests you so much."

Hanleigh gazed at them narrowly. So! They were beginning to suspect him!

"I've told you," he said irritably. "I may buy the place, and naturally I want to look the cabin over."

"Well, there wouldn't be any harm in letting us look it over too. Listen, Mr. Hanleigh—you're up to something, and we know it. If you don't want us to go to Mr. Jefferson and tell him about your visits to the island, you had better kick in with some more money." Tad Carson sat back and winked at his companion.

Hanleigh was almost speechless with wrath.

"Why—why—you young scoundrels!" he spluttered. "This is blackmail. Why, it's a hold-up!"

"Call it what you like!" sneered Nash.

"You can't tell Jefferson anything. I have his full permission to go to the island at any time I want."

"Is that so? Now, look here, Mr. Hanleigh—you've been trying to tell us that you may buy the island. Now, we happen to know that you made Mr. Jefferson an offer for the island and he told you he wouldn't sell at any price. How about that?"

"It's—it's false."

"It's the truth," said Nash.

"Who told you?" demanded Hanleigh.

"Never mind who told us. We know more about you than you think. Now, if you are up to any funny business, we won't put anything in your way, as long as you come through and treat us fair."

"I have treated you fairly. I have always paid you well."

"Ten dollars a trip," laughed Tad Carson. "That's all right if you were just going there to look the place over, as you told us. But you've got a bigger game on, and it will probably be worth a lot of money to you. We want to be in on it. If you're up to something crooked, we're running the risk of being arrested for helping you. We won't take a chance like that for ten dollars each."

"I've told you everything is perfectly fair and above-board," Hanleigh insisted. "Why should you try to hold me up? If I hear any more of this nonsense, I'll hire somebody else to take me to the island."

"Try it, and see what happens," said Nash darkly.

"What will happen?"

"We'll tell Jefferson."

"Tell him. I'm not afraid."

"That's a pretty good bluff, Mr. Hanleigh, but it won't work with us," said Carson. "You have some crooked game on, and you don't want Jefferson to know about it. Why were you so anxious to buy the island? Why won't he sell it to you? That's what we'd like to know."

Hanleigh became more amicable.

"Now listen here, boys," he said smoothly; "it doesn't do any of us any good to quarrel like this. If you think you're not being paid enough, I guess I can let you have a little more. I'll tell you what I'll do. I'll pay you each twenty dollars to take me to the island tomorrow morning. That's fair enough, isn't it?"

Nash laughed scornfully.

"Now we *know* you have some game on," he said. "Twenty dollars won't be enough. We want a hundred dollars apiece."

"A hundred! It's an outrage. I won't pay it."

Nash got up. "All right. Come on, Tad. We may as well go and see Mr. Jefferson now. He'll probably be glad to pay us well for the information we can give him."

The young men got up and were moving toward the door when Hanleigh sprang to his feet.

"Not so fast!" he begged. "Sit down and let us talk this over."

"What's the use of talking when you won't listen to reason?"

Hanleigh regarded the pair for a moment. Then he said:

"You are both very much mistaken. There is nothing crooked about my visits to the island. Still, I wouldn't want you to be running to Mr. Jefferson and bothering him with a silly story that would only cause a lot of trouble. Now, I've changed my mind about going to the island tomorrow. I'll go the day after tomorrow, instead."

"How about our hundred dollars?"

"It's an outrageous price. Fifty dollars—"

"No! A hundred or nothing."

Hanleigh sighed.

"I haven't got that much money with me. You boys seem to think I'm made of money."

"You were willing to spend a good fat sum to buy the island," Nash reminded him. "There's something fishy about the whole affair. Is there a gold mine on that island?"

Hanleigh laughed uneasily.

"You're worrying yourselves about something that doesn't concern you in the least. Give me a day to raise the money and you shall have it."

Nash glanced significantly at his chum.

"Now, you're talking sense," he said approvingly. "You pay us a hundred each and we'll take you there."

"The day after tomorrow."

"Just as you say. But we must have the money before we start."

"And you won't say anything to Jefferson?"

"Not a word. But if you don't come across with the money—"

"I'll pay it to you. Meet me here tomorrow night."

"All right." Nash and Carson went toward the door. "You've saved yourself a lot of trouble, Mr. Hanleigh."

They went away. No sooner had the door closed behind them than Hanleigh laughed sardonically.

"A hundred dollars!" he exclaimed. "The young pups! Thought they could make a fool out of me. Well, they'll have to get up in the middle of the night to get ahead of me. By the time they get wise to themselves I'll be at the island and back, and I won't pay for the privilege either."

Next morning, Hanleigh was up early. It was snowing heavily and there was a bitter wind, but he meant to go to Cabin Island that day. He knew where Tad Carson and Ike Nash kept their ice-boat and he made his way down to the little building unobserved.

The door was protected by a stout padlock, but Hanleigh picked up a heavy iron bar that stood against the side of the building and attacked the lock. He smashed it with a single blow, opened the door, and went inside. He brought out the ice-boat and unfurled its sails.

There was snow on the ice, but the craft moved across the surface under the impetus of a strong wind. Hanleigh sat at the tiller. Within a few moments the boat was scudding down the bay. Hanleigh chuckled to himself as he thought of the way in which he had outwitted Ike Nash and Tad Carson.

The ice-boat sped on down the bay into the driving snow. The storm was increasing in fury. The wind hurtled the craft along at terrific speed. Hanleigh, although he had no experience in managing the boat, got along very well, and within a short time he saw the dark mass of Cabin Island looming out of the storm.

"A good day for it!" he chuckled. "I won't let those boys on the island make a monkey out of me as they did the last time."

CHAPTER XXI

A CRY FOR HELP

When the Hardy boys and their chums awakened that morning they found that the storm of the night before had increased in fury to such an extent that the mainland was no longer visible.

The island was completely isolated. As far as the eye could reach, the boys could see nothing but swirling sheets of snow.

"Looks as if we'll have to stay indoors today," said Frank, as he lit the fire.

"A nuisance!" Chet grumbled. "I thought we could go out in the ice-boat this morning."

"We'd probably get lost out in that storm. It certainly is blowing up a fine blizzard!" Biff remarked.

Joe looked out the window.

"I wonder how our boats are faring," he said. "With a wind like that, they're liable to be damaged."

"I was thinking of that," Frank replied. "After breakfast we had better go down and see that they're all right."

The meal over, the boys donned their outdoor clothes and set out from the cabin. The snow had drifted over the path and they were obliged to break a new trail down the slope toward the little cove in which the ice-boats were left.

"What a dirty day!" exclaimed Chet. "I think we're just as well off indoors in weather like this."

"I should say so," agreed the others.

They found that the ice-boats were weathering the gale well. No damage had been done, but the boys took all possible precautions in making the boats secure. While they were doing this, Joe gazed out into the storm.

"I must be dreaming," he said at last.

"Why?" asked Frank.

"It hardly seems possible, but I'm sure I saw an ice-boat go speeding past, out in the bay. It was just a shadow in the snow."

"What would an ice-boat be doing out here on a day like this?" scoffed Chet. "You certainly must have been dreaming."

The boys gazed out into the blinding wall of snow. They saw nothing, and they were just about to turn away, branding Joe's statement as a false alarm, when they heard a loud crash.

"What's that?"

The noise came from somewhere out in the storm, but it was so loud that the lads knew it had been caused by something not far from shore.

"There *is* something out there!" cried Joe.

"If it was an ice-boat it must have been wrecked," Frank declared. "I guess we had better investigate."

They went on down the shore a short distance, still gazing out into the driving snow, but there was no solution to the mystery. They could see nothing, and they heard nothing but the howl of the wind. Frank turned up his coat collar.

"I don't care to venture very far away from the island," he said doubtfully. "It would be mighty easy to get lost out there."

"I wonder what caused that crash!"

They were just about to give up the search when they heard a faint cry.

"Help! Help!"

It was a man's voice.

"That settles it," declared Frank. "There has been an accident out there and some one is hurt. He'll freeze to death if we leave him out there."

"We'll get him. Listen again, fellows, and see where the sound is coming from."

The cry was repeated. They judged that the man, whoever he was, was out in the blizzard, almost immediately in front of the place where they were now standing.

"Let's go," said Frank.

He took the lead, left the island, and plunged out into the snowy waste. The others followed. Once beyond shelter of the island they caught the full force of the wind. It came howling down on them, flinging snow about them in clouds. They could scarcely see one another, so furious was the blizzard.

"Help!"

"We're coming!" shouted Frank.

In a few moments they could see a dark mass ahead.

"Ice-boat," grunted Joe. "I told you so. All smashed up."

The ice-boat lay on its side, its mast broken in two, its sails torn to ribbons, its understructure smashed. It had evidently been going at a good rate of speed and had overturned when it swung too far over in the wind. They could see the figure of a man pinned beneath the wreckage.

Hastily, the boys knelt down to extricate the victim. When Frank saw who the man was, he gave a shout of surprise.

"Hanleigh!"

"Get me out of here," snarled Hanleigh. "My leg is broken."

The lads wasted no time in dragging their enemy from beneath the wreckage of the ice-boat. He was groaning with pain.

"I can't walk!" he moaned. "You'll have to carry me. My leg is broken."

The boys raised Hanleigh on their shoulders. There was no use trying to save the ice-boat. It was wrecked beyond all chance of repair.

"How did you come to be out here on a day like this?" demanded Frank, as they started the journey back to Cabin Island.

Hanleigh made no reply. He was moaning with pain. His right leg hung limply, but Frank's practiced eye saw at a glance that it was not broken.

"Sprained his ankle, most likely," he said to Joe.

"Lucky I wasn't killed," groaned Hanleigh. "I was going at terrific speed, and I couldn't get the boat stopped. I tried to lower sail and the wind turned the whole boat over on top of me."

"Anybody who goes ice-boating in a storm like this deserves whatever happens to him," observed Chet unsympathetically.

Hanleigh was a heavy man, and by the time the boys reached the island they were forced to stop and rest. Then, puffing from their labors, they raised the injured man to their shoulders again and began to climb up the slope.

"I'm glad you heard me shouting," muttered Hanleigh. "I would have frozen to death out there."

"A lucky chance for you that we heard you at all," Joe said. "If we had been up in the cabin we would never have heard a whisper."

Frank nudged his brother.

"Lucky for us, too," he said. "Now we'll be able to make him talk."

At last they reached the cabin. They put Hanleigh on one of the beds, and then Frank examined the injured leg. As he had suspected, it was not broken, although the ankle was badly sprained. Having bathed it and put liniment and a bandage on the injured limb, Frank looked down at Hanleigh.

"You're all right. Don't make such a fuss. It's only a sprain."

"Lucky it wasn't worse. My, I'm glad you boys heard me calling."

"Pretty nice to have friends near at hand, isn't it?" said Frank. "Now that you're here, Hanleigh, I think you'd better tell us why you were snooping around the island in the first place."

"I wasn't coming to the island," returned Hanleigh lamely.

"As if we'll believe that!"

"Now, boys," said Hanleigh placatingly, "let's forget all our little differences and let bygones be bygones. You have saved my life and I'm very grateful to you. I didn't mean you any harm."

"Why were you coming here today?" insisted Frank.

"I'll tell you. After what happened the other day, I worried a lot. I was afraid you lads might think I was up to something crooked, and I wanted to make things square with you. So I decided to come here and make friends with you. And then I was going to look for that pocketbook I lost."

"Was that the only reason?"

"Absolutely the only reason."

"What interests you here so much?" asked Joe.

"I'm interested in the island because I want to buy it. There is no other reason beyond that."

"Why did you steal our supplies, then?"

"Now, boys," said Hanleigh, "what's the use of going into all that? I didn't take your supplies. I had nothing to do with it. I don't see why you should accuse me of a thing like that."

"Bluff!" said Frank. "Nothing but bluff! Your pocketbook story is a fairy tale. Well, Mr. Hanleigh, you're in a bad fix, you know. You won't be able to get back to town unless we take you there, and I'm warning you that unless you tell us the reason for your visits here, we intend to bring you in and turn you over to the police on a charge of trespass."

Hanleigh's eyes narrowed.

"You wouldn't do that?"

"Wouldn't we? You'd better tell us what you know."

"I don't know anything. You're just persecuting me. I merely came out here to make friends with you this morning and you won't give me a chance."

"We know you too well. What's it to be, Mr. Hanleigh—are you going to talk or are you going to jail?"

The victim groaned miserably.

"I don't see why you try to make everything so unpleasant for me," he complained. "You have me at your mercy and you're just taking an unfair advantage." He rubbed his sprained ankle tenderly. "I'm tired. I want to go to sleep."

"Perhaps after you've had a sleep, you'll think better of it."

Hanleigh shrugged. He removed his coat, folded it very carefully and placed it under his head.

"Do you want a pillow?" asked Chet.

"Hang your coat up on the wall," Frank suggested.

"No. No. I'm quite all right," returned Hanleigh hastily. "I'm quite comfortable as I am. I wish you boys would leave me alone. I want to sleep."

He placed his head on the folded coat.

The boys moved away.

"We can't pump him," whispered Frank. "Better leave him alone for a while."

With a great deal of groaning and muttering, Hanleigh composed himself for slumber. In a short while his heavy breathing told the boys that he was asleep.

CHAPTER XXII

THE LETTER

"Just like a clam, that fellow Hanleigh!" exclaimed Biff Hooper.

"He sure doesn't want to talk," Frank Hardy agreed. "I thought we could scare him, but I guess there's nothing doing."

"He didn't come back here to make friends with us. He was making another try at that notebook, that's what he was doing. It must be mighty important to him." Joe was eyeing the coat Hanleigh had folded so carefully and put under his head. "Wonder why he wouldn't take a pillow. He wasn't taking any chances on letting that coat get away from him."

The boys looked at one another significantly.

"Perhaps he has some important papers in the pocket," whispered Chet.

"Fine chance we have of getting at them."

"I don't know about that," said Frank. "Where there's a will, there's a way. Let him sleep a little longer and we'll see if we can't get at them."

The storm raged fiercely outside the cabin. The blizzard had grown in fury. The trees, bowed before the bitter wind. The boys idled about, waiting for the moment when they could attempt to secure the coat from beneath the head of their sleeping enemy.

At last Frank nodded.

Hanleigh was snoring. Frank went over to the wall and took down his own coat. He folded it carefully, then beckoned to Joe.

Together, the boys tiptoed over to the head of the bed.

While Joe held Frank's coat, Frank gently grasped the coat under Hanleigh's head and began to withdraw it.

The man stirred uneasily. His snoring ceased.

The boys stepped back.

Hanleigh turned over on his side. The coat was almost entirely free. The boys waited a few moments, then went toward the man again.

With a quick movement, Frank drew the coat from beneath his head, while at the same instant Joe slipped the other in its place. They stepped back.

Hanleigh groaned in his sleep, stirred again. His groping hand reached for the coat and he drew it closer to him. In a few moments his snoring again resounded through the cabin.

The boys retreated to the kitchen.

"I don't like the idea of going through a man's private papers," said Frank reluctantly; "but in this case I think there is some excuse. Hanleigh is up to some crooked business here and it's our duty to find out what it is."

"That's right," agreed the others.

Frank felt the inside pocket of the coat. He encountered a bulky sheaf of papers and these he removed. Most of them were letters, but one in particular appeared to be a legal document.

He unfolded this document and brought it over to the window. The others crowded about him.

"Better keep an eye on Hanleigh, in case he awakes," Frank suggested. "Watch him, will you, Biff?"

Biff went over to the door.

"He's still asleep," he whispered.

"Good."

Frank read the document over to himself. Then he gave a low whistle of amazement.

"This clears up a lot of things," he said.

"Read it," whispered Joe anxiously.

Frank read the document. It was a letter addressed to Hanleigh and was from a lawyer in New York City. It was as follows:

Dear Sir:

"This is to advise you that your late uncle, John Sparewell, named you as sole heir in his will, which has just been probated. Under the provisions of the will you will benefit to the extent of all Mr. Sparewell's property, consisting of two lots of ground on the outskirts of Bayport, cash in the bank amounting to three hundred and fifty dollars, and all personal papers and belongings. In his will, Mr. Sparewell made particular mention of a notebook which was to be given into your hands after his death, stressing its importance as containing information of great value. He also gave these instructions:

"My nephew is to take this notebook, with the accompanying key to the cipher which I shall leave in a sealed envelope, and when he has made himself aware of the contents of the message I wish him to go to the place mentioned and procure the object referred to. This is to be returned to its rightful owner. In return for this favor, I name my nephew, George Hanleigh, as my sole heir."

We hereby take pleasure in forwarding to you the notebook and the sealed envelope mentioned by our deceased client and trust you will carry out his instructions to the letter.

Yours very truly,
Flint and Flint, Attorneys at Law.

When Frank had concluded the reading of this document there were expressions of amazement from the other boys.

"So that's how he came to get the notebook!" said Chet. "John Sparewell was Hanleigh's uncle!"

"And Sparewell," observed Frank, "is dead."

"Well, that clears up so much of the mystery," said Joe. "But it looks as if Hanleigh is up against it just as much as we were. We know the secret of the cipher message and it didn't do us any good."

"Perhaps he knows something else. Sparewell may have given him further instructions in that sealed envelope."

Frank looked through the other papers he had taken from Hanleigh's pocket. He was interrupted by a sudden whisper from Biff.

"Be careful!"

"What's the matter?"

"He's waking up."

Frank thrust the papers back into the coat pocket. There would be trouble when Hanleigh learned how he had been tricked. Then Biff sighed with relief.

"False alarm. He turned over again. He's still asleep."

Frank went back to the papers, relieved. He searched through them carefully. But he did not find what he sought. There were no further references to the cipher, to the sealed envelope, or to John Sparewell.

"Nothing else here," he reported finally.

"We'd better put the coat back under his head," Joe suggested.

Frank returned the papers to the pocket in which he had found them.

"We're liable to wake him up if we try to put the coat back now," he said. "I think we ought to wait until he has had his sleep. Then the rest of you can keep him occupied while I slip the coat back where it belongs."

"And we'll ask him what he knows about Sparewell," said Chet.

"Oh, we'll have questions to ask him, never fear. He won't want us to go to Elroy Jefferson with the news about Sparewell."

Outside, the storm was at its height. They heard a distant crash.

One of the trees at the edge of the cliff had fallen before the force of the gale. The wind was sweeping across the island at terrific speed.

"If this keeps up, we'd better watch ourselves!" remarked Biff. "There are a couple of big trees right near the place. If they blow over, they're liable to wreck the cabin."

"Certainly is a wicked wind!" Frank agreed. "And it doesn't seem to be dying down, either."

Hardly were the words out of his mouth than there was a rending, crackling sound immediately above the cabin. Then, with a rush and a roar, something went sweeping past the window. At the same instant there came a grinding noise, followed by a thud and a crash on the roof.

"One of the trees blew down!" shouted Biff, in alarm.

"The chimney is going!" warned Joe.

Crash!

Another impact on the roof. There was a shower of mortar and fragments of stone in the fireplace.

"Back to the kitchen, fellows!" yelled Frank. "The chimney is falling in!"

CHAPTER XXIII

THE CHIMNEY COLLAPSES

Frank Hardy ran over to the bed where Hanleigh was sleeping. The uproar on the roof had already aroused the man somewhat and he was stirring restlessly. Frank shook him.

"Get up!" he shouted. "The chimney is caving in!"

Hanleigh sat up quickly.

"What?" he demanded, rubbing his eyes.

"Get up! It's dangerous here. The storm blew down one of the trees and it struck the chimney!"

There was another crash. Stones and rocks went bumping and rolling down the roof, and more débris came tumbling into the fireplace.

Hanleigh needed no second urging. He sprang out of bed, then halted with a groan of pain.

"My ankle!" he said.

"I'll help you." Frank seized him by the arm, and Hanleigh hobbled out into the kitchen, where the others were gathered. The cabin was creaking and swaying in the violent wind. Every little while they could hear an additional fragment of the chimney come crashing down onto the roof.

"Is the chimney coming down?" demanded Hanleigh eagerly.

They looked at him in surprise. Instead of being frightened, the man actually appeared glad of the mishap.

"If that other tree blows over and hits it, the chimney will be wrecked," said Frank sharply. "I can't see anything to look forward to in that."

Hanleigh was silent, but there was a look of undisguised elation in his swarthy face.

The wind was a hurricane by now.

Wilder and wilder it blew. The snow was so heavy that the boys could not see more than a few feet beyond the window. The chimney was no longer breaking up and the steady thump and clatter of rocks on the roof had ceased. The fireplace was half full of mortar and bits of stone.

"We'd better stay where we are," said Frank. "We're safe enough in the kitchen. If that chimney collapses it will mean trouble for any one in the outer room."

Hanleigh limped over to a chair and sat down.

"Might as well be comfortable," he muttered.

"Certainly," agreed Frank. He swung around to face the man. Then, quite calmly, he said: "When did John Sparewell die?"

Hanleigh was taken completely off his guard by the sudden question.

"About eighteen months ago—" he began. Then he halted. "What do you know about John Sparewell?" he demanded.

"We know he was your uncle. And we know he disappeared from Elroy Jefferson's home with the rosewood box fifteen years ago. We know a lot more than you think, Hanleigh."

"You found that notebook!" shouted the man.

"Of course."

"You had no right to read it. The notebook was mine. I'll have the law on you for reading it."

"The law will be interested in that notebook, Hanleigh. You're none too anxious to let the police see it, or Mr. Jefferson either."

The shot told. Hanleigh's lips curved in a snarl.

"What if Jefferson does see the notebook? What do I care if you turn it over to him or to the police? It won't do any of you any good. The only important thing in the whole book is written in cipher, and I defy you to solve it!"

He sat back, triumphantly.

"We have solved it," Joe told him.

"What?"

Hanleigh started forward, his eyes staring.

"We solved the cipher."

Consternation was written on Hanleigh's face. He groaned.

"You didn't—you haven't found it?" he gasped.

"Found what?"

The man's eyes became cunning.

"Don't you know?"

Frank shook his head.

"We have found nothing, so far. I think you'd better tell us what you were looking for. What should we have found?"

Hanleigh sat back, sighing with relief.

"There is nothing," he said. "Not now."

"Why—have you found it already?"

He nodded.

"Yes. I found it several days ago. There is nothing for you boys to gain by looking further."

"Then why," asked Joe, "did you come back here today?"

Hanleigh licked his lips, and was silent.

"You're bluffing again, Hanleigh," said Frank. "If you had found what you were looking for, you wouldn't have kept coming back to the cabin. You found yourself up against the same problem that we did. We searched that chimney, high and low—and found nothing. Neither did you."

Hanleigh shrugged.

"I've talked too much. You won't get any more out of me. I wish I had kept my mouth shut."

"Just as you wish, Hanleigh," remarked Frank casually. "I think we're all in the same fix. You don't know any more than we do. But I warn you that we will keep an eye on you. If you do learn the secret of the chimney, you won't keep it."

Hanleigh laughed sneeringly.

"Then you'll wait a long time—"

He was interrupted by a startling sound.

The shrieking wind had proved too much for the second of the tall trees that towered above the cabin. It gave way before the gale. With an ominous crackling, with branches snapping like pistol shots, it began to fall. The boys could hear the gathering roar as the great tree plunged down toward the roof of the cabin.

Hanleigh leaped to his feet in fright, then sagged helplessly against the wall as his injured ankle refused to support his weight.

"We're done for!" he shouted, in terror. "The cabin is falling in!"

Crash!

The tree had struck the chimney. There was a deluge of stones on the roof. The boys cowered in the kitchen. If the roof gave, they might be seriously injured. Hanleigh, a picture of abject fright, crouched in the corner.

With a hideous roar, the chimney collapsed.

At the same time, the great tree went sweeping down past the side of the cabin. When it struck the chimney its downward course had been diverted.

The falling stones broke great holes in the roof of the cabin and came crashing down into the living room. A cloud of dust rose from the fireplace. A stone crashed to the floor, rebounded and smashed a pane of glass. It seemed as though the din would never end.

"Let's get out of here!" Hanleigh was babbling, white with fear. "Let's get out. We'll be killed! The whole place is coming down about our ears."

"We're all right!" snapped Frank. "Be quiet!"

Had any of them been in the living room they would probably have been seriously injured. The weight of the fallen chimney had broken in the roof and stones were still crashing through to the floor below. The fireplace was wrecked.

At last the uproar died away. Snow was sifting through the hole in the roof, and when Frank peeped through the doorway he could see the jagged fragments of the chimney rising above the gap.

"I guess it's all over now," he said calmly.

Chet restrained him.

"You're not going in there?" he said. "Frank, don't be foolish! You'll be killed!"

"There won't be any more falling stones. The rest of the chimney is pretty firm. I'm anxious to investigate. Where's that flashlight?"

"I'm coming, too," declared Joe, realizing Frank's motive. "This may be a lucky thing for all of us."

"Lucky?" groaned Biff. "Do you call it lucky to have the chimney fall in and wreck the place?"

"We'll see."

Frank picked up the flashlight. He looked out into the living room again. It was a scene of desolation. Great stones, and quantities of débris, dust, and mortar lay all about. Then, followed by Joe, he left the kitchen and picked his way among the rubbish over to the fireplace.

CHAPTER XXIV

THE DISCOVERY

"Do you think we'll find it, Frank?" asked Joe Hardy.

"I shouldn't be surprised. If there is anything hidden in that chimney, the banging-up it got just now should reveal it."

They peered into the fireplace. It was choked with rubbish.

"Better clear some of this away."

They began moving away the stones and rocks that blocked the entrance. Chet and Biff, after watching the Hardy boys for a few moments from the kitchen, came over to help. They forgot their fears in the eagerness of the search.

Once, while moving away a large stone, Frank dislodged some others that came down with a rush. He jumped back just in time.

"This business isn't safe yet," muttered Chet dubiously.

However, the boys went on with the work, and soon cleared out the fireplace, with no further mishap. Frank entered the opening and peered up.

"Clear daylight ahead!" he called.

The tall chimney having collapsed, he could see the white snow swirling just a few yards above. He switched on his flashlight and examined the interior.

Then he gave an exclamation of satisfaction.

"It's all cracked and broken," he reported. "I'm going up."

"Be careful," advised Biff nervously.

But Frank was already scrambling up into the fireplace. The others waited. They jumped apprehensively when his struggling feet kicked loose some more stones that came plunging down into the rest of the débris.

For a while, there was silence.

Suddenly, there was a muffled shout from the chimney.

"I have it!" yelled Frank, in excitement. "It's here!"

The others heard him struggling for a moment; then came a further shower of stones and mortar.

"Got it!" shouted Frank triumphantly.

Then he came scrambling down into the fireplace again. His hands and face were black with soot, his clothes were ruined, but he bore in his hands an object that brought shouts of delight from the boys.

"The rosewood box!" declared Joe.

Frank nodded.

"Elroy Jefferson's stamp collection!"

The others crowded around him. Frank held the box up. It was a beautiful object, and although it had been hidden in the chimney for many years, its rosewood surface was almost as lustrous as on the day it was first concealed. Great excitement prevailed. The mystery of the chimney had been solved. The boys all talked at once. All clamored that the box be opened.

Frank undid the catch. They looked inside.

There, neatly arranged on sheets, were the rare stamps that had been Elroy Jefferson's pride—the stamps that were worth a fortune!

"Hurrah!" shouted Biff. Chet and Joe did a dance of joy. Frank closed the lid of the rosewood box.

"I found it right at the place mentioned in the cipher," he said. "We didn't discover it before, because the box had been hidden in a hollow right in the middle of one of the stones, and it had been mortared up when they were building the chimney. The shaking-up the chimney got a little while ago had broken the mortar and dislodged the stone. When I turned the flashlight on it I could plainly see the hollow and I knew something was hidden there. I dusted away the mortar, pried the stone up a little—and there was the box!"

A harsh voice interrupted him.

"What's that? You found it? Give it here! That box is mine!"

Hanleigh was standing in the kitchen doorway. His face was livid with rage.

"It belongs to Elroy Jefferson," returned Frank, "and we are going to return it to him."

Hanleigh tried to hobble over toward them, but his ankle gave him such pain that he abandoned the attempt and clung to the wall for support.

"I tell you, it's mine!" he screamed. "You have no right to take it! My uncle left that box to me in his will."

"He left it to you on condition that you return it to Mr. Jefferson, from whom he stole it," snapped Frank. "You haven't a chance to claim it, Hanleigh. We have the box and we intend to give it back to its owner."

Hanleigh glared at them. Then he shrugged.

"If only this ankle of mine was better, I'd show you!" he rasped. "It's downright robbery, that's what it is. I'll take this matter into the courts and make you give it up to me."

Frank laughed.

"You won't go into any court over this affair, Hanleigh. You know it would be the worse for you. We saw the letter you got from the lawyers, telling you that the box must be returned to Mr. Jefferson. Wait until we tell our story. You'll be lucky if you aren't arrested. You never intended to live up to those instructions at all."

This threat frightened Hanleigh. His face was pale.

"I did," he whined. "I meant to give it back to Mr. Jefferson. Let me have the box, boys, and I'll see that he gets it."

"No chance! The box is a lot safer with us than it is with you. We found it and we're going to give it back. You'd better sit down, Hanleigh, and tell us all about it."

Hanleigh hesitated. Then he hobbled over to one of the beds and sat down.

"I guess the game is up," he admitted heavily.

"Tell us what you know about this affair, and we'll let the whole business drop, as far as you are concerned," Frank promised. "If you don't tell us we'll simply let the police take action—and you know what that will mean," he added significantly.

"Well," said Hanleigh, at last, "I suppose there is nothing else for me to do. With any luck at all, I might have had that box, and I would have been miles away by this time."

"How did it get here, in the first place?"

Hanleigh began his story.

"My uncle, John Sparewell," he said, "was a servant in the home of Elroy Jefferson for many years. He was in financial difficulties at one time and when he learned about the valuable stamp collection he thought that if he stole it and sold it he might be able to realize enough money to pay off his debts. He knew that the collection was kept in a small safe in the house, so he watched his chance. He was highly trusted by Mr. Jefferson, so it was not long before he had the opportunity he was waiting for. The safe was left unlocked one afternoon, so my uncle slipped into the study, took the box, put on his hat and coat and left the house."

"And never went back," said Joe.

"He never returned. He had laid his plans very carefully, and he knew he might have to wait until the hue and cry died down before he would be able to dispose of the stamps, so he fled to a little village down on the sea-coast, and he stayed in hiding there for several months. He learned that the police were looking for him and then he found that a full description of the stamps had been circulated and that he would certainly be arrested if he ever tried to get rid of them to any recognized dealer. As a matter of fact, when he left the village where he had been hiding and went to New York, he narrowly escaped being arrested merely because he went to one of the dealers in that city and asked him what the stamps would be worth. The dealer became suspicious and notified the police, but my uncle saw his danger in time and cleared out."

"And he never sold the stamps."

"He couldn't. It was too dangerous. He made up his mind to return them to Elroy Jefferson. So he took the rosewood box and came back to Bayport."

"Why didn't he return them?" asked Frank, in surprise.

"Mr. Jefferson was away. He had gone to Europe on one of his periodical collecting trips. Then my uncle was afraid he might be recognized around Bayport and he knew that if he were arrested and the stamps found on him, no one would believe that he had meant to give them back. So he determined to hide them until he would have a chance to see Mr. Jefferson. At this time, Cabin Island had been purchased, and the cabin was being built. One day, my uncle was prowling about the Jefferson place, wondering if he could steal into the house and return the box without being seen, when Mrs. Jefferson saw him. He did not know if he had been recognized, but he went away. A little while later, he saw her leave the house with the gardener, and he saw them looking for him. He became frightened, and he hired a boat and went out into the bay. But evidently they traced him, for in a little while Mrs. Jefferson and the gardener set out in their own boat."

Hanleigh looked gloomily at the floor.

"My uncle was afraid that they would turn him over to the police if they caught him with the rosewood box. He wanted to talk to Elroy Jefferson and have the charge against him withdrawn. So he decided to flee, but the only place he could think of just then was Cabin Island. So he went there in the boat. The cabin was just being built at this time, as I said, and the fireplace and chimney had not been finished. The masons had the chimney just about half completed. As it was a Sunday, the island was deserted that day. Fearing that he might be trapped on the island, with the box in his possession, he hid it in a hollow of one of the stones and covered it over with mortar, intending to come back for it later. Then he got away from the island before Mrs. Jefferson overtook him."

"Didn't he go back later?" asked Chet.

Hanleigh nodded. "He went back next day. But the masons were back at work, completing the chimney. He did not have a chance to get near the place. He remained hidden on the island all day until they went home that night. Then he went up to the cabin to recover the box. He found that more stones had been placed over the stone where he had hidden the box. They had been securely mortared. The box was sealed up. In spite of all he could do, he could not get the box again. He came back to the island several times that week but he had no success. Every day, the masons did more work on the chimney, and every day his chances grew less. So he left Bayport and went to a little village in Maine, where he lived for a number of years. He did not try to get in touch with Elroy Jefferson again. Then, about five years ago, he determined to make another effort to recover the box and he came back, making several trips to the island, but although he tried to get at the box from inside the chimney, he failed. When he died, the box had not been recovered, although my uncle had repented bitterly of his foolish crime. In his will, he left his property to me and he also left a sealed letter containing the confession I have just told you."

"And he asked you to recover the box."

"Yes. But I wanted it for myself. I had become acquainted with a man who said he could dispose of it for me. He offered me fifty thousand dollars for the collection."

"Fifty thousand dollars!" exclaimed the boys.

"It is worth even more than that, for many of the stamps have increased in value since the year they disappeared. I don't suppose Elroy Jefferson would sell it at any price. My uncle was dead, I was the only person who knew where the stamps were hidden, so I made up my mind to get them for myself. I came to the island, but I soon saw that the only way I could get at the box would be to wreck the chimney. I went to Elroy Jefferson and made him an offer for the cabin. I did not have the eight thousand dollars I offered him, but I thought that if he accepted, I could give him a small cash payment, occupy the island long enough to get possession of the stamps, and then I would clear out. But he wouldn't sell. So then I determined to get the stamps by hook or by crook—"

"Mostly crook!" interrupted Chet.

Hanleigh flashed him a glance of hatred.

"You boys spoiled my game!"

"We were almost ready to give up," Frank told him. "If you hadn't been so persistent we might have left the island and you might have got the stamps after all."

"I was afraid you would find them first," said Hanleigh. "When I lost that notebook, I was afraid you would solve the cipher and get the box before I had a chance. Well, I took a long chance, and I lost. That's the whole story. Now what are you going to do?"

He glared at them defiantly.

"First of all," Frank decided. "We are going to wait until this storm dies down. Then we are going to take you back to Bayport."

"Not to the police!" shouted Hanleigh, in terror.

"No—not to the police. I imagine Mr. Jefferson will be content with getting the stamps back. We promised not to turn you over to the police if you confessed, and we'll keep our promise. But you must get out of Bayport."

"I never want to see the place again," groaned Hanleigh.

"We are going to explain the whole affair to Mr. Jefferson and return the stamps to him. It will be a return for his kindness in letting us have the island for our outing."

"I guess our outing is finished," remarked Chet regretfully, with a glance at the ruined roof.

"We didn't have many more days to stay, anyway," consoled Frank. "And I'd rather get to the bottom of a mystery like this than have all the outings in the world."

"That's right," agreed his brother.

CHAPTER XXV

ELROY JEFFERSON IS PLEASED

The storm died down early that afternoon, and the chums left the island and set out for Bayport, with the injured Hanleigh wrapped in blankets on one of the ice-boats. Hanleigh was completely beaten. When he got back to Bayport he managed to make his way to the railway station, caught the first train, and was never seen in the city again. It was fortunate for him that he left when he did. The Hardy boys made no report to the police, so he had nothing to fear from that quarter, but Tad Carson and Ike Nash, wrathful at the loss of their boat, were anxious to find their erstwhile employer.

The four chums went up to the Jefferson home together. They found Mr. Jefferson in the library, reading. He greeted them kindly.

"Well, boys," he said, "what brings you back from Cabin Island so soon? Haven't you been enjoying yourselves!"

"We've had a fine time, sir," said Frank, who acted as spokesman. "We came back because we found something there that might interest you."

"Something that might interest me?" asked Mr. Jefferson, puzzled. "I can't imagine what on earth it can be. Sit down and tell me all about it."

Frank produced the rosewood box.

"Do you recognize this, sir?"

Elroy Jefferson gazed at the box incredulously.

"My stamps!" he exclaimed. "My precious stamp collection!"

With trembling hands, he seized the box and opened it. When he saw that the stamps were undamaged, and exactly as he had last seen them, his joy knew no bounds.

"Tell me!" he demanded, in excitement. "Tell me where you found them? On the island?"

"We found them on Cabin Island," replied Frank, "hidden in the old chimney, among the stones. They have been there for years."

Elroy Jefferson was amazed.

"But how did you learn they were there? I never suspected for a moment. Why, I had given them up for lost. You can't imagine what this means to me, boys. That stamp collection is priceless. It was one of the tragedies of my life when the rosewood box was stolen."

Then the boys told him the full story of their adventures on Cabin Island, beginning with their first encounter with Hanleigh and concluding with their discovery of the rosewood box after the chimney had been wrecked by the storm.

"I'm afraid the cabin is in a bit of a mess," said Frank; "but I don't think we'd have found the stamps at all if things had not happened the way they did."

"I am of course sorry about the cabin," said Mr. Jefferson. "But these stamps mean more to me than that. The cabin can be fixed up for a few dollars. So that was why Hanleigh was so anxious to buy the place! The rascal! John Sparewell's nephew! I always knew Sparewell had stolen the rosewood box but I never dreamed he had hidden it so near at hand."

The old gentleman's gratification was inspiring. The boys had known that he would be pleased at the return of his treasured stamp collection but they had not expected that it would give him the degree of pleasure which it evidently did. He gazed at the stamps constantly, held them up to the light, admired them, patted the boys on the back, and finally sat down at his desk.

"I can't do very much to express my appreciation," he said, "but I want you boys to accept a little reward. I have spent hundreds of dollars trying to get my collection back. I even engaged professional detectives, who failed. If any one ever has need of a detective I'll certainly recommend the Hardy boys to him."

Frank laughed.

"We're not professionals, sir," he said. "We like tackling a good mystery, though."

"And you tackle them successfully. First, my automobile. Now, my stamps. Very few lads would have made good use of the slim clues you had."

He drew out his check book and wrote busily for a few minutes.

"As for a reward," put in Joe, "we didn't expect anything, Mr. Jefferson. It was fun. And, anyway, you've been awfully good to us, letting us have the cabin for our outing—"

"Nonsense!"

Mr. Jefferson swung around in his chair. He gave each of the Hardy boys a check. Then he wrote again for a few minutes and made a similar present to Biff and Chet.

"But this is for two hundred dollars!" exclaimed Frank, in amazement, as he looked at his check.

"And so is mine," said Joe.

"What of it?" said Mr. Jefferson. "My stamp collection is worth much more than that."

"But," stammered Chet, "I didn't do anything. The Hardy boys deserve any rewards you care to give them, but Biff and I didn't do much. A hundred dollars, Mr. Jefferson—why, I can't take it!"

"Neither can I," added Biff, although he looked longingly at the check Mr. Jefferson had given him. "The Hardy boys deserve all the credit."

Mr. Jefferson quietly waved their objections aside.

"I realize they deserve most of the credit," he said, "because they did the detective work. But you lads helped a lot, too—"

"They certainly did!" Joe interpolated, with great earnestness.

"So you mustn't spoil my pleasure in having my stamps back by refusing what little reward I can give you."

"Gee!" said Chet, in delight. "I can do a lot of things with a hundred dollars! Isn't it great!"

"Furthermore," continued Elroy Jefferson, "I want you boys to understand that Cabin Island is at your disposal at any time. I'll have the cabin fixed up immediately and if you care to go there at any other time during the winter, you are welcome. And I imagine it will be a pleasant place for a vacation outing next summer. From now on, you may consider the cabin as your own. I never use the place, and it will give me a great deal of pleasure if I know good use is being made of it."

Biff forgot himself.

"Hurrah!" he yelled. "Hurrah! You're a prince, Mr. Jefferson!"

The old gentleman beamed with pleasure.

"I can't think of any one I would rather have as my guests on Cabin Island," he said, "than the Hardy boys and their chums."

www.ingramcontent.com/pod-product-compliance
Lightning Source LLC
Chambersburg PA
CBHW011803010726
47498CB00009B/2855